# OASIS 4

Dale Chamberlain

# CONTENTS

# CLOAK-'N'-DAGGER
# AND KORTLAX

**Oasis 4, Quarters of Phillip Ross, Station Manager**

Phil Ross was in that dozing state between being asleep and awake, marveling at the comfort of his bed and how perfectly rested he was.

At 0600, an alarm chimed for a few seconds. It was enough to kick him out of his dozing state and into wakefulness, not fully awake but close enough. The Station Integrated Computer Operating System, or SICOS, decided to find out if Phil was responsive.

"Are you awake, Mr. Ross?"

Phil grunted, "Yeah." He threw off the covers and sat upright. It was at this moment he discovered why his bed was so comfortable. Upon sitting up, his inertia carried him upward until the ceiling stopped his assent.

Now fully awake, and annoyed, Phil massaged the knot forming on his head. He croaked out, "SICOS! What is the gravity level set to?" "One-fiftieth Earth normal, Mr. Ross" came the mechanical reply.

Phil gently pushed off the ceiling and floated downward. When he reached the bed, he grabbed two handfuls of sheets and hung on. "SICOS, increase gravity to Earth Normal over the next two minutes!" There was a glitch in the artificial gravity system on the station; it had a tendency to decrease over time gradually. It acted like a software issue, or at least the software isn't compatible with the controls. The engineers have tried to explain the problem, but they never had to

Phil's satisfaction. He suspected they didn't fully understand the problem themselves.

At least the gravity didn't completely go away. At zero gravity, items around the room that weren't fastened in place tended to float around, then drop when the gravity was restored. At normal gravity, Phil let go of the bedsheets, then he started to dress for the gym.

As station manager, Phil rated deluxe accommodations, which consisted of the main room that served as a sitting room for relaxing and entertaining and an area for dining near the kitchen. He didn't use the kitchen very often, but he had no doubt that his wife would as soon as she arrived. Until then, he was just as happy dining in the company cafeteria or one of the many restaurants on the station. There were two bedrooms: a master bedroom and a smaller one. Phil used the smaller one for an office to do some after-hours work or personal business. The quarters were situated on an outer part of the station, so there was an entire wall that consisted of clear polymer, which gave him a spectacular view of the nebula that dominated this quadrant.

Before leaving, he looked around the room to satisfy himself that nothing was amiss from the partial gravity. Looking about, his gaze focused outside the window, where he spotted the Station Expansion Unit scheduled to be added later that afternoon, which will double the size of Oasis 4 instantly. The new addition will be nearly identical to the existing station, and it was going to be connected directly underneath the existing station via a long cylindrical extension.

The station, known as Oasis 4, is owned and operated by the Stellar Logistics and Freight Company. It consists of a center module, called the CentMod, which was roughly the shape of a flattened sphere approximately 500 meters in diameter, and 150 meters in height. That's where the station's operation center is located, along with the Station System Center. The Station System Center is where the power is generated, and environmental systems are maintained; also, SICOS is housed in the CentMod.

As well as having a utility function, the CentMod is also the social center of the station, having a large open area that is reminiscent of a town square, village green, and suburban mall. There are restaurants, cafés, shops, a hotel, theaters, auditoriums, conference centers, and office centers. Also, a hospital that's as well-equipped and staffed as any on Earth or one if its colonies.

Four of the eight arms that radiate outward from the CentMod go to four cylindrical modules. These modules serve as habitation units, known as HabMods. They measure about 75 meters tall and 150 meters in diameter. Each HabMod has thirty levels, and each level is arranged according to the type of quarters on that level. Deluxe quarters are about 140 square meters all told. As the levels go downward, the quarters get less spacious but still very comfortable. There is a center court in each HabMod, where the quarters that face the center courts have a balcony. The center courts provide air circulation and space for trees and plants, which makes it all seem less sterile. Level 1 of each HabMod is reserved for services, such as a laundry area and a fitness center.

HabMod 1 is reserved for company management. HabMods 2 and 3 are for station personnel who were not management. HabMod 4 is for alien personnel on the station. One major difference in HabMod 4 from the others was the need for separate dining facilities for each alien race.

There were four additional connecting arms radiating outward from the CentMod. These provide access to the storage and docking modules, called CargoMods, which are the reasons for the station's existence. They have multiple docking facilities and accommodations for all types of cargo. Containerized goods, bulk cargo, palletized cargo, and even livestock can be accommodated in the CargoMods. Also, they are used to provide passenger access to cruise and tour ships.

Going out the door, Phil said over his shoulder, "SICOS, secure quarters." The computer replied, "Secure, sir."

He made his way to the Central Core Atrium of HabMod 1 and walked the escalator. Reaching level 1, he walked directly to the Fitness Center. Passing the lap pools, he didn't bother to hide his disgust. They still didn't have water in them because of untrustworthy gravity regulators. He was in the mood for cardio, so he had to settle on the treadmill. His other choice was the rowing machines or stationary bikes, but that was yesterday and the day before.

As he was warming up, he saw that some of his staff and other personal were working out with the weight machines. They weren't exactly "weight" machines since, in space, on a station with flaky gravity systems, the equipment had to be of the resistance type that was computer-controlled and would provide a good workout, even in zero gravity.

After two simulated miles, Phil slowed to a walk to cool down. A minute later, he stepped off the treadmill and made his way back to his quarters for a quick shower and to change into his work clothes. Workwear for Phil consisted of cotton pants with cargo pockets and a cotton shirt. A comfortable pair of lace-up boots and a leather flight jacket, which was a holdover from his days as a shuttle pilot. He started his career ferrying personnel and cargo from Earth to orbiting stations much like Oasis 4. His attire was topped off with a baseball cap with the Stellar Logistics and Freight logo. Finally, he put an earpiece in, and he clipped its mating language translator to his belt.

After dressing, Phil looked at his kitchen and thought a few seconds, *Nah, I'll wait until the better half gets here.*

Out the door again, to an escalator, this time to level 15, where he walked to the connector tunnel that led to the CentMod.

*****

## Oasis 4, CentMod, Eva's Café

Arriving at the CentMod, Phil mused for a second about where to get breakfast. There were quite a few choices to be had, all of them not bad. He finally opted for Eva's Café. It looked as if it was lifted from a European city street corner and plopped down on one of the many levels of the CentMod. Eva's may have looked European, but the food was decidedly North American. Tables were arranged on a walkway overlooking the vast interior of the CentMod, and it was a great place to people-watch.

Sitting at a table were two freighter captains that Phil was particularly acquainted. The one closest was Ed Carlton, captain of the *Bright Star*. He was the youngest at forty-two and was about midway through a very distinguished career. The other captain was Dave Jacobson of the *Atlantis Star*, who was a bit older at fifty-six, he was also in the midst of a distinguished career and loved what he did. Visiting other worlds and experiencing alien cultures is something he truly enjoyed. Dave spotted Phil and waved him over.

After greetings, Eva came over and poured Phil a cup of coffee. "The usual, Boss?"

Phil nodded. "Make 'em scrambled today."

Eva smiled. "Coming up." Then she tapped the order on a touch screen pad as she headed off.

Phil looked at Ed. "Weren't you supposed to be on your way to Celnar by now, Ed?"

"Yup, as soon as they finish loading, we're shoving off," Ed said with a nod. Dave asked, "What's your cargo?"

Ed answered, "Cement and construction materials for the colony." Then he asked, "When are you leaving, Dave?"

Dave sipped his coffee. "In about a week. One hundred and fifty containers of consumer goods and about fifty passengers."

Ed looked at Dave. "Pretars?"

Dave smiled. "Yep. Once the new Station Expansion Unit is in place, the crew that's moving it will be out of a job, so I'll get to take them back to their home planet."

Ed shook his head. "Man! Pretars are hard to get used to."

Dave took another sip of coffee. "That's because you never spent time with them."

Ed considered that and shrugged. "That may be, but I just look at them, and I'm pretty sure that I couldn't spend a lot of time with them." The others stared at Ed, then he got a defensive look on his face.

"I'm not proud of it."

Phil chuckled. "Look around, Ed. Not counting humans, there are six space- faring species that we know of, and most are like humans, more or less. Yeah, there are some noticeable differences. All are bipeds with five of the six having two arms."

Dave frowned. "Finger and toe count varies though."

Ed piped up. "Yeah, but that sixth group bucks all that. The pretars are shocking, amusing, and disturbing, all in the same moment."

Dave chuckled. "You're right about that, but once you get to know them, you learn to appreciate them. I spent a lot of time on the Pretna-Signac run."

Almost as if on cue, there was a rising din coming from one of the connecting tunnels, and all at once about a dozen feathered creatures came pouring into the CentMod. They were four-legged, long-necked, and they were about the size of a large dog. At the end of their long necks, they had a bird's head, with a triangular beak like that of a cardinal. There didn't seem to be a standard color, as some were red, some were blue, and there were yellow ones and green ones. As if the visual features weren't enough, they all squawked and shrieked excitedly as they ran.

Perusing them was a group of pretars. They were indeed a shocking sight to the uninitiated four arms, short squat heads that blended into their bodies. They could turn their heads, but there was no discernible neck. All were each holding a rope or a net, and they were leaping over tables and guard rails in an effort to catch up to their quarry. As they ran, they shouted encouragement and suggestions of strategy to each other, pretty much all at once. Everyone at the table watched both groups race around the CentMod and then disappear into a connecting tunnel.

Phil was getting a feel for what the rest of the day was going to be like, and the look on his face reflected it.

Dave was grinning. "See, I told you there was a lot to like about them."

Ed couldn't quite find the words. It was a few seconds before he croaked out the question, "What were those?"

Dave looked annoyed. "Pretars! What do you think we were talking about all this time?"

It was Ed's turn to be annoyed. "Not them! What were those they were chasing?"

Smiling, Dave answered, "Those are kortlax, the pretars' only meat source."

Ed was starting to look confused again. Dave saw that kortlax needed more explanation. "Pretars don't freeze, can, freeze dry, or preserve meats in any way. They're not opposed to the idea. It just takes them a while to get used to new ideas."

"The company agreed to allow them to keep a small herd…er… flock in CargoMod 4 while they add the Station Expansion Unit," Phil added.

Ed was still trying to work it out and make sense of it. Finally, he said while shaking his head, "Those guys seem to be completely ill-suited to keep those things. They must have farmers or ranchers that know how to control them."

Dave shrugged and answered, "Sure, just not here." Ed was getting exasperated. "Why the heck not?"

Dave shrugged again. "They have a caste system on Pretna. It's not chiseled in stone, but it's what they're comfortable with. Their farmers don't want to go into space to tend a flock, and it wouldn't occur to anyone to ask one if they would be willing to."

Phil started to have an idea. "Dave, have you ever been to a kortlax farm?"

Dave answered, "Sure, it was my ship that brought the kortlax here. I wanted to see what I was getting into before I brought them aboard."

Phil wondered, "How easy are they to catch?"

Dave shrugged. "They're really easy if you know what you're doing."

Phil leaned in. "Don't you think it would be nice if someone showed the Pretar engineers how to catch them?"

Dave considered it for a second, then nodded. "I thought about it, but to be honest, I'm getting a lot of amusement value out of this, and the entertainment system is being serviced on my ship."

Breakfast arrived, and Phil started putting pepper on his eggs. "I would appreciate it if you considered it."

After breakfast, the three went their separate ways. Ed and Dave went to their ships. Phil headed for the platform lift, which was a simple platform with a guardrail, that would take him to the Station Operations Center, located at the top level of the CentMod.

As he ascended, he spotted about half a dozen kortlax racing out of a connecting tunnel, being chased by four pretars, and then disappearing into a different tunnel. At the same moment, about twenty kortlax exited a different tunnel and streaked across the CentMod to dive into a tunnel that led to HabMod 3. The pretars chasing them weren't making any more progress than the first group.

Phil grinned. "How many of those things are there anyway?"

*****

## Oasis 4, CentMod, Operations Center

The elevator slowed to a stop, and Phil stepped through the door into the ops center. The ops center was part airport control tower, part dispatch office, and part city hall. The most interesting part of the ops center, and by far the busiest, was where the controllers worked. The room had a 360-degree view. The controllers guided incoming and outgoing freighters, along with passenger vessels. Most traffic was scheduled, but there were some that just showed up. The freighters varied in size, with the largest usually accommodating roughly thirty thousand tons. The smallest vessel to arrive at the station were shuttles that accommodated four people. These were getting more numerous since the technology to achieve speeds faster than light in smaller vessels was developed.

The lower level of the ops center is where the comings and goings of ships were tracked, along with their cargos, crew, and passengers. When Phil arrived that morning, the night shift was handing over station operations to the day shift. Day and night is a relative concept on a space station; however, chronometers are set to Earth Greenwich Mean Time, also known as Zulu Time. The ships operating from Earth are also set to Zulu Time.

Phil walked into the briefing room, where he found the stations' department heads had already gathered for the daily briefing. He took a sip of the coffee he just poured. "First up, operations."

Virginia Wells checked her pad and reported, "We have four scheduled arrivals and three departures."

"Tell me about the arrivals," Phil ordered.

Virginia consulted her pad. "Two bulk freighters from Quasar lines. The *William Burnside* at 0930 Zulu off-loading twenty thousand tons of bauxite, and the *Roger Blake* arriving at 1300 Zulu off-loading five thousand tons of corn."

Phil looked surprised. "Corn?"

Virginia nodded. "Yup, seed corn for the colonies at Celnar, Altan, and Cordon."

Phil thought a second and asked. "What's the other two?" Virginia answered. "A container, freight, and passenger vessel from

Intersystems Shipping, the *Morning Star*, arriving at 1630 from Flast."

There was a noticeable reaction around the room at the mention of Flast.

Virginia continued, "Number four arrival is a supply vessel, the *City of Akron*, from our benevolent employers at Stellar Logistics and Freight, arriving at 1830 Zulu."

"What about departures?" Phil asked.

Virginia looked down at her pad again. "*Pride of India* leaves at 0820 Zulu bound for Earth with twenty-eight containers of consumer goods. The *Flying Norseman*, a cruise ship, leaves with all twelve hundred passengers at 1200 Zulu. They think the kortlax and pretars were fun by the way. Finally, the *Bright Star* leaves for Celnar, with ten thousand tons of cement, and five thousand tons of construction materials, at 1700 Zulu."

Of course, there were countless other vessels that will come and go throughout the day. These were usually smaller independent operators, dropping off or picking up smaller loads. They were necessary because it was impractical to service small outposts and colonies with large freighters.

Some operators needed repair facilities for their vessels. The station hosted independent vessel repair shops that made a living accommodating the needs of small operators. These repair shops weren't adequate to suit the needs of all their customers, and they were relocating to facilities that were frequented by operators they were better suited to serve. To that end, Stellar Logistics and Freight Corporation was going to add a ship repair department with the station expansion. The new department was going to occupy a significant amount of space, and the corporation felt the customers would be better served.

Some come to bargain with the vendors that make the station home. Still, others stop just for a change of scenery and a chance to interact with people; it makes long voyages more tolerable.

"Up next, facilities maintenance." There was a slight edge in Phil's voice although everyone knew he wasn't actually mad.

Will Dawson, the facilities manager, started his standard briefing. "Up today, docking ports seven through fourteen in CargoMod 4 are being serviced. Fusion reactors three and four will be adjusted for better efficiency. Kind of pointless really. Once the Station Expansion is in place, we'll be switching over to—"

"Gravity Generator Controls," Phil interrupted.

Will looked genuinely uncomfortable now. "Well, there is a container on its way here with enough controls to replace every unit on the station. They're the new upgraded versions, so that should end our problems."

Phil softened. "When?"

"The 1630 arrival, the *Morning Star*." Will was happy to report. "After checking calibration of the units, we'll begin installation. Your quarters will be the very first." Will just wanted to finish his report at this point, so he was hurrying. "I'll have crews working with the pretar engineers, but there isn't very much to do until the Station Expansion Unit is in place," he promised.

Phil seemed satisfied with Will's report, so he then turned to the pretar in the room. "Mr. Selak."

Selak straightened and cleared his throat. Like all pretars, Selak prided himself in the fact that he was a professional and took great pains to reflect that fact in his appearance and manner. As much as he enjoyed how humans could mix humor with work, he could not imagine doing it himself, so he didn't try. "As Mr. Dawson stated, most of the work preparing the station has been completed. It's going to take a minimum crew to tie the two sections together once they're in place. In fact, most of my engineers are idle at the moment."

Phil could barely hold back a smirk. "It's a good thing that there are Kortlax to round up."

Selak's expression suddenly changed to that of someone who was just caught at something naughty.

Phil turned his attention to the woman in hospital scrubs. "What's up, Doc?" Dr. Marie Tillman gave her usual deadpan response, "Never gets old, Phil.

We have twenty-seven patients in bed today. We'll be doing thirty physicals, and as always, we'll be ready for everything from boo-boos to full-on emergencies."

Phil nodded. "Real good. What's new in the area of security?"

Luke Smith, the station security marshal, consulted his pad. "Not a lot to report this morning. We have two freighter crewmen cooling off in our jail after a fight at Sparky's last night."

Phil frowned. "I didn't think that having an establishment that served alcohol was a good idea."

Luke quickly jumped to Sparky's defense, "I know what you're thinking, Boss. The crewmen in question are malnuns."

There was some subdued chuckling around the table. Virginia frowned. "What of it?"

The doctor chimed in, "Malnuns are the galaxy's lightweights. Even the smallest amount of alcohol will get them drunk."

"They're also mean drunks," Luke added.

Phil looked at Luke. "I thought Sparky knew not to serve malnuns?" Luke shrugged. "He does, but he has a new waiter that didn't know it."

Phil nodded. "Make sure he gets a refresher in alien interaction protocols."

"Roger that, Boss" was Luke's reply.

Oasis 4 was solely owned by the Stellar Logistics and Freight Company. It was not subject to government laws since it was located in an area of space that no one has claimed. In fact, like the other Oasis stations, it was located at a crossroads of sorts between several planetary systems and colonies. As a result, it was an attraction for not only legitimate commerce, but some shady characters have tried to use the station for less than legitimate purposes.

Luke and his deputies were more than up to the task of keeping order. Every visitor to the station understands company rules are absolute, and everyone has to comply as if they were in an alien world. As a matter of practicality, that's exactly what the situation was. Most infractions were minor; however, there were mechanisms in place if a severe situation were to arise.

Satisfied that another briefing was successfully dealt with, Phil stood. "All right, folks, let's put another one in the books and make lots of money for the Stellar Logistics and Freight Company."

There was some low chatter around the room, then Virginia called out, "Hey, Will! How about making my quarters number two for the gravity generator control overhaul? I almost drowned in the shower last night." There was some more good-natured banter and chiding as the group left the conference room.

Phil made his way to the upper level where the area controllers and dispatchers were at work. There was a 360-degree view of the area outside the station. He checked his watch, 0818 Zulu.

A controller near him keyed his microphone. "*Pride of India*, docking clamps released, thrust port until clear."

Phil picked up a pair of binoculars and looked through the window. The *Pride of India*'s lights switched on, and there was a short burst from the thrusters, pushing the ship to its left. When the ship had moved about a hundred feet, thrusters gave another short burst stopping its movement.

Satisfied that the ship was clear, the controller keyed his microphone. "*Pride of India*, pitch up twenty-two degrees and thrust forward." The maneuver was done to ensure that the ship's reaction engines wouldn't be pointed at the station when started.

When the *Pride of India* had completed pitching and moved off a distance of five miles, the controller once again keyed his microphone. "*Pride of India*, you are clear to fire your reaction engines and navigate. Have a safe voyage, sir."

Once the ship's computers were satisfied with things, they would switch to light-speed engines; in fact, they would be traveling much faster than light speed. There were smaller vessels arriving and departing the station, and the controllers were doing their usual skillful job of getting them to where they needed to be.

Phil put down his binoculars. It occurred to him that it was going to be a challenge to see the lower section clearly when the Station Expansion is in place. Then he spotted a bank of monitors that were installed to offer a view of the lower section when it was attached. He checked the progress of the Station Expansion and saw it was a bit closer, being guided carefully by tugs piloted by pretars.

Phil went to the area below the controller workstation to the operations center. The amount of information available here was staggering. A complete inventory of all the goods and cargo aboard the station, quarter assignments for station personnel, temporary personnel, and visitors in the hotel were also kept track of here. After scanning the monitors looking for problems, and not finding any, he said aloud to no one in particular, "I'll be in my office."

Reaching his office, Phil sat at his desk. While he adjusted the lighting, he called for his daily task list. "SICOS, pull up my mail." The SICOS display showed several files. Three memos from corporate headquarters in Kansas City. The most important file, which he forwarded to the dispatch office, was a list of ships and cargos due to arrive. The last file was from June Dixon, captain of the *Morning Star*, and her message, if anything, was cryptic. She said she needed to talk to him on a secure frequency as soon as she dropped out of light speed. He was naturally curious, but he didn't dwell on it.

At 0920 Zulu, Phil went back up to the control level to watch the *William Burnside* maneuver into position at CargoMod 3. Thrusters were working overtime, moving the big ship to the docking clamps. When it was close enough, protrusions from the ship aligned with receptacles on the station were extended to enter the receptacles. Clamps built into the docking system gripped the lugs, then they retracted, pulling the ship to the station. Thrusters on the station itself fired to dampen the reaction of several tons of ship bumping into it.

When the ship was securely in place, the station personnel extended an air lock gangway to the personnel hatch on the ship. The gangway air lock was sealed, as well as the access openings, so that station personnel can connect off- loading equipment. The *William Burnside*'s cargo was bauxite ore that is used to make aluminum. A mining company found an asteroid belt rich in bauxite in a nearby star system. In space, nearby is a relative term. The mining company uses the station to store the ore until a buyer can be found; however, finding a buyer isn't normally a problem.

Since the pretars have been introduced to aluminum, they can't get enough. They didn't have a metal with the same strength-to-weight ratio, and they kept coming up with new uses for it; it's solved a lot of problems they've struggled with. The pretars have even come up with a unique method of smelting the ore as well. Using a station of their own that's orbiting a star, they use solar energy to process the ore and alloy it. Then they turn it into sheet material, extrusion, and billet material. Asteroids on the whole are convenient resources, every mineral that can be named can be found in them.

Oasis 4 is made of metal, primarily steel, and the Station Expansion Unit is nearly identical to the existing station but with some upgrades to the systems. The new section will house the power plant, and the existing power plant removed since it's an older model. In less than twenty-four hours, Phil will be responsible for twice as much station as he currently is. Of course, it will take some time to get the new section online but probably not as long as it's going to take for Phil to get comfortable with that much new station.

It will take about twelve hours to complete the joining once the two halves come together. They need to be bolted in place, then the systems are connected, then brought online. Finally, the old power plant will be disassembled and removed. After a few weeks, additional personnel will arrive: maintenance technicians, security deputies, administrative personnel, cargo handlers, and finally, vendors for the additional shop space, custodians, and hotel maids.

There are even older folks moving in so as to use the station as a sort of retirement village.

Phil walked to the operations center. As he passed his administrative assistant, he said, "I'll be in CargoMod 3."

He stepped onto the platform lift and depressed the button labeled plaza level. While he descended, he surveyed the view that the platform provided. People were starting to fill the space: some were freighter crew members looking for diversions while at the station, some were crewmen from small freight operators, making deals with the vendors on the station, and some off-duty station personnel. He noticed that there were a lot of tourists from the cruise liner that was docked. Finally, he spotted a group of pretars in hot pursuit of kortlax, which made Phil grin. "This is getting out of hand."

Reaching the plaza level, Phil headed to the pedestrian walkway that led to CargoMod 3. About halfway to the CargoMod, there is an intersecting tunnel that leads to the HabMods on either side of the CargoMod. At that point, Phil had to move to the edge of the walkway to allow a flock of excited and squawking kortlax to go past. As the pursuing pretars ran past, Phil offered some encouragement, "Give 'em heck, guys."

*****

## Oasis 4, CargoMod 3

In CargoMod 3, the crew from the *William Burnside* that wasn't needed for off-loading cargo was passing through the station's version of customs. Customs was largely a formality since there were only two destinations for this vessel. He noticed that there were already ship's crew assisting the station personnel in off- loading. It was a straightforward procedure. The freighter's cargo holds were at zero gravity, so a conveyor system would be useless. To off-load bulk cargo, an auger system was developed; it wasn't a bad system, just time-consuming. The cargo was mechanically moved into contact with the auger. The auger didn't have to be very long, just long enough to push the material into a tube where it floated to a cargo holding compartment on the station.

The Station Expansion had a newer system, where after connecting to the ship, the gravity would be switched on at low levels, and the bulk material would flow naturally from ship to station. There was another system on the new section that works particularly good for low-mass bulk cargo like food grains. A vacuum was applied to the receiving compartment and the compartment that needed to be emptied was pressurized. Then a valve was opened between the two, allowing the grain to flow. Sometimes the procedure had to be repeated several times to get everything, but there was very little equipment to wear out.

Satisfied that everything was progressing smoothly, Phil turned to leave and came face-to-face with the *William Burnside*'s captain, Yuri Andropov.

Yuri was smiling. "Phillip! How is my good friend?"

Phil smiled back. Yuri was always good for a laugh. "Not terrible. Are you still putting the hurt on the vodka as usual?"

Yuri looked hurt. "Is not nice to stereotype people like that. Just because I'm from St. Petersburg doesn't mean I drink too much vodka."

Phil frowned. "No?"

Yuri straightened up. "Well, this time is true. But is still not nice."

Yuri put his hand on Phil's shoulder. "Are you too important to have lunch with humble freighter captain?"

Phil shrugged. "I guess I can eat with folks below my station."

As they turned toward the connector tunnel, a flock of kortlax raced past. Phil called out to the pursuing pretars. "Hang, tough guys." Yuri quipped, "Usually, one has to wait until after dinner for a show." Yuri had a puzzled look on his face. "How is it that the pretars can enter the secure areas of the CargoMods without slowing down, and the rest of us have to pass through customs?"

Phil shrugged. "They have personnel passes, as long as they're engaged in the station upgrade. It's not fair to say it doesn't slow them down. They have to enter single file, so it gives the kortlax time to catch their breath."

They were about to leave the CargoMod when the intercom paged Phil. He picked up a handset from a com station on the bulkhead and punched a code into the keypad that allowed him to take the call. "Ross here."

The caller identified himself. "Luke Smith, sir. Could you please come down to CargoMod 2 customs desk?"

"Sure. What's up?" Phil asked slightly annoyed.

Luke hesitated. "We have some gentlemen from Flast you need to talk to." Phil frowned. "Flast?"

"Yes, sir. They're after some fugitives," Luke confirmed.

Yuri couldn't hear half of the conversation, but the mention of Flast got his attention.

Phil noted Yuri's reaction and Luke's tone. "Okay, Luke, give me ten minutes." Phil looked at Yuri. "This shouldn't take long. Let's see if we can get a good table before I see the gentlemen."

As they walked along, Yuri said, "I should tell you something before you see the gentlemen from Flast."

Phil lifted his eyebrows. "Oh?"

Yuri went on, "We passed through Flast space on our last run, as you know. We stopped at one of their inspection stations, as is their custom. Usually, they come aboard and do their best to intimidate us. They bluster about and then let us go."

Phil's interest was increasing. "What happened this time?"

Yuri went on, "They tore the ship apart. Every space and compartment was searched."

Phil didn't like where this was going. "Did they say who they were looking for?"

Yuri shook his head. "No, they just growled a bit and made threatening faces. When they came up empty-handed, they were… well, disappointed is not a strong enough word."

When they reached the CentMod, Yuri said, "I'll meet you at café after you give your guests big sloppy kisses."

Phil crossed the CentMod to the connecting tunnel to CargoMod 2. It was nearly noon, and the station was buzzing with activity. People were rushing about from ships docked at the CargoMods to vendors, dealers, repair shops, and back to their ships. The station eateries were doing a brisk business; so far, a normal day. Cargo was moving on the tram system at the lower level, which Phil could see below him from the connecting tunnel walkway.

*****

## Oasis 4, CargoMod 2, Customs Desk

At the customs desk, Phil was greeted by Luke, who was accompanied by two very sour-looking Flaston Fugitive Trackers. He was in no mood to deal with these guys, as flastons had a well-deserved reputation for being difficult to get along with.

Phil nodded as Luke made the introductions. "Mr. Ross, our friends here are trying to locate and apprehend five of their fellow flaston citizens."

Phil wasn't exactly cordial, but he was polite. "Who are you looking for exactly?"

The ranking flaston, who identified himself as Isnod, said, "That is not your concern."

"It is if you want our cooperation," Phil shot back. "This station belongs to the Stellar Logistics and Freight Corporation. It is governed by the rule of law, recognized by your government, which compels you to comply with our regulations."

Isnod was doing his best to keep his temper in check as he wasn't used to having his authority questioned by a petty functionary. "Then you must recall the section in the agreement between my government and your company about the disposition of flaston fugitives found on your station."

Phil said, "That's why you'll provide us with a list of the fugitives and photos along with descriptions of the fugitives, if available."

Isnod handed over a data chip, which Luke took over to a SICOS terminal. Five folders were indicated: "SICOS; download files to security section; wanted folder; this date." Luke waited a couple of seconds until the Operation Completed symbol came onto the screen. Luke removed the data chip and handed it to Isnod's partner, then asked, "What are they wanted for?"

Isnod frowned. "It's not required by the agreement that we have to reveal that information. But in the interest of cooperation, these people are wanted because they are a destabilizing and disruptive element."

Phil was anxious to end this conversation. "Okay, gentlemen, this is the drill. You may stay at the station until your fugitives are in custody. You will be accompanied by one of the station deputies while engaged in your search. Any weapons will have to stay on your ship, and you must submit to customs if you return to your ship and want to reenter the station."

Isnod looked like he was punched in the face. "Is there another option?"

Phil said, "Sure, get back in your ship and wait until we contact you if your fugitives ever show up."

Isnod thought it over for a few seconds then he said, "We will submit to your customs inspection, but I must protest to the deputy following us about. No one else aboard your station has this requirement. It's insulting."

Phil nodded. "Very well, gentlemen. Please try to behave yourselves while you're here."

Luke spoke up, "After processing, one of my deputies will show you to the hotel."

Isnod shook his head. "We will most likely not need those facilities. We have it on good authority that our targets are arriving later today."

Phil nodded. "Which ship?"

Isnod looked embarrassed and admitted, "We weren't given that information."

After Isnod and his partner disappeared down the passageway, Phil looked at Luke. "Let's see who has the world of Flast shaken to its core." Luke chuckled. "SICOS, open security files entered this date from Flast security." The SICOS display brought up five photos of flastons; they were ordinary-looking. Like all flastons, they could easily be mistaken for humans, except that they had mottled skin.

Luke then observed, "They don't look like desperate, hardened criminals to me." Touching the screen brought up biographies and the list of charges for each individual.

Phil didn't like what he was seeing. He frowned and said, "These folks are being hounded for political reasons. I feel a little funny turning over someone for disagreeing with the jerks in charge."

Luke was just as disgusted at the idea. "We don't have a choice. If these folks show up here, we have to turn them in if we want to maintain a working relationship with Flast. There are three different trade routes through their space. If the relationship between Flast and the company is disrupted, the company would make sure we wouldn't even be able to get a job slinging hash on a mining asteroid for the rest of our lives. Even though a government on Flast that's easier to deal with than the current jerks would be welcome, we can't have anything to do with Flast internal problems."

Phil made his way to the CentMod. He passed the occasional kortlax feather and the unmistakable sign of a struggle. Phil decided to press Dave Jacobson a little harder about helping the pretars round up their kortlax.

*****

## Oasis 4, CentMod, Eva's Café

Arriving at the café in the CentMod, Phil found Dave Jacobson, Ed Carlton, and Yuri Andropov sitting at the same table that they had breakfast at that morning. Phil had a bemused expression and hesitated before sitting, "Don't you guys ever do anything else while you're here?" Dave Jacobson feigned insult. "We did lots of stuff. We have ships to maintain and get ready for making revenue for the Great Intersystems

Logistics Corporation." Phil laughed as he sat.

Eva strolled up with a pad in hand. "Fresh tomatoes from the hydroponics garden in HabMod 3."

Phil nodded. "It's settled, Texas toast BLT, onion rings, and iced tea." Eva noted it on her pad. "Be right up."

The four sat and surveyed the crowd in the CentMod. As if on cue, a group of kortlax raced through the crowd while the pursuing pretars chased them, shouting strategy and encouragement.

"I would really appreciate it if you could help the pretars, Dave," Phil said while pouring iced tea from a pitcher Eva just brought over.

Dave shrugged. "Yeah, fun is fun, but this isn't doing anyone any good. I'll see what I can do. Although it would be better to wait until later this afternoon. Kortlax generally value their freedom more than food, but they reach a point where they'll do anything for food. The more they run, the hungrier they get."

As if it were timed that way, a group of kortlax ran through the café tables. A bright green kortlax snatched the top slice of bread from a plate at the next table as it sped past. The pretars pursuing them seemed not to be disheartened in the least.

Ed smiled. "Next time they run past, turn off your translator. It's a riot."

The food arrived, but everyone couldn't fully enjoy the meal, thinking that they might have to defend their sandwich from a hungry kortlax. Yuri spotted the two uniformed flastons. "Are those two the reason you were late for lunch?"

"Yup," Phil confirmed.

Dave didn't try to hide his disgust. "I really don't like those guys." Phil turned to the table. "Have any of you been to Flast?"

Ed nodded. "I have. I spent a couple of years running cargo out of there."

Phil realized that he didn't know anything about the flastons at all. "The flastons I've met have been real jerks. They can't all be unfriendly, can they?"

Ed shook his head. "They're not. Flast is a closed society. Most of the people are kept ignorant of…everything. The rest are busy keeping it that way. Power on Flast is held to a very small handful of people, and those people work hard to keep the population ignorant, compliant, and under control."

Phil was starting to sort it out. "So what incentive is used to keep those at the top of the heap, interested in abusing their fellow flaston citizens?"

Ed answered, "Those in charge have incredible privileges. Minor lapses in judgment, performance under par, or just someone over you doesn't like the way you look, poof, privilege gone. Major screw-ups don't bear thinking about."

Yuri couldn't help but draw parallels between Flast and parts of Earth history. "So what are chances of people rising up and changing things?" Ed said, "I can't speak to that, but I can tell you there is an underground movement that's been growing for years. Everything is so locked down there. It's next to impossible to organize anything that would threaten the status quo."

Dave leaned in, "If it's so closed down, how do you know so much?" Ed answered, "I supervise the loading of my ship. Sometimes I can corner one of the workers. Your average flaston is actually quite friendly, just too terrified to make trouble for himself."

Yuri added thoughtfully, "A more open Flast would benefit everyone, especially us and the corporations we work for. I don't know if that's ever going to happen, though."

Phil pondered, "If these guys are the type they seem to be, it's a wonder they haven't tried to take territory by force."

Dave answered, "They have. About a hundred years ago, they tried to take a planet away from the pretars who were trying to colonize it." Phil was shocked. "You're kidding me! I knew there was some tension between the two groups, but I never thought there were hostilities between them. What was the outcome?"

Dave smiled. "The pretars beat the daylights out of them. Remember, they have a caste system, and their Warrior class is extremely dedicated and professional."

Ed added, "I've met some flastons who had grandparents that were veterans of that misadventure. From what I gather, the flastons have been a lot more circumspect about being aggressive toward other species. They actually had a view toward invading Earth when we first encountered them."

Phil was surprised by this revelation. "How is it that we've never heard of this?"

Ed said, "It's not information that's generally helpful if it's something that could affect trade, and the flastons aren't really proud of the fact that they scouted us out and decided that one savage beating per century is enough."

Dave added, "The flastons are aggressive, but one look at the state of the various military organizations on Earth was enough to take the turpentine out of their bark. I don't think it sits well with the Flast government that they have anger issues and no one to bully."

Ed was watching the two Flaston Fugitive Trackers study the Arrivals and Departures board. He smiled. "Those two are evidence that the word is getting out on Flast."

Phil asked, "What word is that?"

Ed smiled wider. "Change is coming."

Phil replied, deadpan, "That's three words." Ed snickered. "Caught that, did ya?"

They watched as Isnod's partner pointed at one entry on the arrivals board, and both started toward CargoMod 1.

Phil washed down the last of his onion rings with iced tea. "June Dixon of the *Morning Star* will be arriving from Flast at 1630. She wants to talk to me on a secure frequency. I think I know what the topic is going to be."

Ed said to no one in particular, "If she needs help with anything, I will be glad to help." The other two freighter captains nodded in agreement.

Phil looked at his watch. "If the *Morning Star* is docking at 1630, they'll slow to sub-light speed in about half an hour. I don't want to miss June's call. So on that note, I will take my leave of you, gentlemen." Phil left the café and headed to the elevator platform. Before he could step on the platform, some kortlax ran past, and he reached down to his belt and turned off his auto translator. The pursuing pretars were as usual shouting encouragement and suggestions for cornering the kortlax. Phil was grinning and said under his breath, "Ed was right.

That's probably the funniest thing I've heard this week."

*****

## Oasis 4, CentMod, Operations Center

Reaching the operations center, Phil checked the status boards. Of particular interest was the unscheduled arrivals. Of course, he could check the SICOS in his office, but he got a better feel for what was happening if he could see it laid out on a big screen. Not seeing anything to get his interest, he went to his office. After a few minutes, one of the controllers buzzed Phil's office. "Sir, Capitan Dixon of the *Morning Star* is requesting a word with you on secure channel 23 omega."

Phil depressed the push-to-talk button. "Thanks. I'll take it." He turned to the SICOS display and said, "SICOS, open secure channel 23 omega."

A status bar crawled across the screen, and the SICOS responded, "Channel open."

A very frantic June Dixon appeared on the display. "Phil, thanks so much for talking to me!"

Phil smiled. "No problem, June, so what's so important that couldn't wait until you've docked?"

June was looking more uncomfortable by the second. "We picked up some items from Flast that didn't make it to our Manifest or Bill of Lading," she hesitated, "or passenger list."

Phil thought he would have a little fun at June's expense and hurry things along at the same time. "June, are you transporting five flaston fugitives?"

June turned pale. Phil thought he should put her at ease before she passed out. "Relax, June, I couldn't live with myself if I turned anyone over to the goon squad just for having a contrary opinion."

June looked relieved. "I'm sorry, Phil. I don't want to get anyone into trouble, but I couldn't ignore those people. They were a breath away from a reeducation camp. Things are happening quickly on Flast. The only way that'll happen at all is if folks like this are able to continue to have an effect. I'm not saying that we're obligated to help, but I think it's the right thing to do."

June's expression changed. "How did you know about the fugitives?" Phil explained, "We are currently hosting two Flaston Fugitive Trackers. They must have passed you a while ago. They've been here since about noon, and they suspect that their targets are on a ship headed to the station. I saw them checking the boards for likely vessels to check. But I expect that they're betting on them being on your ship." June still wasn't sure where Phil came down on helping the fugitive flastons, and her voice belied that fact, "Phil, we just can't let the trackers take them back to Flast."

Phil put his hands up. "Relax, June, I'm on board, but I'm a little fuzzy on the end game. What's the plan once you get here?"

June shook her head. "We need to figure out a way to get them on a transport to Pentonos. There are other flastons living there in exile. They'll be safe there.

Pentonos doesn't have an extradition treaty with Flast."

Phil's brow furrowed. "Yuri Andropov said he was actually boarded by flaston trackers looking for these folks. I don't recall Flast ever putting this much effort into catching some dissidents."

June started to get excited. "These aren't your ordinary dissidents. These are the Thomas Payne's, Patrick Henry's, and Oliver Cromwell's of their planet. On Pentonos, they'll be a galvanizing element among the other exiled flastons. There's going to be major changes on Flast, and we're going to be part of it."

Phil liked the idea of being at least a footnote in someone's history book. Until then, they had to tread lightly, and he needed June to be sure she understood that. Phil cautioned, "You know that if word ever got out to our respective bosses, there won't be a position low enough in our respective companies for us. I don't know about you, but I'm getting too old to scrub toilets on a mining asteroid."

He paused for effect. "The other freight captains are willing to help. They only have an idea of what's going on, but no details. None of the station personnel have any inkling of anything going on, except my security marshal. Naturally, the Flaston Fugitive Trackers had to brief him about their intentions. Luke doesn't like the trackers, but he also feels duty-bound to uphold corporate policy. He's kind of a Boy Scout in that way. So anything we do, we won't get to rely on his help. I hate going behind his back like this, but I don't see an alternative."

June sounded a bit relieved. "Any ideas about how to get my guest to Pentonos?"

Phil scratched his head. "Ed Carlton of the *Bright Star* is leaving for Celnar at 1700. If we can get your guests on board, they can relax until they get there. Then they can take a transport to Pentonos. The first trick is to get them from your ship to the *Bright Star* without the trackers seeing them. That won't be easy. They check all incoming ships from likely ports and routes. The second trick is to make sure that my security marshal is kept in the dark about this. Finally, the third trick is to throw the trackers off the scent."

June still looked stressed. "I appreciate all this, Phil. I would never ask anyone to take part in anything like this, but I don't see any alternative."

Phil got up from his seat. "As soon as I figure out how to accomplish all this, I'll give you the details when you get here."

June looked considerably better now. "Thanks, Phil. I'll be waiting."

Phil pondered how he was going to accomplish all this. There wasn't a lot of time to get things set. The *Bright Star* was at CargoMod 4 being loaded. The *Morning Star* was going to dock at the opposite side of the station. Staring out of his window, he was weighing the possibilities. The trackers were sure to be watching at the docking port. There weren't very many ways off a freighter at the dock. Anyone leaving the ship will be seen right away. If he barred the trackers from CargoMod, they would be suspicious, and that would damage the relationship between Flast and Stellar Logistics and Freight Corporation. While Phil worked things out in his head, he watched Will Dawson's maintenance crew working outside the station. That's when an inkling of an idea formed in his mind.

Phil turned around. "SICOS, where is Will Dawson?"

"Mr. Dawson is in CargoMod 3" came the mechanical reply. Phil ordered, "SICOS, page Will Dawson."

Will answered in a few seconds. "Dawson here, Boss."

Phil spoke into the microphone, "Will, where will you be in a few minutes?"

"Right here in CargoMod 3, we're upgrading the docking clamps between ports seven and fourteen," Will answered.

Phil checked his watch. "I need to talk to you about something important. I'll be down there in a couple of minutes."

Phil left his office and boarded the elevator where he stepped off at the plaza level. Before he could get to the connecting tunnel to CargoMod 3, he had to duck into the station hair stylist to avoid a stampede of kortlax.

While waiting for the commotion outside the shop to die down, Phil overheard the stylist, who was from Griska, gush over the lady in her chair. "Oh, I love working with human hair. It's so luxurious! Where did you say you were from on Earth dear?"

The lady in the chair, who wasn't used to being fawned over, replied, "Uh… Detroit."

The stylist brightened more, if that were possible. "Detroit! Oh, I've read all about Detroit. It sounds so exotic. When my husband and I go to Earth, we must make it a point to visit there."

As Phil listened to the exchange, he realized that having six fingers on each hand might give a hair stylist a definite advantage, particularly while braiding. When the last of the kortlax and the pursuing pretars passed, Phil turned to the stylist and her customer, nodded, and said, "Ladies."

*****

## Oasis 4, CargoMod 3

Leaving the salon, he walked to CargoMod 3. Reaching the CargoMod, he looked down and saw what looked like blood and a good number of kortlax feathers. Phil walked to docking port 13, where he found Will supervising the clamp upgrades.

"Hey, Will, could I have a word with you?"

Will left his crew to join Phil. Phil kept his voice low. "Will, I need you to get five PEWS, and make sure they make it to the port air lock on the *Morning Star* as soon as it docks."

A PEWS is a Personal Environment Work Suit—a space suit for the maintenance technicians to use while working on the outside the station.

Will stared at Phil. "Sure, is there anything else?"

Phil looked sheepish. "Well, it would be nice if someone made sure the suits made it to the *Bright Star* once they were filled."

Will was having fun now. "I'm guessing the suit filling is flastons." Phil felt a surge of panic. "How did you know that?"

"It's kind of hard to miss those two goons pestering every vessel who came anywhere near Flast space," Will said with a shrug.

Phil leaned in. "I can't order you to do this. If the company found out, it would be a career-ender."

Will smiled. "Then I volunteer. Don't worry, Boss. I'll get those folks moved, and they won't set foot on the station. That should provide some deniability."

Phil smiled. "That's what I wanted to hear."

Will looked concerned. "One thing, though, the port air lock of the *Morning Star* will be in full view of the observation windows. The way those two flaston thumpers hang around, they're sure to see everything that happens, and figure out what's going on."

Just then, Phil and Will spotted some kortlax. Will was shaking his head. "It's going to take weeks to round up all those things."

A smile started to form on Phil's face. "I think I know what we can do for a distraction. It's tricky, and the timing has to be just right, but I think it'll work."

Will nodded. "I'll be ready, Boss."

Phil went to prepare for the upcoming events. He had nearly reached the connecting tunnel when Mr. Selak, the pretars supervisor, entered the CargoMod and approached him.

Selak was speaking, but all Phil could hear was gibberish. Then he remembered he had turned off his auto translator. He held up a finger. "One moment please, Mr. Selak." He reached down to his belt and turned on his auto translator. "I'm so sorry, Mr. Selak. I turned it off earlier to avoid eavesdropping on a group of your colleagues."

Selak smiled. "Oh, Mr. Ross, you always show such kindness and discretion. I have enjoyed working with you so much."

Phil didn't have the heart to tell Selak that he had actually tuned it off for a laugh. He asked, "What can I do for you, Mr. Selak?"

Selak hesitated. "Mr. Ross, I'm afraid I have quite a problem. I thought I could handle it, but it's now quite obvious that I cannot bring this dilemma to a conclusion. Oh my, oh dear. I'm afraid that it may interfere with the joining of the new Station Expansion. Oh dear, dear, dear."

Phil didn't like what he was hearing. Phil wondered what else could happen today. "What could possibly be that bad, Mr. Selak?"

Selak's lower lip trembled; he would rather do anything else than admit he had a problem that threatened to throw off his construction schedule and put a blemish on his professional record. Finally, he took a breath. "It's the kortlax, sir. We won't be able to capture all of them before the new Station Expansion can get here. Oh dear, dear, dear. The technicians I need to integrate the two sections are quite busy chasing kortlax through the station. Oh my, my, my."

Phil was about to reassure Selak when he spotted one of the pretar technicians. He had a shop rag stuffed into one nostril, presumably to stop the blood flow. He also had a blue kortlax he had captured, in tow, on a rope. At the same moment, the fugitive trackers came around the corner. The kortlax began to snap at the flastons, his beak clicking loudly and menacingly. The trackers recoiled and were immediately ready to do battle with the agitated animal. The pretar technician managed to pull the kortlax away from the flastons.

As they strode past Phil and Selak, Isnod's partner growled, "I hate those things."

When the trackers disappeared into the passageway to the CentMod, Selak said, "I don't know why, but kortlax will attack flastons with no provocation."

The pretar technician approached Phil and Selak, obviously pleased with himself for capturing a kortlax. "Selak, Mr. Ross, I've been working the numbers in my head, and I don't see how we could possibly capture all the kortlax loose on the station before we're ready to leave, let alone by the time the new section arrives."

Selak was near panic. Phil couldn't let Selak suffer any longer. "Mr. Selak and I were discussing that very thing. I was about to discuss a plan to get the kortlax rounded up in the next couple of hours."

The technician looked doubtful. In the meantime, the kortlax was chewing the rope with his beak. Selak placed a hand on the technician's shoulder, or at least where most species keep shoulders. "Tonkin, we will get the plans for capturing the kortlax to the rest of you as soon as Mr. Ross and I have finalized them."

As the exchange between Selak and Tonkin went on for a few more minutes, the kortlax managed to sever the rope and started to wander away. Phil couldn't stand it any longer. "Mr. Tonkin."

Tonkin turned to Phil. "Yes, Mr. Ross?"

"Your kortlax is getting away," Phil replied, very deadpan.

Tonkin continued to stare at Phil. Obviously, it wasn't registering what Phil told him. Finally, he looked down at his rope and saw it no longer constrained a kortlax. Frantically looking around, he spotted the kortlax a few feet away and let out a pained wail of frustration. Tonkin bolted after the kortlax that let out its own loud squawk, and both went streaking toward the CentMod.

Phil turned to Selak and asked, "Do all kortlax react that way to flastons?"

Selak replied, "Oh yes, I don't know why, but they're all very aggressive toward flastons."

Phil smiled. "Mr. Selak, I'll have Captain Jacobson get with you to work out a strategy to capture all of kortlax. Apparently, he has some experience with them. I believe he transported them here in the first place."

Selak was visibly relieved. "Oh, Mr. Ross, I cannot thank you enough. You have been very patient with us in this matter. If I had known it was going to be this hard to capture the kortlax, I would never have let them…"

Phil raised his eyebrows. "Never would have let them…what, Mr. Selak?"

Selak was caught, and he knew it, "Oh dear, oh dear, oh my. You must understand, Mr. Ross, my technicians finished their preparations early. They were starting to get restless. I needed to occupy their time. I thought it would be a good way to get them some exercise, so I let a few kortlax loose, but I overestimated their ability to capture the animals." "How many are a few?" Phil wanted to know. Selak was defeated.

"About a hundred and fifty."

Phil's eyes widened. "We had better get to it before they start nesting in the CargoMods."

Selak smiled. "This is most kind of you, Mr. Ross."

While they were talking, a cargo handler walked to a nearby workstation, where he started entering data from the last load of cargo he handled. While he worked, he switched on some music. He bobbed his head in rhythm to the music while he worked. The song was a popular tune on Earth at the time.

Selak was immediately intrigued. "I've heard this before, we have nothing like it. Pretna has other art forms of course but using sound to produce an emotional response has never occurred to us. It's most enjoyable."

Phil smiled. "Mr. Selak." Selak turned to Phil. Phil finished. "Concentrate."

Selak straightened up. "Yes, of course. I will be anxiously awaiting word from Captain Jacobson." He then ambled off.

Phil walked to the workstation. "SICOS, locate Captain Jacobsen." SICOS replied, "Captain Jacobson is aboard the *Atlantis Star*."

Phil turned to the access tunnel to the CentMod. Once there, he made his way to the CargoMod 2 access tunnel. On his way, he tried to work out the timing of the events to come for maximum impact. Reaching the CargoMod, he waved his pass at the customs desk giving him access to the CargoMod and any ship docked there.

*****

## Oasis 4, CargoMod 2

On his way to the *Atlantis Star*, he passed the fugitive trackers. "Any luck, fellas?"

Isnod frowned. "No, Mr. Ross, but there are additional ships to check that could be carrying the criminals."

Phil hesitated. "What are you doing here? There are no ships docking here for some time."

Isnod looked uncomfortable. "We returned for a meal on our ship."

Phil's brow furrowed. "Why didn't you just eat at one of the eateries on the station?"

Isnod shook his head. "We would rather eat food that was accustomed to."

Phil thought it was more likely that they were too cheap to spring for a decent meal, and they would rather eat the rations on their ship. Phil looked around and said, "Wait a second. Your ship is at docking port 28. What are you doing hanging around the access tunnel?"

Isnod now looked embarrassed. "There were a group of those animals near the entrance. I don't know why, but they seem to have a special hatred for flastons."

Phil nodded. "Yeah, I've noticed. Well, they're gone now. Just to reassure you, I'm on my way to enlist the help of an expert to recapture the kortlax."

Isnod grunted, "Good, it can't be too soon for us."

At that moment, Luke Smith entered the CargoMod. On spotting the trackers, he called, "Gentlemen! I've been checking, and I've identified some ships that are arriving over the next hour or so that have been to Flast space recently." That got the tracker's attention, and they followed Luke out of the CargoMod.

Phil continued to the docking port that held the *Atlantis Star*. Even though they were in the secure or bonded area, each ship that wasn't sealed had a crewman assigned to prevent unwanted visitors on the ship. The crewman at the *Atlantis Star*'s air lock desk looked up. "Hey, Mr. Ross. Here to see the captain?"

Phil smiled. "Yup, do me a favor and page him."

The crewman reached out and punched a code into the keypad that controlled the intercom. "Sir, Mr. Ross is here to see you."

A familiar voice came over the intercom. "Send him up, Marty."

The crewman switched off the intercom and said to Phil, "He's in his cabin, just off the bridge, sir."

Phil smiled. "Thanks."

The layout of cargo ships was kept very basic, and each ship was made to a standard pattern although there were usually subtle differences, especially as the ships were modified and repaired over time. Still, once someone was familiar with one, they could get around any of them. The bridge is located at the front of the topmost of the five decks in the forward section. Most of the space here is dedicated to crew and passenger accommodations. The largest section is in the middle section, which is dedicated to cargo. There is a passageway that extends from the forward section through the cargo section to the drive section. On each side of the passageway, there are two spacious bays for palletized cargo. Or they can be sealed and used to carry bulk material. On each side of the cargo section, containers can be attached. Once filled, they're sealed, and tugs are used to attach them.

The air lock entrance is located on deck 3. Phil strode to the end of the passageway where he stepped onto a platform lift. Locking the safety bar in place, he depressed the button for the first deck. At deck 1, he walked toward the bridge but stopped short at a door that was left ajar. He tapped the frame and pushed the door open a little further. Dave Jacobson looked up. "Come on in, Phil. What can I do for you?" "Kortlax," Phil said flatly. "You said you could round them up.

How does` that work exactly?" he asked while sitting down.

Dave leaned back in his chair. "If you know what you're doing, they come running."

Phil looked dubious. "All of them? All the kortlax that are running loose on the station. All at once?"

Dave was grinning. "Yep, they have excellent hearing, and they'll be getting good and hungry. If you call them in the same fashion they've been called to supper their whole lives, they'll come running. They can't help it."

Phil smiled. "That's good information."

Dave said in an "as a matter-of-fact" fashion, "You need a distraction."

Phil nodded, relieved that he didn't have to ask out loud. "I need a distraction."

"When the *Morning Star* arrives, five passengers need to switch ships without those two catching on," Phil said, pointing out a viewport, where they could see the trackers through the CargoMod viewport.

"I don't get it. The connecting tunnels are narrow. They have to pass each other, no matter how many kortlax are there. Unless…they're not going to be inside the station," Dave said, catching on.

Phil thought for a second. "I can make sure that the trackers are not in CargoMod 2 when the *Morning Star* arrives. But they won't want to stay away for long, so you'll have to make it unpleasant to head down the access tunnel to CargoMod 2."

Dave could hardly contain his enthusiasm. "I know what I need to do, and the timing couldn't be easier."

Dave thought for a minute. "I'll get with Selak right now and have him round up a couple of his boys and some netting. Also, I'll need to enlist the help of some of Will Dawson's maintenance guys."

Phil got up from his seat. "You got 'em."

As Dave was rising, Phil turned to him. "You've got a music collection, don't you?"

Dave wondered what Phil was getting at "Sure do. Nothing newer than fifty years old. It goes back to the earliest recordings. I even have holographic recreations of concerts. Mostly rock and roll."

Holographic recreations were computer-generated performances. A song is loaded into a computer; for instance, a song by the Beatles. The computer will generate a holographic performance based on the song itself and archive imagery of the performers. The process is easier if there are video recordings of the performers. The net result is that an entire concert by John, Paul, George, and Ringo can be enjoyed, even if it never actually took place.

Phil shrugged. "Well, I thought it would be nice if the pretars were given a copy for the tremendous job they've been doing. Mr. Selak was admiring one of the station worker's music earlier."

Dave inserted a data chip into a port in the ship's computer system. "Consider it done."

After the program for Selak was downloaded, both men left the *Atlantis Star* and walked through the CargoMod through the access tunnel to the CentMod. Before they parted company, Phil stopped Dave. "I hate to say this, but my security marshal should be kept in the dark about all this. He's not happy about helping the flastons track down these folks, but he's also a company man, and he'll follow company policy to the letter, so I may need to run interference there."

Dave nodded. "No problems."

*****

## Oasis 4, CentMod, Operations Center

Dave went off to find Selak, and Phil took the lift to the operations center. Once there, he went to his office to contact Will Dawson to have him assign someone to Dave and Selak. With that done, he punched a code into the intercom. "Virginia, have you got a second?"

Virginia answered, "Be right there, Boss."

When she entered the office, Phil motioned to a chair. As she sat, he asked, "Do we have any minor ships arriving that have been to Flast space recently?"

Virginia consulted her pad, "Yes, sir, the *Klag*. It's scheduled to arrive at 1600. It's a 125-passenger tour ship. It stopped at Flast…not the last stop but the one before."

Phil frowned. "When did it leave Flast?"

Virginia tapped the screen to retrieve the information. "Wow! They left Flast after the *Morning Star* did, went to Temparna, and now they're going to beat them here by a half hour. That thing is a hot rod."

Phil said, "Perfect. Make sure that our friends from Flast know about this.

What CargoMod are you putting them on?" Virginia glanced at her pad. "CargoMod 3."

Phil nodded. "Good. Thanks, Virginia, and do me a favor and tell Luke about the *Klag*."

She smiled and said as she spun around to leave. "No problem, Boss." Phil also left the office and went to the control center. Using the monitors, he inspected the Station Expansion that was now nearly directly underneath. Pretar tugs were expertly maneuvering the section into position for joining with the existing station. He checked the time, then looked down at CargoMod 3. The *Klag* was maneuvering into position for docking. A quick check of the area plot showed the position of the *Morning Star*, and it was plain to see that it was going to dock on time.

*****

## Oasis 4, CentMod, Plaza Level

Phil left the control center, boarded the elevator, and rode it to the plaza level. There, he spotted Dave Jacobson busy explaining to a group of pretars and Will Dawson's technicians the sequence of events. The pretars in this group were the cooks who normally took care of the kortlax on the station. They had to be trained to do this since the pretars that deal with kortlax on Pretna couldn't be talked into venturing into space.

Phil got Dave's attention. Dave walked over, and Phil asked, "Did our two intrepid trackers go to CargoMod 3?"

Dave nodded. "About two minutes ago."

Phil smiled. "I'll be in CargoMod 2. You have an idea of the timing I take it?" Dave nodded. "Yup, this will be fun."

*****

## Oasis 4, CargoMod 2

Phil made his way to CargoMod 2. On the way, he thought about what Dave said about it being fun. He thought to himself, *I hope this is something I can look back on this and remember as fun.*

Using his identification, Phil passed into CargoMod 2 and went directly to an empty workstation. He punched the intercom code for Will Dawson. Will answered, "What's up, Boss?"

Phil asked, "Are we on schedule?"

You could almost hear the grin on Will's face. "You bet, Boss. I'm on a maintenance tug, transitioning from CargoMod 3 to CargoMod 2 now."

Phil was relieved to see that things were going to plan so far and asked, "Do you have any extra PEWS?"

Will answered, "Yes, I do. I happen to have five with me, and I hope I get a chance to use them."

Phil acknowledged, "We'll see what we can do."

The *Morning Star* was alongside now and inching toward the docking clamps. At that moment, Luke Smith strolled up. "Hey, Boss, have you seen the gentlemen from Flast?"

Phil felt a wave of panic run through him. "Hey, Luke. I saw them heading toward CargoMod 3, I imagine that they didn't want to miss an opportunity to pester the passengers of the *Klag*."

Luke thought a second and said, "Well, a couple of my deputies are there if they find their fugitives. I think I'll go to the CentMod and watch Captain Jacobson catch the kortlax."

Phil grinned. "I think I'll go to, but I have to have a private word with Captain Dixon first. You go ahead. I'll be along in a few minutes."

"See ya there," Luke said while turning to leave.

After Luke left, Phil could finally take a breath. He turned to the viewport and watched as the *Morning Star* inched toward the docking clamps. Since the *Morning Star* had containers attached to the outside the ship as well as internal palletized cargo, it had to be off-loaded in two stages. The ship was docked nosed into the station. Once secure, station workers connected power and communications lines to the ship, as well as a service connection for potable water, and one for wastewater to the station recycling system. After that, an air lock gangway is extended to the personnel hatch to allow crew and passengers to leave the ship.

This is a lengthy process to do correctly, and safety checks had to be carried out. The gangway takes about twenty minutes to a half hour to put in place. The tugs started removing containers from the ship and taking them to the proper CargoMod. Once the containers were removed, larger air lock gangways were extended to offload the palletized cargo. Phil looked up at the video cameras that were recording all movement on and off the *Morning Star*.

A red LED indicator showed that the system was operating, and all data recorded was stored in the SICOS security files. That's one of the reasons they couldn't simply distract the trackers and move the fugitives from ship to ship through the station. The flaston trackers would insist on seeing the data files on any ship they couldn't be there personally to watch the passengers leave. Also, it was impossible to secret them in a cargo container because there was no access to them from the ship. Each piece of palletized material was inspected as it left the ship as well. Phil walked to a work terminal and punched a code into the keypad.

June Dixon appeared on the display. "Phil! I'm sure glad to see you. Do you have any idea how to get these folks on their way?"

"Working on it," Phil said. "Open your port air lock to space. One of my guys will put five PEWS in there. Once your guests are in them, my guy will take them to their next ship."

June looked as if she had a thousand objections. "Phil, the port air lock is in full view of the station viewport, and the fugitive trackers will be sure to be there."

Phil put up his hand. "We're working on a solution to that. They'll be busy with other things when the transfer happens."

June wasn't reassured. "I hope you're right, Phil."

"Don't sweat it, June. They'll be way too busy doing other things to stare out the window," Phil said.

June nodded. "Okay, Phil, I'll be ready. *Morning Star* out."

*****

## Oasis 4, CargoMod 3

Phil powered down the workstation and made his way through the CentMod, then walked the perimeter walkway to the CargoMod 3 access tunnel.

Entering the CargoMod, he went to the *Klag*'s docking port where he spotted Luke Smith keeping an eye on the two fugitive trackers. Phil eased up next to him and said, "I thought you were going to be at the CentMod to witness the great kortlax round-up?"

Luke nodded. "I was, but they're not quite ready, so I thought I should keep an eye on our two flaston friends to make sure they don't make nuisances of themselves."

"How have they behaved so far?" Phil asked.

Luke reassured Phil, "So far, they haven't pestered anyone yet. But they have scrutinized their fellow flaston citizens pretty carefully."

Phil was a bit surprised. "Flastons who are allowed to travel. That's rare."

Luke agreed. "They're on some kind of merit vacation. They probably oppressed more than their quota."

"How many passengers deboarded?" Phil asked."

Luke shrugged. "About seventy-five so far. It should take about ten or fifteen minutes for the rest of them."

Phil turned. "Let's go to the CentMod."

*****

## Oasis 4, Maintenance Tug

Will Dawson was piloting a maintenance tug with five PEWS tied to the back. Reaching the *Morning Star* air lock, he turned the tug around and backed to the open hatch. Once there, he set the thrusters to "Station Keeping," which kept the tug pressed tight to the ship. He unbelted himself from his seat, went to the tug platform where he untied the PEWS, and put them in the *Morning Star* air lock. Will stood on the tug platform while a *Morning Star* crewman closed the outer air lock hatch.

*****

## Oasis 4, CentMod, Plaza Level

Phil and Luke reached the CentMod and then made their way to the area that Dave Jacobson had selected to catch the kortlax. He was accompanied by one of Will Dawson's maintenance technicians and about twenty-five pretar cooks. They had the floor marked in white tape in a large square that measures about fifty feet on each side. The maintenance technician had a portable gravity controller plugged into a receptacle in the floor. The pretars had a mesh net laid out along one side of the square.

Dave approached Phil. "I think we're about ready. What's the timing on this thing?"

Phil made sure that Luke was interested in the preparations sufficiently enough so as not to overhear them. Satisfied that he didn't think Luke could hear him, he answered, "I'd say we wait till our friends get about halfway down the CargoMod 2 access tunnel."

Dave was trying, and failing, to contain his laughter. "That's just mean."

*****

## Oasis 4, *Morning Star* Port Air Lock

In the port air lock on the *Morning Star*, five flaston fugitives were getting into the PEWS. They weren't happy about having to go on a space walk, but the situation was explained to them, and they accepted the fact that it was necessary if they didn't want trouble with the trackers. A *Morning Star* crewman was assisting them with their PEWS, checking seals and setting the environmental controls.

*****

## Oasis 4, CentMod, Plaza Level

Phil and Dave watched as the trackers exited the access tunnel from CargoMod 3, cross the CentMod, and enter the tunnel to CargoMod 2. Phil waited until he thought that they were about halfway there. "I think that should about do it."

Dave picked up a can of what looked like chicken feed. "This is very similar to cracked corn."

He put a little in the can and gave it a good shaking while calling. *Knack, knack, knack, knack.*

All at once, there was a chorus of excited squawking from every corner of the station. Dave gave the can another shake. *Knack, knack, knack, knack.*

Then Dave started to spread the feed on the floor where it was marked out. Some of the pretar cooks did the same. In a moment, the sound of running kortlax feet heading toward the CentMod could be heard. Suddenly, a pair of pained screams came from CargoMod 2's access tunnel. There was a growing din of excited squawking kortlax stampeding toward the CentMod. It was loud, but it wasn't loud enough to drown out the desperate pleas for relief coming from the fugitive trackers who had kortlax swarming around them.

Suddenly, kortlax burst out of every access tunnel into the CentMod. Among them were the two trackers looking for something to climb up on to get away from the kortlax who snapped at them as they passed. Dave continued to spread feed on the floor. *Knack, knack, knack, knack!*"

*****

## Oasis 4, Maintenance Tug, Outside the *Morning Star* Air Lock

The outer air lock hatch on the *Morning Star* opened, and Will Dawson lead each fugitive, dressed in a PEWS, to the tug platform. He made sure that each was securely tethered to the handrail erected in the center of the platform. This type of tug was often used to transport technicians to areas outside the station that was in need of repair or servicing. Anyone looking out the viewport would just see a maintenance crew—nothing special there. When the fugitives were secure, Will remounted the pilot's seat and started to make his way to the *Bright Star*.

*****

## Oasis 4, CentMod, Plaza Level

The kortlax were coming in from every angle and side to the square that Dave Jacobson had laid out, and he was continuing to toss feed into. Dozens of kortlax were enthusiastically pecking away at the feed. Dave waited until all the kortlax were in the square and there was no more heading in. At that point, he nodded to the station maintenance technician. The technician toggled some switches on the control pad that was plugged into the station floor. The kortlax began to float above the floor. The animals panicked at first and began to squawk louder.

Then they realized that the feed was floating with them, and they began to snap away at it.

Dave directed the pretars to float the net above the kortlax. Then the excess netting was pulled under the kortlax, and the edges tied together forming a giant netting bag. The pretars pulled the net away from the square section that had its gravity turned off. As that happened, the kortlax-filled net gently fell to the floor. That done, the pretars pulled the whole thing to CargoMod 4 where the kortlax pen is installed.

Phil looked around and saw that the fugitive trackers had gathered their wits, and they were starting to make their way back to CargoMod 2. Phil thought he should meet them there in case he needed to run interference. To Phil's annoyance, Luke Smith decided to accompany him.

*****

## Oasis 4, CargoMod 2

When they reached the *Morning Star*, Phil was relieved to see that there was no activity at the port air lock. The fugitive trackers were going over the security video at the docking port, and an annoyed Isnod ordered, "Scrutinize everyone that left that vessel, Feldon!"

A rather-shaken Feldon nodded. "Yes, of course, Isnod!"

Luke spoke up before Phil could say anything, "Mr. Isnod, I have something you should see."

Phil was now in full panic mode. They had come too close to getting the fugitives to safety just to have it collapse in on itself by his efficient and well- meaning security marshal.

Luke went to the workstation. "SICOS, open security files twelve alpha." The display brought up five photos of humans boarding a vessel at the station. Now Phil was thoroughly confused. Luke continued, "I was going over video security files, hoping to spot your runaways when I discovered this."

The two Flast officers looked as confused as Phil. Luke continued, "These five boarded the *Shenandoah* before its 1630 departure."

Isnod was very confused. "I don't understand why I should be interested in these people."

"Look at them carefully," Luke urged.

The images showed what appeared to be five humans, three men, and two women. Isnod studied the images carefully and blurted out, "Feldon! They've changed their appearance!"

Feldon's mottled skin paled. "What kind of ship is the *Shenandoah?*"

Luke answered, "It's a three-hundred-passenger cruise ship. They're bound for Earth."

Isnod turned to Phil and Luke. "Thank you, gentlemen." They turned and ran to the docking port occupied by their ship.

When the trackers had gone out of ear shot, Phil slowly turned to Luke who was grinning ear to ear. "You didn't really expect me to turn those people over to those two goons, did you?" Luke said with a grin. Phil was starting to catch up to the fact that Luke, probably, or most likely, knew Phil was going to try to sneak the flastons by the trackers. "Well, it had occurred to me. The truth is, I didn't want to put you in a position that would make you compromise your principles. I also thought that if things went south, the fewer the people in on this, the fewer the careers that would be ended."

Luke shook his head. "I wouldn't worry at all about that. There's plausible deniability all around on this. The most they could get angry about is we had knowledge of the whereabouts of the flastons, that we didn't pass on to the trackers."

Phil said, "I'm afraid I've been a little more involved than that. I made it possible for them to get from one ship to the other. I even managed to make sure the kortlax stampede happened at the right moment."

Luke was laughing. "I've got to hand it to you. That was brilliant."

Phil smiled. "Well, I was inspired, but we should be very careful about making our part in this public knowledge?"

"Well," Luke mused, "unless I miss my guess, the fugitives left the *Morning Star* before the docking procedure was completed. The ship may have been touching the dock, but there were tasks to be completed before anyone could leave the ship through an air lock. Until then, we're not responsible for passengers leaving the *Morning Star* before the air lock to the station is opened. As you know, what happens before docking is completed is not the responsibility of the station personnel." June Dixon probably didn't know she was transporting fugitives until she was underway. So she didn't knowingly break any laws. As far as the shipping company is concerned, there haven't been any agreements broken with Flast."

Phil was feeling relieved. "I was wondering where you got five flastons to put on makeup to pass as humans, then I recognized one of the ladies. She was in the hair salon earlier today. She's from Detroit." Luke explained, "I just picked five humans that loosely fit the descriptions. I knew the trackers would see what they wanted to see. I hope Isnod and his partner don't catch up to her before Detroit."

Both men parted company as they both still had tasks to do. Phil went to the CentMod and rode the elevator platform to the operations center. Once there, he climbed the stairs to the Control Center.

*****

## Oasis 4, CentMod, Operations Center

The operations center was more crowded than usual for this time of day. Among the controllers were Will Dawson and Selak, each with communications headsets, and were communicating with the pretar tugs positioning the station expansion. The expansion section was only a few feet from joining the original station. The new section had an extension at the top of the CentMod where the operations center is located on the existing station. This is to ensure that there was enough room for ship operations between levels.

The pretar tug pilots were doing an exceptional job positioning the Station Expansion. Phil overheard one of the controllers. "*Bright Star*, release docking clamps and thrust aft."

The fact that normal operations could carry on while two enormous space station sections were being joined was a true testament to the skills of everyone involved. Another controller keyed his microphone. "*Flast Security 127*, release docking clamps and thrust port."

The first controller said, "*Bright Star*, pivot port ninety-two degrees and pitch down fifteen degrees, thrust forward."

The second controller said, "*Flast Security 127*, pitch up thirty-five degrees and thrust forward."

In the meantime, Will and Selak were both very busy coordinating the station movement. The first controller said, "*Bright Star*, you are clear of the station and are free to navigate."

The second controller said, "*Flast Security 127*, you are clear of the station and are free to navigate."

Selak keyed his microphone. "All tugs stop thrusting. Let the inertia do its job." Phil heard the telltale sound of metal scraping through the station structure, then a thud.

Will Dawson keyed his microphone. "Connection crew go." Station and pretar technicians descended on the connection junction and started sealing and bolting the two halves together. After a few minutes, the connection was made permanent.

Selak and Will congratulated each other, then turned to Phil. A smiling Selak said, "Mr. Ross, I am pleased to report that the new section is attached. Tomorrow morning, my technicians will begin the task of bringing its systems online and integrating with the current systems then testing."

Phil bowed to Selak. "Mr. Selak, you and your people have done a tremendous job. By the way, did you get a data chip from Captain Jacobson?"

Selak smiled. "Indeed, Captain Jacobson gave it to me earlier. I have reserved the station theater after dinner for some entertainment."

Phil put his hand on Selak's shoulder. "You guys deserve it after the day you've had. I may drop in myself, if you don't mind."

Selak beamed. "Oh, of course, sir. It would be a great pleasure."

*****

## Oasis 4, CentMod, Eva's Café

Phil, Selak, and Will rode the platform lift to the plaza level. Once there, Selak went to HabMod 4 to eat with his own people. Phil and Will decided to eat in the café where they joined Dave Jacobson, June Dixon, Yuri Andropov, and Luke Smith. The six of them sat, ate, and congratulated themselves on a successful series of events.

While having their coffee, Phil asked Yuri, "What part did you play in all this?"

Yuri grinned. "Did you happen to notice that there were more kortlax running out of CargoMod 2 than the others?"

Phil stared at Yuri. "How?"

Yuri went on, "Captain Jacobson showed me how. The trick was getting just some of the feathery beasts and not all of them."

Phil gave Yuri a thoughtful nod. "Glad you could pitch in."

Yuri laughed. "It was worth it to see those two flaston security idiots scream like scared children."

For a time, they sat and laughed about the events of the day. It had been a very long day with the Station Expansion, kortlax, and flastons. One by one, they took their leave and retired to their quarters or ships as the case may be until it was just Phil and Dave at the table. Phil said, "Selak reserved the station theater to watch a concert. Let's go see what selection they decided to take in."

As they strolled to the theater, Dave said, "I suggested something from the mid to late twentieth century."

Phil mused, "Mr. Selak told me that pretna has art. I wonder why they never stumbled on pleasing sounds?"

Dave shook his head as they walked. "The more I get to know the pretars, the more I like them. Yes, they do have art, but their real talents lie in engineering. They can take the complicated and make it simple and turn clunky into something elegant. I'm sure you knew that since they got the contract to expand the station."

*****

## Oasis 4, CentMod, Maintenance Theater

They reached the theater and went inside. They passed through the lobby and through the doors into the darkened auditorium. As they waited for their eyes to adjust, Phil watched the show. On stage was a band he understood to be popular in the late twentieth century into the twenty-first century.

Phil noticed the pretars had removed their auto translators or just turned them off. He understood immediately that the translator wouldn't do the music justice because many words didn't translate directly. They made up for this by putting pretar subtitles at the feet of the musicians. This was actually mostly unnecessary, as most pretars understood English extremely well. They couldn't speak it very well at all because they weren't used to forming the sounds with their mouths. Phil consulted a program prepared by Selak. On stage at the moment was a holographic performance by Bryan Adams. He was singing "Everything I Do, I Do It for You."

Phil looked around and saw that the seats were nearly all full of pretars. A closer look, and he saw they were completely rapt with the performance. Most were busy wiping tears out of their eyes and looked as if they were going to bust out bawling any second.

Phil quickly read through the program. He whispered to Dave, "For Pete's sake, I hope you told them to get used to music before they tried listening to Country and Western."

Dave consulted his program and sighed relief. "I don't see any on tap for tonight, but I'll have a talk with Selak tomorrow." They found seats and watched the rest of the show, which they enjoyed a great deal, and the pretars were visibly moved emotionally by the experience.

*****

## Oasis 4, Quarters of Phillip Ross, Station Manager

Phil and Dave left the theater after the performance, then went their separate ways. Dave to his ship, and Phil to HabMod 1 and his quarters. Upon entering his quarters, he was lifted off his feet and pinned to the ceiling. "SICOS, what is the gravity setting?"

SICOS replied, "Negative point three."

Phil relaxed. "Well, it could be worse, I guess."

The End

# SELAK'S PROBLEM

**Oasis 4, Trading Center Space Station Owned by the Stellar Logistics and Freight Corporation**

0600 came around again, and as always, the SICOS chimed, "Are you awake, Mr. Ross?"

Phil poked his head out from under the covers. "I'm up! I'm up!"

He cautiously pulled off the covers and sat upright on the edge of the bed. Despite the new gravity controllers and the assurances of his maintenance supervisor, there has been a continuance of the glitches in gravity. It was different from the previous problems with the system. Previously, the gravity would decrease over time and would even go to a negative value if not monitored frequently, but lately, it would switch off altogether suddenly without warning.

Phil's morning routine was progressing normally. He had been to the gym where he did some weight training. The lap pools were still waterless, which was a source of genuine annoyance at this point, as he really wanted to add swimming to his physical activity. After finishing his exercise, he went back to his quarters where he showered and dressed. Leaving his quarters, he said over his shoulder, "SICOS, secure quarters."

*****

## Oasis 4, CentMod, Eva's Café

The café was becoming the usual routine for Phil although he was sure that would change as soon as his wife arrived. He arrived at his usual table and saw it was occupied by familiar faces. As he strode up to the table, he was greeted by Yuri Andropov, captain of the *William Burnside*, June Dixon, captain of the *Morning Star*, Dave Jacobson, captain of the *Atlantis Star*, and finally Luke Smith, the station security marshal.

Phil smiled. "Luke, you finally decided to take us up on breakfast." Luke smiled back. "Light day so far this morning."

Eva arrived with a fresh pot of coffee. While she was pouring, she asked the table, "How does the special sound today folks?"

The way she asked made Phil suspicious. "What's in it?" Eva was suppressing a grin. "Something Dave worked out."

Phil was now beyond suspicious. "All right, but I reserve the right to change my order if I get grossed out."

The others at the table nodded assent although they were also equally wary of what they agreed to eat with the exception of Dave who was grinning. "Relax, folks, I wouldn't make anyone eat something I knew they wouldn't be able to stomach."

Phil looked across at Dave. "Shouldn't you be on your way to Pretna by now?"

"Hey, it's only been a week since the "Great kortlax hunt," Dave offered defensively.

Then he changed the subject. "The Atlantis Star is nearly loaded, it's serviced, and all I need is passengers."

The group made small talk until Eva and another server returned with trays piled high with their breakfast. Phil stared at it for a minute. "Scrambled eggs, bacon, and toast. Looks pretty standard to me. That's a lot of egg. How many are there?"

"Just one," Eva answered.

"What kind of egg is that?" Phil demanded.

Dave was holding back a genuine belly laugh now. "That would be kortlax."

At that moment, no one knew if they should be repulsed or not.

June looked at her plate. "The bacon isn't normal." "More kortlax," Dave offered, "it's like turkey bacon."

Everyone stared at their plates until Yuri seasoned his and took a bite. He chewed and swallowed while nodding approval, then everyone started eating.

"Leave it to Dave to introduce us to pretar cuisine," Phil said while eying his toast carefully.

Dave saw that Phil was suspicious. "The toast is just toast."

*****

## Oasis 4, CentMod, Operations Center

After breakfast, Phil and Luke Smith took the elevator platform to the operations center, then Phil walked to his office and checked his watch. Only five minutes until the morning briefing, he grabbed a pad from his desk and went out of the door. Three steps from his office, he realized that he had the wrong pad, turned around, and reentered his office. As soon as he was through the door, he was lifted off his feet, and his momentum carried him to the opposite wall near the ceiling where he smashed his head. He roared, "SICOS! What is the gravity level set to?"

The SICOS responded, "Gravity is at zero."

Phil was having a hard time keeping his temper in check. He ordered, "SICOS, increase gravity to Earth Normal over thirty seconds." At that point, objects started falling out of midair, settling more or less where they started. Settling onto the floor himself, Phil felt a lump growing on his head. He stood and walked to the refrigerator, grabbed some ice, and put it in a cloth napkin that he had dampened, then carefully, he put it to the lump. After grabbing the correct pad, he went out the door again.

Walking into the morning briefing, holding the makeshift icepack to his head, Phil poured a cup of coffee, one-handed. He turned and said, "First up." Virginia Wells lifted her pad, expecting to be first as usual, but Phil decided to change the meeting order this morning. "Gravity Generator Controls!"

The station senior medic, Dr. Marie Tillman, realized what must have happened, went to Phil, and examined his head. "Anything I need to be concerned with, Phil?"

Phil shrugged. "Not really. If I was convinced Will could have prevented this, he might need attention."

Will Dawson, the facility's senior maintenance technician, was starting to question every career decision he had ever made. "I don't know what to tell you, Boss. These new controls are things of beauty, except of course the whole switching-off thing. There are no internal design flaws or weaknesses that we've found. There must be some kind of external influence we haven't been able to identify."

Phil liked Will a great deal, but his patience was wearing a bit thin. "Make this your number one priority."

Will nodded. "We're all over it."

Phil brought the meeting back to order. "Operations next, any unusual doings today?"

Virginia consulted her pad. "Nothing I would call unusual. Just normal freight traffic. Oh, there's a thousand-passenger cruise ship docking this afternoon after they gawk at the nebula. They plan on staying docked for three days for shopping and exposure to alien cultures."

Phil nodded. "Security."

Luke Smith consulted his own pad. "No one in jail. There are no security concerns or consequence. I have my deputies running drills."

Phil made a note on his pad. "Next, what's up, Doc?"

Before Marie could say anything, Phil added, "Yeah I know, it never gets old." Marie smiled. "We're done with station personnel exams. Everyone is in acceptable physical condition by the way. Most of our visits are related to sudden losses in gravity."

Phil adjusted the ice pack on his head. "Yeah, I can relate." Then he turned to the pretar in the room. "Mr. Selak, how is the integration of the two sections coming?"

Selak who maintained a dignified professional persona cleared his throat, picked up a pad, then started his report. "The external struts that aid in rigidity are getting their final adjustment, and the fasteners are getting their final torque. The new power plant is operating and powering both station sections. The old power plant is being removed, and the space will be ready for conversion into whatever you deem appropriate. The work is progressing on schedule. Final test and certification will be completed in approximately three to four weeks." Phil raised an eyebrow. "It's not like you to be that imprecise."

Virginia chuckled. "Hanging around humans has had a bad influence on him."

Selak smiled. "There are variables that cannot be precisely calculated, but rest assured, the four-week limit will not be exceeded. In fact, the merchants and other businesses can start moving into their spaces as long as they realize that they cannot open until final certification."

Phil had reason to smile now. "That is good news."

After adjourning the meeting, Phil returned to his office. Before entering, he grasped the door frame and eased into the room a little at a time. First, he put a foot in, then the leg. Next, he put his full weight on the leg and pivoted his bottom half into the room. With weight on both feet, he straightened up and let go of the door frame. He was inside, but he didn't dare trust the gravity controls. Carefully, he walked to his desk and sat. "SICOS, bring up my correspondence." There were only a few files, and among them, he saw one was a video file from his wife. He opened it and directed SICOS to play. As he watched and listened, he realized that he really missed her. On balance, the time away from each other was probably healthy for their relationship although it really didn't need help.

Alice told Phil about the progress she had closing up the house. They had discussed the possibility of selling the house and putting their housewares in storage. That didn't sit well with them since they had gone through a lot of trouble finding the perfect house, and they pictured themselves staying there forever. They decided to use a bonded service that would do the upkeep and keep an eye on the place, as it were. Alice also said she would be arriving in just over four weeks. Phil smiled at that.

The next file he opened was from the company. As he read the file, he couldn't believe what they wanted him to do. They wanted him to go to Pretna on the Atlantis Star to meet with the firm that built the Station Expansion and is currently finalizing the integration. They needed the schedule for payment worked out. The exact payment was agreed upon, but the timetable to remit needed finalizing. Phil was the logical choice since the payment, in the form of consumer goods and raw materials had to pass through his station. This is last minute, but he had his marching orders. The rest of the day was going to be spent making sure things weren't going to fall apart while he was away.

*****

### Oasis 4, CentMod, Eva's Café

After spending the day making sure things were done that had to be done before he went away, Phil went to his usual table at the café. Waiting there was Dave Jacobson, Will Dawson, and Selak.

"Hey, guys. Mr. Selak, I don't recall ever seeing you here."

Selak looked a bit uncomfortable. "I've been meaning to try some cuisine from Earth. I realized that time was running out to do just that."

Will tossed a menu over to Phil. "We've already ordered."

Phil glanced at the menu and put it down as Eva walked up. "The special today, Eva."

Eva made a note on her pad. "Coming up, guys."

Dave took a sip of ice water. "I understand that you're going to be a passenger on my trip to Pretna."

Phil nodded. "That's right. Sorry it's last minute. I hope it didn't put anyone out."

Dave smiled. "Nope, we had one first-class accommodation left. If we didn't, we could have worked something out."

Eva brought their dinners to them on a large tray. Phil's special was roast beef, mashed potatoes, and gravy with green beans. Dave got the hot beef sandwich, which was pretty much the same thing as Phil's, only on bread. Selak eyed his cheeseburger and fries with curiosity while Dave explained to him what condiments went with what. The conversation stayed away from business for most of the meal, which suited everyone.

About the time Selak started his second cheeseburger, he brought up Phil's business trip. "I will certainly miss working with you, Mr. Ross.

You've made this project quite enjoyable. I wish I could accompany you to my home planet. I'm sure you'll be very impressed with our accomplishments."

Phil couldn't help but be grateful for the compliment "I don't think I could think of a better traveling companion and guide than you Mr. Selak. Although Captain Jacobson, I'm sure, can do an adequate job of showing me the sights."

Selak beamed, "I think Captain Jacobson will do a very fine job of being a tour guide."

Dave nodded. "I can show you some things, Pretna has some amazing attractions. By the way Mr. Selak, are your people ready to depart tomorrow?"

Selak smiled. "Of course Captain Jacobson, they are ready to board at the appointed time. Our tools and equipment, including the tugs that moved the Station Expansion Unit, are loaded into containers and attached to the Atlantis Star."

*****

## Oasis 4, Quarters of Phillip Ross, Station Manager

After dinner, Phil retired to his quarters, where he decided to brush up on the protocols and customs of Pretna. Dave and Selak headed to the CentMod auditorium, where Phil suspected that they were in for another concert. When he arrived at his quarters, he stopped short of entering. He searched his pockets and found a data chip, then tossed it into the room. When he saw that it hit the floor solidly, he entered. After researching Pretna customs and packing a duffel bag, he turned in. In the morning, Phil stuck to his morning routine as normal.

Today, he used the stationary bike with a three-dimensional interface. Back at his quarters, he tossed in a towel that floated to the ceiling. "SICOS, increase gravity to Earth Normal over thirty seconds!"

After the thirty seconds elapsed, he entered while grumbling to himself, "I've got to make sure everything is put in a drawer or taped down before I leave."

After showering and dressing, Phil spent some time shoving things in drawers and cabinets. Finally, he grabbed the duffel bag he had packed the previous night, checked his pockets for the proper travel documents, and went out the door. "SICOS, secure quarters."

*****

## Oasis 4, CentMod, Eva's Café

Arriving at the café, Phil was greeted by Yuri Andropov and Dave Jacobson.

As he sat down, he asked, "Hey, guys, how's the coffee this morning?" Both men shrugged. "It's never undrinkable here," Dave offered.

Eva came over with a pot and poured Phil a cup. "Boy oh boy, pour one bad cup, and you hear about it forever."

"Scrambled today, Eva," Phil put in.

Eva walked away, grinning as she made a note on her pad. Yuri and Dave looked at Phil curiously. Phil said, "She accidentally gave me decaf once."

Both men nodded in understanding.

Dave looked at Phil. "We're leaving at 1400 Zulu. Are you all set?" Phil nodded. "Yup, is that ship of yours going to be ready?"

Dave answered, "I hope so. I think your station has infected my ship." Phil was troubled by that. "What do you mean?"

Dave was pouring syrup on the pancakes Eva put in front of him. "I mean, about a week ago, the gravity controls on my ship started flaking out just like your station."

Yuri chimed in. "My ship has same problem. My engineer has been working on problem almost as long as we've been docked. The trouble is, there is nothing wrong with circuits, and it's very intermittent."

Phil frowned. "Maybe we should get your engineers together with Will Dawson. Perhaps if they did some brainstorming, they could get to the bottom of this. In fact, I'll see if Selak can spare one of his engineers. We'll have them meet at 0830 Zulu in the CentMod conference room number one."

Dave and Yuri nodded assent.

The three were finishing their coffees when Phil looked at Dave. "Say, by the way, what kind of concert did you and Selak go to after dinner last night?" Dave smiled. "An assortment of bluegrass and mountain music."

"How did that go over?" Phil asked.

"The pretars loved it," Dave said. "I think we've started something with those folks, introducing them to music. So far, they've been exposed to twentieth- and twenty-first-century rock and roll, blues, classical, and bluegrass. They take to all of it."

Phil laughed. "I wonder how long it'll be before the pretars start making their own music?"

*****

## Oasis 4, CentMod, Operations Center

Phil went to the operations center after breakfast. He entered his office only after checking for gravity, or rather the lack of it, he retrieved his pad and withdrew to the meeting. Pouring a cup of coffee, he began, "Operations."

Virginia read from her pad. "We have a big day coming today. Four freighters arriving, one from Earth, two from Seltus, one from Pentor, and one from Sotos. Do you want names and cargos, Boss?"

Phil thought about it. "Anything unusual?"

Not looking up from her pad, Virginia answered, "Not really." Phil slowly shook his head. "Not necessary."

Virginia continued, "We have one leaving at 1400 Zulu. Rumor has it that's when a party's starting."

Phil was a little slow at that moment, but then he caught up, "Dang, just my rotten luck!"

After everyone had a small laugh, Phil said, "Next up, maintenance." Before Will Dawson could get a word out, Phil continued, "I was talking to Dave Jacobson and Yuri Andropov at breakfast. Both of their ships are experiencing the same gravity problems we are, so I set up a meeting between you and their chief engineers in CentMod conference room number 1 at 0830 Zulu. It's a priority."

Will nodded. "Excellent notion, Boss. I would also like it if one of Mr. Selak's technicians could join us. They have a unique grasp of that system."

Phil said, "I was going to suggest that very thing."

Phil looked over to Selak. "Could you spare anyone for this, Mr. Selak?"

Selak straightened up to answer in his usual dignified way. "Yes, I will send my best technician. I believe you have met Tonkin."

Phil thought a second and recalled the pretar who had managed to capture a kortlax at the expense of his dignity and a shop rag used to stop a nosebleed just to have the animal get away.

Phil acknowledged Selak's contribution. "Very good."

*****

## Oasis 4, CentMod, Conference Room 1

Will Dawson waited in CentMod conference room number 1. The wait wasn't long before the two ship engineers entered. Each was carrying data chips with their respective ship's specifications, which they had plugged into the SICOS terminal and brought up the gravity controls schematics. Will already had the station specifications and schematics on the display.

Tonkin walked in and greeted the other engineers. "Good morning, gentlemen. I see you are well prepared to troubleshoot this vexing problem."

Tonkin didn't come empty-handed. He had a diagnostic test set with him that he set on the table. The SICOS display in this room took up a whole wall and got Tonkin's attention right away.

Will started the meeting. "Thanks for showing up, guys. You may be familiar with the problems that we've had at the station. Before the Station Expansion Unit was installed, we had an issue with the gravity generator controllers. After the Expansion Unit was installed, my technicians replaced the controllers with upgraded models. Our problems were supposed to disappear, but we still have the gravity cutting out intermittently in unpredictable places."

Tim Hughes, the chief engineer of the *Atlantis Star*, frowned. "I can't understand how just docking could affect our systems. The grav controllers started flaking out at precisely the same moment we docked."

Ned Stevens, the chief engineer of the *William Burnside*, nodded in agreement. "Same thing with us. We had no problems until we docked here. The first instance was about an hour after tying into the station systems."

During this discourse, Tonkin continued to stare at the SICOS display on the wall. "The tie-ins you're referring to are limited to power and computer tie-in. The station is protected by a firewall to prevent any viruses the ship may have picked up. The firewall works both ways, by the way. When a user on a ship accesses the station computer, the ship's computers are isolated to prevent unwanted program anomalies and program glitches. At that point, the ship's terminal is nothing more than an extension of the SICOS. If the ship's computer needs to be tied into a station system, a maintenance computer is tied in. After use, the drive is wiped clean completely or replaced altogether. Nothing like that has happened here."

Tonkin rubbed his chin with one hand and scrolled through schematics with another hand while the remaining two hands rested on his hips. "Is there a log record of the gravity generator anomalies I can review?"

Both engineers helped bring up the maintenance logs for their ships, and Tonkin took in the data. Finally, he started nodding rapidly. "Has there been a change in how the gravity anomalies behaved?"

Both engineers shrugged. Tim shook his head. "No, it would suddenly go away most of the time. Sometimes it would increase."

Tonkin nodded in understanding. "The station's gravity anomalies changed characteristics after the installation of the new controls, which was well after both ships had docked."

Tonkin changed pages on the SICOS display. "The gravity controls on both ships are similar types. The station's new controllers are also similar. They're actually more robust than the controllers used on ships. What they do have in common is the frequency their oscillators operate on. The station's original controllers operated on a much lower frequency. That's one of the reasons they failed. The failures were due to circuit components aging and gradually losing their calibration over a period."

Will Dawson and the ship engineers couldn't help but be impressed with Tonkin. It was all rather a simple exercise in logic, but it would have taken them all morning to work it out.

Tonkin continued, "Since the ships and the station aren't interconnected, we're looking for an outside influence. There is something out there transmitting on a frequency that is at least on the same harmonic as the gravity generator controllers. The anomalous transmissions are sporadic, which explains why the problem is intermittent."

Will interjected, "I've been asking the engineers of the other visiting freighters, and the newer ones are experiencing the same problems. In fact, a couple of them refused to hook up to the station computer, but it hasn't helped."

Tonkin brightened. "Ah! That confirms my theory. I suppose it's possible that somehow the power umbilical is creating the unwanted frequency. It's very unlikely, but I think we should look into it just to say we have eliminated the possibility. Although I remain extremely doubtful, given that the Station Expansion Module gravity controls worked perfectly until it was within half a kilometer. Our engineers who were on board during the move confirmed that fact."

Will was feeling like he had been taken to school by the little pretar. "Guys. I think this has been incredibly productive, thanks to Mr. Tonkin."

Tonkin beamed, "This is a most interesting problem. If you don't mind, I would like to continue to help troubleshoot this issue. It may be interesting enough to get me published in an engineering journal."

Will started grinning. "As long as I get a mention, that would be great." Tonkin reacted, "Oh yes, of course."

Will smiled. "We should get busy, gentlemen. I think we'll test the Atlantis Star's power umbilical first."

Will adjourned the meeting, and the technicians went to work.

*****

## Oasis 4, CentMod, Office of Phillip Ross, Station Manager

After the morning briefing, Phil returned to his office to review the requirements for his meeting with the pretars. While he was reviewing the materials, he felt his stomach do flips, and he started to float above his chair as well as the objects on his desk. "SICOS, increase gravity to Earth Normal over thirty seconds!"

He felt himself settle back into his chair, as well as his desk set. He said to the empty room, "I won't miss that."

At about 1130, Phil decided that he had prepared enough for now. He put a pad in his duffel bag and headed to the door. It was a little early for lunch, so a tour of the control center sounded like a good idea. Setting his bag by the door, Phil went to the stairs and climbed to the control center. Once there, he watched the docking of a freighter. His check of the boards earlier said this ship was from Sotos, and the people of Sotos were called Malnuns.

Phil used an intercom to page Virginia. "Hey, Virginia, could you please call over to Sparky and tell him to remind his wait staff that malnuns have a rather low tolerance for alcohol."

Later, he said his goodbyes then boarded the elevator platform to the plaza level.

*****

## Oasis 4, CentMod, Eva's Café

Phil carried his duffel bag to the café where he sat at his customary table. Eva came over with her pad, and he looked up from his menu. "Any specials today?"

Eva grinned. "It's all special, Boss."

Phil looked back to the menu. "Turkey club, chips, and a big ole root beer." Will Dawson and Dave Jacobson strolled to the table as Eva was tapping Phil's order on her pad. She looked up. "How about you, guys?"

Will ordered the country fried steak with cabin fries and iced tea. Dave opted for the tomato soup, grilled cheese combo with cola. Eva tapped the orders on her pad and then tapped done. When that was done, one of the wait staff came out with a tray with their drinks.

Phil smiled across the table. "Well, guys, what kind of progress have you made in the gravity generator controller glitches?"

Dave motioned to Will. "I'll have to defer to my colleague here. I've been busy with the pre-launch checklist."

Will made an overly animated bow to Dave. "Thank you, sir." He then turned to Phil. "Well, Boss, the meeting was very productive. It would have taken all day to reach the conclusions we came up with if it weren't for Tonkin. That little pretar knows his nuts and bolts. We're still checking to see if the power umbilical is somehow carrying an unwanted frequency. Tonkin is convinced that it's probably a waste of time, but he wants to eliminate all possibilities before moving on to other possible causes."

Phil's eyes narrowed while he tried to reason it out, "I've been led to understand that the gravity generator controllers operate on a frequency that isn't shared by other equipment."

"That's correct," Will confirmed. "The frequency the new controllers operate on was selected to prevent interference. Either there's something on the station that's way out of calibration, or someone is operating something without authorization. The power needed to affect the systems is considerable, so it should narrow down the suspected possibilities."

Phil nodded. "Sounds like the right crew is on this."

The food arrived, and the conversation turned to other topics. While they ate, Phil spotted some Malnuns exit the connecting tunnel from the CargoMod that their ship docked at. Malnuns were similar in appearance to humans, except their ears and eyes were noticeably larger. It was a bit early for the crew since they would be busy shutting down systems and beginning the cargo off-loading. Phil thought they must be passengers. That wasn't unusual since malnuns enjoyed traveling like anyone else, and malnun businessmen also frequented the station.

Phil watched as one of them approached a fellow malnun. He had seen the second malnun around the station for the past month or so.

The malnun had a small shuttle he claimed he used for charter work. He said he would carry freight or passengers to places that weren't serviced regularly by the larger freighters. That wasn't unusual at all. There were several operators of that sort who made the station their base of operations. Phil watched as the first malnun handed an envelope to the shuttle pilot, who looked inside and nodded enthusiastically. It looked innocent enough, but there was something about the way they were acting that Phil didn't like. The malnuns parted company, and Phil put it out of his mind.

Will looked at Dave. "Hey, how come I wasn't told about the Bluegrass review last night?"

Dave shrugged. "I didn't know you were a fan. I'll let you know next time.

Who told you about it?"

Will laughed. "Tonkin has been humming tunes all morning. I asked him what was up, and he told me that the pretar technicians have just discovered music, and they've been sampling different styles."

Will looked at his watch. "Speaking of Tonkin. He's probably back at work. I'll see you, gents, before you launch, I'm sure." With that, Will left a tip for Eva and headed to the CargoMod, where he would find Tonkin.

Phil and Dave stayed behind to finish their beverages and kill a bit of time before they had to board the Atlantis Star. Dave looked at Phil. "Correct me if I'm wrong, but I take it that you've never been to Pretna."

Phil finished his root beer. "That is correct. What can I expect?"

Dave leaned back. "It's hard to describe to someone who's never been there. You've worked with plenty of pretars. No doubt you've noticed that they're friendly, courteous, and hardworking. Picture a whole planet populated with them. That's not to say that there aren't any pretars that are jerks. They're not common, but they do exist. They have their share of internal problems, also like any other species. Their culture, however, compels them to handle things differently than other species."

Dave took a sip of coffee and continued, "I mentioned before that they have a caste system. It's not a legal arrangement, but they're comfortable with it. Trades tend to stay in families, where their skills are developed and encouraged throughout their formative years.

Sometimes, a pretar will show talent in a different area than that he or she was raised in, and they are actually encouraged to choose the career path that they would be best at. Whatever they decide to do with their lives, they endeavor to be the best they could possibly be at it. Everything there is polished, manicured, and well-designed. That's probably the biggest thing that you'll notice, the engineering marvels they have. There is nothing slipshod or thrown together like you see on Earth so often."

*****

## Oasis 4, CargoMod 2

Both men left a tip for Eva and boarded a shuttle tram to CargoMod 2. It stopped at the CargoMod entrance, where Phil waved his pass to clear into the secure area, as did Dave. A short walk later, they approached the air lock that gave them access to the Atlantis Star.

Dave turned to Phil. "Give your duffel to Simon here"—gesturing to a crewman standing at the ship's air lock—"he'll make sure that it gets to the VIP cabin. Let's check on the progress of our gravity issues." A short distance away were Tonkin, Tim Hughes, and Will Dawson.

All three were hunched over the diagnostic test set that Tonkin had earlier, and all three were singing a tune that Phil didn't recognize, "Rocky Top, you'll always be home sweet home to me..."

Dave hated to interrupt, but he thought that he should remind his chief engineer that they were now on a timetable. "Hey, guys. Am I going to have a ship, or are you going to retire tinkering with it?"

All three looked up with an expression like one would give if they were interrupted while reading a really good book. "Sure, Captain. We were just finishing here," Tim answered.

Phil asked, "Did you guys find anything?"

"You'll be relieved to know that there are no unwanted frequencies traveling through the power umbilical," Will answered with a shrug.

"Not even a harmonic," Tim added.

Will noted, "There was an interesting event. The ship's systems recorded two ship's zones lost gravity in the period we were testing."

Tonkin shut down and unplugged his test set. "I think we should look for a transmission of some sort."

Dave interjected, "I'd love to stick around to see how this turns out, but we have final prelaunch checks to make. Come on, Phil. I'll show you how it's done from a perspective you're not used to."

## The Atlantis Star, Freighter Owned by the Intersystems Shipping Company

Dave escorted Phil aboard and showed him to the bridge. "Have a seat in the observer chair."

Phil sat and took in the sights and sounds of the Atlantis Star's bridge while the bridge crew was busy at various workstations. The bridge was located at the top of the ship at the most forward end. The windows gave about a 280-degree view. The only angle one couldn't see was directly aft, so there was a viewer that could be activated that would do just that, if needed.

Dave sat in his own seat, then retrieved a pad from a pocket on the side of the captain's chair. "Okay, folks, time to get serious."

He depressed a button. "Engine room."

Tim Hughe's voice came over the speaker, *"Reactors started, warm, and ready. All ships systems in the green."*

Dave ticked off the first item. "Personnel."

The Atlantis Star first officer read from his own pad. "Ship's crew aboard, twenty-five Pretar passengers, and one human checked in."

Another tick on the list. "Navigation."

"Course is plotted and locked into the computer" came the reply from one of the bridge officers.

Dave continued, "Close and secure hatches." A board on the operations panel showed green.

Dave called the next item on the list. "Switch over to internal power and disconnect umbilical."

Another green light. A station technician depressurized the air locks and retracted them.

The first officer reported, "Ship is ready for cast off."

Dave nodded. "Very well." He toggled a switch. "Oasis 4 control.

Atlantis Star ready for departure."

Phil heard one of his controllers on the speaker on the bridge speaker. *"Atlantis Star; release docking clamps and thrust port until clear."*

Dave gave the orders. "Release docking clamps."

Mechanical thumping could be heard and felt, then the sound of actuators as the clamps released then retracted. A final clunk and thud as the clamps reached the end of their travel and the doors closed.

When the board showed green, Dave nodded and ordered, "Helm, thrust aft fifteen meters."

Phil felt the big ship lurch to aft then thrusters fired to stop its momentum.

The controller's voice came out of the speaker. *"Atlantis Star; yaw to port ninety degrees and thrust forward until clear of the station."*

"Helm, yaw port ninety and thrust," Dave ordered.

The big ship started yawing. As soon as the ninety-degree point was reached, the helmsman tapped the thrusters to full. The ship moved forward, picking up speed.

The Atlantis Star picked up speed slowly, but it did accelerate. After several minutes, a distance of five miles was reached, and Phil once again heard a controller on the bridge speaker. *"Atlantis Star; you are free to maneuver. Have a good voyage."*

Dave ordered a course change to align the ship with their course. This could have been done at speed, but it was easier when the ship was moving slowly. The fewer course corrections needed at high speed, the better.

When the ship was roughly aligned with the final course, Dave pressed a button that warned passengers and crew that they were about to accelerate. A minute after the warning, Dave ordered the reaction engines started. A noticeable jolt was felt as the engines fired. Even at idle, the engines gave a considerable push. The engine thrust was slowly increased to maximum when the Atlantis Star was at maximum velocity and no longer accelerating. Dave ordered the engines cut, and the light-speed engines started.

The ship was surrounded by a bubble of normal space. That's what kept weird things from happening inside the ship while traveling faster than light. Space was then manipulated outside the bubble that pushed the ship faster than photons traveled. The navigation computer confirmed that they were on course within an acceptable tolerance.

Dave called the engine room, "Tim, is everything in one piece down there?" Tim's voice came over the bridge speaker, *"Systems are green."* Dave relaxed a bit. "That's how we do that, folks. Next stop is Pretna Orbiting Station 3."

Phil always liked the jump to light speed. The ship's structure groaned with the strain, and the view of the stars streaking by in the bridge windows never failed to impress.

The next four days passed as quickly as can be expected for a passenger on a freighter. Dave did what he could to keep Phil occupied. He was allowed bridge access; in fact, although Phil was a highly qualified shuttle pilot, he never bothered to get his light-speed endorsement. With that in mind, the Atlantis Star helmsman gave Phil instructions and allowed him a few supervised shifts at the helm. At the end of three days, Phil's logbook contained a light-speed endorsement. Midway through the fourth day, the Atlantis Star approached the Pretna system.

Dave ordered the ship to slow to sub-light speed, which was actually a trickier maneuver than it would seem. Delaying just a few seconds would mean overshooting the destination. Dropping out of light speed too soon could add days of travel at sub-light speed. An indicator at the helm position showed a countdown of sorts to the proper window for dropping to sub-light speed. It was a ribbon-type gauge; numbers would scroll right to left. At zero, the ribbon changed from white to green. As long as they cut the light-speed engines while in the green, the ship would be in the proper position for orbital entry. The indicator reached the green band, and the helmsman let the ship get well into the green before cutting the engines. The further into the green, the less time it takes to reach orbit.

The helmsman cut the light-speed engines, and the stars in view forward of the bridge stopped appearing as streaks and now looked normal. Dave asked, "Navigation, report?"

A bridge crewman at the navigation console consulted his readings. "Primary checkpoints cross-referenced. We are three hours twelve minutes from Pretna orbiting."

Dave was satisfied that his crew put them in a good position. He was convinced that they were capable of coming out of light speed directly into orbit. They couldn't, of course, because near the destination, the risk of collision becomes greater, so ships must be below light speed when entering any solar system.

There were predetermined lanes designated for entering and exiting solar systems that were served regularly by freighters and passenger vessels. There were six orbiting stations over Pretna, and they were heading for number three. The station was identified by the radio beacon that was specific to that station. The ship would have to be put in an orbit that intercepted the station. About an hour from orbit, the ship's speed was adjusted to make sure that that could be accomplished. Approaching Oasis 4 was much easier by comparison since it didn't orbit a planet.

Atlantis Star fell into orbit, and Dave toggled a switch. "Pretna Orbiting Station 3, Atlantis Star has entered orbit."

A very professional-sounding pretar controller answered, *"Atlantis Star; Orbiting Station 3. Please report two-thousand-kilometer approach. Expect docking at tier 2, cargo hub 4, docking port 45."*

Phil was wondering if that was a joke. His own station was large by any standards. If the docking ports were the same size, this station would easily be twice the size of Oasis 4.

Phil was distracted, watching the helmsman maneuver the big ship. Finally, Dave toggled the communication switch. "Pretna Orbiting Station 3, Atlantis Star two-thousand-kilometer-approach."

Phil looked out of the forward viewport and spotted the station. His estimation of it being twice as large was incorrect. It was at least three times the size.

The pretar controller's voice came over the bridge speaker, *"Atlantis Star, continue approach. Please observe speed restrictions."*

Dave acknowledged the instructions.

As the ship neared the pretar station, controllers gave Dave vectors to align the ship with the proper docking port. As they were getting closer, Phil was curious as to where the docking clamps were. Before he could ask, an enormous hatch on the station started to open. The space it revealed was easily large enough to accommodate the freighter. The

Atlantis Star entered the hatch, and the door was closed behind them. Mooring arms were extended to fittings on the ship, and the *Atlantis Star* was gently pulled into the proper position for the docking clamps to engage. The gravity inside the docking bay was only provided on ramps and walkways, so there was no need to provide any sort of cradle for the ship to rest on. Although there were some maintenance docks that have such capabilities. As the ship was being secured, the air was being pumped into the docking bay. Pretar technicians connected the standard umbilical connections to the ship, and Dave ordered ship systems secured.

*****

**Pretna Orbiting Station Number 3**

Dave looked at Phil. "I have to stay here and supervise the off-loading. Besides, you'll be busy for a couple of days with the company business. We'll get together before we leave and do some sightseeing." Phil shook hands with his friend and went to retrieve his duffel from his cabin. After getting his duffel, he went to the boarding hatch. The pretar technicians who shared the voyage were waiting to deboard.

A pretar technician near Phil spotted him and called to the other pretars, "Let Mr. Ross off first, he's a VIP after all!"

Phil put his hands up, "No, no guys. You've been away for a long time, you're anxious to see your families."

The group smiled as one, and thanked Phil. The hatch was opened as soon as the loading ramp was put in place, and the pretar technicians hurried across to a lobby area after clearing the Pretna customs desk. Phil strolled across the loading ramp, which was an odd sensation to say the least. The Atlantis Star was floating suspended in midair in the docking bay. He was now outside a ship that was designed to spend its existence in space.

A pretar cargo tug floated past and latched onto a cargo container. Phil stopped to watch the operation. As soon as the tug was firmly attached to the container, the container automatically disengaged from the ship. The tug gently pulled the container away from the ship and maneuvered it into position to push it to the station storage area. The striking feature of the tug was that it did not have a pressurized cockpit. The pretar tug pilot was using all four hands to maneuver the small vessel, and Phil couldn't help but be impressed with his skill. The container was pushed to a hatch that was barely large enough to accommodate it. The pretar tug pilot pushed the container into the hatch until a mechanism on the station gripped the container and pulled it inside. When the station gripped the container, the tug disengaged and returned to the ship for another. The same operation happens at Phil's station, but it happens in the vacuum of space. Phil looked down at the gangway or loading ramp. It must have gravity generators of its own, or he would have floated off.

Phil walked the rest of the way to the passenger lounge where the pretar technicians were being greeted by their families. It was actually one of the sweetest and weirdest things he had ever seen. The pretars were very affectionate, but the sight of them hugging each other with four arms was actually pretty comical.

A pretar wearing what Phil took as a business suit approached him. "Mr. Ross, I presume?"

Phil smiled back. "Yes, and what do I call you?"

The pretar businessman motioned for an assistant to pick up Phil's duffel. "I'm Billnod, and this is Renfore. We've been sent to escort you to our offices."

Phil raised an eyebrow. "Wow! You guys don't waste any time, do you?"

Billnod recoiled a bit. "Oh no, sir. We wouldn't think of making you partake in a business transaction without proper rest after your voyage. We're just going to have a reception with light snacks and cocktails today. The company officers are anxious to meet you."

Phil felt a little bad about stressing the little pretar. He forgot that they take themselves very seriously and aren't very good at detecting sarcasm. Phil tried to put Billnod at ease. "Please relax, Mr. Billnod. I didn't really expect you to put me to work right away."

Billnod smiled back. He had heard about the human habit of interjecting humor into everyday situations. He didn't expect it to be as subtle as it was. He smiled wide. "Oh, very good, Mr. Ross. I think the company officers will take to you right away."

Without saying it outright, Billnod alluded to the real reason Phil had been sent for. For whatever reason, the pretars wanted to find out what he was like, not just what humans are like but specifically him. That revaluation prompted him to remind himself to be a bit more circumspect.

*****

## Oasis 4, Station Maintenance Shop

Back at Oasis 4, Will Dawson had isolated the frequency that was interfering with the gravity systems on the station. Something was transmitting in short bursts, and they were just long enough to reset gravity controllers to zero. He had devised a way to make the controllers less susceptible to these occurrences by adding a filter and shielding to certain parts of the controllers. He had submitted his proposed design changes to company engineering and was waiting for a response. Tonkin was very impressed with Will's modification and thought that it wouldn't take long for approval.

Unfortunately, the unwanted transmission bursts were too short to trace effectively. Tonkin suggested that Will set up sensors outside the station and use them to triangulate the source. It wasn't as straightforward of an operation as it should have been. The transmission bursts didn't last long enough to effectively trace them. Will used the SICOS to record when there was an event with the gravity generator controllers. On the fourth day after starting this investigation, Will went to the SICOS maintenance terminal and discovered there were four gravity failure events on the station in the time period he specified. Using

that information, he studied the sensor data for those times. There was finally good news. He found an anomalous radio transmission on four of the sensors. He triangulated the source and found that it was coming from HabMod 4 or very near to it. He thought to himself that he shouldn't be surprised. Probably one of the aliens working on the station was using personal equipment he didn't realize was causing problems. Will decided that he would deploy his sensors in positions that would better pinpoint the exact location of the transmission bursts.

*****

## Pretna, Station Commuter Shuttle

Phil, Billnod, and Renfore passed through Pretna customs and boarded a shuttle destined for the city that had the headquarters of the Space Habitat and Systems Corporation. On the way to the surface, Billnod pointed out things of interest on the surface. The shuttle started to slow as they neared the planet's surface. They were over a metropolitan area now, and the pilot configured the shuttle for landing. They slowed even further, and the nose of the shuttle raised and decelerated. The nose lowered as they came to a hover a few feet above the ground. The shuttle lowered and came to rest on the ground outside a terminal. Phil barely felt the landing gear touch. He had made only a few landings that smooth in his life, and he himself had logged thousands of landings in his career.

Billnod and Renfore directed Phil to the terminal, where they boarded a ground shuttle. Billnod entered a destination code into a keypad. The shuttle pod departed the station on rails while the computer selected the optimum route to the destination. Billnod explained that it was rare when they took the shortest path to their destination. The computer selected the route that would get them there in the shortest amount of time, which often meant traveling away from conflicts. Since the computer knew each pod's desired destination, the whole thing flowed amazingly smooth.

*****

## Pretna, Offices of Space Habitat and Systems Corporation

Once at the company headquarters, the three went to the top floor, where the conference room was arranged for an informal gathering. Immediately, he was greeted by the company officers. The CEO, who went by Sten, handed Phil a drink. Phil was delighted that it was a scotch and water and not some kind of strange pretar concoction. Although he was sure that once Dave Jackson joined him, there were a lot of things he was going to try. The pretars were interested in what Phil thought of the expansion unit that the pretars were contracted to add to Oasis 4. Phil assured them that he was absolutely delighted with the workmanship and skill of the pretar technicians.

Phil couldn't help but have the feeling that the pretars were constantly evaluating him. More than once, he saw them give each other a sideways glance and nod approvingly. Normally, pretars are pretty bad at reading people and interpreting body language, tone of voice, and other indicators normally used to gauge someone. He thought it was a bit amusing that it didn't occur to the pretars that there were races that were better at it than they were.

Finally, Sten announced that the initial meet and greet had run its course. "Billnod, I'm sure that Mr. Ross is very tired after his voyage. I do hope the difference in time isn't going to be too difficult to adjust to Mr. Ross."

Phil hadn't even noticed any differences. Then he realized that it was midday or 1200 Zulu when he arrived. Here on Pretna, it was only a couple of hours past midday. Pretna's days were actually twenty-six earth hours long. As a result, in a few days, midday Zulu time will precede midday Pretna reference standard time. Phil made a mental note to reset his programmable watch to Pretna time.

The pretars told time like humans, except the Pretna day was divided into twenty periods comparable to an earth hour, and those were divided into one hundred units, and those were further divided into one hundred units also. Phil nodded.

"Not at all, Mr. Sten. I think I arrived at an opportune time. However, I think that perhaps after a couple of days here, I may feel differently."

The pretars appreciated the difficulty of not only adjusting to a difference in times of days. But the length of days can be devastating until one can get used to the difference.

Sten nodded. "Billnod, please see that Mr. Ross is accommodated comfortably."

Billnod and Renfore then escorted Phil to the shuttle pod, where they departed the company offices for the hotel.

*****

## Oasis 4, HabMod 4, Quarters of Selak

Back on Oasis 4, Selak received a message from the headquarters of the Space Habitat and Systems Corporation, directing him to turn his portable computer over to Tonkin and await a representative from Pretna to arrive with further directives. Selak powered down his computer and put it in its case. As he walked to Tonkin's quarters, he couldn't help but be concerned about why he was to turn his computer over to Tonkin. Any scenario he worked out in his head didn't end well for him.

He reached Tonkin's quarters, and while clutching his computer case with two hands, he depressed the door chime with a third hand. When the door opened, Tonkin stood in the opening with a shaken look on his face. "I received a message concerning that"—he pointed to Selak's computer—"they didn't indicate why I was to do this."

Selak slowly shook his head. "I am also ignorant as to the reason for this. With an absence of more information, we should carry on with the project through to its completion. There are only five earth days left, and we shouldn't allow any delay. Any information we may need, you could retrieve on your own system."

Selak returned to his own quarters, his head buzzing with questions. The project was ahead of schedule, and there were no technical glitches, save the gravity generator controller issues. But it was discovered that an external influence was causing that. Selak went to bed to get plenty of rest because he wanted to be extra alert during the final phase of the project.

*****

**Pretna**

Phil worked with the pretars on the scheduling for remitting payment for the station expansion. Payment was in the form of raw materials and some finished products, as well as the use of the station for shipping and storage purposes for a time. The pretars were to the point and efficient in the way they conducted themselves. The payment was agreed upon, but the timetable to remit payment needed finalizing.

In the evenings, Dave Jacobson came around, and the two of them ate supper, then saw some of the local sights. Phil was absolutely amazed by some of the pretar engineering that he saw. They were masters at building with minimal materials. The structures were also things of beauty and not just thrown up for pure functionality although anything they build is extremely functional.

Midday on the third day, business was completed, and agreements were signed. Phil was still a little in the dark as to why his presence was necessary since this could all have been done by electronic messaging. Plus, Phil always had the impression that some of the things they said were said so they could gauge his response.

As they were having a celebration drink, a serious-looking pretar entered the room.

Sten said, "Ah! Inspector Klon. Please, I would like to introduce you to Mr. Ross, the station manager of Stellar Logistics and Freight Corporation's Oasis 4. Mr. Ross, meet Inspector Klon."

Phil shook hands with Klon, who came right to the point. "Mr. Ross, I will be traveling to Oasis 4 in the morning. My purpose is to take into custody one of the Space Habitat and Systems Corporation technicians aboard your station."

Phil was taken aback. "Before that happens, I need to know why."

Klon replied, "The technician in question is being charged with industrial espionage. There have been trade secrets that belong to this company our operatives have found for sale. We traced the leak to a portable computer used by a technician at your station. We sent technical data to suspected individuals. Each individual received a different version of the data. When that piece of data showed up on the

Black Market, we knew which individual had betrayed their company and people."

Phil didn't like what he was hearing. He knew the pretars that were left on the station, and he liked all of them. Moreover, he didn't think there was any way any of them could betray the trust bestowed on them. He said the only thing that came to mind. "I will have to be there, of course, when you make the arrest."

Klon said, "I have passage booked on the *Lancaster*. I took the liberty of reserving a cabin for you in case you wanted to return with me."

Phil said flatly, "Yes, I would, given the circumstance."

Sten interjected, "Oh, what a shame. I know how much you looked forward to doing some sightseeing while waiting for the Atlantis Star's return trip."

Phil agreed, "It can't be helped. Well, there will be other trips to Pretna." "We look forward to it," Sten offered.

Phil returned to the hotel and left a wake-up call. In the morning, he packed and checked out at the reception desk. When he turned around after turning in his room access transponder, Billnod and Renfore were there.

They greeted him as warmly as ever, "Hello, Mr. Ross. We're here to ensure that you have no problems getting to your ship."

Phil grinned. "I get the feeling that you guys can't wait to see me go."

Both Billnod and Renfore were horrified that their actions were interpreted as anything but helpful.

Phil chuckled. "Don't sweat it, guys. Hey, why don't you just get me to the shuttle that goes to Orbiting Station 3."

Billnod realized that Phil was pulling his leg and smiled. "It would be a pleasure, Mr. Ross."

*****

**Pretna Orbiting Station Number 3**

At the shuttle terminal, Phil shook hands with Billnod and Renfore. Then he boarded a shuttle to the pretar station to meet the Lancaster. The shuttle ride to the station was done with the usual pretar precision.

After docking, Phil gave his duffel to a pretar baggage handler with instructions to have it sent to the Lancaster. Then he went off to the Atlantis Star to have a word with Dave. Entering the docking bay, Phil was again awestruck at the sight of the huge freighter floating in midspace. He saw similar sights every day, but this ship was in an enclosed space surrounded by air. There were pretar station workers floating from the walkway that surrounded the docking bay to the ship.

Some of Dave's crewmen were performing maintenance tasks on the ship.

What made the scene bizarre to Phil's eyes was the fact no one was wearing a PEWS. He spotted Dave near the front of the ship with a crewman and a pretar technician. They were working on the navigation shield array or NavShields. Space wasn't exactly void of debris. It's full of everything from dust particles to asteroids the size of North America. The NavShields created an energy field in front of the ship that deflected everything in the ship's path. If the shields failed, stellar dust could erode the front of the ship off in a matter of seconds.

Phil had had enough of zero gravity to last him for a while, but this was different. He would be expecting the gravity to be gone, and this was a vast space, unlike the cramped conditions of his office or quarters. Phil walked to the platform that was used to transit from the walkway with gravity plating to the zero-gravity zone. Holding on to the handrails, he stepped on the platform, where he immediately felt lighter—in fact, weightless.

There was a cable that was attached between the ship and the handrails. Phil attached the clip on his safety harness to the cable and pushed off the platform. He pushed a little harder than he should have and covered the distance to the ship before he could prepare himself to stop. He bounced off the front of the ship with a thud.

Dave stuck his head around the array and grinned. "Float much, Phil?"

Phil gathered his wits and grinned back. "I came up here to make sure you're earning your pay."

Phil moved his safety clip from the cable to a rail on the ship that was for that purpose. Safety clip was a misleading term. In zero gravity, there was no danger of falling. Its only purpose was to prevent a person from floating away from a handhold, which has been known to happen. Dave knew some great stories about crewmen who got careless on pretar stations and floated just out of reach of a handhold, swearing enthusiastically while their crew mates threw tools at them. Eventuality, they would reach something they could grip. It was actually considered a rite of passage for a new guy because it would teach them to pay attention to what they were doing. There was one case when a crewman was working alone who floated away from a handhold and floated for three days drifting painfully slow until a pretar maintenance crew found him and took pity on him. Since then, protocols were put in place to prevent recurrences of that event.

"What brings you up here, Phil?" Dave asked.

Phil explained to Dave about the pretar law enforcement officer, Klon, and his trip to Oasis 4.

Dave was immediately concerned. "Industrial espionage is a very big deal on Pretna. If there's a pretar on the station dealing in secrets, his life is over. If he doesn't go to prison, he won't be able to work in his profession ever again. In fact, his family members won't be trusted with any kind of responsible position."

Phil didn't like what he was hearing, but there wasn't much he could do about it now. He said to Dave, "I'll be returning to Oasis 4 on the Lancaster. It's leaving today, and you're not scheduled to leave for three more days."

Dave nodded. "I hear ya. I wanted to show you some more sights on Pretna, but this is more important. The Lancaster's captain is a guy named Clive Harrison. He's very professional and runs a tight ship. You probably won't get any helm practice on this trip." Dave and Phil left the crewman to carry on with adjusting the NavShield.

Once back on the walkway, Phil felt like he was laboring to stand and walk. Dave remarked, "This is the payment for floating around, not exerting energy." The two took a tram to where the *Lancaster* was moored.

On the way, Phil said, "I know that the *Lancaster* has been to Oasis 4, but I don't recall meeting the captain."

Dave laughed. "You would remember, Clive. He's the quintessential English ship's captain. In fact, he's the most 'English' person I've ever met."

They got off the tram when it stopped and walked the short distance the *Lancaster's* docking bay. Standing on the boarding ramp was a distinguished man in a jacket with four gold stripes on the sleeve. He turned toward the pair. "Jacobson old man! What brings you here?" Dave shook hands with Clive. "I brought you your stowaway. Clive Harrison, meet Phillip Ross."

Captain Harrison stood straighter. "Ah yes, the station manager of Oasis 4. I've been meaning to make an effort to make your acquaintance," he said, shaking Phil's hand. "Mr. Klon is already aboard. He'll be in the cabin next to yours. Both of you will have dinner at the captain's table, of course. We'll say goodbye to Jacobson here and get aboard."

Phil shook hands with Dave again. "I'll see you in about a week. I hope there's good news when you get there."

*****

## The SS *Lancaster,* Freighter Owned by the Liverpool Shipping Lines

Phil boarded the Lancaster and found his cabin. This ship was a little older than the Atlantis Star, and as a result, the appointments weren't as nice, but it was still quite comfortable. This ship was also faster than the Star Series freighters. Although they didn't hold as much cargo, they were well-suited to transferring small loads to scattered destinations. There were only five passenger cabins, but Phil and Klon were the only passengers on board.

Phil unpacked his duffel and put his shaving kit in the head. He wasn't awfully familiar with this model of freighter, so he looked around the room for a directory. He found the computer terminal and thumbed through the passenger files until he found the ship layout program. Looking it over, he saw the ship was not without amenities. There was a gymnasium, a recreation center, and an observation deck. He decided to make his way to the observation deck to watch the launch. Leaving his cabin, he followed the main passageway to the lift. Boarding the lift, he pressed the button for deck 1. The observation deck was located just behind the bridge and half a deck up. Once off the lift, he had a choice between the bridge and the stairs that lead up to the observation deck. Climbing the stairs, he found himself in a room that afforded a 360-degree view. Even the ceiling was clear polycarbonate. The view from here was spectacular. Unfortunately, they were still in the docking bay, so they would have to wait until they were clear of the station to enjoy it.

From behind him, there was a voice. "Ah, Mr. Ross, how good to see you." Phil turned to see Klon taking the last step into the observation deck. "Mr. Klon, good afternoon."

Klon frowned. "Afternoon?"

Phil smiled. "Remember, once we get underway, we revert to Earth standard meantime."

Klon looked at the watch he wore on one of his four arms. "Oh yes. I must remember to reset this when we leave the station. I'm afraid, travel isn't something I've done a great deal of. To be truthful, this is my first trip away from Pretna."

Phil nodded understanding. "There has to be a first time for everything, Mr. Klon." Phil found the controls that allowed them to hear the bridge conversation and radio calls. Klon was intensely interested as the bridge crew went through their checklists, and Phil explained some items that Klon didn't understand.

Clive started his final checklist. "Engine room."

*"Engines and ships systems are operating nominally"* came the reply. Clive nodded. "Helm and navigation."

The helmsman replied, "Helm and navigation set." Clive continued, "Secure all hatches."

A bridge crewman consulted a panel. "All hatches secure and sealed." "Disconnect all umbilical ties to the station," Clive ordered.

Once again, the crewman consulted the same panel after he pressed the button for the umbilical release. "All umbilical connections secure."

Clive nodded. "Signal the station. We're go for space."

Phil saw the pretar technicians exit the docking bay and seal the station hatches. Warning lights flashed as the air was pumped out of the docking bay and into tanks on the station. When that was done, the bay doors were opened into space. A pretar technician signaled they were ready to launch the *Lancaster*.

Clive was satisfied that everything was ready. "Release the docking clamps." Phil felt a thud accompanied by an audible clunk.

A crewman consulted a panel. "Clamps released, ready for maneuvering." Clive toggled a switch. "Pretna 3, *Lancaster* ready for launch."

A friendly but professional reply came, *"Lancaster thrust aft until clear."*

Clive took a breath. "All right, chaps. Let's begin. Stern thrusters only, thrust aft."

The helmsman operated his controls, and the stern thrusters gave a long blast causing the ship to back out of the bay.

Clive calmly said, "Easy, lad, we have a lot of cargo, but it's not very heavy."

The helmsman already knew that. After all, it was part of his job, but he understood his captain needed to say it anyway. "Aye, sir."

Klon was engrossed with the whole experience. His big eyes scarcely blinked as he took it all in.

The Lancaster was clear of the station, and Clive allowed the ship to continue to drift aft. When they had reached the five-hundred-meter point, the controller called, *"Lancaster, yaw to port ninety-five degrees and pitch up twenty degrees. Thrust forward until clear of the station."* The freighter performed the maneuver and accelerated on thrusters.

The station controller called, *"Lancaster, you are clear to fire your engines and free to navigate."*

Clive ordered the reaction engines started. Even idling, the engines provided an impressive jolt of speed. The helmsman was making small corrections in their course as they traveled further away from Pretna. The navigation computer finalized the course to Oasis 4, but they haven't reached the boundary that allowed them to switch to the light-speed engines. When they were the proper distance, Clive ordered light speed, and the freighter rapidly accelerated past light speed. The view from the observation deck was unbelievable, which made Klon give an audible gasp.

Phil said, "It's a couple of hours until dinner. I think I'll grab a nap before we eat."

Klon agreed that that was a good idea. Phil returned to his cabin and lay down. He didn't have a restful sleep the previous night because he kept thinking about Klon's mission. He wondered which of his pretar friends was being blamed for the data leak. He refused to believe that any of them would betray their people. It seemed out of character for the pretars. Whatever they found, he hoped that they could clear the air. After a couple of hours, the computer terminal woke Phil with enough time to clean up for dinner. After washing the sleep out of his face, he left his cabin and went to dinner. Reaching the dining room, he saw that Klon and the captain were just getting seated at a table in the tiny dining room.

Clive looked up and smiled at Phil. "Don't stand on ceremony, old man. Come in and take a seat." The captain's table was just another table in the dining room. There was nothing special about it. It was just that Clive liked to observe certain proprietaries.

The steward brought the meal, which consisted of roast beef, potatoes, and green beans. Klon wasn't sure he would like it, but he said he wanted to experience as much as he could of alien cultures and cuisine. At first, he tried small bites, but as he decided that he liked what was served, he ate heartily. The steward brought Klon seconds, and the cook was delighted to hear that Klon enjoyed the meal, so he made sure he got a little extra.

While sipping their after-dinner coffees, which Klon was on the fence whether he liked or not, Clive said, "I know it's an odd time to have dinner. Changing over from Pretna Standard Reference Time to Zulu Time is best done at once."

Klon nodded understanding. "I thought it would be tricky to get used to not only a difference in the time of day, but the length of the day is just different enough to make one uncomfortable."

The three finished their coffees, and Clive went to his cabin. He said he wanted to spend time in a book. Phil and Klon went to the ship's recreation center, where Phil taught Klon how to play Eight Ball.

During the voyage, Phil and Klon were trying desperately to fill the time. Klon became quite the Eight Ball player at that time. In the evenings, the crew liked to watch some sort of entertainment on the recreation center's flat-screen display, and popular things to watch were plays. One evening, Clive wanted to watch a concert that featured a particularly accomplished pianist. At first, Klon wasn't very interested, but in short order, he was intrigued.

On the third day, the two of them were in the recreation center with a ship's engineer named Nigel Willoughby. The three were engaged in what became the standard pastime, Eight Ball. Nigel looked at the wall chronometer and said in his cockney accent. "That's gotta be it, Gov. We're almost to your station, and I've got to take my shift in the engine room. If I'm not there sharpish, I'll get a boot in the tradesman entrance. Never mind, then. You gents might want to check the observation deck." Nigel put his cue back in the rack on the bulkhead. "Laters."

Phil had to suppress the urge to bust a gut when he saw that Klon kept trying to adjust his auto translator whenever Nigel said anything. Phil and Klon climbed the stairs to the observation deck. Klon always was in awe at the view from here. The small viewports in their cabins didn't measure up to this room. Phil switched on the speaker, which allowed them to hear the bridge.

Clive just started his checklist for slowing to sub-light speed. The navigation officer consulted the computer. "On course and speed. Optimum window for cutting light-speed engines in two point five minutes. On my mark, mark." A timer on the helm station started a countdown.

When the timer neared zero, Clive ordered the light-speed engines cut. The helmsman pulled back the power levers, and the ship slowed to sub-light speed. The helmsman started the reaction engines and powered them up to maximum continuous power. The nebula that dominated this region of space loomed in the distance, and Klon was having a difficult time keeping his emotions in check. The stunning beauty of this stellar phenomenon was absolutely breathtaking, particularly in the Lancaster observation deck.

Phil took a seat to better take in the experience. Then he realized that they were still a couple of hours from docking. He got Klon's attention. "What do you say we get some lunch? There's plenty of time before we get to the station."

Klon seemed reluctant to leave the observation deck, but he thought that a good lunch would be welcome. The steward and the cook were happy to see Klon, who was becoming quite a fan of earth food.

Phil and Klon were careful not to sit at the captain's table since the captain was not there. Klon was tying a napkin around his neck, or where most species kept their necks, to prevent getting his clothes messy. The steward put a platter of condiments in the center of the table, and Klon was immediately interested. Phil explained that in some earth delicacies, the eater has the option of adding additional flavorings to enhance the food to meet the taste of the eater. The steward placed plates of bratwurst on buns with fries and baked beans. Phil had a cola with his, and Klon had a big glass of root beer, which has become his favorite lunch beverage.

Up to this point, they had avoided discussing Klon's reason for his visit to the station. He could no longer put it off. "Mr. Klon, what is your timetable for placing the suspect under arrest?"

Klon looked up from his activity of adding chopped onions to his second bratwurst. "I will not have a choice. Our laws are very precise on this point. It must be done as soon as practical after my arrival. I will need to enlist the help of your security marshal and two of his deputies. Also, the suspect must be kept in a holding cell until passage back to Pretna can be arranged. It is your station, of course, but I think it would be the best course of action."

After lunch, Phil returned to his cabin to pack. When that was done, he turned to the computer terminal and tied it to the communications system. He entered the frequency to talk directly to his operations office. Virginia Well's smiling face appeared on the screen. "Hi ya, Boss!

We didn't expect you for another couple of days."

Phil gave a half-hearty smile back. "Hey, Virginia, could you patch me through to Luke Smith? We have an issue to deal with."

Virginia noted her boss's tone and decided that small talk would have to wait. "I'll have to locate him first. Give me a minute." With that, her face was replaced by the company logo on the screen.

Twenty seconds later, Luke Smith appeared. "What's up, Boss?"

Phil got right to it. "There's a Pretna security officer coming back with me. He's going to arrest a pretar that they've identified as passing on industrial secrets. He's going to need you and one or two deputies to affect the arrest."

Luke was stunned but remained professional. "Did this officer give you a name?"

Phil shook his head. "No, their procedures preclude doing that. I would like it if your guys understood that whoever it turns out to be, he is to be treated with respect. I'm not fully convinced that any of the pretars are capable of this."

Luke nodded. "I'll make sure they know, Boss."

Phil shut down the terminal, grabbed his duffel, and left the cabin. He made a detour to the hatch and left his duffel on a shelf there. Then he went to the observation deck and found Klon already there. They could see the station looming larger as they approached. The ship was currently below light speed. That's not to say they were traveling slow. Their velocity was still blindly fast. Occasionally, the braking thrusters would fire to slow the vessel. When that happened, an alarm would sound to allow passengers and crew to brace themselves.

Phil said to Klon, "I've contacted my security marshal. He'll meet us at the docking port with deputies."

Klon nodded. "Excellent."

Phil turned up the volume on the speaker that allowed them to hear the bridge. Clive received a distance report from the helm, then toggled the transmit switch. "Oasis 4, *Lancaster*, on the Pretna-alpha approach, inbound."

The station replied, "Lancaster, Oasis 4, continue approach. Expect CargoMod 4."

Clive toggled the transmit switch again. "Lancaster confirms. CargoMod 4, out."

After a few minutes, the station controller gave the Lancaster vectors to help guide it to the proper CargoMod.

The *Lancaster's* helmsman deftly maneuvered the ship to the controller's instructions. "Lancaster, Docking port twenty-six through twenty-eight, clear." The Lancaster was what was called a general freighter. It didn't carry cargo containers or bulk material. Its hold was designed to accommodate cargo on pallets and bins. As a result, there was no need to dock the ship with its nose to the station. They could dock the ship with its side against the station where the cargo hatch aligned with the hatch on the station.

The *Lancaster* inched into place just a few feet from the CargoMod. Instructions and responses were passed between Lancaster and the station. Phil heard metal parts bumping together, then felt a series of thuds as the ship came to a rest against the CargoMod.

Klon wanted to go to the hatch right away, but Phil stopped him. There was no point since it would take about ten minutes for the crew to shut down the ship systems, connect the umbilical, and safety check the hatch seals. Until then, the hatches would remain closed. Klon relaxed, then he turned his attention to the station. Phil answered a dozen questions about his station until he heard over the bridge speaker that the hatches were clear for opening.

Phil said to Klon, "We might as well see if the hatch is open."

Klon followed Phil to the hatch where Nigel and one of the other ship's mechanics were struggling to open it.

Phil and Klon stood back, watching the two technicians. Clive walked up behind them. "I say, Willoughby! What's the hold up?"

Nigel looked up from his task. "I told ya, Gov. The safety locks on the latches are knackered. They've gummed up the works proper. Never mind, then. We'll get it open sharpish." Nigel then said to his partner, "It's a good job that we were able to close this in the first-place in it."

Klon kept trying to adjust his auto translator, and Phil was doing his level best not to laugh.

*****

## Oasis 4, CargoMod 4

Once the hatch was open, Phil and Klon said their goodbyes to Clive and Nigel. They stepped onto the station, where they were met by Luke and two of his largest deputies. Luke wanted to make an impression on Klon. Klon, for his part, tried to seem unimpressed but failed. Then Phil made introductions with Klon and Luke.

Luke got down to business. "Mr. Klon, who are you here to take into custody?"

Klon said, "I must see Selak at once."

Luke and Phil were taken aback. Both men thought Klon needed to confront the pretar that was suspected of espionage before he met with the pretar in charge.

Luke consulted a SICOS terminal, then he turned to the group. "This way, gentlemen." Before getting into the shuttle tram, Phil gave his duffel and Klon's bag to a station worker with instructions to take his duffel to his quarters and to have the station office assign Klon quarters in HabMod 4.

The three went to meet Selak where they found him with Will Dawson and Tonkin in the CentMod maintenance workshop. Selak spotted them first. "Oh, Mr. Ross! What a moment for you to arrive. We've just certified the Station Expansion Unit as complete and functioning."

Phil smiled. "That's great news, Mr. Selak."

Klon stepped forward. "Selak, I am directed to place you into custody."

Selak was instantly thrown into shock. "I don't understand. What am I being charged with?"

Klon responded while maintaining a professional demeanor. "Industrial espionage." He turned to Luke. "Mr. Smith, would you please have your men take Selak into custody?"

Luke motioned to his deputies to do just that. Before they left, Luke told them, "Please escort Mr. Selak to a holding cell. Make sure he's comfortable." The deputies complied, though they thought that they would have to carry Selak.

Luke said to Klon, "I hope you have evidence of this, Mr. Klon."

Klon looked like he was assaulted. "I wouldn't have made this journey if I didn't have compelling evidence. I'm afraid that regardless of your friendship with Selak, I have to perform my duties."

Luke regained his composure. "My apologies, Mr. Klon."

Phil stepped in. "Mr. Selak is still in my station. Any questioning will be done in the presence of Mr. Smith. All evidence will be reviewed by Mr. Smith or anyone he or I deem necessary to review it."

Klon thought about it for a couple of seconds. "That is all very reasonable. Besides, this is indeed your station, and I would be very delighted if evidence came to light that cleared your friend."

Phil felt he may have come across as a bit harsh. Klon said, "I hope I haven't done permanent damage to the friendship we've developed over the last couple of days."

Phil said, "Of course, you haven't. It's just that I'm having a very difficult time believing that Mr. Selak would have anything to do with what he's being accused of."

Klon turned to the other pretar in the room, "Are you Tonkin?" Tonkin looked like he was terrified. "Ye-Ye-Yes, I am."

Klon nodded. "Good, I am to understand that you took possession of Selak's computer?"

Tonkin answered, "Yes, I did."

Klon asked, "After you received the message, how long was it before you did so?"

"I did it immediately," Tonkin told him.

Klon looked like he was satisfied. "Mr. Smith, could you please accompany Tonkin to his quarters and place the computer in an evidence bag."

Luke was feeling flabbergasted. "Yes, of course. After you, Mr. Tonkin."

The two of them left together, leaving Phil, Klon, and Will alone in the workshop. Will broke the silence. "My calendar is clear, Boss. Anything you need to be done to prove Mr. Selak's innocence, I will do or find a way to get it done."

Klon was beginning to sense that if Selak was indeed innocent, his friends would go to any length to prove it. But he had a task to perform. "Mr. Ross, could I please see Selak's quarters."

Phil saw no reason to deny Klon's requests. "Let's go."

*****

## Oasis 4, HabMod 4, Quarters of Selak

They walked from the CentMod to HabMod 4, then a series of escalators to level 30, where Selak's quarters were. Phil and Klon, met Luke and Tonkin in the corridor outside Selak's quarters. Phil explained to Luke they were going to have a look around Selak's quarters. Luke then used his security clearance to gain access to Selak's quarters.

Once inside, Klon surveyed the rooms, looking in drawers, being very careful not to violate Selak's privacy too badly. Klon put two of his hands on his hips, while stroking his chin with a third, "I think that should do for now. Selak's answers to questioning should determine if I need to delve deeper here."

*****

## Oasis 4, CentMod, Security Office

The four of them went to the CentMod. As they were walking to the security office, Klon said, "I would like to question Selak alone, if I could."

Phil protested, "Wait a second, Mr. Klon. Mr. Selak is a friend of ours..."

Klon interrupted, "Precisely, I don't want to give him the impression that you've turned against him. If he's innocent, he'll need his friends to help prove it. If he's guilty, he'll need his friends more than ever."

Luke said, "The interrogation room has an adjacent room with a monitor. We'll be in there watching. If we think of something you should know or ask, it will appear on a monitor in front of you."

Klon nodded. "Very good. Does this equipment collect biometric data?"

Luke answered, "Yes, it does, but I don't have the expertise to interpret anything other than humans."

Klon said, "Not to worry. I am well-versed in interpreting biometric data of my people."

Luke had one of his deputies move Selak from the holding cell to an interrogation room. Klon entered the interrogation room after Phil and

Luke went into the monitoring room and powered up the equipment. Klon was blunt and to the point, but he never badgered Selak. He simply told Selak what the evidence was against him. Selak denied all the allegations although he could not deny that the information came from his computer. Selak couldn't understand how information could have gotten from his computer to the black market.

After the questioning, a deputy took Selak back to his cell. Klon went to the monitoring room to review the recorded interview and examine the biometric data. He replayed all of Selak's responses and examined the data carefully. Heart rate, blood pressure, perspiration, eye dilation, and a half-dozen other measurable parameters were recorded. Klon painstakingly pored over all of them.

Finally, he leaned back in his chair. "Unless I'm very much mistaken, gentlemen, Selak is telling the truth. The problem is that the evidence is solid against him. We need to thoroughly investigate this. I don't want to be the one to arrest an innocent."

Phil said to Klon, "I'd better see Selak and give him some encouragement."

Klon said, "That's a fine idea. Mr. Smith, let's make sure that Selak's computer is secure until we can get an expert to examine it."

Phil added, "After I talk to Selak, we'll get dinner and brainstorm some directions to go in."

Phil had one of Luke's deputies let him into Selak's cell. Selak sat on the bunk with his head down in his hands. He looked up when Phil entered and immediately burst into tears. "Oh, Mr. Ross! You mustn't believe what I've been accused of!"

Phil emphatically tried to comfort Selak. "I don't believe it, Mr. Selak, not for one second." Phil sat down on the cot next to Selak and put an arm around his shoulders.

Selak sobbed uncontrollably. "Even if I don't go to prison, I'll never be trusted with a position of responsibility ever again. My family is doomed. I won't be able to provide for them any longer."

Phil said, "I would never let that happen. If things don't go well, I'll make sure you have a job here. All your friends on the station believe in you."

Selak looked up at Phil with tears streaming out his huge sad eyes. "Mr. Ross, I'm grateful to you and all my friends here, but the problem is much worse than you know. My dependents won't be able to work in a position of responsibility for generations. Because of what happens here, my sons and grandsons will be lucky to get a job cleaning restrooms on mining asteroids."

Phil tried to comfort Selak. "It won't come to that. We'll get this straightened out."

As Phil was leaving the cell, Selak had his head in his hands, mumbling, "Oh my, my, my. Dear, dear, dear."

*****

## Oasis 4, CentMod, Eva's Café

Phil met Luke, Klon, and Will Dawson at Eva's Café. Phil sat and ordered, then turned his attention to the others. "We've got to figure this out, guys. Maybe it would be helpful if we knew where the stolen information cropped up."

Klon consulted a pad he kept in his pocket. "According to my information, proprietary technology concerning heat treatment of alloys showed up for sale by a malnun trader. The data appeared on a Kastian space station."

Will asked, "How was it that Selak had all that data in his possession?"

Klon answered, "Everyone in that company has access to every piece of information. It saves time during projects, and every bit of knowledge a technician has makes him or her a more valuable employee."

Luke asked, "What's the process with Selak's computer?"

Klon said, "We need someone who is skilled in computers to access and review the usage files."

Will looked confused. "Usage files?"

Klon took a sip of root beer. "Yes, the computers used by Space Habitat and Systems Corporation have a program embedded that records the usage history. It cannot be erased by the user without a code sequence. The code sequences are stored by corporate security. Mr. Dawson, do you know of anyone with reasonable computer skills?"

Will didn't hesitate. "Mr. Tonkin is one of the most skilled technicians I've ever met."

Klon nodded enthusiastically. "Ah yes, Tonkin. I've eliminated him as a suspect. He's above reproach."

Phil stood. "Okay, guys. I think we should get a good night's sleep, then attack this thing head-on in the morning."

*****

## Oasis 4, CentMod, Operations Center

After hurrying through his morning routine, Phil went to breakfast at the café. He ordered something that didn't require a lot of time to prepare. Afterward, he hurried to the operations center and started the meeting early. Virginia Wells rushed through her report, as did Dr. Tillman. Everyone knew what today's priority was going to be.

Phil looked at Luke. "Where's Mr. Klon?"

Luke answered, "He's in the security office, trying to give Mr. Selak some comfort and peace of mind."

Phil said, "Have him meet us in the maintenance shop." He turned his attention to Will and Tonkin. "I'll need you two to delve into Mr. Selak's computer." Phil said to the room as a whole, "This is everyone's number one priority. I'm convinced that Mr. Selak is innocent, and we need to prove it."

*****

## Oasis 4, CentMod, Maintenance Shop

Phil, Will, and Tonkin waited in the maintenance shop. After a few minutes, Luke and Klon walked in. Klon had an evidence bag that held Selak's computer. Klon was saying as they entered, "The facility's here are most adequate. Yes, I must say, I'm most impressed."

Phil asked, "How is Mr. Selak holding up?"

Klon looked downcast. "Not well, I'm afraid. There's nothing I could say to give him hope. He just lies there sobbing."

Phil was concerned. "I'll have to see him after we finish here."

Klon set the evidence bag on a work bench and removed the computer.

Tonkin placed his own computer next to it.

Will asked Tonkin, "Do you need a cable to connect the two?"

Tonkin shook his head. "That's not necessary. I can tie the two together without it."

He started his computer and Selak's computer. The computers linked with each other, and a dialogue box appeared on each screen. Tonkin looked at Klon. What is the code, sir?"

Klon handed a pad to Tonkin, who entered the code that was displayed on the pad. Tonkin now had access to the usage history files on Selak's computer. Klon directed Tonkin to find the files that had been copied. Tonkin made some keystrokes and pressed enter.

All at once, they were weightless and started floating as well as the objects in the shop. Will reacted fast. "SICOS, increase gravity to Earth Normal over thirty seconds!"

The gravity slowly returned to normal. Phil asked, very deadpan, "Still haven't figured out the gravity problem?"

Will answered, "I didn't think that I had to. The glitches went away a few days ago."

Phil was flustered. "Well, what made it come back suddenly?" One could almost see the light bulbs light up over Will's and

Tonkin's heads. Tonkin was about to say something when Will blurted out, "I'm way ahead of you."

He ran to a cabinet and came back with a piece of equipment. "This is a radio direction finder. We use it to find where the shielding on circuits has failed." He set up the equipment and oriented the antenna. "Okay, Mr. Tonkin, send another command." Tonkin input another set of instructions and pressed enter. At once, the gravity failed. Will blurted, "SICOS, restore gravity!"

Tonkin and Will stared at each other for what seemed a long time. Tonkin broke the silence, "I believe we have found the source of the gravity generator controller's interference."

Will nodded. "Look at the frequency. It's precisely in the range of the controllers."

Tonkin pointed to the display on the radio direction finder. "Look at the power output. It is much too low to affect anything. It's actually surprising that it even affected this room, and there were failures all over the station."

Will shrugged. "One mystery at a time. Let's compare the time of events with the times the files were downloaded."

Will turned to the SICOS maintenance terminal. He displayed the times there was a gravity failure since the new controllers were installed. Tonkin placed a device on the face of the SICOS. He explained that it would link his computer with the SICOS much like it did with Selak's computer.

Tonkin ran a correlation program and discovered that, indeed, there was a direct correlation between events and times files were downloaded. Tonkin studied them and said, "Look at these times they occurred. At times, I know for certain that Selak was otherwise occupied during these downloads."

"That may be," Klon cautioned. "But it's not quite enough to clear Selak at this point."

For the next three hours, Tonkin and Will pored over Selak's computer. At one point, they moved the operation in a faraday cage to prevent the gravity from switching off every time a new command was input. The longer they dug into files, the more it looked like Selak wasn't present when the files were downloaded. But as Klon continued to point out, that didn't relieve Selak of responsibility. Since it was his computer, it was password protected.

Phil checked the time. "Guys, I'm gonna check on Selak. I'll meet all of you at Eva's at noon."

*****

**Oasis 4, CentMod, Eva's Café**

At noon, Phil made his way to Eva's where he found the others just sitting down. Will asked, "Is Selak doing any better?"

Phil's expression betrayed Selak's condition. "He's not doing well. He just lies there on his cot and mutters to himself. Did you make any progress after I left?"

Tonkin spoke up, "Well, we determined that the data certainty came from Selak's computer. I looked for back doors that we may not be aware of. If one exists, I couldn't find it. As you saw, our computers can be accessed remotely.

That's why it's so important that access codes are kept secret. Selak would never allow anyone to know the passcode, and it's unhackable. A passcode is selected that has no other meanings, like birthdays, or other nonrandom part of the user's life."

Eva showed up with a tray of glasses of ice water. As she put the glasses on the table, she asked about Selak, "Are you gentlemen getting any closer to clearing that sweet Mr. Selak? How is he holding up?" Eva had taken a real liking to Selak, as did her husband, Burt. Eva loved to see someone enjoy their meal, and Burt loved to be the guy to provide it.

Phil managed to wedge a word in, "I think we're further than we were this morning. He's not doing very well at all, though. His breakfast tray wasn't touched."

At that, Eva came unglued. "He's not eating? Oh, he must feel terrible. I can't let this go!" She called to her assistant waitress. "Betty, take over here!" Then she yelled in the direction of the kitchen. "Burt, two cheeseburgers, cabin fries, and a strawberry soda to-go!" Burt handed a to-go container and beverage cup to Eva, who grabbed some napkins, packets of ketchup, and mustard on her way to the security office.

Phil and the others stared at each other for a couple of seconds, then Phil said, "She'll make him eat."

When Betty finally got them their lunch, they ate in silence, thinking about what they knew so far. Phil spotted the malnun trader that's been staying at the station for what seemed like months. "Does that guy ever go anywhere?"

Will looked over to the malnun. "Not that I've ever seen."

Luke furrowed his brow. "Funny way to make a living. Park a shuttle at a space station and do nothing."

Phil said, "I saw him make some sort of exchange with a crewman from a malnun freighter before I left for Pretna."

Luke was starting to smell a rat. "I'll see what I can find out about this guy." Phil turned the conversation back to the maters at hand by asking Tonkin,

"You say someone would need the passcode to access the computer?"

"That is correct," Tonkin confirmed.

Phil continued, "How far away could the other computer be to effectively be linked?"

Tonkin thought a second. "The range is very limited. I would say no further than ten meters."

Phil said to Klon, "After we eat, let's look at Mr. Selak's quarters again."

Klon replied, "I don't know what more you would hope to learn, but of course, we'll go."

*****

## Oasis 4, CentMod, Security Office

Luke had left instructions to the deputy in charge of the holding cells to allow any of Selak's friends to see him anytime they wanted. That allowed Eva to strut into the cell and put the food on the table. Selak didn't stir, save a little shaking from sobbing.

Eva put her hands on her hips. "Mr. Selak, time to eat."

Selak tried to compose himself. Eva was still kind but firm. "Mr. Selak, sit up."

Selak slowly sat up on his cot. Eva let out a small gasp when she saw his condition. His eyes were red and bloodshot, and he looked pale.

Eva sat next to him and put an arm around him. "Now, Mr. Selak, you must eat, and you have to have faith in your friends. Phil, Will Dawson, Mr. Tonkin, Luke Smith, and that Mr. Klon are all working so hard to find who is doing this to you." She got up and slid the table up to Selak. "Now eat."

Selak put ketchup and mustard on a burger and started to eat. Eva made sure he ate every bite. Selak still felt horrible, but he was finally starting to realize that there was a lot of effort happening on his behalf. Before Eva left, Selak said to her, "Please tell everyone that I'm very grateful for the effort they're putting into this."

*****

## Oasis 4, HabMod 4, Quarters of Selak

Phil and Klon entered Selak's quarters. Phil had Tonkin tag along in case they had technical questions. Phil wasn't sure what he was looking for, but he was determined to find it. His gaze rested on the SICOS. "Mr. Tonkin, is there any way someone could use the SICOS remotely to access Mr. Selak's computer?"

Tonkin shook his head. "I'm afraid not, not without a device like I used earlier. There is no interface built into the SICOS that will match the company computers. Our computers are configured that way to prevent unwanted access."

Phil thought he was onto something there for a second. Finally, he asked, "Mr. Tonkin, where did Mr. Selak keep his computer?"

Tonkin pointed to the desk. "Just there."

Phil sat at Selak's desk chair and looked around. He said aloud, "Someone would have to be outside to see the keyboard."

These were top-level quarters, so the polycarbonate windows angled inward as they got higher so that the top of the windows was just over the desktop. Phil started to examine the windows.

Something caught his eye near the very top. It was incredibly small, about three or four millimeters in diameter. It appeared to be a tube with a lens in the end. The tube disappeared out of sight onto the HabMod roof. "Mr. Tonkin, what do you make of this?"

Tonkin climbed up on the desk. "It appears to be a lens. There also seems to be something just out of view on the HabMod roof."

As Tonkin climbed down from the desk, Phil said, "I think we found what we were looking for. I'll get with Will Dawson, and we'll see what that's about."

*****

**Oasis 4, CentMod, Maintenance Shop**

Phil met Will in the maintenance shop in the CentMod, where they both put on PEWS, or Personal Environment Work Suit. In the air lock, they attached a PEWS thruster pack. When they were ready, Will depressurized the air lock and switched off the gravity. Phil was relieved to have the weight of the PEWS and thruster pack removed. Will opened the outer hatch and moved to the threshold, where he pushed off. Phil did the same, and both men fired their thrusters for a short burst. As they floated toward HabMod 4, Phil secretly wished he could come up with an excuse to do this more often. Bouncing off the walls in his office is annoying, but this is different. In a short time, they reached HabMod 4 and went to Selak's window.

As Will examined the object attached to the HabMod, he turned on microgravity units in his boots and knees to keep himself attached to the station to prevent himself from floating away. Phil kneeled next to him. "Well, do you know what this thing is?"

Will went to scratch his head and realized he couldn't in his PEWS. "Well, I can tell you what it isn't. It isn't part of the station." He worked carefully to remove whatever it was without damaging it. Phil handed him tools from a kit they brought with them. Once it was detached, they put away the tools. Will gave Phil the tools to carry back with them, and he carefully put the object in a mesh bag. They turned off the microgravity generators on their suits and pushed off the HabMod gently.

*****

**Oasis 4, CentMod, Maintenance Shop**

Back at the maintenance shop, Will put the object on a workbench where he examined the outer cover. He found the latch and opened the cover. Examining the interior, he identified the function of the components. Klon was looking over his shoulder although he had to use a box to stand on to do so.

Will frowned at the components. "These are Kastian in origin." Phil asked, "Didn't some of the stolen information crop up on a Kastian space station?"

Klon nodded. "That is correct. There are a lot of things about this case that either a remarkable coincidence, or we are definitely getting a direction to go in. Please, Mr. Dawson, can you identify the function of this device?"

Will continued to stare at the device. "Well, this is a transceiver," he said, pointing to a portion of the interior, "and this is a micro camera," pointing to the tubular portion. "The only problem is this wouldn't have enough output to carry very far."

Will put the faraday cage back in use. Using some equipment on the electronics bench, he managed to identify the frequency required to operate the device. He even managed to get the camera operational. "Well, guys, this is a pretty neat bit of spy kit. Someone used the camera to get Selak's password while he typed it. Then they used the transceiver to access the computer at will. They could use it like they were right there, except they were using it remotely."

Luke was confused. "Why didn't Selak turn off his computer as a security precaution?"

Tonkin answered, "He did. That much I can confirm going through the usage files. The problem is our computers can be activated with another computer remotely. Something we should rethink and remedy."

Phil was visibly relieved. "That's great! Selak didn't have any way to know that his computer had been compromised!"

Klon cautioned, "It would certainly seem so. However, according to Pretna law, the existence of this device doesn't prove anything. We need to prove that this was actually used to access the computer."

Luke agreed, "Mr. Klon is right. We need to find the other end of this thing." Phil checked the time. "Hey, it's about dinnertime. Let's continue this at Eva's."

*****

## Oasis 4, CentMod, Eva's Café

At Eva's, Betty took their orders. While waiting, Phil asked, "Did you find out anything about our malnun trader?"

Luke shook his head. "Very little. His name is Fel Nos, a small-time trader. He ferries goods that he feels he can gouge customers with, and there are a few places he's not at all welcome."

Phil frowned. "Maybe you should keep a closer eye on him."

Luke said, "Already done. I've programmed the security cameras to increase their resolution in his direction whenever he's around. Also, I've made sure there's a deputy around when he goes into areas that aren't well covered by cameras."

Phil nodded. "Real good."

Luke added, "There's more that doesn't add up about that guy. The ship he has is top-of-the-line. I looked into that too. Apparently, the former owner just signed it over to him. I asked about that, and the only answer I received is it's suspected that there was some blackmail involved."

Phil said, "I was checking out his ship earlier. That thing is nice. It's also made on Earth. So why does a charter operator and trader just hang around a space station? He doesn't make money hanging around."

Luke shook his head. "I don't know, but I think I'll make him a priority after we clear Selak."

Eva came over from the direction of the security office and sat down. Phil asked, "How's Mr. Selak holding up?"

Eva looked grim. "He's not doing very well at all. I took him something to eat, but he wasn't awfully interested in it."

Phil was concerned. "Did he eat at all?"

Eva nodded. "He ate a chef salad and had some of his favorite strawberry soda pop."

Phil said, "Chef salad?"

Eva shook her head. "I know he loves his cheeseburgers, but he needs to eat something healthier every now and then."

Klon took a sip of the root beer Betty just put in front of him. "Perhaps we could see Selak after dinner to try and cheer him up and tell him about the progress we've made."

Luke, Will, and Tonkin looked at each other, and Will said, "We're in." From behind them, a familiar voice said, "Count me in too."

Phil turned around to see Dave Jacobson standing there. "Holy smokes, you made some good time."

Dave nodded. "It didn't take long to load the ship for the return trip. The pretars are really organized when it comes to that. But enough about that. As soon as I dock, they tell me that Selak is in jail."

Phil said, "I'm afraid so." Then he brought Dave up to speed on the progress so far.

The following morning, Phil went through his usual routine. During the morning briefing, everyone knew he had important business to attend to, so comments were kept to a minimum. In the end, Phil said, "Okay, gang, let's look like we know what we're doing today. If I can, have Will, Luke, Mr. Tonkin, and Mr. Klon meet me in conference room number 1. We'll use that as a base of operations today."

*****

## Oasis 4, Conference Room Number 1

Phil went to conference room number 1 with the others in tow.

As they took their seats, Will remarked, "Man, Mr. Selak looked rough last night."

Klon added, "It's one of the reasons I'm convinced that Selak is innocent. When a member of my race is caught. They simply resign themselves to the fact that they're going to be disciplined. Selak's reaction to these events is very telling to me."

In the conference room, Phil started, "I think the first logical step would be to find out how long that spy device was attached to the station."

Will said, "Let's use the outer recording system." The outer recording system can be thought of as being similar to security cameras.

Will ordered, "SICOS, display ORS Camera 4 Alpha, archive file, yesterday, noon." One of the wall-sized monitors displayed the roof of HabMod 4.

Will thought for a second. "SICOS, overlay grid." A grid appeared over the picture.

Will scanned the image. "SICOS, isolate grid Delta, 7." The selected grid block was now the only one on display.

Will studied it intently. "SICOS, overlay grid, isolate grid Echo, 4." The display showed the small portion of HabMod 4's roof directly over Selak's quarters. The "Spy Device," which is what they were calling the object, was in the center of the display.

Will said, "SICOS, same perspective. Go back one week." The device was still there.

He said, "Again," and the image on display didn't change.

Will repeated the order twelve times before the device wasn't there. Then he went forward a day at a time until the device reappeared. He continued in this manner until he narrowed down the exact time the device was placed there. At first, Phil suspected that perhaps one of his technicians put it there. It would be easy enough to do unnoticed. What they saw surprised them.

Will played a video showing a remotely operated drone carrying the device as it gently maneuvered and placed it on the HabMod, then flying away. Luke was making notes as to pertinent time stamps, camera numbers, and grids. Will said, "Let's see if we can find where this came from." He zoomed out partly. The drone could be seen flying into the frame from the right and left in the same direction.

Will managed to trace the origin of the drone from CargoMod 1. Unfortunately, there was no way to determine which vessel it came from due to camera angles. Luke made a note of that fact.

Tonkin asked, "Mr. Dawson, could you freeze the drone against a dark background?"

Will compiled. Tonkin asked again, "Could you please zoom in as close as possible?"

The drone filled the screen. Tonkin remarked, "This is remarkable resolution on the video system."

Tonkin studied the drone closely. Will said, "Just a minute, Mr. Tonkin." Will had SICOS record the device and use recognition software to find the device on the stored media. This did a couple of things for them. First of all, the drone was in the field of view of several cameras, so Will could provide Tonkin with a complete composite picture of the drone. They could also retrace the path of the device.

Tonkin studied the composite picture of the drone. He used the SICOS controls to rotate the drone digitally. He examined it on all sides, top, and bottom. "This does more than deliver spy devices. It has a repeater on board."

Luke looked puzzled. "I don't understand."

Tonkin explained, "The range of the computer link is very limited. If you wanted to access a computer remotely from more than a few meters, you would need to boost the signal a great deal. Someone unknown is sending a signal from an unknown location through this drone, where it connects to this device." He put up a photo of the spy device. "This connects directly to Selak's computer."

Will said, "Wait a second. You mean this thing has made multiple appearances?"

Tonkin nodded. "Most certainly. It would have to."

Will turned to the SICOS. He had the top and side view of the station displayed on a monitor. Then he had SICOS superimpose the path of the drone on it. Then he had SICOS search the files for the reappearance of the drone and display them on the display.

Collectively, everyone in the group was impressed with the ability of the SICOS to carry out the command so quickly.

Klon said, "Look at the time stamp on each of these events. They mostly occurred during hours where there was minimal activity. These are all during early morning times."

Tonkin pointed to the path of each event. The drone would fly out from its unknown starting point and hover motionless until its mission for the night was over. The point where it would hover was actually pretty random. Tonkin explained that was why the gravity generator controllers were failing at random locations on the station.

Unfortunately, the origins of the drone couldn't be nailed down. Luke stared at the display. "It looks like it could be from CargoMod 1 between docking ports thirty and thirty-five.

Phil asked, "What vessels are there?"

Luke looked at the SICOS display. "There are currently three."

Phil asked, "Have any of them been there for the last eleven or twelve weeks?"

Luke said in almost a growl, "Just one. At docking port 33, owned by a certain Malnun."

Phil said, "That's probable cause." He turned to a communications console. "Virginia, lock down the vessel at CargoMod 1 docking port 33." Luke dispatched two deputies to the CargoMod to detain Fel Nos.

*****

## Oasis 4, CargoMod 1

Phil stood. "Let's go to the CargoMod, guys." Reaching the CargoMod, Luke left the customs inspectors instructions to seal the CargoMod from the rest of the station. The five of them made their way to docking port 33, where they found the ship, operated by Fel Nos, secured, which meant he was somewhere wandering the station.

Luke went to the nearest communications console to call his security office. "Tom! Get deputies to the docking ports of all the vessels under twenty tons."

Tom answered, "That's a lot of folks, Boss."

Luke shot back, "Pull in the off shifts. We have eight CargoMods to cover, and we're not fully staffed yet."

Then Luke remembered that Dave Jacobson was going to visit Selak today. "Is Captain Jacobson seeing Selak?"

Tom replied, "He's back there now."

Luke ordered, "Go back there and tell Captain Jacobson that he's just been promoted to deputy. Put him in charge of keeping an eye on Selak and get yourself to a CargoMod."

While Luke was conversing with his deputy, Will was busy bypassing the security lock on Fel Nos's ship. The hatch finally opened, and Luke stopped the others from rushing in. "Let me clear it before you come in."

Luke pulled out his Tazer and ensured that it was set properly to incapacitate a malnun. He set it to the highest permissible setting for the expected target. The ship wasn't a large one and didn't take long to clear. Tonkin immediately went to the computer terminal in the cockpit and started looking at the files.

*****

**Shuttle Operated by Fel Nos**

Phil, Klon, and Will started to rifle through every space they could, looking for any evidence that would exonerate Selak. Phil got to Fel Nos's personal cabin, where he pulled drawers and dumped the contents on the floor, where he kicked them around. As he was emptying the closet, he came upon a case that was locked. He looked around the room for a hard, heavy object. He found what looked like a small statuette of some malnun Fel Nos admired. Phil took the statuette and pounded the lock until it was shattered. He opened the case and found dozens of data chips. He took the case and carried it to where Klon and the others had gathered.

*****

**Oasis 4, CargoMod 1**

Fel Nos walked along a row of crates and bins on pallets. He was returning from negotiations with a possible buyer for information. He stopped suddenly when he saw the open hatch on his ship. He looked at the docking port door frame and saw the indicators showing his ship was locked down from the operation center, and there was no way to easily override it from the CargoMod. Fel Nos listened intently, and he could hear people inside trashing the interior of the ship. He ducked behind a pallet with a machine part strapped to it, to keep an eye on things.

*****

## Shuttle Operated by Fel Nos

Tonkin took one of the data chips and plugged it into a port on the bridge computer terminal, "This is definitely from Selak's computer. It's engineering details concerning atmospheric filtering systems."

Klon said, "Very good, Tonkin. Please secure that case and contents. I found the drone. It was stored in the air lock used for deploying emergency marker buoys."

Phil said, "I've seen enough." He turned and strode to the hatch.

*****

## Oasis 4, CargoMod 1

The five of them waited as Will placed a security seal on the hatch to prevent anyone from entering the ship. Phil's gaze fixed on a machine tool. In an effort to conceal himself, Fel Nos stumbled backward and crashed into the crate behind him. Phil yelled, "There he is!" Fel Nos bolted out of sight among the crates and bins. Luke rushed to the communications terminal and alerted the deputies that he had previously stationed at the CargoMod entrance.

Phil said, "We don't have enough people to effectively sweep the CargoMod."

Luke went to the communications terminal. "Dave, get the station maintenance personnel to guard the docking ports. Then send deputies to CargoMod 1 to help flush out a malnun."

Dave was a bit out of his element. "According to the security status board, they've already been stationed in the other CargoMods."

Luke was flabbergasted. "That's about, everyone, unless we use freighter crews or cruise ship passengers."

Phil shook his head. "No, we can't do anything like that."

Tonkin pushed a box to the communications terminal and stood on it. He contacted one of his colleagues in HabMod 4. "Cildid, get the others and meet me in CargoMod 1. It concerns Selak."

They walked to the CargoMod entrance and were soon joined by a dozen pretars. Klon addressed the group, "Gentlemen! In this

CargoMod, is the malnun responsible for stealing trade secrets from your company. As a result, Selak has been under suspicion of industrial espionage and has been in custody because of this. We need to comb this facility and apprehend this malnun criminal."

The pretar named Cildid came forward. "We're technicians. What do we know about catching criminals? No, I'm afraid that that's asking too much."

Tonkin couldn't stand it anymore. "I cannot believe what I am hearing! Selak is more than our boss. He's our friend!"

Cildid protested, "We're not security professionals!"

It was Tonkin's turn to protest. "What does it matter! We can overcome our self-imposed limitations to get a task this important done!" Tonkin's fervor was infectious to the other pretars. "Did Pinon the Brave say he was too tired to free his people?" The others answered, "No!"

Tonkin pleaded, "Did Retnor the Unclean complain about not having soap?" The pretar technicians were getting caught up in the moment. "No!"

Tonkin was even more emotional. "Did Glotdopip the Unholy stop when his people said he was too mean to them?"

The pretar technicians were practically foaming at the mouth. "No!"

Tonkin put his fist in the air and turned to the CargoMod. "Then let's get him!"

He rushed into the CargoMod with the other pretars hot on his heels. On their way into the CargoMod, they grabbed anything they could that they thought would help them—lengths of rope, boards pulled from crates, and so on.

Phil, Luke, and Will looked at each other for a couple of seconds before Phil reacted. He let out an "Oh jeez!" Then the three bolted after the pretars.

When they caught up to the pretars, they saw that Klon had organized them and put a plan into action. They were starting at the far end of the CargoMod and pushing to the other end. Luke realized that if they didn't catch Fel Nos, he could conceivably get past the customs desk and into the station. "Let's go along each side and make sure the docking ports are secure."

Phil and Will went along one side while Luke took the other. They did it at a jog to ensure they made it there before the pretars pushed Fel Nos there. Luke beat Phil and Will to the customs desk by a couple of seconds.

Phil looked all right, but Will was winded, which made Luke chuckle. Luke looked at the fence blocking the CargoMod floor from the entrance. It was three meters high, but it left plenty of room between the ceiling and the top of the fence. There were other paths that led to the connecting tunnel, and as a result, the rest of the station but not on this level. The level below him had a tram that moved cargo between CargoMods. Luke knew that the lift that lowered cargo was locked down, so that wasn't a worry. Below that was a maintenance passageway which was also impossible to access at the moment.

The three could hear the pretars getting closer. Luke climbed up on a step ladder to see if he could see the pretars progress. He looked down at his deputy that was posted there. "Get ready, Tiffany. Malnuns are surprisingly agile."

This was the narrowest point of the CargoMod, but there was too much fence to cover. The thought had scarcely gone through his mind when he heard a pretar yell, "There he is!"

The malnun leaped onto a crate to avoid a pretar's makeshift club. Then he started leaping from crate to crate toward the connector tunnel. Luke jumped down from the step ladder, yelling, "Here he comes!

Get ready!" Luke pulled out his Tazer and stood ready. The malnun reached the fence and, without slowing down, leaped the six feet he needed to clear it from the top of the crate. Luke fired his Tazer but missed. The projectiles buried themselves in a bulletin board and discharged.

He yelled to Tiffany, "Open the gate!"

Tiffany complied, and the pretars rushed through. Tonkin grabbed a maintenance equipment case on the way through the gate. Phil watched as the malnun ran into the tunnel. Fel Nos leaped from the connecting tunnel catwalk to the lower level.

Phil rushed to a communications terminal and paged Virginia. "Lock down the whole station! Nothing leaves or docks until we catch this guy!"

Then he paged the security office, "Dave, tell Selak he's off the hook! We're chasing the malnun that's responsible for his problems. I would appreciate it if you let him go."

Dave said, "Consider it done, Phil." Dave looked across the table to Selak who had a look of relief on his face that showed that a tremendous burden was lifted.

*****

## Oasis 4, CentMod, Plaza Level

The malnun managed to reach the CentMod with the pretar posse in pursuit. Phil, Luke, and Will made it to the CentMod where they watched the malnun evade the pretars with unbelievable agility. He leaped from one level to the next like someone would go from one room to the next. Will remarked, "Don't those people use stairs?"

Selak and Dave stepped out of the security office. Selak watched the malnun as he evaded his pursuers. When he reached the plaza level, Selak bolted after him. Tonkin stopped at a maintenance plugin point, extracted a controller from the case he was carrying, and plugged it in. When the malnun reached a section of the floor where he would have to make a quick turn to avoid hitting a wall, Tonkin turned off the gravity in that section.

Fel Nos couldn't stop or turn. He smashed headlong into the wall. Tonkin turned the gravity back on, and Fel Nos crashed to the floor. When he scrambled to his feet and made three steps, Tonkin turned the control until the gravity was three times Earth normal. Fel Nos flattened to the floor motionless. When Selak was about to reach the floor section that Tonkin was controlling, Tonkin switched the gravity to normal. Fel Nos got to his feet just as Selak slammed into him in a flying tackle.

Fel Nos was stunned. Selak grabbed the front of his shirt with two hands and started beating his face with the other two. Fel Nos tried to fend off the blows, but Selak was too quick. Then Selak held on with one hand and increased the beating using three hands. Fel Nos started to beg for mercy. Selak didn't hear him; in all probability, he wouldn't care anyway.

Selak was yelling now while he continued to thrash Fel Nos. "You nearly ruined my life! You nearly ruined my family's lives! All because you're greedy!"

Phil and Dave pulled Selak off Fel Nos, and Luke slapped a pair of handcuffs on him. Selak was struggling to get back at Fel Nos, and in a moment or two, he stopped and broke down. The emotional roller coaster he was on was not something that pretars were wired to experience.

Selak was doing his level best to collect himself. Phil eased his grip on him and said, "Security Marshal Smith." Luke turned to Phil. "If you could please take Mr. Fel Nos to a holding cell and call Dr. Tillman to treat his face." Phil turned to Klon. "I think under the circumstance, the Space Habitat and Systems Corporation may want to drop the charges against Mr. Selak."

Klon straightened up and assumed his most proper demeanor. "Quite correct, Mr. Ross, and I would like to extend my personal apologies to Selak here."

Selak was starting to calm down now. "Thank you, Klon. I don't hold any ill will toward you. You were simply doing your assigned task. In fact, it seems to me that you didn't have to investigate this matter further. I am very grateful that you did. In fact, I'm grateful beyond words for the effort all of you put forth on my behalf."

Luke handed Fel Nos over to Tiffany. "Throw this guy in a cell."

Tiffany grabbed Fel Nos by the arm and spun him around none too gently. "Don't try to screw with me, or you'll regret it."

Fel Nos was thoroughly cowed by the little deputy and was eager to comply.

Dave asked, "Who else is up for cheeseburgers at Eva's? I'm buying."

They all agreed that sounded pretty good. Selak thought for a second. "Perhaps a concert afterward."

Phil nodded. "Sounds good. What are we going to be listening to?"

"I've been doing some research, and I thought I would like to try something called Motown," Selak offered.

Dave, Luke, Will, and Phil smiled and said as one, "Nice choice."

The End

# THE PROSPECTOR

**Oasis 4, Upper CentMod, Office of Phillip Ross**

Phil Ross sat at his desk. It was the end of a long day of administrative duties. His reports were written and filed, so there wasn't much keeping him in his office although he didn't feel like leaving. He sipped his coffee and stared out the window.

There was a freighter approaching the station. It was a new model used by the Trans Galaxy Transport Corporation. He broke his gaze and finished the last sip of coffee. As he set the cup on the desk, his eyes rested on a picture that he had hung earlier that day. It was a group photo of himself, Dave Jacobson, Luke Smith, Will Dawson, Selak, Tonkin, and Klon. It was taken shortly after they managed to prove Selak's innocence.

The pretars have returned to Pretna with a malnun criminal named Fel Nos after a trial was held on the station with Phil as the judge, and Klon acted as prosecuting attorney. It wasn't part of Klon's training as a law enforcement officer, but he did an admirable job. He had been part of enough trials on his home planet, and he confessed that he had a collection of court dramas from various cultures, so from that, he knew the general format. It helped that everyone involved was an amateur at this procedure.

The station wasn't in a star system that anyone could claim jurisdiction in, so company rules of behavior on a space station were the legal system in place. Anyone visiting the station understands this and has signed an agreement that is kept on file.

An officer from a malnun freighter that was docked acted as the defense attorney. Unlike Klon, the malnun had training as a lawyer. Malnun freighters use onboard attorneys to interpret and write contracts and handle other legal entanglements that arise. The malnuns were adamant that Fel Nos was acting on his own and not on behalf of the Sotos government.

Fel Nos was told that it would be considerably better for him if the authorities weren't annoyed by anyone pleading innocent, which he wasn't. The evidence against him was considerable and solid, and in truth, pleading guilty didn't give him any consideration either; it just accelerated the inevitable.

The whole thing put Phil in an uncomfortable and awkward position. He couldn't keep Fel Nos in a cell for any length of time. That would be impractical. Fel Nos didn't actually steal anything from the Stellar Logistics and Freight Company, but it could have a negative effect on a corporation's decision to do business at the station. Phil had to reassure future patrons of the station that their privacy would be protected and to make getting caught stealing information or anything else at Oasis 4 a very unattractive proposition.

Phil decided that the Stellar Logistics and Freight Corporation would take possession of Fel Nos's vessel and ban him from all corporation facilities indefinitely. It was a good deal for the corporation, as they were supposed to provide the station with transport capable of light speed, passenger accommodations, and decent freight abilities. Now they didn't have to provide one. A communication from corporate indicated they were absolutely delighted with the results.

Phil then released Fel Nos to Klon's custody for trial on Pretna. Fel Nos objected because he felt that was double jeopardy. Klon reminded Fel Nos that the trial he just had was for the charge of espionage on the station, and there were additional charges waiting for him on Pretna.

On Pretna, the Sotos Embassy sent the defense council for Fel Nos. The Sotos government was anxious to put the whole affair behind them, so the attorney for Fel Nos advised him that a guilty plea would be the best course of action, given the evidence against him.

For the Space Habitat and Systems Company part, the damage done by Fel Nos couldn't be calculated. It was impossible to put a monetary number on what it cost the company. Fel Nos could never repay them since he sold the information for a small fraction of what it was worth.

Phil looked at the communication he received from Pretna informing him of Fel Nos's sentence. He would be spending the equivalent of twenty-three earth years on a Pretna penal colony mining asteroid. It was dirty, hard, labor, and an effective deterrent.

Phil looked at another communication. This one was from his wife, Alice. She was due to arrive on the passenger liner, the *Odyssey*. Also arriving, was the bulk of the additional personnel needed to staff the station after the expansion was completed.

Phil was feeling the need for nourishment, so he exited his office and went directly to the platform lift then depressed the plaza level button. With the pretars gone, it was an adjustment, as he was getting quite used to evening entertainment. His freighter captain friends were all on voyages at the moment.

In truth, he really wasn't in the mood for a lot of company. Walking through the plaza level, he saw that Eva's was at capacity.

There was a passenger cruise ship docked at the moment so the station businesses, especially the restaurants, were doing a booming business. Phil looked around; all the other restaurants were equally crowded, which made him wrinkle his nose. There was always the company cafeteria, but that didn't hold any interest for him.

******

## Oasis 4, HabMod 1, Quarters of Phillip Ross

Phil walked to the connecting tunnel that led to HabMod 1. Entering his quarters, he looked around the room and realized that when Alice arrived, she wasn't going to be overly impressed with the decor. Then he thought that it would keep her busy turning the place into her home. He retreated to the bedroom and changed into more comfortable clothes, which consisted of sweatpants, T-shirt, and sneakers.

His stomach growled, so he used the SICOS to order a pizza from the pizza parlor on the station which was a franchise restaurant from Earth. While he waited for the pizza to arrive, he decided to take part in another bachelor activity. He engaged the entertainment system and checked the movie list. Finally, he selected an action movie. When the Stellar Logistics and Freight Corporation sent the weekly High-Density Data Stream, which included corporate memos, technical manuals, and personal communications, they would also send what they called the Entertainment Packet. The packet included everything from television series and movies to sporting events.

Phil opened the door when the chime sounded, and there stood a young maldor holding his pizza. He paid for the pie along with a tip, then he settled in with his pizza and beer to watch his movie. After the movie, an early turn-in was sounding good.

The following morning, Phil awoke with some anticipation since Alice was on the passenger liner that was due to arrive later. He dressed for the fitness center. Today, that meant swim trunks and a robe. Since the gravity issues were finally over, he had the lap pools filled with water. You couldn't actually do "laps" in one. The water was circulated to provide a current that allowed the user to swim in place without having to turn around.

Phil started slow, and as he warmed up, the pool controls automatically adjusted the speed of the current, then he found a pace he was comfortable with. After a half hour, Phil had had enough and got out of the pool. It felt good to add a different workout to his routine. He returned to his quarters for a shower to get rid of the chlorine smell.

*****

## Oasis 4, Upper CentMod, Eva's Café

Breakfast was at Eva's again. Phil didn't expect his usual freighter captain friends to be there since they were all off on cargo runs. Luke Smith and Will Dawson arrived as Phil sat at his customary table. The three had breakfast and coffee while talking about nothing in particular. A couple of times, the pretars were mentioned and how dull it was on the station without them. At 7:30 a.m., Phil said, "See you two at eight o'clock."

*****

## Oasis 4, Upper CentMod, Operations Center

Phil went to his office while Will and Luke went to their respective work areas to get any notes they might need before the 0800 briefings. Phil entered his office and reviewed some notes from the previous morning briefing. There wasn't anything worth bringing up today. It was still a bit early for the briefing, so a quick look at the control center sounded like a good diversion. There seemed to be an increased amount of small ship traffic today. The controllers were doing their usual skillful job of getting the vessels to their destinations.

Phil looked down at the displays that gave the controllers the optimal view of the lower CargoMods. They were working perfectly although traffic wasn't going there yet until they could be staffed with dock workers, security, freight handlers, and so on. That was one problem that was being solved today with the arrival of a passenger liner that the company chartered to bring the additional station personnel and their dependents.

A few minutes before 0800, Phil made his way to the briefing room where he poured a mug of coffee, as was his custom. Everyone fell quiet as he sat at the head of the table. He leaned back after taking a sip of coffee. "What's new in the world of operations?"

Virginia Wells took a long look at her pad. "Do you want the details or an overview?"

Phil thought about it for a few seconds before answering. He could get any information that was relevant from the scheduling boards. The traffic to the station was going to double in short order, and after all, having Virginia go over each vessel was just something to fill the time in meetings. Something he was sure they wouldn't have time to do in the future. "I don't think the details are going to be very helpful. Perhaps you can just give me the numbers and any details if there's something unusual."

Virginia was visibly relieved. "It's a deal, Boss. Okay, there's some freighter activity today. One leaving and three arriving. We are at long last getting the additional personnel to make the station fully functional, along with dependents. They will be docking at sixteen thirty Zulu at CargoMod 1. The ship is the passenger liner *Odyssey*." There was applause around the room.

They had never dealt with a huge influx of personnel like this before. "How will they know where to go when they arrive?" Phil asked.

Virginia, indicated to the person on her left. "Our personnel resources director can answer that."

Jim Richardson stood. "We're going to set up tables on the plaza level by the department and alphabetical. There, they will check in and get their quarter's assignments. We'll give them the rest of the day to settle in. After that, it's business as usual."

Phil nodded. "It sounds like you've got a handle on it." Then he looked at Luke Smith. "Are there any security issues this morning?"

Luke consulted his pad. "Not a lot happening this morning. We caught a snoshin pickpocket last night. He's reconsidering his life choices in a holding cell at the moment."

Phil put up his hand. "Refresh my memory, please. A snoshin is from Griska?"

Luke nodded. "That's right, Boss."

Phil looked annoyed. "Why aren't they griskanites?"

Luke couldn't pass up the rare opportunity to make his boss feel silly. "Why aren't we earthers?"

Phil slowly nodded. "That makes sense. Please continue."

Luke smiled. "Anyway, our snoshin is confined to a cell until passage can be arranged for him back to Griska where he's wanted for a lot of petty stuff there. He won't be welcome back at this station in the near future." Luke looked back to his pad. "On a very serious note, there is a great deal of political unrest on Flast. Vessels arriving after traveling through Flast space will be scrutinized carefully."

There was more than one person in that briefing that knew of their role in what was happening on Flast but wouldn't say anything about it for a variety of reasons.

Phil tapped an item on his pad. "Maintenance."

Will Dawson consulted his own pad. "The only thing we have in store for today is going through all the lower-level HabMods and making sure that all environmental settings are as they should be."

Phil frowned. "Didn't the pretars make sure the controls worked?" Will smiled. "Of course they did. They work perfectly, but they didn't set them to a standard setting. My guys have a checklist where they'll check temperature, humidity, and gravity, in addition to lighting and a half dozen other settings."

Phil tapped his pad again. "Last but certainly not least, health care services."

Dr. Marie Tillman consulted her own pad. "We've completed the move from the old infirmary to the new facility in the CentMod lower level. There are currently four patients, two cases of the flu, one appendicitis, and a broken leg. Other than that, we'll probably keep busy for the next week reviewing medical files and scheduling physicals of incoming personnel."

Phil put his pad down. "There's going to be another department added to our staff. Stellar Logistics and Freight Corporation is adding vessel maintenance services to our list of amenities that we offer. That being the case, there will be another staff member in the morning briefing."

Virginia spoke up, "Half of CargoMod 8 is dedicated to vessel maintenance.

Some of us feel that space would be better utilized for cargo handling."

Phil retorted, "Some of us feel that offering this kind of service makes Oasis 4 a desirable destination and invites commerce."

Virginia didn't agree, but she was biased. Phil redirected the subject. "Since we took possession of the vessel that Fel Nos was so good to leave in our care, I thought that we could move it to CargoMod 8 in anticipation of getting it recertified."

Will spoke up, "I'll have some of my guys use a maintenance tug to move it today."

Phil nodded. "Well, if no one has anything else, let's get another day in the books."

When the briefing broke up, Phil retreated to his office where he had reports to review and file. After a couple of hours, he decided that a trip to the control center to stretch his legs was a good idea. Reaching the top of the stairs, he looked toward CargoMod 1 and the vessel that they confiscated from Fel Nos. Phil frowned and said under his breath, "We need to come up with a name for that thing."

While he thought about vessel names, a maintenance tug appeared and headed to CargoMod 1. Maintenance tugs were small enough that they could move about without clearance from the controllers. However, as soon as it started to tow a vessel, clearance would have to be established.

Phil watched as the tug approached the vessel and hovered above it. The tug operator carefully lowered the tug until it came in contact with a flat portion of the small ship's roof. The operator dismounted the tug and connected four cables from the tug to fittings on the ship. Once that was done, he remounted the tug and retracted the cables until the pads on the bottom of the tug were pressing firmly against the ship's roof, essentially making the tug and ship one unit.

An indicator light illuminated, showing the docking clamps have been released. The tug operator was in contact with workers in the CargoMod and had them release the clamps. He could have just as easily had the controllers do it but easing the controller's workload was appreciated wherever it could be done. Even if it was only that one small item.

Phil heard one of the controllers. "*Maintenance tug 3*, free to tow, CargoMod 1 to CargoMod 8 direct." The tug operator acknowledged the instructions then Phil could see the thrusters give a series of bursts to ease the ship away from the station. Both the tug and ship disappeared from view as the operator maneuvered to CargoMod 8.

It would take a while for the ship to reach CargoMod 8, so Phil decided he would go down there after lunch to see if there was anything he could do to help prepare it for the recertification inspection. It would be the first time a hangar bay was used on the station.

CargoMod 8 was different from the rest in one respect. It had facilities for ship maintenance. Not only that; there were also hangar bays similar to those on a pretar space station, only not as big. The hangar bays on Oasis 4 were only large enough to accommodate vessels up to one hundred feet long. The pretar station could accommodate a full-size freighter. The little ship that was being moved into the hangar bay would easily fit with room to spare. It was only sixty-five feet long, so there was plenty of space to accommodate it. Phil returned to his office to grapple with more paperwork until noon. That's when he normally went to Eva's for some lunch.

*****

## Oasis 4, Upper CentMod, Eva's Café

Phil was joined for lunch by Will and Luke, and the three ate and talked about nothing in particular really. Then the subject became the little ship that the station was now in possession of. "What do you guys think we should name the ship we got from Fel Nos?" Phil wondered out loud.

Will grinned. "How about *Selak's Revenge?*"

Luke shook his head. "No, *Fel Nos's Pig Pen* is catchy."

After Phil had a laugh. "Well, whatever the name, the company has to be happy with it."

*****

## Oasis 4, CargoMod 8, Ship Maintenance Shop

After lunch, Phil made his way to CargoMod 8, where the new maintenance department was located at the very end of the CargoMod. He found the maintenance hangar bay that had their new ship. The indicator next to the hatch showed that there was pressure in the hangar bay, so he pressed the entry button, and the hatch opened. Before entering, he grabbed a handful of trash bags.

It wasn't strange seeing this ship resting on its landing gear surrounded by breathable air and gravity. This model was designed to enter a planetary atmosphere and land on the surface. Most vessels spend their entire existence in space as they're much too large to land on a planet, which also greatly simplifies the design and construction of a ship. But this one by design was built to extremely sturdy standards to allow it to operate from planetary surfaces.

The crew that brought the ship from CargoMod 1 to CargoMod 8 didn't have to enter the ship to lower the landing gear since there were controls located outside the ship for that purpose. Phil went to the entry hatch and opened a small door that revealed a control console. With a flick of a switch, a set of steps lowered to the hangar deck.

Phil climbed the steps, and then he operated the hatch locking handle. When the locking lugs disengaged, he swung the hatch door open. He then entered the ship and stood there, trying to decide where to start. Since Fel Nos was alone on this ship, he would have spent the majority of his time in the cockpit, so that's where he decided to start the cleanup.

A ship this size wasn't large enough for a bridge or large crew. In fact, this vessel could be operated solo, which is what Fel Nos did. Ideally, any voyage would have more than one qualified pilot so they wouldn't have to stop to allow the pilot to sleep. It was common practice to get up and move about once a course was established and they were in cruise configuration. However, sleeping while at light speed was inadvisable.

After a working day of cruise at light speed, typically a pilot would establish a stable orbit around a planet so he could get some rest. Occasionally, a lone pilot would simply stop in the middle of nowhere to get some sleep. Phil entered the cockpit and found it surprisingly neat and orderly. There was a small workstation behind the cockpit that had some trash strewn about that Phil cleaned up and threw in the trash bag.

He decided the galley was next to be cleaned. There was an abundance of garbage here that he stuffed into bags. The pantry had goods stored, as well as the refrigeration unit. There was also a suspended animation unit on this ship. It wasn't particularly large, as these units get larger, they consume more power. These are desirable to have for foods that couldn't be frozen or preserved in other ways without compromising the nature of the food. Fruit was a popular thing to store this way, as well as bread so it wouldn't get stale while in one of these. All the food was malnun, so Phil used a communication panel to contact the malnun cafeteria in HabMod 4 to have a kitchen worker come down and take it away.

A look at the staterooms revealed that they have been used, but it's been quite some time since anyone has even been in any of them. That left the captain's cabin yet to be cleaned. Phil walked in and looked around. It was in a sorry state indeed. It wasn't all the fault of Fel Nos, as it was Phil who rifled through it thoroughly in his search for evidence that he was mining information from Selak's computer.

Phil took a fresh trash bag and started to fill it with clothes. Fel Nos wouldn't need them where he was. The pretars were sure to provide him with prison togs. When Phil ran across something that appeared to be personnel or sentimental, he put it in a separate container. Four trash bags were filled before he felt he had everything that belonged to Fel Nos gathered.

He decided to make another check of the drawers and closet. The drawers were empty, as was the closet. He looked up and saw that there was a shelf above what he thought was the topmost shelf. He found a step stool and placed it in the closet. Standing on the top step, he peered into the dark recess of the upper shelf and started pulling various items off and letting them drop to the floor. He came upon a metal box with a lock, similar to the one Fel Nos used to store the data he had stolen from Selak. There were obviously items in it, but the lock was a good one and wouldn't budge.

Phil quickly sorted the items from the shelf. There were a couple of things for the box of personnel items; the rest went into a trash bag. Before leaving the cabin, he put the box of personnel things back in the closet and then carried all the trash bags to the hatch, where he threw them in a pile on the hangar deck floor.

Back on board the ship, Phil walked to the cargo hold and found it to be completely empty. Well, he didn't really expect to find anything, since Fel Nos didn't actually do any trading. Looking at his watch, he saw it was getting close to sixteen hundred and he should get to the operations center. On his way out of the ship, he grabbed the small lockbox.

*****

## Oasis 4, CentMod

Phil secured the ship and went to the CentMod. He saw that the personnel director had tables set up and manned. He rode the platform lift to the operations center where he went to his office and deposited the lockbox on his desk. Up the steps to the control center, he checked the plot to see if the *Odyssey* had dropped out of light speed yet.

Seeing that it had indeed begun its approach to the station, he picked up a pair of binoculars and searched in the direction indicated by the plot. The big passenger liner was rapidly approaching the station. Phil could hear the conversation between the controllers and the captain of the Odyssey. As a passenger liner, the *Odyssey* wasn't nearly as heavy as a freighter so it could maneuver much quicker, and it was something Phil had to get used to. They didn't have as much mass as a freighter, but they were just as large, which was very deceiving.

As he watched, the *Odyssey* fired its engines and deployed the thrust reversers to slow its velocity. The ship glided toward the station, and thrusters fired to position it. After a few minutes, the ship remained stationary just a meter or two from the docking ports. Thrusters fired for a second or two, and the liner eased toward the docking clamps. Soon, the clamps engaged and an indicator light in the control center showed the docking was complete.

Phil descended the stairs and left the operations center where he stepped onto the platform lift and took it to the Upper CentMod Plaza Level. He crossed over to the connecting tunnel that leads to CargoMod 1, where he boarded the station shuttle that whisked him off to the CargoMod. At the customs desk, Phil used his pass and continued to the docking port. The station workers were just finishing connecting the umbilical and checking the seal on the hatch. The indicators were all green, so a worker released the safety and opened the station hatch. A crewman on the liner opened the ship's hatch and stepped aside.

*****

**Oasis 4, CargoMod 1**

Passengers started exiting the liner as a purser bid them farewell. A station worker helped direct the flow of people toward the customs desk. Seasoned travelers weren't anxious to exit the liner as it had the effect of crowding the customs desk and shortening tempers.

The passenger lines were long used to the difficulties of moving a large number of people through a single hatch, so they provided a schedule to leave the ship. Where you were on the schedule was determined by what cabin you were in. The purser came up with a method to determine the order. As part of the entertainment one evening, chits with a time block were put in a hat, and a representative from each cabin pulled a chit. The time blocks were announced and recorded on a view screen, everyone catcalled and laughed when unpopular time blocks were pulled and applauded when prime time blocks were pulled.

Phil had no idea what time block Alice had, so he stood there and smiled at the newcomers. Every now and again, he would spot someone who he knew, and there would be a quick reunion. He had to admit that the off-loading was going very smoothly. Baggage was brought out of a hatch on a conveyor system, then met their owners at the customs desk, and customs went quickly since the newcomers were company employees or employee dependents.

After about two-thirds of the passengers had departed the liner, Alice finally emerged. She was slightly shorter than Phil, slender, and with red hair. She spotted Phil right away and let out a squeal, which, in turn, delighted and embarrassed him. Alice threw her arms around Phil and planted a big wet kiss on him.

Phil held her away from him. "Hey, lady, what's the big idea? I'm a married man!"

She put her hands on her hips. "And I'm a married woman!"

Phil had a puzzled look on his face. "I'm not sure where that leaves us." Alice was grinning. "It's a good thing we're married to each other."

Phil nodded in a very animated fashion. "Well, maybe dinner and take you back to our place."

Alice smirked. "Are you sure you can handle it?"

Phil had a smirk of his own. "I'm pretty sure I won't be able to handle it. But what a way to go."

*****

## Oasis 4, Upper CentMod

In anticipation of Alice's arrival, Phil had made reservations at Maurice's, the poshest restaurant on the station. They walked to the customs desk and passed through by waving their passes and proceeded to the connecting tunnel that led to the CentMod. Alice was awestruck with the size of the CentMod and the variety of shops and vendors that were there.

They entered Maurice's, and the maître d' brightened. "Ah, Mr. Ross, how nice to see you. We have a very special table for you near the window." The maître d' sat them at an elegantly set table that had a spectacular view of the nebula, which made Alice gasp.

As Phil sat, the maître d' held Alice's chair. "Timothy will be your waiter." He then explained what the specials were that day.

Phil said, "Thank you, Donald."

A maldor waiter placed menus in front of Phil and Alice. "Hello, I'm Timothy. Can I get you an appetizer?"

Without looking up, Phil said, "I think I'll just have a salad. Hey, weren't you the guy who delivered my pizza last night?"

Timothy smiled. "Yes, sir, I am. I deliver pizzas on nights I don't work here."

Phil asked, "Are you ambitious or really hard up?"

Timothy answered, "It's actually part of a study I'm doing on food service. I plan on opening my own eating establishment someday."

Phil said, "Well, good luck with all that." Phil and Alice enjoyed the meal, and Phil rounded out the evening with a tour of the CentMod.

*****

## Oasis 4, HabMod 1, Quarters of Phillip and Alice Ross

The baggage arrived while they were at dinner. Alice inspected their quarters carefully and finally pronounced them suitable. Although she did say what was needed was a ladies' touch. Phil had to admit that things were a bit Spartan in their lodgings.

The next morning, both awoke at six, and Phil escorted Alice to the fitness center. Alice also liked to start the day with exercise. It's not that she or Phil were fitness fanatics. It was important to establish a routine that promoted healthy habits. It was too easy to let oneself get complacent about exercise in an enclosed environment like a space station. Alice was pleased with the fitness center facilities. Like Phil, she enjoyed a variety of different exercises to prevent her from getting bored with a routine.

After their workout, the pair returned to their quarters for showers and a change of clothes. Alice showered first, then when Phil showered, she used the opportunity to check the kitchen. She thought it was well-equipped but not well-stocked.

When Phil emerged freshly showered and in his work clothes, she stared at him with her hands on her hips. "I don't expect that you have anything we can turn into breakfast, do you?"

Phil looked at Alice with a sheepish expression and muttered, "No, ma'am."

Alice had to suppress a laugh. "Then, pray tell, what have you been doing for meals?" She didn't give Phil time to answer. "I can just guess, judging by the leftover pizza in the refrigerator."

Phil put up his hands. "Why don't we go to my favorite breakfast venue and you'll see for yourself I haven't been completely corrupted by bachelor living."

The couple walked out of their quarters. Phil looked over his shoulder. "SICOS, secure quarters."

*****

**Oasis 4, Upper CentMod, Eva's Café**

They took the escalator to level fifteen and walked the connector tunnel to the CentMod. Phil led her to Eva's where they went to Phil's customary table.

Already sitting there was Captain Dave Jacobson. "About time you rolled out."

Phil smiled. "Dave, when did you get in?"

Dave tossed a couple of menus across the table. "About four-thirty. Introduce me to your young lady."

Phil held a chair for Alice. "My bad. Alice, this is Captain David Jacobson of the *Atlantis Star*. Dave, this is my 'much better half ' Alice." Alice smiled. "Ah yes, one of the fine vessels of the Intersystems Shipping Company."

Dave was surprised. Phil explained, "Alice was a controller on Earth Station 3. That's where we met." Eva came over with her pad, and Phil made more introductions.

After breakfast, the three had coffees and brought Alice up to speed on their roles regarding Selak and Fel Nos. It was getting close to eight o'clock. Phil looked at Alice. "We need to hustle." They bid Dave a good morning and took the platform lift to the operations center.

*****

**Oasis 4, Upper CentMod, Operations Center**

A quick stop at Phil's office to pick up a pad, and then it was off to the conference room. Phil grabbed his customary mug of coffee and turned to sit at his place at the head of the table, only to see that Alice had taken his seat. Phil stood there staring at her, not sure if he should have her move or not. The others in the room were trying not to reveal how amused they were, and they were failing.

Finally, Phil sat at the seat next to Alice. For her part, Alice's expression didn't reveal her amusement until Phil said just loud enough for her to hear. "You did that on purpose." Alice was smirking unashamedly now. The others in the room were getting a sense of the kind of relationship their boss had with his wife.

Phil consulted his pad. "Operations."

Virginia Wells cleared her throat. "Today, there's just the standard freighter traffic today. Nothing special actually. We'll be doing New Arrival Orientation this morning for the ops center folks right after the orientation meeting for all new arrivals."

Phil tapped his pad. "Security."

Luke Smith glanced at his own pad. "We're doing the same orientation schedule as everyone else. Afterward, we'll be bringing the customs desks in CargoMods 5 through 8 online."

Phil tapped his pad again. "Maintenance."

Will Dawson didn't need a pad. "After orientation, we'll be fully powering up the new CargoMods and addressing the little glitches that arise with new equipment."

Phil interrupted, "I wouldn't expect a lot of that. The pretars were pretty thorough."

Will nodded. "Took the words right out of my mouth." Phil gave his pad another tap. "Medical."

Dr. Tillman didn't have a pad. "We have a bunch of physicals to perform. Plus, it'll be the longest period on a space station for the new arrivals, so there's sure to be a rash of nausea cases, especially with the dependents."

Phil looked confused. "Didn't they just spend a month and a half on a spaceship?" The doctor nodded. "Yes, but the ship was moving. There's something about being in motion that kills nausea. It sometimes takes a little time to get used to station life."

Phil put down his pad. "Well, today is the first day that we'll have all the new sections of the station up and running. The conversion of CargoMod 1 to a dedicated passenger terminal and passenger liner service facility will start immediately."

Phil continued, "The outer half of CargoMod 8 is a facility designed for servicing and repairing vessels, and it's complete with four maintenance bays that will accommodate one-hundred-foot-long vessels. It's a different additional set of operations than what we're not used to doing, but I think it's a good fit for what we do out here."

Phil gestured to Alice. "Finally, I would like to introduce everyone to my wife, Alice. Both of us will be at the orientation for dependents and the luncheon for new personnel and dependents. By the way, I do expect all of you to be there. I wish all the company employees could be there, but we need someone to watch the store. Well, if no one has anything further, I think we'll adjourn."

Phil made personal introductions for Alice before everyone left the briefing room, then he and Alice left together. Phil saw her to the platform lift where they parted company. She wanted to explore the CentMod before the dependent's orientation.

Phil went to his office and checked his pad to see if his notes for the orientation were in order. He went through the notes point by point. Satisfied that everything was there, he put the pad in a pocket. In truth, the orientation would only be useful for the personnel who were new to living on a space station. Actually, the dependents would especially find the orientation useful. Phil thought the biggest problem would be the boredom that grew from living in an enclosed environment.

Phil got out of his chair and glanced down at the lock box on his desk. He thought a second or two and decided that he would go to Will Dawson's workshop after the luncheon and open the box. The orientation for all new company arrivals was held in the CentMod theater. He didn't really like to address crowds, but it was part of the job.

*****

## Oasis 4, Upper CentMod, New Arrival Orientation

The orientation was mostly to introduce himself and put a face on station upper management. In many ways, Oasis 4 was the least desirable of assignments because of the location and distance from Earth, but the word about Phil's management style had gotten around, and as a result, when word got out within the company that positions were available, a bidding process was put in place. The result was Oasis 4 got some of the most experienced personnel in Stellar Logistics and Freight Corporation.

Phil finished his contribution to the new arrival orientation and then walked to the orientation for dependents. It was held in an auditorium much like the theater but smaller. Most of the dependents were the wives and husbands of company employees. In attendance were some parents of employees, as well as a few children. There wasn't a company policy about kids living on a space station, but Phil thought there should be because kids needed open spaces and sunshine to play in. The confined environment of Oasis 4, even with its enormous proportions, wasn't an ideal place to raise kids.

Thankfully, most of the new arrivals were "empty nesters." Folks with grown kids but too young to retire themselves. In fact, spending the last years of one's working career on Oasis 4 was an ideal way to bolster the retirement fund. Housing was free, and a premium was paid to workers on remote stations. Also, it was hard to spend money out here. Alice was just finishing her remarks to the dependents that were gathered in the small auditorium when Phil entered. He strode down the aisle and climbed the steps to the stage. He kept his remarks brief and to the point. The kids and teenagers looked like they appreciated not sitting there any longer than they had to.

The orientation being over, everyone filed out of the theater and made a beeline to one of the banquet halls in the CentMod. The buffet meal was provided by the station employee cafeteria staff. After everyone ate, coffee was provided, then Phil and the department heads got the opportunity to finally have a conversation with the new arrivals.

A familiar voice came from behind Phil. "Hey, Phil, won't they let you bounce shuttles off space stations anymore?"

"Boy oh boy. You wreck one shuttle and scratch a space station. They won't let you forget it," Phil said as he turned to find himself face-to-face with Gus Condent.

Gus was a shuttle pilot who worked with Phil for several years before Phil was moved to management. Phil had about ten years of seniority more than Gus, but Gus has always been just as competent as Phil as a pilot.

Phil was genuinely confused as to why Gus was there. "What are you doing here, Gus?"

Gus smirked. "Corporate decided you needed a copilot. There's a betting pool back in Kansas City, whether you actually read the new personnel organization chart. Officially, I'm the assistant station manager, but I received a corporate memorandum en route to here, saying that the station is now in possession of a light-speed capable shuttle. I'm listed as the principal pilot, and you're listed as the backup."

Phil frowned. "Nice! You go through all the good trouble of sending an alien to a labor camp for a quarter century to get his shuttle, and corporate won't let you keep it."

Phil and Gus spent a few minutes catching up, and after a while, another new arrival strolled up. Gus said, "Oh, Phil, this is Jeremy Cole. He's the director of maintenance in the station's new ship maintenance shop."

Phil smiled. "Ah, I have a customer for you already when you settle in."

Jeremy smiled back. "Let me guess. A slightly used shuttle, acquired from a malnun with a flexible sense of morality."

Phil nodded. "That would be the one. It seems to be in good condition. Although there have been some unusual modifications, and I'm not sure if the certifications are current."

Jeremy said, "I'll make it a point to go over the maintenance logs thoroughly before we take any action. By the way, what's the name of the vessel?"

Phil thought a second. "I thought that we would name it the *Aurora*."

*****

## Oasis 4, Upper CentMod, Operations Center

The luncheon wound down, and Phil told Alice he would see her that evening, and he left her talking to some of the other new arrivals. He retreated to his office and grabbed the lockbox that he removed from the ship he had just dubbed the *Aurora*.

When he had just reached the platform lift to go back down, one of the platforms was rising with Gus holding a box under one arm. Phil saw it held some framed photos, a desk nameplate, and other items that one would put on a desk.

Gus was grinning. "No time like the present to move into my office." Phil felt like he should have anticipated Gus getting an office. "Er, right, you get an office. Come on, we'll see Virginia."

Phil found his operations director. "Hey, Virginia, did you set aside an office for the new guy?"

Virginia suppressed a chuckle. "Of course, I did. I read the new organization chart. This way, Gus."

Virginia then led Gus to the office next to Phil's and went through the door with Gus and Phil trailing behind her.

Gus put his box of belongings on the desk. "Well, this is homey." Virginia nodded. "I think it's the nicest office on the station."

Phil looked puzzled. "It's exactly like my office, which is exactly like your office."

Virginia turned to Phil. "Exactly."

Virginia then had Gus register his voiceprint in SICOS while giving him access authorization to station files. She turned to Gus again. "We'll fast-track you through in-processing, then I'll give you a tour of the operations center and the control center."

Gus protested, "This isn't my first time on a space station. I can find my way around."

It was Virginia's turn to protest. "Yeah, but it's your first time on this station. It's your first assignment on a station that's not part of a planetary system. There are operational differences involved. Finally, we have some procedures that differ from corporate norms, some are out of necessity given our location and clientele, and some are changes that Phil or myself have instituted."

Gus put his hands up in mock surrender. "Okay, the new guy's been knocked down a peg. I will submit to my new overlords."

Phil slowly nodded and said sarcastically, "Well, okay, just don't do it again."

Virginia said, laughing, "Come on, Gus, let's get your security pass first. Luke Smith will want to go over a couple of specific items personally since you're the assistant station manager."

The three of them boarded the platform lift. After Virginia pressed the button for the plaza level, she looked at Gus. "I couldn't help but overhear you at the luncheon. Something about bouncing a shuttle off a space station."

Phil blurted out, "I move to the most remote station in the system, and I'm still getting grief over that."

Gus leaned over to Virginia. "I'll tell you later."

As the platform lift slowed to a stop at the plaza level, Phil said, "I'll be in Will's maintenance shop, so you two can talk freely."

As Phil strode in the direction of the maintenance shop while Virginia and Gus chuckled. They knew Phil wasn't really upset. Virginia said, "Okay, I still haven't heard the dented station story yet."

Gus shrugged. "Phil was piloting an old Delta 7 shuttle with twenty-five passengers. He was easing up to the docking clamps when the thruster controls failed. Unfortunately, they didn't fail in a predictable manner. The proportioning circuitry malfunctioned, causing the amount of thrust to be variable. The same amount of control input would result in different outputs, making it nearly uncontrollable and unpredictable. The thrusters would also fire on their own just to make things interesting. The shuttle slammed into the station a bunch of times before Phil could stop it from beating itself to death."

They stepped onto an escalator to an upper tier. Gus continued, "Phil kept his head and dealt with the problem. The shuttle was beaten up to scrap, and he was kept pretty busy for a while with a roll of reinforced tape, stopping leaks. The station couldn't contact him because the antennas were all snapped off, so they finally sent a tug to pull them to a docking port. That particular malfunction was put into the simulator, and there were only about 3 percent of the pilots who could successfully resolve the problem."

Virginia asked, "What's so problematic about resolving the thruster malfunction?"

Gus thought about his answer. "The main problem is you're being thrown around the cockpit in about the most violent manner you could possibly think of, and guessing the thrust you're going to get is impossible."

Virginia said, "I've never heard that story before. I wonder why?"

Gus shrugged. "Pilots are an odd breed. We'll brag about things that we should be doing all the time, but getting out of a bad situation by the skin of your teeth barely gets a mention."

Virginia frowned. "Give me an example of something pilots brag about that should be routine."

Gus thought for a second, "The perfect landing. Being at a position fix at exactly the planned time. Going through reentry without any control corrections because you've set up your pre-reentry profile perfectly. Stuff like that."

Virginia said, "Still, it's funny I've never heard that story before."

Gus said, "It probably has something to do with us nicknaming him Crash."

*****

## Oasis 4, Upper CentMod, Maintenance Shop

Phil entered the maintenance shop. He looked around and saw, in one corner, Will was issuing tool kits and lockers to new arrivals. He indicated to Will's work bench, and Will nodded approval, so he carried the lockbox over to the bench and set it down. After examining the locking mechanism, he could see it was a particularly sturdy lock but not as sturdy as the box itself.

Phil was studying the box when Will walked up. "Where did you get that, Boss?"

Phil kept scrutinizing the box. "The ship we got from Fel Nos. He had it squirreled away in his closet. It struck me at the time that he was trying to hide this, and I thought it would be worth looking into."

Will looked over the box. It was made of a material that was extremely resistant to cutting and heat. The weakest part of it was indeed the lock. He then picked up the box and glanced at Phil. "May I?"

Phil nodded. "Sure."

Will walked over to a milling machine and clamped it to the table, ensuring that the surface of the lock was parallel to the table. This wasn't precision work, so he didn't have to be real fussy. He looked in a cabinet and selected an end mill.

As he was installing the tool in the mill's collet, he said, "These tools haven't changed much at all in the last few hundred years." He adjusted the table height and made sure it was aligned the way he wanted it. When he was satisfied, he turned on the mill and engaged the mechanism that fed the work into the cutter. Will had the cutter adjusted to shave off the surface of the locking mechanism a couple of thousands of an inch at a time.

Will was right about the lock; the tool steel cutter went through the metal lock like it was butter as it was shaved down. After several passes a layer of the lock was removed, exposing the interior mechanism. Will used fine needle nose pliers and picks to pull the workings out of the lock. With that done, he could pull the bolts out of the way and disengage the lock.

Will opened the case and found that it was filled with foam that had cutouts for data chips. Phil and Will examined the data chips. They were labeled in malnun, which made Phil frown. Will had an idea, "SICOS, display the malnun alphabet and numerical system." Malnun symbols filled the screen, and they began comparing them with what was on the data chips.

After a minute, Will said, "Wait a second, we're doing this the hard way. Help me lay these out on the bench." They laid out the chips, being careful to keep them in the same order they were in while in the box.

Will used a digital camera and photographed the chips. After he downloaded the photo to SICOS, he ordered, "SICOS, translate writing in image and overlay translation on the image."

The SICOS didn't find that task difficult in the least. Phil pulled out a sheet of labels and a permanent marker then began making new labels in English.

Phil remarked, "This hasn't changed in a few hundred years either." Will laughed as he peeled the backing from the labels that Phil finished and stuck them to the appropriate data chip. Once the chips were labeled in English, Phil selected the chip labeled Background Information. He plugged it into the SICOS terminal; an image appeared on the screen. Phil tapped the image, and several file indicators appeared. Studying the file names didn't offer any clarification.

The first file was titled "The *Prospector*," so he tapped the file indicator, and the file opened. What he saw was a Shipping Registry Vessel Profile for a ship called the *Prospector*. It was a 123-foot-long mining vessel. It was designed to land on asteroids. A mining crew would extract the ore and load it into the ship's hold. It had a crew complement of five officers, including the captain and eight crewmen. There were also twelve miners assigned to the *Prospector*. The equipment on board included rock-boring drills, rock crushers, ore separators, loaders, and instruments to assay minerals. Phil read the profile with interest. Then he saw the registration status that read "Vessel lost."

Reading further, Phil saw that it simply disappeared seventeen years ago. It was owned by the captain and not by a corporation. As a result, there were no records kept as to previous ports of call. Apparently, there weren't even any flight plans filed to give a clue as to the final resting place of the *Prospector*.

Will finally said, "This is fascinating and everything, but I need my SICOS and shop back."

Phil smiled. "Okay, hint taken."

Phil closed down the SICOS program and removed the data chip. He put the chip back in its place in the lockbox and headed toward the door to the CentMod public area. Once in the public area, he took an escalator to the plaza level then the platform lift to the operations center. On the way up, Phil was lost in thought. He wondered why Fel Nos was interested in a mining ship gone missing seventeen years. A guy like Fel Nos wasn't going to do historical research for personal knowledge. Phil had done some research on Fel Nos a few weeks ago. From what he could determine, Fel Nos had an aversion to making a living honestly. He was always involved in some sort of scam or get-rich-quick scheme. Phil's interest was definitely piqued.

*****

**Oasis 4, Upper CentMod, Operations Center**

Once in the operations center, Phil saw Virginia showing Gus some of the finer features of the status boards. He retreated to his office and deposited the lockbox on his desk. Then he went back to the ops center lower level in time to see Virginia introduce Gus to the chief controller, Bret Pinkerton. Bret led Gus to the control level, and Phil followed. It wasn't Gus's first time in a control center, but there were several features of this one that was unique to Oasis 4.

Phil was grateful to see that Gus was very attentive and serious. He didn't joke around or try to impress Bret with his credentials. He had to admit that even though Gus was a professional, he was still a pilot. It was part of a pilot's persona to not take anything very seriously. While Bret continued to orient Gus, Phil picked up a pair of binoculars and took a look at some of the vessels approaching the station.

When Bret finished, Gus shook his hand and turned to Phil. Phil smiled. "Well, what do ya think?"

Gus smiled back. "I think we're in over our heads."

Phil shook his head. "Na, there's actually not a lot to do if you have quality folks to run things for you. The trick is to let them do what they do best and allow them to function."

Phil checked the chronometer on the wall and got a look on his face. "What do ya say we go to Sparky's for a drink?"

Gus liked the idea. "Why don't we get dinner too?"

Phil shook his head. "Can't. The Old Ball and Chain will skin me alive if I screw up and miss a dinner she prepared."

*****

## Oasis 4, Upper CentMod, Sparky's Taproom

Fifteen minutes later, they were walking into Sparky's. The interior looked as if an American Midwestern corner bar was picked up, moved a couple of thousand light-years, and plunked down on Oasis 4.

Phil's eyes adjusted to the dim light, and he spotted Alice with one of her friends at a table. He just stood there, staring. "How does she do that? I haven't been to Sparky's since I've been here. The second I give in, she's there." Alice spotted them and waved them over.

When Phil and Gus approached the table, Alice asked, "Is this what you do before dinner?"

Phil felt cornered. "No! I thought Gus and I could get caught up over a beer.

I've never even been here before today... Hey, wait a second, you're in here."

Alice was laughing now. "Relax, Phil. Brenda and I were having a glass of wine before dinner and catching up ourselves."

Gus recognized Brenda from his earlier arrival at the ops center. "How do you two know each other?"

"Alice was my supervisor on Earth Station 3," Brenda offered.

A server took Phil and Gus's order as they sat. Alice looked at Phil. "There is no food to speak of in our quarters. Honestly, I don't know what would become of you if I didn't come here to make sure you got a home-cooked meal every now and again. Tomorrow, I'll order groceries. Meanwhile tonight, you'll have to take me out to dinner."

Several times during Alice's little fake rant, Phil tried to get a word in to defend himself. When Alice finally stopped, he hesitated and finally just said, "Yes, ma'am."

Brenda and Gus were thoroughly amused by what was happening. Alice enjoyed putting Phil on the spot, and Phil knew better than to fight it.

The drinks arrived, and the conversation shifted to Phil's relief. Gus remarked, "I've had a full day with the orientation, in-processing, and the briefings."

"How did the briefings go?" Phil asked.

Gus took a sip. "Very informative. You have a well-oiled machine here. That Luke Smith is a thoroughly professional individual. I guess he has to be with the riffraff that visits the station on occasion. While I was in the security office, they discovered that someone had broken into the Aurora last night."

Phil nearly spit out his beer. "That's news to me. What do you know?" Gus shrugged. "Not a lot. I just know what I overheard."

Phil thought a second or two and finally said, "Whoever it was must not have got away with much. I removed all of Fel Nos's belongings. There's nothing there. Did they steal ship parts?"

Gus shook his head. "It didn't sound like it. They were saying it looked like all the personnel spaces were rifled through."

Phil took another sip. "The only thing I can think of that Fel Nos may have had that would have any interest is a lockbox full of data chips."

"Where's the box now?" Gus asked.

Phil answered, "In my office, on my desk."

Gus took a sip of beer and slowly nodded. "I believe I would put that under lock and key."

Phil agreed. "That is a good idea."

"Did you check out any of the chips?" Gus asked.

Phil said, "Just one. It was a Shipping Registry Vessel Profile for a ship called the Prospector. I couldn't tell you what was valuable about it. It's been listed as missing for seventeen years."

Alice interrupted, "Yeah, yeah, quite a mystery. We're done with our drinks.

Take me to dinner."

Brenda thought she should strike while the iron was hot. She looked at Gus. "Buy me a nice meal at an elegant establishment."

Gus felt he shouldn't give in easily. "How about a standard meal in a whimsical setting?" He looked at Phil. "What's the policy on dating coworkers?"

Phil shrugged. "It's acceptable if you're not allergic to pepper spray. I have just the place."

The four of them left after Phil paid the tab. They didn't notice the grunst sitting at the table behind them, hanging onto every word of their conversation.

*****

## Oasis 4, Upper CentMod, Plaza Level

Tiffany Waters was on patrol in the CentMod. Although the station was a twenty-four-hour operation, a day/night routine was established to simulate normalcy. During the hours between 2000 hours Zulu and 0700 hours Zulu, the lights were dimmed, and the shops were closed. Of course, there were station personnel at work for the benefit of arriving vessels; however, the operations were generally shut down.

Tiffany was walking the plaza level when she had a security breach alert on her communication pad that all security personnel wore. It indicated that there was someone trying to enter the station manager's office without authorization. Instantly her five-foot-four-inch frame was sprinting to the platform lift.

Once on the lift, she pressed the button for the operations center. Near the top, she reached down and extracted a baton from her belt. It was about as old- fashioned a weapon as there could be found, but it was one of the few things that were effective on all the species that inhabited the station. Firearms weren't a viable option, given that a stray bullet could spell disaster for all concerned. Energy weapons were being developed that held some hope, but so far, they were too difficult to dial down the power to prevent vaporizing a perpetrator.

The platform lift stopped, and Tiffany stepped into the operations center. She turned in the direction of the management offices, then proceeded slowly at a crouch, with a baton at the ready. The station manager's office was around the corner, and Tiffany stopped to listen. She could hear someone disassembling the electronic lock. Glancing down at the communication pad on her wrist, she saw on the display that her backup was just stepping off the platform lift.

She pressed a button to show she was ready to confront whoever was in the office. One security deputy stayed at the hallway entrance while another crept up next to her, then he glanced in her direction and nodded. Tiffany was first through the door, followed by her fellow deputy. There at Phil's desk stood a grunst stuffing the lockbox in a rucksack.

He reacted instantly at the interruption and bolted for the door. Tiffany and her fellow deputy were surprised that he thought he could make it past them. All at once, the grunst leaped to the ceiling and stuck there. He scurried along like a spider on the ceiling toward the door. The other deputy reacted to try to block his way, then the grunst swung his feet down and kicked the deputy in the head while swinging through the door.

Tiffany rushed through the door in pursuit, prompting the grunst to leap to the ceiling again and scurry away. She caught up and swung her baton, catching the grunst in the arm, causing him to lose his grip and fall to the floor. Tiffany took another swing and smashed his knee, making the grunst howl in pain. Then he tried to find a position that offered him the most protection while she swatted him several more times with her baton.

The deputy that entered the office with Tiffany ran up and fell on the grunst full force, finishing the process of subduing him. The deputy that remained at the hallway entrance heard the commotion and rushed in to offer any assistance if needed. The grunst was far too distracted by the deputy he kicked, now putting cuffs on him, and Tiffany standing there with her baton raised, ready to crack him again. They pulled him to his feet and pushed him face-first to the wall.

His pockets were checked and emptied. Tiffany bent down and picked up the rucksack. "Are you okay, Bill?"

Bill had blood pouring from his nose. "Yeah, I should have been on the ball with this guy. Good job knocking him off the ceiling."

They took the grunst to the security office and called a medic to make sure Tiffany didn't do any permanent damage and to treat Bill's nose.

*****

## Oasis 4, Upper CentMod, Eva's Café

After Phil and Alice's morning exercise, they showered and went to breakfast. Sitting at Phil's customary table at Eva's, Alice asked, "Do you eat all your meals here?"

Phil quickly answered, "No, no, just most of them."

Alice smiled. "Actually, it's not bad if you don't always get the comfort food on the menu."

Alice was adding cream to her coffee. "Dinner tonight will be in our quarters.

That is if the grocery on this station is stocked halfway decent." Phil said, "I haven't had any complaints."

Luke Smith strolled to the table. "Hey, folks, can I join?"

Alice beat Phil to the draw. "Please sit. Don't stand on ceremony."

Eva brought Luke a cup and took his order. He took a sip and said, "That tastes good after the last couple of hours."

Phil looked annoyed. "What about the last couple of hours?"

Luke took another sip. "My deputies caught a grunst breaking into your office."

Phil was in now even more annoyed at being kept in the dark about the break in of the *Aurora* and now his office and relieved that they caught the culprit. "Why am I just learning about this? I was told the Aurora was ransacked also."

Luke put up his hands. "Whoa, Boss. We were still investigating to see if there was indeed a crime committed on the *Aurora*. Nothing was missing, and it looked for all the world like you might have come back and opened all the hatches and drawers. As far as the incident this morning goes, we're still processing the perpetrator. Besides, there was no point in waking you since there's nothing you can do until we interrogate him."

Phil backed off. "Okay, what was he after anyway?"

Luke scratched his head. "He tried to make off with that lockbox on your desk."

Phil leaned back. "I'm beginning to suspect that Fel Nos was into something lucrative. I'm wondering whether it was legal or not."

"Judging by what we know about Fel Nos, probably not." Luke laughed.

*****

## Oasis 4, CentMod, Briefing Room

Phil walked into the briefing room and poured a cup of coffee at 0800 as normal and sat at his usual seat. He saw there were two people in attendance that were in addition to the normal complement. There was Gus sitting to Phil's right and Jeremy Cole at the opposite end of the table. Phil started, "I'd like to start by welcoming Gus Condent, our new assistant manager, and Jeremy Cole, director of maintenance of the new ship maintenance division."

Everyone gave a short round of applause. Phil continued, "I'd also like to thank the security division for the tremendous job in arresting the grunst that broke into my office. Please, get everyone up to speed on what happened yesterday."

Luke cleared his throat. "Yesterday early, it appeared that someone had broken into the station's new shuttle and ransacked it. Then this morning, three of my deputies arrested a grunst who had broken into the station manager's office. The only thing he appeared to be interested in was a lockbox that was removed from the newly acquired shuttle."

Phil asked, "Has he made a statement yet?"

Luke shook his head. "Not yet. He wouldn't even tell us his name. We had to use his DNA to get information on him from the Multi-World Commerce Cooperative Database. His name is Jitec Kilonoct, and he had a room in the Star Lodge Suites."

"How did you get his DNA?" Phil wondered.

Luke tried to keep from laughing. "He wouldn't cooperate at first, but Tiffany convinced him that it would be in his best interest if he let us have a saliva sample."

Gus started to ask, "How did she—"

Luke interrupted, "She scares the daylights out of him."

"She scares the daylights out of a lot of us," Phil added. "Well, anyway, Luke, I'd like to be there when you interrogate him. What else is new in the world of security?"

Luke looked at a pad. "Really, only one item sticks out. Flast is in the middle of a revolution. It's actually one of the least violent revolutions I've ever heard of. The ruling class there is in exile, and the new government is deliberating and writing a new constitution and Charter of Rights. Before you wonder how this affects us, let me help you. Any arrivals from Flast may be in a desperate frame of mind. Unless they're wanted by some authority somewhere, they're welcome here, but a heightened security profile would be appropriate."

Phil heard the reports from Operations, then medical and station maintenance. He then said, "I don't expect you to have a huge report today, Jeremy, but what are your plans for today?"

Jeremy leaned back. "We'll be organizing the shop, and I'll have a crew evaluating the Aurora. Stop by the hangar bay this afternoon, and we'll have a report for you."

Phil turned off his pad. "Okay, folks, let's have a great day."

As everyone was filing out, Phil stopped Luke. "Luke, I want two things. First, I want to know how this grunst made it past the station security measures. Then I would like first crack at interrogating Jitec Kilonoct."

Luke looked concerned. "Look, Boss, I know you're mad, but I don't think it's a good idea for you to be in the same room with him."

Phil said, "I have some experience with grunsts. I think I can squeeze something out of him."

*****

## Oasis 4, Upper CentMod, Security Office

In the security office, Phil sat in the interview room while Luke settled in the observation room. Phil had the lockbox that Jitec Kilonoct tried to steal on the table in front of him. The door opened. Jitec was led into the room and thrown into the chair opposite Phil. The deputy removed the handcuffs and left the room. Jitec sneered at Phil in obvious contempt, and Phil had to work at not smiling. Grunsts are so predictable, and this one is a textbook example.

Phil looked at the pad he had in front of him. "Jitec Kilonoct." Jitec curled his lip. "Yes, what is it you want, human?"

Phil kept his tone very even and reasonable. "I would think that would be obvious."

Jitec shot back, "Well, it isn't. I tried to steal something, and you people are thinking that there is more to this than there is."

Phil looked at him across the table. "You could hardly blame us for that." Phil slowly opened the lockbox, exposing the data chips inside. "After all, you can get data chips anywhere. There must be something very special about these particular chips."

Jitec stared at the lockbox. "Why don't you look at them yourself?"

Phil answered, "I plan to. I thought it would save time if you filled us in with what you know."

Jitec was starting to really get contemptuous. "I wouldn't tell you if my life depended on it! If those chips have any value, you'll need to determine that for yourself!"

Phil was thinking that Jitec was nearly ready. "I looked at the first chip. There was just information about a mining ship. I doubt if it's even still commissioned. Even if it was, I can't see how it could be valuable." Phil knew full well that the ship was listed as missing. He didn't want Jitec to know how much he knew.

Phil pressed a button that was not in view of Jitec. A deputy entered and put down a plastic pitcher of ice water and two plastic glasses. Without looking away from Jitec, Phil said, "Thank you, Roger."

Roger picked up the lockbox and left the room.

Luke sat in the observation room, wondering why Phil thought he was more qualified to wring information out of Jitec. Phil poured ice water into both glasses. Jitec picked his up and took a sip.

Phil continued, "I'll ask one more time. What is it that makes the data chips so valuable that you would risk getting caught?"

Jitec snorted in derision. "So far, getting caught hasn't been that much of an inconvenience."

All at once, Phil flew out of his chair and swept the pitcher and glasses from the table with his hand. "I'm sick and tired of screwing around with you! If I don't get some answers, you'll go out an air lock!" Phil started climbing over the table.

On cue, three deputies rushed into the room. Two held back Phil while the third rushed over to Jitec and shielded him. "Spit it out, grunst! What do you need those chips for! What were you and Fel Nos up to?"

Jitec was confused, scared, and wishing he had made better life decisions. "They're everything that Fel Nos had collected on a mining ship called the *Prospector*."

Phil was red in the face. "I know that! What about the *Prospector*? What do a pair of losers like you and Fel Nos need information about a missing mining vessel for?"

Jitec couldn't get the answer out of his mouth fast enough. "We were going to salvage the ship. The ore in the hold alone will get us enough to buy our own space station."

Phil strained against the deputies. "No one knows where the Prospector is. It's listed as missing!"

Jitec was sobbing. "One of Fel Nos's partners found it. He was hiding in an asteroid belt and happened upon it. The asteroid belt was rich in paxtite ore, and Fel Nos's partner reasoned that the hold must have been nearly full judging by the condition of the asteroid."

Phil kept the pressure on Kilonoct. "What was the name of this partner of Fel Nos?"

"He's a human named Marcus Pointer," Kilonoct cried. "Where is this Marcus Pointer now?" Phil spat.

Jitec stammered, "H-H-H-He was arrested by the pretars for trying to steal a shield array for an asteroid mining facility."

Phil considered what Jitec told him. "Did Pointer happen to tell Fel Nos where this asteroid belt is?"

Jitec shook his head. "No, I suppose he adhered to the old earth axiom that there's no honor among thieves."

Phil softened. "What do you bring to the party?"

Jitec continued, "I have some experience in towing vessels." "Yeah, I read that. Most of them without the owner's knowledge,"

Phil shot back. "So what did you and Fel Nos need additional funds for?"

Jitec shook his head. "Fel Nos said we needed additional equipment and supplies."

Phil wasn't buying that explanation. It may be partly true, but it didn't explain everything. Phil stared at Jitec for a few seconds then turned to the deputy standing near him. "Take Mr. Kilonoct to a holding cell."

Phil stepped into the hall where Luke was laughing and wiping tears from his eyes. "Okay, you'll have to explain how you managed to get him to talk."

Phil smiled and said, "Let's talk about this in your office."

Once in Luke's office, Phil explained, "Grunsts are pretty predictable once you know how their brain works or, more precisely, what they haven't trained their brain to accept. He charged right at Bill because he knew what to expect from him. Kilonoct could have probably given Tiffany a fight, but everything in his experience told him that there should be no way a human female her size could possibly do anything to cause him pain. When she proved that theory wrong, Kilonoct couldn't process it in his head. If he was wrong about that, what else could he be wrong about."

Phil grinned. "In his eyes, I'm just a functionary, middle management type.

Nothing to fear here. I played into that for a while. When I sensed that Kilonoct was feeling smug, I shifted gears. Suddenly the rules changed. Kilonoct didn't see it coming and couldn't catch up."

Luke shook his head while chuckling. "I'll have to write that down. Each culture has its own quirks. It's useful to know what buttons to push. By the way, how in the heck does he climb the walls and scurry along the ceiling like that?"

"The same way a gecko does it," Phil offered. "I'm sure you noticed he wasn't wearing shoes. A grunst's fingertips and toes are bulbous and covered with microscopic hairs called setae. These hairs get into the tiniest imperfections in a surface. It's such an intimate fit Van Der Waals force takes over."

Luke's expression changed to understanding, "Let's go to the crime lab."

They walked into the crime lab, which wasn't large, but it was well-equipped. They spotted a deputy at a workstation who was busy going over data and video. Luke announced his arrival, "Hey, Carl, are you having any luck?"

Without looking up, Carl said in a perplexed tone, "Not much, Chief, but I did find out how he defeated the security video monitor in CargoMod 8, though. He tapped into a data cable at maintenance access."

Carl tossed a small device on the table next to him. "He installed this device on the cable, and it fed us a video loop of an empty corridor." Carl continued, "How he made it to the operations center without showing up on any of the monitors long enough to track him is a genuine mystery."

"I can help you with that," Luke offered. "Display the CentMod plaza level security camera coverage plot."

Carl complied, "I've been over this a dozen times. There's simply no way he could get to the platform lift without being recorded."

Luke studied the areas that didn't have coverage. "The central column has a couple of areas without coverage."

Carl protested, "Yes, but there's no need for it. No access, no need for coverage."

Luke studied the plot. "Bring up the number 6 column camera." Carl did as he was told. "That points away from the Central Column."

Luke said, "Yup. Zoom in to the window at Sparky's. Now start at the time index twenty minutes before the alarm."

Carl played the video at two times the normal speed. He watched carefully until he saw motion reflected in the window. He stopped the video and backed it up until the figure he saw came back in view, then he paused the image.

Luke smiled. "Well, look at that. It's Mr. Kilonoct."

Carl straightened up. "Give me a second." He tapped instructions into the computer. He had the program isolate Kilonoct in both the window reflections and the raw video, where he couldn't manage to avoid being recorded. Next, he created a composite of Kilonoct's movements and selected a point of view to observe how he managed to get to the operations center. All three watched the playback from the time Kilonoct appeared in the CentMod.

Kilonoct stopped at the center column at a point he selected. Carl gasped. "That's how he did it. He just climbed the wall to the landing at the top."

Phil said, "Now you know something else about grunsts."

*****

## Oasis 4, Upper CentMod, Eva's Café

Phil and Luke went to Eva's for lunch. After ordering, Luke looked over to Phil. "I thought Alice was going to put the brakes on you eating out every day?"

Phil shrugged. "She hasn't said anything about lunch yet. But I do suspect I'll either be brown bagging it before too long or going to the company cafeteria."

In a few minutes, they were joined by Will Dawson, Jeremy Cole, and Gus Condent. After ordering, Gus asked, "How did your little chat with Kilonoct go?"

Phil answered sarcastically, "Oh, he's doing great. He would like a larger cell to practice his wall climbing, though. Seriously, however, he and Fel Nos were into something potentially lucrative. I'll have to go over these data chips carefully and see if I can figure out what they knew."

Luke looked down at the lockbox on the table. "I would put those in the vault in your office tonight."

Gus frowned. "Didn't you get Kilonoct to spill his guts?"

Phil replied, "Yeah, I'm convinced that he told us everything he knew. There's a lot apparently that Fel Nos didn't fill him in on."

Will asked, "What exactly were they into?"

Phil said, "A 123-foot-long mining vessel with a hold full of paxtite ore."

Gus and Will started laughing but stopped suddenly when they realized that Phil wasn't kidding. Will pulled a pad out of his pocket and started tapping. "Do you know how much that much ore would be worth?"

Luke nodded. "More than this station brings in revenue in a year."

Then Luke wondered aloud, "So why was Fel Nos raising revenue in the unsavory fashion that was eventually his undoing?"

Jeremy said, "I think I can help you with that. He needed to make modifications to his ship. The modifications he made weren't cheap, and there are still one or two things he would have needed to do before he could do what I suspect he wanted to do."

Gus looked at Jeremy. "I won't ask you to repeat that. Because I don't think it would make it any more understandable."

Jeremy laughed. "I've had my best guys going over the *Aurora* all morning. It's in unbelievably good condition. Recertification won't be a problem at all. This Fel Nos guy has had some modifications done that made no sense until you told us what he was into. If you stop by this afternoon, we'll have a complete report for you."

Gus shook his head. "I don't get it. This Fel Nos guy knew where to find enough paxtite ore to live like a king in any colony in the known galaxy. Even if he brought in an investor and had to give up the lion's share, his portion would be more than any one person could burn through in a lifetime."

Luke was putting ketchup on the burger Eva just put in front of him. "Greed. It doesn't make sense to us to run the risk of not being able to cash in on something like that. But Fel Nos obviously couldn't stand the thought of having to share this with anyone. I'd be willing to bet that Kilonoct was going to be cut out the deal somehow."

Phil crushed some crackers into his soup. "You're probably right about that.

Kilonoct didn't contribute a lot to the plan."

Phil took a bite of his sandwich and thought while he chewed. He swallowed and took a sip of iced tea. "You know, that ship is just a taste of the wealth that's out there. Kilonoct said the asteroid belt is rich in paxtite."

You could almost see the lightbulb click on over Gus's head. "You know, if we were to find that ship and asteroid belt, we would be in line for one heck of a finder's fee."

Phil stared over the heads of those across the table from him. "Let's think about this. We tumbled onto this information in the course of our duties working for the Stellar Logistics and Freight Corporation. We would have to use the *Aurora*, which is a company-owned asset. As employees, we wouldn't be entitled to any of the proceeds in a legal sense. However, the company has been pretty good to us over the years, and screwing us over on a deal like this would be bad publicity. Even if we didn't get anything out of it, it would be a hoot to do this."

"I wouldn't count my kortlax before they hatched," Will cautioned. "The last time I looked out a viewport, I noticed the galaxy is still a rather large place."

Phil smiled. "You're right about that. But on the other hand, Fel Nos and Kilonoct were willing to take all kinds of risks to bring in the Prospector."

*****

## Oasis 4, Upper CentMod, Office of Phillip Ross

After lunch, Phil retreated to his office with the lockbox. He sat at his desk and examined the contents. Then he selected the data chip he had viewed previously, labeled Background Information. He had already viewed the ship profile. The next file was labeled Bills of lading, so he opened it and saw that it contained a list of the cargo manifest reported by the *Prospector* going back several years. He decided to start at the earliest entry.

The minerals delivered were nothing out of the ordinary. There was a lot of bauxite, which was a good bread and butter material. It made sense since bauxite, or aluminum ore, and was in high demand. There was also iron, nickel, copper, zinc, and occasionally loads of hard-to-find ores like tungsten, lithium, and carbide. The last entry was very interesting. The *Prospector* delivered a thousand tons of nickel and four tons of paxtite to Oasis 3.

That was the last entry, so Phil closed that file and ejected the data chip. He inserted the next data chip. It contained the communications records of the *Prospector*. They weren't the records of the *Prospector* exactly, but what was recorded by monitoring stations. All of it was considered public information, and there wasn't anything illegal. However, there were some messages that were coded and not intended for public consumption.

Phil reasoned that the coded messages must have been purchased from unscrupulous individuals in possession of them. The interesting thing about the communications records was most of them had a code that indicated the direction the signal originated from. Phil made it point to remember that little bit of knowledge. It may prove to be useful. Phil inserted a third data chip and examined the single file it contained, which was information on an asteroid mining facility. He was a bit confused by this. According to Kilonoct, the asteroid in question didn't have any facilities on it at all. Then he realized that the file detailed a prison facility. Phil didn't grasp the significance of the file at all. Then he realized that the information anyone needed to break someone out of the facility was all there.

So if Fel Nos couldn't figure out where the Prospector is, he would just go and grab Marcus Pointer. The pretars would be very interested to learn how Fel Nos got ahold of this information. The fourth chip was inserted, and Phil knew immediately that this one was definitely going to be useful regardless of how this business with the Prospector turned out. It was all the manuals on the modifications made to the Aurora. Some of them, he wasn't sure why they needed to be done, but at least he had the manuals on them. He decided to have a talk with Jeremy Cole before he drew any wrong conclusions.

Phil pocketed the data chip with the records of the modifications made to the Aurora. The rest of the data chips, he ensured that they were back in the lockbox, then he placed the lockbox in his office vault and secured it.

*****

## Oasis 4, CargoMod 8, Ship Maintenance Shop

Jeremy Cole was in the hangar bay that held the *Aurora*, and he was sitting at a workstation using the SICOS to complete the inspection report.

Phil strolled up. "Hey, Jeremy, what kind of shape is she in?"

Jeremy looked up from his work. "Hey, Boss, it's in great shape overall. In fact, it's in fantastic condition. This Fel Nos guy got a hold of a very clean vessel. I did some checking on the registration history and found it was originally owned by a gentleman from our planet who was under suspicion for various nefarious activities. He signed over ownership of the ship we now call the *Aurora* to Fel Nos. I asked some colleagues in the industry why the ship was signed over, and no one really knows. It's suspected that there was some blackmail involved. That's more a question for Luke Smith. What I can tell you is this ship was no slouch when it was in its original configuration, but Fel Nos had some interesting modifications done."

Phil put up a finger. "That reminds me, you'll need this. It was in a lockbox Fel Nos had hidden." Phil dug the data chip out of his pocket and handed it to Jeremy.

Jeremy inserted the chip into the SICOS and viewed the files. "Ah, yes, this is good to have. We didn't have any documentation on who did the modifications or how they did it. We could see it was quality work, but it's good to have it written down, so to speak."

One of Jeremy's technicians strolled up. "I never thought that I'd see the day.

The Astrodyne 65 is a serious machine in the first place, but the mods on this thing turn it into a legend. The light-speed engines are Victor 150s. The reaction engines are Detroit, ion-injected 750s. Thrusters are twice the size as original."

Jeremy smiled. "Phil, meet Chad. Chad's one of my lead technicians. He's in charge of the recertification of the Aurora. Here, Chad, make sure you save these documents in the usual places."

Chad looked at the SICOS display and brightened. "Great! This saves me about a week's worth of work."

He looked at the file menu. "These mods were done at New Oslo Shipyards." "Is that a good thing?" Phil asked.

"That's a great thing," Chad confirmed.

Chad ejected the data chip and went to another SICOS terminal to download the data. He would also put it in the ship's maintenance database. After that, he would make two more data chips, one would be stored on board the *Aurora*, one filed on the station, and finally, Chad was going to send the data to company headquarters on Earth, where they were going to make similar precautions.

Jeremy chuckled. "Chad's one of a dying breed. He's right, though. This ship is impressive. In addition to the engines and thrusters, there have been some interesting additions to the hull. First, the navigation shield array has been upgraded. It'll throw a protective bubble around a ship more than four times as large as this one. Also, the bottom half of the bubble can be turned off."

Phil frowned. "What use would that be?"

Jeremy answered, "It's a common feature on mining ships. While parked on an asteroid, occasionally, smaller rocks will collide with the rock the ship is parked on. If one of those rocks smashed into the ship, it's all over."

Phil was trying to recall his classes on asteroids. "I'm not well-versed in mining vessels or asteroids. I would have figured the small asteroids would just float there next to the big asteroids. What motivates them to move around?"

Jeremy said, "I'm not an expert either, but from what I understand, there are a number of things that could do it. The most common is comets passing in close proximity. If the comet collides with an asteroid, it'll put things in motion. The ones with the least amount of mass move easier. I've heard of some asteroid belts having clouds of smaller rocks weaving in and out of the larger rocks. Eventually, they'll smash into each other until there are just a few rouge travelers in the belt."

Phil absorbed the new information. "What else is different?" Phil asked. "There are towing clamps installed. You can see them there and there,"

Jeremy said while pointing to fittings and clamps on the side of the ship.

Phil had noticed them before but didn't know their function. Only now he saw that they were recent additions. "Okay, let me get this straight, Marcus Pointer finds the *Prospector*. He hooks up with Fel Nos because Fel Nos has a ship that can be modified to tow the *Prospector*. Fel Nos recruited Jitec Kilonoct because Kilonoct knows how to tow ships, usually without the owner's knowledge."

Jeremy pondered on the new information. "This ship is ready right now to grab the *Prospector* and cash in. Now I understand that this Fel Nos guy was caught stealing information from the pretars. Why? It seems like a stupid and unnecessary risk."

"I think I can help with that," Phil and Jeremy turned around to see Luke. "What's going on, Luke?" Phil asked.

Luke said, "We just had a twenty-passenger shuttle dock about two hours ago. The occupants were a motley collection from the Soldier of Fortune community."

"What is a group of mercenaries doing on my station?" Phil asked pointedly.

Luke smiled. "Funny. I asked that very question. In fact, the head guy approached me and said he was supposed to meet Fel Nos."

Phil's expression changed to that of understanding. "That's why Fel Nos needed funds. He was planning a jailbreak. Marcus Pointer has the location of the *Prospector*. Fel Nos had the ship. The pretars have Marcus Pointer. Now the pretars also have Fel Nos. Now we have nearly everything we need to cash in on a finder's fee. Everything except a location."

The three turned to see Gus approaching. Gus was shaking his head. "Those mercenaries didn't know why Fel Nos wanted to hire them. They had a meal at Eva's and cocktails at Sparky's. Now they're doing prelaunch checks. They have another job offer at a flaston colony."

Luke looked crosswise at Gus. "Cocktails?"

Gus replied, "I was being kind. What passes for potables with those guys is quite a thing. I'm surprised Sparky had that stuff in stock."

Phil brought the conversation back to the *Aurora*. "Okay what's the next phase in getting this in service?"

Jeremy leaned back. "There's not much left to do. We need to establish a maintenance routine. That'll be easy now that we have the shipyard records. Also, all the placards and labels need to be changed back to English. I'll put in a work order to have the ship thoroughly cleaned inside and out, including the bedding, mattresses, upholstery, and linens. After that, the only thing you have to do is stock the galley and go."

*****

## Oasis 4, HabMod 1

Phil and the rest went their separate ways. He couldn't help but wonder what Alice was planning for dinner. He missed her cooking almost as much as he missed her. He made the walk to HabMod 1 while deep in thought. Whenever his mind went back to Fel Nos, he got an uneasy feeling. A guy like Fel Nos wasn't a prime example of someone willing to stay put and call it quits. Combine that with the fact that he was studying the very facility he was sentenced to spend twenty-three years in to bust out his former partner. He made a mental note to have Luke Smith inform the Pretna authorities what they had learned.

*****

## Oasis 4, HabMod 1, Quarters of Phillip and Alice Ross

Phil found himself standing in the corridor, staring at his door. He was trying to refresh his memory. The two things Alice wanted to do were restock the pantry along with the food preservation and refrigeration unit, then "girl up" the quarters. He was concerned that Alice wouldn't like the selection at the station food store, or she wouldn't be able to find the right knickknacks to doll up their quarters. His concern mostly centered on the fact that if she was unhappy, she would make sure he was unhappy.

Phil took a deep breath and pressed the door button. The door slid open, and the pleasant aroma of Alice's cooking met him. He tried not to get excited, as there were still a couple of possible obstacles to marital bliss to overcome. Cautiously, Phil called out, "Honey? I'm home."

Alice walked out of the kitchen wearing an apron and smiling. Phil breathed a sigh of relief, one hurdle past.

Alice planted a big wet kiss on Phil. "About time you decided to come home." Phil checked the time. "What do ya mean? I'm right on time."

Alice grinned. "That's what I said. It's about time."

Phil knew better than to try to match wits with his wife. "Well, I'm glad we got that right." Alice grinned and had him clean up and sit at the table in the dining area.

After dinner, Phil helped Alice clear the dishes, and then they sat down to watch a movie Alice selected from the entertainment system database. During an intermission, Phil prepared some drinks while Alice made popcorn. Phil observed, "You haven't done any redecorating yet."

Alice walked in with a huge bowl of buttered popcorn. "Give me some time. I seem to have plenty of it available."

Phil was afraid of this. Life on a space station was challenging if there wasn't something to occupy your time. "I'm finding out on this station. Boredom is not an option," Phil observed.

Alice laughed. "I'd keep the kortlax off the station if I were you." Phil nearly spit out his beer. "You heard about that, did you?"

Alice nodded. "Yes, I got together with some of the other ladies for lunch. It seems they'll be talking about the great kortlax round-up for years to come." Alice then shrugged. "I wouldn't worry about keeping busy. Something will come up. If not, I'll make something happen." Of that, Phil had no doubts.

In the morning, Phil and Alice went through their morning routines of exercise and showers. Alice let Phil shower first then she took hers. Alice came out of the bedroom, buttoning her shirt cuff. "I thought we could have breakfast at Eva's this morning. We'll split up the week between breakfast at Eva's and here. I've noticed that you take care of a lot of business then."

Phil smiled. "I knew I married you for some reason. Let's get our favorite table."

As they left their quarters, Phil looked over his shoulder. "SICOS, secure quarters."

*****

## Oasis 4, Upper CentMod, Eva's Café

They arrived at Eva's to find Ed Carlton and Dave Jacobson sitting at their customary table. "Alice, I think you remember Ed Carlton, captain of the *Bright Star*, and you met Dave Jacobson, captain of the *Atlantis Star*."

Alice sat in the chair Phil held for her. "I sure do. I haven't seen you, Ed, since I was a controller at Earth Station 3, Ed. What runs are you guys on?"

Dave took a sip of coffee. "I've been going to Pretna a lot lately." Ed said, "I just returned from Flast yesterday."

Phil asked, "I thought you went to Celnar?"

Ed nodded. "I did. We off-loaded in record time and loaded with food."

Phil was surprised. "What kind of food?"

Ed answered, "You name it, we hauled it. Celnar is truly the galaxy's breadbasket. The holds were full of grains of all kinds. Some of which I never heard of. We had preservation containers full of fruits and vegetables. Some had meats of every description. The flastons diet is very close to ours."

Phil pressed, "Why are the flastons buying food?"

Ed shrugged. "The change in government there threw some things into chaos and exposed other shortcomings in their system. June Dixon of the Morning Star is also busy bringing them supplies."

Alice's interest was piqued. "What's the mood there?"

Ed smiled. "Pretty positive. The average flaston acts like a two-ton weight has been lifted from his shoulders. The funny part is, they didn't make a purge of personnel like expected. The supervisors I've dealt with acted like the hammer was going to fall any second. Their treatment of their underlings was a lot kinder than I've observed in the past."

Luke Smith joined them. "Morning all. What's the topic today?" Dave answered, "Flast."

Luke nodded. "Ah yes, the source of many security bulletins these days."

Ed added, "Man, that escalated quickly. It's only been a few weeks since our little incident. From what I gather, change was bubbling below the surface for a while. The incident we're familiar with was just one of the triggers."

Alice looked confused and looked like she was about to ask a question when Phil decided they shouldn't be talking about their involvement in the present situation on Flast. He thought that he should change the subject. "Luke, I was thinking that the authorities on Pretna should be made aware of the fact that one of their inmates was studying the facility with an eye on busting out another inmate."

Luke nodded. "Way ahead of you, Boss. I sent a message to them last night."

Phil nodded. "Real good."

*****

## Oasis 4, Upper CentMod, Operations Center, Briefing Room

After breakfast, Phil said goodbye to Alice and took the platform lift to the operations center. A quick stop at his office to check his vault and grab a pad, then he was off to the morning briefing. He walked into the briefing room and poured a cup.

Phil sat and took out his pad. "Up first, operations."

Virginia Wells looked at her own pad. "Too much to name individually. The freight companies are putting our new capacity to the test. There's nothing out of the ordinary, with the exception of two passenger liners making extended visits."

Phil was satisfied with how Virginia ran the operations department, so there was no need to micromanage her. He checked his pad. "Facility maintenance."

Will consulted his own pad. "Docking port maintenance continues. This will be the last week for that scheduled task. Other than that, we're keeping busy with the little problems that arise."

Phil checked off an item on his pad. "Okay, vessel maintenance."

Jeremy Cole smiled. "Apparently, a vessel maintenance and repair facility is long overdue in this neck of the woods. We have maintenance, repairs, and inspections scheduled for weeks to come."

Phil liked what he was hearing. Jeremy continued, "The work on the Aurora continues. Chad Kowalski is tasked with making sure all the labels and placards are in English. Also, he'll be powering up systems and doing final checks. The ship will be ready for a test flight later this afternoon."

Phil looked over to Gus. "I think we can fit that into our schedule. What do you think, Gus?"

Gus smiled. "I think I can wedge it in somewhere," he said sarcastically.

Jeremy continued, "I'd like Chad to go along for good measure.

Besides, he'll never be happy until he experiences the *Aurora*." Phil checked off an item on his pad again. "Medical."

Dr. Marie Tillman shrugged. "Everything is as routine as can be." Phil made another check. "Security."

Luke didn't look happy. "I just received a communication from the Pretna authorities. They thanked us for passing on the information, but Fel Nos and Marcus Pointer escaped from the mining penal colony they were in. The pretars have put out the word to law enforcement agencies everywhere, plus bounty hunters. They want these guys bad." Phil didn't react well to the news. "I want all arrivals double- checked with facial recognition, and when there's any doubt, DNA analysis until those guys are back behind bars. Also, I want the *Aurora* locked down. In fact, put a guard on it whenever it's at the station until

Fel Nos and Marcus Pointer are locked up again."

"It'll be done, Boss," Luke promised. "They just escaped yesterday.

Even the fastest ship would take three days from the penal colony." Phil didn't want to be the guy that told people how to do their job,

but he was tired of being one step behind these criminals. "We didn't know anything about Jitec Kilonoct before yesterday. We don't know who else is running around here connected with this caper."

Luke didn't like being caught off guard either, and it didn't help that Phil had to tell him what his next action should be. "It'll be done, Boss."

*****

## Oasis 4, Upper CentMod, Operations Center, Office of Phillip Ross

Phil adjourned the briefing and retreated to his office. He retrieved the lockbox from his vault and checked the contents. He was relieved to see they were still there, as the events of the last couple of weeks had left him quite paranoid. He remembered that the second data chip contained communications records, so he decided to check that one again. He put the chip in the SICOS terminal and opened the file menu. The communications of the *Prospector* were what was expected.

Most of the communications were from the captain looking for the best prices for the ore they were hauling—that was the good news. Many of the communications had data attached that indicated the direction of the signal source. The *Prospector* was owned by the captain, so there were no records available as to where they picked up their loads. There were only records of loads delivered.

Phil used the SICOS to compile a composite of directional data from the records. He tried to pinpoint the location of transmissions by asking SICOS to indicate areas where multiple transmissions were made within half a light-year of each other. There were several places indicated where multiple transmissions were made.

Phil pondered it a bit. If an independent mining ship had exclusive knowledge of a source of a valuable commodity, it would take measures to keep it secret. To that end, the captain would make his transmissions well away from the source of wealth. Phil studied the display and saw that the last years' worth of communication from the *Prospector* came from an area of the galaxy that has been largely unexplored to this date. At least no one has published any findings about the area. The area in question was actually fairly close to Oasis 4. It's not that no one thinks the location is not worth looking into, but rather, there are millions of other places to explore. It's unlikely that more than 1 or 2 percent of the known galaxy will be explored.

Back when the *Prospector* was in service, there were no legal provisions or treaty agreements to honor claims or mineral rights. Phil pondered further what he would do if he were captain of the *Prospector*. He certainly wouldn't start looking for buyers at a prime location and practically invite competing mining ships. There were three general locations the *Prospector* used for communications. Phil reasoned that the location of the lost ship would most likely be in a triangle formed by those three points. He had the display zoom in on that area, which immediately deflated him.

The highlighted sector was not only vast but held thousands of star systems. Leaning back in his chair, he refused to give in to an impossible situation. Then he had an idea. "SICOS, page Luke Smith."

In a couple of seconds, Luke answered the page, "What can I do for you, Boss?"

Phil said, "Luke, find what you can about Marcus Pointer. Particularly, any information about any and all transports he may have been in possession of."

Luke answered, "Will do, Boss. In fact, it's already in progress." Phil wondered why Luke was compiling data on Marcus Pointer.

Then he realized that Luke took it very personnel that there was a criminal enterprise on the station, and he not only had no knowledge of it, but he didn't tumble onto the fact there were multiple players. So Phil reasoned that Luke was busy making sure that Marcus Pointer, Fel Nos, and Jitec Kilonoct didn't have a fourth partner.

*****

## Oasis 4, Upper CentMod, Security Office

Luke prepared a file on the SICOS and labeled it Marcus Pointer. He was in the dark as to why Phil needed info on the vessel Pointer was in possession of, but he was sure his boss had his reasons. Luke sent a request to the Pretna authorities to enquire about the vessel that Pointer was using when he got nabbed. In the meantime, he started to organize the file on Marcus Pointer. He first added a subfile he labeled "biographical data." Then another subfile labeled "arrest," "felony," and "misdemeanor" records. This was by far the thickest file. Then he loaded a subfile labeled known associates. Luke scanned the list and discovered that it didn't exactly read like a "who's who" of crime, but it was distinguished.

He had the SICOS compare that list with list of all the people that have ever set foot on the station. SICOS spit out a list of twenty-four names that Luke studied. Then he frowned. "SICOS, eliminate the names that were in a correctional facility in the time Marcus Pointer was on Oasis 4." SICOS removed eighteen of the names. "SICOS, display the location of the remaining names." Of the six remaining names, three were labeled deceased, one was labeled unknown, and one showed up as currently residing on Oasis 4. The name was Brin Os, another malnun.

Luke asked SICOS for information on Brin Os, and there was very little. Brin Os was a qualified pilot with a light-speed endorsement. Apparently, he went afoul of the law in a scam of some sort. He was Marcus Pointer's cellmate for about six months after Pointer committed a minor felony on Sotos. It also seems that Brin Os and Fel Nos were old friends. They were persons of interest in more than one investigation. Apparently, the two had never had enough evidence against them to warrant an arrest, but they certainly felt the heat more than once.

Luke directed SICOS to alert his deputies whenever Brin Os moved about the station. The alert was a class three, which meant that Brin Os wasn't to be alerted to the fact that he was being monitored. The information was transmitted to the deputies via the communications pad they wore on their forearms.

Luke sat back and reminded himself not to get too smug. He had already had his pants figuratively pulled down by these guys, and he was determined not to let it happen again. Luke ordered, "SICOS, display known associates file of Marcus Pointer, Fel Nos, Brin Os, Jitec Kilonoct. Eliminate files of deceased associates." The list narrowed to a small amount.

Luke then ordered, "SICOS, using facial recognition, compare this list with all visitors to the station. Start the search from the current time and run backward."

It was going to take SICOS a long time to make those comparisons. SICOS was up to the task, but there have been thousands of people passed through the station in the last couple of months alone. With that in mind, Luke considered his next move. "SICOS, start a second search. Using facial recognition, compile all security imagery of Marcus Pointer."

After a couple of minutes, the SICOS reported, "Second search completed."

Luke responded, "Display results." The display listed the time indexes that Marcus Pointer was being recorded by station security sensors.

Luke thought about how to narrow the search. "SICOS, display only time indexes where Marcus Pointer was within one meter of other personnel." The list was narrowed considerably.

Luke rubbed his chin while he thought about how to narrow the search further. "SICOS, display only time indexes when Marcus Pointer was within one meter of other personnel more than once." Luke was grateful the list was now down to a manageable size.

Luke had the SICOS display the locations on the station where Marcus Pointer was in proximity of anyone else. It was no surprise that there were a handful of places that Pointer had multiple encounters. He had SICOS display visual stills of the location that had the most hits. The stills were scrutinized carefully by Luke. He felt silly because this location was Eva's. Of course, he would be in close proximity to people. He almost discarded this location, then he thought about it again. Eva's was a good place to have a meeting and not arouse suspicion.

Luke thought a second or two. "SICOS, drop the following indexes." He started tapping the screen on the images where there was only Pointer or if there was only Pointer and Eva or one of her wait staff. That left a series of images with Pointer and persons yet to be identified. Luke studied the images; for most of them, he was with Fel Nos, Brin Os, or Jitec Kilonoct. A couple of times, he was with all three. In one image, he looked at the background and saw himself sitting at a table with Phil Ross and Will Dawson.

Luke continued to study the images; he saw that there was a face unknown to him. Before he had SICOS identify him, Luke looked at the other locations that Marcus Pointer had encountered. Most of them were in the CentMod, often in seating areas on the plaza level or at an observation area where visitors would often gaze at the nebula. Luke was again grateful that there weren't any new players in this little drama. Pointer was often with Fel Nos, Brin Os, Jitec Kilonoct, and this other guy, whoever he was.

Luke thought that he should tie up some of the searches. "SICOS, what is the progress on the first search?"

SICOS responded, "Five point three years previous to this date." Luke nodded. "That's good enough, SICOS. How many of Marcus

Pointer's known associates have visited Oasis 4 in that period?" SICOS indicated that there were three. However, two of them predated Pointer's arrival at Oasis 4. The third was here at the same time.

Luke ordered, "SICOS, is this the same subject as indicated in the previous search?"

SICOS responded, "Affirmative." Luke asked, "What is his name?"

SICOS again responded, "Thatt Voffyes. Biographical information as follows, Thatt Voffyes, thirty-six Earth years in age. Home planet, Griska. Species, snoshin. Criminal record, extensive. Would you like to have the list of offenses and convictions read?"

Luke responded, "No, save data. Where is subject at present?" SICOS replied, "Last known location, Kempeck colony. Status, incarcerated."

Luke smiled. At least all the subjects were contained or under observation. Then he frowned when he remembered that Pointer and Fel Nos were on the loose. Luke saved the data he had compiled thus far in a file. He then saw that there was a notification from SICOS that there was an answer to the request sent to Pretna.

He opened the file and saw that Pointer was in possession of a Pulsar 621. It was a five-passenger, one-pilot, light-speed capable shuttle. It was small but very fast. Luke supposed it had to be since the galley only held enough food for three weeks for six people, and there was a generous amount of space for freight. It was, at best, a way to move people long distances quickly but had no room for cargo, which limited its usefulness.

Luke loaded the data in the file he was preparing for Phil and sent it to him. He then paged Phil, who answered, "What have ya got, Luke?"

"The Pretna authorities sent that info you wanted. I sent you a file," Luke replied.

There was a pause, and Phil said, "Okay, this is great. Let's meet for lunch. Eva's in ten minutes."

*****

## Oasis 4, CentMod, Operations Center, Office of Phillip Ross

Phil quickly opened the file Luke sent him. He scanned the background information on Pointer and decided that he would let

Luke fill him in on him. Next, he opened the file sent by the Pretna authorities. "Ah, the Interstellar Station Wagon."

Phil was familiar with the model although he had never personally flown one. It was a light-speed version of the Pulsar 600. Reading on, he saw that the shuttle had been stolen, and the Pretna authorities had it returned to its rightful owner at the Unisystems Incorporated Research Colony.

Phil got up. "I told Luke ten minutes."

Gus stood up. "I could do with some lunch and a stretch of the legs. A change of scenery would be good too."

Phil put on his cap. "Come on." They took the platform lift to the plaza level and walked to Eva's. Luke had just sat down when Phil and Gus strolled up. Luke's attention was on someone in the distance. Phil was used to Luke's mannerisms and recognized the look.

*****

## Oasis 4, Upper CentMod, Eva's Café

Luke was casting a suspicious eye on a malnun. Phil cleared his throat, making Luke realize he wasn't alone and glanced at Phil and Gus. "Hey, Boss, I've dug up some info on Marcus Pointer you might find useful. But the most immediate thing I found was Mr. Pointer had two additional partners we didn't know about. One is a Snoshin named Thatt Voffyes, who is now a guest of the correctional facility at Kempeck colony. The other partner is named Brin Os. He's another malnun, and his last known location is right over there," he said, pointing to a malnun some distance from them who was purchasing a fruit cocktail from a kiosk.

Phil looked at Brin Os but looked away when he realized that he shouldn't make it obvious that they were onto him. "Do we know what his part in all this is?"

Luke shrugged. "He must be the pilot. He has a light-speed endorsement. I think the others have had a hand at interstellar flight, but Brin Os is the only one with credentials."

Phil thought a second or two. "Piloting a ship like the *Aurora* takes a more practiced hand than piloting a six-place shuttle. What about this Thatt Voffyes guy, any idea how he fits in all this?"

Luke shook his head. "No idea. I just know that he was seen with the others while on the station."

Gus took a sip of ice water then observed, "You know, with those two escaping the pretar facility and this guy running around the station, we need to be real careful about leaving the keys to the *Aurora* lying around."

Luke chuckled at the absurdity. "Look over to the right of Brin Os, in front of the bookstore."

Phil and Gus looked. They saw a pair of deputies. At first glance, it seemed that their attention was on anything but the malnun. On closer inspection, Phil saw that one deputy had at least one eye on Brin Os. When he was about to look away, he would tell his partner where to look to pick up a visual.

Luke continued, "Check in front of Sparky's," there were two additional deputies, "and the level two walkway in front of the Galaxywide Freight Forward office." There was a deputy supervisor leaning on the rail, watching in Brin Os' direction.

Phil nodded approval. "Has he done anything here that would warrant picking him up?"

Luke shook his head. "No, in fact, we wouldn't have even known about him if it weren't for the 'Known Associates' search on Marcus Pointer."

Phil mused about the situation. "I wouldn't mind if this guy disappeared.

Maybe we can get him to leave before he causes mischief."

Luke added, "He's kept his nose clean for a while. He needs a nudge in the right direction."

Gus chuckled. "Or a swift kick in the seat of the pants."

Phil nodded. "I agree with Gus. We need to scare the daylights out of this guy. That might change the vector his life is on, and he might encourage other criminals to avoid Oasis 4."

Luke nodded. "We'll work on that."

Eva brought their lunches, and the conversation paused while they passed ketchup and other condiments back and forth. Luke asked while stuffing French fries in his mouth. "What did you need data on Pointer's shuttle for?"

Phil swallowed a mouthful of burger and held it up. "Did you see what Eva's calling this meal? The two cheeseburgers, cabin fries, and strawberry soda pop meal? It's the Selack."

Luke rolled his eyes. "Boss, shuttle."

Phil regained his focus. "Oh, I was thinking if we could get a hold of Pointer's shuttle, we could get a look at his navigation logs."

Gus nodded. "That's not a bad idea. Assuming someone hasn't wiped the records."

Luke frowned. "How do you know someone else hasn't downloaded the logs and found the *Prospector?*"

Phil smiled. "Did you hear about the lost ship that was recovered from an asteroid that was rich in paxtite?"

Luke smiled back. "You make an excellent point. By the way, what were you doing while I was cyber sleuthing?"

Gus answered, "Phil and I are giving the *Aurora* a shakedown flight after lunch. There aren't any instructor pilots out here familiar with the Astrodyne 65. Let alone one that's been modified like this one, so we've been going over cockpit layout and procedures."

June Dixon strolled up, sipping a cola through a straw. "You two cowboys plan on flying an Astrodyne 65 without a familiarization course?" "The Astrodyne 65 is just a light-speed version of the Astrodyne Shorthauler," Phil objected. "The cockpit layout is the same."

June rolled her eyes. "Do me a favor, do your company's insurance carrier a favor, and let me tag along. I flew the 65 for three years before they gave me the Morning Star."

Phil was relieved, but he didn't want to show it. "Well, okay, if you think it would be best."

June smiled; Phil wasn't fooling anybody.

*****

## Oasis 4, CargoMod 8, Ship Maintenance Shop

Phil, Gus, and June arrived at the maintenance hangar bay in CargoMod 8, where they were met by Jeremy Cole and his lead technician Chad Kowalski.

Jeremy greeted the three. "Right on time. I see you brought someone who knows what she's doing. Good afternoon, Captain Dixon."

June smiled. "Good afternoon to you too, Jeremy."

Jeremy smiled. "I would like you to take Chad with you. He has a maintenance checklist to go through just to establish some parameters and trend monitoring."

Phil looked at Chad. "Welcome aboard."

The four of them boarded after Phil and Gus did a prelaunch walk-around check. This check is impractical to do if the ship is docked. However, in the hangar bay, the exterior is readily accessible, and the flight manual strongly recommends the check be made in circumstances where it can be done. That would include sitting on a planet's landing pad. Chad wasn't at all bothered that a couple of button pushers were looking for flaws on a spacecraft that he had just gone over every square inch of. Actually, he would have thought a lot less of Phil and Gus if they hadn't.

*****

## The *Aurora*, Astrodyne 65, Owned and Operated by the Stellar Logistics and Freight Corporation

When all four were aboard, Chad shut and sealed the hatch. Phil took the pilot's seat, much to Gus's annoyance. After all, the company did assign him to be the lead pilot, but he took it in stride and took his seat in the copilot position.

This vessel was actually designed so that it could be operated by a single pilot. However, a second pilot decreased the workload considerably in certain phases of a flight. That was why this class of vessel had a cockpit. Larger, more complex ships had a captain, a helmsman, a navigation officer, and a crewman that handled engineering systems.

These ships had a bridge. June took a seat in the observer's position. Chad sat at the systems station and powered it up.

Gus picked up the checklist and read the prestart portion. He read each item and waited for a response from Phil. As each item was read off, Phil would make sure it was in the proper configuration for launch. Every switch and control were set precisely. Once that was done, Gus started the engine start checklist. When they reached the portion where the engines could be started, Phil pressed the Reactor Start button.

There was a low hum as the reactor came to life. Phil checked the gauges and made sure they were all in the green. He looked back at Chad, who nodded his approval after checking his own gauges. Phil switched power to internal and keyed his microphone switch, "Maintenance bay, *Aurora*; disconnect umbilical."

A technician outside the ship disconnected the power umbilical and exited the hangar bay. A reply came back on the communications set, *"Aurora, umbilical disconnected, hangar bay clear."*

Phil keyed the microphone button. "Maintenance bay, configure for launch." The station technician started by ramping down the gravity level in the bay.

As the gravity decreased, the ship started to rise as the weight on the nitrogen- charged struts decreased. They had to be careful because if the gravity disappeared suddenly, the struts would extend just as suddenly, and the ship would bounce off the ceiling.

As the maintenance bay gravity decreased, the gravity inside the *Aurora* gradually increased. The *Aurora* was now floating in the center of the bay and rising slowly. The air was pumped out of the bay, and when that was done, the technician opened the bay doors. Phil made sure the thrusters were set to "fine maneuvering," which limited the output at the same time, increasing the control sensitivity. He bumped the forward thruster, and the *Aurora* moved to the open bay doors.

Phil retracted the landing gear. This was completely unnecessary in space, but it was standard procedure. If they entered atmospheric flight and forgot that the gear was still extended, they could be damaged. The navigation shields would protect them from the plasma. However, once reentry is over, the shields are switched off. The landing struts shouldn't be extended at too high a speed, or there may be structural damage.

The *Aurora* inched forward until it was clear of the bay doors. Phil looked back at June. "Is there any place special you want to go?"

"Don't tell me didn't you file a flight plan?" June said sardonically.

Phil and Gus looked at each other sheepishly. "Well, I don't want to tell you I didn't file a flight plan," Phil offered.

June looked back to Chad. "Three hundred fifty light-years enough to satisfy your needs, Chad?"

"Yes, ma'am" was Chad's response. There was a bit of mirth in his voice. June quickly used a computer station to input a flight plan and then transmitted it to the station ops center.

Phil turned back to the controls and sheepishly uttered, "Thank you, ma'am."

He put the station control center frequency in the comm set and keyed his microphone. "Oasis 4, this is the *Aurora*. CargoMod 8, bay 1. Ready to depart station."

The controller responded, "*Aurora*, pitch down thirty degrees and thrust forward."

As Phil completed the maneuver he was starting to feel right at home. He thought it had been too long since he was behind the controls of a shuttle.

After the ship was at thousand yards distance, the Oasis controller contacted them again, "*Aurora* pitch up twelve degrees yaw left forty degrees and thrust." Phil acknowledged the instructions and then completed the maneuver crisply.

When the *Aurora* was established on that heading, the station controller called, *"Aurora, you are free to navigate."*

Phil checked the navigation display and made a small correction then he engaged the reaction engines. June's eyes widened. "Whoa! That's quite a kick!"

Phil made sure the engines were set to idle. Chad was grinning ear to ear. "That's those Detroit 750s. There's twice as much low-end power as the original engines."

Gus glanced at Phil. "I believe I would take it easy with the throttle." Phil gripped the power levers. "You read my mind."

Chad consulted some performance charts. "Let's do this in four stages. First, ease it up to 25 percent." Phil advanced the power levers until the thrust indicator read 25 percent.

Chad checked his display and was satisfied with what he read. "Okay, 50 percent." Phil pushed further and was starting to feel more comfortable with his new ride.

Chad nodded. "Seventy-five percent." Phil eased the power levers forward.

Chad made a quick check of his display, "Let's see one hundred." At 100 percent, the *Aurora* didn't show any signs of any bad habits.

Chad double-checked the display and found it hard to believe they were getting the performance they were getting. It was the result of having engines that were incredibly oversize. Chad took a deep breath. "Okay, push 'em full. Let's see what we get."

Phil eased the power levers forward until they were at the mechanical stops. The speed indicator showed acceleration until they reached the maximum speed. Chad was checking the display, and June broke the silence. "Feel how smooth this is."

Chad sat back. "You're right. This is one amazing machine."

The factory put a practical limit on the engines and called it 100 percent. They could be operated over this limit but only for short periods time and then only if necessary. The amount of time they were over the maximum was recorded by the onboard computer, and when a predetermined amount of time over maximum was reached, the engines had to be inspected.

Chad turned back to his display. "Okay, number one engine is holding at 126 percent. Temperatures are well below maximum. Engine number two is at 124 percent. Temperatures also below maximum."

Chad went back to his checklist. "One more check at sublight speeds. Ease the power down to idle."

Although they were in a vacuum, space is rarely devoid of matter. The navigation shields are constantly colliding with interstellar particles. If it weren't for the navigation shields, the front of the ship would erode away in very short order.

When Phil lowered the power setting, the ship immediately started slowing. It was an unperceivable amount, but it was there.

Phil asked Chad, "What's this next check?"

Chad explained, "Acceleration check, this ship seems to be very controllable, so I don't expect any surprises."

He had Phil use reverse thrust to slow the *Aurora* and then cruise at idle to allow the engine temperatures to stabilize.

When Chad was satisfied that the engines were ready, he said, "Prepare yourselves for a jolt. Anytime you're ready, boss." Phil pushed the power levers forward to 100 percent.

Gus let out a rare display of emotion. "Geez o Pete's." All four were pinned back to their seats as the *Aurora* picked up speed.

When they stopped accelerating and resumed sublight cruise, June remarked, "I still can't get over how smooth this is." Everyone nodded in agreement.

Chad said, "Let's try the Victor 150s."

Phil shook his head. "I'm not sure if I want to after the 'Ion-injected Detroit 750' experience."

Gus smiled. "No guts, no glory, Crash."

Phil looked at Gus. "Just make sure you close your eyes if it gets too scary." Phil switched on the light-speed engine's power master and engaged the start sequence initiator. Gus kept an eye on the display, "Bubble formed." The "bubble" was an envelope of normal space that surrounded the ship; it was needed to keep the ship and its occupants in the same time continuum. Phil never pretended to be a physicist. He just knew it was important to keep the passage of time inside the ship the same as outside.

Phil slid the power selectors forward, and the fabric of space was manipulated outside the ship, causing it to accelerate.

Gus called out the speed, "LS 0.6, LS 0.7, LS 0.8." LS, being sort hand for light speed. "LS 0.9, LS 1.0."

Chad stared at his display. "Looks good here. Keep it going."

Phil shut down the sublight engines, then pushed the slides on the light-speed engines. Acceleration was rapid past LS 1.

Gus continued to call the speed, "LS 2, LS 3, LS 4, LS 5."

The LS numbers weren't simply multiples of the speed of light. LS 1 is the speed of light; LS 2 is the speed of light squared. LS 3 is the speed of light cubed, and so on.

Phil continued to push forward the power slides. At LS 8, the hull started to groan.

Chad switched his display from engine to system mode. He studied the structural integrity monitors. Finally, he smiled. "It's just talking to us. Everything's well below nominal stress."

June nodded knowingly. "Usually, the Astrodyne 65 does that at LS 5."

The speed topped out at LS 11.5. After looking over the readings on the engine display, Chad agreed with the engineers at New Oslo Shipyards that cruise speed should be limited to LS 9. That's the power level that offers the longest service life and most economical return.

June had Phil slow to a cruise setting of LS 9 and execute some course corrections. At these velocities, the maneuvers had to be done with an extreme level of precision and required accurate astronomical charts. Phil saw they were nearing the destination that June had filed on their flight plan. The Astrodyne 65 had an exceptional navigation computer. Phil input the data into the computer, and the navigation display provided a countdown with the course information. Phil started the sublight engines and idled them. When the countdown reached zero, Phil cut the light-speed engines. The view in front of the ship suddenly came into focus, and they found themselves rapidly approaching a planet.

Phil saw immediately that it was a Gas Giant. "I thought we were going to practice some landings?"

June reached past Phil and highlighted one of the planet's moons on the navigation display. "Set a course for this moon. There's a practice pad on a mountain top there."

Phil put the *Aurora* in an orbit around the moon, which was actually somewhere between Earth and Mars in size, then identified the mountain with the landing pad. After Phil made a quick check of the navigation database, to his surprise, he found the practice landing pad. Intersystems shipping company put the pad there for their personnel, and they even published approach and landing procedures.

Phil started his first approach. As he came closer to the landing pad, he aimed the engine nozzles downward and adjusted the thrust to maintain his decent angle. He was constantly manipulating the controls to stay on a stabilized glide path while slowing the ship. At a distance of a kilometer, Phil called, "Gear down."

Gus pulled the landing gear lever to get it off the lock and pulled it down to the gear-down position. Vibrations and bumps could be felt as the hydraulics moved the gear and locked them into the extended position.

When the gear locked, indicators illuminated, and Gus confirmed, "Gear down and locked."

Phil continued the approach until he was hovering motionless over the landing pad. The first thing he noticed was the mountaintop location made it a challenge due to the fact that his visual references diminished as he got closer. Easing the power levers back an almost unperceivable amount, the Aurora lowered and settled onto the pad. June tried not to reveal how impressed she was with how Phil handled it. Phil made four additional landings and turned over the controls to Gus, who also made five landings. June had Gus fly the return trip. She made him do the same course corrections Phil did, and he performed them flawlessly. Chad didn't need to do any more engine checks, so he occupied himself by roaming the ship and checking systems.

Chad walked to the engine room. After leaving the cockpit, he walked through the crew and passenger accommodations, then through the cargo hold until he reached the engine room hatch. A check of the indicator near the hatch showed that there was no radiation. The reactor being a low-time unit, he didn't expect there would be any leakage, but procedures had to be followed.

A press of a button gave him access to the engine room. The reactor was operating normally. It was almost completely silent, save a low hum. Chad leaned his backside against a railing staring at the engine gauges. There was a slight rumble followed by a groan. He checked his display and confirmed they were passing through LS 8. The velocity indicator showed they reached a cruising velocity of LS 9.

Chad was happy with the engine operation, so he decided to check the rest of the ship. First, he checked the cargo loading hatches and confirmed there were no leaks. He checked the lighting and artificial gravity systems. Finding those systems acceptable, he looked around, and it struck him that there was no cargo- handling equipment anywhere. Usually, there was at least one antigravity unit on a vessel this size.

The gravity controllers on the Astrodyne 65's cargo hold are on or off. Some ships have aisles where the gravity can be shut off, and the cargo moved along those aisles by hand. When the cargo is in place, the gravity is switched on then the cargo is secured. But that's not the case here. Looking at the deck, he noticed that it was still new looking. Even on a vessel this new, the cargo deck would be a bit beat up. There were a series of lockers along the bulkhead that he decided to investigate. He expected to find cargo tie-downs and other necessary items for securing cargo.

Opening the first locker just served to confuse him. It was full of metal bowls, and each bowl had a spoon attached to it with a length of cable. He closed the locker and opened the next one. This one had stacks of filthy blankets. He thought to himself that they were out of place on this ship, especially after the cleaning crew gave this vessel the once over. Then he reminded himself that they only cleaned the cockpit, crew, and passenger spaces.

Chad was starting to get an uneasy feeling. He opened the third locker, and his blood ran cold when he examined the contents. Chad reached in and pulled out a set of shackles. "I thought this sort of thing didn't happen anymore." Each shackle was designed to fit around the ankles, and a short length of chain was used to lock them to the fittings in the floor.

There was also a neck collar that was attached to the ankle cuffs by a chain. The other lockers had buckets and other items necessary for providing for basic needs. Chad felt dirty just looking at this stuff. He made sure the lockers were closed and proceeded to carry on, checking the rest of the ship.

Chad finished his checks and reentered the cockpit just as Gus was ready to drop out of light speed and start his approach to the station. Gus cut the Victor 150s, and suddenly, the view in front of them came into focus. The occupants of the ship had to brace themselves to prevent them from falling forward.

Phil looked at Chad. "How come we feel the inertia on these smaller ships, but on the larger ones, you don't feel as much?"

Chad shrugged. "These smaller vessels only use what they need. They don't exactly produce an excessive amount of power, especially this one. All the power is being routed to these massive engines. Space available is also a consideration. The systems on this ship are enough to prevent the occupants from becoming grease spots on the back bulkhead during acceleration."

Phil thought about it for a second or two and decided that Chad probably dumbed it down considerably for him.

Gus contacted the station and received approach vectors. Gus recognized the voice of the controller and realized that it was Brenda, so he made a conscious effort to ratchet up the professionalism. The station was visible, and they were rapidly approaching it. Gus used the thrust reversers and decelerated. He repeated the operation at regular intervals while adjusting his heading. Brenda assigned Docking Port 1 of CargoMod 2 to the *Aurora*.

Gus followed the vectors he was given precisely, and they found themselves hanging stationary a dozen or so feet from the docking port, where Phil engaged the monitor that had a view of the docking port. The image had a reticle in the center that the pilot would align with a target on the station. Gus used the thrusters to ease the Aurora toward the station. Probes that were extended from the ship slid into receptacles on the station. When they had penetrated deep enough, clamps were engaged, and the *Aurora* was pulled into position, and indicators lit when the hatch seals were engaged.

Gus kept the reactor idle while station personnel connected the umbilicals. Chad made some notes on a pad, and June stood up. "Gentlemen, that was surprisingly well done."

Phil turned to her. "Thanks, June. I was a little nervous because it's been a while since—hey! What do ya mean by surprisingly?"

June had a laugh. "Gotcha. Actually, I meant the part about 'nice job.' That being said, I'll see you two around the station, and you can buy me dinner." She then got up and headed to the hatch.

Chad cleared his throat. "Hey, Boss. Did you get a chance to go through the cargo hold?"

Phil was confused. "It's completely empty."

Chad shook his head. "Not completely. You really need to see this." All three walked back to the cargo hold, and Chad opened the lockers. A picture of what may have occurred on this ship was forming in their heads.

Phil looked like he was going to be physically ill. "Whoever had this shuttle before Fel Nos got a hold of it was into some evil stuff."

Gus eyed the contents of the lockers with disgust. "I don't think we should throw any of this away. Luke Smith will want to hold it in some sort of evidence locker."

Phil concurred, "We'll talk to Luke directly." The three of them walked to the hatch, where Phil and Gus thanked Chad for his expertise, and Phil added that perhaps he shouldn't tell anyone about what he found just yet. They didn't want to let everyone know that they knew about the *Aurora's* checkered past. Chad said they could rely on him.

Phil used the SICOS terminal near the docking port to page Luke.

Luke appeared on the display. "What's up, boss?"

"You need to get down here to CargoMod 2, Docking Port 1. We found something on the *Aurora*," Phil responded.

Luke took notice of Phil's tone. "I'll be there in just two minutes." It took Luke just a minute and fifty seconds to reach the docking port. "There's something in the cargo hold you need to see," Phil said, motioning Luke to the boarding hatch.

In less than a minute, Luke stood in front of the lockers staring and doing his best to suppress his rage. After a couple of minutes, he lifted his left arm and paged the security office. "Carl, grab someone to help you and bring the evidence handling cart. Oh, and bring extra evidence bags to CargoMod 2, Docking Port 1."

While waiting for Carl, they turned their attention to other matters. Phil asked Luke, "So what do you suggest we do to smoke out Brin Os?"

Luke pushed his cap back a bit. "First thing we do is secure the docking clamps. I talked to Will earlier, and he said that we could disconnect the indicators and make it appear that the ship was easy pickings."

Gus nodded. "We could probably give him a little urging too." Phil furrowed his brow. "How do you suggest we do that?"

Luke smiled. "Unguarded, open conversation close enough for him to overhear. I wouldn't overdo it, though. Just enough to assure him that we don't suspect a thing."

Phil nodded in understanding. "Gus and I can take care of that. By the way, I'm guessing that you still have Brin Os under surveillance?"

Luke nodded. "Yes, we do. He looked pretty stressed when the Aurora left, and he thought it went away forever. When he saw on the boards you were returning, he was extraordinarily relieved."

While they talked, Gus realized that getting the evidence cart in the cargo hold would be easier if the cargo loading hatch was open, so he set about opening the hatch. He checked the seal integrity, then pressed the button to open the hatch door. The door opened, and he pressed the call button to summon a station worker to open the docking port doors. The station doors slid open as Carl showed up with a deputy pushing the evidence cart.

Gus showed Carl to the lockers, with the deputy pushing the cart and following along. Carl knew right away what he was looking at. There were rumors about the slave trade. Now he was staring at evidence. Every government in the known galaxy, including both colonies and home planets, had condemned the practice and had strict laws forbidding it, as far as anyone knew. That didn't stop criminals from doing it. A mining operation that produced low yields or an agricultural concern that barely existed could be made downright profitable when you didn't have to pay your labor. The trick was to separate the product from the operation without the end user knowing its origin.

Carl cleared his throat. "Benjamin, I'll take photos of the lockers. Get the number four bags ready. We'll put each item in its own separate bag."

Carl and Benjamin used gloved hands to handle the evidence. Each bag was marked with a description of the contents, which locker they came from, and where in the locker the item was located.

There was quite a pile of evidence bags on the floor. Carl went to the SICOS terminal outside and arranged to have station workers bring antigravity carts to move the bags to the security office. He examined the lockers themselves and saw that they weren't part of the original ship's equipment, so he used large plastic bags to seal them, and he had them loaded onto the cart to be moved to the security office.

Luke said to Carl, "Make sure that stuff gets secure and get a fresh start at processing them in the morning. We'll secure things here. You make sure you get a good night's sleep."

As they were closing and sealing the hatches, Phil asked, "Where is Mr. Brin Os now?"

Luke consulted his communications pad. "He just bought a sandwich at Oscars Deli, and he's eating it in the sitting area on the plaza level near the platform lift."

Phil nodded. "Okay, let's make a suggestion."

*****

## Oasis 4, Upper CentMod, Plaza Level

They walked to the CentMod, where they spotted Brin Os eating his sandwich. Phil leaned toward Gus. "Remember what to say?"

Gus nodded. "Oh yeah." They started walking at a businesslike pace. The route they selected ensured that they would walk past Brin Os. When they were near enough, Phil said to Gus, "I want the *Aurora* kept in just that condition. Make sure you have the galley stocked with basics and the ship ready for a trip within thirty minutes' notice."

Gus had a hard time "not grinning." "You got it, Boss. Everything will be kept on auto-launch."

Auto-launch was a function that allowed the ship to be launched without aid from station personnel. Umbilicals can be disconnected remotely from the cockpit and docking clamps released. Saying that in front of a guy that wanted to steal your ship was practically ordering him to steal it.

Phil and Gus took the platform lift to the operations center. They retreated to Phil's office, where he used SICOS to page Luke. "Did he react?"

Luke nodded. "There's no mistake. He was very uninterested in whatever you guys said."

Phil let out a breath. "Okay, you know what to do. If he takes the bait tonight, put him on ice until morning. You won't have to wake me or anything." Phil paused for effect. "Why break precedent?"

Luke rolled his eyes. "Point taken, Boss."

Phil turned to Gus. "We might as well call it a day. If I don't see you at breakfast, I'll see you at the morning briefing." Phil went to his quarters, and Gus went to find Brenda to see if she had dinner plans.

Luke decided to overnight on the Aurora. He made arrangements with his deputies on where to position themselves in CargoMod 2. At 0200, Zulu Brin Os left his room at the hotel and waited for the desk clerk to be distracted by something before hurrying through. The desk clerk used the SICOS terminal to alert security that Brin Os was on the move. He made his way to the connecting tunnel to CargoMod 2. There are times that there's no activity in the public spaces on the station, but obviously, Brin Os checked the boards and selected a time that there were arriving and departing ships. That way, he would likely pass unnoticed. There was a group of freighter crewmen entering the tunnel to CargoMod 2, and he fell in behind them. As he passed the deputies on patrol, they appeared to pay him no mind. After he passed, one of the deputies used his communications pad to alert Luke. Brin Os ducked away from the crowd of crewmen while the deputy at the customs desk was busy checking them into the secure area.

Brin Os saw his opportunity to jump the fence and took it. He leaped from crate to crate until he was near Docking Port 1. He jumped to the deck with the grace of a cat and went to the hatch of the *Aurora*. He was grateful to see that the station doors were open, but the ship hatch was shut. Brin Os pressed the button for the hatch to open, and his efforts were rejected. A chime informed him that the hatch was locked.

A voice behind him made the blood drain from his face. "Thinking of taking her out for a spin?"

Brin Os spun around and saw one of the largest humans he had ever seen, staring at him. There were no crates or catwalks nearby to leap to nearby so as to make his escape.

He turned to his right and took a step when another oversize deputy stepped into view. "Can I help you find your way, sir?"

Brin Os considered fighting the deputies, but he decided to try getting away before resorting to violence, which he was perfectly willing to do at this point. In fact, he almost wished they would try something. Besting two human security deputies would do wonders for his reputation. He turned to his left and took another step when Tiffany walked into the light with a baton in hand. Brin Os recognized her as the girl who cowed Fel Nos and beat Jitec Kilonoct into submission. He fell to his knees and started sobbing.

The hatch of the *Aurora* opened, and Luke stood there, trying not to laugh when he processed what he was looking at. "Take this guy to lockup and process him."

The two deputies lifted Brin Os to his feet while Tiffany put handcuffs on him. Luke stepped closer to Brin Os and faced him. "I'm going to my quarters to finish sleeping. I would recommend that you try to get some rest, Mr. Brin Os. You have a big day tomorrow. Tiffany, take him to a cell." Luke secured the *Aurora* and headed to bed.

*****

## Oasis 4, HabMod 1, Quarters of Phil and Alice Ross

0600 found Phil and Alice crawling out of bed and getting ready for their morning workout. Phil chose to use the lap pool. Alice didn't think that was such a bad idea and decided to do the same. He suspected that Alice was up to her old tricks by subtlety getting him to compete with her. He knew what was going to happen, so he resolved not to play her game. He was just going to set a pace he was comfortable with. He thought she would say something that would call his masculinity into question. Then she'll match his pace, causing him to pick up his pace. The result will be sore muscles and a gloating wife. Well, he wasn't going to play that game. Alice would just have to be disappointed—that's all.

Forty-five minutes later, they returned to their quarters. Alice threw her towel in the hamper. "Wow, you really came out of the gate hard today!"

Phil, trying to be nonchalant, said, "I just wanted a decent workout today." Alice gave him a peck on the cheek. "I'll be right out."

When Alice disappeared into the bathroom, Phil let out a groan and collapsed onto the bed. He lay there and said, "Why did I let her do it again? She didn't even have to say anything. I just set the water current to the highest speed. She thinks she's so clever. I showed her."

Alice came back to the bedroom and started to dress while Phil showered off the chlorine. After he dressed, they looked at each other. Alice asked, "Eva's?"

Phil nodded and smiled. "Hard to beat Eva's place for breakfast."

Alice laughed. "I'm not complaining. If I insisted that you eat in quarters, you would probably have eaten nothing but doughnuts and soda pop. At Eva's, at least the food is healthier."

*****

## Oasis 4, CentMod, Eva's Café

At 0700, Phil and Alice ere taking their seats at Phil's customary table. Eva poured them coffee and took their order on a pad. June Dixon and Gus Condent strolled up from two different directions. Alice smiled. "Sit, sit." Eva poured two more cups and took their orders. June talked about how it was good to be back in an Astrodyne 65. The fact that the *Aurora* had monster engines was a plus.

They were halfway through their breakfast when a very tired Luke ambled up to the table and sat. Eva poured coffee, and Luke said, "The usual Eva, and keep the coffee coming."

Luke took a sip of coffee and Phil finally had enough. "Are you going to make me wait until the briefing to tell me whether we caught another malnun?"

Luke grinned. "0200 Tiffany strikes again. Mr. Brin Os is sweating it out in a four-by-six cell at the moment.

Phil nodded. "We'll have a chat with him after the morning briefing."

Phil never told Alice about the developing saga concerning the Aurora. June was only vaguely aware there was some intrigue. Both

Alice and June listened intently and were completely caught up in the saga. Both ladies also were repulsed by the idea of the slave trade actually existing in this day and age.

"What kind of work is being done by slaves?" Alice wanted to know. Phil shrugged. "You name it, farming, mining, manufacturing, even domestic help."

Alice was quite flabbergasted. "I hope merchandise and bulk goods coming through this station aren't products of the slave trade!"

June answered for Phil, "No one would knowingly deal in goods that had anything to do with slavery. But the hard truth is, it's impossible in most cases to tell what's the product of honest effort or forced labor." Phil checked the time. "We need to go." With that, Phil, Gus, and Luke went to the morning briefing.

*****

## Oasis 4, Upper CentMod, Security Office

The briefing was satisfyingly short. Phil and Luke headed directly to the security office to see what Brin Os had to say for himself. Luke led Phil to the area off the interview room called the observation room. They watched as a deputy led Brin Os into the interview room. Luke cast a critical eye on Brin Os. His oversize eyes were bloodshot, and he appeared to be in a daze as a result of last night's misadventures and lack of sleep.

Phil let out a sigh. "Except for Fel Nos, I don't have a lot of experience with malnuns, so I'm more than happy to let you take the lead on this."

Luke looked down at a pad. "Except for last night, he's kept his nose clean since his short stint in jail on Sotos with Marcus Pointer. He's not wanted by anyone at the moment, so there's no one we can fob him off on. What do you suggest?"

Phil thought a second or two. "See what information you can wring out of him, and I'll come in and offer him some hope."

Luke entered the interview room, which startled Brin Os and made him start to shake. He managed to get himself under control but not before Luke noticed. Luke sat at the table and pulled out a pad. "Brin Os, malnun. You were arrested on Sotos for…selling real estate on Utex 4. I understand that you were offering the property at a very reasonable price. The problem was, Utex 4 is a Gas Giant."

Brin Os didn't try to defend himself. Luke exhaled. "What happens to you after this depends entirely on how honest you are with me."

Brin Os resolved to be very honest right then and there. Luke continued, "Okay, let's see. You're a pilot with a light-speed endorsement. You were caught early this morning trying to steal an Astrodyne shuttle. You planned on meeting your buddies, Fel Nos and Marcus Pointer. You guys were going to use the ship to retrieve a derelict mining vessel and live in the lap of luxury the rest of your lives."

The color was draining out of Brin Os' oversize ears. Luke stared at him. "Am I close?"

Brin Os sheepishly nodded. Luke made a note on his pad. "Where were you to meet Fel Nos and Marcus Pointer?"

Brin Os choked out. "Kempeck colony. There is an associate of theirs in prison there. We were going to arrange for his release."

Luke already knew the answer to his next question, but he had to ask. "What's this associate's name?"

"Thatt Voffyes," Brin Os replied.

Luke made another note. "What was the plan for Jitec Kilonoct?"

Brin Os shook his head. "Nothing. Pointer was looking for a way to cut him out anyway. I told him going after those data chips was foolish. The information they contained wasn't vital, and it would only raise suspicion if they were stolen."

Luke made a note. "You got that right. Where did Fel Nos get ahold of the *Aurora*?"

Brin Os was confused. "I'm not sure what you're talking about."

Luke clarified, "That's what we renamed the Astrodyne 65 we confiscated from Fel Nos."

Brin Os nodded in understanding. "Oh yes, I forgot. He was a crewman on it. He compiled a body of evidence against the owner of the vessel. When they were at a space station whose owners took those particular offenses very seriously." Brin Os took a sip of water Luke poured or him, then continued, "Fel Nos threatened to expose him unless he signed the title of the vessel over. The old owner complied, but I suspect Fel Nos is playing a very dangerous game."

Luke pressed, "Evidence of what?" Again, he knew the answer, but he wanted to hear it.

Brin Os didn't want to say it aloud. "Slave running."

Brin Os knew he was getting into territory that was provocative, but he kept talking and said, "The vessel's former owner, a human named Borislav Lovanova, had agents who would gather "stock," they then showed up and whisked off the victims to the auctions. Marcus Pointer was one of the agents. He and Fel Nos reconnected after Pointer found the derelict mining ship. Marcus knew I was a pilot familiar with the ship's design, so they brought me in afterward. I had nothing to do with the slave trade, I swear!"

"Why bring Jitec Kilonoct into this?" Luke asked.

Brin Os replied, "He knew what modifications we needed to make to retrieve the derelict ship."

Luke checked his pad. "I still don't understand what they needed this Thatt Voffyes guy for."

Brin Os shrugged. "He provided us with intelligence we needed. We avoided arrest on the information he provided. To be honest, I think Thatt Voffyes knew too much about Marcus Pointer and Fel Nos to leave it to chance that he would just sit in prison and sulk while the others enjoyed newfound wealth."

Luke put down his pad, signaling to Phil that he was done with the interview. Phil left the observation room and entered the interview room and took a seat. Brin Os was concerned about this new development.

Phil moved the pad on the table around with his fingers. "Brin Os, you tried to steal a spaceship. Normally, we would ship you off to a law enforcement agency that you were wanted by. That would get you out of our hair, and justice would be served. But that's not an option since you're not wanted by any law enforcement agencies. I guess we could lock you up in a cell for a few months."

More color drained from Brin Os's ears. Phil continued, "I don't think a lot of that option. We would have to expend resources to keep you fed and guarded. Then there's no guarantee that you'll walk the straight and narrow when we let you out. There's another option I think you'll like and would be wise to take advantage of. Check out of your room at the hotel, go to the Shipping Union Office, get your dues up to date and sign onto a freighter. With your references, you won't be able to sign onto a premium vessel, but there are three ships leaving this afternoon. They have honest captains who will treat you fairly."

Brin Os was visibly relieved. "Mr. Ross, that's very generous. I'm grateful for the second chance."

Phil nodded. "This isn't without negative effects. Your name and photo will be distributed not only to stations owned by the Stellar Logistics and Freight Corporation but all other operations that do business with us. It's a sort of probationary period. If you keep your nose clean, you'll be all right." Phil got up. "Luke, I think Mr. Brin Os can see to these details himself."

A very relieved Brin Os thanked Phil and Luke several times while he was leaving. Phil and Luke went to Luke's office. Luke poured two cups of coffee. Phil asked, "Do you think he'll reform?"

Luke shrugged. "I hope so. I'm finding out there are too many horrible people out there. If we had a hand in helping him change the vector his life was on, I'll feel better. I don't think he's a hardened criminal. He just got caught up in a bad situation. He was tempted by the idea of fast money. Then he was suckered into a scheme headed by Marcus Pointer. It seemed reasonable at first, but they had to do one illegal thing after another until he was in too deep. He needed a way out, and we provided it."

Phil gave his coffee a smell. "Unless I miss my guess, Marcus Pointer, Fel Nos, and Jitec Kilonoct are probably beyond redemption."

Luke nodded in agreement. "Speaking of jerks. I did some research on Kilonoct, and he's wanted on more than one world."

Phil nodded. "Great, which world offers the longest sentence on conviction?"

Luke laughed out loud. "It doesn't really matter. There are extradition treaties that guarantee that once he's done serving time in one place, he'll be handed over to the next group he's offended."

Phil smiled. "Okay, is he wanted anywhere near the Unisystems Incorporated Research Colony on Triptous?"

Luke looked at the list of planets that wanted Kilonoct. "Yes, there is. Yunnar is quite anxious to have Mr. Kilonoct as a guest, and it's only half a day's travel from Triptous."

Phil nodded. "Okay, we'll transport Kilonoct to Yunnar as soon as we can."

After finishing their coffees, Phil and Luke went to the crime lab. Upon entering, Luke greeted Carl in a whisper, "Hey, Carl, what kind of progress are you making?"

Carl had the evidence they had removed from the *Aurora* laid out on tables. He looked up from the instrument he was adjusting, "Oh hey Boss. I'm just about done getting samples. About the only useful thing I can get from this stuff is DNA, and there's plenty of it."

Phil asked, "What kind is it"?

Carl didn't have to consult a pad. "Every race we know of, malnun, grunst, flaston, snoshin, pretar, maldor, and human."

Carl motioned to a terminal. "I have SICOS searching databases to see if we can put a name to these samples. If our database comes up empty on a sample, I'll make inquiries. There are eleven hundred and twenty-two separate samples unless these last few items reveal additional samples."

Luke frowned. "Is there any way to tell the difference between victim and criminal?"

Carl nodded. "Indeed there is. The victim's DNA will be only on one set of shackles, the criminals DNA will be on multiple sets of shackles."

Carl saw the look Luke and Phil were giving him, "I know it's thin, but it will stand up in court on any world."

Phil saw that Carl had four shackles separated from the rest. "What's the story with these?"

Carl replied, "Those were never used. They were at the bottom of the locker, so their evidence value is nil."

Phil thought about it. "Put these four back on board the *Aurora*." Luke was puzzled. "What do you want those for?"

Phil answered in a menacing tone, "In case we run into slavers."

Phil and Luke went to lunch at Eva's. Afterward, Phil had station business to attend to, which thankfully took his mind off the events of the last couple of days. He was walking past the Shipping Union Office when Fedir Makhno, a Ukrainian captain, stepped out with Brin Os in tow. Fedir was a highly respected captain of an independent freighter. Brin Os had a duffel bag over his shoulders.

Fedir was talking away as he led Brin Os. "You will like *Odessa Dream*. Is good ship, not as new or fast as Star series but is good, dependable ship."

Phil felt better about being lenient with Brin Os. Fedir was an honest man and had a reputation for taking raw crewmen and turning them into first-class ships company.

At about 1730 Zulu time, Phil had enough for one day. He retreated to his quarters, where Alice had dinner waiting. They ate dinner and decided to go for a stroll instead of watching a movie or playing a game on the entertainment system. They walked through each HabMod, only stopping to chat with friends for a few minutes. It seemed they spent more time in HabMod 4, where the alien races were housed.

Everyone who spotted Phil wanted to bid him and Alice a pleasant evening. Word had gotten out quickly about Phil's compassionate handling of the Brin Os incident. Most of the details were unknown to the general public, but it was generally understood that Brin Os got a break that Phil didn't necessarily need to give him. As a result, Phil was held in very high regard by the nonhumans. The pretars particularly had a fondness for Phil, knowing of his friendship with Selak, Klon, and Tonkin. They also knew he didn't have to put in the effort he did to prove Selak's innocence.

Back in the CentMod, Phil and Alice bought an ice-cream cone each, then sat down to enjoy them, and people-watch. Alice licked a drip from her cone before it could run down onto her fingers. "This station feels different from the others."

Phil considered what she said but didn't quite get what she was getting at. "What do ya mean?"

Alice wasn't quite sure how to articulate what she meant. "Well, on other stations, you can jump on a shuttle and visit the nearby planet to do business or just get a change of scenery."

Phil nodded in understanding. "I wondered when you would crack." "I'm not cracking up," she said, punching him in the arm playfully.

Phil uttered, "Ow," then he finished his cone. "You know you could jump a freighter or even a cruise ship to some pretty awesome places. There's enough traffic that you could take a two-week vacation if you really needed to."

Alice said, "I know that. We're not to that point yet. I was actually thinking there was something on the station I could do."

Phil stopped her. "You know as well as I do that you could be reinstated as a controller anytime you want."

Alice shook her head. "I've thought of that, but I don't want to get back into doing that every day. I wouldn't mind helping out in a pinch. But full-time? No. Actually, I was thinking there might be something I could do here in the CentMod."

Phil thought a second. "We already have an ice cream vendor."

Alice play-punched him in the arm again. "Ow" was Phil's deadpan response. Alice continued, "I'm not sure what yet. I've got to think about it."

Phil got up. "Well, there's no hurry."

*****

## Oasis 4, Upper CentMod, Operations Center, Briefing room 1

In the morning briefing, Phil announced his intention to take the Aurora to Yunnar. Jitec Kilonoct needed a ride to his next residence, and Phil said he was more than happy to help. He also told his staff that he was going to make a side trip to Triptous. He didn't offer any details, but most suspected it had something to do with the events of the last couple of days.

There was plenty to do before leaving. Phil sent a communication to Triptous to inform them that they would be there in a few days, and it would be appreciated if they could have the shuttle that the pretars returned standing by. Luke sent a communication to Yunnar law enforcement to inform them that Jitec Kilonoct would be back with them. Gus was given the task of stocking the *Aurora* galley with food and filing a flight plan. Luke informed his deputies, Tiffany Waters and Ian Mackenzie, that they were doing the prisoner transfer.

The next morning, Alice walked with Phil to the ship. Gus was already on board powering up systems and checking them. Tiffany and Ian showed up with a manacled Jitec Kilonoct in tow.

Phil gave Alice a hug and kiss. "Are you sure you don't want to tag along?"

Alice shrugged. "I would, but I'm still getting used to being here on the station. Besides, I want to do girl stuff."

That raised Phil's hackles. "Wha-What are you calling 'girl stuff'?" Alice knew she was going to make him wonder what she's up to. "Oh, you know, afternoon tea, brunches, garden parties, that sort of thing."

Phil turned to board the ship. "I'm coming back to lace curtains and fussy tablecloths, I'll bet."

Alice chuckled, then said, "Hurry home."

*****

## The *Aurora*, Astrodyne 65, Owned and Operated by the Stellar Logistics and Freight Corporation

Phil closed the hatch and checked the seal. He decided to check the ship spaces to ensure that everything was secure. The first thing he encountered was Jitec Kilonoct secured to a fitting on the bulkhead. Tiffany and Ian were in the cabin assigned to Jitec Kilonoct. They were rifling through the drawers and closet, looking for anything that Kilonoct could use to try to escape or even harm himself.

Kilonoct was wearing the bright orange jumpsuit that prisoners on Earth wore for centuries. He had already been scanned with medical instruments to ensure he wasn't hiding a weapon or a tool.

Just when Phil thought they were happy, Ian pulled the mattress from the bunk. "I'll secure this in the cargo hold if that's not a problem."

Phil nodded. "Sure, no problem. Just one thing, what's wrong with letting him keep the mattress?"

Tiffany answered, "Standard procedure. The mattress can be used for any number of things."

Kilonoct objected from his position at the bulkhead. "Yeah, like sleeping on." Phil, Ian, and Tiffany looked at Kilonoct and, in unison, replied, "Shut up!"

Ian disappeared with the mattress, and Tiffany put the few items they found in a plastic bag and placed it on the deck in the corridor.

Ian returned and released Kilonoct from the bulkhead fitting. He led Kilonoct into the cabin and started to remove the manacles with Tiffany. The moment the last handcuff was released, Kilonoct pushed Tiffany roughly aside and lunged for the door.

Ian was lighting fast and pulled his baton. The batons the deputies carried had a Tazer built into it. Ian jabbed Kilonoct in the side and pulled the trigger.

Before he could crumple to the deck, Tiffany came up with her own baton and put it across Kilonoct's back. Next, Ian caught a knee, then Tiffany used her baton to sweep him off his feet. Then one last hit across the stomach made Kilonoct's eyes widen.

The whole thing took less than two seconds to happen. Ten seconds later, Kilonoct had the wrist and ankle cuffs back on. Only this time, behind his back with the chain shortened, effectively hog- tying him. Ian picked him up and threw him unceremoniously on the hard mattress-less cot.

Tiffany and Ian secured the cabin serving as a brig on this trip. Then they retreated to their own cabins to settle in. Phil went to the cockpit to help Gus do the prelaunch checks. He sat at the copilot position and picked up a copy of the checklist and helped Gus finish the checks. Gus started the reactor and signaled the station workers to disconnect the umbilicals. Next, he called the station controllers, where they had him release the docking clamps and thrust away from the station. When they had sufficient distance, Gus idled the reaction engines and eased the power levers forward.

The *Aurora* picked up speed, and Phil busied himself, inputting the data into the navigation computer. When they had traveled the minimum distance from the station, Gus powered the light-speed engines. He pushed the light-speed engine's power selector forward, and Phil called out the velocity, "LS 1, LS 2, LS 3…" At LS 8, there was a low groan from the hull. Gus continued to accelerate and set the velocity to LS 9.

Phil did some calculations on the navigation computer. "According to the nav computer, we will establish orbit in twenty-five hours."

Phil and Gus agreed on a piloting schedule. It was never a good idea for the pilot to leave the cockpit on a trip although in most vessels with a single pilot, that's exactly what they do when they need to get a meal or use the head.

Twenty-four hours thirty minutes after they left the station, Phil cut the light- speed engines and powered the reaction engines. Yunnar could be seen in the distance, and Phil adjusted their course to intercept the planet and enter orbit with as little fuss as possible. The landing pad the Yunnar authorities assigned to them wouldn't be open for another four and a half hours. That allowed both Phil and Gus to get some rest. Orbit was considered an acceptable place to leave the cockpit and let the autopilot keep an eye on things.

After a four-hour nap, Gus fired the thrusters for atmospheric reentry. The navigation computer was in approach mode, which provided directional and pitch cues on the primary navigation display. At five kilometers distance on the final approach, Phil lowered the landing gear. Near the landing pad, Gus slowed the *Aurora* by pitching the nose up and adjusting the thruster angle while constantly tweaking the thrust level.

He showed his usual skill in handling the *Aurora*. He did notice that the combination of oversize thrusters and a ship with no cargo made for a touchy situation. He couldn't be very aggressive in controlling the *Aurora*. At last, he found himself hovering just a few feet over the landing pad. He slowly eased up on the thrust, and the *Aurora* settled gently on the ground. Gus shut down the thrusters and the reactor after a ground crewman connected a power cable to the external power receptacle.

*****

## Yunnar, Capital Shuttle Port

Phil went to the hatch and opened it. There were three grunst law enforcement officers waiting with restraints in hand. The officer who seemed to be in charge approached Phil. "Hello, Mr. Ross. I understand that you have a prisoner for us."

Phil nodded. "My security personnel is bringing him out now."

The grunst officer started to walk to the hatch. "Perhaps you should let my men handle Kilonoct. Your people are very capable, I'm sure, but as you may know, grunst can be…"

The officer stopped when Ian and Tiffany emerged carrying a hog-tied Jitec Kilonoct and dropped him on the landing pad. The officer and his subordinates stood and stared for what seemed like minutes. The two subordinate officers started to laugh, and a few seconds later, the officer in charge started to belly laugh. He motioned his officers to put their own restraints on Kilonoct and remove the shackles that Ian and Tiffany had on him.

Once their restraints were secure, Tiffany walked over to hand over the key for the shackles. Kilonoct started screaming, "Please don't let her near me!"

The officer in charge nearly doubled over in laughter. When he finally caught his breath, he said, "It seems I was a bit condescending where I had no cause to be."

The officers finally removed the shackles and led Kilonoct away.

The officer asked Phil, "Are you going to stay with us for a visit?"

Phil shook his head. "I'm afraid not. We have pressing business at Triptous colony. Otherwise, I would be absolutely delighted to see what your world has to offer. Perhaps if my wife needs a break from living on a space station, we can visit."

The officer smiled. "We look forward to that. By the way, my name is Supervisor Linbus Nuhfrez. If you ever need anything while you're here, please do not hesitate to ask."

Nuhfrez turned and walked to the spaceport terminal building. Gus exited the *Aurora* and had a word with the ground crewman, then walked over to Phil, Tiffany, and Ian. "There's no huge hurry to leave. If we leave now, we would arrive at Triptous at about 0530 local time.

The fella who is assigned to this pad says there's an excellent restaurant in the terminal. There's also a shop filled with souvenirs and trinkets."

Phil, Ian, and Tiffany thought that sounded like a good idea. Inside the terminal, they discovered that the restaurant was on the other side of the terminal, where they had to pass through customs. They made sure they had their passports and identification cards with them and headed to the customs desk. They saw that the restaurant wouldn't be open for about an hour, so the four of them went to the souvenir and gift shop. They noticed that the selection was very good. There were reasonably priced tourist souvenirs to top-of-the-line items.

The four of them spent a good deal of time in the shop. They made their selections and had their purchases packaged. Then they took advantage of a service that had the purchases delivered to their ship. During their meal, they compared their purchases. Phil bought Alice a necklace made from a gemstone found on Yunnar called finelds. It was a very common, therefore inexpensive gem, but it's an incredibly beautiful gem. In fact, everyone bought finelds in one form or another. They did notice that everyone at the terminal kept a wide berth from Tiffany. Finally, Phil asked the waiter in the terminal diner why. He told them when the officers led Kilonoct through the terminal. He was ranting about the "dangerous human female" and how we should keep our distance. Gus said, wiping tears from his face, "I can't wait for this to get around the station."

*****

## The *Aurora*, Astrodyne 65, Owned and Operated by the Stellar Logistics and Freight Corporation

Phil paid for the meal and started the prelaunch checks and walk-around check while Gus filed the flight plan. Back in the *Aurora*, Phil thought he would pilot the first part of the flight to Triptous. With all aboard, Phil started the reactor and signaled the ground crewman to disconnect the power umbilical. With the area outside the ship clear, Phil powered the thrusters and hovered over the landing pad. He increased the power to the thrusters and adjusted the thruster angle to start moving forward.

The *Aurora* picked up speed as it rose upward. Once outside the atmosphere, Phil established an orbit and fired the reaction engines, then set them to idle. Once they intercepted their desired course, he made the necessary adjustments and increased power.

They accelerated and cruised at the maximum sublight speed until they were at a distance that was safe for transitioning to light speed. Phil started the light- speed engines and increased power, then established a cruising velocity of LS 9 where he could relax after setting the autopilot.

The leg to Triptous was uneventful, with Phil and Gus taking turns at the controls. It wasn't entirely necessary in cruise configuration, but they were both professionals, and it wouldn't do to develop bad habits. Ian and Tiffany joined them in the cockpit, and the four of them passed the time telling stories and laughing at shared experiences.

Gus didn't hear the full story about the fugitives from flaston or the tale of the "Great Kortlax Round-up" and how they relate to each other. He was, of course, familiar with the story of Fel Nos and his crime spree at Selak's expense.

Halfway through the journey, Ian made a trip to the galley and brought four meals to the cockpit. They could have retreated to the galley to eat, but that would have either left the cockpit unattended or the pilot at the controls alone. Phil didn't like the idea of eating in the cockpit, but there were only the four of them, and it seemed wrong to do anything else.

The conversation was so pleasant that the time to cut the light-speed engines nearly took them by surprise. Phil was back at the controls, and he cut the light- speed engines. He fired up the reaction engines and checked his course. Some small adjustments were needed, which Phil made in an efficient manner while Triptous grew larger in their view.

Phil found the frequency for the Triptous orbiting station navigation beacon and put it into the navigation receiver. After making positive identification of the beacon, he put the *Aurora* in an orbit that intercepted the station's orbit.

When the station was near, he fired braking thrusters and slowed to a crawl relative to the station. The station controllers assigned a docking port, and he carefully aligned the *Aurora* then eased it into the docking clamps.

*****

## Triptous Orbiting Station

The *Aurora* was shut down after the umbilicals were connected. Gus opened the hatch and waited for the station hatch to be opened. Phil and the others arrived just as there was a clunk from the station hatch as the locks were released and the door slid open. Phil and the others stepped through the hatch, and they were greeted by the station manager and the shuttle fleet maintenance manager.

The station manager smiled brightly. "Gentlemen and lady," he said while bowing slightly for Tiffany.

Phil got a read on the manager immediately. The way he acted said volumes. For one thing, Phil figured that he was trained from early on to be management. Just looking at him, one could tell he wasn't technically minded at all. "Hi! I'm Eric Hornsby. You must be Phil Ross."

Eric put out his hand, and Phil shook it. "This is Gus Condent, the assistant manager of Oasis 4."

Then Phil motioned to Tiffany and Ian. "This is Tiffany Waters and Ian Mackenzie, two of my security deputy marshals."

Eric was taken aback. "I hope that you're not here for any of my personnel." Phil shook his head. "No, we moved a fugitive from our station to Yunnar."

Eric smiled. "Ah, of course. Oh, this is Klaus Mueller. He's our shuttle fleet maintenance manager."

As Klaus shook Phil's hand, he said, "We have that shuttle standing by that the pretars returned. We haven't had time to inspect and put it back into service. I'm not sure what information you can glean from it, but it's yours to inspect."

Eric smiled. "Let's take a shuttle to the surface, where the maintenance facility is located. Phil can get his data, and we can all have a meal or refreshment."

Phil nodded. "A light meal and a stretch of the legs is what the doctor ordered."

Eric led them through the station. "I must apologize for the walk. There were no docking ports that would handle the *Aurora* near the available shuttle to the surface."

Phil chuckled. "Nothing new in my experience. By the way, the *Aurora* could have landed on the planet. Why did we have to stop here?" Eric kept smiling. "We have very limited facilities on the planet.

There is hardly enough room for what we have now. In fact, we are currently in negotiations with a pretar firm to expand the station and add a shuttle maintenance facility. When that's done, we can use the space on the planet for other things."

Phil found it hard to imagine that a planet this size with a very small population would have space issues. Phil said, "Well, if you're thinking of having the Space Habitat and Systems Company do the work, I can give them my personal recommendation."

Eric was pleased to hear that. "Well, that's excellent news. We've had a lot of anxiety about hiring an alien firm."

Looking around and recalling what the station looked like before they docked, it was very obvious this station wasn't near as large as Oasis 4. It was really only a place to dock and unload passengers and cargo, then shuttle both to the surface.

The six of them reached a shuttle docking port and took their seats in a Pulsar 600. Klaus took the controls. After releasing the docking clamps, they started thrusting away from the station. The procedures for launching from the station were somewhere between more relaxed to nonexistent. That's not to say Klaus wasn't an excellent pilot. Phil was quite impressed at his skill.

When they were close enough to the ground, Phil could see what Eric was talking about. Triptous was very Earthlike in many ways. The planet itself was nearly the same size. As a result, gravity was within 2 percent of Earth's. The planet's rotational axis was slanted like Earth's giving them seasonal changes. There were seas, but they only covered about 35 percent of the planet. The most striking thing about Triptous is the amount of it that's nearly vertical.

Most of what came to Phil's eyes was mountains and forest-covered hills. He spotted some farms where terrace farming was possible. Klaus flew into a mountain valley that opened onto a large lake. Eric explained that the lake was actually a fjord. On the far shore, there was a landing pad cut into a mountain.

To their right was the capital city actually built onto the sides of the mountains. It was constructed to either blend into the landscape or enhance it. Klaus aligned the shuttle with a pad marking and started his final approach. He slowed the shuttle and came to a hover, inches over the ground momentarily, and settled on the pad.

*****

**Triptous, Research Colony Shuttle Port**

Eric opened the hatch, and everyone exited. He then turned to Klaus. "Could you show these folks to the shuttle in question? I'll arrange transportation to the restaurant."

Eric turned and strode toward the terminal. Klaus led the others to a hangar carved into the mountain. Phil had never seen anything like that before and was very impressed. Once inside, Klaus had a technician connect power, then he motioned to Phil. "After you."

Phil pulled a data chip from his pocket. "It'll only take a minute." Inside the shuttle, Phil turned on the power and then powered the navigation computer. Selecting the history function, he copied the files for the period that Marcus Pointer was in possession of the shuttle. With that done, he removed the data chip and powered everything down.

Once outside the shuttle, Klaus smiled at Phil. "Well, that didn't take long." Phil shrugged. "Well, I didn't need much."

The group went to the terminal and passed through the customs desk then rejoined Eric. He turned to them. "Ah, our transport is just arriving."

Eric led them through a set of doors at the back of the terminal, and they found themselves in a tunnel carved out of the rock. A vehicle large enough to accommodate all of them pulled up, and they piled in. Phil realized the reason he didn't see roads from the shuttle was because they were all underground.

Eric saw the looks on everyone's faces. He saw that they needed more explanation, so he volunteered. "We put the buildings on the outer face of the mountains and the roads inside. It solves all kinds of problems, such as problems with weather and maintenance."

Gus asked, "Aren't you afraid of earthquakes?" Eric laughed. "You mean Triptousquakes?" Gus reddened slightly. "I suppose I do."

Eric continued, "Triptous is very stable, seismically speaking."

The driver moved out as soon as everyone was sitting. Eric continued to explain the road system, "We're in the process of modernizing the road system. The desire is to convert to an 'on demand' rail type system similar to the system on Pretna."

Gus was immediately impressed. "This is pretty spectacular, but what does a person do if they feel like a walk or jog?"

"Oh, we have footpaths, stairs, and footbridges where needed. There's a scenic walk close to the restaurant we can explore after we eat," Eric offered.

The meal indeed hit the spot and the short walk to a park with a scenic overlook of the fjord. Phil had to remind the group that they had other places to be. Eric summoned transport, and they rode to the spaceport terminal building.

Entering the terminal, they were greeted with the sight of two flastons pleading with a Triptous security official. The flastons had two individuals on their knees with their hands tied and cloth sacks over their heads.

Phil edged closer so that he could hear. The flaston that seemed to be in charge was saying, "Look, these two are wanted fugitives. We need to get transportation to Pretna."

The security official sounded flustered but sympathetic. "Gentlemen, I would be more than happy to let you take these two to Pretna. But you must understand. You don't have extradition papers. You don't have warrants. You're not registered bounty hunters. I'm sorry, but a judge will have to sort this out."

It suddenly occurred to Phil who the flastons were. "Isnod? Feldon?"

The flastons turned. Isnod recognized Phil. "Mr. Ross, we wondered if we would see you here."

Phil looked down at the two fugitives that Isnod and Feldon had cuffed and on their knees. "You know, I'm very suspicious of coincidences. Who do you have to take to Pretna?"

Feldon yanked the sacks off the head of the two captives. Phil stared down at the very bruised and swollen faces of Marcus Pointer and Fel Nos. Keeping his stare fixed on the two pathetic individuals at his feet, Phil said, "Officer, I'm the station manager for Oasis 4. In that capacity, I would like to make an official request for the custody of Marcus Pointer and Fel Nos."

Isnod and his partner looked angry. They thought they were going to miss out on a bounty.

Phil continued, "Mr. Isnod and Mr. Feldon are now agents of Stellar Logistics and Freight Corporation, Oasis 4 security division."

The security official smiled. "Oh. I didn't know it was Stellar Logistics and Freight Corporation initiative. I'll just need to scan your identification so the judge will be satisfied."

Phil handed over his identification, and the official scanned it into the computer. He had a short conversation with a judge on a communications terminal, and a printer next to the computer spit out an official document.

Phil saw it had an official seal embossed into the paper. The security official took the documents and handed them to Phil. "These are the extradition papers for these two."

Phil took the papers and leafed through them. "Still using paper here, huh?" The official shrugged. "Our laws require physical documents for such things.

When you get back to Oasis 4, you will probably want to scan those into a file and discard the physical paperwork."

Phil smiled. "Maybe I'll have Isnod give them to the pretars. They would probably get a kick out of this stuff."

The official turned to Isnod and Feldon. "Gentlemen, both of you are quite welcome to return to Triptous. However, if you return in your capacity as bounty hunters, make sure you're on the registry, and I would recommend getting new passports from your new government."

*****

## Triptous Research Colony Shuttle

There was a passenger shuttle returning to the station, and Eric secured passage for everyone. On the flight to the orbiting station, Isnod leaned toward Phil. "I'm afraid I don't understand completely what's happening. Are you offering to facilitate our trip to Pretna?"

Phil smiled. "Yes, I am. We have as much interest in locking these two up as you do. They've been breaking laws all over the galaxy. That one"—Phil pointed at Fel Nos—"caused all kinds of problems on my station and almost ruined the life of a friend of mine."

Isnod nodded. "I'm afraid they're nothing more than a business transaction to us."

Phil asked, "What happened to your shuttle?"

Isnod shrugged. "It wasn't really ours, was it? The Flast embassy on Earth confiscated it when they informed us. We were no longer employed. The new government had no use for our profession at this time. Feldon and I did some soul-searching and decided that it might be best if we didn't return to Flast for a while."

Phil nodded in understanding. "We'll see what we can do to get your prisoners to Pretna. I'm sure the pretars will be happy to compensate you guys. They're very honorable when it comes to things like that."

Isnod smiled. "Of that, I have no doubts. They have a reputation for being very honorable people." Then he furrowed his brow. "What sort of things have these two been doing to get in so much trouble?"

Phil proceeded to explain the whole saga about Fel Nos, the others, and what brought them to this point. He didn't offer any information about the *Prospector,* though.

Isnod tried to work it out in his head. "What information did this Fel Nos have that would compel that human to sign over a fine vessel like the Astrodyne?"

Phil answered, "They were all slave traders. Fel Nos blackmailed himself into a ship."

Isnod didn't say a word on the rest of the trip to the space station. He simply glared at the two cuffed figures with sacks over their heads, sitting across the aisle from him.

*****

## Triptous Orbiting Station

Reaching the station, Phil turned to the others. "Gus, why don't you start the prelaunch checks? Isnod, Feldon, Tiffany, and Ian will get you two settled."

Pointer started pleading, "Please hurry. These wrist ties are cutting into me." Before Isnod could respond, Phil jumped in, "By all means, hurry. Tiffany, there are shackles left over from the Aurora's slave ship days. Please make sure that they get put to use. Don't waste a cabin on these two scumbags. Lock the shackles to a floor fitting in the cargo bay."

Isnod smiled. "Mr. Ross, I think we're going to enjoy this trip." Phil nodded. "I'm going to file the flight plan."

Phil left to visit the operations center to file the flight plan, and the others went to the *Aurora*.

At the operations center, a clerk approached Phil. "Mr. Ross, there is a communication for you."

Phil read the pad the clerk gave him. He rolled his eyes. "You've got to be kidding me."

Back at the *Aurora*, Phil secured the hatch, and then he summoned everyone to the galley. Isnod and Feldon were sitting at a table across Tiffany and Ian. Gus entered, "What's up, Boss?"

Phil held up a pad. "Corporate threw us a curveball." Isnod and Feldon didn't get the curveball reference. Phil continued, "They want us to go to Reynolds Planet and pick up forty passengers."

Gus protested, "We don't have the berths or rations for forty people."

Phil shrugged while looking at his pad. "It says here they'll be bringing their own rations and cots. They'll set up in the cargo bay, and we won't have to deal with them at all."

Gus furrowed his brow. "I wonder who these people are that they couldn't charter a passenger shuttle?"

Phil replied, "That's the best part. The leader of this group is called Major Henson."

Gus blurted out, "Mercenaries? Funny that we run into more of these guys in such a short space of time."

Phil shrugged. "It seems to be a growth industry these days. The fact is our corporation is providing transportation tells me that whatever is happening benefits us. Speaking of rations, this detour will add two days to our wanderings. Ian, I would like you and Feldon to pick up additional stores. Actually, make sure you get more than what we need in case there are more surprises. Feldon, I'm sending you along to see if there are any flaston delicacies you would like to get."

*****

## The *Aurora*, Astrodyne 65, Owned and Operated by the Stellar Logistics and Freight Corporation

Ian and Feldon returned from the station rations store and set to work, putting the rations into storage. When they were done, Gus started the launch procedures. They made sure everyone was sitting before thrusting. Once they were a sufficient distance from the station, Gus adjusted his course, then powered the reaction engines.

This was his favorite part of the flight. The Detroit 750's pinned him to the back of the seat. The inertia neutralizers weren't exactly up to the task with the engine upgrade. Once he was satisfied with his course and distance, he started the light-speed engines and increased speed until he reached LS 9. Gus and Phil took shifts at the controls for the one-day journey to Reynolds Planet.

Gus entered orbit and contacted the spaceport they were assigned to. They were assigned to a landing pad and a course to intercept. He deorbited and entered the atmosphere and then intercepted the course he was provided. Phil brought up the published approach and landing procedures for this spaceport. Gus followed the vectors that the controller gave him until he established himself on the glide path and followed it to the spaceport.

Breaking out of the clouds at a thousand meters altitude above the ground, he called the controller and reported he had the visual. In a few minutes, he had the *Aurora* hovering motionless over the landing pad and slowly lowered the ship until its full weight rested on the pad. Gus shut down the thrusters, and a ground crewman connected a power cable to the shuttle.

*****

## Reynolds Planet, Shuttle Port

Phil went to the cargo hold and started to open the cargo loading hatch. When the hatch was fully open, he extended the loading ramp. They were supposed to be only picking up passengers, but the message he received from corporate didn't specify if they had any equipment or not. He looked over to Pointer and Fel Nos, wondering how the mercenaries would react to these two.

Gus and the others entered the cargo bay, and Phil said, "You might as well stretch your legs and get some fresh air."

Pointer raised his sack-covered head. "I'd like to stretch my legs too." Isnod gave him a kick in the side. "Shut up."

Gus was standing next to Fel Nos and kicked him for good measure. "You shut up too."

Phil went to the terminal building with the others in tow. Inside the terminal, Phil went to find the operations office while Gus and the others went to find a souvenir shop.

Phil found the operations office, where he inquired about his passengers. The clerk behind the desk checked a screen, "They're scheduled to arrive in a half hour or so. They'll be in two large transports. I'll send them to your landing pad as soon as they arrive."

Phil sent a message to the Pretna authorities informing them that they'll be bringing Fel Nos and Marcus Pointer to Oasis 4. Hopefully, they'll send someone to the station to fetch the fugitives back to Pretna.

Finally, Phil filed a flight plan to Oasis 4. Then he went to join the others in the souvenir and gift shop.

Phil found a figurine that he thought Alice would like. Gus, Tiffany, and Ian all found similar items to purchase. Isnod and Feldon didn't see the need although they did seem to enjoy browsing. After making their purchases, they retreated to a seating area outside the terminal building to wait for their passengers.

They didn't have to wait long. The voice of the clerk in the operations office came over the public address system. *"Mr. Ross, your passengers have arrived. They'll be at your ship momentarily."* They rose and made the short walk to the landing pad.

As they reached the ship, two ground transports arrived. A human stepped out and shook hands with Phil. "I'm Major Henson. You must be Phil Ross."

Phil smiled. "That's right. This is my assistant manager, Gus Condent." Then he indicated to the others. "This is Tiffany Waters and Ian Mackenzie, two of my deputy security marshals." Then he added, "Finally, this is Isnod and Feldon. They're bounty hunters."

Major Henson raised an eyebrow. "Your people didn't mention these two."

Phil said, "Actually, they're a last-minute addition. We ran into them on Triptous. They have two fugitives that we're very interested in making sure the Pretna authorities get their hands on again."

Major Henson asked, "What are they charged with?"

Phil replied, "Escaping from a penal colony mining asteroid. The original charges are theft. However, we found evidence recently that proved that they were slave traders. In fact, this is the ship they used to smuggle their victims."

Major Henson's eyes narrowed. "Interesting. Well, with your permission, I'd like to get my people aboard and settled in."

Phil nodded and smiled. "I'd like nothing better."

With that, Major Henson turned to the first transport. "First Sergeant Thack! Get 'em loaded!"

Phil watched the roughest and meanest-looking pretar he had ever seen, get out of the transport, and turn around. "Okay, you devils! You heard the major!" The paid soldiers exited the transports and started unloading equipment boxes. Phil said to Major Henson, "If you follow me, I'll show you to some quarters for you and your officers. How many officers do you have?" Major Henson answered, "Myself and two others."

Phil led the Major on board, then showed him where his cabin was, and assigned a double for his officers. They went to the cargo hold to check on the loading, where they found the soldiers standing in a semicircle staring at the two shackled figures on the deck.

Major Henson cleared his throat. "Men, these two are fugitives being transported back to Pretna via Oasis 4. They are thieves, and I just learned that it's recently come to light that they have also run slaves."

The mercenary's expression turned from curiosity to loathing in an instant. Although they had sacks over their heads, there was a noticeable reaction from Pointer and Fel Nos. They thought that their career in running slaves was a well- kept secret. They didn't like the fact that it was now known publicly, particularly by the men that surrounded them at the moment. Fel Nos started to weep softly, and Pointer was trying to keep his shaking under control.

One mercenary slowly stepped forward. He had a face that was hard and gaunt for a young man. He pulled the hoods off Pointer's and Fel Nos's heads, then squatted in front of them and stared. Fel Nos and Pointer stared back at the man in front of them with expressions of terror.

In a low voice, the mercenary said, "If the pretars don't end you, I will. If you two ever get out of the pretar prison, I'll hunt you down and make it last for days."

First Sergeant Thack cleared his throat. "Corporal Evans, get yourself squared away." Then he looked around. "That goes double for the rest of you!"

One of the officers stepped forward. "Major, all personnel and equipment are aboard."

Phil stepped to the cargo hatch, where he retracted the ramp and closed the hatch. Then he turned to the major. "Oh, by the way, we have oversize engines on this, so your guys will want to hang on when we accelerate."

The major nodded. "We're used to things like that. We'll put straps in the floor fittings."

Phil added, "Sorry about the accommodations. We'll be getting under way in a few minutes."

*****

## The *Aurora*, Astrodyne 65, Owned and Operated by the Stellar Logistics and Freight Corporation

Phil turned and went to the cockpit. As he was strapping into the copilot seat, Gus said, "I'm through with the prestart checklist."

Phil turned to the reactor start page on the checklist and read each item off while Gus checked the items as Phil read. When they were ready to launch, Phil announced over the intercom they were ready for takeoff. Then he contacted spaceport control and received clearance to launch. Gus powered the thrusters, and the ship rose into the air. He pitched upward and increased forward speed.

It took several minutes to leave the planet's atmosphere. Once they were in space, Gus adjusted his course, then fired the reaction engines. As the speed increased, he fine-tuned his course. Once the maximum velocity that the reaction engines could provide was reached, Gus engaged the light-speed engines. The hull gave its customary groan at LS 8 and kept accelerating until the *Aurora* settled in at a velocity of LS 9.

Phil got up. "I'm going to check on our passengers."

He left the cockpit and walked the corridor between the cabins to the cargo hold. Entering the cargo hold, Phil saw the mercenaries had an equipment container open and were busy pulling out cots and bedding. First Sergeant Thack was supervising the setup, ensuring that they were arranged according to which squad they were in.

Major Henson spotted Phil and smiled. "You weren't just whistling Dixie about the acceleration of this thing."

Phil smiled back. "I'm delighted with this ship personally. It's turning out to be quite an acquisition. By the way, how exactly did you secure yourselves?"

Henson stepped to a pile of harnesses and picked one up. It looked like a standard cargo tie-down strap, only shorter. "We treat ourselves like cargo. We sit cross-legged with this over our laps."

Phil couldn't help but admire the simplicity. "How did these two do during the launch?" He asked, pointing to Pointer and Fel Nos.

Henson chuckled. "Those shackles are no one's friend. I truly hope the rest of their miserable lives are filled with despair. There is absolutely no honor in what they did."

Phil nodded. "I don't think the pretars are going to kiss them when they get them back. By the way, why don't you and your officers join me for coffee in the galley at about 1400 Zulu? Oh, and your First Sergeant Thack, of course."

Henson smiled and said they would be there.

1400 Zulu rolled around, and Phil made sure there was an urn of fresh coffee and cups. Tiffany got out a small platter and arranged some cookies on it. Phil looked at what she was doing and had a laugh. "Tiffany, they're mercenaries, not a garden club."

Tiffany looked at the table, then started chuckling herself. "All the more reason to observe and maintain civil behavior."

Major Henson walked in with his officers behind him and First Sergeant Thack trailing. Phil smiled. "Gentlemen, come in. We don't stand on ceremony. There are cups there by the coffee urn." He said, pointing to the counter. "The cream and sugar is on the table. Help yourselves."

Henson grabbed a mug and started filling it. "I have to apologize to you, folks. I didn't introduce my lieutenants. These are Lieutenants Greene and Yondlyn, and this is First Sergeant Thack."

Greene was obviously human, but Yondlyn was flaston. They weren't chatty, but they weren't especially aloof either. When everyone had something to drink, Phil took a sip. "I don't suppose it would do any good to ask what your mission is, would it?"

The major chuckled. "First, we'd have to know what the mission was."

Phil was flabbergasted. "You mean you have no idea where you're going or what you're doing?"

The major shrugged. "For security reasons, our superiors keep a lid on the details. We can tell you, however, our mission is related to those two jackasses chained up in the cargo hold. There are some worlds that are tired of their citizens coming up missing. We're going to meet a Snoshin at your station. Apparently, he has a line on a location of a slave market. These men I have with me are elite forces. It sounds like we'll be conducting a raid. Probably an intelligence gathering mission with a possibility of rescuing slaves."

Phil asked, "Why doesn't Griska use their own troops?"

Henson shrugged. "There are several reasons. They may not have the political will to risk their own troops in something that may become embarrassing. We can also be horribly vicious without political fallout. Security is generally tighter with us. If they deployed their own people, politicians would have to be informed, and historically, they have always had big mouths. Usually, some elected officials will try to show how important he or she is by crowing about what they know. If they're the first to spill the beans about something like this, they think it makes them look important. Finally, we're short-notice operators."

Ian was silent up to now, but his curiosity prompted him to ask, "What makes a man become a paid soldier?"

Lieutenant Greene answered, "Every one of us has our own reasons. The lowest level of our profession is in it strictly for the money. They will work for anyone and do anything. They usually don't last long in this business. If they don't get killed on the job, they usually wind up getting greased in a seedy bar fighting over a female or drinking themselves into absolute uselessness or worse. Then there are those who are born to do this. Being in the company of elite soldiers, the adrenaline rush you get in combat, and the satisfaction of crushing some oppressive jerk. Then there's a third group. Those who are there for their own reasons that range from revenge to wanting to have a part in a victory over a group that you have a personal animus against."

Phil peered across the table. "What group are you in, Lieutenant Yondlyn?" "I'm in that third group," answered Yondlyn. "I grew up in a flaston colony.

Our home planet refused to provide protection because we decided to structure our government as a Republic with democratically elected officials. You can imagine how it would make them feel if we were successful. The slavers would show up and grab everyone from a village.

They would leave the old and the children too young to work. I've had friends and family disappear without a trace. So you can say that I'm here to make the slavers pay, and then there's also the pride one gets in being with a group of men like this."

Phil grabbed a cookie from the platter. "Your Corporal Evans is definitely in the third group."

First Sergeant Thack put down his mug after taking a sip. "Indeed he is. He started a farm in New Iowa. Things were wonderful for him until the slavers showed up in the middle of the night and took his young bride. They would have taken him too, but he was repairing an irrigation pump to try to save his crop. He was kilometers away that night and didn't know they had been there until he came home."

Phil absorbed what he heard. "What about you, First Sergeant? I can't imagine there's a mercenary caste on Pretna."

Thack smiled slightly. "You would be right, Mr. Ross. My family is actually part of the artistic caste. My father was an architect, but I never felt the pull to that life. The Pretna military is very difficult to enter if you're not in the proper caste. So I left home and found a purpose in being a soldier of fortune. It's been my good fortune to associate with Colonel Devonport and Major Henson here. But I've got to say, I'm here for the men. They're my men, and I love those murdering devils."

Phil finished his coffee. "It's a well-known fact that there's a slave trade in the galaxy. How bad is it?"

Major Henson answered, "It's small but growing. Demand is rising, and slavers are growing bolder. Every government on earth is dedicated to eradicating it. Colonial governments are tired of their citizens disappearing, but they don't always have the resources to stop it from happening. The best way to discourage the slave traffickers is to make being found an extremely undesirable outcome. That's where we come in."

"Well, I'd like to wish you guys the best of luck, but how did my company get involved with all this?" Phil asked.

Henson finished his own coffee. "I thought that would be obvious. Tons of goods and materials go through your station daily. If just a tiny percentage of it was from slave labor and became known, the consequences for your company would be huge."

Phil nodded. "I see what you mean."

Lieutenant Yondlyn looked at Isnod and Feldon. "I imagine you two found yourselves unemployed suddenly and turned to bounty hunting." Isnod and Feldon were suddenly uncomfortable, then Isnod sheepishly said, "We were fugitive trackers on a mission when Flast changed governments. We decided to become bounty hunters to support ourselves until we could determine which way the wind blew on Flast. The Flast embassy on Earth confiscated our transport, but we managed to get ourselves to Triptous, where we were lucky enough to catch up to Pointer and Fel Nos."

"How did you know to find them at Triptous?" Phil asked.

Feldon laughed. "It was a pure guess. We knew Pointer had stolen a shuttle from there. Then we saw on the flight plan registry that you were making a stop there. Combine that with the events at your station recently. We wondered if there was some sort of connection, and it turns out there was. We caught them while they were looking for a way to break into the shuttle port hangar."

Phil smiled. "That's actually pretty clever."

Isnod held back a laugh. "We didn't exactly dazzle anyone with our skills on your station. After all, you managed to sneak those people past us when we were there."

Isnod saw the expression on Phil's face. "That's right, Mr. Ross. We figured out what you did that day."

"We followed that one lady to a place called Detroit," Feldon put in. Isnod continued, "After we figured out what you did, we were in a rage. Then we thought about it for a time and laughed ourselves sick. After the government we worked for collapsed, we decided to just start again with a new perspective. Believe me. We don't hold any ill will toward anyone."

The next day and a half were uneventful, with Gus and Phil trading places at the controls. Isnod and Feldon made sure Pointer and Fel Nos received some food, which was really just runny porridge, and they took them to the head so they could relieve themselves. The mercenaries made it a point to terrify Fel Nos and Pointer on those trips.

In addition to making sure Fel Nos and Marcus Pointer didn't forget how much they were despised, the soldiers traded notes with

Ian and Tiffany on subjects that ranged from hand-to-hand combat to nonlethal weapons. There was one incident where the soldiers were curious about the stun batons that Tiffany and Ian carried. After Tiffany bruised a couple of them and gave one a bloody nose, First Sergeant Thack put a stop to the demonstrations.

Phil was getting ready to relieve Gus at the controls when his conversation with his passengers kept rolling around in his head. Something was bothering him, and he couldn't put his finger on it. Then it occurred to him. Why couldn't he look in the *Aurora's* navigation history? Perhaps Fel Nos was careless and left the history intact. He was feeling kind of stupid since he traveled more light-years than he cared to count just to download the history of Pointer's shuttle. He grabbed a data chip and went out the door.

Phil entered the cockpit, and Gus looked in his direction. "You're early."

Phil sat at an observer seat and powered a workstation. "I know. It occurred to me that the navigation records on this ship would be a real boon to anyone who was trying to put an end to the slave trade. After all, it was used for that purpose."

Gus thought about it for a second and shook his head. "Boy! We're a pair, aren't we? That's so stupidly obvious it didn't occur to us to check our own ship."

Phil scrolled through the navigation computer menu and found the historical records. The historical records were kept to make going to frequent destinations easier. Particularly when there were complicated courses to be followed, some pilots use the function so infrequently that it slips their mind that the function exists. That was what Phil was banking on.

After finding the historical records, he saw that they were intact. The records were all there from launch and test flights at the factory to their latest flight. Phil inserted the data chip into the computer and copied all the files.

After taking the controls, Phil let Gus get a couple of hours of rest before they had to drop out of light speed. They wanted to arrive at the station at an hour that drew the least amount of attention. Checking his navigation computer, he calculated the exact moment to cut the light-speed engines to give them exactly one hour of sublight speed to the station.

Most pilots and helmsmen don't like to cut it that close, being as the calculations are extremely precise, and the closer you get to the station, the danger of a collision greatly increases. When they were ten minutes from cutting the light-speed engines, Phil activated a chime that was heard throughout the ship. Then he announced over the passenger address system they had ten minutes to prepare for the transition to sublight speed.

Gus sat in the copilot position and strapped in. The time to cut was a few seconds away, and Gus provided a countdown over the passenger address system. When the timer read zero, the navigation computer cut the light speed engines automatically. The scene out of the viewport in front of them came into sharp focus. Phil started the reaction engines and set them to idle. A quick check of the navigation data reassured him that they were precisely where they had to be.

Major Henson entered the cockpit and sat in an observer seat. Phil contacted the station to announce his arrival. They gave him a warm greeting and vectors to follow. Phil asked the controllers to have Luke Smith contact him on a secure frequency. In a few minutes, the communication set announced that there was a secure transmission ready to be responded to.

Phil activated the proper code sequence, and he was greeted with Luke's image on the monitor. "Welcome back, Boss."

Phil smiled back. "It's good to be back. Are you familiar with our passengers and their requirements?"

Luke answered, "Yes, I am. They have reservations at the hotel. I'll have one of my guys escort them there. I've also arranged to have their equipment off- loaded and put in secure storage."

The major stood up. "Well, it sounds like you guys have everything situated."

Phil said, "Just a second, Major. I checked our own navigation computer and discovered that the historical records were intact from the day this vessel rolled off the line until present."

It took the major a second or two to grasp the significance of this piece of news. After thinking about it, he slowly nodded. "That will most likely prove to be extremely useful. But don't give me the information. Pass it on to your security marshal. That's the proper channel. He will forward it up the chain, and the proper intelligence agencies will collect the data and best decide what to do with it." After a bit, the major excused himself and retreated to the cargo hold.

Phil continued the vectored approach to the station. The controller steered him to a perfect alignment with his destination, which was CargoMod 2, Docking Port 1. He brought the *Aurora* to near-perfect alignment with the docking port by adjusting pitch, roll, and yaw in minuscule proportions. When he was happy, he thrust port until the docking clamps engaged and were retracted to bring the ship into intimate contact with the station. Station personnel connected umbilicals and opened the air lock hatch after ensuring that an airtight seal was affected, then the cargo hold hatch air lock was also opened. Phil and Gus completed the shutdown checklist and secured the cockpit. Power from the umbilicals kept the ship systems operating that was necessary to have on while the ship was docked.

Gus went to the personnel hatch to open it, with Tiffany and Ian in tow. Phil went to the cargo hold to open the cargo hatch. Major Henson and his men were dressed in normal clothes. The major explained that they didn't want to draw attention while at the station. Phil opened the ship's cargo hatch and was greeted with the sight of Luke Smith with three of his deputies. "Welcome back, Boss!"

Luke stepped into the hatch and shook hands with Major Henson as Phil introduced them. He said, "Gentlemen, if you'll please follow Roger. He'll show you to the Star Lodge Suites."

As the soldiers were moving toward the hatch, they had to walk past Pointer and Fel Nos. One of the soldiers gave Pointer a swift kick in the sides as he walked past. It was delivered in the same manner that a person would give an annoying little dog a kick. Fel Nos tried to make himself as small as possible while waiting for his kick. A soldier reached down, grabbed the chain to his neck shackle, and gave it a couple of quick yanks. "Pray you never run into me out there, Nos."

After the soldiers were gone, Luke stared at the figures in shackles on the floor. Pointer was trying to collect himself, and Fel Nos was sobbing. Luke said to his deputies, "Get those slave shackles off them and put on standard restraints. We can't parade them through the station in those. They smell like they forgot how to use a toilet too. Run them through the wash and get them clean jumpsuits." Phil knew that the wash Luke had in mind wasn't going to be gentle.

The deputies lead their prisoners away, leaving Luke, Phil, Isnod, and Feldon in the cargo hold. Luke said to Isnod and Feldon, "Guys, we'll hold your prisoners for you until the Pretna authorities get here. Until then, we've made arrangements to put you up in the hotel. By the way, welcome back to Oasis 4."

*****

## Oasis 4, HabMod 1, Quarters of Phillip and Alice Ross

Isnod and Feldon followed Luke while Phil retrieved his own small duffel and headed to his quarters in HabMod 1. It was 2300 hours Zulu, and activity in the common areas was minimal. He reached his quarters and stood at the door, then he asked himself, "I wonder what she has in store for me."

He entered their quarters and said in a quiet voice, "SICOS, turn on lights to very low."

The lights came on just enough to keep himself from tripping. He put the souvenirs he bought for Alice on a sideboard. Quietly, he went into the bedroom, where he put down his duffel then took off his clothes and crawled into bed next to Alice. She stirred slightly, then mumbled, "Hey, big fella, my husband's coming home tonight."

Phil smiled in the dimness. "I'll watch it. SICOS, lights out." Alice smiled as the lights dimmed out.

In the morning, SICOS turned on the lights and announced, "It's time to wake up, Mr. and Mrs. Ross."

Alice threw off the covers, rolled up onto her knees, and started shaking Phil while hopping up and down. She rapidly started firing off questions without giving Phil time to respond. "How was your trip? Where did ya go? Who did ya meet? What did you bring me? Huh? Huh? Huh?"

Phil poked his head out from the covers. "Mom was right. I married a crazy woman."

He sat up and gave Alice a smooch, then he replied, "The trip was fine.

Yunnar, Triptous, and Reynolds Planet. Lots of people. Stuff from gift shops, I put them on the sideboard."

Alice jumped up, threw on her robe, and ran into the sitting room. Phil heard a squeal of delight when she saw what he had brought her. He got up and put on sweats in anticipation of going to the fitness center this morning. He was thinking that perhaps there should be something on the Aurora he could use to get in a cardio workout while on a trip. Just a couple of days was enough to throw him off his rhythm.

He went into the sitting room and saw Alice admiring the figurine he bought on Reynolds Planet. Then she picked up the case with the fineld gem necklace.

She squealed again when she opened it. "Here, here, here, put it on me, put it on me!"

Phil took the necklace from her and put it around her neck while she held her hair out of the way. After frantically looking around the room for a mirror, she darted into the bedroom. He followed her and saw her admiring the necklace in the mirror.

He came up behind her and said, "It's just something from a terminal gift shop."

Alice replied, "Well, I think it's pretty special."

He helped her remove it and put it back in the box. "Now get dressed for the fitness center," he said as he swatted her on the backside. Then he retreated to the sitting room before she could retaliate.

*****

**Oasis 4, CentMod, Eva's Café**

After their workout and showers, the pair went to breakfast at Eva's. They sat at their customary table, and Eva came up with a pot of coffee and filled their cups. She entered their orders on a pad and went to another table.

Alice sipped her coffee. "Did you get the information you were after?" "Yes, we did," Phil replied.

He took a sip of his own. "After I take care of station business, I'm going to analyze it to see if I can nail down the final resting place of the *Prospector.*"

Phil gave Alice the condensed version of the events of the past couple of days. She was unhappy to learn how widespread the slave trade was becoming but was glad that someone was trying to do something about it.

Major Henson walked into the café with First Sergeant Thack. Phil motioned them over. "Major Henson, First Sergeant Thack, please sit." They both happily sat, and Phil introduced them to Alice while Eva filled their mugs.

Then Eva asked, "What can I get for you two, dears?"

Major Henson scanned the menu. "I see you have biscuits and gravy. I'll have that with hash browns."

First Sergeant Thack put down his menu. "I'll have a soldier's breakfast, chip beef on toast, and scrambled eggs."

Eva entered it on a pad. "Soldiers breakfast. You sound like my husband.

What kind of toast do you want with that?" Thack replied, "Whole wheat please."

Phil asked, "Did you gentlemen have a pleasant evening?"

Henson answered, "The hotel was very comfortable, and the fitness center is first rate."

Thack nodded in agreement. "The beds are much more comfortable than what I'm accustomed to, but the major is quite correct about the fitness facilities."

Eva brought their breakfasts, and they spent a pleasant period enjoying their meal.

After some time, Eva refilled their coffees after the busboy cleared the tables. "How was it, gentlemen?"

Thack replied, "That was most excellent. The only thing that would make this better would be if the eggs were kortlax eggs."

Phil finished his coffee. "Guys, I'm hoping to have some information about your length of stay here. Right now, I have to take my leave and attend the morning briefing. Why don't you gentlemen come up to the Operations Center at 0900 Zulu." He gave Alice a kiss and headed to the operations center.

*****

## Oasis 4, CentMod, Operations Center

Before the briefing, Phil had time to go to his office and check his correspondences. There was only one letter worth looking at before the briefing. It was a memorandum explaining the corporate interests in the current intrigue. He read through it and grumbled to himself, "You know they could have condensed this to one sentence, 'Slavery bad, help stop.'" Then he thought, maybe a few more words to make it less awkward.

Entering the briefing room, everyone broke into applause and congratulated him for bringing the *Aurora* back in one piece. Phil put up his hands. "Please, please, Gus was there to take the blame if anything went wrong."

Virginia started her portion of the briefing. "There's only one item of interest this morning. A five-hundred-passenger ship is docking the day after tomorrow to pick up our guests that are currently residing at the hotel."

Phil made a note on his pad. "What's the name of the ship?" Virginia consulted her own pad. "The *Overlord*."

Marie Tillman gave her report next. She didn't have anything special to report, so she was done quickly. Will Dawson reported on today's maintenance activities. There was nothing that would alter operations there. Jeremy Cole gave his report on vessel maintenance being performed at the time. They were starting to develop a backlog of work. If things kept going the way they were, the next station expansion would have to be dedicated to maintenance.

Phil saved Luke's briefing for last. Luke took out his pad. "Okay, first up, Pretna authorities are sending some officers to take Pointer and Fel Nos back to Pretna for adjustments to their sentences."

Phil interrupted, "What does that mean?"

Luke continued, "Well, they beat up a pretar guard pretty bad during their escape. Escaping alone is bad enough, but that added a horrible new dimension to their prison term. It not only automatically doubles their sentences. They'll be put in the pretar version of maximum security. Before you ask, the cell is roughly six feet long, four feet wide, and four feet tall. They go in, and the door is sealed shut until their release date. I have to tell you, not many survive long in those conditions, and those that do are quite broken."

Marie Tillman shook her head. "That's barbaric!"

Luke replied, "No, ma'am. The way Pointer and Fel Nos violated the basic freedoms and rights of innocent people for their own gain was barbaric. They made people miserable and stripped them of their dignity due to no fault of their own. Then when they were given the opportunity to atone for their transgressions, they repaid the people trying to correct their behavior by nearly killing one of them. In my opinion, the Pretna government is absolutely correct. They've demonstrated that it's unlikely that they will be rehabilitated, so the only option is to put them away so they won't harm anyone else."

Marie couldn't argue with the logic presented. Like a lot of people, she felt that criminals should be able to be rehabilitated with proper counseling, but the truth was that attempts at rehabilitation for individuals like Pointer and Fel Nos, who have dismissed the possibility of earning an honest living, were rarely effective. The only real effective deterrent would be the threat of a horrible existence if they were caught. Luke saw the look on Marie Tillman's face and thought it would be wise to mend fences. "I'm sorry if I came across harsh, Doctor, but I'll reserve my sympathies for their victims."

Marie nodded and put up her hand to indicate understanding. Phil asked, "When will the Pretna representative be here?"

Luke checked his pad. "Arriving tomorrow on the *Atlantis Star*."

Luke found the next item on his pad. "Second, my evidence technician, Carl Stewart, has matched the DNA he found on the shackles recovered from the *Aurora*. A complete list has been compiled. We'll be sending it along to interested parties."

Phil added, "I have some additional data to add to that." Luke was puzzled. "What do ya have, Boss?"

Phil replied, "The flight history of the *Aurora* from the first flight to present." Luke smiled. "That may make things easier for our side."

Phil Looked around the room. "Does anyone have anything to add? Gus, how about you?"

Gus answered, "I think I'll track down Isnod and Feldon. They'll want to open an account at the bank. The Pretna government will want to have a place to transfer the bounty."

Phil stood. "Okay, let's do what we do best."

The briefing adjourned, and Phil retreated to his office. He reached into his pocket and pulled out a data chip. Putting the data chip into the SICOS terminal, he said, "SICOS, copy the data chip and store it in memory under the file name '*Aurora* voyage history.'"

The SICOS indicated the task was completed, and Phil ordered, "SICOS, send a copy to Station Security."

With that done, Phil contacted Luke to make sure he received the data. Luke acknowledged he got it and said he sent Phil the DNA files from the shackles. Phil opened the file, and the display filled with over a thousand names.

Looking at the names, he felt overwhelmed. There was something deep down that bothered him. Some of the mercenaries lost family to slavers. He wondered if the very vessel he used to transport them here was used to kidnap their loved ones. "SICOS, display only the humans."

The list shortened considerably. "SICOS, display only those abducted from New Iowa."

The display showed about a hundred names. He scrolled down the list until he found what he was looking for. He tapped the name he found on the screen, and a photo appeared along with the particulars of the disappearance. Rosanne Lisa Evans, age twenty-five, so on, and so on.

There was a knock at the door. Phil looked up to see Major Henson and First Sergeant Thack. "Come in, gentlemen. Have a seat."

Phil offered them coffee, and they declined. Then he filled them in on what he knew about the ship they were waiting for.

First Sergeant Thack lamented the fact that on a space station, his men wouldn't have the benefit of training while stuck there. Major Henson reminded him that there was training they could do that wouldn't draw attention. It wasn't all tactical training, but it's still extremely valuable. Things like first aid and map reading could be practiced. Phil offered them the use of the same banquet hall where the new arrival orientation was held in. Major Henson thought that would do just fine.

Henson glanced at the SICOS display. "Excuse me, but why is Corporal Evans's wife on your display?"

Phil explained about the DNA they found and compiled a list of the abductees that were transported by the ship they now call the *Aurora*. Corporal Evans's wife was certainly carried off by Pointer and Fel Nos. If anything, it gave the soldiers a fresh resolve.

As they stood to leave, Thack spotted the picture on Phil's wall with himself, Dave Jacobson, Luke Smith, Will Dawson, Selak, Tonkin, and Klon. He studied it for a second or two. "This looks recent."

Phil smiled. "That's right. That was taken a few weeks ago. There's quite a story behind it. I'll tell it to you some time."

Henson and Thack left to organize some training for their men. Phil was frustrated by the fact that he couldn't take a more active role in finding the folks that were abducted. He was comforted with the knowledge that there was an active effort to put an end to a despicable practice. Even though they had the destination, it was likely that it was only an auction site or relay station.

Phil pulled the data chip out of his pocket that he had removed from the shuttle Pointer stole from Triptous. He inserted it in the SICOS terminal and opened the file. Pointer was in possession of the shuttle for a very short time, so it shouldn't be a problem to nail down where the *Prospector* is. Studying the files, Phil found what he was looking for. It seemed too easy, but there it was. He only strayed into unexplored space once. That was about a year and a half ago.

The star system he stopped at appeared to be inside the nebula. Phil reasoned that he used the nebula to confuse and elude his pursuers.

Then hid in an asteroid belt until he was sure they had lost him. Now that Phil had a location, he needed to make sure that the *Aurora* had everything needed to retrieve the derelict ship. He also needed a carefully laid-out plan. Whatever he did, it would have to wait until the soldiers left and someone took Pointer and Fel Nos off the station.

*****

## Oasis 4, CentMod, Eva's Café

Noontime came without warning. Phil's gut started rumbling, so he shut down the SICOS in his office and headed to the platform lift. Arriving at the plaza level, he stepped off the lift and looked around. There was a good deal of activity today. He wandered over to Eva's and found Luke sitting at their usual table. Before sitting down, he passed Eva and quickly gave her his order.

He sat down and asked Luke, "Everything still on schedule for transferring Pointer and Fel Nos?"

Luke didn't even look up. "Did you see what Eva's calling this meal? The two bratwursts on a bun, fries, and baked beans meal? It's called the Klon."

Phil rolled his eyes. "Luke, prisoners."

Luke looked at Phil. "Oh yeah, things are on schedule. I had Marie Tillman send down a medic to look at them. There were a lot of bruises on them, and they seemed to be in a lot of pain. Isnod and Feldon must have really worked them over good because there weren't three square inches on either of them that wasn't bruised, but no serious damage."

Phil chuckled. "Those two are lucky to be alive. I think the only thing keeping the mercenaries from pushing them out of an air lock was that it would have been over too quickly."

Phil's lunch arrived; Phil opted for "The Selak." After Eva left, they continued the conversation. "Do you have any idea what those mercenaries were doing on Reynolds Planet?" he asked before biting into his burger.

Luke was actually pretty surprised Phil didn't know. "That's their home base. The residents of Reynolds Planet don't want to develop their own military, but it leaves them vulnerable. Having a mercenary force in-house solves a couple of problems. The mercenary force pays their own way, so it doesn't cost Reynolds Planet anything to have them there. In return, the mercenaries are obliged to protect them. Only a fool would screw with a planet protected by them."

Phil absorbed what he heard while he ate. He took a sip of strawberry pop. "How big is the force on Reynolds Planet?"

Luke swallowed a bite. "That's a fairly well-guarded secret. However, most estimates put them at thirty to forty thousand. That doesn't sound like a large number considering the number other militaries field, but you have to take into account the type of missions these guys go on. They rarely have need for a huge infrastructure organization. Logistics only need to hold out for the duration of the action. That's probably the greatest weakness of the mercenary unit. An opposing force could outlast them in a protracted engagement. That's why they plan their battles for brevity. Their engagements are usually short and extraordinarily violent."

Phil was way out of his element with this sort of thing, but he was catching on. He asked, "First Sergeant Thack mentioned a Colonel Devonport. Do you know anything about him?"

Luke replied, "Colonel Devonport is legendary. He's the guy who organized the Special Forces for the mercenary group on Reynolds Planet. His unit is under the larger mercenary organization. This Major Henson is the commander of the reconnaissance element. These guys who are our guests are the elite of the elite."

Phil dipped a fry in ketchup. "This might be a stupid question, but those guys that showed up a few days ago because Fel Nos wanted them to help break Pointer out of prison. How do they stack up?"

Luke laughed. "They're not even in the same league. They're not the least little bit concerned with who they work for or what they do. They're little more than pirates really. Our current guests are true professional soldiers, and they're very picky about who they work for and what they do."

*****

## Oasis 4, CargoMod 8, Ship Maintenance Shop

After Phil and Luke finished their lunches, they went their separate ways. Phil headed to the platform lift to go to the CentMod lower level. Reaching the lower level, he made his way to CargoMod 8 and the ship maintenance shop, where he found Jeremy Cole in his office putting the finishing touches on a maintenance logbook for a passenger shuttle they had performed a service inspection on.

Jeremy looked up. "What can I do for you, Boss?"

Phil replied, "If you have a few minutes, I'd like to go over a couple of things with you."

Jeremy leaned back. "Anytime. Have a seat."

Phil sat. "First, I'd like to report that the *Aurora* performed flawlessly. Incredible machine."

Chad Kowalski walked in, wiping landing gear grease from a wrench. "That Fel Nos guy has his flaws, but he knew how to trick out a spaceship."

Jeremy was about to chew out Chad for the interruption, but Phil waved him in. "Come on in, Chad. I think you might have some insight into this."

Chad took a seat, and Phil continued, "You just touched on what I wanted to ask. When you first inspected the *Aurora*, you said it was basically ready to retrieve the *Prospector*, but it just needed a couple of odds and ends. Exactly what are those odds and ends?"

Jeremy scratched his chin. "Well, the fittings were installed on the *Aurora* hull, but you need the tension struts to attach to them and then attach to the *Prospector* basically making them one ship. With that in mind, you need the fittings to attach to the *Prospector*. To do that, you'll need a welder. PEWS to do this work outside of the ship. Some special tools to adjust the tension struts. Finally, sensors to install on the *Prospector* to monitor it in flight. Easy peasy."

Phil thought about it. "What kind of crew do we need to do this?" Jeremy answered, "I'd say two qualified pilots and two mechanics."

Phil was surprised at the confidence Jeremy had in his answers. "You seem pretty sure of yourself. How is that?"

Jeremy chuckled. "When you've done this for a living long enough, you've pulled your fair share of mining ships off rocks."

Phil could scarcely believe that they could actually this close to pulling this off. "How long would it take you to get that stuff together?"

Jeremy stood up. "Follow me."

The three of them left Jeremy's office and went to a corner of the shop area.

There were pallets of equipment boxes. Jeremy pointed to each box in turn. "Tension struts, fittings, welder, towing sensors, PEWS, and tools."

Phil stared at the collection. "We're making a big assumption that corporate will sign off on this adventure."

Jeremy shrugged. "Even if the *Prospector* turns out to be a big nothing, the *Aurora* gives us a unique capability. Being able to retrieve broken down ships is a big deal."

Phil smiled. "I never considered that. When we're ready to go, who would you recommend go with me?"

Jeremy didn't hesitate. "Chad here has the most experience at this sort of thing. He also has a pilot certificate with a light-speed endorsement. The best welder we have is Helmut Schultz."

Phil was impressed with not only how fast his maintenance guys put all this together but how they worked out an explanation that corporate would be happy with. He rubbed his chin and said, "We're not going to do anything until our guests that are currently with us have left. But I would like to move as quickly as possible."

Both Jeremy and Chad said, "You got it, Boss."

*****

**Oasis 4, CentMod, Operations Center**

Phil left Jeremy and Chad and returned to his office, where he brought up the navigation data from the shuttle Pointer stole. His picture of the situation was still pretty weak, and after staring at it for a time, he finally pressed an intercom button. "Gus, you in there?"

"Sure am" came the reply.

"Come into my office. I want to bounce a couple of things off ya," Phil said. "Be right with ya," Gus replied.

Gus walked in and filled the mug he brought with him. "What's up?" Phil transferred the navigation data from the SICOS display on his desk to a large display on the wall of his office. "This is the only time Pointer left explored space. As a result, we don't have any idea what's in this star system."

Gus used the SICOS control to highlight the star in question. "Well, that's interesting. This star is named. It's called Anna Mae."

Phil furrowed his brow. "How can that be? I thought that was unexplored territory."

Gus laughed. "No one went there. At least until the *Prospector* went there, but you can certainly see it. Even from Earth with a good telescope. There was a bit of a fad in the early twenty-first century where you could name a star for a small fee. Apparently, someone thought enough of a girl named Anna Mae to register a star in her name."

Phil laughed. "Well, that's interesting."

Gus studied the display and sighed. "I see your dilemma. There's limited information here. The asteroid belt appears to be orbiting that star at a distance somewhere around the distance Mars is from our sun. That would mean the *Prospector* is somewhere in a circular line of rocks several billion miles in circumference and probably about a hundred million to three hundred million miles wide. Did I put too fine a point on it?"

Phil slowly nodded. "No. I think you've got a handle on the difficulties we're facing."

Gus brought up a three-dimensional image of the area surrounding the star system and had Pointer's track highlighted. He zoomed in and was immediately disappointed. "That shuttle's recording system wasn't designed to record data of new systems. However, it did record its position in relation to known checkpoints." Gus zoomed in tighter on Pointer's track.

After staring at it for what seemed a ridiculously long time, Gus nodded. "Well, it's definitely an asteroid belt and not a planet or moon."

Phil was flabbergasted. "Okay, impress me. How could you possibly know that?"

Gus smiled. "Check Pointer's track. You can see where he entered the belt. His velocity slows dramatically, and he does a lot of maneuvering. Then suddenly, he stopped. Two days later, he does a lot of maneuvering again. Then he hightails it for known space."

Phil said, "Okay, I get it. The erratic maneuvering probably means he's dodging rocks. What else?"

Gus continued, "Look at the period where he was motionless for two days. He wasn't actually motionless. For two days, his shuttle was orbiting Anna Mae. If he landed on a planet orbiting Anna Mae, you would see his track as a spiral as the planet spins on its axis. I suppose he could land on a planet that had the same rate of rotation as its orbit. That would keep one face of the planet toward the sun constantly. Mercury is almost like that. I don't think that's the case, though. Not with all that erratic maneuvering. Landing on a moon would give you an even crazier course track."

Phil said, "All that doesn't tell us how to find the Prospector when we get there."

Gus zoomed in tighter on Pointer's track. They were now looking at the period where Pointer waited to see if he had eluded his pursuers. In a two-day period, he actually moved several thousand miles. A closer examination revealed that the course was curved exactly to match the orbit of Anna Mae. They used the distance traveled in that period along with the distance from Anna Mae to calculate where the *Prospector* should be. Gus shook his head. "That's the best we can do for now with the information we have, but it's a place to start."

Phil considered the task ahead and realized that follow-up expeditions would need better navigation data than what they were currently using. "Do you think the *Aurora's* nav data system is enough to record what we need to?"

Gus was deflated immediately. "The Astrodyne has a standard nav data system. It wasn't designed to record large amounts of new data."

Phil made a note to ask Jeremy if the *Aurora's* system could be upgraded or replaced.

Gus thought a second. "You know, it may be possible to add a stand-alone system instead of screwing around with changing the existing system."

Phil agreed that was a good idea. After a while, they realized that it was close to quitting time. As if on cue, Alice paged Phil. "Honey bunny, I don't feel like cooking tonight."

Gus grinned at "honey bunny," then he said, "Why don't I see what Brenda is doing, and we could get something together? Maybe drinks at Sparky's afterward."

Alice gushed. "Ooh, that sounds fun! I'll meet you in the CentMod sitting area near the platform lift."

Phil looked at Gus. "I guess I told her."

Gus turned to leave. "I'm going to find Brenda."

*****

## Oasis 4, CentMod

The two pairs decided on Mexican cuisine, so they went to Baja Juan's. Their meals were the usual excellent fare found at Juan's. While they ate, they discussed the events of the last couple of days. Phil noticed Brenda was wearing a new bracelet with finelds in the settings. The conversation steered to the *Prospector* and the possibility of retrieving it.

Alice normally didn't concern herself with cargos and their values. She simply wasn't interested in that sort of thing. "What's so special about this particular ship?"

Phil dipped a chip in salsa. "It's not so much the ship as the cargo. Apparently, it's sitting on an asteroid that's chock full of paxtite ore."

It was Brenda's turn. "I've never heard of paxtite. What is it, and why are people willing to risk so much to get it?"

Gus answered, "It's a metal that has very useful properties. In short, it's nearly as strong as steel but close to the same weight as aluminum." Brenda nodded in understanding. "So you could replace a steel structural member with a paxtite part of the same dimensions, and the only thing that changes is the mass of the part?"

Phil smiled. "I think you have a major understanding of it. But the really neat thing about it is the corrosion resistance of it when it's manufactured correctly. Up to this point, there's only been very limited quantities of it available, which gives me pause because we're proceeding on the word of Marcus Pointer, a known felon and person of low character."

After leaving a tip for the service and settling the bill, the foursome decided that an ice cream dessert was in order. Phil and Alice got cones while Gus and Brenda enjoyed sundaes. Alice spotted Brenda's bracelet and admired it. She then showed off the necklace that Phil gave her. Their conversation about the various gift shops that seemed to be at every space terminal was giving Alice an inkling of an idea. She'll keep it to herself. For the time being, it'll be better to flesh out her idea before springing it on Phil. Besides, he has enough to worry about at the moment. Phil stared at Alice. He recognized the look on Alice's face and wondered what was in store for him in the future.

After finishing their ice creams, it was off to Sparky's for a drink. When they walked in, Phil noticed it was more crowded than usual. Then he thought about it. Since he had only been there once, he really didn't know what a usual crowd consisted of. A more careful survey and he saw that many of the faces were Major Henson's men. They found a table for four and sat. One of Sparky's waitresses took their drink order. Phil then said to her that Stellar logistics and Freight Corporation was buying a round for Major Henson's men. She entered the order on a pad and went to retrieve the drinks for Phil's table.

When Sparky's wait staff delivered the drinks that Phil bought for the mercenaries, they were confused until it was explained to them that it was Phil's treat, then there were smiles. First Sergeant Thack stood and raised a mug of dark lager and announced, "Huzzah, Mr. Ross!"

The rest echoed, "Huzzah!"

Phil looked closer at Thack's table and saw that he was sitting with Eva's husband, Burt. The two were talking and laughing in a very animated fashion.

Gus was looking at Burt like he had just spotted something about him that had until now escaped his notice. "How much do we really know about Burt?"

"Quite a lot, really." Gus spun his head and saw Luke standing there with a mug of beer. He motioned for Luke to grab a chair and sit with them.

Luke sat and sipped his beer. "Did you happen to see the tattoo on Burt's arm? He was in Special Forces, Delta Force."

Phil looked over to Burt and Thack. "Kindred spirits, I suppose."

Phil spotted Isnod and Feldon at a table, talking to Major Henson's lieutenants. Phil had to hold back a chuckle when he saw Feldon was wearing a Detroit Red Wings jersey. "How have those two been behaving?"

Luke shrugged. "Pretty well, actually. After Gus helped them open accounts at the bank, I assisted them in registering as bounty hunters."

Phil finished his drink. "You know, I have a feeling that those two are going to be really busy in the future. I think breaking up the slave trade is going to expose a lot of really bad people."

*****

## Oasis 4, CargoMod 8, Ship Maintenance Shop

The next day, Phil went to the maintenance hangar bay, where he found Jeremy calibrating engine instruments on a malnun freight shuttle. Phil's timing was pretty good because as he strolled up, Jeremy shut down the calibration equipment and said, "That finishes that."

Phil jokingly said, "Well, that's a relief."

Jeremy turned around. "What can I do for you, Boss?"

"Well, it occurred to us that we'll need to chart the star system that we're headed to," Phil answered.

Jeremy frowned. "The Astrodyne's systems aren't nearly enough to do all that."

Phil nodded. "I had a feeling you'd say something like that."

Jeremy thought a minute while he put his tools away. "You know there's a mining company exploratory vessel docked at docking port 23. They carry just the equipment you need. The nice thing is they have repairs that need to be made and a very tight budget."

Phil frowned. "I don't think that a captain of an exploratory vessel is going to give up its charting systems. It would render them useless."

Jeremy smiled. "The repairs they need are going to take at least a week. We could negotiate to borrow the equipment."

Phil smiled. "That's not a bad idea. I think I'll go over and visit with their captain. Do you recall what his name is?"

Jeremy checked a pad. "Captain Hastings."

Phil went off in search of Captain Hastings of the *Goldfield*. Half an hour later, Phil looked up Jeremy again. Jeremy was surprised that the negotiations were over so quickly.

The exploratory vessel captain was eager to make a deal. It not only helped solve his problem, Phil also promised that his company would get first consideration when there were contracts to be had for the mining rights of the asteroid belt. Not only was the mining company going to loan equipment but a technician to operate it. Phil told Jeremy to get ahold of *Goldfield's* cartographer and get a schedule for transferring the equipment. With that done, he decided that he really should check in with the office to take care of station business.

*****

## Oasis 4, CentMod, Operations Center

There wasn't a lot to be done that afternoon. Phil smiled when he realized that he didn't have to deal with much of the petty little day-to-day tasks anymore. He had an assistant for that now. He decided to tour the operations center. His first stop, as always, was a check of the boards. When he saw who was arriving at 1600 Zulu, he smiled. The Atlantis Star, with his good friend Dave Jacobson, was arriving from Pretna. A check of the chronometer revealed that the *Atlantis Star* should be visible by now.

He climbed the stairs to the control center and picked up a pair of binoculars. He searched in the direction the plot indicated that the *Atlantis Star* was approaching. The ship was closer than Phil expected it to be. The *Atlantis Star* was already firing its braking thrusters in preparation for accepting vectors for their approach to the station. In less than an hour, the *Atlantis Star* was sliding into the docking clamps. Phil decided to meet Dave Jacobson.

*****

## Oasis 4, CargoMod 7

When Phil reached the *Atlantis Star* at CargoMod 7, Luke Smith was already waiting, the umbilicals were already connected, and crews were removing containers from the hull and putting them in the CargoMod. The station crew checked the air lock seals and opened the hatch. At nearly the same moment, a crewman on board the ship did the same.

Phil's mood went from good to great when he saw who was ready to enter the station. "Mr. Klon!"

Klon beamed back. "Mr. Ross! Mr. Smith! It's so good to see you!" Klon shook Phil and Luke's hands warmly.

Klon had two uniformed pretar security officers with him. "Please allow me to introduce Biknid and Osich. They will be restraining Marcus Pointer and Fel Nos on our return voyage to Pretna."

Phil smiled. "I can't wait to be relieved of those two."

Klon looked apologetic. "Rest assured, Mr. Ross, they will not have the opportunity to do any more mischief."

Phil said, "Of that, I have no doubts."

Then Phil had a thought. He took a couple of steps to a SICOS terminal and paged Alice, "I hope you didn't start dinner. There's someone I'd like you to meet."

Alice replied, "When and where?" "Eva's, about a half hour," Phil answered.

Then he paged Gus, "If you don't have dinner plans, there's a get-together at Eva's."

Gus came back, "Can I bring Brenda?"

Phil said, "Absolutely, in about twenty minutes."

In a short time, everyone met at Eva's, where Eva spotted Klon and gave him a big hug. Even Burt came out of the kitchen to greet Klon. Phil made the introductions for Alice and Brenda. Naturally, Klon ordered the bratwurst, fries, baked beans, and Root beer. The two pretar security officers weren't sure about human food. Klon reassured them and steered them toward menu items that he was sure they would enjoy. Biknid ordered the Selak, and Osich ordered the country-fried steak meal. The conversation was so pleasant that no one brought up anything even remotely to do with business.

*****

## Oasis 4, CentMod, Security Office

The next day, after the morning briefing, Phil met Luke, Klon, Isnod, Feldon, and the two pretar security officers in the security office. Luke led them to the holding cells where Pointer and Fel Nos were waiting.

Klon stood there and stared, "Well, Fel Nos certainly hasn't improved with age. In fact, he looks a bit 'shop worn' to me. This is obviously Marcus Pointer. Please look at me, gentlemen."

Pointer and Fel Nos looked up and stared at Klon through swollen sleep- deprived eyes. Klon continued, "You will be turned over to me as soon as I can arrange passage on a vessel returning to Pretna. I have to inform you that your actions have been added to your sentences. A magistrate will make that official."

Klon then turned to Isnod and Feldon. "Gentlemen, we have business at the bank. Please let's conclude your part in this. By the way, we are very grateful to you for bringing these two to justice."

Klon led Isnod and Feldon to the bank, where he saw the transfer of funds into their accounts. Outside the bank, the two flastons heartily shook hands with Klon. They were, in turn, relieved to be done with the business, and it was hugely satisfying to be paid such a handsome amount.

*****

## Oasis 4, CentMod, Eva's Café

Lunchtime came, and Phil found himself at his customary table at Eva's. Will Dawson was eating with him. They were discussing the difficulty of unloading ore from a derelict ship. Phil asked, "If we can't power the ship, how will that affect the unloading process?"

Will held up his sandwich with a bite taken out of it. "Did you see what Eva's calling this meal? The barbecue pulled pork and slaw sandwich with fries? It's called the Tonkin."

Phil rolled his eyes. "Will, unloading without power."

Will looked up. "Oh, that's not a problem on the station side. If there's equipment on the ship that needs power, it could be patched into station power. That's more of a question for Jeremy."

*****

## Oasis 4, CargoMod 8, Ship Maintenance Shop

After lunch, Phil checked on the progress of the charting equipment being installed on the *Aurora*. Jeremy had moved the *Aurora* back into the maintenance hangar bay in CargoMod 8. Chad Kowalski was busy installing a high-resolution sensor array on the hull. He was lying on his back, helping to tighten the fasteners, and there was a technician with him that Phil didn't recognize.

When Chad spotted Phil, he made the introduction. "Boss, this is Beverly Ashton. She's the chief cartographer on the *Goldfield*."

Phil shook hands with Beverly. She gave Phil the general rundown of her résumé. Phil thought she was immensely qualified to accompany them on this trip. When the sensor array was bolted in place to Chad's satisfaction, she gave Phil the tour of the equipment she was going to employ. Things were starting to come together, and Phil was getting excited about it. He then told Beverly and Chad that they were going to leave the day after tomorrow. They both nodded and said they would be ready.

The following morning, the *Overlord* docked, and Phil had made sure that it was done with as little fanfare as possible. He was pretty sure Major Henson didn't want to call any more attention to them as necessary. Phil was in his office when he received a page from Luke asking him to see him in the security office.

*****

## Oasis 4, CentMod, Security Office

Phil went into Luke's office and was greeted with the sight of Luke, Major Henson, and a snoshin that looked familiar. Then it struck him who the snoshin was. "Thatt Voffyes!"

Voffyes couldn't suppress a grin. "It's good to be back, Mr. Ross. Mr. Smith tells me that my association with Marcus Pointer and company has put me on your short list of undesirable visitors to your station."

Phil nodded. "Uh-huh, and you're supposed to be locked up in Kempeck Colony."

Voffyes smiled and nodded. "It was a necessary deception. Certain parties couldn't be made aware that I'm actually an operative with Griska intelligence. Putting the word out that I've been arrested was a necessary fiction. I've been working undercover in an effort to gain intelligence about the slave trade."

Phil was trying to catch up. "I hope our actions here on the station haven't ruined things."

Voffyes shook his head. "No, just the opposite. Having Pointer, Fel Nos, and the others running loose could have had an adverse effect. As you humans say, they could give gummed up the works."

Klon entered the office, and Voffyes turned to him. "Ah, Mr. Klon. I have something for you."

He handed a data chip to Klon. "You'll find on that all the evidence you need to make additional charges against Pointer and Fel Nos."

Klon looked confused. "Exactly what else have these two done." Voffyes gave Klon the condensed version of Pointer's and Fel Nos's actions.

Klon was speechless for a moment, then, finally, the words came to him. "I hope you make this information available to all the governments, where these two have operated. I doubt if they'll ever leave confinement on Pretna. But there's always the unexpected." He then thanked Voffyes for the information and took his leave.

Phil turned to Voffyes. "Exactly what are you doing here, Mr. Voffyes?" Voffyes took a breath. "I'm here to brief Major Henson here on his mission.

That's going to be done on the *Overlord* after we're underway. I'm meeting with you and Mr. Smith as a courtesy. You've done a tremendous job supporting our efforts to this point, and I wanted to pass on my government's gratitude as well as my personal gratitude."

Major Henson added, "My men and I will be leaving at 0400 Zulu. It seems prudent to leave at that hour so as not to draw attention to ourselves."

Henson then stood and shook hands with Phil. "You have my personal thanks, Mr. Ross."

Phil made sure that the equipment Major Henson's men brought with them was transferred to the *Overlord*. After lunch, Phil had half a dozen administrative tasks to attend to before he could knock off for the day. It was too early to head back to his quarters, but there was nothing that needed his attention, so he thought he would tour the CentMod. There were establishments that he frequented of course, but there were plenty that he seldom even glanced at. On one of the upper tiers, he spotted Klon and his subordinates going into Sliders Pool Hall. Phil shrugged. "I've got a few minutes."

*****

## Oasis 4, CentMod, Tier 2

He strolled over to the pool hall and went in. Phil hadn't realized it before, but he could see that this establishment was popular. A quick scan of the hall and he spotted Klon and his subordinates at two tables in the corner. There was also a human with them that he recognized from somewhere, then it hit him where he knew him from. He walked back to them as Klon was explaining to Biknid and Osich how to play Eight Ball.

When Phil reached them, Klon turned to him and smiled. "Mr. Ross!" Phil smiled back. "Mr. Klon, Mr. Biknid, Mr. Osich, Nigel." Biknid and Osich nodded politely, and Nigel grinned. "Evening, Governor." Klon selected a cue from the rack on the wall and started chalking the tip.

"You'll be pleased to learn, Mr. Ross, that I've secured passage for our return voyage to Pretna on the *Lancaster* tomorrow afternoon."

Phil nodded. "That's good news indeed."

He looked over to Nigel, explaining the finer points of Eight Ball to Biknid and Osich. Both pretars were trying to adjust their auto translators, which made Phil suppress a chuckle.

Klon had his own grin. "It took me a while, but I'm getting better at human slang. It can be most baffling since the slang changes from region to region on Earth, even when the language is the same. I have to admit, though, that watching Biknid and Osich try to figure it out can be entertaining."

Phil said, "Enjoy your game, gentlemen. I'll make sure to be there to see you off tomorrow."

The following day was divided between station business and getting ready for the expedition to recover the *Prospector*. Gus made sure the Galley was stocked. Chad and Helmut loaded the equipment on the *Aurora*. They also checked each PEWS for proper operation. Phil double-checked the route he was going to take to Anna Mae. The route went directly into the nebula. Phil saw that Pointer didn't take a straight line into the nebula. He penetrated it to approximately the halfway point and then changed directions. He shrugged and thought that the reason for doing that would probably become apparent.

*****

## Oasis 4, CargoMod 6

At 1630 Zulu, he went to CargoMod 6 and waited with Klon and his subordinates until Luke and some of his deputies brought Pointer and Fel Nos. The deputies removed the restraints, and Klon's subordinates replaced them with their own. The restraints the pretars used didn't look much different from the ones Luke's guys were using, save a small module on the waist belt.

Klon fingered a button on a controller on his wrist. Pointer and Fel Nos instantly fell to their knees. They were still convulsing long after Klon released the button. Klon stared down at the pair. "I trust, gentlemen, that it won't be necessary to do that again."

Pointer and Fel Nos rose to their feet and allowed the pretar security officers to lead them away.

Phil and Klon said their farewells and parted ways. That evening, Phil spent a quiet night with Alice. She didn't say it, but she was uneasy about Phil assuming the role of explorer. He managed to reassure her by saying that if Pointer could do it, he shouldn't have a problem; besides, Gus was going to be there. Phil didn't know how to feel about her being more comfortable with Gus along.

In the morning, the routine went as usual with exercise, breakfast, and the briefing. Phil, Gus, Chad, Helmut, and Beverly Ashton met at Docking Port 1 CargoMod 2. Phil looked at the group. "Well, let's not stand on ceremony. Let's get rolling."

*****

## The *Aurora,* Astrodyne 65, Owned and Operated by the Stellar Logistics and Freight Corporation

An hour later, Gus powered the Astrodyne's light-speed engines. They were following the track that Pointer followed while trying to elude his pursuers. They settled into a cruise speed of LS 9.

Chad and Helmut were gushing over the overpowered Astrodyne while Beverly powered her equipment and checked the performance. She explained that she couldn't do a full test at light speed although they could do some very accurate charting even at this speed. The vastness of space is on full display in these conditions. They were heading directly toward the most overwhelming feature in this part of space at multiples of the speed of light. Even then, it didn't appear they were getting any closer. It wasn't until the afternoon of the third day they had reached the edges of the nebula.

This particular nebula was extremely dense. It was impossible to discern any features beyond it. As they flew on, they discovered that this nebula was unusual in that it wasn't one big, dense cloud. The best way to describe it would be pockets or clumps of gasses. They were traveling in the clear areas between the clumps. This particular passage was nearly impossible to spot. It was definitely the wildest stroke of luck that not only the *Prospector* found it, but Pointer stumbled on it in a desperate bid to elude his pursuers. Beverly was careful to record their progress as they traveled.

Chad asked, "Why is it no one has traveled through this before?"

Gus replied, "No profit. There's enough on the outside of the nebula to keep us busy for many years to come. There's really no point in traveling through this nebula with no knowledge of what hazards might be there for a 'Pig in a Poke.' As I said earlier, there's enough to deal with in space that's charted to last many lifetimes. The captain of the *Prospector* must have had a nose for finding ore, or he felt particularly adventurous."

Phil checked the navigation display. "We're getting close to the point where we need to make that turn."

Gus nodded in agreement. "It looks like a box canyon in front of us. I don't relish the idea of penetrating those clouds with no clue of what's in there."

The navigation computer started a countdown. At zero, Gus cut the light- speed engines. The navigation computer prompted a pitch up of twenty-five degrees and a turn to the right forty-seven degrees. When the maneuver was completed, Gus and Phil stared out the front viewport.

Gus finally broke the silence. "Are you seeing this?"

Phil slowly nodded. "I think I understand what Pointer did. He was desperate to elude whoever was after him, so he thought he would hide in a nebula. He found out this thing was more porous than it looked and flew into it until he couldn't maintain a straight course. Right here, he turned."

Gus engaged the light-speed engines and pushed it up to LS 9, then he said, "Makes sense. He would have slowed down when it became apparent that the course he was on was a dead end. He would have started looking for another route. At lower speeds, he could have spotted the route we're on."

From the point where they turned, they could see an open area inside the nebula. It was like looking down a very long tunnel, but it was definitely an open area they were looking at. Beverly was checking her own equipment. "Even if this turns out to be a fool's errand, we've been getting great data. We've been in the nebula a full day, and it looks like we'll be clear in about eight hours."

Phil checked the navigation computer. "According to this, Anna Mae is about an hour past that."

They decided that it would be best if they were all reasonably well-rested when they arrived. To that end, they divided the remaining time at the controls among themselves, including Chad. In fact, Chad talked them into letting him take the lion's share. His special skills wouldn't be needed right away when they arrived.

Chad was at the controls when they broke out of the nebula. He thought of it as a nonevent. "Broke out" was overstating it. The passage they were traveling through gradually widened until they were clear. Beverly had him take a position above the pole of Anna Mae at a distance of three hundred million miles. Gus and Phil relieved Chad at the controls. Chad and Helmut went to the cargo hold, where they put on their PEWS.

Among the equipment Beverly brought, there were three canisters that held sensors that would deploy and were programmable to fly in a pattern and send data back to a receiver on the *Aurora*. They placed a canister in the starboard side cargo hold air lock. They closed the air lock and depressurized it. Once it was ready, they opened the outer hatch and pushed it into space. They closed the outer hatch and repressurized the air lock.

When they were back inside, they secured themselves, and Gus repositioned the *Aurora* off the opposite pole of Anna Mae and the process of putting a sensor pack in space was repeated. Beverly activated the sequence that launched one hundred sensor probes from each container. The skin from the cylindrical containers was jettisoned, and one by one, a series of one-and-a-half-foot-long probes would drop out of each one.

Once clear of the container, the probes would power its engine and streak off on their preprogrammed courses. The probes would travel away from the containers on headings that were 3.6 degrees from each other. A plot of the probes would look like the spokes of two wheels parallel to the system's plane of rotation. When the probes reach a distance of three billion miles, they're programmed to make a left turn. When they reach a point where they're halfway to the adjacent probe, they make another turn and return to the point of release. This is to make up for the fact that the distances between the probes at the end of their journey are too great for usable resolution.

Chad and Helmut put the third and final container in space. Beverly started receiving data, and she began her analysis. "Well, let's see. Anna Mae is a 'main sequence star,' but we knew that. The first planet is located at 62 million miles from Anna Mae. The second planet is at 150 million miles. Ah! Here we go. At 250 million miles, there's the asteroid belt. It's a whopper! Densely packed, it goes out to 370 million miles. It's approximately 30 million miles deep."

She programmed the final volley of probes to make their way to the asteroid belt at 3.6-degree intervals and then circle the belt in a spiral pattern. The probe speed will be greatly reduced to get optimum performance of the sensors. Once the programming was complete, the probes were launched.

By this time, Chad and Helmut were out of their PEWS and made their way to the cockpit. Chad looked over Beverly's shoulder. "I hope your ship is better equipped to launch those things than ours is."

Beverly chuckled. "Yeah, we have those containers loaded in launchers. I'll say this, though. It would have taken weeks to get here on the *Goldfield*."

Helmut was intrigued with the whole process. "What happens to the containers and probes? It seems to me they would pose a navigation hazard."

Beverly nodded. "A small hazard, but a hazard nonetheless. The containers will align with Anna Mae and fire a thruster. It'll take a while, but eventually, they'll be consumed. The probes will do the same at the end of their mission."

It took until the afternoon of the next day for the probes circling the asteroid belt to complete their mission. Beverly compiled the data and started to analyze it. "Well, let's see. The composition distribution is a bit abnormal. The C-type, or carbonaceous type, only makes up 63 percent of the total mass of the belt. S- type, or silicate type, makes up about 15 percent. That leaves a whopping 22 percent M-type, or metal-rich. There are six dwarf planets ranging in size from 450 nautical miles in diameter to eleven hundred. There is a high number of objects above one nautical mile in size but don't have sufficient mass to create gravity."

Phil studied the display. "I'd be willing to bet that the Prospector is sitting on one of the dwarf planets."

Gus turned his head and stared at Phil. "I thought we weren't supposed to use the term Dwarf Planet. We're supposed to use the term Planetoid."

Phil took on an annoyed expression. "It's spherical, has gravity, orbits a star. How is that not a planet? It's a fine example of eggheads arguing over nothing."

Beverly laughed. She agreed with Phil, though, but she was curious. "Why do you think the *Prospector* is on one of the dwarfs?"

Phil took a few seconds to articulate his thoughts. "Gravity. A ship sitting on an asteroid or any body without gravity would have floated off by now."

Beverly looked at her display and said, "I hate to disagree with you, Phil. The metals on the dwarfs aren't in high enough concentrations to make landing on one worthwhile."

Phil was annoyed again. "Then where would you recommend that we look?"

Beverly studied the display, and finally, she started to slowly nod. She assigned the M-type asteroids a red color, and she started to nod faster. "The highest concentration of metal-rich asteroids is here."

Phil looked at the display. "There's a bunch of them big enough to land on too. But what keeps a ship in place with no gravity?"

Helmut offered an explanation, "Das landing gear on mining vessels will have drills that bore into the rock and insert wedges that hold the ship in place."

Phil was learning more than he bargained for on this trip. He gave Gus the coordinates to the concentration of M-type asteroids.

The *Aurora* approached the first of the asteroids on their course. Beverly examined her display. "This one is roughly fifty by thirty by forty nautical miles, high in metals. Oh, hey! Confirmed high concentrations of paxtite ore."

Phil relaxed. "Well, that's a load off my mind. Up to this point, the paxtite was just a rumor started by a couple of criminals."

Beverly was smiling. "It looks like both of our companies can forget getting out the reprimand paperwork. I'm not picking up any readings that would indicate a ship."

Gus set a course for the next asteroid. The next three asteroids had similar results although they varied in size. The next body was a dwarf planet.

Phil thought about it, then he said, "I wouldn't feel right if we didn't check this out."

Gus grinned. "I hear ya." Then he put the *Aurora* in a slow orbit.

As Beverly examined her instruments, Phil mused, "Hey, we get to name this thing, don't we?"

Beverly, without looking away from her instruments, said, "That's the tradition."

Phil looked at the cratered surface. "I can't think of a more appropriate name for this one than Prospector. We'll argue about the others on the trip home."

Beverly shook her head after the orbit was complete. "I'm not detecting any signs of a ship. There's not enough metal to make a landing here worthwhile either."

Gus broke orbit and visited the next five asteroids, which were all very similar to the first four. They were occasionally detecting asteroids that ranged in size from pea-sized and larger. Some were actually moving at a pretty fast pace. The ones they couldn't see they could easily be handled by the navigation shield. Beverly remarked that there were a lot of bodies in this system that are traveling in a manner contrary to a harmonious system.

They were approaching the sixth asteroid past the dwarf planet they named Prospector when Chad, who was monitoring the communications system, said, "Whoa! I've got an emergency signal on the comm. It's an analog signal on the VHF band, very faint."

Gus said, "I was wondering why you were fiddling around with the comm." Phil smiled. "That's how Pointer found the *Prospector*."

Beverly frowned. "It still seems very lucky to me. We're nearly on top of the asteroid, and we're just barely getting a signal."

Phil said, "Pointer was in a Pulsar. The comm system in Pulsars has incredible receivers. He probably picked up the signal as soon as he entered the system."

The asteroid came into sharper view. Gus slowed the *Aurora* until they were relatively motionless to the asteroid. Beverly gave him vectors, and suddenly, there it was. The *Prospector* was there, sitting on the surface. Chad had Gus hover over the *Prospector*, and he studied it carefully with the aid of the image processors that were normally used to aide in docking. Finally, he showed Gus where to touch down on the *Prospector*.

Gus lowered the landing gear and bumped the thrusters to ease the *Aurora* into place. A slight scraping could be heard as the *Aurora's* gear rested on the *Prospector's* roof. Gus was getting a lesson in the importance of gravity as an aid in landing a spaceship.

The landing gear struts would slightly compress. When Gus killed the thrusters, the Aurora would rebound, forcing Gus to bump the thrusters again. Chad chuckled. "Set the thrusters to station, keeping Gus. They'll give just enough downward push to keep us in place. Come on, Helmut. Let's get us strapped together before Gus pushes the whole asteroid back to the station."

After Chad and Helmut left the cockpit, Phil looked at Gus and jokingly asked, "Could we do that?"

Chad and Helmut put what they needed in the cargo hold air lock, then Chad depressurized the air lock and opened the outer hatch. After lowering the loading ramp, they examined the *Prospector*, and Chad declared it fit to move. His headset started crackling, and he heard Phil ask, "Hey, Chad, what's the placement like?"

Chad looked around. "Tell Gus he did a pretty decent job centering the ship, and it looks like fore and aft placement is good. Keep the thrusters at station keeping until we can get this tied down."

Chad used the fittings on the *Aurora* as a reference to make markings on the *Prospector* where he wanted Helmut to weld reinforcement plates. The plates had fittings in the center of each of them. When

Helmut finished a plate, Chad would get a tie strut from the air lock and attach it to the fittings.

Once all the struts were attached to the *Prospector*, Chad had Gus relieve the pressure from the landing gear struts, lowering the *Aurora*. Once Chad had all the struts attached to the *Aurora* as well, he had Gus kill the thrusters so that he could fine-tune the positioning of the *Aurora* on the *Prospector*. Then he tensioned the tie struts, essentially making both ships one solid unit, removing the pressure from the landing gear shock struts aided in this process. If the landing gear shock struts were left pressurized, the tension on the tie struts could be variable under certain conditions.

Depressurizing them essentially made them a solid unit. Using a tool to measure the tension on the tie struts, he made sure they were all the same. Helmut used a hand scanner to check the welds. Any weak welds would show up on the screen in a red hue. At a flip of a switch, he could examine the internal strains on the metal hull. The plates Helmet welded in place were round so that there were no points for stresses to concentrate.

Chad helped Helmut put the welder back in the air lock, and because they finished their tasks for the day, they closed the air lock and pressurized it. Phil met them in the cargo hold where they were getting out of their PEWS. Chad looked exhausted, and Helmut didn't look much better.

Phil said, "Let's get some dinner in you guys and a night's sleep. Did you happen to see anything out there that would provide an explanation of what happened here?"

Chad shook his head. "Not a thing, Boss. We'll hopefully have a better idea when we get inside."

Phil wasn't an expert on ship recovery by any stretch, so he asked, "What exactly do we need to do inside the *Prospector?*"

Chad hung his PEWS on a rack and then pointed to an equipment container. "That has sensors that get attached to different parts of the Prospector to monitor it in flight. We need to attach them and run the wire harness to the Aurora. Then we need to jettison the *Prospector* reactor core for safety. Then finally break the grip the *Prospector* has on this rock."

In the morning, Phil and Gus suited up in PEWS along with Chad and Helmut. The equipment was loaded into the air lock, and after closing the inner hatch and depressurizing, they stepped out. Phil had to remember to turn on the microgravity units in his boots. The asteroid they were on wasn't nearly large enough to have enough gravity to keep them from floating off. Chad started work by drilling a hole into the Prospectors hull near the electrical connector he installed back at Oasis 4. When that was done, he inserted a red bar with a cross piece welded on end. While he did that, Helmut led Phil and Gus to a maintenance access hatch on the *Prospector*.

While Helmut worked to open the hatch, Phil took the opportunity to look over the side of the *Prospector*. There was mining equipment scattered around. Phil pondered why there weren't piles of spoil lying around. Then he realized that after separating the ore from the rock, they would jettison the spoil away from the asteroid.

Examining the mining equipment, he could see where the raw material was loaded into the separator, and there was a tube that led to the *Prospector* cargo hold and another outlet that sent the unusable material into space. There was rock-boring equipment near the ship. As the name implies, these machines were designed to bore into the asteroid and send the extracted material to the separator via a tube.

Chad walked up while Phil was studying the mining operation. "We'll have to load that stuff up before we leave."

Phil turned to him with a flustered expression. "Why do we need to make work for ourselves?"

Chad shrugged his shoulders in his PEWS. "Treaties and agreements stipulate that there won't be a bunch of junk lying around after salvage operations."

Phil pointed to the drive section. "What about the reactor core you plan on jettisoning?"

Chad chuckled. "Yeah, you can send a nuclear pile into space, but you can't leave a drill on the surface of a rock in that space." Chad paused for effect. "Actually, boss, we'll use a thruster pack to direct it to collide with Anna Mae."

Phil pondered what Chad said and had a chuckle of his own. "Collide would be overstating it. I'm pretty sure the reactor will be long gone before it reaches the sun's surface."

Gus looked over to Phil and Chad. "Hey, guys, we're in." They walked over to the hatch where Helmut was peering into the ship's interior using the flashlight built into the arm of the PEWS.

Helmut switched on the light built into his helmet. "There's no point in standing on ceremony." Then he descended into the ship with Gus following him.

Chad lowered equipment boxes through the hatch. Phil could never get over the fact of how much a lack of gravity can be a useful thing. Chad stepped on the top rung of the ladder in the hatch. "Coming down!"

Phil followed him and was again surprised by an unexpected effect of the artificial gravity created by his boots. They didn't work so well on the narrow ladder rung, so he stepped off with both feet and floated there. Then he used his hands on the rungs to lower himself to the ship's interior.

Chad picked up an equipment box. "Boss, you'll work with me forward, and Gus, you can give Helmut a hand."

Below the hatch, they went through there was the companionway between there cargo hold and the engineering spaces. Helmut led Gus to the engine room to start the process of disconnecting the reactor core. Chad started walking forward stopping occasionally to get his bearings. The deck they were on was just above the space where the actual mining equipment would be stored when not in use.

Going further forward, they had to go through the main cargo hold. They were actually walking through a passageway that ran through the center of the hold. The hold itself was unpressurized during loading and unloading operations. The passageway that ran through it was sealed to allow the crew to get forward and aft when the holds were unpressurized.

Chad opened an access hatch to look inside. It was a vast space, and it appeared to be completely full of ore. Phil realized that he was looking at paxtite ore floating in space. It wouldn't be obvious how much was actually there because there was no gravity to make it settle. Chad looked around and grabbed a rod that was fastened to the bulkhead. It was about six feet long, and he pushed it into the floating mass of ore. He repeated the action a few times and said, "Not exactly a calibrated method, but I'd say it's about four-fifths full."

Continuing going forward, they came to the crew and passenger accommodations. Phil checked the first crew cabin he came to and was greeted by the sight of two crewmen in PEWS of the style that was in use at the time. They were floating freely in the two-man cabin. Phil looked around and found data chips that were simply labeled "When someone finds us." He made a mental note to organize a way to match up the body with any goodbye letters or journals.

Each cabin was a similar story. Phil checked the PEWS controls on each and saw that their occupants chose to meet their end in different ways. Some cracked open the valve to vent the atmosphere in the PEWS suddenly and get the inevitable over quickly. Others lowered the oxygen level and drifted off to sleep. Phil could see the trauma in the faces of those who chose to end things suddenly. Those who chose to drift off to sleep looked more at peace. In both cases, the bodies were preserved in the vacuum of space.

Phil and Chad went into the captain's office and found the captain and a crew member floating without PEWS. As soon as Chad saw that, he remarked, "Well, now we know whatever happened here was sudden."

The *Prospector* was a large enough vessel for a full bridge. There was an area just aft of the bridge for mechanical and electronic systems on each side of the passageway to the bridge entrance. Chad saw it, and it took his breath away. "Wow! That's what happened."

Phil stood next to Chad and stared at the mess in front of them. "Meteorite, do you suppose?"

Chad nodded then realized that Phil couldn't see that with his helmet on. "Yeah, right through the side of the hull. Funny you don't expect to see meteorites collide from the side like that. I don't know why. Maybe we're used to seeing movies where they crash straight down."

Phil looked at the mess. "It looks like they tried to make repairs but gave up."

Chad agreed. "There's too much damage to fix without a maintenance bay and a whole bunch of spare parts that aren't normally part of a ship's supply."

Phil took a breath. "Okay, we know what happened. But why did it happen?"

Chad shook his head. "It shouldn't have happened. They would have a deflector shield operating at all times while parked here." An examination of the bridge revealed that it was unoccupied.

Chad and Phil attached sensors to various parts of the hull. Chad chose locations on main structural members to place the sensors, which measured strain, vibration, and heat. They ran cables to each one and connected them to a junction box.

Chad checked his work and declared it acceptable. "Okay, boss. Now we just need to find where I drilled that hole in the hull. Hopefully, it's not in a cargo hold."

Chad knew better because he had studied the *Prospector's* mechanical engineering drawings and knew there was a service area where he drilled the hole.

They found the ladder to the service area, where Chad picked up a coil of multiconductor cable and headed up. Phil followed, bringing the tools Chad asked him to bring. At the top of the ladder, Chad opened a hatch and went through with Phil still following him. After a brief search, Chad found the red bar that he had inserted into the hole he drilled in the hull. He carefully pushed the bar back out of the hole and inserted the wire harness connector and secured it. With that done, they ran the wire harness to the junction box and connected it.

When Chad was satisfied, he said, "Let's go and see if Helmut and Gus need any help."

In the engineering section, Helmut was just disconnecting the last item of the reactor, and he said, "Das ist the last connection. Release the locks at the corners."

The four each took a corner and climbed ladders to the ceiling, where they each released a safety and pulled on a handle that unseated the reactor from the ship. At this point, the reactor and the ship were separate entities.

They turned to leave when Helmut said, "You need to see this, Boss." He led them to a hatch labeled "Deflector control room." Helmut opened the hatch. "The deflector shield failed. These two were in the midst of repairing it when something breached the hull." There were two crew members floating near an open junction box. They showed signs of trauma from sudden depressurization but otherwise preserved.

Chad said, "Yeah, we found the hole made by a meteorite. Let's go topside."

Back on the *Prospectors* hull, Chad and Helmut pulled a remote thruster pack from an equipment box, and they attached it to the reactor top. With that done, they pulled the reactor out of the hull. Again, Phil was pleased with the help the lack of gravity gave them.

Once the reactor was free, they flipped it upside down and left it floating there. Gus looked around. "I wonder if our deflectors are up to the task."

At that moment, the shield started sparkling from a thousand individual impacts. Chad smiled. "I'd say they were working fine."

Chad ran a wire harness from the connector on the *Prospector* to the connector on the *Aurora*. With that done, they took the equipment boxes back to the *Aurora* air lock and reboarded.

Once back inside, they removed the PEWS. Hanging up the PEWS on racks would automatically recharge the power cells and download the memory cards. Small cameras located on the helmets would record everything they saw. This was handy in cases where a visual record needed to be checked on a maintenance task. But Phil realized that historians would be very interested in what they saw, not to mention insurance companies and mining companies.

The four of them made their way to the galley, where they found Beverly had made coffee, soup, and sandwiches. Phil looked at the spread and remarked, "Beverly, this is great, but I hope you didn't think we expected you to do this."

Beverly laughed. "You mean because I'm the only woman on his trip?" Phil was put back on his heels. "No, I meant—"

Beverly cut him off. "Relax, Mr. Ross," she said with a chuckle. "I've been crunching numbers and analyzing data all morning, and

I needed the break. Besides, you guys have been working hard all morning yourselves."

All five of them started chowing down. Phil asked between bites, "Beverly, how is the mapping project going?"

Beverly replied, "It's getting close to complete. The probes have started their return trip to Anna Mae. The amount of fresh information they gather from this point will diminish as they converge."

Gus polished off his sandwich. "Tell me, Chad, how's our progress?"

Chad had to swallow his bite of sandwich. "We're actually ahead of schedule. After lunch, Helmut and I need to get a small number of systems on the *Prospector* up and running."

Phil was flabbergasted. "You're kidding me? Like what?"

Chad said, "Four items really. The navigation shield array, the inertia neutralizers, gravity generators, and finally, the landing strut anchors." Gus was as baffled as Phil. "I thought the shields were down on the *Prospector*.

That's the reason we're here."

Helmut had his own laugh. "Das ist der deflector shield used when conducting mining operations. Der navigation shield ist a separate system on the *Prospector*."

Chad continued, "We'll run power and control cables to the individual systems and secure a portable power unit to supply power. Control cables will be run to the *Aurora* along with the sensor cables we ran this morning."

Phil nodded and asked, "Same as this morning? Gus and I shadowing you guys?"

Chad shook his head. "No, some of the spaces there won't be enough room for two. Besides, you two need to load all that mining equipment and secure the hatches."

Beverly jumped up. "Oh, that reminds me." Then she rushed out of the galley. In less than a minute, she returned with two canisters. "Could you get me a sample from the hold and one from the asteroid before processing?"

Phil took the canisters. "That shouldn't be a problem?"

After lunch and a restroom break, the four were back in the cargo hold, putting on their PEWS. Chad and Helmut put two equipment boxes in the air lock. When all four were in the air lock it was depressurized, and the outer hatch opened. Phil and Gus walked to the edge of the hull to survey the scene below. Gus nodded. "That doesn't look so bad."

Phil furrowed his brow. "Did you happen to notice if there was equipment on the other side?"

They walked to the other side, looked down, and were immediately deflated. Phil just laughed. "Well, where would the challenge come from if it was only one side."

Chad and Helmut overheard the conversation and were laughing as they descended through the hatch. Phil and Gus followed. When they reached the bottom, they located a hatch that led to the level below. As luck would have it, they found themselves in the space used to store the mining equipment.

The equipment bay hatches on this vessel served as the ramps. It was an efficient design but was considered unsafe since there were no air locks. They were open, and the ramps rested on the surface of the asteroid. Phil and Gus picked a side and started evaluating what they needed to do. First, they disconnected the tubes and stored them into racks they found in the equipment bay.

Next, they went to the drilling rig and studied it. It wouldn't budge, and that didn't make sense. Gus finally found the culprit. "Check this out. It's anchored like the ship."

There were foot pedals on the pads that rested on the ground. Gus stepped on one, wedges popped, and spring-loaded bolts retracted from the rock. The drill rig was now free from the asteroid.

Phil said, "Hold up a second," as he pulled a canister off his PEWS that he had attached with hook and loop strips. He filled the canister with rock fragments from a drill bit guide. "Okay, let's move this thing." They gently raised the drill rig. In a gravity environment, it would weigh about a ton and a half. Even in a weightless environment, they had to exercise caution because there was still a great deal of mass, and a ton-and-a-half object had a great deal of inertia.

Phil and Gus spent the next three hours gathering the mining equipment. When they were done, they closed the hatches. Without power, they had to engage the latches by hand. Phil looked around and declared their work acceptable and climbed the ladder to the next level. He was starting to get used to coordinating the microgravity generators in his boots with climbing ladders. The trick was to step on the first rung and step off and let the lack of natural gravity take over. He would simply hand over hand climb the ladder. That was mostly for control since he could simply float up.

Once on solid footing again, the microgravity units in his boots would be attracted to the decking. Outside the hull, they had to be very careful to keep at least one foot on a solid surface. A person could jump up and find themselves floating away from the surface. Phil thought it was a good thing modern PEWS were equipped with tiny emergency thrusters in case they tripped or something similar happened.

On what they came to call the main deck, Phil went to the small hatch that Chad used to probe the ore to check how much was there. He opened the hatch and took out the second canister Beverly gave him and scooped up an ore sample. While he was fiddling with the lid, there was a sudden pull on their bodies, and the ore in the hold suddenly settled.

Phil and Gus couldn't hear anything in the vacuum of space, but they could certainly tell the effect of tons of ore settling. Phil threw the switches on his PEWS communications system to connect him with Chad and Helmut. Gus saw what Phil did and followed suit. Phil said, "Chad, was that you?"

Chad replied, "Sure was Boss. Sorry, we didn't warn you. That was a calibration test."

Phil nodded. "That was some test. Are you guy's going to need a hand?"

"Actually, Boss, things went surprisingly smooth. The meteorite didn't damage any of the systems we needed, so we're about done," Chad replied.

Phil and Gus exited the *Prospector* with Chad and Helmut right behind them. They secured the hatch for the last time, and Chad said, "Helmut and I are going to connect the systems control to the *Aurora*. Why don't you and Gus take the opportunity to do a preflight check since we have the chance."

Phil nodded inside his helmet. "Okay, Gus. You take the left, and I'll grab the right."

Gus started toward the left side of the *Aurora*. "Roger."

Phil hadn't had an opportunity to look at the struts and fittings that were attached when they first arrived. He couldn't help but be impressed with the quality of the welds Helmut made. Not finding anything to concern him, he met Gus at the cargo hold air lock. They stood there staring at the nebula in the distance. Gus finally broke the silence. "It still baffles me that no one tried to find a passage through that."

Phil thought a minute. "Well, the crew of the vessel we're standing on did. So did Marcus Pointer."

Gus chuckled. "I hope it works out better for us than it did for them." Phil continued to stare at the nebula. "Amen, brother."

Chad and Helmut finished their tasks, and the four of them went through the air lock and entered the *Aurora*. The PEWS were stored in their shipping containers and secured with the equipment boxes. They met in the galley and had a meal that, again, Beverly was kind enough to prepare. Chad poured himself a mug of coffee. "Man, I'm beat."

Gus took a sip of his own coffee. "Tell me about it. Doing anything in PEWS is exhausting."

Phil asked the question everyone wanted to be answered, "When can we leave?"

Chad looked at Helmut, who nodded. Chad put down his mug. "We can leave right now if you want. I would recommend that we all get plenty of rest before that happens. It's going to take all of us to get this thing off this rock and headed in the right direction."

Phil nodded. "Okay then. We go in the morning."

The last couple of days were exhausting, and sleep came easily. Everyone awoke early, as they were all anxious to see the end of this adventure. At breakfast, Chad presented a modified checklist for the launch. Beverly mentioned that they needed to place a claim marker before they left, which caught everyone flat-footed.

Beverly saw their expressions and laughed. "Sorry, guys. Prospecting isn't your line. I brought a beacon that's programmed to announce the claim on this system in the name of the Stellar Logistics and Freight Corporation. If someone showed up after we left, they could make a claim, and it would have as much legitimacy as ours. A beacon will record the time and date of our claim, and it will be respected by agreements and treaties."

Phil saw that the beacon wasn't very large at all, and he suggested that they could launch it from the air lock Fel Nos used to launch his little spy gadget. After breakfast, Beverly loaded the beacon in the air lock and turned on the power switch. Gus and Phil were powering systems in the cockpit while Chad and Helmut were making sure the systems were operational on the *Prospector*.

When everything was set, Chad said, "Okay, let's get rid of the *Prospectors* reactor core. Please put the reverse view on the monitor."

Helmut threw a switch, and the monitor showed the view behind the Aurora, and they saw the reactor core where they left it suspended just above the *Prospector* hull.

Chad used the controls for the thruster pack they installed to rotate the core roughly in the direction of Anna Mae. Thrusters then fired to push the core away from the hull.

Gus shut down the shields to prevent the core from bouncing back at them. Once it was far enough away, he restarted the shields. It looked for all the world that the core was being flown by a drunk monkey. Chad explained that the onboard computer was calculating mass and center of mass so that it could maintain positive control. When it was satisfied that it knew enough, the main engine fired and sent it on its programmed course to destruction at Anna Mae.

Chad took a breath. "I'm ready to release."

Phil gave the thumbs-up, and Chad threw a switch that relaxed the wedges and retracted them back into the *Prospector's* landing gear. A push of a button gave a blast of compressed air under the landing gear pads lifting the ship off the asteroid. Phil remarked, "I felt that, and it felt good." Gus nodded. "I've got to agree."

Gus fired the thrusters to pitch up and away from the asteroid. At first, Gus thought the thrusters were not operating. Chad reminded him they now had a mass that was at least five times their original mass. Gus shut down the shields again to launch the beacon. Beverly made sure it was operating normally, and Gus restarted the shields. A long blast of the thrusters sent the piggy-backed Aurora away from the asteroid, and the navigation computer gave him vectors to exit the system.

When they were on a vector that gave them a straight line to the point on the nebula that offered them passage, he started the reaction engines and set them to idle. They didn't give them the kick they were used to, but the acceleration was unmistakable. Chad gave the thumbs-up, and Gus increased power. He was monitoring the sensors they had installed the previous day. He had Gus increase power in increments until they were at full power.

Chad nodded. "So far, so good. When the speed stabilizes, start the light- speed engines."

Acceleration was painfully slow with all the mass. Finally, Gus took a deep breath. "Well, here goes nothing."

Chad remarked, "If anything bad is going to happen, it'll be in the next few minutes." Gus engaged the light-speed engines, and Phil called out the velocity. When they reached LS 1, everyone breathed a sigh of relief. Chad's eyes were glued to the readout from the sensors they installed. He didn't say if he liked what he saw, but he kept telling Gus to increase velocity.

At LS 6, there was a low groan from the hull. Everyone broke out in a sweat except for Chad. "Keep pushing, Gus. It's just talking to us." At LS 7, the groan changed pitch. Gus looked at Chad anxiously.

Chad knew the others were getting nervous. "It's okay, guys. All the readings are well into the acceptable range."

The pitch changed with velocity until it was gone at LS 8.5. Gus settled the velocity at LS 9. "Please tell me we'll be able to stop this thing when we have to."

Chad said, "Sure, we have to be just as cautious stopping as we were when we were accelerating."

Entering the nebula was just as much a nonevent in this direction as it was in the other. Phil and Gus agreed on a schedule for duty behind the controls, as did Chad and Helmut for monitoring the *Prospector* sensor data. They didn't want to ignore the sensor data because there have been accidents in the past involving ships being towed that happened because seemingly minor glitches became major problems.

Sometimes a vibration would occur that was a harmonic of a critical structural member. Other times repeated stresses would heat a component to the point it couldn't be trusted to perform its designed function. Phil was at the controls when they reached the turn. Gus took the copilot's seat, and both Chad and Helmut were monitoring the additional instruments. Chad recommended that they put the brakes on slowly.

Phil eased the power off and slowed to LS 8. Then continued to slowly back off the power. At LS 4, there was a quick shudder that disappeared before he could even ask Chad what was happening. At LS 1, Phil cut the light-speed engines and started the reaction engines. He left the reaction engines idle and allowed the ship to coast.

Gus was calling out the time to make the turn. He also gave Phil some advice. "In this configuration, we have our thrust line above the center of mass, so you can't make any assumptions about controllability," he cautioned.

Phil smiled and said, "I would love to say, 'Here, hold my beer and watch this.'"

Before Gus could ask what he meant by that, Phil started a slow right roll. He held it for a time until he thought they reached the right moment, then he pushed the thrust levers forward until the high centerline thrust pitched the ship down. When they had aligned with the return heading, Phil adjusted the thrust vectors to stop the pitching motion. He brought the reaction engines to full power and waited for the ship to accelerate to maximum sublight speed.

Phil was suppressing a grin. "That's how we do it downtown." Gus was flabbergasted. "Show off."

Chad was grinning ear to ear. "Sweet."

The *Aurora* was pushed back to a cruising velocity of LS 9. During the rest of the journey, Beverly did an analysis of the ore samples Phil got for her. She said the results looked very good to her, but she wasn't trained for a fine analysis. That would have to wait for a more qualified individual to complete. Even so, her company committed to projects on a lot less.

Phil was preparing his own report to corporate headquarters when he wasn't at the controls. All five took turns at the cooking duties.

Although Chad and Helmut insisted on doing the lion's share, both technicians knew their way around the galley. Before they knew it, they had cleared the nebula and were in open space. After three days of travel since leaving the nebula, they were ready to cut the light-speed engines. Again, it was all hands on deck for the deceleration.

Gus was at the controls, and he took his cues for power reduction from Chad. At LS 1, they cut the light-speed engines and fired the reaction engines. Chad started to relax. "Guys, we do good work. I've been on new freighters that didn't behave as well as our composite ship."

Phil nodded in agreement. "Still, in all, I won't feel entirely relieved until I hear the docking clamps engage."

That last statement took a minute to sink in, and everyone in the cockpit looked at each other. Gus broke the silence and asked the question everyone wanted to be answered, "Can we dock with this pig strapped to our belly?"

Chad looked embarrassed. "I've been so preoccupied with getting us back I didn't even consider how we were going to get back on the station."

Gus shrugged. "We could always use PEWS."

Phil shot that down. "Last resort. That would be too embarrassing. Besides, we only have four PEWS on board."

Chad thought about it and offered a solution. "When you make initial contact with the station, tell them to have Jeremy contact me on the maintenance frequency." Phil made initial contact with the station, and a very relieved controller welcomed them home. After accepting vectors for their approach, Phil relayed Chad's request.

In a short time, Jeremy contacted Chad, and after a brief conversation, Chad signed off. "Relax, guys, we've got it handled."

At the station, Jeremy got things organized and talked to the controllers about the requirements for what they needed to do to dock. Chad explained what they were going to do when they arrived.

Gus groaned, "Separate the ships! It took you and Helmut hours to put them together."

Chad shook his head. "Relax, Gus, we had welding and adjustments to make and only two people. Jeremy is going to have teams of people disconnecting us from the *Prospector*."

Gus followed the vectors that the controller gave him, and he brought the *Aurora* to a stop a hundred yards off CargoMod 2. The word had gotten out about the arrival of the *Prospector*, and a crowd of people gathered at the viewing areas to get a glimpse of the salvaged ship. Four maintenance tugs loaded with technicians in PEWS approached them, and the tugs clamped themselves at the upper corners of the *Prospector*. The technicians disembarked the tugs and set to work disconnecting the *Prospector* from the *Aurora*.

Gus felt a little silly about fretting about the time it would take to separate the two ships when Jeremy contacted them on the maintenance frequency. "Ships are separated. Stand by and give us time to get some clearance."

Phil and Gus watched as the technicians reboarded the tugs, and they gave a long blast from their thrusters to push the *Prospector* downward. Once a safe distance was achieved, Gus was given clearance to go direct to CargoMod 2, Docking Port 1.

Gus eased the *Aurora* into the docking clamps, and the station crew connected the umbilicals. The ship's systems were shut down, and then the passenger hatch opened.

*****

**Oasis 4, CargoMod 2**

Phil expected to be greeted by more people than the station crew that connected the umbilicals. He stepped off the ship and looked around. There was a station crewman verifying the power connection settings. Phil asked, "Where are they putting the *Prospector*?"

The crewman checked the display at the workstation SICOS. "It's at Docking Port 15, Boss."

Beverly decided that she should check in with Captain Hastings. Phil extended an invitation to her and Captain Hastings to attend the morning briefing. Phil, Gus, Chad, and Helmut started walking to Docking Port 15.

As they approached Docking Port 10, there was a small crowd at the passenger air lock. Phil saw Will Dawson down on one knee giving a young malnun girl a hug. She hugged him back, saying, "Thank you, Mr. Dawson, for taking care of Bosto."

Will said to her, "It was no trouble, sweetheart."

Then he shook hands with two adult malnuns, who were obviously the young girl's parents. The malnuns boarded the ship and docked at Docking Port 10, and the crowd dispersed as the foursome arrived.

Phil asked, "Hey, Will, what was all that about?"

Will turned toward Phil and the rest. "Oh, hey, Boss! I'll tell you later. Let's see how they're making out with the *Prospector*."

At Docking Port 15, Jeremy and three of his technicians were putting on PEWS. He looked over to Phil and the rest. "Welcome back, Boss."

Phil wondered, "Couldn't this wait until tomorrow?"

Jeremy shrugged in his PEWS. "We have some time today. I thought maybe we could get things powered so that the night shift can off-load the cargo."

Phil looked concerned. "Are you aware that there's meteorite impact damage?" Jeremy nodded. "Yes, I am. I saw it as you were approaching. Chad, Helmut, what can you tell me about the damage?"

Chad scratched his head. "From what I could see, the damage was to the control systems. I didn't even have to bypass any of the systems I needed to get us back here. I pulled the breakers anyway in case there were any sneak circuits."

Jeremy thought about what Chad said and finally nodded. "I think we can pressurize this. Do you agree?"

Chad smiled. "Except for the hole in the hull, it shouldn't be a problem."

Jeremy said, "I've got guys putting a temporary patch on the outside. I'll confirm the reactor room is secure so that the hole created by the missing core isn't a problem."

Helmut asked, "Why are you putting a temporary patch on the hull?" Jeremy grinned. "Mrs. Ross wanted it preserved."

Gus had to turn away to stifle a chuckle while Phil furrowed his brow. "You'll have to run that by me again."

Jeremy blurted out, "It'll have to wait until later, Boss. I've got a lot of work to do."

Before Phil could protest, Jeremy put on his helmet. Phil told one of the technicians before he could put his helmet on that the *Prospectors* crew was still on board, and he should tell Jeremy. He would call the medical clinic and have someone come down and recover them. The technician gave him the thumbs up.

Phil went to a workstation and contacted Dr. Tillman. "Hey, Doc, could you send a team to recover the crew of the *Prospector?*"

Marie was embarrassed to admit that it hadn't occurred to her that there was going to be a body recovery. She asked, "How many?"

Phil answered, "Twenty-five."

Will took a breath. "How did they go?"

Phil thought about it. "Not a pleasant experience for any of them. It looks like the crew was busy making repairs to the deflector shield when they were struck by a meteorite. It was nearly instant for them. The miners were in PEWS and lived through the event, but the folks who knew how to repair the ship and fly it was gone. Chad here says it was unlikely they had the parts to make a repair anyway."

Marie Tillman arrived with the necessary things to recover the crew of the *Prospector*, and Phil explained they were waiting on Jeremy to make sure that it was safe to pressurize the ship. A technician at the workstation was in contact with Jeremy, and he was carrying out tasks as they were needed. Phil overheard Jeremy ask for power, and the technician closed the switches and monitored the output. When Jeremy was satisfied, he asked for a valve to be opened, and a rush of air could be heard as air from the station filled the *Prospector*. The technician switched off the valve and waited for word from Jeremy.

Phil said, "That couldn't have been enough to fill the ship, could it?"

Chad shook his head. "Not by a long shot. Jeremy pressurized it just enough to make sure the seals were holding."

Gus wasn't convinced. "I wouldn't think that the seals would be any good after all these years."

Helmut chuckled. "You're forgetting that it's been in a perfect vacuum, and the seals were made of very high-quality material originally."

The technician reopened the valve, and the air started rushing into the *Prospector* again. After a few minutes, the sound of rushing air couldn't be heard. Suddenly, the air lock hatch opened, and Jeremy stepped out with his helmet off.

Phil, Gus, Chad, and Helmut led Marie Tillman and her staff on board to show her where the crewmen of the *Prospector* were. It was still very cold on the *Prospector*, so Jeremy had his technicians busy checking the environmental systems so they could turn on the heat while others tested the ore off-loading equipment.

When Dr. Tillman and her staff were finished, the four of them went back to the CargoMod. Phil turned to the other three, "Guys, I think you went above and beyond on this one. For that, I would like to personally thank you."

At the CentMod, the four of them parted company where Chad and Helmut made their way to HabMod 8 to their quarters while, and Phil and Gus walked to HabMod 1.

At the top floor, Phil stood outside his quarters. "Eight days. She's had eight days. Am I going to recognize the place? Be strong, Phil. Be strong."

He went in and was greeted warmly by a very relieved Alice. She tried not to show it, but she missed him and was worried. She stepped back and put her hands on her hips. "What did ya bring me?"

Phil was caught flat-footed. He just muttered the first thing that came to mind. "I couldn't find the gift shop on the asteroid, but I did name a planetoid after you."

Alice acted disappointed, then smiled and gave Phil another kiss. "Wash for supper."

The End

# BOSTO

**Oasis 4, Lower CentMod, Station Maintenance Shop**

Will Dawson was in his shop. Having handed out the day's assignments to his technicians before the morning briefing, he checked his job board and wondered which technicians would need his help first. It's not that his technicians were incompetent, just the opposite, in fact, but there were sometimes problems that needed a fresh perspective to solve.

There was a station replenishment ship docked on CargoMod 2 Docking Port 20 at the moment. The replenishment ship was delivering the four things that were always slowly diminishing on a space station, oxygen, nitrogen, and hydrogen to make breathing air and potable water. Water could certainly be made on the station by simply mixing oxygen and hydrogen in the correct proportions. In fact, there was equipment on the station to do just that in the event it was needed. It was just easier to bring water to the station, premixed, as it were.

The oxygen, nitrogen, and hydrogen come in cryogenic form. Technicians connected tubes from the ship to the station. Piping carried the cryogenic liquid from the ship to holding tanks in the CentMod. Before the ship arrived, technicians checked and tested the piping for leaks. They were taking delivery on twice as much of all three liquids as they usually receive. The recent doubling of the size of the station made that necessary. The added station section had its own storage tanks that needed filling. Piping connected the tanks to allow fluid to be transferred when needed.

There were systems called scrubbers that removed carbon dioxide from the air and purified it. There were also plants in the HabMods and the CentMod that kept the air smelling fresh. But there were always small amounts of air lost whenever a ship docked and undocked or someone used an air lock to work outside the station in a PEWS. A mixing valve would combine nitrogen and oxygen in the right proportions and make air when necessary. Wastewater was normally filtered and recycled, but like the air, it needed occasional replenishing.

Will wasn't disappointed, as he was summoned to CargoMod 2 to help resolve a small issue. Truthfully, he could have given some advice over the intercom, but he was looking for an excuse to get out and about. At the docking port, there was a small issue with the liquid nitrogen flow rate. Will stayed at the workstation and monitored the flowmeter while he sent his techs to "tweak" the valves downstream. He was engrossed in what he was doing, but suddenly, he sensed movement behind him. That wasn't unusual, as station personnel and ship's crew were bound to be in the area. Then there was purring behind him, which got his full attention. The volume of the purring is the main thing that gave him alarm.

He slowly turned, unblinking. Perched on a shipping crate was a cat. It looked to all the world like a normal yellow house cat, except that it was about the size of a mountain lion. Will slowly backed up until he bumped into the workstation. He fumbled around, feeling for the proper button on the intercom. He didn't dare take his eyes off the huge cat in front of him. Finally finding the button he wanted, a voice came over the intercom. "Station security, what's your emergency?"

Will struggled to find the words. Finally, he croaked out, "Send someone here immediately. There's a huge animal loose."

The cat sitting on the crate was staring at Will, and after a few seconds, it stood and dropped to the floor. Will was feeling doomed as the cat slowly walked toward him while he wondered what was keeping security. The cat started doing that "rubbing against his legs" thing that nearly bowled him over, and the purring increased in volume. Will was starting to realize that this cat wasn't looking at him like a snack. He reached down and scratched him behind the ears, then the big cat rolled over and exposed his belly, which Will carefully scratched.

Ian Mackenzie's thundering steps were getting nearer, then he rounded the corner and spotted the big cat and suddenly stopped. "Bloody hell!"

Luke Smith was close behind Ian. "Will, are you all right?"

Will looked up with a relieved look and a smile. "I think so. He's a friendly guy."

Luke reached down and scratched the cat under the chin. The cat responded by purring louder and playfully batting at Luke's hands. Luke stood. "We can't have him running loose. Let's find out where he came from."

He used the SICOS terminal to look at the security monitors in the CargoMod. Soon, he smiled and said, "Look at this."

The monitor showed the image of Docking Port 10. In a few seconds, the big tomcat appeared. He leaned into the doorjamb and rubbed it as he exited the air lock. Will said, "That's the malnun shuttle. It belongs to some kind of research scientist. Apparently, he's traveling around collecting samples of some kind, and he has his wife and daughter with him."

Luke nodded. "Let's get their kitty cat back to them."

Ian left them to continue patrolling. Luke and Will strolled to Docking Port 10 with the cat in tow. Will peeked into the air lock. "Hello? We found your cat wandering the station!"

Not hearing a response, Luke looked at Will. "Wait here. This doesn't seem right."

Luke entered the shuttle. In a few seconds, he rushed out and fingered a button on the communicator he wore on his wrist. "Dr. Tillman, we have a medical situation in CargoMod 2, Docking Port 10!" Marie's voice came over the speaker. "What's the problem, Luke?" Luke tried to maintain a professional demeanor. "I have unconscious malnuns, two adults, a male and a female. Also, there's a malnun child approximately eight earth years old. As I said, they're unconscious, very warm, and their breathing seems labored."

Marie responded, "Isolate yourself, and don't let anyone inside that ship."

Will edged himself away from Luke. He went to a locker on the bulkhead and removed a roll of yellow caution tape. He secured the end of the tape to the bulkhead and stretched it across the walkway, then repeated the process on the other side of the air lock. The big cat was playing with the loose end of the tape as Will tried to put it away. Dr. Tillman arrived with several of her staff. She was dressed in a Biohazard protective garment. When she arrived, she put on the head covering and sealed it. She told Luke and Will to stay put. It was just then she spotted the cat. "Oh my heavens!"

Luke reassured her, "Relax, Doc. He's a friendly guy."

Marie shook her head as she entered the shuttle. When she came out, she had her helmet off, and she directed her staff to enter the shuttle and carry the malnun family to the infirmary. A malnun doctor on Dr. Tillman's staff arrived. Marie turned to him. "They're bringing out three, two adults and a child."

She approached Luke and Will while keeping one eye on the enormous cat sitting next to them. "I tested them, and it seems to be some kind of virus. They're past the contagious part of this particular virus."

The medics brought the family out of the shuttle on stretchers which were placed on gurneys. The malnun doctor descended on them, and he gave the medics orders that they carried out. IVs were started, and the gurneys were wheeled to the infirmary. Marie followed the medics back to the infirmary leaving Luke and Will standing there with the cat.

Luke walked to the air lock. "Come on, let's see what we can find out about this cat."

The shuttle interior was typical of the type. There was a small cockpit and an open area in the rear. The open area served as a combination sitting room and galley. There was a semiprivate sleeping area in the rear, and the seats in the main room converted into bunks. On the floor next to the bulkhead was a basket with padding in it. Hanging on the bulkhead above the basket was a piece of paper that was obviously labeled by a child. The writing was in malnun, which neither Luke nor Will spoke. Luke pulled a scanner out of a pocket. "Let's see what they're calling this thing."

He scanned the paper and had the scanner translate it. "Well, the kitty cat's name is Bosto."

Will said, "That's nice. What does it mean?"

Luke tapped the screen. "There's no single word that's a direct translation. Basically, a combination of words to express an overall trait, cuddly, lovey, furry, soft."

Will was nearly bowled over by Bosto rubbing on his legs. He looked down at the cat and said, "Well, he's appropriately named."

They looked around for food for the cat and found a supply and the biggest litter box they had ever seen. Other than the size, it was a standard litter box. It had a mechanism that raked the litter after use and deposited the waste in a hopper. There was also a pad that cleaned and sterilized the cat's feet as he stepped out. Luke furrowed his brow. "How do they carry enough food to keep Bosto happy?"

Will stood upright and scratched his head. "They must resupply at each stop."

Luke protested, "Not many worlds stock cat food. Particularly when the cat weighs about a hundred pounds."

Will pondered for a second or two. "I've never been to a world that didn't have fish or fowl on the menu."

Will shrugged his shoulders. "Well, someone has to take care of Bosto here."

They grabbed the bed, litterbox, food, and the two bowls on the floor and carried them to the CargoMod where they put them on a cart. Will put Bosto's things in his quarters, much to his wife's consternation. Bosto didn't seem hungry, but he also didn't want to be away from Will.

For the next two days, Will and Bosto were inseparable. The cat food situation was holding out, but Will didn't want to run into the possibility of running out. To that end, he went to the cafeteria to see if they could help. The head cook was delighted to help because sometime past, he had purchased five hundred pounds of fish filets from a maldor trader. There wasn't anything wrong with the fish. It just had a strong taste that didn't go over well. When he heard that it could be put to good use, he put one of his cooks to work processing the fish. First, the fish was cooked then shredded. There was equipment that could put meal-sized portions in cans they found very useful.

In the afternoon that day, there was some good news. The malnun family was showing signs of getting better. They were regaining consciousness, and their temperatures were near normal. Will decided that he should pay them a visit. Naturally, Bosto followed along. Will stepped into Marie Tillman's office. "Hey, Doc. I came to see if your patients could stand a visitor."

Marie smiled. "I think Dr. Tu Vos is ready to see folks." Will had to ask, "What kind of doctor is he?"

Marie punched up a bio on her SICOS display and turned it toward Will. "He's a well-known genetic scientist. He took his family with him on a trip to 'collect samples.'"

There was an outbreak of Tineckian Fever on Trosic while they were there. This particular illness is particularly nasty to malnuns. It has three distinct stages: the germinating stage, the fever stage, and the recovery stage. After the germinating stage, they're no longer contagious. Even if a human contracted Tineckian fever, we would probably only get a bad cold—if a human was really unlucky, a low-grade fever. We have a better-equipped immune system for that sort of thing."

Will asked, "Did you say that he worked in genetics?"

Marie laughed and looked at the enormous tomcat happily napping on the chair next to Will. "You think?"

Will left Bosto with Marie and headed to Dr. Tu Vos's room. He knocked on the open door lightly and poked his head inside. "You're looking better today than you did when you arrived, Doctor."

Dr. Tu Vos looked at Will. "I cannot argue with that statement, Mister…"

Will smiled and came the rest of the way in. "Dawson. Will Dawson, I'm the station maintenance chief."

Will related how he had discovered Bosto and that led him and Luke Smith to their shuttle. Dr. Tu Vos nodded as he tried to recollect what happened. "We were very sick when we arrived. I managed to get the shuttle docked and the air lock open. I told the young man that connected the umbilicals that we would check in after a rest. It was between 0300 and 0400 Zulu, as I recall. That's the last thing I remember," Dr. Tu Vos said tiredly.

Will said, "Well, you can thank Bosto for getting my attention. By the way, what's the deal with the size of Bosto?"

Dr. Tu Vos laughed with some difficulty. "Bosto is an experiment, or at least he was. During a visit to Earth, I became enamored with felines. I wanted to adjust their genetics to remove some of the more unpleasant traits associated with cats and enhance some of their more fun aspects. I think you'll agree I was quite successful. Bosto is playful but not aggressive, and he doesn't feel the need to mark his territory like male cats are apt to do, and I managed to make him hypoallergenic."

Will nodded. "He's a sweetheart, but why is he so big?"

Dr. Tu Vos laughed. "Everyone makes mistakes. I inadvertently triggered a genetic marker that allowed him to achieve, shall we say, a larger-than-normal size. I was going to have the animal destroyed for that reason, but my daughter spotted him, and they took to each other instantly."

Will assured him that taking care of Bosto was no trouble. Even his wife was becoming fond of him. Will left the infirmary with Bosto in tow to allow Dr. Tu Vos to continue resting. The next morning after the briefing, he was in his shop with Bosto when Alice Ross and Brenda Walters came in, and they immediately started petting and scratching Bosto under the chin. Bosto didn't object until the petting slowed. The ladies were so taken with Bosto they almost forgot why they came there. Will thought he should remind them that they were in a workspace.

"Ladies, what brings you here?"

Alice gave Bosto a final pat on the head. "I understand that the original reactor and other mechanicals have been removed from the Upper CentMod when the station expansion was added."

Will wondered where she was going with this. "That's right. The new systems were more efficient."

Alice continued, "Has the space been spoken for?"

Will shook his head. "No, the space is in an awkward place on the station.

Tenants want more accessibility and exposure."

Alice smiled. "I understand that there's an access hatch that was designed to allow large pieces of equipment to be taken on or off the station."

Will nodded again. "Yeah, that's how we removed the old reactor?"

Alice and Brenda shared a look. "Will, if you don't mind, we're going to go look at the space."

Will cautiously smiled. "Help yourself."

Later during lunch, Will was walking through the CentMod. He normally ate at Eva's, but having Bosto constantly in tow made that impossible. He glanced in the direction of Eva's where he saw Alice with Brenda talking excitedly with Jeremy Cole, and he was wondering what they were up to. Alice had a reputation for being a bit impulsive. Whatever she was planning involved Jeremy and the equipment hatch in the Upper CentMod reactor room that was vacated when the station was expanded.

There was a kiosk that sold pizza by the slice on the plaza level, so he bought a couple of slices and a cola. Will found a place to eat in a sitting area. After he finished the first slice, he wadded the foil the pizza came in and tossed it on the floor, where Bosto batted it around the floor, to the delight of some children from a cruise ship.

The next morning started normally with the morning briefing. After Virginia adjourned the meeting, Marie Tillman approached Will. "Could you make time this morning to come to the infirmary?"

Will was puzzled. "Sure, Doc. What is it you need?"

"The little malnun girl is awake, but she's showing very little progress. I thought that if she saw Bosto, it would go a long way toward getting her better," she replied.

Will smiled. "You can count on it, Doc."

After Will checked on the progress his technicians were making on the morning assignments, he took Bosto to the infirmary. Marie led them to the malnun girl's room and said, "Wait here a second."

Marie put her head in the room. "Pin Vos, are you in the mood for another visitor?"

Will could hear the little malnun girl say in an exhausted, tired voice, "I guess so."

Marie turned her head to Will and nodded, so he went in and saw Pin Vos's parents there. He could see that they were feeling much better, but they were still quite obviously recovering themselves. They were momentarily confused as to why Will was there. Then they spotted the cat following him. Pin Vos looked down and saw the cat. The color returned to her face, and she excitedly said, "Bosto!"

Bosto started purring as loud as ever, and he jumped up on the bed, soaking up every bit of affection Pin Vos could lavish on him.

Marie told Dr. Tu Vos and his wife that they were discharged, but Pin would have to stay an extra day. She was extra encouraged when she saw the instant improvement when Pin spotted Bosto. Dr. Tu Vos and his wife said they were getting a room at the Star Lodge Suites, and they promised that they wouldn't leave until they were feeling a hundred percent. Will promised to send Bosto's bed, litter box, and food to the hotel. Also, Pin Vos insisted that Will showed up to say goodbye when they left the station. Naturally, Will couldn't say no, so he said he would be there.

Lunchtime came, and Will thought Eva's sounded like a good idea since he didn't have Bosto in tow anymore. He found Jeremy Cole sitting at a table, so he joined him. They had just ordered when they heard Alice Ross. "See, Brenda, I told you they would both be here."

Both ladies didn't stand on ceremony. They each took a chair at Will and Jeremy's table. Jeremy was a bit taken aback at first but recovered quickly. "What can we do for you ladies?"

Alice smiled in a way that raised the hackles on Will and Jeremy. "Guys, we've picked your brains a little bit, and you need to be aware of what we're going to propose to corporate headquarters. With the increased cruise ship traffic, we thought a museum would be an appropriate attraction."

Will and Jeremy asked in unison, "What kind of museum?"

Brenda jumped in, "We were thinking that there was an opportunity to have a little of everything. Mainly local stuff."

Will still needed more explanation, "We're not part of any planetary system. How can anything be local?"

Alice looked annoyed at Will. "Oh, you know what she meant. The planets and systems that we regularly do business with. My thinking is we can feature both the history and art of those planets in displays. I thought we could also feature the station's history from construction to the recent expansion. I think it would be great if we could even  have a gift shop that sells souvenirs from the systems we do business with.

There are a lot of shops on the station, but there aren't any that sell tourist trinkets."

Jeremy took in the information and finally took a breath. "That all sounds great, but you were asking about the *Prospector* earlier. How does that fit in?"

Alice paused to articulate in her head what she was thinking. "Correct me if I'm wrong, but if Phil gets here in one piece with the *Prospector*, salvage laws make it the property of Stellar Logistics and Freight Corporation."

Jeremy nodded. "Yeah, but that particular model is considered not only obsolete, but it's also considered hazardous to operate. The *Prospector* was an antique when it came up missing. I'm sure you know that having a derelict ship taking up a docking port so that tourists can walk through isn't practical. What exactly are you proposing?"

Alice said, "I never had any illusions of keeping the whole ship around. I studied the ship's design, and I discovered that it was built in modules. I think it would be great if we could take sections of the ship and put them on display."

Will grinned. "That's why you were asking about the access hatch." Jeremy looked thoughtful. "That would actually solve a couple of problems. That thing needs to be scrapped anyways. The more we don't have to grind up, the quicker we can free up a docking port."

Will took out a pad and brought up a station diagram. "What parts of the ship were you thinking of?"

Brenda pulled out a pad of her own. "We were thinking the bridge, galley, and some of the cabins."

Will and Jeremy compared the ship sections on Brenda's pad with Will's diagram. Finally, they declared the project was within their capabilities.

Phil had been gone with the *Aurora* for eight days. Some station personnel started to wonder if their boss was going to return at all. They were careful not to mention anything around Alice or Brenda, but there was a concern. The little malnun girl has been out of the infirmary for a couple of days and was getting stronger and making good progress while staying at the hotel with her parents. In the afternoon, Will was in his maintenance shop when Virginia Wells called him from the operations center. "Will, the *Aurora* just dropped out of light speed. They'll be here in about an hour and a half."

Will was relieved. "That's great news, Virginia. Are they towing?"

Virginia answered with an obviously upbeat tone in her voice. "I'll say they are. It's quite a sight."

Will nodded. "Thanks, Virginia. I'll make sure I get my best people there.

What docking port are you putting them in?"

Virginia answered, "CargoMod 2 Docking Port 15." Will said, "Thanks for the heads-up, Virginia."

He had just switched off the intercom when Dr. Tillman called, "Will, the Vos family is recovered, and they've scheduled a departure for about an hour and a half from now."

Will thought the timing could have been better. "Thanks, Doctor." Will thought for a minute about where he might get the best view of the *Aurora* piggybacked on the *Prospector*. He left his shop and found himself on the plaza level. Looking at the observation areas, he saw that there was a crowd already forming. With that knocked out of contention, the control center was the only choice left. It was actually a better choice, being that the view was better. The view from the platform lift revealed that there were more people making their way to the observation areas. Once he reached the operations center, he climbed the stairs to the control center, where there was an excessive number of people there. Controllers going off shift were lingering, and those going on shift came in early.

Alice Ross was there using a terminal to download images from the station image processors. She had a hard time concealing her relief as she watched the two ships make their approach. Will watched until the ships were separated, and they were cleared to the docking ports. He looked at the time. "Oh my goodness, I've got to go."

He hurried to the platform lift, descended to the plaza level, and jumped on a station shuttle to CargoMod 2. A jog to Docking Port 10 got him there just in time. Bosto was the first to spot Will and start purring. The big Tomcat started rubbing his legs, and Will scratched behind his ears. Will got down on one knee and gave Pin Vos a hug, and she hugged him back. "Thank you, Mr. Dawson, for taking care of Bosto."

Will said to her, "It was no trouble, sweetheart." Pin Vos then ran into the shuttle with Bosto trailing her.

Dr. Tu Vos and his wife gave Will warm handshakes and entered the shuttle closing the hatch. Will heard behind him. "What was that about, Will?"

Will turned to see Phil, Gus, Chad, and Helmut. "Oh, hey, Boss! I'll tell you later. Let's see how they're making out with the *Prospector*."

The End

# RESCUE

**Oasis 4, Trading Space Station of the Stellar
Logistics and Freight Corporation**

Phil Ross was sitting at his desk, staring out the viewport. He was
watching a mining ship ease into a docking port in CargoMod 5. It
was the *Goldfield* under Captain Hastings, which was a prospecting
and mining ship that belonged to the Superior Mining Corporation of
Duluth, Minnesota.

Phil had borrowed sensors and one of their stellar cartographers
when they recovered a derelict mining ship called the *Prospector*. As
a result, Stellar Logistics and Freight Corporation had a claim on
the system with the mineral-rich asteroids, and the Superior Mining
Corporation of Duluth, Minnesota, was given exclusive rights to
conduct mining operations in the system.

The Superior Mining Corporation was a small operation; in fact,
they were teetering on bankruptcy when Phil approached Captain
Hastings for the loan of equipment and a cartographer. The deal
for exclusive mining rights in the Anna Mae system turned their
fortunes around.

At first, the corporate officers at Superior Mining were upset that
Captain Hastings had made the deal in the first place. When they found
out how lucrative the deal actually was, they started shopping for newer
vessels. According to Jeremy Cole, that was a good thing because the
*Goldfield* was only one generation newer than the Prospector, which
wasn't saying much.

This was the first load of ore brought back by the *Goldfield*. They left for the asteroid belt as soon as the borrowed equipment could be removed from the *Aurora* and returned to the *Goldfield*, which was ten weeks ago.

The *Prospector* was gone, so to speak. Alice had Jeremy's crew save the bridge and the spaces immediately aft of the bridge on the starboard side. The ship was cut along the centerline behind the bridge, leaving the entire bridge and the starboard side spaces. She also had the section of the hull saved that the miners connected the tubes to.

The rest of the *Prospector* was ground up, and the metals were separated and put into containers. Before all that happened, the surviving family of the crew members of the *Prospector* visited the station and claimed the remains and personnel effects. Each was given a tour of the ship and given a chance to have a final reflection on the lost. Phil made a mental note to be sure that he saw Captain Hastings while he was at the station. He took in a deep breath and let it out, then he said, "Might as well see what the 'Old Ball and Chain' is up to." With that, he left his office and started making his way to the platform lift.

Alice was in the new museum space, trying to work out the general layout. The centerpiece of the museum was the bridge of the *Prospector* and the spaces behind the bridge. Directly behind the bridge was the compartment that was damaged by the meteor. The damage was left intact to illustrate what it took to render the *Prospector* inert on an asteroid. Behind that was the galley kitchen, then a crew cabin. It would have taken too much space to include any more of the ship. Also, there wasn't a lot to be gained by adding more crew cabins.

The museum was the old Station System Center. When the station was expanded, the new section had improved systems that made the old, less efficient systems redundant, so they were removed and scrapped. As a result, this space had an access hatch of considerable size that was designed to accommodate large pieces of equipment. They used this hatch to bring in the *Prospector* sections and the mining equipment that Phil and Gus had to stow while on the asteroid.

Alice was fussing with the equipment all day, and she finally had it situated the way she wanted it. She was going by images that Phil and

Gus recorded while on the asteroid. There were two identical sets of equipment. One set would work on the starboard side of the *Prospector*, and the other would work on the port side. Alice arranged one set of equipment as it was found by Phil and the others. A volunteer artist managed to make the floor look like the surface of an asteroid.

The hull section with the ore loading chutes was mounted to the wall and had the tubes from the chutes to the separators connected. All in all, it was very realistic. The other set of equipment was displayed in its stowed configuration.

Alice was standing back admiring her efforts when she heard behind her. "It might have been easier to just take the museum visitors to the asteroid."

She turned around to see Phil checking her handiwork. "Don't think that I haven't thought of that more than once."

Phil took Alice back to their quarters, where he made dinner. After they ate, they settled in and watched a movie that arrived in the latest data stream. Alice decided that she wasn't going to make it through to the end, so they retired early.

A good night's sleep reenergized Alice. Most of the heavy moving was done, so really, the rest of the work was putting up partitions and deciding how the displays should be arranged.

In addition to the Prospector remains, there were volunteers busy creating information cards with photos and text relating to the salvage of the Prospector. Also, there were efforts made to create displays to show the Prospector and its crew on happier days. The families of the crew were more than happy to provide photos and artifacts when they heard what Alice was doing.

Phil, in the meantime, went to the ops center after his morning workout and breakfast. After the morning briefing, he went to his office and sat at his desk. He turned to the SICOS display. "SICOS, download correspondence." His eyes bugged out because there were more than the three or four company memos he normally received.

He had a lengthy letter from corporate and a letter from the foreign department of each of the worlds they did business with. There were also letters from the cultural departments of each of those worlds.

Obviously, he had to open the letter from corporate first. As he read, he wondered if his life was going to be more complicated or less. The Stellar Logistics and Freight Corporation has extended an invitation to the worlds that regularly did business at Oasis 4 to open a consulate on the station.

Phil opened the letters from the foreign offices, and indeed, most of them were requests for office space on the station.

Phil leaned back in his chair. "SICOS, page Virginia Wells." In a few seconds, Virginia answered, "What's up, Boss?"

Phil said, "You're going to love this, Virginia. I got a communication from corporate that you need to see. Come to my office so we can discuss this."

You could almost hear the dread in her voice. "I'll be right there, Boss."

Phil next paged Gus. "Hey, Gus, get in here."

Both Virginia and Gus entered Phil's office in a few seconds. As they sat, Phil moved the corporate letter from his desktop SICOS to the wall display. "How does this first item affect us?"

Gus and Virginia quickly scanned the letter, and finally, Virginia said, "I don't see any problems. In fact, I can see one or two advantages to having representatives from these planets on the station."

Phil thought a moment. "Yeah, you may be right. Where do you suggest we put the offices?"

Gus was feeling left out of the conversation, and he thought he should say something. "There's a row of office space in the lower CentMod on tier 5 that's unoccupied. It's not a prime retail location, and it's far enough from us to keep self-important dignitaries from pestering us."

Phil nodded and said, "That's not bad. I'm going to dump this in your lap, Virginia."

Before she could object, Phil added, "Gus here will be happy to help you with the details." Then he showed them the letters from the foreign offices. "These are the responses from interested parties. I'll have SICOS copy them for you two. From what I can see, these are their requirements."

Virginia and Gus stood up, and Virginia said, very deadpan, "Thanks, Boss," and they went out the door to carry on with their assignments.

Phil turned his attention back to the company letter. Reading on, he saw that corporate decided to assign a senior instructor pilot to the station. His function would be to provide currency training for station customers and to act as flight crew on the Aurora as needed.

Corporate wasn't comfortable with the two highest-ranking company personnel being away from the station whenever the Aurora was needed. Phil wasn't happy about sharing the Aurora with anyone else, as he was starting to think of the shuttle as his own.

Reading on, he saw that the pilot they were sending was named Dwight Needles from Casper, Wyoming. Phil checked Dwight's bio, and that provided few answers and produced more questions. This guy had impressive credentials, but he never advanced past instructor.

In Phil's mind, this Dwight was qualified to be an examiner, which was a pilot that administered the practical exam to hopeful pilots. Now he was limited to teaching primary and advanced flight training along with administering flight reviews to pilots to keep their certification current. It was a lot less demanding than the other areas that he could get involved in. In fact, it was quite easy to make a living without drawing a lot of attention. Unless the pilots that came to him for review were terrible, he could just coast through life without a lot of effort. Phil told himself not to make any judgments until he met Dwight Needles. The letter also heaped loads of praise on Phil and all that were involved in finding the Prospector and a rich source of paxtite. Finally, the corporate president informed Phil that he intended to pay a visit to Oasis 4 in the near future. Phil sat back and thought to himself that this was the downside of retrieving the Prospector. Now the corporate bigwigs will want to meet everyone involved and probably make giant nuisances of themselves. Actually, it was just the corporate president arriving, and Phil actually thought very highly of him.

Next, Phil opened the letters from the cultural departments of the various worlds that they did business with. They had generously committed to donating representative pieces of art or placing them on permanent loan. There were also displays prepared to educate museumgoers about the worlds that do business at the station. The biggest surprise was Flast had committed to the project. They had only just thrown off their previous government, and they're still not used to being an open society.

In Phil's mind, the most helpful feature the letters had was a list of the items being sent and the dimensions of each artifact and the lighting requirements. Phil sent copies of the letters to the museum SICOS, he was going to meet Alice for lunch, and he would tell her about them at that time.

*****

## Earth, Home of Borislav Lovanova, Near Plovdiv, Bulgaria

Borislav Lovanova sat on a patio chair outside his home on a mountainside. It was a remarkably clear day, and he stared across the valley at the city of Plovdiv, Bulgaria. He was still fuming over losing his Astrodyne 65 to that ungrateful Fel Nos. If it wasn't for that betrayal, his obligation to the Syndicate would have been paid ahead of time, allowing him to move up in the organization.

As it is, he had to use some of his earnings to acquire a new vessel. It wasn't as fast or nice as the Astrodyne, but it'll get the job done. The hold on the new vessel, he figured, would be able to accommodate about twenty-five individuals.

He had to put together a new crew that he could trust. It was a tall order, but he had a line on some men in the Syndicate that was ready to move up in the organization. He didn't think there was any way he was going to be able to replace his best gatherer, though, an eager up-and-comer named Marcus Pointer. Pointer was the best at gathering stock than anyone he's ever heard of. After Fel Nos stole the Astrodyne, Pointer went off on his own. He stole a small shuttle and immediately found himself on the run.

Borislav's information is a little sketchy after this point. He heard Pointer disappear into a nebula while eluding authorities. Then he heard that he reconnected with Fel Nos afterward. Now the report is that both of them screwed up and ended up in a Pretna prison. He was sure that Fel Nos most likely did something stupid to end up in prison, and he wasn't sorry in the least. Marcus Pointer being locked up, however, was a reason to be sad. Pointer was an excellent earner, and he was always enthusiastic about doing what he was hired to do.

There wasn't any point in dwelling on what was or what could have been.

There was work to do. He had been sent word that there was going to be an auction on Sisten, and he had to gather stock then deliver.

Timing of these things was critical for maximum profit. The stock had to be gathered, shipped, and delivered before the auction, but not too early, as the traders were responsible for feeding the stock before they were sold. Also, it didn't pay to stay too long where such activities were taking place in case someone objected to the manner of commerce taking place.

There was a report that the Griska government raided a market that he had done business with before. It was bound to happen, but it was of no great concern. For now, he had to select a source for the gathering operation. After selecting a target, he would take his crew there. Once in position, his crew would gather the stock. He would land the ship for loading and be off before the authorities could respond. Ideally, he would be on the ground for less than fifteen minutes. He stood and gazed across the valley toward Plovdiv and took a deep breath. There was planning to do.

*****

## Holid 4, Slave Trader Auction Complex

Major Henson surveyed the destruction his men inflicted on the compound. By any measure, the mission was a success as the principal targets were captured alive, along with six slave ships and their crews. The crews will be turned over to the government on Griska, where they'll be put on trial and sentenced. The shuttles will be turned over to the Stellar Logistics and Freight Corporation since they were paying for a large portion of the operation. It's unlikely the slavers will ever breathe free air ever again. If they outlive their sentences on Griska, they'll be extradited to other governments where there have been offenses.

This planet was barely habitable in Henson's opinion. It was hot and humid, and there wasn't anything here worth being here for. What wasn't rocky was swampy, and even the trees were quite useless, which was exactly the reason the slave traders used it for their transactions. It was remote enough to prevent visitors but not so isolated that it discouraged motivated buyers. Equipment was brought in, and a large area was flattened and a compound was set up.

There were facilities to store the stock and get them presentable for sale. An administration building where the auctions took place and syndicate business were conducted. A luxury resort for the use of buyers and landing pads for transport vessels.

The nature of the layout of this place dictated that the raid had to be carefully planned and executed. Henson divided his men into three groups. Lieutenant Greene led the group that assaulted the complex with the administration building and stock quarters. Lieutenant Yondlyn led the group that secured the landing pad and Luxury hotel. Major Henson set up a command post with First Sergeant Thack and two runners.

The major landed on the landing pad with lieutenant Yondlyn and his group in an Astrodyne 35. It appeared to those on the ground that they were late- arriving buyers, so they didn't raise suspicion. Once the shuttle was secure, the doors flew open, then Yondlyn and his men spread quickly around the ramp securing it and making sure the vessels parked there couldn't leave.

The ground personnel were taken completely by surprise and didn't have time to raise the alarm. Lieutenant Greene and his group suddenly dropped into the compound courtyard in an assault vessel. Greene and his men were on the ground and spreading out within seconds of touching down. The assault vessel was speeding off before the slaver's guards could respond.

Greene's men had the guards neutralized when the slaver's small garrison went into action. By then, the mercenaries had the upper hand. They knew where the garrison guard force was likely to counterattack. The mercenaries had interlocking fields of fire set up, and the guard force was pinned in place. They were actually in several locations that Greene and Yondlyn started methodically neutralizing one at a time. The guards put up a spirited, albeit hopeless, fight.

There were over a hundred guards, and now there were less than ten left to tell the tale. What was left of the guard force was put in the courtyard and cuffed? Yodlyn's men were herding the vessel crews into the courtyard and cuffing them. Greene's men were rounding up everybody that wasn't a slave and dragging them to the courtyard.

During the fighting, there was some damage done to the buildings. The guard barracks were on fire, and a guard shack was in shambles. There were about three hundred people rescued from the slave market who were being attended to by medics that were shuttled down from the *Overlord*. They were in good health, unsurprisingly, since it was impossible to make money selling a person that was sick or injured.

Shuttles were employed to move the rescued to the *Overlord* while Thatt Voffyes and some of his associates were interrogating the operators of this complex. The bosses were separated from the handlers and the shuttle captains from their crews. The crews and handlers were further separated between those who were known/wanted and those who were unknown to authorities.

In the unknown group, the interrogators wrung out as much information as they could in the time they had. Most were so anxious to tell what they knew; the interrogators could barely record everything they related. The more experienced individuals were a different story. In the end, it really didn't matter since the others talked.

After the victims were transported to the *Overlord*, the criminals with warrants were transported. The commander of the *Overlord* had crews retrieve the slaver's vessels that were worth keeping. Major Henson watched as First Sergeant Thack directed his men in placing explosives in the shuttle's damaged to the point they couldn't fly again and the remaining buildings after they were stripped of anything that could be used for intelligence. When they were done, they boarded transports to return to the *Overlord*.

Major Henson strolled to the final transport and turned before boarding to face the slavers that didn't have warrants. They could bring them to Griska for trial and conviction, but they would only get minimum sentences being as they were first-time offenders as far as anyone knew. The official position was they were being released on their own responsibility. The fact is, they were being left on a planet with no food or shelter. Even a survival expert would succumb in due course.

Henson boarded the shuttle and closed the hatch. The shuttle lifted off the pad and pulled away from the surface. Five minutes later, the buildings and remaining shuttles were reduced to rubble and scrap.

*****

## Gostis, Snoshin Agricultural Colony (Independently Governed)

Rosanne Evans was in the fields with a harvester's bag over her shoulder. She was picking what the snoshins called falta. It was a fiber much like cotton in many respects, but it had qualities that were superior to cotton. There were a few problems with it, though.

For one thing, there was no implement devised to harvest the pods that contained the fiber. It seems absurd, but the nature of the plant made it difficult to pick without destroying the plant. The plant would continue to produce the pods as long as they stayed healthy. The pods themselves had a rough texture that cut the hands of the harvesters.

Once picked, the pods were sent to the processing house, where workers would split them and extract the fiber. The extracted fiber was fed into a machine that functioned like a cotton gin from Earth. The resulting product was very much like cotton, except it was tougher and more rot-resistant. The fibers were bailed and sent to markets well away from their source.

All that didn't matter to Rosanne. The only thing she knew was she was doing this very much against her will. The work was hot, and the humidity made the air heavy and difficult to breathe. She wasn't alone in this field as there were dozens of other slaves laboring to harvest the falta.

Every known race was represented although the planet's population in charge was snoshin. There were also snoshin slaves, so who was master and who was slave wasn't a racial issue. The snoshins that colonized this planet believed that they were destined to rule supreme over all they surveyed, and whoever was too weak prevent themselves from getting in the position they were in. Rosanne looked down at her bloody and sore hands. A flaston girl picking falta in the next row hissed a warning. "Boss is looking. Better look busy!" Rosanne resumed her picking before boss could object.

*****

## Oasis 4, Station Manager Office

Phil saw that the day had come when his new instructor pilot was due to arrive. He checked the boards and saw that the ship Dwight Needles was arriving on had been docked for two hours. It wasn't required that new personnel report to the station manager, but he expected that the only instructor pilot would want to make his introductions.

Phil went to the outer office and asked his executive assistant, Jay, "Have you seen the new instructor pilot due in today?"

Jay didn't look up from his work. "I saw Miss Wells directing someone that meets his description about an hour ago."

Phil was a little annoyed that he didn't get a chance to meet the guy he was sure he was going to be working with a great deal. He wanted to get an idea of what he was like before he had a chance to settle in. He went to operations center to find Virginia. Phil found her with her dispatchers, working out a plan for docking freighters.

Phil waited until she finished. "Virginia, could I see you for a moment in Gus's office."

Virginia had an idea what Phil wanted and wasn't anxious to get into the upcoming discussion." She smiled nervously at Phil. "Be right there, Boss."

Phil turned and went to Gus's office and tapped on the doorjamb. "Gus, you, me, and Virginia are going to have a chat about Dwight Needles."

Before Gus could respond, Virginia walked in. "What's happening, Boss?" Phil turned. "Tell me about Dwight Needles."

Virginia didn't hesitate. "He arrived and came to the ops center. I assigned him quarters in HabMod 1 and told him to expect to start work tomorrow."

Phil nodded. "That's great. I don't expect to meet every new arrival, but someone I'm supposed to be personally working with I expect to greet so I can get an idea what he or she is like."

Virginia was starting to feel uncomfortable. "Boss, I didn't think that it was a good idea if you saw him after his long voyage."

Phil could tell she was trying not to divulge too much. "Go on."

Virginia was cornered, and she knew it. "Like I said, Boss. He just had a long voyage, and I thought it would be best if he had a chance to freshen up before you met…"

Phil was starting to get a little irked. "Is there a particular reason for that line of thinking?"

Virginia took a deep breath. "He smelled like he had been drinking. I didn't think it was a big deal since he was just on a passenger liner."

Phil took a breath himself. "I know you're just trying to run interference for him, but he's a big boy. He doesn't need you compromising your integrity."

He looked at Gus. "Feel like doing a flight review tomorrow?"

Gus nodded. "I'm almost due anyway. Might as well get it done early."

Phil turned to Virginia. "Put it on Needle's SICOS that he's doing a flight review tomorrow for three on the *Aurora*."

Virginia frowned. "Who's the third?"

"Chad Kowalski in vessel maintenance. He has a light-speed endorsement, and I want as many company personnel kept current as I can. Chad seems a logical choice being what he can do for us," Phil replied.

Phil thought a second or two, then said, "Jeremy Cole would be another one I'd like kept current. That is if he's a pilot. I'll make it a point to find out."

Virginia sighed. "What time tomorrow, Boss?"

Phil said, "Right after the morning briefing, 09:30 Zulu. I'll go down to CargoMod 8 and talk to Jeremy and Chad when we're done here."

Virginia nodded. "I'll get it scheduled, Boss." Then she turned and left.

Phil was about to leave, and Gus stopped him. "Hold up, Phil. I got a personal letter from Norton Parker yesterday. He wanted me to know that he was well aware that Dwight Needles had issues. The hope is that one of two things will happen. Either we can straighten him out or let him coast."

Phil didn't like the second option. "We'll shake him up. I still have final authority, so he'd better be anxious to do his job or find himself out of a job."

Phil went to CargoMod 8, where he tracked down Jeremy and Chad, who were putting the final touches on a navigation shield array. He waited until he was sure he wasn't interrupting something important, "Hey, guys. We'll be taking the Aurora out tomorrow morning. Is there anything keeping that from happening?"

Jeremy considered it for a second. "No, not a thing. What's the mission, if I may ask?"

Phil had a hint of a smirk. "Our new instructor pilot has arrived, and I'm looking to get the measure of him. Gus and I are going to get our flight reviews in the morning. I wanted Chad to come along also because I want to put a little pressure on him."

Chad nodded. "I'm game. My flight review is getting near due anyway."

Phil smiled. "That's great. We'll be launching at 09:30 Zulu. Jeremy, it would be helpful if there was a list of qualified pilots that we can keep current." Jeremy said he would put one together. Phil left to see if Alice was done playing with her museum so they could go to dinner.

Today was Brenda's day off, so she was helping Alice as she was committed to helping in the museum on her off hours. There were quite a few people involved with the museum project. Mostly dependents of company personnel. There were even a couple of retirees who had made the station home that was helping.

Alice and Brenda were putting the polish on a display when they heard Phil's footsteps behind them. Phil tried to work out what the display was and finally said, "What is that supposed to be?"

Alice smiled in a way that gave him chills. "It's a presentation from Pretna.

You'll see what it is at the opening."

Phil knew better than to press further. He was relieved when Gus walked in and provided an excuse to drop the subject. Gus ambled up. "Are we going to eat or what?"

Alice and Brenda both looked like fine dining was the last thing on their minds. Alice looked at the state of her clothes. "Do you suppose Eva would toss us out?"

That drew a chuckle from Phil. "We would be the first. Come on, let's get a burger."

The foursome sat at their customary table at Eva's having their after-dinner coffees. The subject of their new instructor pilot came up. Gus repeated what Norton Parker had related to him.

Alice smiled. "I haven't seen Nort in a long time."

Gus nodded. "He was made chief pilot for the Stellar Logistics and Freight Corporation after you left the company."

"Nort and I worked together for a short time. I was offered the choice of chief pilot position or manager of Oasis 4. When I took this job, he was offered the chief pilot position," Phil added.

Gus said, "Nort is generally a pretty good judge of character. If he wants us to give Needles some slack, I've got to think he has pretty good reasons."

Phil took a sip of coffee. "I'm trying not to develop any preconceived notions of the guy, but it's hard to ignore what his behavior has been like since being here."

Before Gus could object, Phil continued, "I know I haven't even met him yet, but that, in itself, is telling. I'm reserving judgment until I work with him, and that's the bottom line. We have to work together, and anything that disrupts the working relationship has to be dealt with or jettisoned."

Gus looked up. "Oh, hey. Speak of the devil, here he comes. Over there, wearing tan pants and nylon flight jacket."

Phil and the rest turned and had a look. Dwight Needles was lanky, as you would expect someone to be that hailed from Casper Wyoming.

He was also a bit scruffy looking with at least two days' growth of facial hair.

Phil and the rest watched as Needles stopped at the CentMod Plaza Level and looked around. Gus said, "He looks okay to me."

Then Needles smiled, crossed the CentMod, and went into Sparky's. Gus said in a very deadpan manner. "I'm not saying he won't be a bit of a project, though."

*****

## CargoMod 2, Docking Port 1

In the morning, after the briefing, Phil met Gus and Chad at CargoMod 2 near the docking port occupied by the Aurora. Phil said, "We'll use the landing pad June Dixon had us use, then we'll return for docking evaluations." He checked his watch. "That is if Dwight ever gets here."

Gus frowned. "I hope he didn't spend too much time at Sparky's."

Phil said, "I checked the security monitors before the morning briefing and saw him leaving at 02:00 Zulu."

Gus was downcast. "I hope he gets here soon. I hate to think that he's so far gone that he blows off his first assignment at his new posting." Phil thought a minute and said, "However this goes, whatever my reaction is, let me deal with it. Just trust me to know how to deal with him."

Gus didn't like being restrained like that, but he had learned to trust Phil and his intuition when it came to dealing with people. At 09:35 Zulu, Dwight Needles finally showed.

Phil smiled brightly and grasped Dwight's hand. He couldn't help but notice that Dwight didn't manage to improve his appearance, and he smelled like a combination of alcohol, mint, and aftershave, "Hi, you must be Dwight Needles. I'm Phil Ross, and I'm told you've worked with Gus Condent here."

Dwight attempted to smile through the hangover and greeted Phil back in his western drawl. "Shore nice to meet you, Phil."

Then he shook Gus's hand. "Haven't seen you in a coon's age, Gus."

Phil motioned Dwight to the Hatch. "There's one more on board, Chad Kowalski from vessel maintenance. He's on board now, warming the systems. It's completely up to you, but there's a moon orbiting a gas giant that has a practice landing pad we've used before. It's about 350 light-years away. Then we can return and take turns docking."

Dwight stopped in the passageway and turned to Phil. "That all sounds like a right smart way to do things, fellas. If you don't mind, I'd like to use one of these cabins to get a couple of winks in. I'm still a might outa sorts from traveling."

Phil nodded. "That sounds fine, Dwight."

*****

## The *Aurora,* Astrodyne 65, Operated by the Stellar Logistics and Freight Corporation

Dwight found a cabin while Phil and Gus joined Chad in the cockpit. Chad went to give up the pilot's seat, and Phil stopped him. "You take the first shift, Chad. I want you to get a feel for how it handles thrusters. It occurred to me that you never had a chance to do anything other than cruise."

Chad nodded assent and started going through the checklist. Gus sat at the copilot's position. "Are you letting him play out a little rope?"

Phil smiled. "Just a little. I think we can salvage him with the right kind of encouragement."

Gus stared at Phil with a bemused expression.

Phil smiled and shrugged. "What can I say? I like the guy."

Chad got clearance to launch, and the docking clamps were released. He used the thrusters until he was given clearance to fire the reaction engines. He started the Detroit 750s and set it to idle. There was the customary lurch they were getting used to. Chad eased the power levers forward to maximum. There were a couple of course corrections necessary that Chad made efficiently. When he was satisfied that they were on the correct course, he engaged the light-speed engines. Phil and Gus exchanged looks of approval at Chad's handling of the *Aurora.*

After a while, they had reached the gas giant and identified the proper moon. Then Chad set the approach vectors in the navigation computer. Phil looked at Gus. "Go ahead and get Dwight."

Gus asked, "Why do I have to be the one to get him?"

Phil grinned. "'Cuz I ain't his buddy who ain't seen him in a coon's age." Gus stood up. "That's fair."

Gus returned shortly with Dwight. Phil started to get up to give Dwight his seat when Dwight motioned for him to remain there. "I want to assess how you guys handle cockpit management. I know this vessel can be handled by a single pilot, but since there are three of you, it's a good opportunity."

Chad relaxed in the pilot's seat. "Okay, before landing, checklist, please."

Phil read off each item, and Chad made the proper responses. Chad put the *Aurora* on a decent path to the landing pad. At just a few feet above the landing pad, Chad idled the thrusters and gave them gentle pulses when the Aurora's descent accelerated faster than he wanted. The *Aurora* eventually settled gently on the pad.

Dwight was making notes on a pad at the time. "Chad, be gentle with the thrusters when you get near the landing pad. I noticed back at the station that you were a little heavy-handed with them." Chad reached up and cut power to the thrusters.

Dwight jerked his head up. "Don't cut those until we land, boy!" Chad was, in turn, annoyed and amused at Dwight's admonishment.

"We've landed about fifteen seconds ago, Dwight."

Phil and Gus exchanged looks; Chad just made them look like a pair of rookies. If their eyes were closed, there's no way that they could have known they had landed.

Dwight was momentarily speechless. "Good job, Chad. Lift off and trade seats with Phil."

Chad reached up and powered the thrusters, then he gently lifted off, and once above the moon's surface, he traded seats with Phil. Phil successfully set up the approach and landed squarely on the pad. It wasn't as smooth as Chad's landing, but Phil deemed it in his top ten.

Gus' landing was also one for the books, which made him grin. After Gus took off from the pad, Phil said, "Your turn, Dwight."

Dwight looked defensive. "Hey, I'm not under evaluation."

Phil leaned back. "Actually, you are. As the manager of Oasis 4, I'm obligated to evaluate the performance of incoming personnel."

Dwight slowly nodded. "Okay, okay, I'll take the seat."

As he sat, Phil saw his hand had a slight tremble. Dwight established a glide path to the landing pad. He was starting to regret admonishing Chad about being heavy-handed on the thrusters. The thrusters on the Aurora were oversize and required an extremely light touch. Fel Nos had them installed in anticipation of salvaging the *Prospector*. The result was a very touchy set of controls.

Beads of sweat were forming on Dwight's forehead. The aft right landing gear was the first to touch. Dwight tried to adjust the attitude but overcompensated. The *Aurora* bounced and danced on the pad until Dwight could get the oscillations dampened, and the *Aurora* settled down. Chad was in the copilot seat. He looked over to Dwight and explained about the thrusters. Dwight said, very deadpan, "Well, that would do it."

Phil and Gus were grateful they were behind Dwight, so he couldn't see them smirking. Phil said, "Dwight, why don't you take off and take the leg back to the station."

Dwight was eager to prove he wasn't a completely incompetent individual, so he readily agreed. He powered the thrusters and performed a shaky but acceptable liftoff then set the *Aurora* on a course back to the station.

Dwight was determined more than ever to show he knew what he was doing. "All the Astrodyne's I've ever flown, you had to boost the reaction engines to 25 percent right away to get any kind of speed out of them."

Chad said, "Hold up, Dwight—"

Dwight cut him off, "Listen, son. I've been flying Astrodyne's while you were building plastic models of them."

Before Chad could protest again, Dwight engaged the reaction engines and pushed the power levers to the 25 percent position. Just idling, the reaction engines on the *Aurora* pinned the occupants in their seats. At 25 percent, the inertia neutralizers were nearly useless. Dwight's eyes bugged out. He was quite overwhelmed and knew it. He tried to move his arms but immediately knew he wouldn't be able to until they were done accelerating. He said the only thing that came to mind. "Gaaall Daaang!"

When the Aurora stopped accelerating, Chad looked over to Dwight. "One of the modifications made was swapping out the stock reaction engines for Ion injected Detroit 750s."

A wild-eyed Dwight stared straight ahead. "That would do it."

Dwight gently eased the power levers forward. When they were at maximum velocity, he was about to engage the light-speed engines and hesitated. "What am I in for with these?"

Chad reassured Dwight. "The light-speed engines are more powerful than the originals, but they're smooth."

Dwight engaged the light-speed engines and accelerated to LS 1. He moved the slides forward and watched the velocity indicator. At LS 5, he started to frown. As they passed LS 8, the *Aurora* started rumbling. Dwight relaxed slightly. "The 65 usually does that at LS 5."

Chad nodded. "There's a few things that are different on the *Aurora*. The most efficient cruise setting is LS 9."

After Dwight set the *Aurora* on a course back to the station, Gus went to the galley and brought up box lunches and coffee.

Dwight cut the light-speed engines and restarted the reaction engines when they had reached the proper checkpoint. Phil was actually impressed with the precision Dwight displayed in coming out of light speed.

Dwight contacted the station and received vectors. The controller assigned them CargoMod 3, Docking Port 15. Phil explained that the controllers were asked to give them four different docking assignments, with the last one being at CargoMod 2 Docking Port 1 so that everyone could demonstrate a docking maneuver. Dwight took a deep breath, "I guess I'm first."

The controller vectored him into position, and he bumped the thrusters inching the *Aurora* closer to the docking clamps. Dwight still tended to overcontrol the thrusters. Phil thought that the *Aurora* must have looked drunk with all the wobbling it was doing. Finally, Dwight managed to get the docking clamps engaged.

After Dwight relaunched, Phil took his turn, then Gus took his. Chad took the controls for the final docking, and he didn't fail to impress. They couldn't feel the docking clamps engage; he had done such a smooth job of it. The engines were shut down, and the power source was switched over from internal to the station.

Phil said, "Well, guys, let's do the logbooks in the galley dining room, that is if Dwight is going to approve us."

Dwight signed all three logbooks. Paper logbooks were a throwback to a bygone era since electronic logbooks have been acceptable for centuries, but most pilots prefer to put ink on paper. When that was done, Gus and Chad shook hands with Dwight.

Phil put his own logbook in his flight bag. "Guys, this has been a good day. Gus, let's see if the ladies are ready for dinner in a few minutes. Chad, you're welcome to tag along."

Chad chuckled. "Don't want to be a fifth wheel, Mr. Ross." Then he took his leave.

Phil continued, "I'd like to have a word with you if I could, Dwight."

Gus left Phil and Dwight in the galley. Dwight couldn't look Phil in the eye. He suspected that Phil wasn't happy with first impressions. Phil poured a cup of coffee for both of them and sat across Dwight.

Dwight just said, "I know what you're going to say, Phil. I'll make it easy for you. I'll book passage on a freighter and be out of your hair. After the dis-play I put on today, I can't blame you."

Phil sighed. "I don't want you to leave, Dwight."

That got Dwight's attention, and Phil continued, "I'll admit I was put out when you didn't report to me when you arrived yesterday. Then I learned why you were steered away from me. I watched you go into Sparky's last night, and after checking the security monitors, I learned you didn't leave until two in the morning. Five minutes late for an appointment with the new boss. I could smell the booze on you. To be frank, I can still smell the booze on you."

Dwight interrupted, "My flying didn't impress anyone today." Phil nodded. "You had a couple of things going against you. First, the *Aurora* is a touchy machine, and you're not familiar with it. Being hung over didn't help."

Dwight took a deep breath. "What do we do next, Boss?"

Phil took a sip of coffee and considered his answer. "I don't throw people away. Particularly those that show some talent. Yes, you flew like a rookie today, but I saw enough to see that you had some genuine skills, even if they weren't on dis-play today. Here's what's going to happen. Tomorrow, you'll report to Virginia Wells and finish your in-processing. You'll be in Virginia's department. I don't know what else to do with you since we don't have a flight department, per se. We're going to get you straight Dwight. Nort Parker thinks you're worth the effort. I've known Nort for a while now, and I know he's a pretty good judge of character."

Dwight looked relieved. "You haven't asked me why I fell into a 'self- destructive cycle' as they would say."

Phil polished off his coffee. "I don't figure it's my business. My business is the operation of this station and the welfare of everyone in it. As long as your personal life doesn't affect those two things, your business is your business."

Dwight finished his own coffee. "I owe it to you. I'm not a drunk. At least I didn't start that way. About six months ago, I took a hit in my personal life."

Phil interrupted, "It's not hard to guess what happened. Only a woman can make a guy want to turn his life into a shuttle wreck."

Dwight laughed, probably for the first time in a while. "You got that right, Hoss."

Phil stood up. "You're the most qualified pilot on the station. You're welcome to get into the other areas that are in your purview. For now, get yourself cleaned up, rested, and report to Virginia Wells tomorrow morning after the briefing, about 08:30 Zulu. By the way, she stuck her neck out trying to cover for you yesterday, I think you owe her an apology."

Dwight nodded. "You can bet the ranch I will, Hoss." Phil grinned. "Sober."

"Sober," Dwight confirmed.

*****

## Gostis, Home of Toanin Zisros

Toanin Zisros stood on one of the many balconies that adorned his home on Gostis. The balcony overlooked one of the vast falta fields that he owned. The troublesome fiber was making him rich along with his associates. Toanin was truly the master of all he surveyed. He was ruthless enough to dominate those around him and establish himself in the upper tier of society on Gostis called the elite class.

There were other free snoshins here that were in a class called the taskmasters. The taskmasters made sure the slaves did their jobs. Yet another class of snoshin on Gostis was the warrior class. They could never rise to the level the elites were at, even the officers. Their function was to protect the way of life that has been established on this planet.

Toanin and his peers had a genuine concern: to truly establish a hierarchy, the slave class had to be indigenous. Slaves that were captured elsewhere and brought here had an independent streak; the humans were particularly troublesome.

The discussion among his peers was to establish breeding centers. Slaves with qualities that were desirable would be paired with the opposite gender and produce offspring. There was some resistance among the others in the elite class concerning this plan. They didn't like the fact that they would have to wait at least until the slave reached puberty before they could get any use out of them.

They were finally swayed when they realized that the slaves wouldn't be as independent-minded. Another thing that's driving the push to start breeding their slaves was the rumors circulating of an effort building to end the activities of the slave vendors. After they start their breeding program, that wouldn't be a concern.

Some of Toanin's peers expressed concern that the activities of the slave vendors would draw attention to their planet, and their way of life would be put to an end. Personally, Toanin thought that possibility was remote. As far as he was concerned, aliens had no right to demand how they conducted themselves on their own planet. If the offended aliens decided to make war, that was also of little concern. Invading a planet was an immensely difficult task.

The flastons tried to take a planet from the pretars in the distant past and regretted it. Apparently, getting an invasion force on a planet isn't the only hurdle; supplying that force is critical. The flastons were brave, but all the courage in the galaxy wouldn't defeat an enemy when the supplies ran out.

All in all, Toanin felt secure that even if the social order on Gostis was discovered, there wasn't much anyone could do about it. In fact, he thought that they would serve as an example of how to properly structure a society.

*****

## Oasis 4, Lower CentMod, Office of I&F
## Investigations and Retrievals

Isnod and Feldon had worked a deal with Phil on a small office in the Lower CentMod plaza level. They were now officially licensed bounty hunters. Due to agreements, they had to be licensed, registered, and have an official office.

There were still some items that they needed to acquire, most notably a shuttle. Their new office had a desk, each with computer terminals that were tied into the SICOS, and there was also some furniture that Will Dawson scrounged up for them. The pair had plenty of funds left over from the bounty the pretars paid them for recapturing Fel Nos and Marcus Pointer, but that wouldn't hold forever.

Feldon was going over the files he had downloaded, which were the modern versions of wanted posters. One of the postings caught his attention, and he started additional searches. After some checking, he looked over to Isnod. "I think I found one that meets our needs."

Isnod rolled his chair over so he could see Feldon's display. He read the posting and furrowed his brow. "Losnic Rullot, thief. Why this guy?"

Feldon smiled. "Look at what he was fond of stealing."

Isnod wasn't impressed with Feldon's find yet. "I see he liked other people's shuttles, but that doesn't do us any good. He's a grunst, who is known to do business at Kassnins trading colony."

Feldon said, "Look at what they're offering for reward."

Isnod continued reading and started to smile. "Mr. Losnic Rullot must be a thorn in the side of whoever he keeps stealing shuttles from."

Feldon thought a minute and added, "We might as well see if there is anyone else wanted at Kassnins colony that we can profit from."

Isnod chuckled. "This might turn out to be a good trip. That is if we can get there. I'll start checking for vessels that are going in that direction."

*****

## Gostis, Falta Plantation of Toanin Zisros

Rosanne Evans struggled with her harvest bag in the waning Gostis sun. She handed it to a malnun, who emptied it into a wagon and tossed the bag back down. Every bone and muscle in her body ached and protested each movement. Falta was harvested whenever there was enough light, which was eighteen hours on Gostis. Thankfully, there were nine hours of the nighttime to rest. A typical day started before dawn with a trip to the restroom and then a crude breakfast, which was usually a runny porridge. Then they had to be in the fields before the sun came up, ready to pick falta pods. A lunch was provided or what passed for lunch. It was usually a soup made from a local bean that Rosanne loathed. She ate it anyway because she knew it was a good source of protein. After they consumed a bowl of the bean soup, it was another nine hours in the fields. Thankfully, when the sun set, they would be led back to their quarters, where they had a meal, cleaned up, and went to bed.

When she first arrived, she would often break down at night and sob uncontrollably. She was past that for the most part. Now she concentrated on surviving until the day she could leave. It's been just over two years since she was kidnapped. At that time, the only true friend she made was a flaston girl about her age named Tillya. That's not to say she didn't get along with the other slaves, as they all reasoned that they were in the same predicament and needed to cooperate with each other.

Rosanne and Tillya made a connection soon after they arrived at this farm. After she picked up her empty harvest bag, she saw Tillya struggling to lift her own bag to the malnun loading the wagon. Rosanne reached up and helped Tillya push the bag up to the malnun. The bag was emptied and thrown back down to Tillya, who clutched it tightly. Rosanne put her hands on Tillya's shoulders. "Common, let's get cleaned up and fed."

Tillya smiled and said sarcastically. "I hope I don't eat too much."

*****

## Oasis 4, Office of Phil Ross, Station Manager

Phil was checking his correspondence before the morning briefing. There was a letter from the corporate president, Elias Gilmore. Phil and Elias were friends from Phil's shuttle pilot days, and Elias was station manager of Earth Orbiting Station number 3.

Phil quickly scanned the letter and saw that Elias was going to be at the station to welcome the dignitaries that had opened consulates on the station and also for the opening of the museum. He was bringing Norton Parker and an executive assistant with him.

Phil was also made aware that he had to organize a reception for the dignitaries that were opening consulates at the station. The most surprising thing Phil saw was they purposely timed their visit to coincide with the arrival of the *Overlord*.

Checking the chronometer, he saw it was time for the morning briefing, so he grabbed a pad and headed for the briefing room. Entering the room, he poured a cup of coffee and took his seat at the head of the table. After hearing the department reports, Phil handed out assignments regarding the upcoming visit from the brass. The last of the consulate dignitaries had already arrived, and Alice had the museum ready for its grand opening.

*****

## Kassnins Trading Planet

Isnod and Feldon sat at their seats on a shuttle, ferrying them from the orbiting freighter that brought them to Kassnins to the planet's surface, and they were anxious to get to work. Isnod looked at Feldon, who was busily checking his equipment. He couldn't carry the tools of his trade openly since they were trying to pass unnoticed while they were here.

Isnod furrowed his brow. "Have you ever been here, Feldon?"

Feldon didn't look up from his activities. "No, I haven't, but I've heard that this place can be a challenge."

Isnod smiled. "That's something of an understatement. This place started as a legitimate trading colony, and there's still a great deal of above-board business here, but as with many places like this, a seedy element was attracted. After a few decades, the local government became so corrupted they were unable and unwilling to clean itself up. As a result, we cannot count on any official assistance if we need it. In fact, we have to be careful, as we don't know if our targets have paid the local authorities for protection. We may find ourselves in a cell."

That got Feldon's attention. "It would have been nice to know that ahead of time."

The shuttle landed, and the passengers went their separate ways. Isnod and Feldon went to the terminal lobby, where they consulted an informational computer terminal. Feldon entered the name "Losnic Rullot," then he started to smile thinly. "He didn't even use an alias."

Isnod nodded. "He doesn't feel the need. Bounty hunters generally avoid this place. What pad is his ship on?"

Feldon ran his finger down the display "Pad 26," then he smiled. "It's a Pulsar 1250."

Isnod nodded. "Let's see if he's there."

They walked to Pad 26 and found the shuttle unoccupied. The pair approached the shuttle and discovered that it was left unsecured. Feldon frowned and said, "This one is either very confident or very stupid."

Isnod considered it and said, "Probably both. Let's check inside."

They went through the hatch and looked around. Feldon shook his head. "It doesn't look like he's residing on board, and I'm not seeing anything here that indicates where he might be staying."

Isnod nodded. "It looks like we have more work to do. Come on, let's see if there is someone here who can point us in the right direction." They exited the shuttle and closed the hatch. Isnod spotted a ground crewman several pads over and smiled. He leaned over to Feldon. "Follow my lead. Act like we're looking this shuttle over."

Feldon suppressed a grin. "I'll make it look good."

When Isnod had judged the ground crewman was close enough, he said in a voice that wasn't overly loud but just loud enough to show he wasn't concerned with who heard him. "Feldon, this Rullot fellow said this vessel had low hours."

Feldon was peering into an access panel. "This appears to be what was advertised. I would recommend we purchase this vessel."

Isnod made sure the approaching ground crewman was paying attention. "Very good, Feldon. Mr. Rullot is supposed to be here to finalize the transaction."

The ground crewman strolled over. "Excuse me, gentlemen, but I don't recognize you. Are you certain Mr. Rullot is expecting you?"

Isnod turned to the man and acted like he was surprised that he was there.

Then he made a show of collecting himself. "Ah! You know Mr. Rullot then?"

The ground crewman was now caught a bit off guard. "Well, I've only dealt with him here in regard to his vessel."

Isnod now had a feel of the temperament of the man. "Sir, it would be helpful if you knew where we could find Mr. Rullot. He has obviously been detained."

The man straightened. "I suppose he would be upset if he couldn't complete a deal. I heard him say he was staying at Morrok's Inn. I understand he meets clients there also."

After Isnod thanked the ground crewman and gave him a tip, they left the shuttle port for the village nearby. Calling it a village is being kind. It was a motley collection of seedy bars and warehouses. The warehouses were full of largely stolen goods, and the bars was full of riffraff of every description. Oddly, Isnod felt comfortable here, not quite at home, but familiar surroundings gave him confidence.

Feldon was the first to spot Morrok's, and they entered. The interior was dimly lit, and it took a few seconds for their eyes to adjust. Isnod spied Rullot sitting at a table in the corner and gave Feldon a nudge. They both bought tankards of a frothy drink a human would call an alcoholic version of root beer, then strolled to Rullot's table and sat.

Rullot looked annoyed. "I don't remember inviting two flastons to drinks."

Isnod lifted his drink and stopped just short of his lips. "We're not in the habit of drinking with grunst. But we have need of a man of your talents and resourcefulness."

Losnic was the kind of man that could smell money. Once he had the scent of precious metal in his nose, all other considerations went by the wayside. He grinned and took a sip of his drink. "Which of my talents are you in need of, and how resourceful would I need to be?"

Isnod had to suppress a smile. "We are in need of a shuttle and a pilot. But we can't use a junker that its owner would gladly pay us to take off their hands."

Losnic chuckled. "I have one in inventory that might suit your needs."

Isnod nodded. "It would have to be at least a five-passenger model with a small area for cargo or equipment storage."

Losnic finished his drink. "You're in luck. I have a low-time Pulsar 1250 that would suit your needs about right. It's an eight-passenger model with a decent amount of cargo area."

Isnod looked disappointed. "We were hoping to find an Astrodyne 23 or 25.

I'm not familiar with the Pulsar."

Losnic shook his head. "The difference between the two is minimal for most applications. The Astrodyne is a fantastic utility machine, a real work animal, but the Pulsar is more stylish. Don't get me wrong. It's still a very good machine for work, but they've put a little more into style and creature comforts."

Isnod leaned over to Feldon, and they whispered to each other. Finally, Isnod nodded. "We would have to see the machine before we commit."

Losnic stood. "That's very wise. Why don't you gentlemen finish your drinks, and we'll go to the shuttle port together?"

They found themselves back at the Pulsar in less than an hour. After pointing out features on the shuttle's exterior, Losnic opened the hatch. "Follow me, gentlemen. The real selling point is the interior."

Losnic led them inside and started pointing out features when Feldon interrupted, "Excuse me, Mr. Rullot." Losnic turned, and Feldon grabbed his hand, twisted it palm up, and bent his wrist back toward him. Losnic immediately went to his knees and brought up his free hand to try to free himself, which made Feldon apply more pressure.

Isnod pulled an instrument out of his pocket and put a portion of it in Losnic's mouth. A push of a button and a clamp was applied to Losnic's cheek. Isnod stared at the instrument's display until a green indicator illuminated. He nodded. "DNA confirms that this is indeed Mr. Losnic Rullot."

They applied shackles to Losnic's wrists and ankles. Feldon looked at Losnic. "Why don't we take a page out of the human security officer's book."

He then trussed up and hog-tied Losnic. With that done, Isnod stuffed a gag in his mouth and stood back. He then looked at Feldon, "That went pretty smooth. There are three more here we can grab and really make this venture profitable."

Before the day was over, they had managed to locate and lure the three additional targets back to the shuttle. Isnod and Feldon were becoming well aware of how valuable someone else's greed could be. When the four fugitives were secured, Isnod and Feldon powered up their new Pulsar shuttle and left the surface. The bounty offered by the Pulsar Corporation was the shuttle that Losnic was trying to sell, so it was indeed a profitable day.

*****

**Caravel 500 Owned by Borislav Lovanova**

Borislav Lovanova was orbiting a moon of the eighth planet in in the Nitus star system. It was out of the way and a good place to wait until his stock gatherers could do their job. He had dropped them in a fairly remote location on the third planet in this system, the inhabitants called Ashbury.

The operation was simple enough: first, have a scout identify a likely target; an isolated village was best. The scout would select a target that was easily subdued. The slave gatherers had to be able to control the population.

They would swoop in, subdue the population, and select the most likely stock for maximum profit. Profits were going to be down following his latest business model. His new shuttle doesn't hold as much as the Astrodyne he had to sign over to that ungrateful Fel Nos. That also meant that he had to use a "contractor" to gather stock instead of a crew he brought with him. He had crewmen of his own to attend to the slaves en route. The crewmen were on the target planet, aiding the contract gatherers.

Checking the chronometer, he saw that he had about half an hour before he had to make his way back to Ashbury.

*****

**Ashbury, Human Colony**

Jason Gannet stood on a hilltop, overlooking the target village. The lead contractor stepped up next to him and asked in a low voice, "Are you sure about this place?"

Jason grinned. "As sure as I could possibly be. These people are real throwbacks. They've rejected technology of any kind and definitely, no weapons."

The contractor chuckled. "This place is too good to be true."

Jason used night vision binoculars to survey the village. "That large buividing off the village square looks like some sort of community center. We'll do the sorting there." He paused. "Well, let's get started."

The contractors worked quickly and efficiently, going silently from house to house. The villagers made it easy for them by not bothering to lock the doors.

The gatherers used stun guns to make sure their quarry remained compliant. When they awoke, they found themselves gagged and shackled. Once they were satisfied that everyone was under their control, they would bring them to a central location for sorting. The building the contractors were using for sorting was indeed used as a community center and meeting hall.

Jason started by separating the children under ten from the rest. Their monetary value was nil as they were too young to be of much use. That's not to say there wasn't a market for kids, but they didn't bring top price, so it wasn't worth the effort to transport them although he had heard Borislav say there may be increased demand for children in the future.

As Jason worked, he saw that most adults had dilated pupils. He laughed. "Do all of you get stoned every night?"

One of the contractors continued with what he was doing and remarked, "Judging from the crops they're growing out there, I'd say they were probably baked most of the time."

He tore the adhesive gag off one of the male adults. The man was frantically trying to make sense of what was happening. "Hey, man! You guys need to get centered, and you need to learn to live in balance, man!"

The contractor pulled his firearm from a holster and put the muzzle against the villager's forehead. "Am I going to have trouble with you?"

The man's eyes widened. "Hey, man! Guns aren't allowed here!" Jason overheard the conversation and laughed. "Yeah, I know.

What's your name?"

The man kept his cross-eyed stare at the gun placed between his eyes. "It's Oliver, man."

Jason laughed and said, "Well, Oliver, where you're going, you won't have to worry about guns."

When the sorting was nearly done, a shuttle landed in a field just outside the village, and another one landed in the village square. Jason smiled. "That sounds like Caravel 500 to me."

Lovanova stepped out of the shuttle, carrying a small duffel. He went into the community building, where Jason greeted him. "There they are, Mr. Lovanova." Lovanova cast a critical eye on the ones that Jason selected. "Very good. I count twenty-five."

He looked closer. "What's wrong with their eyes?" Jason laughed. "They've been self-medicating." Lovanova had his own laugh. "Get them loaded."

He handed the duffel to the lead contractor, who opened it and smiled, then he directed his men to help with the loading. The villagers that the slavers weren't interested in were left in the community building. The contractors boarded their own shuttle parked in the field outside the village and left in a cloud of dust and noise.

When Borislav was satisfied that he was ready, he lifted off out of the village square, accelerated to the upper atmosphere, and then to space. The newly acquired slaves were wedged in tight, but that wasn't a concern. He would have grabbed the whole village if he could have, but the shuttle wouldn't hold all of them.

*****

## Oasis 4, Office of Station Manager

Phil sat at his desk, going over paperwork and generally catching up on filing reports that corporate was always demanding. One of the motivations he had was the arrival of corporate bigwigs today. The president of Stellar Logistics and Freight Corporation, Chief Pilot Norton Parker, and other assorted VIPs and their executive assistants.

Phil decided that they would be most comfortable in HabMod 8. The quarters there were configured for visiting dignitaries and their attendants. Phil made sure the quarters were stocked with potables and enough food so that the occupants could have a snack.

The corporate VIPs were arriving in the afternoon shortly after lunch, where Phil was going to greet them and take them on a tour of the station, then afterward, dinner at Maurice's. He wondered if cocktails afterward were appropriate, then he decided after some thought that he should play that by ear.

Tomorrow was going to be a busy day indeed. In the morning, there was going to be a short ceremony to officially open the consulates on the station, followed by a meet-and-greet luncheon afterward. After that, Alice and the other museum volunteers were scheduled to have a ribbon cutting and grand opening. Having done everything he needed to do, he decided it was lunchtime.

Passing Gus's office, he tapped on the doorjamb. "Hey, Gus, lunch?"

Gus put down a pencil. "You read my mind." They decided to eat at Eva's, of course. While eating, they discussed the upcoming visit from the corporate brass. Phil spotted Virginia going into Baja Juans with a gentleman, and he furrowed his brow. "Who is that going into Juans with Virginia? I don't reco—oh my goodness! That's Needles!"

Phil was flabbergasted. Dwight was clean-shaven, pressed, and sported shined boots. He was even wearing a bolo tie. Phil remarked, "He cleans up halfway decent."

Gus nodded. "I've been keeping an eye on him. He's done a bunch of flight reviews, and I saw he was studying for the pilot examiner's test. I don't know what you told him that first day, but it seems to have had an effect."

Phil chuckled and said, "I just helped him realize that there were things worth doing besides spiraling down to oblivion. What you just saw was all him. By the way, where does Dwight spend his time when he's not doing reviews?"

Gus sipped his coffee and said, "Virginia had Jeremy find an office for him in CargoMod 8. There were already classrooms there and testing facilities. It seemed a natural move. Dwight is also getting pretty tight with Jeremy and his crew."

Phil finished his coffee and checked his watch. "Let's see if the *City of Akron* is on the approach."

Phil and Gus stood in the control center and watched through binoculars as the *City of Akron* made its approach. The controller assigned them CargoMod 1, Docking Port 2. When the *City of Akron* engaged the docking clamps, Phil put down his binoculars and said to Gus, "Well, let's go see the boss."

They arrived in time to be there when the air lock was opened. The first to step onto the station was Corporation President Elias Gilmore. He smiled broadly. "Phil, my boy!"

Phil smiled back. "Good to see you, sir."

Elias gripped Phil's hand and shook it warmly. "It's been too long. You've been doing great work for us, both of you." Then he gripped Gus's hand and shook it enthusiastically.

Next out of the air lock was Norton Parker. "Hey, Crash, it's good to see you!"

Phil grinned. "Holy smokes, Nort! It's been a long time." He shook Norton's hand. "I thought we were friends until you sent this guy." He chuckled, nodding toward Gus.

Norton grabbed Gus's hand. "Have you learned how not to run a space station yet?" he asked jokingly.

Gus smiled. "Not everything yet. It's a pretty steep learning curve."

Phil was surprised to see three more people he knew stepping out of the air lock. There was Erica Gainsly, the station manager of Oasis 1, Thomas Grandall, the station manager of Oasis 2, and Victor Higgins, the station manager of Oasis 3.

Phil was good friends with all of them and greeted his friends. Erica even gave him a hug. "Phillip Ross, where's your better half?"

Phil was caught flat-footed and offered an explanation. "If I had known you were coming, I would have made sure she was here. As it is, she's busy putting the finishing touches on her latest pet project. I'll make sure you two sit next to each other at dinner."

Erica smiled. "That would be great."

Erica was a controller who worked with Alice some time ago. She and Alice were contenders for the station manager position on Oasis 1 when Alice decided that being married to Phil was challenging enough.

Elias apologized. "Sorry, I didn't give you any warning, Phil. At the last minute, I came on the idea of bringing these three. They were all able to catch transports to Raytheon, where we all met for the last leg here."

Phil was grinning. "I'm certainly glad you did. This is an unexpected treat."

Phil went to the nearest communication terminal and paged Virginia, "Hey, Virginia, we need three additional quarters prepped in HabMod 8."

Virginia, who was well aware of Elias's habits, suspected something like this would happen, so she had several extra quarters prepared. She replied, "No problem, Boss."

Phil conducted the tour of the station. Oasis 2 and 3 were similar in design to Oasis 4, but it was different enough to hold the interest of the other managers. Oasis 4 was not only the newest of the four. It was the largest before the station was expanded. Now it's by far the most impressive station in the Stellar Logistics and Freight Corporation system. Phil mused that if they had ever seen a Pretar orbiting station, they would be less impressed with his.

When they reached CargoMod 8, Elias and the rest were immensely interested in the operation there. They could readily see the advantage of offering repair services on this scale. They passed the classroom facilities, and Norton Parker saw through a window that there was a class being conducted. Then all at once, he recognized who was conducting the class. "Oh my goodness, that's Dwight Needles!"

Phil edged up next to Norton and said, "He cleans up halfway deceit, doesn't he, Nort?"

Norton chuckled. "You'll have to tell me how you managed that." Phil shrugged. "I can't take much credit for it. I just made him take a hard look at himself and offered a path for him to get himself together. Distance and change of scenery did the rest."

Dwight dismissed his class and started to straighten the things on the desk. Phil tapped the glass, and Dwight looked up and grinned when it registered with him who Phil was standing there with. He came out the door and gave Norton a very warm handshake. After the greetings, Dwight asked, "We going to see you at supper, Nort?"

Norton nodded and smiled. "You bet I am." He couldn't quite believe that this was the same guy that he had sent here.

After the tour, they went to Maurice's for dinner, where Phil and Alice had a busy evening entertaining and catching up with old friends. They saw their guest at their quarters in HabMod 8 before going to their own in HabMod 1.

In the morning, Phil and Alice went through their usual routine then it was breakfast at Eva's. Shortly after they ordered, Elias and Norton were passing, and Phil called them over, "Please sit. This is the best breakfast and lunch venue on the station."

The four of them ate and enjoyed each other's company. Phil's known Elias for most of his career at Stellar Logistics and knew him as an effective manager. Elias's specialty was business administration, and Phil thought he was the best at it than anyone he ever knew. In fact, Phil tried to pattern his own management style after Elias.

Finally, during their coffees, Elias said, "Phil, there's a bit of business we might as well talk about now. It might save some time later. That was a great bit of work you did in retrieving the *Prospector*. I realize that much of it was luck and circumstance, but a lot of people in your position wouldn't have taken the chance."

Elias took a sip of coffee. "With that being said, everyone involved deserves some sort of bonus. What percentage everyone gets has yet to be decided. It's fair to say that there will be a few people who won't have any financial problems, ever. Oh, and I'm not forgetting, Captain Hastings of the *Goldfield* and his cartographer, Beverly Ashton."

Phil smiled. "I had forgotten all about any finder's fee. I'm sure the others will appreciate the consideration."

When breakfast was over, Phil extended an invitation to Elias to attend the morning briefing that Elias declined. He said he would see the Oasis 4 management at the reception later.

The presentation welcoming consulate officials was held in the upper CentMod theater. Phil acted as master of ceremony, introducing Elias, who made some remarks, then each one of the station's department heads had an opportunity to introduce themselves. Alice then invited everyone in attendance to the ribbon cutting and grand opening of the station museum.

The attendees mostly included the consulate staff that was opening offices at the station. Alice thanked all of them for the individual contributions made by their worlds, and she acknowledged the individuals who helped with the museum creation.

They all left for the banquet hall for the luncheon, where a buffet lunch was waiting for them. After eating, they mingled and sipped coffee. Phil had a chance to meet the consultant's staff, who it seemed all wanted to meet Phil. The delegation from Pretna, who was briefed on the events that occurred on the station, was especially warm toward him.

Before everyone filed out, a flaston lady approached Phil. "Mr. Ross, it's a great pleasure to meet you face-to-face. My name is Lynuna, Flast consular general. It's also a pleasure to be back at Oasis 4 although I would have preferred to switch ships inside your station instead of on the back of a maintenance tug during my last visit."

While Phil shook her hand, he was working out the last thing she said, and it hit him that she was one of the fugitives he helped transfer from the *Morning Star* to the *Bright Star* to elude Isnod and Feldon. "It's a pleasure to meet you."

Lynuna smiled broadly. "I want to thank you for making it possible to get us to Celnar then Pentonos. I was talking to Mr. Smith earlier, and he said it was quite an eventful day."

Phil chuckled. "I'm glad it worked out the way it did. There were at least half a dozen things that could have gone horribly wrong that day." Lynuna looked apologetic. "You'll have my eternal thanks for that day, as well as my colleagues. By the way, I understand that the two fugitive trackers who were after us have opened an office on the lower CentMod as bounty hunters."

Phil was caught flat-footed. "Look, Isnod and Feldon are just trying to make a living—" Lynuna cut him off with a laugh. "Please relax, Mr. Ross. Mr. Isnod and Mr. Feldon were simply carrying out their assignment."

Phil was puzzled, and he looked at Lynuna. "They were going to drag you and your friends back to Flast where your fate was less than ideal."

Lynuna took a deep breath. "It's complicated. Mr. Isnod and Mr. Feldon didn't normally track political dissidents. They were criminal trackers. From what I understand very good ones. When my colleagues and I fled Flast, the former government sent out political fugitive trackers. When it became apparent that it wasn't enough, they assigned our case to as many criminal trackers as they could."

Lynuna took a breath. "As far as Mr. Isnod and Mr. Feldon knew, we were just another enemy of the state. They weren't fully aware of the political nature of who they were chasing, and I tend to look at them as victims every bit as much as the average flaston. Actually, I'm looking forward to meeting them, but I understand that they're tracking down a bounty."

Phil grinned. "I hope I'm there when you meet them."

*****

## Oasis 4, Upper CentMod, Museum

After the luncheon, everyone met at the museum for the ribbon cutting. Phil was still not used to addressing crowds, but he reluctantly made some remarks and introduced Alice, who was even less used to making speeches. After a few words, Alice and Brenda used a pair of ceremonial scissors and invited everyone in.

First impressions of the museum were stunning. The first section of the museum was a history of the station. It had displays and photos of the initial construction and the station expansion. There were pictures and biographies of previous managers, and here, Alice made sure to leave room for additions as new managers came and went.

As it was, there were only two managers before Phil. Pictures and biographies of the current station management staff were next. Then Phil spotted the display donated by the pretars. There was a crowd gathered around it who were giving it their complete attention.

The display appeared as an ordinary round table with a solid base but projected above it was a holographic projection of the station. The station slowly rotated, and vessels were shown coming and going. Then the Station Expansion Module appeared, being pushed along by pretar tugs. Everyone watched as the module was maneuvered into position and connected to the existing station.

Phil chuckled, remembering that day. He thought to himself, If only they knew what was going on inside the station when this was going on.

Another popular exhibit was the *Prospector* recovery exhibit. Many people weren't prepared for how emotional the experience would be. There were photos of the crew of the *Prospector* and some of their personal effects that the crew's families graciously agreed to put on permanent loan. The recovery operation took up a good deal of exhibit space which Elias and Norton found very interesting.

The last exhibit that featured the station was a mock-up of a portion of the Control Center, which floored Phil. He leaned toward Alice. "Where did the equipment come from?"

Alice answered, "Will Dawson. Most of the equipment in the control center is replaced periodically. It isn't cost-effective to rebuild it, so it just gets replaced with new. Everything you see here is used. Will supplied power to the panels, so they appear to be operating."

The really impressive bit was behind the tall windows. Will had managed to put three-dimensional projections on the other side of the glass. If one didn't know better, one would swear that one were standing in the control center watching ships dock. He watched as he saw the *Aurora* with the *Prospector* strapped to its belly approach the station.

The rest of the museum was dedicated to exhibits from the various worlds that did business with the station; most of it was artwork. There was a gift shop that sold souvenirs like one would find in a shuttle terminal on any world. Many items in the gift shop Phil recognized, like the fineld jewelry that was quite popular. He smiled when he saw that there were models available of the *Aurora* and the *Prospector*, both in finished and kit form.

One kit that seemed to get a lot of attention was the one that had both the *Aurora* and the *Prospector*. The builder had the option of putting them together or separating them. There were also books available with every description. To Phil's surprise, there was a coffee table book full of illustrations and photos of the *Prospector* recovery. Picture books of ship recognition and space station operations were also a hit.

*****

## Pulsar 1250, Newly Acquired Shuttle of I&F
## Investigations and Retrievals

Isnod and Feldon were easing their newly acquired Pulsar 1250 into the docking clamps at CargoMod 6, Docking Port 3. When the station worker connected the power cables, Feldon shut down the shuttle's reactor and relaxed.

Isnod stood and opened the hatch that led to the passenger compartment, then he turned to Feldon. "I'll contact the security office while you get our friends ready to move."

Feldon smiled. "It's good to be back. With the consulates opening on the station, we can avoid traipsing around the galaxy delivering criminals."

Isnod and Feldon had brokered a deal with Phil and Luke to house the fugitives that they managed to catch. The government that held the warrant would be responsible for reimbursement to the station for keeping the fugitives. The whole process was simplified with consulates on the station.

Isnod returned in a few minutes and helped Feldon remove some of the restraints from their prisoners. The four restrained prisoners were allowed to get the blood flowing back into their limbs. In a few minutes, Tiffany Waters and four more deputies arrived. Isnod smiled. "Ms. Waters, it's so good to see you. I see you've been given a promotion."

Tiffany smiled and nodded. "Welcome back, gentlemen. Yes, I have. I've been made the lower section security supervisor. Thank you for noticing."

She stepped over to the prisoners. "Let's see, two grunst, one malnun, and one human." Tiffany had the deputies lead the prisoners to their holding cells.

She noticed that they had difficulty walking and chuckled. "If they want to avoid being trussed up, they should give up doing illegal things."

*****

**Oasis 4**

The *Overlord* dropped out of light speed and started its reaction engines en route to Oasis 4. An Astrodyne 65 dropped out immediately behind it, followed by a second Astrodyne 65, then an Astrodyne 85, followed by a Pulsar 5500.

The controllers on duty were caught off guard as ships the size of the *Overlord* normally could be found on the schedule. There was ample time to determine the Overlord's needs and assign a docking port. They managed to find room for the *Overlord*, Astrodynes, and the Pulsar at CargoMod 7.

Elias tapped on Phil's doorframe. "Hey, Phil, I'd like you and Gus to join me in the control center."

Phil furrowed his brow. "Sure, Elias. What's happening?"

Elias hesitated, "Let's do this first. Afterward, I'll go into more detail." Phil stood and walked out of the office with Elias following. Phil tapped on Gus's doorframe. "Gus, we're needed." A confused but compliant Gus followed Phil and Elias to the control center.

Norton was already there staring through binoculars. Elias asked, "Are they on time?"

Norton nodded while lowering the binoculars. "They just dropped out of light speed."

Elias picked up a headset and put it on. He plugged into the station communications system and keyed the microphone. "*Overlord*, this is Oasis 4. Could I speak to Major Henson, please?"

Major Henson was obviously standing by because he replied immediately, "Go for Henson, Oasis."

Elias keyed his microphone. "Received your message, congratulations. How many can we expect?"

Henson answered, "Three hundred plus. There are no serious medical issues, so that's not a worry. We also have a number of prisoners, but they can be kept on the ship."

Elias smiled. "That's great news, Major. You and your guys did a fantastic job.

We'll see you when you get here."

Elias removed his headset. "Phil, Gus, could you grab Virginia and meet Norton and me in your briefing room?"

Phil nodded. "Right away, Elias." Phil asked Gus to get Virginia then he led Elias and Norton to the briefing room. Phil pressed the button on the coffee maker, and a pot was brewed.

While the three were filling mugs, Gus and Virginia entered. Gus got his own mug, and Virginia made a cup of tea, then they sat at Elias' invitation. Phil put his cup on the table. "I take it from your conversation with Major Henson that they've struck a blow in the war on slavery."

Elias smiled. "In a big way. The major and his group broke up a major trafficking organization and destroyed the auction site."

Gus chimed in, "Why is it I'm getting the feeling that our participation in this business is far from over."

Elias nodded. "Very perceptive, Gus. After the raid, Thatt Voffyes and some of his associates managed to sweat out some information from the slave traders. They've identified a planet that's structured its society around slavery."

Virginia was flabbergasted. "An entire planet? No one knows about it? How does that happen?"

Elias shrugged. "They don't allow visitors, and they don't have diplomatic relations with anyone."

"What's their product?" Phil asked.

Norton joined the conversation. "Falta. They use their own ships to move the product to brokers at different locations. The Falta is quite separated from the source by the time legitimate buyers get a hold of it."

Virginia felt slightly ill. "Do you know how many tons of falta have come through the station?"

Phil asked, "So what's next?"

Elias sipped his coffee while he considered his answer, "Decorum demands that diplomatic efforts are tried first."

Gus was perplexed. "I thought that they didn't have diplomatic relations with anyone?"

Elias continued, "The Griska government is sending an envoy. They think that they might be more receptive to fellow snoshins. If those efforts fail, there are preparations being made for military operations.

If that happens, this station becomes essential in those efforts because the location of Oasis 4 makes it an ideal center of operations."

Phil asked, "Exactly what planet is this that we're talking about?"

Norton turned to a terminal. "SICOS, activate holographic projector and display this sector."

The room lights dimmed, and a holographic image of the section of space that Oasis 4 was near the edge of. Norton continued, "Highlight Oasis 4."

A tiny dot of light suddenly glowed brighter. Norton said, "Highlight Gostis." A planet some distance away glowed.

Norton continued, "The following worlds have committed troops to this effort." As Norton named the different planets, they would glow. The last planet Norton named shocked Phil, Gus, and Virginia.

Phil could hardly repeat the name, "Earth! Which country?"

Elias fielded the answer. "The United States, Great Britain, France, Germany, Russia, Ukraine, New Zealand, and Australia are sending troops. Japan is handling some of the shipping."

Phil nodded and asked, "When will we find out if the negotiations fail?" Elias took a breath. "The Griska envoy should be contacting us very soon."

*****

## Gostis, Council Chambers of Teanon Council

There was an emergency meeting of the Teanon Council of Gostis, which is the governing body of Gostis. Toanin Zisros was a member of the council and enjoyed considerable influence on its other members. The council president, Olunic Noynin, called the meeting to order and didn't hesitate to get to the purpose of the meeting.

After the council came to order, he said, "Our fellow snoshins have sent a delegation to demand that we give up our time-honored practice of benevolent treatment of the lower classes."

The council members flew into a rage. One member shouted above the rest, "Who are they to come here and make demands of us!"

Another shouted, "Our social order must be protected!"

Olunic restored order to the meeting. "Gentlemen! I have no intention of allowing outsiders to come here and dictate policy. Our way of life will be preserved."

One of the council members stood. "What would they likely do when we say no?"

Toanin leaped to his feet. "What could they possibly do? In all of known history, a planet has never been successfully invaded."

Olunic looked at the military officer seated next to him. "What say you, General Peintoc? What are our chances if these other worlds decide to invade?"

The general stood and cleared his throat. "I believe our chances are excellent. As Mr. Zisros said, there has never been a successful invasion of a planet. We have systems that prevent unwanted shuttle landings, and if they do manage to land troops, we can determine the location instantly and employ countermeasures."

A different council member stood. "I couldn't help but notice that you said our chances are excellent and not certain."

The general bristled slightly. "Nothing is 100 percent certain. But I can promise you that any unwanted visitors will be dealt with. The possibility that casualties will be at unacceptable levels will most likely dissuade any invasion."

Zisros growled, "I hope that's true for your sake, General." General Peintoc didn't like the last comment from Toanin Zisros,

but he hid his displeasure.

Olunic Noynin quickly steered the meeting in a different direction. "So I take it, gentlemen, that we can tell the delegation from Griska that we reject their demands?"

The council voted in the affirmative enthusiastically. Secretly, they all were concerned about how this would affect the falta trade.

*****

## Oasis 4, Tier 6 Upper CentMod

Isnod and Feldon were coming out of the bank located on an upper tier of the upper CentMod. They were shaking hands with the malnun consular general. The malnun was grinning and vigorously shaking hands. "I can't tell you, gentlemen, how badly we wanted this criminal. I do hope the reward is adequate. I mean, I wouldn't want you gentlemen to be dissuaded from bringing in more felons wanted by my government."

Feldon smiled. "Mr. Gos, we wouldn't have bothered if we thought it wasn't worth our effort."

Isnod put his hand on Feldon's shoulder. "Quite right, Feldon. We're quite satisfied with the bounty."

Pel Gos beamed. "I'm so happy to hear that. I take it then that you gentlemen will be receptive to any offers from my government to assist us in locating and capturing any felons in the future?"

Feldon smiled back. "We're looking forward to doing more business with your government in the future."

Pel Gos bid the pair a good day and went back to his consulate to arrange transportation for the criminal that had been a pain in the side of his government.

Isnod and Feldon returned to their office to plan their next business venture. The bounties for the human, the malnun, and one of the grunst were secure in the business account of I&F Investigations and Retrievals. Part of the bounty for Losnic Rullot was also in their account. It was offered by Yunnar, and their consular general was very pleased to pay the bounty and arrange for Rullot's transportation to Yunnar. The other half of the bounty was offered by the Pulsar Corporation. They were losing so much in stolen shuttles to Rullot that they considered it well worth the price of a shuttle to put him out of business.

Isnod was at his desk, checking their daily communications when Lynuna appeared at the door. He was too engrossed in what he was reading to notice. He then smiled. "See here, Feldon. The Pulsar Corporation sent us a title for the shuttle. It's officially ours now."

Feldon looked up and saw Lynuna. He slowly rolled his chair over to Isnod. While keeping his gaze on Lynuna, he tapped Isnod's shoulder. Isnod looked at Feldon then Lynuna, then he recognized her, and his expression changed, exposing the fact that he wasn't sure how this new development affected him.

Lynuna was amused at their reactions and had trouble hiding it. She smiled brightly. "Gentlemen, I've been looking forward to meeting you. I understand that you were away on business."

Both Isnod and Feldon simultaneously uttered, "Uh-huh."

At this point, the pair wasn't sure if Lynuna knew if they were pursuing her and her friends just a short time ago.

Then Lynuna decided to remove all doubt. "I understand that our paths crossed at this station not long ago while I was traveling with friends," she said as she took a seat across Isnod.

Isnod stammered, "Uh…er…it's nice too…er."

Lynuna laughed. "You gentlemen could arrest me, but the warrant is no longer valid."

Feldon said, "Ma'am, we were assigned too—"

Lynuna put up her hand. "I'm not here to air grievances. I've been inquiring about you, gentlemen, and I decided that I would like to get to know you better. Could I buy you lunch?"

Isnod shook his head. "No. I insist that we buy you lunch."

She smiled broadly. "Excellent! They told me I would have a difficult time finding fellow flastons to spend time with, but I've been here scarcely a week, and I'm going to lunch with two very handsome former fugitive trackers." Feldon and Isnod's mottled skin blushed.

*****

## Upper CentMod, Eva's Café

Phil, Gus, Elias, Norton, and Luke just sat down at Phil's customary table at Eva's. The Overlord wouldn't dock for another hour or so, so they took the opportunity to have a meal and discuss some of the particulars of upcoming events.

Phil heard a familiar voice behind him and turned to see Lynuna, Isnod, and Feldon. Lynuna said, "This is so wonderful. I've wanted to try human food for a while now. I've tried some things, but nothing more than some appetizers and such."

Feldon held a chair for Lynuna and Isnod looked over to Phil's table, then turned to his companions, "Excuse me, I need to see Mr. Ross and Mr. Smith for a second."

He walked to Phil's table. "Excuse me, Mr. Ross."

Phil turned to him. "Hello, Mr. Isnod. I understand that your business trip to Kassnins was a success."

Isnod smiled. "Indeed it was, thank you for asking." Isnod continued, "I must apologize for the interruption, but I have something for Mr. Smith."

Isnod handed Luke a small case that Luke opened. It contained three data chips. Luke looked at the chips then up to Isnod. "What exactly are these?"

Isnod smiled. "Three of our last business contacts had shuttles. If I'm not mistaken, they were used in the same manner that the Aurora's original owner did. These are the downloaded navigation records."

Luke smiled. "That's good thinking, Isnod. We need to collect as much information as we can get."

Elias cleared his throat. "Excuse me, Mr. Isnod, but what is the status of the shuttles?"

Phil interrupted, "Oh, I'm sorry, Isnod. This is Elias Gilmore, corporate president, and Norton Parker, chief pilot. Gentlemen, Mr. Isnod is one of two bounty hunters who have opened an office on the station."

Isnod politely nodded at Elias and Norton's introduction. "Sir, I inquired on that very thing. The shuttles are now the property of the agency executing the arrest warrants. However, there are fees to be paid at the shuttle port on Kassnins. Feldon and I don't have the resources to bring the shuttles back and make a decent profit. It's too bad too because they're low-time shuttles."

Elias pondered it for a second. "What kind of shuttles are they?" Isnod replied, "Two Astrodyne 65's and a Caravel 3500."

Norton was grinning, and Elias leaned back with a smile of his own. "Mr. Isnod, if you provide us with all the information and paperwork we need to pick up the shuttles, we'll pay your company a finder's fee. Perhaps we can come to some kind of arrangement concerning your office rent."

Isnod nodded with a smile. "That would be more than acceptable. Feldon and I will have everything in order when you're ready. Now you'll have to please excuse me, gentlemen. Feldon and Ms. Lynuna are awaiting my return." Isnod returned to the table and rejoined Feldon and Lynuna.

Phil furrowed his brow. "I'm not sure if it's any of my business, Elias, but what does the company need all these shuttles for?"

Norton answered for Elias. "You should know the answer to that, Phil. We've been knocking around the idea of equipping each of our stations with a shuttle. Mr. Isnod's good fortune is our windfall. Besides, we're going to need the shuttles in the short term for the events that are brewing."

Elias continued the thought. "Major Henson captured the shuttles that are accompanying the Overlord. Since we paid for the raid, the shuttles belong to us."

Gus nodded in understanding. "Any military action on Gostis would require moving personnel from orbit to the surface. Keeping troops supplied is the biggest challenge in any military operation. I've heard a saying that said, "Amateurs study tactics, professionals study logistics."

Norton nodded. "Getting troops from space to the surface is hard enough. The first wave is usually pretty understrength and vulnerable. Keeping the troops supplied has always been the key to success."

After lunch, Phil and the rest went to CargoMod 7 to meet the *Overlord*. It occurred to Phil that the people that were rescued would need accommodations while at the station. There were just over three hundred, which would just overwhelm the hotel, so Phil had station personnel prepare quarters in HabMod 7. They put in bedding, edibles, and potables in a number of quarters.

Virginia was standing by with about a dozen people from her department to escort the rescued people to HabMod 7 and to hand out bracelets that had credit chips embedded that allowed the wearer to eat in any restaurant or cafeteria on the station for free.

The indicators at the air lock turned from red to green showing a positive seal allowing a station worker to pressurize it. The hatch opened, and Major Henson was standing in the air lock, smiling.

"Gentlemen! It's good to be back. We have about three hundred folks anxious to disembark."

Phil stepped forward and shook the major's hand. "Good to see you back safe and sound. If you have the folks file off, Virginia and her people will get them settled."

Major Henson turned to a crewman from the *Overlord* and nodded. The crewman started leading the people rescued from the slave traders off the *Overlord*, where Virginia's people led them to a terminal and assigned them quarters.

After the rescued people were on their way to quarters, Major Henson's men started filing off. Elias made a point to shake hands with each and every one of them. He kept repeating, "Make your way to the Star Lodge Suites, guys, and just sign in."

Finally, Lieutenants Greene and Yondlyn, along with First Sergeant Thack, emerged from the air lock and joined Major Henson and the others. Elias shook their hands enthusiastically. "Guys, after you check into the Star Lodge Suites and freshen up, get something to eat, then drinks are on me at Sparky's."

*****

## Sisten, Slave Auction Complex

Borislav Lovanova landed his Caravel 500 on pad 6 of the Sisten shuttle port that serviced the slave auction complex here. Like Holid 4, Sisten was a rather useless planet. It did have a nitrogen/oxygen atmosphere provided by an abundant amount of plant life and an ocean.

About the only good thing the plants do is take in carbon dioxide and expel oxygen. There were no trees large enough for lumber. The soil was too rocky for anything of size to grow, which also made crops out of the question. The ocean was teeming with sea life and had a healthy amount of plant life. Like Holid, the fact that Sisten had a breathable atmosphere but was otherwise undesirable made it an ideal location for the slave traders.

A ground crewman plugged in a power cable, and Borislav powered down the shuttle systems. He left the cockpit and said to Jason and his other crewman, "Get them ready."

He opened the cargo hatch to see there were handlers waiting. The lead handler stepped forward. "Borislav! It's been too long."

Borislav smiled upon seeing the Snoshin handler. "Snit! It's good to be back." Snit had his men move the newly acquired slaves to the processing shed.

When they were gone, he looked at Borislav. "This bunch is being sold as a lot." Borislav was surprised. "That's not how things are normally done."

Snit shrugged. "They want to speed operations here because no one has heard from Holid 4 lately. There are rumors that someone has taken exception to the operation there. As a result, they're most anxious to conclude things here and get back to Gostis."

"Is the auction going to take place as scheduled?" Borislav asked.

Snit nodded. "Of course. For now, you and your men come to the main house for a meal and enjoy Mr. Untocks's hospitality."

Entering the main house, Snit led Borislav, Jason, and Jason's assistant, a Malnun named Pil Jos, to a large dining room where they were greeted by a well-fed snoshin named Yidlin Untocks. "Borislav! I'm so glad you could be here. This is indeed a good day. Come in, my friends, and sit."

As Borislav took his seat he introduced Yidlin to Jason and Pil Jos. Human and maldor slave girls brought trays of food and drink to them while Yidlin continued talking, "Eat well, my friends. The auction starts later. The prices should be very good today."

That got Borislav's attention. "I wouldn't have expected that with slaves being sold in lots instead of individually."

Yidlin took a breath. "Undoubtedly, Mr. Snit told you about Holid 4. I'm afraid that it's more than a rumor. A stock-buyer friend of mine stopped there and found it in shambles. All the buildings were destroyed and…"

He hesitated, "Apparently, there were survivors from the small garrison there. They were left there without food or drinkable water.

By the time my friends arrived, there was nothing that could be done for them. The buyers here would like to conclude business and be back to their home planets as soon as possible. About three hundred slaves were taken off the market, and some excellent stock gatherers are out of circulation. That's what's making the price rise on stock, that, and decisions being made on Gostis."

Borislav felt his blood run cold. He was pleased to hear that he was getting top price for his stock, but the rest of it didn't sound so great.

*****

## Oasis 4, Eva's Café, Upper CentMod

Phil sat with Luke Smith, Major Henson, First Sergeant Thack, and Elias Gilmore at Phil's customary table at Eva's. They were just about ready to make selections from the menu when Lynuna walked up. Elias stood and motioned to a chair. "Please, Miss Lynuna, this table could benefit from the civility and grace of a lady."

Lynuna smiled broadly. "That's a very kind offer, Mr. Gilmore. I wouldn't want to interrupt important business."

Elias grinned. "Nonsense. You could never be considered an interruption." The others stood, and First Sergeant Thack held her chair for her.

When she settled, she remarked, "One of the niceties we have to reestablish on Flast is politeness and manners. Earth and Pretna should figure out how to export such commodities." Elias introduced Lynuna to Major Henson and First Sergeant Thack.

Major Henson furrowed his brow. "I couldn't help but catch your use of the word reestablish, my own Lieutenant Yondlyn is from Treest, a flaston colony. I've observed that he has exceptional manners and habits. Has the society on Flast declined due to conditions that were there?"

Lynuna took a breath. "That is a very astute observation, Major. A long time ago, Flast was very different. There were rules of etiquette and politeness that were both spoken and tacit. After decades of increasingly oppressive policies, laws, practices, and conditions, my people have lost the part of themselves that makes them dignified and more civilized.

On top of the marked degradation of civility on my home planet, I'm ashamed to admit that there are those on Flast that are enthusiastic purveyors of the slave trade."

Major Henson sipped the coffee Eva brought, then he said, "I suppose what's happening on Flast is brutal, but it's not unique. Would it shock you, Ms. Lynuna, to learn that my ancestors were slave owners?"

Lynuna was indeed shocked. "I thought you were from Earth!"

The major smiled. "An Earth history lesson might sour your opinion of humans. The fact of the matter is, slavery existed throughout our history. It occurred on every continent, and there wasn't a culture on Earth that wasn't slave or slaveholder. My own country was one of the last to have legalized slavery, and it only ended with a great civil war."

He paused to take a sip of coffee. "My family owned a plantation in the slave-holding south, and a distant great-grandfather of mine fought in that war. He survived the troubles only to come home to destruction. He set about rebuilding the family plantation, and during that time, he had a lot of time for reflection. He came to realize that for generations, his people tolerated slavery because it made them money."

Henson gathered his thoughts. "Slowly, they convinced themselves that they were doing the slaves a favor by taking care of them, and it was the natural order of things. Finally, no one wants to admit they're wrong, and they would rather take a path to destruction than mend their ways. Since then, Henson men have been taught never to accept oppression. I don't accept responsibility for events in the past, but I believe all of us have the responsibility to learn from it."

Luke Smith spoke up, "My ancestors were those slaves. After the war, they were free to make whatever they could for themselves. It took a long time to achieve true equality, but eventually, my people and the people who held us in bondage came to consider ourselves one people. As the major already said, there hasn't been an innocent group of people in our history, my ancestors included."

Luke paused. "I acknowledge what happened and let it serve as a lesson, something not to repeat. I get steamed when I see someone like Marcus Pointer. We're both Americans of African descent, but he refused to learn anything from the past. I don't know if it's because he's ignorant or because he's angry and looking for some kind of social justice, tit for tat, or maybe he's just plain greedy and doesn't care who he hurts to line his own pockets."

Luke took a second to calm down. "I won't use past events to define me in a negative way. In my estimation, you either conduct yourself honorably or not. Anyone who uses ancient injustices to justify dishonorable behavior is intellectually dishonest, and anyone who lets them get away with it is a fool."

First Sergeant Thack nodded. "It seems every planet has a less than ideal record where the treatment of different groups is concerned. On my own planet, we have a caste system. There was a definite social order while some castes were in the elite class. Some were considered unclean. It affected everything from finances to receiving services. We've managed to remove the more negative aspects of the caste system, but there are still lingering attitudes and policies that affect everyday life on Pretna."

Thack smiled. "I myself have felt the pull to be a solder since I was a child, but my family is in the Artistic Caste. I chose a different direction from what was expected of me, my family isn't hostile toward me, but I can sense the disappointment. Then there was the resistance from the Pretna military to accept anyone, not from the warrior caste."

*****

## Sisten, Slave Auction Complex

Yidlin Untocks led Borislav and his companions to the auction house, where buyers were busy inspecting the newcomers. They seemed pleased with the latest arrivals, being that it was obvious that they were no strangers to agriculture.

When the buyers were satisfied that they knew what they needed to know about the last lot, they filed into the Auction room. Yidlin said, "Let's watch the proceedings."

He had seats for Borislav and the others in the back so as to afford the best view for the buyers. The other slave gatherers were already seated and anxiously waiting for the main event.

An auctioneer stepped to the lectern and rang a bell. "Welcome, ladies and gentlemen, to the Sisten Auction. Today's stock will be sold in lots. Lot number one consists of twenty-eight malnuns, eight adult males, nine adult females, six adolescent males, and five adolescent females. I'm asking for an opening bid of five thousand goaners."

A goaner was a monetary unit worth just a little under an ounce of gold. Borislav found the opening bid encouraging. Buyers picked up pads at their seats and entered their bids on them. The bids were shown on a large display behind the auctioneer.

A buyer entered the opening bid, and the auctioneer nodded. "We now have an opening bid of 5,000. Can I get 5,500? Very good, Let's see 6,000."

The bids came up in 500 goaner leaps. When the bidding slowed, the auctioneer cut the increases to 100. "There is a bid on the board for 12,500. Can I get 12,600?"

When that slowed, he decreased the raises even more. "13,100, can I get 13,110?"

When it seemed that the buyers would go no higher, the auctioneer added, "These are malnuns. Very good for working in mines and other dark places."

That garnered a couple of additional bids. Finally, the auctioneer rang his bell.

This lot was sold for 13,140 goaners."

Each lot was sold in a similar fashion. A sociologist would probably find it interesting which species commanded more money than the other and why. Humans were possibly the most adaptable, but their independent streak makes them the most troublesome.

Pretars make excellent builders. It didn't matter if they were building roads, bridges, structures, or any number of public works. The quality of work was always first-rate. The other races had their uses, but general labor was usually their purpose. The lot Borislav brought was herded out to the platform.

The auctioneer rang his bell. "Final lot of the day. Twenty-five humans, ten male adults, five female adults, six male adolescents, and four female adolescents. They were acquired from an agricultural colony. They know the soil and would be an asset to any agribusiness.

The bidding will begin at 5,000 goaners. I have 5,000 on the board. Can I get 5,500?"

The bidding continued until Oliver stepped forward. "Hey, man, do you know how much damage you're doing to your inner being? If you just did a little herb, you would mellow and realize that this isn't necessary, man." The buyers laughed and resumed bidding.

Yidlin laughed. "He probably did more to boost the bids than the auctioneer ever could. Some of the buyers delight in watching new slaves 'adjust' to their new life."

The auctioneer continued, "I see a bid of 12,500. Can I get 12,600? 12,700?"

The auctioneer finally rang the bell after several more bids and said, "This lot is sold for 14,360 goaners."

The usual protocol was for the buyers to meet with sellers to partake in a cocktail party and negotiate transport for their new acquisitions. It wasn't long before a snoshin approached Borislav to make a deal to transport the same stock he brought. Borislav readily agreed, being as the time would be pure profit. The buyer worked for a falta plantation on Gostis. Borislav thought that he would spend time there and see if he could do some networking.

*****


**Oasis 4, Conference Room Number 1**


Elias had called a meeting with the corporate management and other personnel he thought should be there. Major Henson and First Sergeant Thack were also in attendance.

When Elias thought everyone was there, he began speaking, "Thank you for being here, folks. As everyone is aware, Stellar Logistics and Freight Corporation paid for Major Henson and his men to conduct a raid on a slave auction site. The results were outstanding as you well know. One benefit to the venture was, we got to keep the spoils. In this case, two Astrodyne 65s, an Astrodyne 85, and a Pulsar 5500. We've had Jeremy Cole and his guys going over them since they got here. Jeremy, what's their status?"

Jeremy pulled out a pad. "The first 65, hull number 2665, is a clean machine.

Relatively low time and free from deficiencies of any consequence. The second 65, hull number 3462, is newer but has more operational hours on it. There are some deficiencies but mostly related to wear and tear. There are also some things that should have been dealt with, but laziness prevented that. The engines are about three quarters of the way to needing overhaul. When the time comes, maybe we can have it modified like the Aurora. The 85 is really clean. We got very lucky with this one, as it's brand-new. The Pulsar is everything you would expect from a Pulsar. This one was also lightly used and had a lot of time left on it before it needs anything major."

Elias smiled. "Thank you, Jeremy." He then turned to Major Henson. "Excuse me, Major, but I was given to believe that there were six shuttles at the slave complex."

Major Henson nodded. "Yes, sir. Indeed there was. However, two of them were damaged in the fighting. We didn't think it would have been prudent to take the time to try to repair them, so we destroyed them in place. To be honest, I don't think you would want them anyway. One was a forty-year-old Caravel, and the other was a well-used Delta 850."

Elias laughed. "I'm no pilot, but from what I understand, even undamaged, it wouldn't have been a good idea to bother with either of them."

Those in the room that have had experience with both of those models nodded assent. Elias smiled because he didn't often get it right when it came to an understanding the hardware end of things.

Elias continued, "We've made a deal with I&F Investigations and Retrievals for two Astrodyne 65s and a Caravel 3500. I've been told they were very clean, but I propose that we send a couple of technicians to make sure, just in case. I'd like Norton Parker, Gus Condent, Dwight Needles, Thomas Grandall, and Victor Higgins to go to Kassnins and bring back the shuttles. Norton will handle paying the fees and probably greasing the right palms. Jeremy, which technicians would you like to go along?"

Jeremy thought for a second. "Well, there are four shuttles involved, and you would want two pilots each, so you need three of my guys to get an even eight. My first choice would be Chad Kowalski, Helmut Schulz, and Roy Ingle. They're all pilots and first-rate technicians."

Elias nodded. "If you gents could get a start in the morning, that would be great. Phil, I know you would like to go along and get behind the controls of the *Aurora*, but we're going to need you here." Phil didn't argue, being as there was a lot happening at the time.

Elias adjourned the meeting, then looked at Phil. "Hang back for a second, would you, Phil?"

Phil stopped. "Sure, Elias."

Elias waited until everyone filed out, then closed the door. He warmed his coffee with a bit of fresh. "I received news that the envoy to Gostis got an answer."

Phil nodded. "I don't imagine the good people of Gostis have seen the errors of their ways."

Elias smiled. "You got that right. It's not a surprise, so with that in mind, everyone involved has been preparing for military intervention. Stellar Logistics will be handling transportation from the troopships to the Gostis surface. Intersystems provided troopships and cargo ships. Oasis 4 will be used to store supplies needed for the invasion."

Phil was taken aback. "I don't think we have enough ships for that."

Elias shook his head. "We're only doing transportation for the American effort. However, Oasis 4 will be handling the supply containers for everyone, so it's going to get very busy around here."

Phil nodded. "The station can handle the containers. Now I know why the company is going on a light-speed capable shuttle buying spree." Elias nodded. "That's right. We'll have to bring in a few people from within the company, but we can get it done. My biggest concern is we may not have enough shuttles to put guys on the ground fast enough for their own security."

Phil asked, "How is it you know so much about this stuff, Elias?" Elias shrugged. "I had a career before coming to Stellar Logistics.

I was in the Army myself. I specialized in logistics. There's one other thing, the organizers of this little venture are going to meet here in a few days to work out the details."

*****

## Cargo Hold of Caravel 500 Belonging to Borislav Lovanova

Oliver shifted around, trying to get comfortable. It was impossible to sit cross- legged in the shackles he was wearing, which made meditating difficult. Oliver's wife was having a difficult time. She was sobbing at the moment, which she did often.

Their teenage son was trying to comfort her. "It'll be okay, Ma. We'll try to escape or get the word out or something."

Oliver interrupted, "George! We ain't doing anything like that, man. We just need to find some people who are open-minded, man. We can show them how to get centered and find balance. I've got some seeds in my pocket. We'll just talk them into letting us grow some herb, man, and we'll be all right."

George looked at his dad. "It feels like this situation is going to require a little more than 'herb,' Dad."

*****

## Kassnins Trading Planet

Dwight eased the *Aurora* onto the landing pad at Kassnins. Norton smiled at Dwight. "It's nice to have the old Dwight Needles back. Let's go to the terminal and conclude our business here."

Dwight nodded. "I'm with ya, Nort. This place gives me the creeps."

The pair grabbed a ride on the courtesy transport after the ground crewman connected power. They had made it a point to work out how to approach the shuttle port authorities. Officials on Kassnins were notorious for being corrupt and greedy. Once they realize they can squeeze someone, they get even greedier. Norton and Dwight looked at each other and nodded. Then they went into the outer office of the shuttle port manager.

Norton strode to the receptionist's desk, where he put his briefcase on the counter. He opened the briefcase and pulled out three bundles of paper. "We're here to pick up two Astrodyne's, hull numbers 5698 and 6254, and a Caravel hull number 25688. If you'll tell us what the fees are, we can be on our way."

Norton delivered his line in a manner that was calculated to throw the receptionist, a maldor, off his game. The maldor wasn't used to strangers walking in and being this direct, which flustered him.

He went to a terminal and said, "What are those hull numbers again?" Norton read them off, and the receptionist entered them in the terminal.

"5698 is on pad fourteen, 6254 is on eight, and 25688 is on pad twenty-two." The man punched some keys and said, "Fees come to 525 goaners." Norton looked at him. "Goaners, huh. I'm prepared for that."

At that moment, the inner office door opened, and an older maldor came out with a younger maldor trailing. He looked directly at Norton. "There are some additional fees you'll need to pay before I can let you take those shuttles."

"It doesn't say anything about additional fees here," Norton said, pointing to the terminal screen while suppressing a grin.

The maldor smiled. "I haven't had a chance to enter the additional fees yet."

Dwight stepped up. "Nort, our clients on Reynolds Planet won't be happy about additional fees."

The younger maldor's head came up at the mention of Reynolds Planet. Norton looked at Dwight. "Don't you think they'll be more upset if we came back empty-handed?"

Dwight leaned toward Norton. "The colonel wouldn't be happy about us spending his money over and above what was understood."

The younger maldor was nearly in a panic. He pulled the older man aside, and it was obvious that he was frantically trying to explain something to him. It was equally obvious when the older man finally understood what his younger companion was trying to get across.

The older man hushed his friend, then smiled nervously. "Gentlemen, I think we can forget the additional fees. Just pay the fees that are currently in the system, and that should be sufficient."

Norton gladly paid the fees and even gave the three maldors an extra goaner each, which they seemed grateful for.

Norton and Dwight rode the transport back to the *Aurora* and told the others where to find the other shuttles so they could do their preflight checks. The decision was made not to file a flight plan in an effort to expedite their departure. One by one, the shuttles departed Kassnins and took a heading to Oasis 4.

*****

## Oasis 4, Eva's Café

Alice managed to tear herself away from the museum long enough to have a meal with Phil. During the last couple of days, military commanders from the various participating worlds were arriving. Phil and Elias made a point to meet them as they arrived and to escort them to quarters. The commanders from Earth were scheduled to arrive the next morning.

Phil was doing his normal "people watching" when he spotted some of the people that were rescued from Holid 4. Phil could see they were humans who made him wonder where they came from. Most of the rescued people were transported by now. They must have been from an out-of-the-way colony to have to wait this long for a ride home.

Alice saw Phil's gaze and commented, "Those poor people. They've been through a lot lately."

Phil looked at her. "Have you had a chance to talk with any of them?" Alice dipped a fry in ketchup. "Yes, I have. I think most of them have been through the museum. None of them were used to life on a space station, so they looked for distractions wherever they could find them."

At that moment, Corporal Evans walked to their table. "Excuse me, Mr. Ross."

Phil looked up at him. "It's Corporal Evans, isn't it?" The corporal nodded. "That's right, sir."

Phil introduced him to Alice and invited him to have a seat.

Evans sat, and Eva brought him a cup of coffee. He took a sip and said, "First Sergeant Thack was telling me that the Astrodyne that brought us here was the same one that was used to kidnap my wife."

Phil nodded. "That's right. My security division used DNA that was found on the shackles that were stored in the shuttle. That gave us a pretty extensive list of victims. During the investigation into all this, we uncovered the name of the original owner. I forget the guy's name, but my security marshal would know it. All the information on this has been passed up the line to all interested law enforcement."

Evans took a sip of his coffee, then put down his cup. "Do you know if this guy has been arrested yet?"

Before Phil could answer, someone behind him said, "I can help you with that."

Phil turned to the newcomer. "You have us at a disadvantage."

The man apologized. "I'm sorry. I'm Special Agent Tim Davis of the Federal Bureau of Investigation."

Phil said, "Well, take a seat, Mr. Davis."

Then Phil motioned Eva over to fill a cup for Tim.

Tim continued, "The original owner is a Bulgarian national named Borislav Lovanova. He's involved in kidnapping and trafficking his victims as slaves. He hasn't been arrested yet because we've been tracking him, gathering intelligence on the slave trade. Quite frankly, Corporal Evans, the amount of useful information we can get surveilling him is now minimal. If he were to get caught in the crossfire, it wouldn't break anyone's heart. I shouldn't say things like that, but he's a real scummer. It would save everyone a lot of trouble."

Evans furrowed his brow. "How do you know my name?"

Agent Davis answered, "It's my job. You're Charles Evans. You're a native of Wisconsin. You have a farm in New Iowa you've been working with your wife, Rosanne, Lisa Evans. She was kidnapped about two and a half years ago. Thanks to Mr. Ross here, we know that it was Borislav Lovanova who did it, along with Marcus Pointer and Fel Nos."

Evans's anger was bubbling to the surface. "Those two that were being transported to Pretna when we came here the first time?"

Davis nodded. "That's right. But don't be upset about not using the opportunity to exact a little revenge. They've only been in the Pretna prison for six months when I saw them. Normally, the pretars won't open the cell door once closed, but they were very accommodating when I explained that I needed information. You see, the cells are completely dark and soundproof. I thought Pointer was going to die when the pretars opened his cell and dragged him out. He looked ghastly. There was no color in his skin. Light and sound caused him extreme agony.

Fel Nos just screamed himself horse. I couldn't get anything out of him at all. I did find out from Pointer that your wife is somewhere on the charming planet that we're talking about visiting."

"Pointer and Fel Nos were in pretty bad shape, were they?" Phil asked.

Davis nodded. "You got that right. I wouldn't count on them making it to the end of their sentences."

"It's impossible to feel sorry for them. What they did to innocent people was just horrible, and they knew what the consequences would be when they were caught," Alice said, shaking her head.

Evans took a deep breath. "I don't think I could think of a worse way to deal with those two if I had to."

Alice furrowed her brow. "How did the FBI get involved in this? Let alone the United States?"

Davis said, "You would be right in thinking that no one has knowingly come up missing to slavers in the US, but there have been plenty taken while off- world. Mostly, people working at outposts, sometimes tourist groups are targeted, and don't forget, New Iowa is a US territory. The present administration feels that enough is enough. The best way to discourage the slave trade is to wipe it out."

Phil looked at Evans. "I'm looking forward to meeting Mrs. Evans." Alice wiped a tear. "As am I."

*****

## The *Aurora*, Astrodyne 65, Operated by the Stellar Logistics and Freight Corporation

Gus checked the navigation display and waited until it indicated the optimum moment to drop out of light speed. He cut the Victor 150s and idled the Detroit 750s. He slowly brought the power levers to maximum and checked his position. Norton turned the communication radio to the company frequency and said, "Let's give them a little time to catch up."

The Caravel 3500 had the fastest cruise speed of the four shuttles. It was even faster than the *Aurora*, but they had all agreed upon a time coordinate to arrive at the station. Since they were all traveling on the same route, it was necessary that no one deviated from the plan to avoid collisions. The proximity warning display indicated a vessel dropping out of light speed just behind them, then another, followed by the last shuttle.

Norton keyed his microphone. "Flight, this is *Aurora*. Check in."

Thomas Grandall was with Helmut Shultz. "Astrodyne five six niner eight right behind you."

Victor Higgins with Roy Ingle. "Astrodyne six two five four is number three." Finally, Dwight Needles with Chad Kowalski. "Caravel is in trail."

The three newly acquired shuttles were assigned Docking ports on CargoMod 8, and the *Aurora* was given its customarily docking port on CargoMod 2. One of the Astrodyne's and the Caravel had restraint shackles stored on board, so Luke sent his forensics expert Carl Jenkins to collect any evidence.

*****

## Oasis 4, Eva's Café

Phil and Alice went to Eva's for breakfast and found Elias, Norton, Gus, Dwight, Thomas, Victor, Chad, Helmut, and Roy sitting at tables they had pushed together. Phil smiled when he saw the group. "Hey is there room for two more?"

Elias waved them over. "Right over here, folks."

Phil grabbed a chair for himself while Elias held a chair for Alice. Phil sat and asked, "When did you guys get in?"

Gus put down his cup after taking a sip. "About a half hour ago. We didn't feel like getting fleeced on Kassnins, so we beat it back here."

Phil laughed. "Is it as bad there as I've heard?"

Norton and Dwight related their experience in the Kassnins shuttle port. Elias was pleasantly surprised that it only cost the corporation an additional three Goaners over and above the legitimate fees that were required to secure their release.

Phil moved his coffee so that Eva could put his breakfast in front of him. He picked up the pepper and asked, "How do the new shuttles look?"

Chad chimed in, "Whoever said crime doesn't pay didn't know what they were talking about? Those machines are all prime, every one of them."

Elias said while buttering a slice of toast, "Oasis 4 has the *Aurora*. The other 65s should be distributed to the other stations, and I think the Pulsar would make an excellent corporate executive transport. The Astrodyne 85 and the Caravel can be kept in the system and used as needed to shuttle supplies and personnel."

Norton nodded. "We may consider sending the 65s to the New Oslo Shipyards and have them modified like the *Aurora*. I think we can agree that it's been proven that the ability to tow a stranded ship is useful."

Chad added, "Not to mention the performance boost."

Elias smiled. "I've heard all about the *Aurora's* performance. I think perhaps you have to be a pilot to appreciate that sort of thing."

Victor asked, "Phil, what made you choose *Aurora* for the name of your shuttle?"

Phil put down his coffee cup and said with a smile. "Well, first, it's not my shuttle. It belongs to the Great Stellar Logistics and Freight Corporation." Elias grinned at that. Phil continued, "I chose *Aurora* because I always think back to something I saw early in my career. I was ferrying freight from Kansas City to Orbiting Station Number

One when the Northern Lights were on full display. I thought it was the most incredible thing I've ever seen."

Elias was smiling. "Vic, if the sixty-five you brought back suits you, what name do you want for it?"

Victor leaned back in his seat and considered his answer. Finally, he said, "Considering the current circumstances, I think I'll call it the *John Newton*."

Everyone at the table struggled to remember who John Newton was. Finally, it dawned on Dwight. "That's a right fine idea, Vic."

Phil added, "I'd agree with Dwight, except I have no idea who John Newton is."

Dwight smiled. "Come on, Phil. I'm sure you've at least heard his work." Phil frowned. "Huh?"

Victor chuckled. "John Newton was a slave ship captain in the 1700s. He was so distraught at the practice. He gave up the slave trade and then became an Anglican clergyman and abolitionist. He's best known for a hymn he wrote called 'Amazing Grace.'"

Everyone's face lit up with understanding. Alice remarked, "That's one of my favorites. I never knew there was a story behind it, though."

Victor nodded. "It's an interesting story. In 1743, he was pressed into service in the Royal Navy. Apparently, he was deemed too much trouble, and they transferred him to a slave ship. He didn't get along with the slave ship's crew, so they left him with a slave trader in Africa. The slave trader made Newton a slave and gave him to his wife, Princess Peye, of the Sherbro people as a gift. Apparently, she abused him along with her other slaves. In 1748, he was rescued by a sea captain sent by his father. He then went into the slave trade himself until the mid-1750s. Sometime in that period, he had a religious conversion and became an outspoken opponent of slavery."

Elias looked at Thomas. "What about you, Tom?"

Thomas smiled broadly. "The *Abraham Lincoln*. I don't think I need to go through a history lesson to explain why."

Elias said, "Don't feel obligated to name it after a great name in abolition just because that's what we're involved in now."

Thomas smiled. "I'm not. I would have anyway since I've always admired Mr. Lincoln."

Phil spotted some pretars in military uniforms. Elias saw Phil was distracted and turned to see what held his attention. "Ah, there's the pretars. They're the last group to arrive. They watched as the flaston representatives entered the CentMod and approached the pretar group." Phil remarked, "This might be tense."

The ranking flaston exchanged some words with the ranking pretar. The group sitting at Eva's held their breath, waiting to see what would happen next. The Ranking flaston put out his hand, and the pretar shook it warmly.

Phil exhaled loudly. "That's a relief." Norton asked, "Why do you say that, Phil?"

Phil took a sip of coffee. "Apparently, a while back, the flastons and the pretars clashed, and since then, the relations between the two groups have been icy, to say the least."

Elias nodded. "I remember studying that incident. I think the changing power structure on Flast is going to go a long way toward easing tensions. Besides, we have a common cause that's bigger than any minor differences or ancient wrongdoing."

Elias continued, "The first briefing the military planners have scheduled is at 0900 Zulu. I'll be there, and I'd like Norton and Phil there." Both Phil and Norton nodded in compliance.

*****

## Oasis 4, CentMod Auditorium

The 0900 meeting was called to order by Elias. "Gentlemen, on behalf of Phillip Ross, the station manager, his staff, and myself, I'd like to welcome you to Oasis 4. While you're here, if you need anything, please don't hesitate to ask anyone of us. I won't waste any more of your time. Now I'd like to introduce General Hosnes Lingur of the Griska Defense Force."

A distinguished Snoshin took the stage. "I'd like to add my thanks to Mr. Gilmore and Mr. Ross, along with his staff, for hosting this event. It has made things much more convenient for everyone involved. The Griska government has taken the lead in the effort to end the slave trade. The reason for this is simple. Our fellow snoshins on Gostis are the largest purveyors of this despicable trade. It is to the everlasting shame of my race that it has been allowed to get out of hand."

Lingur paused for effect then carried on. "We have a very small amount of time to finalize and execute invasion plans. Before we proceed further, we should make the goals of this effort crystal clear. We are going to Gostis to secure the release of slaves. If we have to take down their government to do that, that's fine. If they agree to release the slaves before that, then that's fine also. Either way, the slave trade on Gostis ends. We will concentrate our efforts on separating the government from their army. If we capture the Teanon Council and the council president, perhaps they'll stop fighting and negotiate. If we're lucky, just threatening the council will be enough."

The ranking pretar in attendance raised a hand. General Lingur looked at him. "Yes, General Bortas?"

The pretar General stood. "Even after eliminating the opposition's air assets, our best projections calculate 35 to 40 percent casualties. I'm still unclear as to how we're going to maintain the tempo necessary to achieve our goals."

Lingur nodded. "To bring everyone up to date, I'll explain some things. The Pretna contribution brings an excellent system to deny the opposition of air assets. They will deploy orbiting platforms that will, when activated, launch weapons that will fly to pre-targeted destinations. Once the opposition air assets have been located along with their facilities, the appropriate device will be assigned to destroy those assets. The system will hold a number of weapons in reserve to protect against the unexpected. We can predict with 100 percent certainty that the air threat will be eliminated before we put any soldiers on the ground."

He took a sip of water and continued, "As you know, the opposition has systems to detect the signature of landing assault vessels and blanket the landing zone with ordnance designed to destroy everything in a large area. The control facilities for that system are housed in extremely hardened bunkers. No one possesses ordnance that is up to the task of destroying these facilities from orbit. Human contribution promises to negate that threat. When on the ground, they will neutralize those systems in the zones we'll need to use to land troops and equipment."

The ranking flaston raised his hand. Lingur said, "Yes, Colonel Grast."

The colonel stood. "The humans have a reputation for being some of the best soldiers to be found, but I fail to see how they plan on getting from shuttles to the surface without landing. Would you please enlighten us,"

Lingur grinned. "I think I'll let Colonel Kline explain."

Colonel Kline got out of his seat and climbed the steps to the stage. He took his place behind the podium and activated the wall-sized monitor display behind him. "Gentlemen, we'll be leading the assault using technology that's centuries old on earth. It does not involve landing in a shuttle or other device that will trigger the planet's defense system, allow me to demonstrate." Kline pressed a button, and a screen lit up.

Kline narrated while a video of paratroopers played. "To get troops in an enemy's rear area, a system was developed to allow soldiers to jump out of aerial vehicles and float to the ground using a decidedly low-tech device. The troops sent by the earth contingent are proficient in using this method." The video played out, and Kline walked off the stage.

The rest of the soldiers in attendance stared straight ahead without blinking.

Finally, the malnun ranking officer said, "Better you guys than me."

Laughter broke out and some friendly banter. The general consensus was that humans are inherently insane. After they settled down, the rest of the meeting was spent adjusting timetables and assigning objectives.

Noon came around, and Lingur decided that a lunch break was in order, and smaller groups should reconvene in conference rooms. Phil used the SICOS to contact Virginia and assign a number of conference rooms for use after lunch.

*****

## Oasis 4, CentMod

Eva's filled fast with the visiting military staff members, so Elias, Norton, and Phil decided that the company cafeteria would be less crowded. Norton said, "I couldn't help but notice that the Paratroopers were jumping from Astrodyne Shorthaulers."

Elias nodded. "That's right. The 65s we acquired will be used to drop them since they're similar to the Shorthauler. Astrodyne Corporation has some used 65s that they're bringing out to boost the number of ships in this effort. We'll have to mount troop seats in the cargo area and run a pair of cables that'll need to connect their static lines. Astrodyne sent drawings that I forwarded to Jeremy Cole for the static line cables, and they're bringing seat assemblies."

Phil remarked, "This thing is happening fast."

Elias nodded. "Yes, it is. We'll need every pilot in the system to make this work smoothly."

Phil, Elias, and Norton stepped onto the plaza level after lunch. Phil stopped cold. He was staring into the face of his son, who was wearing the uniform of an Army Ranger, which added to Phil's confusion.

Finally, he croaked out, "Michael?" Michael grinned. "Hey, Pop."

Phil was feeling that he had missed important information and was trying to decide which question to ask first. He finally blurted out, "What are you doing here? What happened to graduate school? How long have you been in the Army? Does your mom know about this?"

Michael answered, "I took classes for a semester and had second thoughts. I enlisted two and a half years ago, then I was accepted to OCS. No, Mom's in the dark about this. I was hoping you would help me break it to her."

Phil's eyes widened. "You're out of your cotton-pickin' mind! No way! You are on your own on that score!"

Michael nodded. "I understand, Pop."

Phil was still trying to catch up. "Why didn't you say anything about joining the Army? How did you keep it a secret?"

Michael took a breath. "Well, it wasn't all that hard with you moving here and Mom closing the house. I would make sure I called when I should. When I had leave, I saw you and Mom."

Phil was starting to get his breath under control. "What's your role in all this?"

Michael said, "I'm a platoon leader with First Battalion Seventy-Fifth Rangers. Colonel Kline heard my pop was station manager and offered to bring me for a visit."

Phil asked, "How is it that I missed you getting off the ship?"

Michael shrugged. "The colonel asked me to hang back until after the briefing so as not to distract you."

Phil turned to Elias and Norton. "If you'll excuse me, gentlemen, I have to watch my son give my wife a heart attack."

Phil led Michael to the level below the plaza level and the museum entrance. Alice was busy planning an expansion of the exhibit from Sotos. Phil cleared his throat, and Alice turned around.

Phil and Michael held their collective breaths, waiting to see what the reaction would be, and Alice didn't disappoint. She eyed Michael up and down, and it took a few seconds to realize who it was. That's when the show started. She squealed in delight, "Mickey!" Then she threw her arms around him, giving him a tight "mom hug."

Suddenly, she grabbed his arms and held him at arm's distance, "What are you doing here? What are you doing in that uniform? What happened to graduate school?"

Michael rolled his eyes. "Geez, Mom, you sound like Dad."

Alice put her hands on her hips. "You don't have to get insulting!"

Phil furrowed his brow when it registered with him what Alice said. Alice left one of the volunteers in charge of the museum, and the three of them went for a walk in the CentMod and finally stopped in a seating area where Michael got his parents fully caught up on the last two and a half years.

Alice was having a hard time making the adjustment to Michael's new profession. He was studying civil engineering the last she knew, and now her son was a soldier and a platoon leader in a ranger company no less.

That's not to say Phil was having an easy time of it. There was a lot to bite off all at once. That night, Michael stayed in Phil and Alice's quarters in the spare bedroom at Alice's insistence because she didn't want to miss a second with Michael while he was on the station.

The next morning, all three went through Phil and Alice's standard routine although they didn't even try to keep up with Michael. Afterward, breakfast time found them at Eva's.

Phil asked, "Where is the rest of your unit?"

Michael answered, "They've moved the regiment to New Iowa for staging and training. The other members of the Earth contingent are on different planets in the area. The plan is to arrive at Gostis at a preplanned time and execute our individual parts of the plan in a timed sequence. Each group brings a different talent to the party, and the operation is being planned to exploit that. After the initial assault, I'm sure it'll be a series of reactions to whatever the opposition offers."

At that moment, Colonel Kline and his staff showed up for breakfast. Phil invited them to sit at their table, which they gladly accepted. Colonel Kline introduced his officers and asked Michael, "Did you manage to surprise your folks yesterday?"

Michael was uncomfortable rubbing elbows with a staff officer, being he was a first lieutenant at his first posting. Michael straightened in his seat. "Indeed I did, sir."

Alice shot a look at her son. "Mickey arriving here was not as surprising as his new vocation. I'm still miffed at him for not telling us."

Phil said to no one in particular, "I'm delighted and very proud of him." He looked up to see Alice glaring at him, and he looked right at Michael. "But I'm very put out that you didn't tell your mother!"

Colonel Kline was clearly amused at the family dynamic.

Phil thought it would be a good idea to change the subject. "Colonel Kline, aren't you concerned with what you soldiers call operational security? It seems to me that there's an awful lot of information in the open about this. We were cautioned not to discuss the operation in general, but it doesn't seem to be a lot of effort in keeping this secret."

The colonel took a sip of coffee. "It's as secret as it needs to be. The details are being held close to the vest. As far as the operation itself, they know we're coming. What they don't know is when or how we plan to defeat their defenses."

Alice asked, "Can you at least tell us how long it will take for those people to come to their senses?"

Kline shook his head. "Impossible to tell. The plan we have laid out now has a high degree of success. That is if the intelligence report on those guys is accurate. The pilots from Astrodyne Corporation are going to be here this afternoon. We're going to brief all the shuttle pilots taking part in this. For now, we have a morning to kill. I suggest we take in that museum. I've been hearing good things about it."

Alice gave Colonel Kline, his staff, and Michael a personal tour of the Museum, which impressed them, especially given its newness. They spent a good deal in the gift shop, which pleased Alice. They mostly bought things to take back to their families. Fineld jewelry was, of course, a popular item. Michael bought a coffee table book that documented the salvage of the *Prospector*.

Phil had station duties to perform, so he couldn't spend time with Michael that morning. All the pilots that could be spared in the Stellar Logistics and Freight Corporation system have arrived that morning along with thirty-five Astrodyne 65s and two pilots each from Astrodyne Corporation. They also brought along a number of Air Force pilots to ensure that the civilian pilots flew the correct profile and crewmen familiar with the requirements of carrying paratroopers.

The Astrodyne's had to be "stacked" to avoid taking up excess docking space. One shuttle would put its starboard hatch against the station's docking port. Then the next shuttle would put its starboard hatch to the first shuttle's port hatch. There were seven stacks made, and the pilots assigned quarters.

*****

## Oasis 4, CentMod Auditorium Number 2

All the shuttle pilots gathered in CentMod Auditorium number 2 for the briefing on the upcoming operation. It wasn't a stretch to realize that the majority of the assembled shuttle pilots had never participated in anything like this.

An Air Force training officer briefed the assembly on the proper flight profile. The most ticklish part of the whole thing is going to be keeping the drop zones a surprise. Low-flying shuttles appearing near sensitive military assets are bound to raise the alarm.

A plan was revealed where formations of shuttles would make low passes on random vectors. This would raise alarms in the Gostis defense forces initially and cause them to go on a heightened alert status. After a while, they would come to get accustomed to the flights. When they saw that the shuttles weren't attempting to land, they would possibly relax their alert profile. The other participants from Earth will be operating on similar lines. Of course, the plan depends entirely on the pretars ability to eliminate the anti-air threat.

The invasion plans were finalized, and each representative went to brief their individual units. Colonel Kline, his staff, and Michael boarded a transport to New Iowa to rejoin their unit. Major Henson took his men back to Reynolds Planet to refit and rearm. Erica Gainsly boarded a transport bound for Oasis 1 with the last of the humans rescued from Holid 4. Freighters began to arrive with containers full of supplies that would be needed for the invasion.

*****

## Gostis, Falta Plantation of Toanin Zisros, Slave Quarters

Rosanne and Tillya ate breakfast, then went outside to board the tram that would take them to the field they would be harvesting today. They walked out of the housing building and took a seat on the waiting tram. The tram was similar to a train, except that it wasn't on rails. A tractor pulled a dozen cars that each had a bench along the centerline that the field-workers would sit on while being taken to their tasks.

When they were all seated, a taskmaster walked along the cars with a device they called a counter. He held the counter in one hand while he held an antenna in the other. The antenna was waved near the neck collars that each slave wore. When the taskmaster was done, he checked the display and made sure that all the slaves that were supposed to be there were actually there. When he was satisfied, he boarded a seat on the last car and pressed a button signaling the tram operator that they could leave.

They bounced along in the dark until they arrived at a building that all recognized but haven't seen since their arrival. All new slaves purchased by Toanin Zisros were processed in this building. Processing consisted of a medical exam, and their collar was coded and affixed permanently around their neck. The collars fitted to the pretars had straps attached that went under the top two arms since their necks were generally about the same size as their heads. Their clothes were issued to them in this building also.

The taskmaster got off the tram and said loudly, "The following slaves will get off and stand on this line facing the building."

The line he mentioned was a white line painted on the pavement in front of and parallel to the building. He pressed a button on his counter, and Rosanne's collar started vibrating. She stepped off the tram and stood on the line. Tillya stood next to her and tried not to show how anxious she was.

The processing building was brightly lit, and the glaring lights dazzled the confused slaves. About a dozen slaves were standing on the line when the taskmaster walked the line passing his antenna past their neck collars. He checked his display and nodded in a satisfied fashion. He went to the building entrance and, after pressing a call button, said into a speaker, "They're assembled."

As the taskmaster went back to his seat on the tram, the building door opened, and a different taskmaster opened the door. "Enter and stand on the line in the first room." The slaves complied although they were concerned with the change in routine.

A snoshin doctor entered with an assistant in tow. The doctor started with the first in line by waving an instrument at the neck collar and then performing medical scans. The scan results were recorded by the assistant, and the doctor would occasionally have the assistant make further notes. When he had a question about a scan result, he would stop and make a more careful examination. Occasionally, he would consult a database when he had a question about alien physiology.

After the general examination each slave was brought into an examination room and the doctor performed a more thorough exam that was decidedly more personal. Rosanne knew better than to ask questions, but it was eating at her not knowing what these tests were for.

*****

## Gostis, Capital City Shuttle Port

Borislav Lovanova guided his Caravel 500 to the pad assigned to him and touched down. He looked toward the terminal building and spotted a group of soldiers scrutinizing him carefully. A ground transport arrived. Snit got out and waited until Borislav opened the hatch.

Borislav stepped down to the ramp, and the Snit smiled. "Mr. Lovanova, it's good to see you made it all right." Borislav opened the cargo hatch to reveal Jason, and Pil Jos removing the shackles from the new slaves.

Then Snit turned to the transport. "Go ahead and help Mr. Lovanova and his men get the new stock unloaded." Three snoshins got out of the transport and approached the shuttle.

One of the snoshins walked up the ramp to the cargo hatch. "We won't need to put restraints on you. There's nowhere you can go. So you might as well cooperate and bend to the inevitable. Now file off the shuttle and get on the transport. You are now the property of Toanin Zisros, a member of the Teanon Council and one of the most important suppliers of falta."

Oliver walked to the hatch and turned to the rest. "Do what he says, man. They'll take better care of us if we cooperate." Oliver and the rest filed off the shuttle and onto the ground transport.

When the ground transport disappeared, Snit asked, "Are you leaving right away, Mr. Lovanova?"

Borislav shook his head. "I thought I would stay for a short while and enjoy your local climate. Perhaps meet with some of the more important buyers and talk about customizing stock orders."

Snit furrowed his brow. "What do you mean by customizing?"

Borislav considered his answer. "There are things happening that make me suspect that my profession will be shut down, as far as Gostis is concerned anyway."

Snit nodded. "Our proper social order seems to be unpopular in other cultures." After securing the shuttle, Snit took Borislav, Jason, and Pil Jos to a hotel to rest from all the traveling and to acclimate to the local time.

*****

## Oasis 4, CentMod Briefing Room

The standard briefing was over, but it had become procedure lately to have what they called a war meeting.

Norton had the task of collecting the information needed and sorting out what was relevant. He stood and looked at his pad. "Things are coming to a head. The *Atlantis Star* and the *Bright Star* have arrived with full loads of supplies. The *Morning Star* is at New Iowa loading supplies and vehicles that will be used by the Rangers. It'll arrive when the Rangers are ready to jump off. There have been containers full of supplies stored here for the other members of the Earth contingent. The rangers are being shuttled to cruise ships that are being pressed into service as troop transports. There's an orbiting station that needs to be secured. The grunsts are going to take care of that in a few hours. When that's done, the pretars will deploy their system for neutralizing the air threat. Our little Astrodyne fleet is leaving tonight for Griska."

That last statement caught everyone off guard. Phil raised his hand. "Excuse me, Nort. Did you say tonight?"

Norton smiled. "Indeed I did. It had to come eventually. It occurred to the folks in charge that if we announced our timetables. It might have a negative effect. Anyway, there will be a pilot's briefing at 1600 Zulu, and launch will be at 1700 Zulu. By the way, all the shuttle pilots have been given commissions in the Air Force Reserve for the duration of this effort. Those who are assigned as pilots are captains, copilots are first lieutenants. I'm a major, of course."

*****

## Gostis, Falta Plantation of Toanin Zisros, Processing Building

After four hours of humiliating tests, the exams were completed. Rosanne and the rest were standing on the line in the main room when a door opened, and a taskmaster led a group of new slaves into the room and had them stand in line. This bunch consisted of twenty-five humans, ten flastons, and five maldors.

It was a scene Rosanne and Tillya were familiar with. The new arrivals were clothed in new slave clothes, which were off-white shorts and pullover shirt, rubber-sole sandals, and a wide-brim cloth hat. They carried two additional sets of clothes, plus bedding and a towel for their personal use. They were all made to stand on white lines painted on the floor in rows behind the front row that Rosanne and Tillya were standing in.

A taskmaster said loudly, "If your neck collar vibrates, stand in the first row!"

He pressed a button on the counter he carried, and thirteen of the new arrivals stepped forward and stood on the first row line. They were all female, consisting of six humans, three flaston, and four maldors.

When the front row was completed, the taskmaster loudly said, "All except the first row, exit the building and stand on the line outside."

Oliver stepped forward. "I don't think we should be separated, man. We'd like it a lot better if we were in one group, man."

The taskmaster stepped over to Oliver. "Why do you think you'll be happier in one group?"

Oliver smiled, thinking that he finally found someone who would listen to reason. He smiled and answered, "We find it a lot easier to stay centered, man. You know, maintain balance."

The taskmaster's face had a puzzled expression. "Balance?"

Oliver smiled. "Yeah, man, balance. It's how we keep in harmony with our surroundings, man. If you want, we can show y—"

The taskmaster fingered a button on the counter. Oliver and the rest of the new arrivals shrieked in pain and fell to the floor in agony. The taskmaster had a grin on his face when he said, "That's how I find balance, man."

Oliver's son lifted his head and yelled, "For pity's sake, shut up, Dad!" The taskmaster yelled, "Get up, all of you! I will only repeat this once! Pick up your things and go outside! Wait on the white line! The slaves in the front row stay here!"

Oliver and the rest did as they were told without a word. When they were gone, the taskmaster went to a communication panel and pressed a button. "The twenty-five selected females are in the main room Madam Zisros."

A door opened, and a snoshin woman with a sour expression entered. She was dressed in fine clothes and wore a tasteful amount of jewelry. She eyed the twenty-five slaves in the same fashion that one would use to evaluate a row of garden tractors in a showroom. One could tell that she felt that interacting personally with slaves was distasteful but necessary in this case.

Finally, she took a breath. "It has been decided that slaves will be bred here on Gostis instead of bringing in slaves from other worlds. I have been tasked by my husband, Mr. Toanin Zisros, to oversee that effort on this plantation. You have been selected to be breeders. Do not concern yourselves with raising the offspring. There will be rearing centers established and staffed by slaves who are too old to be productive. You, twenty-five breeders, will be paired with a male sire and produce offspring."

Rosanne was horrified. "I'm a married woman! I can't be with another man. I have a husband!"

Madam Zisros angered instantly, strode over to Rosanne, and slapped her across the face. "I don't see him here, you stupid girl! I would think you would be grateful to be a mother. We provide you with food, clothing, a bed, and a sense of purpose. Your culture was too weak to prevent you from being brought here, so I would think you would be a little more grateful for being cared for!"

Madam Zisros collected herself. "You'll go back to the fields until we're ready to breed you."

With that, she turned on her heel and left the room. The taskmaster had them go outside where a tram was waiting to take them back to the housing building to assign the newcomers a bunk and to have a meal. Afterward, they would be in the fields picking falta.

On the tram ride, Rosanne's face was still stinging, and she said in a low voice, "My husband will straighten these people out."

The way she said it made Tillya take it as a matter of fact. Rosanne didn't know exactly what Charles Evans was doing. She didn't even know for a fact if he even escaped the slavers. She didn't think he was taken, at least not on the night she was taken. Somehow, she felt he was going to be here for her.

*****

## Gostis, Orbiting Station

The station controller on duty was bored, as there was never a lot of traffic this time of day to occupy his time. This wasn't the bustling trading center that could be found on other worlds. It was simply a place to shuttle falta to, then transfer it to freighters. The ship proximity alert indicator on a panel lit and got the attention of the controller. He picked up binoculars and scanned in 360 degrees. When he didn't see any traffic, he frowned and checked the sensor plot, but it didn't reveal any traffic. He made a note to have the maintenance crew check the calibration of the proximity alert unit in the morning.

A grunst shuttle was directly under the station and backing away. They dropped out of light speed under the station and coasted into position. When they were near enough, they ejected commandos in PEWS and used thrusters to back away from the station. The commandos floated to an access hatch and engaged microgravity generators to attach themselves to the station outer wall.

A commando opened a maintenance assess panel and attached a control. He toggled a switch on the control, and a cargo loading hatch opened. The cargo air lock was large enough to accommodate all the commandos. They entered and closed the outer hatch. Once they repressurized the air lock, they removed their PEWS and readied themselves. There were no viewports in the hatch, so there was no way to tell if there was a welcoming committee on the other side. They crouched with their weapons at the ready and then opened the hatch.

The fact that they were on a space station severely limited the choice of weapons they could use safely. As a result, they used special ammunition that was developed for this exact scenario. It could be used in a standard submachine gun of the type they carried, but the projectile didn't have the needed inertia to penetrate the outer hull of the station. On impact, the projectile emitted a powerful energy burst that had a stunning effect on whoever it struck.

The commandos opened the door and found a dimly lit space with bales of falta. They spread out to clear and secure the room. Then they happened upon a group of slaves moving bales of falta under the watchful eye of a taskmaster.

The slaves immediately put up their hands while the taskmaster had other ideas, and he bolted toward a falta bale to press a panic alarm on the bulkhead behind it. The alarm was installed to alert station security in the event there was a slave revolt. Before he made it safely behind the bale, a human slave tripped him, sending him sprawling on the deck.

Before the taskmaster could react, the slaves grabbed wooden pegs that were used to secure falta bales and used them to beat the taskmaster. The commandos were so surprised at what happened that it took them a few seconds to pull the taskmaster away from the slaves. The taskmaster was properly subdued by binding his hands and feet, then a strip of adhesive tape was put across his mouth.

The commandos swept through the station pushing aside the security personnel. Station security was geared toward subduing unruly slaves and were out of their depth when it came to confronting professional soldiers. Once cleared, the commander sent the message that their assigned task was complete.

A pretar freighter dropped out of light speed and quickly established orbit around Gostis. When it reached predetermined points over the planet, it would jettison what appeared to be cargo containers. It became evident that they were actually more than cargo containers. Thrusters would fire and precisely position the objects.

When the last of the containers were positioned, the ship approached the station and docked. The hatches were opened, and pretar technicians started unloading equipment onto the station. The process was made easier by the station workers who were suddenly emancipated.

Controls were mounted in the control center and the interface to the containers tested. When that was done, General Hosnes Lingur and General Bortas left the freighter and went to the control center. They both congratulated the grunst commando leader for a job well done.

General Lingur looked at General Bortas. "If you would please do the honors, General."

Bortas smiled and looked at one of his soldiers. "Captain Ostic, please contact the Gostis authorities and deliver the message."

The captain had a soldier establish communication which wasn't difficult since they took over the station. The people on the ground were going crazy trying to figure out why they lost contact with their station. The recorded message sent by the pretars basically stated the facts at hand. Their station was taken over, and they should be prepared to endure military action.

Bortas ordered the anti-air brought online. A pretar technician threw switches, lighting up his display, and a map of the Gostis surface appeared. The containers they put in geosynchronous orbit were now collecting data using multiple passive systems. When something needed clarification, an active system would activate and determine the nature of whatever was questionable.

Bortas and Lingur watched the screen as indicators popped up showing locations of bases where the Gostis defense forces kept their interceptors. The pretar technicians put the system in full active mode and collected far more detailed data. The Gostis defense forces started launching interceptors, and that made Bortas smile "You're right. They are predictable."

Lingur nodded. "Arrogance in your opponent can be a powerful ally."

When Bortas was satisfied that they had enough data, he authorized the technicians to activate the neutralizing systems. The computer assigned the appropriate weapon for each target. The canisters launched a series of weapons that were targeted at the facilities that launched the interceptors. The weapons were ejected, and when they were the proper distance away from the canisters, the motors on the weapons ignited, and they streaked to their targets.

The anti-facility weapons were essentially identical, but they were configured according to the specific target they were assigned to. Normal high explosive ordinances were used on buildings, and time-delayed penetrators destroyed hardened targets. Next, more weapons were launched to knock down interceptors that were airborne.

Generals Lingur and Bortas watched as the air defense system on Gostis was decimated. Within an hour, there were no interceptors or bases to threaten the invasion. It was time to neutralize the next threat.

Unmanned vehicles were launched and entered the atmosphere flying preprogrammed courses. The planet's air defense sensing system went into active mode. The sensor arrays were identified and targeted. When the defense system launched anti-aircraft missiles at the drones, the pretar system detected the launch and targeted the launcher. The drones themselves were quite capable of eluding the anti-aircraft missiles largely because there  wasn't a biological pilot to limit the maneuvering required.

The Astrodyne 65s started dropping out of light speed and entering orbit at a slightly higher altitude than the orbiting weapons containers the pretars deployed. Norton Parker keyed his microphone. "Coalition commander. this is Minuteman Transport Six. Are we go for phase three?"

Lingur keyed his microphone. "Stand by Transporter Six."

Bortas looked at the display and asked, "Do we have all the ground-to-air defense facility's detected?"

The pretar technician nodded while not looking away from his screen. "They're all targeted, and weapons assigned."

Bortas ordered, "Launch weapons."

The canisters ejected more weapons that streaked toward their targets. There were explosions all over the planet as the weapons caused secondary detonations. Bortas turned to Lingur and nodded. Lingur keyed his microphone. "Transporter Six, you are go."

Norton switched frequencies and keyed the microphone. "Flight, this is lead, execute plan A."

The Astrodyne's broke into groups and entered the atmosphere. Each group was assigned a route to fly at varying altitudes. The Gostis defense forces could track them, but there wasn't a thing they could do about it.

Phil was leading a flight of three Astrodyne's through a valley with Chad acting as his copilot. An Air Force transport pilot was sitting in the observer seat behind him critiqued his flight. "Altitude and speed are spot on. This is the exact flight profile you need maintain."

Phil nodded. "Keep your hands on the reaction engine controls, Chad. If we set off the anti-landing countermeasures, by the time we get the word about it we'll only have seconds to get out of Dodge."

*****

## Gostis, Council Chambers of the Teanon Council

The council members were fit to be tied. Olunic Noynin continually rang the bell at the head of the council chamber trying to get order. He finally managed to bring the assembly to order. "As you are well aware, we are being attacked. If you'll be patient, General Peintoc is going to give us a briefing from military headquarters."

He pressed a button, and a grave-looking General Peintoc filled the screen facing the assembly. He took a breath. "As you are undoubtedly aware, there has bee—"

Toanin Zisros stood. "I'll save you some time, General! Our orbiting space station has been taken over and is being used as a base for our attackers. There have been reports of our military interceptors being blotted out of the sky at will! Their bases obliterated! Our ground-based air defense system has also been removed from existence! There are alien vessels making bold, low-level flights over our planet with impunity! What can you offer as comfort to ease our minds about these developments?"

The general was genuinely uncomfortable now. "It is a fact that our air defense no longer exists. However, they haven't tried to land troops. They are undoubtedly aware that we have defensive systems to prevent just that."

Zisros interrupted again, "We had air defense systems just this morning, General! As you pointed out, they were obviously vulnerable!"

The general was doing his best to keep his voice even. "Those were active systems and fixed bases. Our opposition used detection methods that were able to exploit that feature. The systems in place to prevent unauthorized landings are passive and detection proof. The fact that they haven't landed troops is evidence of that. We suspect that the low flights are an attempt to trigger the system and get us to expose it."

Zisros decided that he was too much in a rage to engage the general any further, so he sat down. Noynin took the opportunity to try to calm things. "General, please remind us how this system operates that prevents unauthorized landings."

The general nodded. "The Automatic Intruder Countermeasure System is activated when there is an alert situation. There are sensors placed in likely landing areas that will trigger a response if a set of conditions are recorded. Then a series of weapons are launched which will blanket the area of perceived threat."

One of the council members put up a hand. "Excuse me, General. I find it difficult to believe that the entire planet is covered by this wonderful system of yours."

Peintoc shook his head. "It's not because it's not needed everywhere. We only need it in areas of military value. It does an attacker no good to land if they must cross mountains or deserts. By then, we'll have forces in place to counter such a move on our terms."

Toanin said in an exhausted tone, "You've given us reassurances before, General."

Peintoc had a tone of his own. "So far, there hasn't been one enemy soldier set foot on Gostis."

Noynin quickly interjected, "Thank you, General, please keep us informed." With that, he ended the transmission and managed to adjourn the meeting.

The council members were upset, but they decided that there was little to gain in the meeting. They had to settle on being satisfied with daily briefings.

*****

## Gostis, Orbiting Station

The falta bales that were stored in the orbiting station, were transferred outside the station to make room for military supplies. The bales were tied to each other and attached to the station structure. There was no point in throwing away perfectly good falta. After all, Gostis was going to need every goaner to pay reparations. Besides, the bales would store nicely in the vacuum of space.

Phil and the other Astrodyne pilots from the US effort were taking a break from making their low passes of Gostis to have a meal and get some sleep. The *Bright Star*, the *Morning Star*, and the *Atlantis Star* freighters were docked and unloading supplies at the moment.

Meanwhile, other members of the Earth coalition took over the task of making low passes over Gostis. Phil ate dinner with his freighter captain friends, Dave Jacobson, Ed Carlton, and June Dixon. He was encouraged to hear that public perception of what they were engaged in was overwhelmingly positive.

Phil wondered. "How long have you been docked?"

Ed checked his watch. "About five hours now. They'll have me unloaded in about an hour."

Phil was flabbergasted. "That fast! Even the pretars can't unload a ship that fast."

Dave nodded. "The station workers here are extremely motivated to make this a success. I'm thinking we can expect more of the same cooperation from the people that suddenly find themselves free."

June used a napkin in her mouth. "Whatever ends this as quickly as possible. I hope people who are of a mind to use slave labor will see what lengths we're willing to go to will think twice."

Dwight nodded. "Amen, sister."

Phil stood, stretched, and said, "The troop ships will be in orbit in a few hours. Get some rest so we can be at our best tomorrow."

Everyone slept on the Astrodyne that they were assigned to because there weren't accommodations on the station for bunking. After a few hours' rest, the Astrodyne pilots met in the spacious cargo area of the station along with the shuttle pilots from the other members of the Earth contingent. An officer presented the outline and timetable. These things were already worked out and disseminated, but it was always good to reinforce information, particularly since this was the first time all the Earth contingent shuttle crews were in the same room. Generals Lingur and Bortas made short comments, and General Lingur said, "Good luck, gentlemen. This couldn't be done without you."

*****

## Gostis Orbit, Freedom Flight

The Astrodyne pilots went through the hatch that held all forty stacked shuttles. Docking space was at a premium at this station, so the shuttles had to park hatch to hatch. As a result, Dwight had to walk through thirty-nine shuttles before reaching his assigned ship.

When every shuttle was manned with the hatches shut and sealed, indicators switched from red to green. Dwight keyed his microphone. "Freedom flight, lead, disengage in sequence and reassemble at point Alpha."

Each Astrodyne disengaged the docking clamps and thrust away in turn, starting with the outermost shuttle. Dwight waited until the flight formed up and set a course for the two cruise ships being used as troop transports.

The shuttles docked with the transports. Twenty shuttles per ship, ten on each side, four stacks of five for each ship. Colonel Kline was the first to board when the hatches were opened. The rangers were indeed a frightening-looking group of soldiers. Their faces were camouflaged, and their composite helmets sported ragged multi-colored cloth attached to the cover.

Most carried for their personal weapons, an M-56 carbine that uses the standard 6.5-millimeter caseless ammunition. The fact that the ammunition was caseless meant that each round was only slightly longer than the projectile itself, which also meant that each man could carry an impressive amount of ammunition. Each ranger also had a supply of fragmentation grenades. Each squad had two grenade launchers and one machine gun. The machine gun also used caseless ammunition, but it was 7.62-millimeter and in a belt.

After discharging the paratroopers, the shuttles were going to return to the station where they were going to load additional equipment for redeployment to the final objectives, most notably the ninety-millimeter mortars. When all the rangers were boarded and settled in, they disengaged the docking clamps and formed up on Dwight.

*****

## Gostis, Capital City, Hotel Yund

Borislav Lovanova sat on the patio of the hotel near the swimming pool. He was enjoying a cup of tea after his breakfast along with Jason Gannett and Pil Jos.

A snoshin slave wearing the white jacket of a hotel waiter stepped onto the patio with Yidlin Untocks walking behind him. The waiter stopped a few feet from the table. "Excuse me, Mr. Lovanova, there's a Mr. Untocks here to see you."

Borislav waved Yidlin to an empty seat. "Yidlin, please sit." Then he said to the waiter, "Bring Mr. Untocks a beverage."

Untocks barely acknowledged the waiter's presence. "Bring me a hot guthar with extra crystals."

The waiter bowed and backed away.

Borislav smiled at the newcomer. "It's nice to see you, Yidlin. Have you been able to talk to Toanin Zisros about what we discussed earlier?"

The waiter returned with Yidlin's drink on a tray along with fresh drinks for Borislav and the others. Yidlin added the crystals to his drink and stirred with a wooden stick. "Indeed I did. He and his colleagues are planning to breed slaves here because they feel that slaves born into that condition will be more controllable. However, before any such slaves are old enough to be useful, the current stock will be worn out. With the current efforts off-world to curtail the accusation of fresh stock, this would be a problem. Your proposal of filling in that age gap with children has piqued some interest."

Borislav sipped his tea. "I'm looking forward to meeting this Toanin Zisros.

By the way, what were those explosions we heard yesterday?"

Yidlin waved his hand. "Off-worlders, they're just trying to intimidate us."

At that moment, a flight of ten Astrodyne 65s in V formations flew past, barely a hundred meters over their heads.

*****

## The Aurora

Phil and Chad were laughing because they were flying low enough to actually spot persons on the ground and see their reactions. They were flying lead in the second group; Dwight was flying lead in the first group. Phil suddenly stopped laughing. He wasn't sure why, but there were several things happening at once, and each was demanding a different emotion. First, there was the concentration required to complete the task at hand, and the excitement it generated. Then there was the concern for his son Michael who may be in the back of this very shuttle.

It was decided that they would make more low-level passes to confuse the enemy before the final pass over the drop zone. Phil checked his position and saw he was precisely where he had to be on this leg of the flight.

When they were ten minutes from the drop zone, the Air Force officer used the ship intercom to inform the jump master. Two Air Force crewmen partially opened the cargo doors on each side. The jump master had the troops stand and check equipment. Chad threw a switch that illuminated a red-ready light, indicating that they were one minute from the drop zone.

The rangers would have normally preferred to jump at night, but it was decided that since the snoshins had no experience in dealing with paratroopers, jumping at night added an additional risk that was most likely unnecessary.

The jump master yelled over the noise of the open door, "Hook up!"

The paratroopers hooked their static lines to the cable that ran the length of the cargo area along the sides. Only the troops along the sides could hook up. As they exited, the ones seated in the center would file into line, and when they reached the cable, they would hook up. The jump master yelled, "Stand in the door!"

The company commander stood in the door, then turned to his men. "Rangers, lead the way!"

The rangers replied, "All the way!"

Chad threw a switch illuminating a green light. The jump master yelled, "Go!"

The company commander leaped out of the shuttle, and his chute opened while the rangers filed out behind him one after the other in good order.

*****

## Gostis, Orbiting Station

Cameras were set up to record the event, and the signal was transmitted to the orbiting station where Generals Lingur and Bortas were watching on monitors. They switched to the view taken from the trail shuttle. They watched as paratroopers streamed out of each shuttle, and the chutes opened.

Bortas was immensely interested in the mechanics of the operation while Lingur shook his head. "Part of me didn't believe Colonel Kline when he told me about this."

*****

## Gostis, Falta Plantation of Toanin Zisros

Tillya stopped at the sound of ten Astrodyne's in formation. They had been admonished the previous day, not to look up at the low-flying shuttles, but something caught her attention. The sight of men falling from the ships was shocking. She whispered, "Rosanne! Look!"

Rosanne stopped her picking and stood straight. "Do you know what that is?

That's our ticket home."

The taskmaster they called boss saw them not working and gave them a warning jolt on their collars. He bellowed, "I won't warn you again! Get back to work! Those activities don't concern you!"

*****

## Gostis, Orbiting Station

After a few minutes, a communications technician sitting at a console nearby reported, "Sir, the human units are checking in. The American Rangers are on the ground and moving to their objectives. The British SAS is on the ground and heading toward their objectives..."

The report was identical for the French, Russians, Ukrainians, Germans, New Zealanders, and Australians. Lingur shook his head.

"Amazing."

Bortas smiled. "I'd say absolutely brilliant."

*****

## Gostis, Hill 567, Overlooking Gostis Defense Network Data Processing and Command Center

Colonel Kline selected this position for his command post because it was in sight of both Ranger objectives, and it was relatively easy to defend. The first objective was a data processing and command center for the planet's defense network. The second objective was a military shuttle port. The main problem was there was a garrison of ten thousand enemy soldiers ten kilometers to the south.

The processing center was located in a narrow valley with the shuttle port about three kilometers to the south. Both facilities had substantial forces to guard them, but Kline calculated that they could deal with them with relative ease.

A radio operator reported, "Sir, all units report that they're at their phase lines."

Kline checked his watch. "Everyone, go."

The radio operator relayed the signal, and there was an instant response.

It sounded like two sustained explosions coming from the directions of the shuttle port and the data center. The rangers used grenade launchers to throw special rounds that covered the fence with det cord that, when it exploded, completely disintegrated the fence in wide sections. Rangers rushed through the gaps and began the task of clearing the detachments that were tasked with defending those facilities.

The data center was a series of buildings not unlike any such facility anywhere. As with all such places, once past the outer perimeter, most defensive plans tend to fall apart. The defenders were confused but put up a fight; however, they didn't have a plan to fight a force that got inside the facility. That much was obvious.

Another thing that struck the rangers as odd was the choice of uniform the opposition was wearing. They were wearing white uniforms with dark red jackets that looked like they would be more at home on a parade ground than on a battlefield.

They found the building that housed the equipment they needed to destroy. A squad set to the task of getting inside the building, which was the only true obstacle up to this point. The door was sturdy, and there were no windows, so getting in was tricky and dangerous. Shaped charge explosives were placed on the door perimeter, along with a high explosive charge in the center of the door. The detonator was triggered, and the shaped charges sliced through four inches of solid nickel steel. After a delay of less than half a second, the high explosive detonated and threw the door into the building, then the team followed the door in and started clearing rooms with small arms fire and hand grenades.

Once cleared, explosives were placed on three cable bundles: one was on the power cable, one on the data bus from the sensor network, and one on the weapons control bus. When detonated, the defense system in their sector was rendered inert.

The battle for the shuttle port was having similar success. After the objectives had been accomplished, the commanders of both attacks radioed success to Colonel Kline, who relayed the news to the orbiting station.

Several shocked and confused prisoners were taken, then they were secured in a makeshift stockade at the shuttle port. The rangers then started preparing for an expected counterattack from the garrison located ten kilometers to the south. The Astrodyne's returned to the orbiting station and picked up containers full of additional equipment and brought it to the shuttle port. The rangers used ground transports that they captured to move the equipment to the rest of the unit, which was deployed to meet the counterattack.

*****

## Gostis, Council Chambers of the Teanon Council

Olunic Noynin was trying desperately to get the Teanon Council to come to order. The council was understandably upset. Finally, Toanin Zisros stood, and the others calmed down. Olunic put up his hand. "We have General Peintoc standing by."

Toanin was seething, and he shot a hateful glare at the monitor. General Peintoc started to say, "I'm sure you've heard that enemy soldiers have been landed on Gostis soil."

Toanin roared in as sarcastic a voice as he could, "Oh really! Is that what all the noise was?"

Olunic asked, "Tell us, General, how many of the enemy transports have been destroyed?"

Peintoc uttered, "None."

Toanin turned red. "You assured us that our defense system would be effective!"

Peintoc nodded. "It would have been if they actually landed."

Toanin roared, "How does one get from a flying shuttle to the ground without landing? Are these aliens a winged species we haven't heard of?"

Peintoc shook his head. "They're humans. The reports are confusing, but witnesses said they jumped out of the shuttles and floated to the ground using some sort of device."

Olunic asked, "What is the military situation at present?"

Peintoc looked grave. "The humans attacked with the express purpose of neutralizing our defense system, which they've accomplished. They are anticipating our counterattack, and they're making preparations. There is one sector that they didn't attack, and the defense grid is intact there."

Olunic asked, "Why did they leave that one sector intact?"

Peintoc shook his head. "One can only guess, but I would say that sector isn't necessary for their plans. I've ordered the Fifth Armored Motorized division there for two purposes. First of all, the humans wouldn't be able to destroy that facility with the Fifth Motorized sitting there. Also, it's in a good position to attack in several different directions if needed."

Toanin growled, "I don't need to remind you, General, that failure here would be catastrophic. As it is, you need to be very impressive to avoid being moved to the lower classes."

Peintoc said, very deadpan. "I'll keep you, gentlemen, informed as best as I can, but I'll be extremely busy for the next few days."

The monitor went blank, and the council was silent for the first time. Olunic turned to Toanin. "I don't think he's used to people talking to him that way."

*****

## Gostis, Supreme Military Headquarters, Outside Capital City

General Peintoc was seething after his conversation with the council. Being treated like a second-class citizen was getting tiresome. Then the reality of the social order became crystal clear; he was indeed a second-class citizen. No matter how brilliantly he performed his duties, he would never be viewed as an equal to the men that sat on the Teanon Council.

Olunic Noynin was possibly the most amiable of the council members. The member he truly hated the most was Toanin Zisros, of all the haughty, condescending, spoiled elites. He made up his mind right then and there. If he wins this fight, he'll make sure there's a different social order on Gostis.

He stood and went to the situation room. Entering the room, he stopped to stare at the map displayed on a monitor that took up an entire wall. He ordered, "Show the enemy positions in red."

An aide stepped up to the map. "The enemy landed their troops near sensitive strategic facilities and attacked those facilities. As you know, our defense network has been neutralized except sector nine."

Peintoc was short on patience at the moment. "How is the enemy redeploying?"

The aide was uncomfortable. "We haven't been able to determine that. They attack and destroy, then they just disappear."

Peintoc studied the map and said, "The shuttle port and data processing center to the south of Capital City is destroyed, as is the identical facilities to the southeast. The facility to the southwest was left intact. There must have a reason."

The aide cleared his throat. "Sir, if you'll permit me. The centers that they eliminated in the outer provinces were necessary to their plans. Once they've established themselves there, they could reinforce and tie up our forces to prevent them from driving on to Capital City and protecting the Teanon Council."

Peintoc nodded. "That makes sense, except the facility to the southwest is a higher value target. It would have made more sense to ignore one of the outer province facilities."

The aide said, "We don't think they had a choice in the matter. The location of the facility makes it very difficult to approach. With the speed the enemy has demonstrated, they needed to be effective. We've analyzed the method they used to put troops on the ground, and we've concluded that they need large areas of open country to make it work. The facility to the southwest is in a narrow valley with thick forest surrounding it for extremely long distances."

Peintoc nodded. "While we're on the subject, how exactly did they manage to land troops?"

The aide almost smiled. "It took some research, but we saw the first wave was human, so a search in the Earth database revealed something very interesting." He tapped a file symbol on the display screen and several files opened.

Peintoc stood and looked at each file in turn, including a video. He stepped back and put his hands on his hips. "How does one predict something like that?"

Finally, he said, "What's done is done. We must deal with what's in front of us. What's happening in this sector?"

The aide checked his data, and he put up a topographic map of the sector. We know the enemy has a detachment at the shuttle port as guards until the pretars can land enough of their own soldiers to take over. They've begun to shuttle down just a short time ago. We believe the humans have taken positions to block the advance of the Dagger Infantry Division."

Peintoc rubbed his chin and asked, "Where is the Dagger Division now?"

The aide said, "They should be in action anytime now. General Kolunoc reported his scouts were entering the valley."

Peintoc nodded. "They're a force of ten thousand. That should be sufficient.

After all, I can't imagine there being half as many enemy soldiers there."

*****

## Gostis, Rondoli River Valley

Lt. Michael Ross positioned his men in a fashion to inflict the most damage on their enemy. The Gostis defense forces were sure to attempt to retake the shuttle port the rangers held, even if they did realize that it didn't really matter who held the shuttle port since landings could continue at a makeshift location. The fact of the matter was, the rangers were sitting between the Gostis defense force infantry division and their capital city.

The river snaked through the valley, which made things easier for the Rangers. From his hilltop, Colonel Kline had an excellent view of the expected battlefield. Earlier, there were explosions coming from the direction of the oncoming infantry division. A communication from the orbiting station told them that the Gostis defense forces tried to launch aerial assault shuttles, but the pretar system detected and eliminated them. Their own shuttles could continue delivering troops and supplies due to the use of transponder codes programmed in the shuttle's communications systems.

Kline knew how many troops he had against him and how many he had. Peintoc was more correct than he knew. The Dagger Division was nearly three times the strength of the rangers that opposed them.

The portion of the valley that they dug into was where it narrowed considerably. The Dagger Division would enter the valley from a wide plain, funneling them together and restricting their ability to maneuver. Kline smiled and remarked, "This setup is page one from the textbook."

Movement at the mouth of the valley caught Kline's eye. He raised his binoculars and saw what he assumed was the division scout. The vehicle stopped at a point of higher elevation, and a hatch opened on top where a soldier's head appeared and took a good long look with his own binoculars. He lowered his binoculars and talked into a microphone. Moments later, nine troop transports motored up and took position behind the scout. The scout then motored forward, crossed a bridge, and continued into the valley.

The scout repeated the process of stopping and making observations. The troop transports crossed the first bridge and again took up position behind the scout. The scout was halfway across a second bridge when a missile streaked out of the tree line and slammed into the side of the vehicle. Flames poured out of the vehicle, and it became a fiery roadblock. The transports behind it reversed, and a second missile tore open a transport as it mounted the first bridge attempting to escape.

The transports were now trapped between the two bridges. Not having a choice in the matter, the troops dismounted the vehicles and attempted to reach cover. They rushed toward the tree line, but before they reached safety, Michael ordered "open fire," and his men cut down the opposition. There were about a dozen that made it back to the vehicles, but it was plain to see the initial engagement was handily won by Michael's platoon.

The Dagger Division commander, General Kolunoc, watched through binoculars as his lead element was chopped to pieces. He consulted a map and determined where his opponents had to be positioned and ordered his artillery battery in position to cover an assault. He was feeling confident that the enemy position could be overrun if properly prepared.

He wasn't feeling confident in his troop transports, though. The armor plate might not as well be there, for all the good that it did. While the artillery battery was setting up, he ordered two battalions to reposition themselves before the first bridge and dismount.

Kline could see what was happening and ordered his units to reposition to secondary locations. They repositioned in time to avoid the Gostis preparatory artillery bombardment. The area nearest the first attack was saturated with high- explosive fragmentation ordinance. To mask their movements, the Dagger Division commander had smoke rounds mixed with the other ordinance.

A battalion from Dagger Division moved into the area occupied by the disabled troop transports under the cover of the barrage. The battalion commander ensured that his leading assault units were in place then he ordered them forward.

Kline watched from his position as the leading elements of the new attack approached the position formally held by his rangers. It almost amused Kline that he could tell what his opponents were thinking by the way they maneuvered. It was painfully obvious that they weren't encountering what they expected. When they reached the edge of the area that received the artillery bombardment, they stopped.

Kline watched as an officer used a radio to report to the rear then have his men take positions. Kline's aide was also watching and commented, "I wonder who thought it was a good idea to make their soldiers wear white uniforms?"

Kline grinned. "You have to admit, the red jackets are snazzy."

Kline lowered his binoculars. "Did we get a position fix on their artillery?"

The aide lowered his own binoculars. "Yes, sir, and a platoon of rangers are ready to deal with it."

Kline raised his binoculars again. "They won't use their big guns again on this assault, but they could be a problem later. Have them dealt with before light tomorrow."

*****

## Gostis, Rondoli River Valley Shuttle Port

Pretar shuttles have been arriving and unloading troops and equipment from the moment Kline's Rangers secured the facility. The last shuttle carried General Bortas and his staff. On touchdown, he exited and was led to a makeshift command center that was set up in the shuttle port administration building. He looked around to take in the layout his people set up. Finally, he strolled over to the map and studied it. After a few minutes, he ordered, "Give me a rundown of the situation thus far."

An aide consulted his notes. "Yours was our last shuttle. Our units are taking position in preparation to drive on to Capital City. The units from Reynolds Planet are landing as we speak. They will be on our left flank, except their reconnaissance element, who will be well forward of all our units. The flastons will be landing after Colonel Devonport's men are on the ground and they will be on our right flank. The humans who landed in the outer provinces have effectively neutralized the Gostis forces there, or they're in the process of securing their areas of responsibility. The shuttle port and data center to the southeast was captured by the humans from the British SAS. The Griska troops are landing there and preparing to drive onto Capital City with the malnuns covering their right flank and the maldors on their left flank."

Bortas nodded in approval. "What is the status of Colonel Kline's Rangers?"

The aide reported, "They've taken position at a narrow point in the Rondoli River Valley. There was a skirmish earlier with the leading elements from"—the aide checked his notes—"the Dagger Division. There has been a pre-attack artillery bombardment and the Dagger Division counterattack is expected any moment."

*****

## Gostis, Rondoli River Valley

An entire battalion of infantry was moving toward the rangers who had taken cover in fighting positions along the steep slope on the right side of the valley when facing upstream. The left side of the valley had a sheer cliff that went right down to the river, limiting options for General Kolunoc. If he wanted to take the shuttle port back and engage the pretars, he had to clear out these human demons.

His men were in chevron formations headed toward the steep sides of the valley. When they reached the foot of the hill, Michael ordered the remotely detonated mines fired. The first two chevrons were mowed down. The battalion commander responded instantly by ordering his men to go up the first draw. As they proceeded up, a squad of rangers, along one side of the draw, opened fire and cut down the attackers. Those who weren't cut down took cover.

Reinforcements poured into the draw to press the attack on the rangers along the side of the draw. The rangers on the opposite side of the draw opened fire, allowing those opposite of them to take up new fighting positions further up the draw. When the Gostis troops reached the positions, they were being decimated from. They would find them abandoned, and they were under withering fire from higher up.

After two hours of fighting, there wasn't enough of the Gostis fighting force to press the attack. Those who could surrender did. The ones that could flee, fled. Prisoners were rapidly transported to the shuttle port to prevent them from being a burden.

Kolunoc put down his binoculars. "Contact that battalion commander! I must know how the attack went!"

The communications officer was genuinely flummoxed. "Sir, they're not responding!"

After some time had passed, some of the survivors made it back to safety and reported on the failure of the effort. The division commander's blood ran cold, and he envisioned his fate if he were to fail in his assignment. He turned to his aide. "I want to see the commanders of the second brigade in half an hour."

*****

## Gostis, Rondoli River Valley Seventy-Fifth Ranger Regiment Command Post atop Hill 567

Kline checked his watch and saw it was time for the platoon that was assigned to deal with the enemy artillery to begin their attack. It was the early morning hours, and he wondered how his opposition was going to react to a night attack.

So far, they haven't impressed him as being very good soldiers, and he seriously doubted that they were proficient at night fighting.

A radio operator nearby reported, "Sir, Postlethwaite reports he's at the phase line."

Postlethwaite was the platoon leader assigned to relieve the Dagger Division of its artillery. The phase line was the predetermined reporting position for this mission.

Kline nodded. "Give them the green light." The response was relayed to the platoon leader, and Kline raised his binoculars in anticipation.

*****

## Gostis, Dagger Division Rear Area Artillery Firing Point

A platoon of rangers had marched to their objective under the cover of darkness. They had climbed steep hills to go around the flanks and reach the Dagger Division artillery firing point. Lt. Postlethwaite waved his men forward and they rushed into the artillery firing point.

There were only a handful of guards that were dealt with in short order. Postlethwaite had the bulk of his platoon stand overwatch while teams placed charges on the stored ammunition. Next, they put an incendiary grenade in each cannon tube. When all the charges were set, everyone faded back to defensive positions. Once they were a safe distance, the incendiary grenades were triggered remotely, and great plumes of smoke poured from the muzzles until the white- hot flaming mass burned through the bottom of the tubes.

A sentry some distance away raised the alarm, and there was instant chaos. The cannon crews rushed out of their tents and ran to the guns. Lieutenant Postlethwaite yelled for his men to take cover then triggered the charges on the artillery ammunition. The ensuing explosion could be felt all the way to Capital City.

As part of the plan, Postlethwaite had his platoon take the most direct route back to their own lines. The Dagger Division soldiers were confused and disorganized. As a result, the ranger platoon was in a two hour long, moving firefight to get back to a point where they were covered by the rest of the rangers.

*****

**Gostis, Dagger Division Field Command Post**

Kolunoc was in a rage. His artillery was gone, and the attackers managed to make it back to their own lines. His officers were in front of him with sheepish expressions while he berated them, "Did it not occur to any of you that they may be motivated to deny us of the one major advantage we possessed? Then they strolled back to their lines while we ran in circles screaming, "Please don't shoot me!"

A colonel tried to plead his case, "Sir, they're using tactics that we've never remotely considered training for."

Kolunoc refused to hear any explanations. "Don't make excuses! We're going to attack at first light, and I expect to be eating my midday rations in the enemy command post! Get your units in position to begin the attack!"

*****

**Gostis, Rondoli River Valley, Area of Operations, Alpha Company, Third Platoon**

Michael was in the location of his first action, and the first hint of sunup was visible behind him. He didn't have long to wonder when the counterattack was coming. He could see movement in the distance. The

Gostis defense forces white uniforms stood out in the dark, denying them of any kind of surprise. Michael watched as they deployed their units to positions where they could begin their attack. Michael used his radio to report his observations.

The balance of the Dagger Division aligned themselves against the rangers and prepared for a frontal assault. When they started moving forward, Michael keyed the microphone on his radio. "Thud Bud Alpha, Alpha three-six. Requesting barrage at presighted targets Bravo through Echo."

The mortar crews at the top of the hill consulted a table they made upon arrival and adjusted their tubes to put ordinance on the requested targets.

Michael heard behind him the unmistakable thudding sound of mortar rounds leaving the tubes. The units to his left and right made similar requests and the mortars assigned to them went into action. Each tube had a crew of three. One adjusted the fire control system, changing the point of aim between each round while the other two fed rounds to the mortar. The firing rate was so rapid that an experienced crew could put thirty to forty rounds down range in a minute.

The oncoming enemy formations hesitated at the sound of the mortars leaving the tubes. The rounds started raining down on the white uniformed soldiers, and it had the desired effect. Michael watched in awe as the rounds dropped in among the oncoming snoshins at an incredible rate. The Gostis units that weren't as far forward were spared from the barrage, so they rushed forward in an attempt to close with the rangers before the mortar crews could readjust. Most were successful and got uncomfortably close.

Michael's platoon sergeant set off the remotely detonated mines, shredding scores of attackers. Dozens of firefights broke out along the axis of attack as the Gostis forces tried to force their way through the rangers.

By midmorning, the Dagger Division had had enough, and they started to surrender. At first one or two individuals would give up, then larger groups. Finally, General Kolunoc came forward with his staff. He had tears streaming down his face as he waited for Colonel Kline to arrive. Kline faced Kolunoc and presented a crisp hand salute, which Kolunoc returned by putting his fist on his shoulder in the fashion of the Gostis Defense Forces. Then with Kline's permission he instructed his men to attend to the wounded under the watchful eyes of the Rangers.

Not only was there wounded to attend to, but those who were killed in action. There was an ever-increasing number of slaves who had taken the opportunity to escape and found themselves seeking sanctuary with the rangers. After assuring the escaped slaves that they were indeed free, they were utilized in the task of policing the battlefield. The pretars anticipated the requirements of the rangers after the battle, and they sent trams they liberated from falta plantations to move the wounded and the prisoners to a POW enclosure they set up at the shuttle port.

After the battle was won, there was no reason to stay in the Rondoli River Valley, so the rangers boarded the trams and went to the shuttle port where they took over a maintenance hangar to get some well-deserved sleep.

*****

## Gostis, Supreme Military Headquarters, Outside Capital City

General Peintoc stared at the tactical map. "What is the situation in the Rondoli River Valley?"

The aide approached General Peintoc. He inhaled and, in a trembling voice, said, "Sir, we just received a report about the Dagger Division."

Peintoc didn't like the way his aides voice sounded. "Carry on, Captain."

The aide continued, "Sir, the Dagger Division has been neutralized. Their attack failed, and the survivors have been taken prisoner."

Peintoc was staggered and speechless. Finally, he looked over the map and nodded. "Sector 9 is quiet. I think I'll put additional units there to keep the Fifth Motorized Armor Division company."

Peintoc's aide hesitated. "Yes, sir. It'll be done right away."

The aide was loyal and obedient, and he was always eager to learn his craft. "Sir. I can't help but wonder why."

Peintoc slowly nodded. "The Fifth Motorized is our most capable unit. They project the most offensive potential. If they were augmented with additional infantry, they could be quite affective. The enemy can't land shuttles in that sector yet, and it's unlikely they'll ever be able to with an armored division sitting there. All the enemy has is light infantry. We could frustrate them with the correct mix of tactics and unit composition."

*****

## Gostis, Rondoli River Valley Shuttle Port

Colonel Devonport was on the last shuttle of the Reynolds Planet contingent. He was gray-haired, tall, and lean, but mostly, he was very British. It was easy to pick up on the fact that he was a very no-nonsense person, except for the swagger stick that he carried. He strode into the administration building and General Bortas's staff directed him to the situation room that they set up.

Bortas looked up. "Ah, there you are, Colonel. Welcome to Gostis."

Devonport shook hands with Bortas. "Good to be here. Are we on schedule?"

Bortas smiled and nodded. "Indeed we are. Please come over to the map, and I'll bring you up to date."

Bortas pointed out the disposition of the units on the ground and what had been accomplished thus far. Devonport nodded and smiled. "Kline's lads did a bang-up job. Sturdy chaps."

Bortas nodded. "The Earth contingent is what made this venture possible. I shudder to think what our casualties would be like if we landed the old- fashioned way."

Bortas paused and said, "Your Major Henson is pushing toward Capital City, and he reports that there are Gostis infantry units filtering to the sector to the southwest of Capital City."

Devonport furrowed his brow. "That's not good news. There's a motorized unit there now. If they reinforce, they could be a real problem. They can counterattack in the direction of our flanks."

Bortas nodded. "It is worrisome that they're reinforcing that position now. When Colonel Kline's Rangers are rested, I think I'll ask him to position themselves to counter any moves they may make."

Devonport nodded. "You know, looking at this, their reserves to the southwest of Capital City can only attack to the north and northeast. Attacking south and west of their position gains them nothing since there's nothing there. Attacking east toward the Griska forces isn't possible due to the mountain range between the two positions."

Bortas agreed. "Those were my conclusions. So as it is, the Griska troops, malnuns, and maldors will have secure flanks as they drive to Capital City. That means that it will fall to us to deal with the Gostis forces to the southwest."

*****

## Gostis, Ten Kilometers South of the Rondoli River Valley Shuttle Port

Major Henson was in a reconnaissance vehicle standing on the passenger seat with his head out of the roof hatch. They were parked at the edge of a wooded area overlooking a field of falta. His mission wasn't to engage in combat but report the position of the Gostis forces.

So far, his men haven't encountered any, but they didn't expect to yet. The intelligence he had told him that the opposition was pulled in tight to Capital City. That was both good news and bad news in that it gave the attackers time and space to organize. But it also gave the defenders time to prepare for the coming attack.

His men were in ten vehicles spread out over several kilometers along the axis of attack. His first responsibility was locating any enemy lookouts and neutralize them. He didn't want to lead his men into an ambush, but he didn't think that was a realistic possibility since the reports he had so far didn't paint the Gostis defense forces in a professional light.

He did have reason to be concerned, though. The troops tasked to guard the seat of government were bound to be better equipped and trained than the troops in outlying districts. He reminded himself that he couldn't make assumptions about the capabilities of the people he was facing.

Each of his vehicles had four men each. Where necessary they'll park, three of them would dismount and scout ahead. When they were satisfied that they weren't heading into trouble, they would remount their vehicles and continue. Henson made it back to the vehicle before his two scouts, so he was using binoculars to closely examine the terrain ahead. From the corner of his eye, he saw his two scouts hurry back to the vehicle, and before he could ask, they grabbed the camouflage netting that was secured on the hood and pulled it over the whole vehicle. One scout took a position to the left where he had a view of the falta field in front of him.

The second scout edged up next to Henson. "Some workers just entered the field from our right." The scout then found his own position and waited. Henson was understandably nervous. Although the vehicle was well- camouflaged and in an excellent location, spotting it would be difficult enough if you were looking for it. If your attention was on other things, it was easy to miss.

Henson kept his head through the roof hatch, as he had his face painted camouflage, and his hat was adorned with foliage to break up its shape and help it blend into the background. A line of field-workers was making their way through the falta. Henson saw they were cultivating the crop with what looked like Gostis versions of hoes. The workers on their end of the field would pass within feet of them.

As the field-workers chopped away at the weeds, Henson saw two individuals lagging behind the workers that he immediately identified as the taskmasters, which he understood was the equivalent of overseers on Earth. The taskmasters were a decent distance away, so all they had to do is sit tight and wait for them to pass.

The line of workers was as close as they could get. The closest was a malnun who was busy chopping away at the weeds. Suddenly, the malnun stopped, then, while he remained hunched over, turned his head and looked directly at Henson. He wasn't surprised to see soldiers because everyone in the vicinity of Capital City could hear the previous days battle.

While making hoeing motions, he asked in a low voice, "Are you looking for Gostis soldiers?"

Henson answered in as low a voice as he could, "Yes, we are. Do you know where they are?"

The malnun shook his head. "I don't know. I haven't seen any between here and the slave compound, about five ligins straight off your nose. Get in the field and go to your right then follow the tree line. You'll avoid meeting anyone."

At once, the closest taskmaster yelled, "Who are you talking to!"

The malnun stood straight, then lowered his eyes. "No one, Boss. I was just complaining about these stubborn weeds."

Henson saw the malnun casually move to get the taskmasters line of sight away from him and his men. The taskmaster pressed a button on the counter he carried, and the malnun let out a scream. The taskmaster yelled, "This is the only thing you need to complain about! Now get back to work!"

The taskmaster strutted off after making sure the malnun started hoeing again. The malnun turned his head while chopping away at the weeds, then he looked at Henson and smiled. Henson smiled back.

The driver asked, "How far is a ligin?"

Henson consulted a pad. "According to this, it's about a kilometer and two- thirds."

When the line of workers reached the end of the field, they boarded a tram and were transported away. The two scouts stowed the camouflage netting, and Henson had the driver follow the tree line as suggested by the malnun.

*****

### Gostis, Rondoli River Valley Shuttle Port

Kline went into the makeshift headquarters set up by the pretars and was led to General Bortas. Bortas turned and smiled. "Ah, Colonel Kline. Are you and your men rested?"

Kline smiled back. "Yes, we are and were itching to get back in action."

Bortas led Kline to a large-scale map and said, "I think we can accommodate you. You see here that the Gostis defense forces have a motorized division to the southwest of Capital City. They've been reinforcing since yesterday. From their position, they can attack our flanks. In fact, if they move quick enough, they could even get behind us."

Kline studied the map. "If I read this correctly, what you could use is a roadblock."

Bortas gave Kline a sideways look. "A roadblock with teeth."

Kline rubbed his chin. "We have a lot of anti-armor, but I've studied their composition, and we didn't bring enough to take on that whole division."

Bortas nodded. "Perhaps it would be enough to slow them down."

Kline nodded. "We can do that. If we can disable enough vehicles in strategic locations, they'll have to stop and clear the road. I still wouldn't mind if the odds were cut down a bit more."

After studying the map, Kline asked, "What's the progress so far?" Bortas answered, "The report I have from General Lingur is the Griska troops are driving toward Capital City, and they have started to meet resistance. My troops are driving north. Major Henson of the Reynolds Planet contingent is scouting ahead, and he reported the position of the enemies' forward positions. When my units are situated, we'll go on the attack."

Bortas smiled. "There's a problem we didn't anticipate. As our troops move forward, we liberate falta plantations. It's very difficult to carry on operations and organize the liberated slaves. We've been detaining the plantation owners and taskmasters to prevent them from communicating with their friends. The slaves have been most helpful in agreeing to keep an eye on their old masters and stay out of our way. Have your vehicles been unloaded yet?"

Kline nodded. "Yes, they have, and my guys have figured out how to operate the personnel carriers we captured in the first engagement. With all that, we've become quite mobile. What kind of terrain are we looking at?"

Bortas said, "The ground to my front is sparsely populated woodland with falta plantations sprinkled around and some gentle hills. You'll be going over your original drop zones, which is pastureland and falta plantations. That gives way to dense woodland and steep hills, which is where the reinforced motorized division is located."

Kline saluted Bortas and said, "Rangers lead the way." Bortas smiled and returned the salute. "All the way."

*****

## Gostis, Capital City, Hotel Yund

Borislav Lovanova stood on the pool patio next to Jason Gannett and Pil Jos. They were staring to the southeast and the columns of billowing smoke that was dominating the skyline. Borislav tried to leave the previous day, but he was warned not to due to the fact that any shuttles trying to leave Gostis without permission was subject to destruction.

Yidlin Untocks strode up and joined them in staring at the horizon. Borislav asked while not taking his eyes off the smoke rising on the horizon. "Yidlin, do you have a place to hide us if that makes it to the city?"

Untocks nodded. "Mr. Zisros has graciously offered to secret you at his plantation until this crisis can be resolved."

Borislav was relieved in the short term, but he was looking at the long view. "My shuttle is at the civilian shuttle port. If they check the registration, I'm done. I'll be on the run the rest of my life."

Untocks shook his head. "If they make it this far, there's a long way for them to go yet. At any rate, Mr. Zisros's plantation is in the opposite direction of the fighting. You and I are welcome there because of our status in the syndicate. Your friends however aren't high enough for consideration with Mr. Zisros, but do not fear, Snit has graciously offered to accommodate them in his home until the present troubles are over."

Borislav looked relieved. "When can we leave?"

Yidlin smiled. "Anytime you're ready. Snit is waiting with a transport now.

We can leave as soon as you can gather your things." Borislav asked, "Is Mr. Zisros going to be going with us."

Yidlin shook his head. "He has important business at the Teanon Council. He will do what he can to join us later."

Borislav, Jason, and Pil Jos went to their rooms and quickly packed their belongings and climbed into a transport with Yidlin and Snit doing the driving. The road they took went directly west and skirted along the edge of the operating area of the Fifth Motorized division.

After they've traveled west a good distance, Snit turned north and traveled about half an hour more.

This is the most traveling Borislav has done on Gostis, and he was getting a bit of an education. It was actually a very pleasant planet with its woodlands and farms. The open-aired transport allowed all the smells to be experienced, which Borislav and the rest enjoyed.

After a while, Snit turned off the main road and drove through an impressive gate. Yidlin explained that they just entered the Zisros Plantation. The drive to the main house went through field after field of falta. They passed one of the wagons that moved the falta pods from the field to the processing house. As they passed, more than one field-worker saw who was in the transport as it passed. They finally reached the main house, where they were greeted by Madam Zisros.

*****

## Falta Plantation of Toanin Zisros, Slave Quarters

Rosanne sat at the communal table where all slaves took their morning and evening meals. Tillya sat next to her and stared at her plate. Rosanne asked, "Did you see who was in that transport?"

Tillya shrugged. "Just some snoshins, humans, and a malnun." Rosanne said, "One of them was there when I was taken off New Iowa. He was the one in charge."

The teenager on the other side of the table whispered, "The two humans and the malnun were the guys who took us from Ashbury."

Tillya frowned. "I wonder what they're doing here?"

Rosanne said, "You saw the soldiers parachuting from those shuttles and the sounds of the fighting. I'm telling you, we're not going to be here too much longer."

Tillya shook her head. "I want to believe that, but I'm not optimistic. I know from my own planets history that invading a planet is near impossible."

The teenager thought a second. "If I get the chance, I'll do what I can to make it possible."

Oliver was sitting next to the teenager. "George, man. That means doing things that could get you out of balance man."

George shook his head. "I don't even know what that means anymore, Dad. Frankly, right now, I'm beginning to think that it's nothing more than an excuse to knuckle under and not take a stand for anything."

Oliver was downcast. "That hurts, man."

*****

## Twenty Kilometers North of the
## Rondoli River Valley Shuttle Port

After quietly eliminating the Gostis Defense Force pickets, Major Henson reported to Bortas and waited for the pretars to get themselves in position for an attack. When they arrived at the position occupied by Major Henson, the pretars began the attack in earnest. Pretar tactics dictated that they concentrated their attack at points along a front. Once resistance was eliminated, they would exploit the break and raise havoc in their opponents' rear areas. Where the attacks came was dictated by a variety of factors like terrain, roads, and the ability to defend the location. Major Henson moved to the west of the pretar axis of attack to join the rest of Colonel Devonport's unit.

*****

## Rondoli River Valley Shuttle Port

Astrodyne 65s crowded the shuttle port and were being off-loaded with the enthusiastic help of the slaves that had been freed. Phil went to the makeshift operations center to find out what his next load was going to be. All the vehicles were delivered now, but they were sure to need food, water, and ammunition. Once in the ops center, he found Dwight, Gus, Norton, and all the other company pilots.

Kline was at a map studying it carefully when he asked a nearby aide, "Tell me about these armored vehicles of theirs."

The aide replied, "They're like the ones we first encountered. Our anti-armor missiles cut right through them. The problem is that they have so many of them. We didn't bring near enough missiles with us to deal with all of them. Even if we get a 100 percent hit rate, it won't take out half of them.

Kline didn't like what he was hearing, and a look at the map made him not like what he was seeing. "I don't see any choke points where we can take out a vehicle or two and strand them in bunches."

The aide was sympathetic. "No, sir, unless we can keep them in the deep woods where they sit now."

Kline shook his head. "We have to approach on this flat, open terrain while they stay under concealment in the woods. Anything we do is going to be spotted immediately."

One of Kline's Battalion commanders remarked, "It's too bad we couldn't take out that data center the first day."

Kline nodded. "The woods and hills made that impossible since there were no drop zones close to it."

Dwight cautiously stepped up. "Excuse me, sir." Kline turned to him. "Yes?"

Dwight continued, "I know we can't land guys in that area because of the defense system there. How does that work?"

Kline could see that Dwight was working up to something, so he nodded to an aide.

The aid explained, "There's a sensor network that detects landing shuttles and launches weapons to blanket the area and destroy the perceived threat."

Dwight frowned. "This all happens automatically?" The aide nodded. "Yup."

Dwight asked, "Exactly what does the system need to sense to trigger a reaction?"

The aide furrowed his brow. "Landing thrusters have a unique signature. I'm not a pilot, but I do know that there's no way to put a shuttle on the ground without using its thrusters, and you won't have enough time to land, discharge passengers, and take off before the system blots you out. In fact, you wouldn't even get on the ground because the defense missiles will arrive while you're on approach."

Dwight inhaled and turned to Phil. "Hoss, I'm wondering if I can trade shuttles with you for this next run. Oh, can I have Chad too?"

Phil frowned. "Dwight, you heard the man. That wouldn't get us anything but a new smoking crater on Gostis."

Dwight smiled. "I don't plan on landing, but I would like to trigger that system."

Kline grinned. "Could that work?"

Dwight rubbed his chin. "I get the feeling that the real tricky part is triggering the system in the first place. That's why I asked to borrow the *Aurora*. It has oversize thrusters and those Detroit 750s."

Phil nodded. "I'll buy that. Why do you need Chad?"

Dwight replied, "Because that kid is a prodigy. He's the best pilot I've ever seen, and I want the best I can get with me. Besides, he knows the *Aurora* the best."

Phil grinned. "I couldn't argue with any of that, okay Dwight, you've convinced me. What do you need to make this work?"

Dwight thought for a second. "I'll need to make the *Aurora* as heavy as possible. We'll load up with ammunition since it'll give us the most weight."

Kline asked, "Is that it?"

Dwight nodded. "That's it." Then Dwight turned to the map. "Where's those rascals that are frettin' ya."

*****

## Gostis, Supreme Military Headquarters, Outside Capital City

Peintoc was giving a briefing to a very upset Teanon Council. Olunic Noynin with the rest of the Teanon Council behind him was on the screen in front of Peintoc. Noynin looked like he hadn't slept in days, and the rest of the council was equally haggard looking.

Noynin asked, "General Peintoc, could you please tell us what the military situation is, please?"

Peintoc looked directly at the monitor. "Our fellow snoshins along with the maldors and malnuns are driving toward Capital City from the southeast. The pretars with the flastons and mercenaries from Reynold's Planet are attacking from the south. Our forces were staggered, but it seems we've stalled their progress. I'm organizing a counterattack before they can resume their efforts. I'm also ordering the Fifth Motorized to attack the pretars flanks."

Behind Noynin, Peintoc could see Zisros who said sarcastically, "Oh, good, you didn't forget about them."

Noynin jumped in, "Thank you, General. We look forward to hearing of your victory over the invaders."

The screen went blank, but Peintoc continued to stare at it. An aide eased up to him. "You know, sir, if you wanted a change in the planet's leadership, most of the commanders are more loyal to you than the council. The others would hesitate to back the council when they see the support you have."

Peintoc smiled thinly. "That's dangerous thinking, but I'll keep it in mind. The commander of the Fifth Motorized is related by marriage to a member of the council. Any move I make along those lines would be countered by them, but you're right. The way I feel right now, though, that's an attractive idea."

*****

## The *Aurora*, Astrodyne 65, Operated by the Stellar Logistics and Freight Corporation

Dwight reentered the Gostis atmosphere and checked his position on the navigation computer. Chad did some quick calculations. "We'll be over the valley that Colonel Kline marked out in thirty minutes."

Dwight nodded. "I think we'll do this in two runs. I don't know how wide a swath that system will cut, so I want to do it right."

In twenty-five-minutes, Dwight had the *Aurora* aligned with the length of the valley. Chad scanned the instruments and asked, "Maybe you mentioned it, but…what exactly is the plan?"

Dwight kept his stare straight ahead. "This is going to be tricky. We have to be low enough to the ground to trigger the system, but if we're too slow, we get knocked out of the sky. We'll keep the speed up, I'd say about eighty knots, then I'll use pitch and power to maintain altitude.

At the end of the run, we'll fire the reaction engines and get out of Dodge. Use the aft viewer to keep tabs on what's happening behind us. If their weapons get too close to us, that's also a good time to fire the reaction engines."

The *Aurora* dropped into the valley, and when Dwight judged the altitude to be what he wanted, he pitched the nose up. Then he used the landing thrusters with pitch and power to maintain the flight profile he wanted. The *Aurora* would occasionally sink a bit, and Dwight would pulse the landing thrusters to maintain altitude.

This actually helped the Gostis defense network make up its mind that there were unauthorized landings taking place and assigned weapons to neutralize the perceived threat. The computer programmed each missile with a location, then it made sure that enough ordinance was assigned to annihilate everything in a wide area around the center of the spot the landings were calculated to be.

The launchers ejected their covers, and hundreds of missiles were launched at blinding speeds. The missiles went to an altitude of three thousand meters, changed directions, and streaked downward. Chad was watching the aft monitor and was about to tell Dwight that they drew a blank when a series of explosions started erupting behind them.

The blasts were following them at an incredible rate; in fact, they were gaining on the *Aurora*. Chad had a cautioned tone in his voice.

"Dwight…they're getting close."

They had reached the end of their programmed run anyway, so Dwight fired the reaction engines and pushed the power levers to 25 percent. Their nose high attitude did two things. The exhaust knocked down trees in a wide swath behind the *Aurora*, and it helped them clear the area immediately.

Dwight managed to idle the reaction engines before they left the atmosphere. He turned the *Aurora* and flew a course that allowed them to view the results of their efforts. He nodded. "One more time oughta be about right."

He used the width of the destruction path to gauge how far he needed to fly on a parallel course to inflict the most damage. The second pass went precisely like the first, except that they were more relaxed. About two-thirds through their run, the explosions behind them stopped. Chad reasoned, correctly, that the defense system ran out of ordinance.

*****

## Fifth Motorized Armor Division, Field Headquarters

From his position, General Rogutts could see the extent of the damage. There was smoke billowing from wrecked vehicles the length of the valley. He was clueless as to what was happening until the Astrodyne started its second pass.

What really put him in a rage was that their own weapons were used against them. The good news was, the weapons were designed to knock down relatively fragile space ships. They actually had minimal effect on his armored vehicles, but the soft skinned vehicles were a different story. He could continue mission without them, but it made things very inconvenient.

The armored vehicles didn't escape unscathed in the incident entirely. Most had sustained some sort of damage. A third of them required repairs to make them operational while another third was operational but had restricted capabilities. The real damage was the personnel he lost. There weren't enough crews to fully man the vehicles he had, and there was chaos in his division.

His division was well-trained and disciplined, so the reaction to this disaster came automatically although the scale and suddenness couldn't be trained for. Rogutts turned to his aide. "Inform General Peintoc of what just happened, but we will carry out his orders as soon as practicable."

*****

## Gostis, Supreme Military Headquarters, Outside Capital City

Peintoc stared in disbelief at the monitor. The defense system detected an attempted landing and expended weaponry to deal with that threat. The display said the weapons magazines were emptied, but there were no vessel crashes reported. After he studied the disbursement pattern of the defense weapons, his heart sank.

An aide approached him. "Sir—"

General Peintoc cut him off, "Let me guess. General Rullot is reporting."

The aide replied, "Yes, sir. They've lost a number of vehicles and a significant number of soldiers. General Rullot reports that they will carry out your orders to drive on to Capital City as soon as they can organize themselves."

Peintoc sighed. "Our forces around Capital City will have to hold a little longer until the Fifth Motorized can get into action."

*****

## Forty Kilometers North of the Rondoli River Valley Shuttle Port

The Gostis defense forces actually managed to stop the pretars on their drive to Capital City. There was an inordinate number of pretar officers and NCOs that became casualties during operations. Bortas was at a loss as to what to do about reestablishing a command structure in his hardest-hit company-sized unit. He decided to break with tradition and pay Colonel Devonport a visit. After they conferred for a short time, Devonport sent for Major Henson and First Sergeant Thack.

When they arrived at Devonport's mobile command post, Devonport said, "Gentlemen, General Bortas has a problem that First Sergeant Thack can help him solve."

Bortas said, "Yes, indeed. I have urgent need for experienced leadership in one of my forward units, and I'd like you to take charge of one of my company-sized units. You will be given the rank of superior sergeant and have 250 soldiers under you."

Thack was caught completely by surprise. "I'm flattered and appreciative, but I already have men who rely on me."

Henson spoke up, "You trained your guys well, First Sergeant. We can advance people in rank without a lot of disruption. The level you trained them to make that possible."

Thack was still hesitant, and Devonport put his hand on his shoulder. "We'll be fine, lad. Your people need you."

Thack stood ramrod straight and said to Bortas, "I accept your offer, sir." Then he turned to Henson. "I would recommend that Sergeant Tyson move into my position and promote Corporal Evans to sergeant."

Henson smiled. "My thoughts exactly."

Thack saluted Henson and Devonport. "It's been the honor of my life to serve with you, gentlemen."

Henson and Devonport returned the salute. Devonport smiled. "The honor has been ours."

Henson lowered his salute and grasped Thack's hand. "Indeed."

Bortas used the opportunity to confer with Devonport and Henson on the next phase of the operation; after which, he returned his own sector with Superior Sergeant Thack.

*****

## Fifth Motorized Armor Division Area of Operations

The three ranger battalions took a different area of responsibility in the effort to deal with the Fifth Motorized. Each battalion had a number of scout vehicles that they used for fast hit-and-run operations. There weren't enough of the vehicles made by Jeep Corporation for everyone to be able to ride, but it gave them a lot of capabilities.

They also were able to figure out how to operate the transports captured from the Dagger Division, which they repainted with paint they found in the maintenance hangars. The transports were no longer the Gostis defense forces blue; they were now camouflaged. That turned the elite light infantry unit into a highly mobile task force.

The valley that the Fifth Motorized occupied ran roughly southwest to northeast in a line directly to Capital City. The valley itself is approximately thirty kilometers long and ten kilometers wide at its widest. The steep hills on each side of the valley were thickly wooded as was the valley itself. Toward Capital City, the woodland gradually gave way to a wide plain with open pasture and farms until it reached the outskirts of Capital City.

The rangers mounted up and drove southwest from the shuttle port. They passed the original drop zones and continued on for another hour or so until they reached the point where the valley emptied onto the plain. Kline had his units with Jeeps take position to fire their missiles on any transports that exited the dense woodland.

The mortar crews set up at points that allowed them to cover half of the valley. Kline considered setting up his units in an ambush and letting things happen, but he felt that plan didn't give him as much control of the situation as he would have liked. After studying the map, he decided that a multilevel approach was probably the best course of action.

The woodland that the Fifth Motorized occupied was dense, but it had an extensive network of roads and trails they could take advantage of. Ranger units filtered into the woods and carried out hit-and-run attacks. The first thing the rangers noticed was their opposition was better trained than the soldiers they were against previously. They still weren't on the same level as the rangers, but they were tenacious. In fact, the rangers were starting to take their first serious casualties.

Eventually, though, General Rogutts grew tired of reports of units coming under attack suddenly and effectively. The sound of mortar rounds pounding positions at will filled his soldiers with dread. Finally, he had had enough. He ordered his division to drive on to Capital City, and they would simply leave their troubles behind them. His men weren't trained to fight the kind of war these humans were waging, so he would simply turn the tables. Once he had his armored vehicles in relatively open country, they would see what his people were capable of.

Armored vehicles started filtering out of the tree line then formed up in chevron formations and slowly crossed the open area between fence lines. At a point where the formation was most exposed, a missile would appear from nowhere and reduce the lead vehicle to an inert flaming mass. A second missile in the formation would usually encourage the soldiers to get as much distance between them and the potential cause of becoming an entry on a casualty list. The net result was the Fifth Motorized, and the add on units were caught in the open and decimated. The battle itself from first engagement to the surrender of the remnants of the Fifth Motorized lasted five and a half days. Another full day was spent policing the battlefield and transporting the prisoners to a holding facility that they set up on the outskirts of Capital City.

The pretars were making progress although it was at great expense. Several times, they let units become surrounded and vicious fighting ensued. The shuttle port near the city was captured and put into operation almost immediately. The Australian and New Zealand units had finished operations in their sectors and were shuttled to Capital City to reinforce the pretar position. The New Zealanders found themselves against a particularly stubborn Gostis Defense Force unit that allowed both sides to run dangerously low on ammunition.

The Gostis soldiers rate of fire diminished severely, which gave the kiwis a sense that they could take charge of the situation and end the hostilities in their area of operations. One of the New Zealanders slung his weapon over his shoulder and stepped into the open between the opposing forces and started shouting at the astonished snoshins.

The rest of the Kiwi unit stepped out behind him and joined in the Maori haka, which is an ancient ceremonial dance with exaggerated movements. The centuries-old ritual had the designed and desired effect of unnerving the Gostis soldiers who put down their weapons after they were assured that the kiwis wouldn't eat them. General Bortas witnessed those events and made a note to send a personal letter of thanks to the officers and men of that unit.

*****

## Gostis, Supreme Military Headquarters, Outside Capital City

General Peintoc sat silently after reading the report on the screen. The commander of the Fifth Motorized sent him a coded message, informing him that he could see no other alternative but to surrender. His offensive capabilities were reduced to zero, and continued operations would only result in more dead Gostis soldiers.

Peintoc took a deep breath and turned to his staff and said, "Gentlemen, it's painfully obvious to me that we are not going to prevail in this endeavor. Does anyone disagree?"

His staff stood silent with the haggard expressions of men who haven't slept in a long time. Peintoc nodded. "If anyone is uncomfortable with me dissolving our present government, I'll understand if you want to step down."

Peintoc's personal aide looked around the room at the other faces and stepped forward. "Sir, the longer we discuss this, the more of our men will die."

Peintoc stood. "Get Colonel Otsrod on the communications set. Have him execute plan number one."

*****

## Field Headquarters, Fristus Guards

Colonel Otsrod put down his communication dispatch and smiled. "It's about time."

Otsrod actually was Peintoc's superior for most of their careers, but Otsrod actually had questioned the Teanon Council about certain policies; as a result, his career stalled at colonel. Otsrod and Peintoc were actually good friends and had confided with each other about what they considered to be shortcomings with the system they had on Gostis.

Officially, the Fristus Guards were held in reserve in Capital City for the protection of the Teanon Council. Peintoc and Otsrod planned to overthrow the Teanon Council if the opportunity arose. They couldn't do it though, as there were too many defense forces commanders loyal to the council. The council saw to it that loyal officers were put in command of their forces. They weren't completely comfortable with Peintoc, but he didn't give them an excuse to scrutinize his career, and he didn't do anything to incur their wrath so he could advance through competence.

Otsrod, however, was never comfortable with the system on Gostis, and he was more than willing to become a conspirator. For a long time, he was in a position to fill the leadership positions in his brigade with men he could rely on.

He turned to his aide. "All battalions execute plan number one."

Events progressed rapidly after that. Otsrod strode to his vehicle and said over his shoulder, "Contact General Peintoc and inform him that he'll be hearing from me in a short time."

Troop transports rolled up to the council building and soldiers dismounted. The council guards could hear the fighting getting closer as the day wore on and were relieved to see that they were getting reinforced. When the soldiers brushed past them, they were understandably confused.

As the Fristus Guards soldiers filled the council building, sergeants approached the council guards and convinced them that their best course of action was to keep their weapons on safe and let things happen. Otsrod's vehicle pulled up. He dismounted then strode into the building. He arrived just as his men were ready to enter the Council Chamber. He stopped and said, "Do it."

A soldier kicked in the door, and a squad rushed in. Toanin Zisros jumped to his feet. "This is an outrage! Only the elite class is permitted to be in the chamber!"

Otsrod walked down the aisle and stopped in front of Zisros. Looking him in the eye, he said in a very deadpan manner, "Shut up." Otsrod then continued to the front of the room, where he waved Noynin aside. "Excuse me, sir."

He activated the communications system and the wall-sized screen lit up, and General Peintoc's face stared back at them.

Otsrod said, "Sir, it's done."

Peintoc nodded. "Excellent job, Colonel. Please ensure that they're kept comfortable while we put an end to this current foolishness."

Then he fixed his gaze on the council. "You're position of authority is over, gentlemen. I'm hoping that the forces arrayed against us will eventually allow us to govern ourselves again. For now, I'm putting an end to this pointless war."

*****

## Gostis, Supreme Military Headquarters, Capitol City

Peintoc sent out an order to all his commanders to cease all hostilities immediately, then he and his aide boarded a vehicle. After he directed his driver to make his way to the snoshin axis of attack, he asked his aide, "Didn't they indicate what the proper signal should be if we wanted to call a truce to confer?" The aide nodded and pulled a white cloth out of his pocket. "Yes, sir.

Apparently, there's a human tradition for such an occasion. We tie this to our communication antenna, and it will act as a signal that we wish a conference."

The driver stopped dand said, "We should tie that on before going further."

After attaching the white flag, he remounted the vehicle and drove into the battlefield. In a short distance, a snoshin officer stepped in front of the vehicle. They stopped, and Peintoc saluted. "I need to see your commander."

The officer returned the salute. "If you'll follow me, sir."

Both vehicles went directly to General Lingur's headquarters. Peintoc dismounted and entered the building where he met with Lingur. An agreement was made where the Gostis forces would turn in their weapons and report to assembly areas for temporary internment. In all likelihood, many of the soldiers would remain in the service or law enforcement after some sort of new government was established. In the meantime, there was a general stand down of hostilities.

*****

## Gostis, Capital City Shuttle Port

The rangers were billeted at the shuttle port and started the process of getting their equipment back in serviceable condition after they had a chance to rest. The first phase of the operation was now over. Now the daunting task of returning the slaves to their home worlds was about to begin.

The first step in this stage was to communicate to the slaves and slaveholders, informing them of the efforts to bring slavery to an end on Gostis. Since the normal lines of communications were badly disrupted, information had to be distributed in person. To that end, Lingur had squads of soldiers go from farm to farm getting a count of slaves to get a sense of how much transportation they would need to get people back to their homes. The mercenaries from the Reynolds Planet contingent occupied some hangar facilities on the opposite side of the shuttle port that the rangers occupied. The Astrodyne fleet was parked in rows on the ramp, and their crews sleeping in the staterooms and cabins.

Special Agent Tim Davis was going through the shuttles that were parked when they got there to determine who owned them. He approached a Caravel 500 and stopped. Something about it made him scrutinize this vessel more carefully. He consulted a pad and compared the hull number on a list he had. Finding what he was looking for made him smile.

He walked directly over to the mercenary area of operations and found Colonel Devonport and Major Henson enjoying cups of guthar with Colonel Kline. Devonport looked up. "Davis, get yourself a cup and enjoy Old Man. It's called guthar. You add some of these crystals and stir with a wooden stick."

Davis smiled. "No, thank you, sir. I've tried it already. It's delicious, but it doesn't seem to agree with me."

Henson leaned back. "What can we do for you, Mr. Davis?"

Davis smiled. "I think I can do something for one of your men. I was checking hull numbers on shuttles, and I ran into something very interesting. It seems that the man who kidnapped the wife of your Corporal Evans is on this planet somewhere."

Devonport and Henson put down their cups, and Henson said, "It's Sargent Evans now. What makes you say that?"

Davis pointed across the ramp to the Caravel 500. "That's owned by a Mr. Borislav Lovanova. He's the wonderful man that took it upon himself to relocate people around the galaxy to help them find work. Sergeant Evans' wife was one of his victims."

Henson stood. "I'll get him and Lieutenant Yondlyn."

Kline turned to his aide. "Have Lieutenant Ross report with his platoon sergeant and a driver right away."

Michael Ross pulled up in a Jeep about the same time that Henson returned with Evans and Yondlyn. Davis explained to the newcomers what he related earlier, which left Evans trying to maintain his composure. Lieutenant Yondlyn asked, "What are the mission parameters, sir?"

Devonport put down his cup. "The mission is simple. Find Mrs. Evans." Kline added, "Mrs. Evans is an American, which is why I'm having Lieutenant Ross accompany you. You may not need the backup, but they'll be there if you need them."

Davis said, "I'll go along also to lend a hand if you need any sleuthing."

Yondlyn nodded. "I'm glad to hear that because I haven't the first idea how to begin."

Davis said, "Right now, the only connection we have is that shuttle. Lovanova would have to have interacted with the ground crew."

Evans said, "Those guys are being held in the ground crew shed next door." Davis shrugged. "Let's go have a chat."

Davis, Evans, and Yondlyn left to see the ground crew while Michael went to his Jeep to brief his platoon sergeant and driver.

Evans and Yondlyn walked into the ground crew shed and looked around. The crewmen locked worried eyes on them, and Evans asked, "Who can tell me about the owner of that Caravel 500?"

The ground crewmen didn't want to do or say anything that would upset the two men in front of them. They had heard that soldiers from Reynolds Planet didn't have any reservations about shooting sources of annoyance.

For Evans and Yondlyn, they knew that reputations could be useful, and they weren't about to do anything that would go toward dispelling that reputation. A snoshin stood. "T-T-T-T-That belongs to M-M-M-Mister Lovanova. He arrived with a load of new slaves some time ago. He had another human with him and a malnun."

Evans pressed. "Where can we find this Lovanova?"

The snoshin started to shake. "P-P-Please, I don't know. They don't tell me their plans. I j-just service their shuttles."

A crewman behind him, who was obviously amused that his superior was scared out of his mind, stood and said, "Tell him about Snit."

Evans stepped closer and said in a low menacing tone. "Yes, tell me about Snit."

The snoshin was pale, shaking harder, and near passing out. "Snit met them when they arrived."

Tim Davis was standing in the doorway and asked, "Does this Snit belong to the Syndicate?"

The crewman nodded. "I think he w-works for someone of middle ranking in t-that organization."

The crewman who first mentioned Snit said, "If the directory is working, I can tell you where he lives."

He then walked to a computer terminal and entered Snit's name. "Here it is, and there's a map also."

Evans pulled out his own map and started making notes. While he worked, he asked the ground crewman, "What does this Snit do?"

The crewman answered, "He works for a big important slave trader.

I don't know which one."

Evans nodded. "You gentlemen have been very helpful."

*****

## Gostis, Toanin Zisros Falta Plantation,
## Home of Toanin Zisros

Madam Zisros stared at the monitor in disbelief. It directed all slaveholders to cease working with their slaves and keep them comfortable until they could be returned to their homes. She was as close to going into a rage as she had ever been. How dare off-worlders demand that we change our social order. She thought about it for a time and decided that perhaps there was a way to preserve their way of life even though their slaves were about to be taken away.

There was a possibility that she could secret a number of slaves from the authorities and proceed with the breeding program. In her mind, she had no choice but to preserve slaveholding, secretly at first, but she was sure that, eventually, the wisdom of their structured society would prevail. To that end, she called her head taskmaster to her office, and she gave him a list of slaves that she wanted in the breeding program. She had to reduce the number of slaves in the program from fifty to twenty because there weren't accommodations for a larger number in the location where she planned on hiding them.

*****

## Gostis, Falta Plantation of Toanin Zisros,
## Slave Quarters Common Area

Rosanne and Tillya had started their day before sunrise as normal, but the taskmasters didn't take them to the fields. Everyone couldn't help but notice that the sounds of fighting disappeared, and the taskmasters were on edge. They ate the midday meal and discussed the events of the last few days. There were too many theories and not enough facts to suit anyone. They heard a tram arrive outside the slave quarters then the door opened.

The head taskmaster stepped in. "If your collar vibrates, get in the tram!"

Rosanne felt her collar vibrate, so she went to the tram and took a seat. Tillya sat next to her, and they watched the others get on the tram. Rosanne couldn't help but notice that the females were ten of the twenty-five that were selected to be breeders. She looked at Tillya, who looked back with an expression of dread. They both realized what might be happening, but they knew better than to discuss it.

*****

## Gostis, Village of Tinnetti, Seventy-five Kilometers West of Capital City

Evans drove into the village of Tinnetti and then stopped in the center, where there was a fountain and small village green. Michael was in a Jeep right behind Evans and Yondlyn, with every eye in the village on them. Evans consulted his notes that he made earlier and drove slowly down one of the streets that radiated from the village green like the spokes of a wheel.

When he spotted the house that belonged to Snit, he stopped. There was a group of snoshins standing nearby who were dressed similarly, which made Evans reason out that they were slaves who were used as domestic help. He pointed at the house and asked the snoshins, "Snit?"

The snoshins smiled and nodded.

The six of them dismounted the vehicles and approached the house. The three rangers slipped into an alley and covered any potential exits at the rear of the house while Evans and Yondlyn went to the front door. Evans kicked in the front door, and Yondlyn threw in a distractor.

A distractor was a grenade that acted like an old-fashioned flash-bang grenade. The difference was a distractor's initial flash and bang threw dozens of submunitions into every corner of the room, where they, in turn, made their own flash and bang. The result was a confusing terror-filled existence that incapacitated the room's occupants long enough to enter and take command.

Evans rushed in with Yondlyn close behind, where they found a snoshin trying desperately to gather his wits. Evans kicked the snoshin in the chest, knocking him to the floor, and Yondlyn quickly started to clear the rest of the house, but before he finished, he could hear a commotion at the rear of the house. Michael and his platoon sergeant entered the room dragging Jason Gannett and Pil Jos. "Look what we found."

Davis walked into the room and took stock of the scene in front of him. Then he pulled an instrument out of his pocket. He clamped the instrument on the cheek of Gannett. "Well! Mr. Jason Gannett. I see you're moving up in the syndicate. Although I wouldn't count on any promotions for a while." Then he used the instrument on Pil Jos. "Ah, Pil Jos. I see you're also upwardly mobile. Well, at least up until now."

Evans reached down and roughly pulled Snit to his feet. "This, I'm sure, is Mr. Snit."

Davis used the instrument a third time. "You would be correct."

Michael said to Davis, "Why don't we find a way to secure these two while Lieutenant Yondlyn and Sergeant Evans have their little chat with Snit?"

Davis thought that was a good idea, and he led them out of the room, leaving Evans and Yondlyn to work things out with Snit.

Michael decided that the best place to secure Gannett and Pil Jos was to lay them facedown on the hood of the Jeep, then bind their wrists and ankles then lash them to fittings on the Jeep. Michael's platoon sergeant suggested that they also gag them before they go into the next phase of the mission so they wouldn't give away their position or shout warnings at inopportune times.

Evans and Yondlyn came out of the house dragging Snit, who was clearly incapable of making his way to Evans's vehicle. When they saw how they planned on transporting Gannett and Pil Jos, they laughed. Yondlyn said, "That's a fine idea. It'll keep the stench out of the vehicle." After strapping Snit to the hood, they went to Michael to brief him and his men on the next phase. Evans pulled a map out of his pocket. "According to Snit here, he dropped off Lovanova and the stock trader he works for, named Yidlin Untocks, at the home of Toanin Zisros." He pointed to a point on his map. "It's just here, about fifteen minutes away."

Davis said, "If anyone knows what happened to Mrs. Evans, it'll be Untocks, and I've heard of this Zisros guy. He's a big-time falta grower, and get this. He's a big deal in the syndicate and a ranking member on the Teanon Council. He was taken prisoner when Peintoc dissolved the government."

Michael said, "It sounds like this Zisros has a lot of slaves." Yondlyn nodded. "I'm looking forward to making him a pauper."

*****

## Gostis, Falta Plantation of Toanin Zisros

The tram stopped in front of the processing building, and the taskmasters ordered them off. Rosanne and the rest were herded into the processing building where Madam Zisros was waiting. "Events have forced us to accelerate our breeding program. There are ten quarters adjacent to this building. A taskmaster will assign a room to the pairs I have selected." She then turned and left the room.

The taskmaster they called Boss said, "I will now pair you. When you feel your neck collars vibrate, step forward." Before he could touch the button on his counter, Rosanne rushed him and knocked the counter to the floor. He was too shocked to respond at first.

After he processed what had just happened in his brain, he was angered and bent down to retrieve the counter, yelling, "You troublesome woman! You're going to regret you did that!"

Rosanne kicked the counter to a corner of the room and then kicked Boss in the face, who fell backward, roaring in rage.

Tillya joined the struggle by grabbing his arm and preventing him from getting up. Boss put his free hand on the floor to push himself up. That's when Rosanne stomped his fingers, breaking them. He howled in pain and tried to protect himself from Rosanne and Tillya's repeated kicking.

The taskmaster that was assisting Boss heard the commotion and rushed into the room. He saw what Rosanne and Tillya were doing to his superior and started to go to his aid when George tripped him, sending the taskmaster to the floor in a heap. George and one of the flaston men started beating him with their fists. Both beatings stopped when they realized that the taskmasters weren't resisting them anymore. They stood around the battered snoshins, wondering how much damage had been done when they saw both were breathing. George pulled at his collar, then he said, "I don't know about the rest of you, but this thing is coming off."

He then walked to the door, cautiously opened it then looked outside. "The tram is still there. Boss keeps a tool set under his seat for the collars."

George crept to the rear of the tram where Boss sat and lifted the seat. He reached in and grabbed a canvas bag full of tools. He went back to the others, where they spread the tools on a table. They found the exact tools they needed to remove the collars, but there was a problem. The collars had an auto translator built in, and once removed, they couldn't understand each other.

George pulled a collar module apart and found the auto translator. From there, it was no problem to remove it and discard the rest of the collar. They stood there and stared at each other for a few seconds, then a malnun asked, "Now what do we do?"

George started packing up the tools. "We go back and remove the collars from the rest, then we do what we need to."

A pretar covered her mouth. "Oh my, my, my, goodness, dear, dear, dear. Yes, that's the best course of action."

It was by no means a popular decision. Some had been slaves so long. The idea of starting an uprising scared them, and they were reluctant. But they also yearned to be free, and that idea pushed them passed any doubts. They started toward the door to the outside when the door leading to Madam Zisros' office suddenly opened, and she stepped through.

It took her a couple of seconds for her to reason out what she was seeing. When she realized what was happening, she retreated back through the door to her office. A malnun suggested that it might be a good idea if they hurried back to the quarters and removed the collars from the rest.

As Rosanne and the rest boarded the tram for the short trip to the slave quarters with George driving, Madam Zisros ran to the main house, yelling, "Mr. Untocks! Mr. Lovanova! You must help. The slaves are revolting, and I fear that they may wish to harm us!"

It really wasn't an unreasonable assumption seeing the condition they left Boss and his assistant taskmaster in. Borislav and Yidlin rushed to her and tried to calm her. After a couple of minutes, she was able to relate to them what she saw, and both Borislav and Yidlin didn't like this new turn of events at all.

They helped Madam Zisros to a chair in the sitting room, where a servant brought her hot guthar. Borislav looked at Yidlin. "What do we do now?"

Yidlin looked back at Borislav with a confused expression. His face was flush and finally answered, "We must do what we can to put a stop to this."

He went to the foyer, where there was a weapons locker. Most slaveholders on Gostis kept a locker like this for uprisings that may occur. Yidlin opened the locker just as some assistant taskmasters entered the house. He reached in and pulled out two carbines and ammunition. He handed one carbine to Borislav with a bandoleer of ammunition.

The assistant taskmasters were selecting their own weapons when one of them asked, "Did you set the alarm, sir?"

Yidlin gave him an annoyed expression. "What good would that do? Our forces were ordered to stand down."

The taskmaster answered, "Mr. Zisros has a small garrison nearby that's independent of the regular forces. I don't know what their current status is, but I suspect that they're still willing to deploy here as they're very loyal to Mr. Zisros."

Yidlin looked at Borislav, who shrugged. "I'd say try it. I don't relish the idea of facing dozens of slaves with just the five of us. Even if we are the only ones with firearms."

The taskmaster nodded and opened a panel on the wall and pressed a button. Then he turned to the rest. "They should be here shortly. I would recommend waiting for them."

*****

## Gostis, Capital City Shuttle Port

Kline and Devonport were contemplating whether they wanted another cup of guthar or not when a snoshin entered the room. "Excuse me, sirs, but there has been an alert from the Toanin Zisros falta farm. We understand that you sent a detachment there to look for a particular slave trader."

Kline looked at him. "That's right. What kind of alert are we talking about?"

The snoshin answered, "Members of the Teanon Council had garrisons of about a hundred soldiers, called a reaction force, near their homes for their security. They are fiercely loyal to the council members, and there was concern that they may not heed the surrender order. The homes have panic buttons that summon the garrison and inform a central threat monitoring center. That's how we found out."

Kline nodded. "Thank you. We'll keep General Lingur informed."

Devonport picked up a microphone. "Henson, Yondlyn, this is Devonport.

Come in, please."

Yondlyn was surprised that Henson was out and about. Yondlyn and Henson answered the call. Devonport continued, "There's a good chance that you're running into trouble. Meet at the crossroads five kilometers east of your objective. Colonel Kline has the balance of Lieutenant Ross's platoon on the way also."

Kline relayed the same information to Michael. Then he turned his attention back to his beverage decision. Devonport put a kettle on. "It's a good job that we decided to send those two platoons when we did."

*****

## Gostis, Crossroads, Five Kilometers
## East of the Toanin Zisros Falta Farm

Evans and Michael reached the intersection and stopped. Henson pulled up with his men in their scout vehicles with Michael's platoon in captured armored transports. Everyone dismounted, and the officers worked out a plan. The map showed an extensive road and trail network surrounding the Zisros Plantation, so they decided that the rangers would circle the plantation and approach the main house from the rear. Henson's men would make a frontal assault. The plan was simplicity itself. The soldiers remounted their vehicles and started to make their way to the Zisros Plantation.

*****

## Gostis, Falta Plantation of Toanin Zisros,
## Slave Quarters Common Area

In the slave quarters, George was busy removing collars from the others. The slaves that were relieved of their collars grabbed farming tools and went outside. They were naturally worried about facing trained troops with nothing more than farm implements, but most were determined that, one way or another, this was their last day in bondage.

A series of reaction force personnel carriers rolled up to the main house, and soldiers dismounted. Yidlin and Borislav came out of the main house with the taskmasters in tow. The commander of the reaction force looked at the weapons they carried and said, "Don't use those unless your life is in jeopardy. Slaves are an expensive commodity. We need to resolve this without killing any of them."

The soldiers carried stun batons and carbines, but the rifles were slung over their shoulders, as the firearms were only to be used in dire circumstances.

The soldiers broke into squads and made their way to the slave quarters. There was a low wall that surrounded the quarters, which formed a courtyard. As the soldiers hunkered down behind them, an officer raised a megaphone to his lips. "Come out in the open, and we won't harm you. If we have to come in there, we will do what is necessary to end this!"

Oliver opened the door and stuck his head out. "Hey, man! We're cool here, man. We just need to get centered, and all this isn't helping."

The officer with the megaphone had a confused expression. While he was working out what Oliver said, Major Henson's voice boomed behind him, "Surrender!"

The officer turned his megaphone outward. "Who are you to demand my surrender?"

Henson replied, "The guy who's going to kill you if you don't!"

Oliver quickly pulled his head back in. "There's a lot of people out of balance out there, man!"

The reaction force soldiers put away their batons and unslung their carbines.

Henson warned, "Don't do it!"

The reaction force commander was arrogant and conditioned from birth to believe in the righteousness of their mission. He was no fool either. He knew he was in a tough spot, but in his mind, he couldn't back down.

Rosanne, Tillya, and the rest hunkered down below the windowsill but kept watching. They could see the soldiers weren't reacting well to the latest development. They couldn't see Henson or his camouflaged men, so they weren't sure if the reaction force could see them. They certainly weren't aware of Michael and his Rangers sweeping up from the rear.

The reaction force commander shouted a single command, "Attack!"

The soldiers fired blindly into the trees and brush. Henson's men had the advantage of having an excellent view of their targets and fired effectively, mowing down the reaction force soldiers nearest them. The rest of the soldiers took cover as best as they could and returned fire.

They were at a distinct disadvantage since they were never trained to fight other soldiers. Their plight was magnified by the fact that they were against two groups of the most elite soldiers in the known galaxy. Some of the reaction force soldiers tried to get behind the slave quarter's compound to try to flank Henson, but they were immediately cut down by the rangers.

While Henson had his men advance in a tactic called fire and maneuver, Yidlin was lying prone next to a stone wall a short distance from Borislav. At that point, there was nothing that could convince him to get up. Borislav, however, was in a more desperate state of mind.

Evans had just advanced and raised his weapon to cover his squad members when Borislav raised his weapon and started to point it. Evans recognized Borislav from a photo that Special Agent Davis had shared with him. He took careful aim and put three into Borislav. He was careful not to hit him anywhere that would be immediately fatal. Borislav was thrown to his back, and the carbine flew out of his hands.

The reaction force soldiers, realizing that they were hopelessly outmatched, gave up the fight. The chaos and incredible noise of the battle suddenly ceased. Rangers and mercenaries started gathering prisoners and taking stock of what was accomplished.

Evans stood and went over to Borislav, who was holding his hands to his abdomen, trying to stem the blood flow. He squatted in front of him and stared with an expression of loathing that was impossible to miss.

Borislav looked back at Evans, but his expression was a mixture of curiosity, confusion, and disdain. He finally said, "You killed me. Why don't you go away and let me die?"

Evans glared at him. "Because you don't deserve to die in peace, Lovanova.

How many raids have you made on New Iowa?"

The look on Borislav's face revealed he now understood why Evans had a particular animus toward him. However, he had no clue how Evans knew who he was or how he knew his name. Evans kept his eyes locked on Borislav. "I wanted you to know the day you kidnapped my wife, it was the beginning of your end. I'll find my wife, and we'll get on with our lives, but no one's going to miss you at all."

Borislav couldn't stop the blood from flowing, and no one rushed to help him. In less than a minute, he closed his eyes for the last time. Evans stood and looked around. He saw Yidlin lying next to the wall, and he assumed he was dead. Then he saw Yidlin shaking, and he turned to his corporal and nodded toward Yidlin. The corporal gave Yidlin a kick in the ribs. "Roll over and show us your face!"

Yidlin groaned loudly, then rolled over. Evans smiled. "Why, it's Mr. Untocks! The very man that we're looking for!"

Yidlin was lifted off the ground with quite a bit of effort. Tim Davis strolled up to the group of men. "Well, this just makes my day. Mr. Untocks here is an up-and-comer in the Syndicate, and now he's heading to a particularly uncomfortable cell with food of questionable quality. If you, gents, would be so kind as to strap Mr. Untocks to the hood of a vehicle with those other three idiots. Sergeant Evans is going to have a word with him later."

Evans watched as Untocks was dragged off. Tim Davis went to the slave quarter's common area door to talk with the people who were starting to filter out. Lieutenant Michael Ross, Major Henson, and Lieutenants Yondlyn and Greene were comparing notes for their after-action reports.

Suddenly, Evans heard a familiar voice. "Charlie!"

Evans turned, and he saw Rosanne running toward him. He ran to her, and they threw their arms around each other to make up for all the embraces they had missed out on. There were tears streaming out of both of their eyes. Finally, Charles held her at arm's length. "Rosie, let me look at you."

There were still tears coming out of her eyes. Two and a half years of hardship showed on her face. Her hands and arms were rough and scared from picking falta. She was still the most beautiful woman he had ever seen. Tillya slowly approached Charlie and Rosanne. Rosanne saw her and pulled her to them, and there were hugs anew.

All at once, there was a commotion on the path coming from the main house. A group of house servants was forcing Madam Zisros down the path, and she was loudly objecting. They stopped the group of officers and demanded that she be arrested. Madam Zisros still hadn't caught on to the fact that there wasn't anyone in the galaxy that was willing to take orders from her, and she was demanding that the soldiers leave and the slaves get back to work.

Rosanne smiled. "Excuse me, hon."

She walked over to Madam Zisros and looked her in the eye. "Do you remember what I said to you when you told us about your little breeding program?"

Madam Zisros glared at her. "Yes, I do. You went on about your husband." Rosanne asked, "Do you remember what you said to me?"

Madam Zisros was still as haughty as ever. "I reminded you that your husband wasn't here."

Rosanne smiled and said, "You also called me a stupid girl. Well, I have someone here you need to meet."

Rosanne then reached up and grabbed a handful of Madam Zisros's hair and walked her over to Charlie. Everyone who watched thought it was one of the funniest things that they ever saw. Madam Zisros was hunched over, trying to break Rosanne's grip on her hair as she was dragged to where Charlie Evans was standing.

Rosanne stopped and lifted Madam Zisros's head by pulling up on her hair. Madam Zisros found herself face-to-face with Charlie Evans. Rosanne said, "Just for your information, this is my husband."

Rosanne then twisted Madam Zisros's head by her hair and used her free hand to deliver a slap to her face hard enough to give her a nosebleed.

Rosanne then said, "Now get out of my sight, you stupid old hag," as she released her hair.

Michael told a shocked and confused Madam Zisros, "You'll have to do things for yourself from now on. I'd suggest going back to your home and get used to the idea."

Rosanne then gave Charlie another tight hug. She suddenly released him when she spotted Lovanova lying on the ground. She pointed at him. "He's the guy, Charlie. He's the one who grabbed me on New Iowa!"

He said, "Yeah, I know, babe. That's why I put a couple of pills in him." Evans wasn't sure how Roseanne was going to react to what he just said.

When she last saw him, he was a farmer working two thousand acres of ground in New Iowa. Now he was quite different. He was a member of one of the most elite military units ever assembled and obviously very skilled in that position. She processed what he said, then turned to Tillya. "See, I told you my husband was going to straighten these people out."

Tillya's emotions were all over the place. On one hand, she was overjoyed at the developments of the last couple of days. On the other hand, this left her with few attractive options for her future. Rosanne saw the look on Tillya's face, and it wasn't the expression of someone who just had an enormous weight lifted from her shoulders.

Rosanne put her hands on her shoulders. "What's wrong, Tillya?"

Tillya was trying to make sense of what she was feeling. Finally, she croaked out, "I can't go back to Flast."

Rosanne felt like she had a bucket of ice water thrown on her. "Why would you say that? You have to go home. You told me you missed your family terribly."

Tillya had a tear stream down her face. "That's why I can't go home. I wasn't kidnapped. I was sold outright."

Charlie shook his head. "But there was never slavery on Flast."

Tillya inhaled. "Never officially. My village was under the control of a crime syndicate. They stayed in business by bribing or intimidating the officials they needed to. If I return, I could identify the men who sold me, and that would put my family in jeopardy. Even if word gets out that I was given my freedom, my family would be in danger. They told me this to keep themselves safe."

Charlie looked at her. "There's a new government on Flast. Any deals the syndicate had died with the outgoing government."

Tillya was still crestfallen. "Then it's probably even worse than before. As a student of history, I know full well that the new government, good intentions notwithstanding, is probably too week to keep the crime syndicates from getting stronger."

Charlie considered what Tillya said. "We'll talk to Lieutenant Yondlyn. He may know what to do."

He started to escort Tillya and Rosanne toward the group of officers when George strutted to the officers with Oliver behind him. Rosanne sighed. "Oh, jeez."

Oliver was trying to get George to see things his way. "Hey, George, man!

You're talking like some kind of out-of-balance crazy, man!"

George spun around on his heels. "Stop it with the out-of-balance and centered garbage! Where has it gotten us? I'll tell you where! It landed us on a plantation as slaves! But hey, we're actually better off here than in Ashbury. Here, we get fed. That wasn't always the case in Ashbury! But oh, we always had plenty of herb! The last thing I saw as we were getting dragged out of the community center was my baby sister bawling her eyes out because her family was being taken from her, and there was nothing we could do to stop it or even prevent it in the first place!"

Oliver looked like he was punched in the face. "George, I don't know how to live anyway else."

George looked at his father. "I'm sorry, Dad. I just want more than what Ashbury offers, namely security."

Oliver had tears in his eyes. "I'm sorry, George. But there has to be a different direction."

George had tears of his own. "I'm sorry too, Dad. But I think I have to find that out for myself."

George wiped his face and turned to Major Henson. "Sir, are you from Reynolds Planet?"

Henson nodded. "That's right, son."

George straightened up. "I'd like to join up."

Henson glanced at Oliver, then asked George, "How old are you, son?" George answered, "Fifteen, sir."

Henson smiled. "We'd be glad to have you, son."

George started to beam, but Henson continued, "But I've got to make you wait another year."

George started to protest, but Henson cut him off, "From what I just heard, your family needs you right now. Go back to Ashbury. Help your folks rebuild. Do that, and you'll show me that you've got the character we're looking for."

George agreed, but he was still very determined to join the Reynolds Planet Unit.

Charlie then approached the officers and introduced Rosanne, who gave them all hugs. Then he introduced Tillya and explained her predicament. Yondlyn considered it and said, "I'd suggest taking her to Treest, but the syndicate is sure to be entrenched there also."

Michael spoke up, "Maybe my pop can help. At the very least, Miss Tillya can stay on the station."

Henson smiled. "That's not bad. He's also acquainted with some flastons that are somewhat indebted to him."

Yondlyn chuckled. "I'll bet things are going to get very interesting on Oasis 4."

Charlie said to Tillya and Rosanne, "Mr. Ross is the station manager of Oasis 4, and he's good people."

Henson said, "We'll bring Miss Tillya and Mrs. Evans back with us to Capital City."

Tim Davis said, "If you don't mind, Miss Tillya, I'd like to question you. There's also an investigator from Flast that would also like to have a word with you."

Tillya was visibly shaken at the thought of a representative from Flast knowing she was free. Tim reassured her, "I've been working with this gentleman for some time, and I trust him implicitly."

Tillya agreed, then Charlie turned to Rosanne. "You two get your things and hurry back out here."

Rosanne frowned. "There isn't one thing that I want to bring back with me." Charlie smiled. "Trust me."

Then he pulled a digital camera from his pocket. "This is going to sound weird, but take pictures of everything in there. Things like your bed, where you eat, everything."

Rosanne was about to question Charlie about the unusual request when an intelligence sergeant said, "It's already being done."

Charlie smiled. "Could you do me a favor and make sure that Mrs. Ross on Oasis 4 gets copies of those?"

The sergeant smiled when he realized why. "You bet I will, Sarge." While Rosanne and Tillya were gathering their things, Henson called George and Oliver to him. He said to them, "We can't take everyone back to Capital City today. I don't have room to transport all of you or a place to put you in Capital City."

He handed George a pad. "Have everyone put down their name and what planet they're from on this. They'll use that information to organize and schedule your departure. It may take a while because there are a lot of you. In the meantime, they're going to see about getting all of you decent food."

While George gathered names, the small battlefield was policed, and the dead and wounded were taken care of. Michael and Henson used radios to report on their success and order transportation for the prisoners.

When the transports arrived, they discovered that Lingur had ordered rations for the slaves that they couldn't transport right away. Oliver organized the unloading of the food. Then the prisoners were loaded and moved out. When that was done, Rosanne and Tillya climbed into the scout vehicle with Charlie and Yondlyn after they had some tearful goodbyes with some of the other slaves.

Snit and Untocks were still strapped to the hood of the vehicle. As the mercenaries walked past, occasionally, one would give one of them a slap upside the head. When everything was ready, the convoy moved out to their destination of Capital City Shuttle Port. Rosanne was feeling probably the most joy she had ever experienced. Even Tillya was feeling better.

*****

## Gostis, Capital City Shuttle Port

The convoy arrived at the shuttle port, and the vehicles were put in the parking area. Michael dismounted and approached Charlie, Rosanne, and Tillya. "I'll see what time my pop is free tonight, and we'll come and see ya."

Charlie took the girls for their first decent meal in over two years while Tim Davis went to find his flaston counterpart.

After eating, a pretar staff officer sought out Colonel Devonport and whispered into his ear. Devonport leaned over to Henson and said something into his ear. Henson stood and walked to Charlie. "Sergeant Evans, First Sergeant Thack was wounded two days ago. He's in the pretar field hospital.

Let's go see him."

Charlie stood and said to Rosanne, "We need to see this guy, Rosie."

Henson, Charlie, and Rosanne left Tillya with Tim Davis and a Flast criminal investigator. They climbed into a scout vehicle and headed to the field hospital. When they arrived, a clerk told them where Thack was. They found him but had to wait until the medics that were attending him finished what they were doing. While they waited, a pretar colonel spotted them and came over and greeted them.

Henson asked, "What was the situation that put Thack in here?"

The colonel shook his head. "A unit was cut off and in danger of being annihilated. Superior Sergeant Thack led a detachment to break through to the cutoff unit. Once they reached them, he stayed behind and held off scores of enemy soldiers while his soldiers redeployed. He demonstrated leadership, skill, and true courage."

The medics finished, and Charlie took Rosanne's hand. "Superior Sergeant Thack, there's someone here you have to meet."

Thack opened his eyes, and Charlie smiled. "Please say hello to Rosanne Lisa Evans."

Thack's eyes opened wider, and he focused on Rosanne's face. When it registered with him what Charlie said, a smile formed on his face. "Evans, that alone makes this whole effort worthwhile. I'm so very happy for both of you."

Rosanne knelt next to Thack and took his hand. "Is there anything we can do for you?"

Thack patted the back of her hand. "You two can take care of each other. Go back to New Iowa and be the best farmers on that planet. If Sergeant Evans is half the husband as he is a soldier, you two should be happy for the rest of your lives. I've had the privilege of serving with the finest soldiers in the galaxy, and I've led soldiers of my own people in a desperate battle in which we were victorious. Now I see you two here, reunited, and it all makes me so incredibly happy."

The medication that the medics gave him started to take effect, so Charlie and Rosanne said their goodbyes to let Thack get some sleep.

*****

## The *Aurora*, Astrodyne 65, Operated by the Stellar Logistics and Freight Corporation

Phil touched down on the parking pad that was assigned to him, and Chad read the shutdown checklist. An Air Force loadmaster opened the cargo door so that a load of freight they just delivered could be off-loaded.

Norton Parker met Phil and Chad when they stepped out. The other Astrodyne pilots and crew joined them, and Norton said he had an announcement. He waited until he was sure that everyone could hear him. "Guys, today was the last load of freight for most of us. The volume of freight required from this point on will be severely diminished. All the Stellar Logistics crews will return to our regular jobs, and a small number of Astrodyne Corporation crews will stay here to move the freight as needed."

Norton wanted to record the moment that this portion of their participation in this venture came to a close, so he arranged for all the Astrodyne crews to pose for a group photo in front of the *Aurora*. Then the Stellar Logistics crew posed for one that was meant to be mostly for themselves.

Michael pulled up in a Jeep. "Hey, Pops!"

Phil turned and saw Michael for the first time since leaving the station. He was relieved to see Michael was in one piece. Norton couldn't pass up the opportunity to have Phil and Michael pose for a photo.

When everyone went their own way, Michael said, "Pop, I actually had a second reason for coming here. One of the mercenaries from Reynolds Planet found his wife at a Falta Plantation."

Phil brightened. "Evans? That's great! What do you need from me?" Michael continued, "She has a friend here, a flaston girl, who apparently can't go back to Flast without putting her family in danger."

Phil frowned. "I don't get it."

Michael shrugged. "She was actually sold to the slavers by some kind of crime boss. There's a very real possibility that he'll harm her family if word gets out that she's free."

Phil furrowed his brow. "So what do you want me to do?"

Michael answered, "This girl needs a place to go until things can get sorted out."

Phil thought about it and nodded. "Yeah, why not. I'm not sure what kind of job we can give her. Maybe one of the vendors on the station can put her to work, but there's plenty of time to figure that out."

Michael smiled. "That's my pops. Let's go see her." They climbed into the Jeep and drove to the mercenary compound.

Phil and Michael went into the operations room to find Henson, Devonport, Charlie Evans, and Rosanne Evans. Charlie looked up and said, "Davis and a flaston investigator named Prendle are back there interviewing Tillya. I think they're about done.

As if on cue, the door opened that led to the small room they were using for the interview.

The flaston investigator led them out, saying, "You're quite right for being concerned about letting these criminals know you're no longer held in bondage. I cannot stress enough the importance of keeping your whereabouts secret. Even I shouldn't know where you're living. If I need to get information to you, I'll contact Mr. Davis. The number of people between you and Mr. Davis is completely up to you."

He bid them all good day and left the room. Davis turned to Tillya. "Do you trust me?" Tillya nodded. "I think so."

Davis nodded. "I take it from what Lieutenant Ross said back at the Zisros Plantation, and seeing Mr. Ross here makes me think that Miss Tillya will be residing on Oasis 4 for the time being."

Tillya looked at Phil, then back to Charlie and Rosanne. Charlie said, "Mr. Ross is good people, Tillya, and he surrounds himself with good people."

Davis smiled. "Excellent. I can contact Mr. Ross, or his security marshal, Mr. Smith, so I can avoid contacting you directly, which may compromise your whereabouts."

Phil said, "Speaking of Luke Smith, send him as much information on these bad players as you can. The station has tech that uses facial recognition."

Davis laughed. "I checked on your security team. They have a reputation for being tough on crime. I'll send him as much information as I can get a hold of."

Tillya was near tears. "Mr. Ross, I can't say how much this means to me. All of you have been so kind to me. I don't know how to respond."

Phil put his hand up. "Employees usually reserve their opinions of me for a few weeks."

Tillya laughed. "I promise that you'll get maximum effort from me."

Henson said, "Before you all run off, we need to talk to Sergeant Evans and Mrs. Evans. Charlie, you have a year and a half left on your obligation to us, but you know how I feel about married men in the reconnaissance platoon. To that end, when you report back at Reynolds Planet, we'll get you housing and put you in the training unit. We think you'll make a great training cadre. But first, it has come to our attention that you have a lot of leave saved up. Take the missus back to Earth, visit family, and get to know each other again."

Phil added, "You know, you two could come back with me and help get Ms. Tillya settled, then jump a cruise ship to earth."

Phil waited for his offer to sink in, then continued, "I'm leaving tomorrow morning, and I have space for three more."

Charlie, Rosanne, and Tillya said in unison, "Deal."

*****

## Gostis, Capital City Shuttle Port, Seventy- Fifth Ranger Regiment Briefing Room

Colonel Kline checked himself in a mirror. He was going to record a briefing for transmission to Earth. There was a news blackout for security reasons, but there was no longer a reason to maintain it.

A press presentation packet was prepared by his staff that laid out the operation. It included maps, a time line, and combat footage. He stood behind a podium with the flag behind him. He organized his notes on the podium, and an officer from his headquarters company said, "Anytime you're ready, sir."

Kline cleared his throat. "Greetings, my fellow Americans. I'm Colonel Gregory Kline, commanding officer of the United States Army Seventy-Fifth Ranger Regiment. Undoubtedly, you have been made aware that there's an ongoing effort to end the slave trade that's been growing in recent years. A major player in the slave trade was identified, and the Seventy-Fifth Ranger Regiment was deployed along with other units from a coalition of assorted countries on Earth and other worlds to confront the offenders. A little more than a week ago, we landed on the snoshin world of Gostis with the intent of securing the release of all people held in bondage. Two days ago, the Gostis military leadership dissolved the Teanon Council, which was the ruling body of this planet. Within minutes, hostilities ceased, effectively ending the conflict. The next phase of the operation will involve taking a census of the slave population and arranging for their transportation to their home planets. I would be remiss if I didn't mention that this hasn't been a bloodless affair. The Seventy-Fifth Ranger Regiment has suffered some casualties in dead and wounded. Our numbers lost were blessedly light. However, any loss of one of my rangers is a cause of great sadness. We look forward to returning home and being with family. See you all when we return home."

That evening, General Lingur hosted a dinner party for the senior officers of the coalition forces. Kline was hesitant about the cuisine as it was mostly a mixture of traditional snoshin and local Gostis dishes, but it proved to be quite delicious.

During the after-dinner drinks, the conversation steered toward the previous operations. Kline mentioned off-handedly that he thought the Gostis soldiers weren't exactly up to scratch when it came to fighting. The others in the room fell silent. The cessation of conversation was very noticeable to the point that Kline thought that he made some kind of faux pas. He looked around, and the others were looking in his direction. He quickly added, "That's not an indictment of snoshins."

Lingur smiled. "I didn't take issue with that, but there are two reasons why you would think that. First, I'm sure that you've noticed that the uniforms our opposition was wearing weren't well-suited for the tactical situation they found themselves in."

Kline nodded. "That was unmistakable. They looked as if they would be better at marching in a parade or part of an honor guard."

Lingur smiled. "Or it may be effective in intimidating rioting slaves. It's an odd situation our opposition found themselves in. They had the equipment necessary to prevent military action against them, but their training was more suited to what they considered the more immediate and realistic threat."

Kline's expression changed to understanding. "So very little of their training was devoted to fighting other soldiers, but a lot was devoted to keeping the population that was in bondage from uprising."

Lingur smiled some more. "That's a big part of it."

Kline sensed that there was more. "Well then, sir. Please tell me, what's the rest of it?"

Lingur hesitated, "I don't want this to upset you, but…humans have a reputation, which is now well-deserved for being a warrior race."

Kline was flabbergasted. "What brings you to that conclusion? We haven't been remotely hostile toward other races."

Lingur said defensively, "I wasn't making that assertion, I promise. When two races meet for the first time, it's prudent to study that race's history, customs, practices, and attitudes. A study of your planet's history revealed some interesting contrasts, but the one thing that stood out to those of us that study such things is how good humans were at making war."

Kline processed what Lingur said, "Everyone in this room is a professional soldier. We've dedicated our lives to the service of each of our countries."

Colonel Grast from the flaston defense forces answered, "That's very true, but each of us came into this with our own ideas of how to fight a war. We used tactics that were developed by our individual experiences in combat. Humans have proven to be exceptional soldiers, and your performance here hasn't gone unnoticed. Everyone in the Earth contingent has proven to be incredibly good at combat."

Kline considered what the others told him, and he thought to himself that it would make an interesting footnote in his report.

*****

## The *Aurora*, Astrodyne 65, Operated by the Stellar Logistics and Freight Corporation

Phil cut the light-speed engines and started the reaction engines, then pushed the power levers to full. Chad tuned the radio to company frequency and started monitoring the proximity warning system. They counted as the Astrodyne's started dropping out of light speed behind them. Phil pulled back on the power levers to 50 percent to allow the trailing Astrodyne's to catch up and get into formation.

When the last one was in position, Phil eased the power levers forward to a sublight cruising speed that was comfortable for the other 65s that weren't modified like the Aurora. Phil contacted Oasis 4 and received approach vectors to the station. At the station, the *Aurora* was given its customary parking spot at CargoMod 2 Docking Port 1. The other Astrodyne's were assigned CargoMod 2 as well.

After docking, power was switched from internal to station supplied. Chad opened the hatch and looked into the CargoMod. He saw the station worker who connected the power walking away. Chad turned around to see Phil, leading Tillya and the Evans. "There's no one out there."

Phil could feel his hackles rise. "What's she up to?"

Chad started grinning. Charlie furrowed his brow. "What's 'who' up to?" Phil looked up and down the CargoMod aisle and said, "Mrs. Ross."

The other crews started arriving, then Gus said, "I expected a warmer welcome than this."

Phil inhaled and slowly let out a breath. "I have a feeling that they're laying for us in the CentMod."

He shrugged. "Let's get this done."

They walked the connector tunnel to the CentMod. Phil saw it was early evening, and the lights were dimmed. As the group entered the CentMod, the lights came up, and military marching music played. Everyone on the station had gathered in the CentMod and applauded and cheered. Most were on walkways that overlooked the plaza level. Phil spotted Alice standing next to Elias, and he led the rest to them.

Alice ran up and gave Phil a huge wet smooch on him, then she asked, "How's Mikey? Tell me he's okay."

Phil smiled. "He's more than okay. You should have seen him there. I made him promise to write."

He then said, "I have three people you need to meet."

He led Alice to Charlie, Rosanne, and Tillya. "Hon, you know Charles Evans already. This is Rosanne Evans, and this is Tillya."

Alice ran over and gave Rosanne and Tillya hugs, which surprised both of them. Alice said, "Phil sent a communication telling me to expect you. Tomorrow, we'll get better acquainted."

Elias was busy shaking hands with everyone and nearly forgot about the crowd still applauding. He finally came out of his reverie and looked at the crowd. He held a microphone up to his mouth, and the crowd fell silent. "I want to personally congratulate everyone who participated in this venture and returned safely to us. All of you must be exhausted, so please get to your quarters and get some well-deserved rest. Tomorrow, you can thrill us with stories of your adventure."

Elias purposely omitted to mention Tillya and Rosanne to prevent them from getting too overwhelmed but also so as not to draw a lot of attention to Tillya. Alice said to Charlie, Rosanne, and Tillya. "We reserved rooms for all of you at the Star Lodge Suites, Phil and I generally have breakfast at about seven in the morning at Eva's Café."

Phil and Alice walked them to the Star Lodge Suites and checked them in. Rosanne and Tillya found that Alice and Brenda had made sure that the ladies had new nighties and underwear, along with dresses, shoes, and socks to wear in the morning. Both Rosanne and Tillya broke down and cried a little, both at the kind gesture and holding in their hands the simplest of personal items, but now they seemed like an extravagant luxury after having been denied for more than two years.

In the morning, Phil and Alice reestablished their morning routines. After a workout and dressing, they went to Eva's for breakfast, where they were met by the Evans and Tillya. Rosanne and Tillya jumped up and gave Alice simultaneous hugs.

Alice was appreciative of the affection but was unsure why it was being lavished on her. She said, "This is really nice girls, but are we going to do this every time we see each other?"

Rosanne laughed. "We just might."

Tillya said, "The clothes that you made sure were in our rooms are so beautiful, and it was so thoughtful."

Alice said, "Nonsense. We couldn't have you, girls, running around in those coveralls you were wearing when you got here. I wanted to make sure that you had something decent to wear. I was pretty sure the stores on Gostis would be closed."

Alice then stepped back and scrutinized their clothes. "It looks like I guessed the sizes about right. After breakfast, we'll get you two a fresh wardrobe."

Rosanne protested, "You've been too kind. We can't possibly take advantage of you like this."

Alice put her hand up. "More nonsense. Phil and I are quite wealthy. Besides, I haven't had an opportunity to go on a shopping spree for quite a while. So both of you, just relax and let me have fun." Phil was digesting what Alice told Rosanne and Tillya. He then furrowed his brow. "I'm all for getting the girls new outfits, but what did you mean by wealthy?"

Alice smiled. "We received the first installment of the bonus from finding the Prospector."

Phil had quite forgotten about that. "Oh, I guess I'll have to talk to Elias about that. Hey, speaking of Elias."

At that moment, Elias arrived with a big grin on his face. "Morning, all!" Everyone said in unison, "Morning, Elias."

Eva took Elias's order and poured him a cup of coffee. Elias took a sip and smiled at Tillya, enjoying her first taste of pancakes and maple syrup. After two years of eating tasteless porridge for breakfast, she was overjoyed at this table.

Eva saw the same thing, and it brought a smile to her face. She went to Tillya and put her hand on her shoulder. "Would you like a little more, dear?"

Tillya realized that everyone was amused at the attention she was giving to her breakfast and broke out with her own grin. Then she said to Eva, "Oh, thank you for offering, but I'd better exercise some self-control. I never thought I would taste anything this wonderful ever again."

Eva smiled and went to the kitchen to get Elias's breakfast and tell Burt that his pancakes were a big hit.

In a couple of minutes, Elias was putting pepper on the eggs Eva just brought to him. "Miss Tillya, after you have your breakfast, Alice has volunteered to help you get settled into your new quarters. We'll give you a few days to get used to the place. Then we'll put you to work."

Tillya suddenly felt nervous. "What kind of job will I be doing?"

Elias shrugged. "Our operations manager, Virginia Wells, has some ideas about getting you trained in her department. Don't concern yourself. Virginia has a way of figuring out where folks can best be used."

Phil smiled and asked Elias, "When am I going to get back to running my station without the boss lurking about?"

Elias sipped his orange juice. "In two days. There's a passenger liner leaving direct to Earth. Major Henson sent a message asking me to make sure that the Evans have a cabin on that ship, which was my pleasure to do. Now I have traveling companions besides my personal assistant. Today, though, I expect you to relax and spend time with Alice and our guest."

After breakfast, Alice left with Rosanne and Tillya, which left Phil and Charlie some time to kill. They decided that a stroll through the station was a good idea, so they started there at Eva's and visited every level in the upper CentMod. When they passed Slider's pool hall, Charlie smiled and said, "You know, Rosie was a pretty decent eight ball player in high school."

Phil laughed. "Challenge accepted. Maybe after dinner, we can get the girls and make an evening of it."

They made their way to the lower CentMod and explored the plaza level. Phil noticed that there was still some shop space available for occupancy and wondered how long it would take to rent the space and what kind of businesses would move in. He also noticed that I&F Investigations and Retrievals was empty, and the lights were off.

They walked to the level that had the consulate offices that had taken on the unofficial title of Embassy Row. All the consular generals knew Phil's role in the action on Gostis. Also, word had gotten out about Charlie and Rosanne. As a result, it seemed they all wanted to greet and congratulate them on a very positive outcome.

Lynuna greeted Phil as warm as ever. Then she invited both Phil and Charlie into her office, where she closed the door. They could tell that Lynuna had something she wanted to discuss. She had them take a seat on a sofa she had in her office then she sat in an armchair across them. Her assistant brought in a tray of flaston tea.

As she poured, Phil noticed that the tea set wasn't flaston. She saw Phil looking the set over and said, "I ordered this set from a catalog of an Earth retailer. I thought it was more elegant than anything from Flast."

After taking a sip, both Phil and Charlie decided that they liked flaston tea.

When the assistant left, he closed the door behind him, and Lynuna quickly got to the purpose of asking them to her office. "I couldn't help but notice when you arrived, there was a flaston girl with you."

Both Phil and Charlie felt a wave of panic, and Lynuna quickly put her hand up. "Please don't get excited, gentlemen. I was given a briefing concerning some of the flastons who have found themselves slaves and the circumstances that brought them to that condition. The new government on Flast is dedicated to annihilating the organization that profited from the misery of others. One of the reasons the old government had to go was it had become so corrupted. It used the crime syndicate to consolidate its power. To that end, as far as this girl is concerned, the fact that she's a former slave will be a well-guarded secret until those that did this to her are locked up."

Charlie nodded. "I'm glad to hear that we're all on the same page on this."

Lynuna smiled. "Everyone on my staff has had negative encounters with the Syndicate. The other flastons on the station, Isnod and Feldon, have also had horrific experiences with them, so we can trust them in my estimation, but I'll leave that up to the young lady."

Phil smiled. "I don't think she could find a safer place to be than right here. Luke Smith takes his responsibilities very seriously, and I know he'll have the SICOS positively identify any flastons using facial recognition. Also, Isnod and Feldon can be scary. I can't imagine they would pass an opportunity to protect one of their own. By the way, where is the dynamic duo? Their shop is closed."

Lynuna sipped her tea and put her cup on its saucer. "They had a job come up. They seemed motivated to complete their task, as their client sought them out."

Charlie said, "I'm sorry I missed them. I kind of like those guys."

Lynuna sighed. "They're a bit overdue. I hope they haven't gotten into trouble."

Phil shrugged. "Those two are capable of taking care of themselves. I would hate to be the one they were after."

After their tea with Lynuna, Phil and Charlie continued their tour of the station until lunch. Of course, they ate at Eva's, where Rosanne and Tillya excitedly told Charlie about their morning and gushed at the new clothes they had. After lunch, Phil used SICOS to contact Virginia Wells to see what quarters she assigned to Tillya.

Alice had Tillya's things sent up from the hotel to her quarters then they all went to HabMod 4 to help her settle in. On arrival, they all stood back and let Tillya enjoy her big moment. She took a breath. "SICOS, allow entry."

An indicator next to the entry button went from red to green, and she pressed the button. The door slid open, and she cautiously stepped in and stood in the sitting area, where she stared out of the window.

The others timidly stepped in, Tillya turned, and they saw tears running down her cheeks. Rosanne quietly asked, "Tillya, what's wrong?"

Tillya shook her head. "Nothing at all. This is all so wonderful. Three days ago, I was sleeping in slave quarters with dozens of others. If you would have told me then that I would have these fine clothes, this luxurious place to live, I would have told you to stop telling wild stories."

Phil and, for the first time, Alice was at a loss for words. They were just grateful they could help her in any way they could. There was another round of tears and the girls hugging. After they composed themselves, Alice explained to Tillya that the quarters came with a standard complement of items like bedding and kitchenware. As time went on, she could replace them with items that she was more comfortable with, and the standard items could be put back in supply.

After settling Tillya into her quarters, the five of them went to Maurice's, where Rosanne and Tillya had a difficult time keeping their emotions in check. Tillya absolutely loved the cuisine, but she decided that it really was too fancy for her to eat more than once every now and again on special occasions. Even growing up on Flast, the food she was raised on was simple and healthy.

The diet she was forced to endure on Gostis was calculated to keep her and her companions alive and nothing more. She learned that the food court in HabMod 4 had a flaston serving line, and she was actually quite anxious to sample a taste from home.

When they had finished their desserts, they took a stroll in the CentMod to help their digestion. Gus and Brenda were coming out of Baja Juans, and Phil suggested that they cap the evening with a couple of games of pool at Sliders.

Rosanne grinned. "Are there table stakes?"

Phil's hackles raised. "Absolutely not! You've been hanging around my wife too much!" Then he turned to Alice. "Stop being a bad influence."

Charlie was laughing out loud. "Don't blame your wife, Mr. Ross. Rosie gets this way when she starts thinking about eight ball."

On their way up to Sliders, they met Elias and begged him to tag along. Elias beamed. "I haven't played in years. I'd be happy to join you, folks."

It turned out that Rosanne was indeed very good at eight ball once she warmed up. The surprise was, Elias was also very good. He and Rosanne battled it out more than once. Neither one could claim they were the better player since they split their wins and losses evenly. Tillya had a wonderful time and became quite a player herself.

The day had finally arrived for Charlie and Rosanne to board the passenger liner with Elias, bound for Earth. Naturally, Phil and Alice were there along with Tillya. It was the picture of a bittersweet moment. For the first time in years, Tillya and Rosanne would be separated, and it was harder on everyone than they anticipated. For that reason, Alice decided to take it upon herself to make sure Tillya's transition to a normal life went smoothly.

After Charlie and Rosanne boarded with Elias, the liner's hatches were shut and sealed. Phil, Alice, and Tillya then strolled from CargoMod 1 to the CentMod. Phil immediately noticed some excitement near the security office. Luke Smith came out of his office, spotted Phil, and hurried over to him. "Hey, Boss, we have a possible developing situation in CargoMod 6."

Phil grinned and said, "Ah, it's good to be back and in charge."

He turned to Alice and Tillya. "Why don't you two girls go to Sparky's and get a glass of wine? I'll meet you there after I take care of this."

Phil left with Luke and took the platform lift to the lower CentMod. Sparky's was having a slow night, and it was agreeably quiet. Alice and Tillya were about half finished with their first glass when Gus and Brenda arrived.

Alice invited them to share their table and, soon after, Dwight and Virginia. In short order, Phil arrived. Alice asked, "What did Luke have for you?"

Phil took a sip of the lager the waiter put in front of him, then said, "Isnod and Feldon have returned with a shuttle full of felons. From the looks of it, they're lucky to be alive. Marie Tillman has her people working on them now."

Gus shook his head. "I knew those two were nuts. Do you think they're in the habit of biting off more than they can chew?"

Phil slowly shook his head. "I don't think they were after fugitives this time. I think Lynuna sent them after something. They had a case on board that she had me secure in my office vault. I'll see if I can get some answers tomorrow."

Alice looked at Phil. She saw something in his eyes that she hadn't seen in a while. "How are you feeling, Phil?"

The question caught Phil off guard, but he recovered, and his lips slightly curled into a self-satisfied smile. He nodded and said, "I feel good. We've just helped right a tremendous wrong. Thousands of people have their lives back. Other than my kids, I can't imagine a group of people I would rather be with right now. I'm not suggesting that there isn't any more evil in the galaxy, but we exposed and eradicated a big chunk of it. I'm not sure if it's possible to overstate how I feel right now although it seems right somehow that the simplest answer is the best. I feel good."

The End

# ARTIFACT

### Pulsar 1250, Owned by I&F Investigations and Retrievals

Feldon cut the light-speed engine and started the reaction engine. A very groggy Isnod entered the cockpit and handed Feldon a cup of coffee after taking a seat. Feldon took a sip and smiled. "At first, I thought this human concoction was vile, but now I can't imagine having to do without it."

Isnod took a sip of his own coffee. "There's a lot of things about the humans that are like that."

Feldon contacted the station and received approach vectors while Isnod was savoring his own coffee.

A voice in the rear compartment called out, "Hey, guys? Whatever you're drinking smells good. Do you think I could have some?"

Isnod looked slightly annoyed. "Why would we share anything with you?" The voice was insistent. "Aw, come on, I haven't been trouble, have I?"

Feldon grinned. "He has a point. In some ways, he's probably the easiest bounty we'll ever collect."

Isnod slowly nodded and said to the voice in the back, "All right, whatever shuts you up."

He then stood up, went to the rear compartment, poured a cup of coffee, and handed it to the pretar that was sitting there with an ankle cuff secured to a fitting on the deck. The pretar took a sip and made a yummy sound. "Mmm, that's tasty."

Isnod had to work to suppress a grin of his own. "Wasn't there honest work you could do? You seem intelligent, and the way you manipulated that banking computer to transfer funds was inspired. It just seems to me that you would be a lot better off right now if you had a job that didn't involve taking things that weren't yours."

The pretar smiled. "Then where would the challenge come from? Or the fun?" Isnod had to admit that he liked the little pretar.

Feldon eased the Pulsar into the docking clamps and switched power from internal to station supplied as soon as it was available. Isnod opened the air lock and used a terminal to contact the security office. In a few minutes, Tiffany Waters arrived with a deputy, and Isnod handed her a data chip, "This is the warrant for Mr. Gotic here. We'll be contacting the Pretna Consulate directly."

Tiffany took the chip. "I hope you two didn't put yourselves in too much danger with this one."

It took Isnod a second or two to catch the joke. He chuckled and nodded toward the deputy. "With that being said, did you bring enough muscle?"

As he was being led through the air lock by a deputy, Gotic said, "I'm picking up on the sarcasm."

Isnod grinned and said, "I hope so. We were being pretty obvious."

Isnod and Feldon grabbed their duffels and headed to the lower CentMod. After throwing their bags in their office they took an escalator to the sixth level and walked to Embassy Row. Entering the Pretna Consulate, they were subject to curious stares.

The consular general's assistant approached them and asked, "How can I help you, gentlemen?"

Isnod politely replied, "Hello, I am Isnod, and this is Feldon of I&F Investigations and Retrievals. We have just returned from a business venture with an individual that's wanted by your government for various crimes."

The assistant pressed a call button and told the consular general what Isnod told him. In a few seconds, a distinguished-looking pretar emerged from his office. "Hello, you can call me Ungnas. I understand you gentlemen have another fugitive wanted by my government."

Isnod bowed ever so slightly. "Indeed we do, sir. He's a pretar named Gotic."

Ungnas said, "Oh my! This is indeed good news. Gotic has been a genuine nuisance for some time now. Oh yes, yes, this is indeed welcome news after the events that have occurred this week."

Feldon frowned. "We've been out of contact for some time. To what events are you referring to?"

Ungnas replied, "Oh dear, dear, there's been a major blow struck against the slavery institution. All the major worlds are participating in an invasion of Gostis. The last news I received indicates the humans have landed three days ago, and there's been one vicious battle after another. A large contingent from Pretna is landing now, and they'll be fighting alongside forces from Flast."

Isnod shook his head. "That all happened remarkably fast. We'll have to check with our own consulate to see if there's any way we can help."

Ungnas accompanied Isnod and Feldon to the security office, where he made positive identification of Gotic. Luke Smith couldn't help but kid them back in his office. "I'm glad both of you decided to go to retrieve this one. A man could get hurt if he resisted."

Feldon grinned. "I suppose it was fortunate for us that Mr. Gotic is a peaceful man."

Gotic was out of sight, but he said loud enough for everyone to hear. "You know I can hear you back here."

Ungnas, being a pretar, wasn't quite as adept at recognizing sarcasm and humor among other races furrowed his brow and said, "Gotic has never had a history of violence."

Isnod nodded. "The quiet ones have a tendency to snap sometimes." Gotic said from his cell, "Again, I'm right here!"

It finally became obvious to Ungnas that they were having fun at Gotic's expense, but he wasn't comfortable chiming in, so he simply said, "Thank you, Mr. Smith, for your time."

Luke politely nodded. "Always my pleasure, Mr. Ungnas."

Then Ungnas turned to Isnod and Feldon. "Gentlemen, I suggest we go to the bank before it closes and conclude your involvement in this affair."

After ending their business at the bank, Isnod and Feldon retrieved their duffels from their office, and then it was a walk back to their quarters in HabMod 4 for a good night's rest.

*****

## Oasis 4, HabMod 4

As was their habit, they awoke early and met in the HabMod 4 fitness center. They had a strict routine of both cardio and weight training. Being they were former fugitive trackers and their current profession required it, they would also practice flaston martial arts called micton.

Of the two, Isnod was better at the ancient flaston fighting style than Feldon, but Feldon was gradually getting to the point where he could stalemate Isnod, which is to say the pair of them were extremely formidable. Afterward, they returned to their individual quarters for showers and then to the HabMod food court for breakfast.

After filling their trays at the flaston serving line with breakfast fare, they found a table and sat. Feldon looked around. "There's a lot of flastons on the station."

Isnod lifted his eyes. "There's more than the consulate staff here. I was told there were going to be some flaston-run businesses open on the station. I guess they arrived while we were tracking down Gotic."

At that moment, Lynuna arrived with her tray. "Gentlemen, can I join you?"

Isnod and Feldon stood, then Isnod pulled a chair and held it for her. "Of course, it's always a pleasure."

Lynuna sat and started removing the meal from the tray. "Was your business trip a success?"

Feldon nodded. "Indeed it was. We've handled more dangerous fugitives, but rarely have they been more elusive." Then he grinned. "Present company accepted."

When it registered what Feldon said, Lynuna nearly spit out her morning tea. Then she laughingly said, "A gentlemen would have waited until after I finished my sip of tea before saying that."

Isnod had trouble keeping a straight face. "Quite right. You should be ashamed of yourself, Feldon."

After they collected themselves, Isnod said, "I understand that there have been developments with ending the slave trade."

Lynuna smiled. "Oh yes, indeed. There is even a unit of our brave soldiers from Flast participating. I get updates on their progress every day. There are also some of the station personnel involved in this business."

Feldon asked, "Who exactly?"

Lynuna answered, "Well, for starters, Phillip Ross, the station manager, then there's Gus Condent and several others in the Stellar Logistics and Freight Corporation."

Isnod said very seriously, "If there's anything Feldon and I can do, we're more than willing to do it. We probably aren't the two most popular people on Flast, but we're both patriots."

Lynuna smiled. "Of that, I have no doubts. As far as your popularity goes, I think you're thinking that the new government is like the old regime. We're taking great pains to transition to a new society without reprisals on those who were in positions of power. Your names were mentioned by my colleagues on more than one occasion, and the consensus is the embassy on Earth was a little heavy-handed in how they treated you."

Isnod and Feldon had never heard that before, and they were at a loss for words. Feldon finally broke the silence. "The offer is genuine. Anything we can do, we're more than willing to do whatever is necessary."

Lynuna nodded. "I'll keep my ear to the ground."

Isnod frowned. "That's a curious saying. Undoubtedly, it's human. I have to tell you, Ms. Lynuna, I think they've been a bad influence on you."

The three of them laughed and made small talk for the duration of their meal. After their breakfasts were consumed, they went their separate ways. Lynuna went to the consulate, and the pair of bounty hunters to their office.

*****

## Oasis 4, CentMod Lower Section, Office of I&F Investigations and Retrievals

The bounty hunters started their workday trying to find as much information they could on the war being waged on Gostis. After about an hour and a half, they didn't learn much more than what Lynuna already told them.

They were about to check the wanted bulletins when Lynuna appeared at their door, which was usually a happy occasion, but it was immediately apparent that Lynuna was deeply troubled. Isnod leaped to his feet and helped her to a seat. "What happened since breakfast to bring you to this state?"

She took a sip of tea that Feldon brought her. "I just received disturbing news from Flast. An artifact of great importance has been stolen."

Isnod asked, "What was stolen?"

Lynuna took a breath and answered with a hitch in her voice, "The Faldos Charter."

Isnod and Feldon exchanged looks, then Feldon shook his head. "The Faldos Charter is a legend!"

Lynuna shook her own head and said, "That's what they wanted us to believe. The Charter was secreted away at the end of the Colavar Rebellion and hidden for generations."

Isnod and Feldon were floored. To this point, the Faldos Charter was something that reformers had pointed to as a blueprint for forming a new government and outlining a modern Charter of Rights. The Colavar Regime had denied the existence of the Faldos Charter to consolidate its hold on the population. The Charter had to be kept hidden because it would be immediately destroyed. Knowledge of the Faldos Charter would give an incredible amount of legitimacy to a Charter of Rights based on it. Flast still had opponents to a change in the government who would take any opportunity to sabotage efforts to establish a Republic.

Both bounty hunters knew the weight of what was at stake. Isnod asked, "Where was the Charter stored?"

Lynuna replied, "There was a secure secret facility built in the Utis Mountains. They built vaults in an abandoned salt mine, caretakers kept guard on it, and other important artifacts for generations."

Feldon asked, "How was it stolen?"

Lynuna put down her teacup. "It was being transported to the capital archives. They were going to unveil it at the conclusion of the ratification of the new charter. The convoy was ambushed, and the Charter stolen."

Isnod furrowed his brow. "If the Charter is that damaging to the old regime, why didn't they destroy it instead of stealing it?"

Lynuna shuddered at the thought. "One can only guess."

Feldon leaned back. "It would be helpful if we knew a little about who stole it."

Lynuna said with a shake of her head. "No one has claimed responsibility, and there have been no demands. There is some security camera footage of the attack, but the investigators have stated that there wasn't any useful information they can get from it."

Isnod asked, "Who's the lead investigator?" Lynuna answered, "His name is Pindon."

Isnod sneered. "I know him, I consider him a friend, but he's a lazy investigator. He makes the right friends and insulates himself from criticism. He doesn't have a great case resolution record in the Law Enforcement Brigade."

Lynuna scowled. "Why would they give such an important assignment to a man with such a poor performance record?"

Isnod shrugged. "Like I said, he makes friends in positions that can do his career the most good. Also, I hate to mention this, but the new government is probably quite disorganized and most likely isn't in a position to make the best selection. Besides, Pindon might be a mess when it comes to investigating himself, but he does have some strong suits. For instance, he's a very good administrator, and he does have a sense of who the best investigator would be to carry out a given assignment."

Lynuna stood. "Gentlemen, the proposition is simple. Find the Faldos Charter, and you'll be rewarded handsomely."

Feldon nearly shouted, "It's off-world?"

Lynuna sighed. "That's just a guess, I'm afraid. Shortly after the criminals stole the Faldos Charter, a shuttle took off and left our system. There were no identifying codes transmitted or flight plan filed. Pindon feels that the shuttle was a ruse, and the Charter is still on Flast."

Isnod furrowed his brow. "That's a possibility, but I wouldn't count on it."

Lynuna continued, "I've sent you all the information we have on this to your SICOS terminal. Anything you can do would be appreciated." After Lynuna left, Isnod found the files that she had sent to them.

After going over the various reports, which didn't tell them much, Isnod turned his attention to the footage of the actual crime. Feldon observed, "This bunch is very careful. They're wearing masks. The clothes they're wearing don't offer any clue as to who they are."

They viewed the footage over and over, scrutinizing over every detail. Finally, Isnod stood and rubbed his eyes. "I need a break. The flaston serving line in the HabMod 4 food court is closed, so I wouldn't mind having a Klon at Eva's."

Feldon stood. "I think I'll have a Tonkin."

After they ate, they returned to the office and again started reviewing the video of the ambush. Feldon suddenly said, "SICOS, pause replay!"

Isnod frowned. "You can only see his back."

Feldon continued to stare unblinking at the monitor. "SICOS, reverse play, slow."

The video slowly played backward until Feldon said, "SICOS, pause, overlay grid."

A grid appeared on the screen, and Feldon examined it, then ordered, "SICOS, isolate grid delta eight and enhance."

The picture tightened on the criminal's hand. Feldon smiled. "He has dermal ink markings on his left arm, part of it is protruding from under his sleeve onto his hand. That looks like a dragon's tail to me."

Isnod looked closer and smiled. "Well, we haven't run into these guys in a while."

Feldon leaned back in his chair. "Where do we start?"

Isnod rubbed his chin. "Let's work on the assumption that they took the Charter off-world. Probably the planet they feel the safest on would be Treest. At least that's where they've been the most active."

"Do you have any contacts there?" Feldon asked.

Isnod nodded. "Just one. We'll drop in on him. First, though, I have more questions for Lynuna."

*****

## Oasis 4, Flast Consulate

A few minutes later, the pair found themselves at the Flast Consulate, where Lynuna welcomed them into her office. Isnod came right to the point. "If we find the Charter, how can we be sure it's the genuine artifact?"

Lynuna thought for a second. "That's a good question. I'm sure there's experts on Flast that will be able to determine its authenticity." Isnod shook his head. "We may not have the option of returning to

Flast. Is there a way you could tell?"

Lynuna frowned. "I've never considered there might be a reason to create a forgery."

Feldon interrupted, "What good would a forgery do anyone?"

Isnod thought about it, then he said, "Consider what would happen if a fake were presented as genuine, but later, it was revealed as a fake. People who are still loyal to the old regime would claim that the Charter was nothing more than a myth, and the present government is trying to deceive the people. If that happens, the whole process of writing a modern Charter of Rights would be undermined. If we're successful, we'll bring the Charter back here and determine its authenticity before returning it to Flast."

Lynuna nodded. "I'll educate myself on how to do just that. I wish you, gentlemen, luck."

*****

## Treest, Flaston Colony (Self-Governed), Capitol City Shuttle Port

After putting fresh provisions in the Pulsar 1250, they boarded and set a course for Treest. The journey to Treest lasted a week as it was one of the most remote inhabited worlds from Oasis 4. After landing at the capital shuttle port, Feldon shut down the engines and stood. "I'm so glad the Pulsar is as fast as it is."

Isnod nodded in agreement. "I concur. If this vessel was slower, I'd want a bigger one just to be able to move around a little more."

They took a courtesy tram to the terminal, where they were scrutinized by the customs inspector. Satisfied that Isnod and Feldon weren't up to mischief, the customs inspector allowed them to proceed. On the street side of the terminal, they waited for the public transportation ground shuttle.

They didn't have long to wait, as a shuttle came by every ten minutes. Feldon sat and looked for a map. Not finding one, he asked, "How does one get to a specific part of the city."

Isnod answered, "Did you notice the number on the shuttle was on a blue background?"

Feldon shook his head. "No, it's not something I expected to be important."

Isnod nodded. "I wouldn't say it's important so much, but it does help get you around. Blue backgrounds indicate direct service between a ground shuttle hub and a major destination like a shuttle port or retail center. Red backgrounds indicate service from a hub to a route called a loop. A loop has several stops in specific sectors of the city. We'll consult a map at the hub to see which loop we need to be on and which stop to get off on."

The ground shuttle pulled into the hub and stopped. When everyone exited, the shuttle moved forward to a boarding area to take on passengers. Isnod and Feldon went to a large map, and Feldon said, "You know, I never did ask who your contact is here."

Isnod said, "His name is Yesnic. He's not an out-and-out criminal, but he does enjoy his shady activities. It's useful to foster relationships with guys like Yesnic for information. He has a talent for getting involved with criminal activity without actually doing anything illegal. That way, he's not in much danger of being arrested. Those doing the real crimes are careless what they say around him because he presents himself as being generally harmless and living off their scraps. He can take seemingly unrelated bits of information and find the connection. Sometimes he can use the information to put goaners in his pocket, or he offers the information to interested parties, sometimes for profit and sometimes for future consideration."

Feldon was finding it hard to imagine how anyone could operate that way for very long. He shook his head. "It sounds like he would make a good investigator."

Isnod grinned. "He would, actually. He has a talent for putting together information for his own enrichment. I think he would be good at doing what we do."

After Isnod consulted a transit map and selected a loop, they went to the proper platform to board the ground shuttle. The shuttle departed on its preprogrammed route automatically. They were rushed at breakneck speed to the section of the city serviced by this particular shuttle.

Not all loops were serviced by red shuttles, but it was possible to get to an adjoining loop by getting off at an overlap stop. An overlap stop was shared by adjoining loops serviced by yellow shuttles. One would simply travel from overlap stop to overlap stop until the destination loop was reached.

Isnod and Feldon got lucky. Yesnic had a house near the loop they were on. Isnod peered out of the window, found the station number, stood, and said, "This is ours."

They stepped off the shuttle and onto the station platform. Isnod pointed to the right. "He's this way a short distance."

The section of the city they found themselves in was on the outskirts. The homes here were relatively humble but well kept, and the inhabitants were, for the most part, hardworking laborers and honest. Feldon looked around as they walked. "I would have expected this Yesnic to live in a seedier part of the city, perhaps somewhere near warehouses."

Isnod smiled as they walked. "Part of the secret to his success, separate where you operate from where you live. He doesn't tell them where he lives, and he doesn't give them a reason to ask."

They walked a short distance further, and Isnod nodded toward a neat little dwelling. "That's his, right there."

They entered the small yard through a gate and approached the door. Isnod pressed a call button, and a red indicator illuminated, then a voice from the speaker asked, "Who's there?"

Isnod rolled his eyes. "You know very well who it is."

The door slid open, and a flaston about Isnod's age was framed in the doorway. "Isnod, I didn't recognize you without your uniform."

Isnod feigned annoyance. "Surely even you couldn't have missed the news that Flast is now under new governance."

Yesnic nodded. "Indeed, I have heard, but I would have expected you to be tracked down by a different pair of fugitive trackers by now."

Isnod was having difficulty suppressing a chuckle. "If that's the case, are you going to invite us in before we're spotted?"

Yesnic grinned and motioned them inside, saying, "Why not?" Once inside, he eyed them up and down. "Who's your friend?"

Isnod introduced Feldon to Yesnic. "Yesnic, this is my partner and friend Feldon. Feldon, this is Yesnic."

Yesnic motioned them to a courtyard in the middle of his home. "Here, have a seat, and I'll bring out some tea."

The pair sat as Yesnic busied himself, putting tea service on a tray. Feldon looked around at Yesnic's home, which was nothing like anything on Flast. "Your home is really quite nice, Mr. Yesnic."

Yesnic returned with the tea. "Thank you, but please, just call me Yesnic. This home is quite typical of homes on Treest. From its inception, this colony has gone to great lengths to make ourselves unique and not a copy of Flast. We've borrowed elements from other worlds to enhance our culture. This courtyard, for instance, is an architectural element inspired by homes from certain regions on Earth. But you, gentlemen, didn't come here for a cultural tour. You said you were partners?"

Isnod quickly related the events that brought them to their current profession. Yesnic nodded approvingly. "You took your government profession and turned it into a business. You probably  should have pulled the trigger on that idea a long time ago."

Then Yesnic asked, "What brings you to my door?" Isnod simply said, "The Faldos Charter."

Yesnic started to belly laugh but stopped suddenly when he saw the expression on Isnod's and Feldon's faces. He looked at the bounty hunters. "Hey, you're not laughing."

"It's real," Isnod said. He then detailed what Lynuna had told them. Yesnic absorbed the information. The ramifications of the Charter's existence weren't lost on him. He finally asked, "What can I do to help?"

Feldon said, "There's a video of the crime."

Yesnic rubbed his chin. "I'd like to see that video."

Feldon pulled a data chip from his pocket and held it up. Yesnic smiled and took the chip. "Please accompany me to my workshop."

They followed him to a door at the corner of the courtyard, and he used his thumb on a biometric lock. Entering the room, he motioned Isnod and Feldon to a pair of chairs while he started a computer terminal and inserted the data chip.

Yesnic scrutinized each video segment, pausing occasionally to take a closer look at something. Several times Feldon wanted to point something out to Yesnic, but Isnod stopped him. He then replayed the video that provided Feldon with the clue he found.

Yesnic then had the computer tighten on the left hand. "So that's why you thought to come here. The Dragons have been a genuine nuisance here. Some of my acquaintances still do business with them." Isnod said, "I'm afraid that's all we have to go on." Yesnic nodded.

"It should be enough."

Feldon frowned. "I will be very impressed if you can get more than we already have."

Yesnic grinned. "We'll see."

He had the computer create a composite of what little of the tattoo was visible. As it turns out, different pieces of the tattoo were visible in different segments of the video. When that was done, he nodded and said, "There aren't any two of these that are identical."

Then he ordered, "Computer, compare image with known Loyalty Brand Dermal Ink Markings for the Dragons."

The computer started going through file images of tattoos that were recorded by members of the Dragons. The Dragons are an organized crime group with ties to the Syndicate. Once someone is confirmed as a member, a dragon is inked onto their left forearm as a sign of lifelong loyalty.

The computer found a matching Loyalty Brand, which it rated 98 percent positive match. Yesnic smiled. "Can't do better than that. His name is Brinot. Now let's see whose crew he's in. Computer, show known associates."

The computer put up a large list of names that immediately deflated Isnod and Feldon.

Yesnic shook his head. "Don't give up now, guys."

He went back to the ambush videos and assigned each individual involved a number for the computer to track. Then he said, "Computer, using physical trait analysis archive data and known associates list from previous search, identify individuals tagged in the video."

The computer started the search, and Isnod shook his head. "Exactly what are you doing?"

Yesnic leaned back in his chair. "They covered their faces, and they tried to obscure their markings, but they can't do anything about height, weight, and physical stature. Even the way they move is unique. Their stride, hand movements, and the way they stand can be measured and compared with known parameters."

Feldon frowned. "I've never heard of such a thing. How did you get a hold of something like this?"

Yesnic shrugged. "I have a friend developing the program for law enforcement. He needed as much data as he could get on some of my…shall we say…less-upright associates. I get video of them walking, talking, standing, and sitting, then add it to the database. Along with archival data from other open sources, a fairly complete behavioral picture can be created. My fee for doing this for him is the program itself and access to the database."

The computer chimed, and Yesnic peered at the monitor. "There's one match."

A rectangular block labeled "Biographical Information" appeared on the screen, with a photo on the left side and data on the right.

The data block provided links that could be selected if more detailed information was desired.

The computer chimed again, and another biographical information block appeared. One feature built into the program was the ability to narrow the search parameters automatically using the known associate's feature as more identities were uncovered.

In a few minutes, Yesnic smiled. "That's all six."

He studied the names and let out a breath. "So that's what they were talking about."

He could see Isnod's and Feldon's expressions and explained, "This fellow here"—he tapped an image on the monitor, which made it expand to a larger size—"his name is Hindor. I cannot stress enough how dangerous he is. Some of my acquaintances were tasked with providing him with support. I heard enough to figure out that they were going to offer something to the highest bidder. I didn't know what it was, but I also got the definite impression that no matter what the outcome was, one party was going to be double-crossed. The Dragons are part of the Syndicate, and the Syndicate would be a lot better off if the former regime was back in charge. The Faldos Charter is safe for now, but as soon as payments are made, it gets destroyed. I can guarantee that."

Isnod asked, "You wouldn't happen to have heard where they were going hole up until they get payment, did you?"

Yesnic tapped another image on the monitor. "This is Tonbor. He has a small warehouse at Kassnins Trading Colony. That's the first place I would look. It's near a place called Morrok's."

Feldon smiled and said, "We're familiar with Morrok's."

That evening, Isnod and Feldon spent the night at Yesnic's to rest up before they continued their mission. Yesnic accompanied them on the shuttle tram to the hub. After sitting, he said, "I'll keep an eye and ear tuned. If I come across information I think you could use, I'll send it to you."

Isnod and Yesnic exchanged codes to enable them to contact each other discreetly.

*****

## Kassnins Trading Colony, Shuttle Port

It was four days to Kassnins, and Isnod was at the controls when they arrived. He touched down on the pad assigned to him, and he switched the power from internal to ground supplied. Feldon opened the hatch, and the ground crewman was standing there. He had an expression on his face that gave Feldon pause.

Isnod came up behind Feldon and stopped. He saw that the ground crewman, and Feldon were both searching for words. The ground crewman finally said, "I wondered if I would see you two. Mr. Rullot isn't usually away for this long, so I checked an open-source database and found out he had been incarcerated. I take it then that you two are bounty hunters?"

Isnod and Feldon were caught flat-footed. Their profession wasn't illegal, but they didn't want it generally known who they were here on Kassnins. The ground crewman could sense their discomfort. "Relax, gentlemen, as far as I'm concerned, that makes us friends."

The pair climbed down the steps, and Isnod asked, "So where does that leave us?"

The man said, "Well, for one thing, if you plan on bringing your prisoners back here, it wouldn't be a good idea to let those two see you do that." He motioned toward the shuttle port office.

Then he continued, "I can help you keep things discreet." Feldon asked, "What's that going to cost us?"

The man shrugged. "Whatever you think is fair. I don't think gouging you would make for a healthy business relationship."

Isnod and Feldon looked at each other and nodded. Isnod shrugged and said, "That sounds good to us."

The crewman smiled. "There's one more thing. The clerk in the office is amenable and willing to run interference as needed. It might be a good idea to show him consideration."

Feldon reached into his pocket and produced two goaners and handed them to the crewman. "Give one of these to the clerk."

The crewman looked at one of the goaners and smiled. He was looking at ten days' wages working for the shuttle port authority. He pocketed the goaners. "I'll make sure the clerk gets his share. Making sure he's properly compensated is good insurance for all of us."

Isnod nodded. "Now that we're all friends, what do we do?"

The crewman said, "Exit through the terminal after paying your landing fees, conduct your business, but when you return, don't go through the terminal."

He pointed to a gate near the shuttle. "Come back to that gate. There's a call button that will summon me. I'll let you in through there. It's out of sight of the terminal, and you can board without a lot of fuss and bother. Your last visit didn't go unnoticed by the port manager. He's unaware of what happened then, but if he even suspects that you're making profit from your activities, he'll want a sizable kickback. When you go through the terminal, inquire about Losnic Rullot and act a bit desperate. That will give the impression that things aren't going well for you and probably not worth trying to squeeze extra goaners out of you."

They did as instructed and walked the short distance to Morrok's. On the way out of the terminal, Feldon said, "Those two looked awfully disappointed."

Isnod chuckled. "That ground crewman certainly knows how to manipulate them. That's a useful thing to know how to do."

*****

## Kassnins Trading Colony, Morrok's Inn

They went into Morrok's and let their eyes adjust. Feldon frowned. "Why are these places always so dimly lit?"

They found a table in the corner and waited. Yesnic told them Tonbor had a warehouse close by, so it was very likely that at least one of them would come in, and they didn't have long to wait.

Five flastons walked in, took a table, and ordered food and drinks. The bounty hunters saw the dragon markings on their left forearms, and they started to put their faces with the names of the men that stole the Charter. Isnod nodded. "That's them for sure."

Feldon took a sip of his drink and said, "You know, the bounty money at that table alone would be enough to get us halfway through this year's projections."

Isnod smiled. "Let's not get greedy. Our priority is the Charter." They finished their drinks and left the bar. It was now dark outside, so it was an easy task to find a place to hide in the shadows. Again, they didn't have long to wait. The five flastons exited Morrok's and turned left. One was carrying a container that Feldon reasoned was a meal for their partner they left behind to guard the Charter.

The bounty hunters followed at a very discrete distance until the five Dragons stopped at a warehouse door and entered. Isnod and Feldon circled the warehouse paying attention to doors and windows. They saw a bank of windows that were lit and positioned themselves so they could see inside without getting too near.

Isnod pulled a monocular from his pocket and started scanning the lighted offices. He could see the group sitting around a table playing a gambling game while the one they brought the meal for ate. Isnod scrutinized every bit of the room and was starting to wonder if they made a wasted trip.

The dragon that Isnod recognized as Tonbor got up from the table and went into an adjacent room. While he busied himself getting drinks for his companions, he left the door open. Isnod suddenly smiled. "There it is, on that table."

Feldon was looking through his own monocular. "There's a door leading to the warehouse. We can get in through there and not even deal with the Dragons."

Isnod nodded. "Let's find a way in there."

They crept to a side door that led into the main warehouse and defeated the lock. Once in the building, they made their way to the interior doors that led to the offices. Feldon put his ear to the door and whispered, "They're still playing their game."

Isnod went to the door that had the Charter behind it and worked the lock.

Once it was open, he crept inside, grabbed the case, and darted back out into the open warehouse area. At that moment, the lights came up and froze the two bounty hunters in place. The six Dragons rushed to form a semi-circle around Isnod and Feldon.

Isnod looked at the six felons, exhaled, and said, "We had hoped to avoid this and leave you, boys, without bruises, but if you insist."

He put the case on a packing crate and took up the classic micton defensive stance while Feldon followed suit. Brinot laughed. "All six of us? You two must be desperate. I'll tell you what, we'll make sure what's left of you two makes it back to Flast."

The largest of the six lunged at Feldon and took a swing at his head, which would have been devastating had he been able to land the punch. Feldon expertly deflected the punch and brought the heel of his left hand under the right side of the Dragons jaw sharply in an upward direction. The Dragon's eyes rolled into the back of his head, and he crumpled to the floor in a heap. The entire encounter took less than three seconds, and the outcome took the other Dragons quite by surprise.

Isnod instantly switched from defensive mode to offensive and leaped into the air while spinning in a 360-degree turn. During the spin, he brought up his foot, which had gathered a great deal of momentum and landed it upside Hindor's head, bringing him down. Simultaneously, he brought both hands down in a chopping motion on either side of Tonbor's neck just below the ears.

Feldon had a short but spirited duel with Brinot, which he won. That left two to deal with. These two were much more of a challenge for the pair, as they were better at fighting than the other four. They weren't familiar with the micton disciplines, but they were very skillful brawlers nonetheless.

At one point, Feldon's opponent got a hold of a club and managed to land a couple of blows on him before Feldon could render him unconscious. Isnod's opponent was also dangerous, as he was powerfully built and doing his level best to win.

Finally, he made a mistake, and Isnod gave him a chop to the neck at a point that short-circuited his nervous system, rendering him useless. Both Isnod and Feldon were hurt, and they knew it. Isnod was limping, and Feldon held his arm tightly to his ribs. Isnod said, "Look around for something to tie them up with. We weren't prepared to take prisoners."

Feldon started searching the warehouse and found a spool of cord. When he brought it back, he said, "I found this on a utility transporter."

That got Isnod's attention. He smiled and said, "We might as well collect a bonus."

They bound the hands and feet of the six Dragons and heaved them up onto the flatbed of the transporter. After putting a tarp over them and lashing it down, Isnod put the case holding the Charter into the cab and climbed in while Feldon turned off the lights and opened the door. Isnod drove the transporter out, and Feldon carefully closed the warehouse door, then climbed into the cab.

After sitting, Feldon shook his head. "That last guy did some damage."

Isnod looked concerned. "Can you hold out until we get back to Oasis 4? I wouldn't trust the doctors on this planet."

Feldon shifted uncomfortably in the seat. "That shouldn't be a problem, as long as I can stay relatively immobile for a day or two."

They found their way to the back gate of the shuttle port, where Isnod pressed the call button. The ground crewman arrived in a few minutes and let them in. Isnod drove directly to their Pulsar 1250 and stopped.

The ground crewman stopped his own vehicle and got out. He approached Isnod. "I wasn't expecting you to be driving a transporter. I'm not sure if I can accommodate this."

Isnod carefully climbed down and said, "It couldn't be helped.

We're bringing back more than we planned on."

The man could now see Isnod limping and Feldon walking very carefully himself. Feldon carried the case holding the Charter to the Pulsar, opened the hatch, and went inside, where he put the case in a cabinet. Isnod said to the crewman, "Give me a hand with this."

They removed the tarp, and the crewman could see why they had to use a transporter. He backed up and said, "They look angry."

Isnod nodded. "They'll get over it."

He started to pull their prisoners off the flatbed. As he worked, he said to the ground crewman, "If you want it, the transporter is now yours. In fact, it belongs to this one," he said, pointing at Tonbor.

Feldon walked over to help load the prisoners, then said, "He also has a warehouse full of goods whose ownership is in question. It's up for the taking if you want it also, warehouse twenty-two near Morrok's."

The ground crewman smiled. "I'm familiar with it. We all do all right on this, except these six, of course."

Feldon was in too rough of shape to manhandle the prisoners, so he did a quick preflight check, then went to the cockpit to warm the systems. Isnod stood each of the Dragons and made them hop into the Pulsar, as they couldn't walk, having their ankles tied. After loading, Isnod shut the hatch, and the ground crewman took his new transporter to see what awaited him in Tonbor's warehouse.

*****

**Pulsar 1250, Owned by the I&F**
**Investigations and Retrievals Company**

Feldon took off and set a course for Oasis 4. The station was four days travel in the Pulsar, and they were anxious to get there. They were obligated to make sure their prisoners were fed and allowed to relieve themselves. Isnod saw to these duties since Feldon couldn't move without experiencing pain. Isnod also fed them one at a time to minimize the risk of them trying to overpower them.

After two days, both Isnod and Feldon were exhausted. Feldon used the autopilot and took long naps while Isnod did the same in the back. He tried to time his downtime to when the prisoners were sleeping, but that was difficult at best.

Brinot was working the heel of his shoe with the toe of his other foot. The heel came loose and dropped away, revealing that it was actually the handle of a short blade. He kicked it toward Hindor, who looked at him and smiled as he rolled his body around to grasp the blade. Once he had it in his hands, he did some more positioning and carefully cut the cord binding Brinot's hands.

Once Brinot was free, he quickly cut Hindor loose and started working on his ankle ties. Hindor cut the ties on Tonbor, and in short order, they were all free. The blade slipped from Brinot's fingers and rattled on the deck. Isnod's eyes snapped open, and he saw his worst nightmare coming true. "Feldon, they're loose!"

The prisoners lunged at Isnod. At the same moment, Feldon cut the light- speed engines while simultaneously using the reaction engines in reverse thrust. The bounty hunters had worked out a plan for just such an occasion. As with all vessels, the inertia neutralizers weren't 100 percent effective on the Pulsar. The prisoners smashed into the bulkhead, stunning them. Isnod had his back to the bulkhead, so the event didn't affect him like the others.

The prisoners recovered quickly and descended on Isnod, who was learning that the confined space of the shuttle was not a good place for a fight, and six opponents were beyond his abilities. They were swinging away at Isnod's face and landing punches. Feldon made his way out of the cockpit and took some pressure off Isnod.

As with the fight at the warehouse, the bounty hunters used micton techniques to battle their opponents. The bad news was their opponents had a couple of days to think about their fight and come up with countermoves that might be effective, at least in their heads. The thing that they really had going against them was the uneven odds. Feldon already had broken ribs. His adversaries knew it and tried to use it to their advantage.

The bounty hunters' conditioning and discipline were finally paying off. Each had managed to render opponents unconscious and were gradually wearing down the rest. In an additional few minutes of intense fighting, the prisoners were once again lying in a heap. Isnod grabbed the spool of cord and growled, "I've had enough of these guys."

They proceeded to bind the prisoners' wrists and ankles again, but they went a step further dand hog-tied them. An observer who didn't know the circumstances would have said it was cruelty to treat them in such a fashion. For their part, Isnod and Feldon were not going to take another chance that they could get loose. Isnod could feel his face swelling from the beating, and now he feared that some of his own ribs were fractured. Feldon made his way to the pilot seat, saying, "Two more days."

They finally dropped out of light speed after two days and contacted the station who gave them vectors and eventually a docking port assignment. Isnod managed to send Lynuna an audio message, telling her they had returned.

*****

## Oasis 4, CentMod, Lower Section

Lynuna heard the message and noted Isnod's voice sounded tired and labored. She wondered what she should do. In any case, security should be summoned. If they have the Charter, it should have the highest level of security that could be provided. If they have prisoners, they'll need escorting to a security cell. She rolled her chair to the SICOS terminal next to her desk and paged the security office. Luke Smith answered, "What can I do for you, Miss Lynuna?"

She explained as much as she thought she could to Luke, who reassured her. He said he would have a team at the docking port when they arrived. He checked with the controllers and found out when they were expected to dock and where. He called down to the lower section and informed Tiffany Waters what was happening, then summoned additional deputies.

After sending deputies to CargoMod 6, Luke stepped out of his office. He spotted Phil with Alice, and the new flaston girl named Tillya, then hurried over to them and said, "Hey, Boss, we have a possible developing situation in CargoMod 6."

Phil grinned and said, "Ah, it's good to be back and in charge."

He turned to Alice and Tillya. "Why don't you two girls go to Sparky's and get a glass of wine? I'll meet you there after I take care of this."

Phil left with Luke and took the platform lift to the lower CentMod. On the lift, Phil asked, "What's going on?"

Luke said, "Miss Lynuna contacted me. Apparently, Isnod and Feldon have returned from their latest adventure, and they may have run into a little trouble."

Phil frowned. "What kind of trouble?"

Luke shook his head. "She didn't say, but she sounded pretty stressed." Reaching the CentMod Lower Section, they boarded a tram to CargoMod 6.

When they reached the docking port assigned to the Pulsar 1250 owned by the I&F Investigations and Retrievals Company, they found Helmut Schultz busy trying to override the air lock controls while Lynuna and a handful of security personnel stood by.

Helmut looked up when Phil arrived. "There must be something wrong, mit Herr Isnod und Herr Feldon. They had a very difficult experience docking, and now they don't respond."

Luke said, "Hold up, Helmut."

He turned to his deputies and pointed to an equipment locker. "Roger, you and Bill put on biohazard gear from that locker. Tiffany, you and Ian use caution tape to isolate this area."

Luke then went to a terminal and punched a code for the infirmary and explained the situation to Dr. Tillman who started gathering emergency personnel. When Roger and Bill were ready, Luke said, "Go ahead, Helmut."

Helmut let them into the air lock and closed them in. This allowed them to enter the shuttle without an air exchange with the station. Dr. Tillman arrived at that moment with her team.

In a few seconds, Roger opened the air lock and took off his mask. "They're not sick. They're beat up. There are half a dozen detainees tied up in the back. They're beat up too, but they don't look as bad."

Luke said to the group, "Make sure the prisoners are secure and help Dr. Tillman with Isnod and Feldon."

They found Feldon in the cockpit, slumped at the controls, and Isnod was in a seat behind the cockpit, barely conscious. Luke knelt next to him while one of the medics started to tend to him. Isnod looked at Luke and, in a weak voice, said, "Lynuna."

Luke said, "She's right outside. Do you need to see her?" Isnod slowly nodded with a great deal of difficulty.

Luke called out the hatch, "Miss Lynuna!"

Lynuna rushed in and gasped when she saw Isnod's swollen and bloody face.

She knelt next to him. "Did you get it?"

He nodded and pointed to a cabinet. Lynuna opened the cabinet and pulled out a case. She opened it and let out a relieved sigh. "Isnod, this is amazing—"

Dr. Tillman interrupted, "Please, Miss Lynuna, we need to tend to Mr. Isnod." Lynuna stood and left the shuttle while holding the case. She approached Phil.

"Mr. Ross, do you have a safe or vault I could use to store this?" Phil nodded. "Sure, Miss Lynuna. What is it?"

Lynuna hesitated, "I would rather tell you later, Mr. Ross, but rest assured, it is of vital importance to Flast."

Phil nodded. "How could I say no to that?"

They left the CargoMod with a security detail and went to the CentMod, then boarded the platform lift to the ops center.

*****

## Oasis 4, Operations Center

In the morning, Phil and Alice went through their morning routines as normal, and Phil found getting back to his regular duties was easier than he imagined. He went to his office to retrieve a pad, and on his way through the ops center, he saw Tillya beginning her training.

Phil grabbed his pad and made his way to the briefing room, where he poured a cup of coffee. When he took his seat, everyone, in unison, said, "Welcome back, Boss."

Phil smiled and started the briefing. After hearing reports from Virginia, Will, and Jeremy, he said, "Now, if Luke could enlighten us as to exactly what happened to Isnod and Feldon, that would be great."

Luke slowly shook his head. "I'd like to be able to tell you, but there are more questions than obvious answers. We checked the DNA of the prisoners they had tied up in the back, and they're all wanted felons. All of them have similar tattoos on their left arms, so we checked on that too. They're called Loyalty Brand Dermal Ink

Markings. These charming gentlemen belong to a criminal organization called the Dragons, who happen to be part of the Syndicate. I think what happened was, the Dynamic Duo went to retrieve a stolen item of some importance and had to deal with the Dragons."

Phil nodded. "I'll see Lynuna later this morning. Hopefully, she can shed some light on what's going on and tell me what that thing is that she had me lock in my vault."

Phil checked off an item on his pad, then said, "Next up, medical." Marie Tillman said, "Nothing unusual in the infirmary except for

Isnod and Feldon."

Phil asked, "If it doesn't violate patient/doctor confidence, what is their condition?"

Dr. Tillman smiled and said, "They're resting. Whatever their physical conditioning routine is, it helped them tremendously. Both have fractured ribs, bruises, and slight concussions. I want them to rest for at least three days before I even think about releasing them from the infirmary."

Phil thanked her for her report and adjourned the meeting.

As Phil walked through the ops center, Lynuna stepped off the platform lift with one of her staff. She spotted him, and they walked directly to him. "Oh, Mr. Ross, I'm wondering if we could have a few minutes of your time."

Phil smiled. "Of course, you can, Miss Lynuna, I imagine you want that case you had me lock up."

Lynuna nodded. "Actually, Mr. Ross, if we could examine it in the privacy of your office, that would be most helpful."

Phil nodded. "Of course, please step this way."

Phil caught Luke before he left for the security office. "Hey, Luke, I'm getting into the vault."

They went into Phil's office, and he started to open the vault when Lynuna said, "Excuse me, gentlemen, could you please close the door?"

Luke sensed Lynuna was very nervous about keeping the contents of the case safe and walked to the office door and closed it. Phil opened the vault, removed the case, and placed it on his desk. Lynuna looked at the staff member that was with her. She nodded  and said, "Please examine the document, Palnit."

The man removed a pair of white gloves from his pocket and put them on. He unlatched the case, opened it, and slowly removed what looked to Phil like a large ancient folder. Palnit's hands were slightly trembling as he opened the folder, exposing what was obviously a flaston document.

Phil and Luke could see that Lynuna and Palnit were having what could be described as a religious experience. Palnit then examined the document with a magnifying device he produced from a pocket. Both Palnit and Lynuna scrutinized the document carefully while Phil and Luke watched in silence. After discussing items that they found worth noting, they both stood straight, and Palnit said with a hitch in his voice, "This appears to be the genuine artifact."

Lynuna was speechless for a few moments. She looked as if she really needed to sit, so Phil led her to a chair. She finally collected herself enough to say, "Please put it back in the case, Palnit."

Palnit lifted the document while Luke put the case on Phil's desk and opened it for him. Once the case was reclosed, Luke put it back in Phil's vault at Lynuna's request.

Phil thought both Lynuna and Palnit could use a cup of tea, so he went to his coffee corner and made two cups for his guest, and he got coffee for himself and Luke. When Lynuna took a couple of sips and appeared to calm down, Phil asked, "Exactly what is it that's in my vault, Miss Lynuna?"

Lynuna took another sip of tea and answered, "It's called the Faldos Charter. To put it in terms, you and Mr. Smith will understand it's the flaston equivalent to your Constitution or perhaps the Magna Carta."

She then detailed for them the events on Flast and how Isnod and Feldon became involved.

Luke furrowed his brow. "I understand that losing something that has that important of historical significance would be tragic, but even if it did get destroyed, the underlying idea would be intact."

Lynuna nodded. "That's undeniable. However, because the previous regime denied the Charter's existence for decades, many of our people are skeptical that we have a historical heritage of such a thing. There are those on Flast that are trying to convince the population that the Charter never existed, and we as a people don't have experience with the kind of freedoms that are in the Charter. Existence of the original Charter will establish legitimacy and give reformers more solid ground to stand on."

Phil started to shake his head and smile. Finally, he said, "Once again, we find ourselves putting our nose in Flast history."

Lynuna frowned, and slowly, her lips curled into a smile. "I never considered that. I suppose all of you on this station will be a curious study for future historians on Flast."

She took a last sip of tea and suddenly put her hand over her mouth. "Oh my goodness, Isnod and Feldon will undoubtedly be the subject of a lot of school essays."

Phil stood. "Speaking of Isnod and Feldon, shall we see if they're ready to have visitors."

They stood, left the ops center, and boarded the platform lift. The platform lift stopped at the Lower Section plaza level, where Palnit went back to the consulate, and the rest made their way to the infirmary. A quick check at the nurses' station to make sure the pair was ready for visitors, and they went to Isnod and Feldon's room.

Entering the room, Phil saw someone had sent them a Mylar helium balloon each that said, "Get well soon." Phil read the card attached to one of them and saw they were sent by the Lower Section security office. Lynuna cleared her throat, which made Isnod and Feldon open their eyes.

There were still bruises and cuts, but the swelling was down. The pair smiled, and Lynuna rushed over and carefully gave each a hug.

Phil chimed in, "You guys look a lot better than you did yesterday."

Luke added, "You ain't kidding. I thought we were going to be feeding you two through a tube for months."

Isnod asked, "Did you get a chance to examine the artifact?" Lynuna smiled. "We just examined it, Palnit from my staff and me.

From what they told us, it's the true artifact. Experts from Flast will have to verify it, of course."

Luke said, "We also had a look at those thugs you brought with you. They're about the worse thing I've ever seen in our little jail.

Killers, every one of them. What made you think that putting the bag on six gorillas was a good idea?"

Feldon furrowed his brow and asked, "What's a gorilla?"

Isnod looked over at him. "You remember Feldon. We saw some at the Toledo Zoological Park on Earth."

Feldon smiled. "Oh yes, I remember."

Feldon then connected the inference that their prisoners were more like the brutish animals they observed in the zoo on Earth than civilized persons, and that made him laugh at the expense of his ribs.

Isnod nodded. "To answer Mr. Smith's question, it wasn't our intention to bring anyone back. We had the Charter in our hands when those charming gents objected. After we established our claim on the Charter, we thought it would be a shame to pass up an opportunity to profit. Besides, having six Dragons know what we look like and letting them go would have been a bad idea."

Lynuna nodded. "Add the bounty for those six monsters to your reward for recovering the Charter, and it's quite an impressive payday."

Isnod objected, "We only want the bounty for the felons. Recovering the Charter is our gift to Flast."

Lynuna was speechless and stumbled for something to say. Then Feldon said, "We told you before, Lynuna, we're patriots."

The End

# NEW GUYS

**Oasis 4, Trading Center Space Station Owned by the
Stellar Logistics and Freight Corporation**

Phil Ross had been doing paperwork all morning, and he was
starting to feel sorry for himself. Leaning back in his chair, he fixed his
gaze out the viewport of his office and watched the ship and shuttle
traffic for a time. As he studied the traffic to and from the station, he was
becoming aware that something was not right. Vessels were changing
course seemingly for no reason—one was in a holding pattern about
five miles distant, and another one was just sitting a mile away. He
thought he might ask Virginia or Bret Pinkerton, the chief controller,
if there was something he should be aware of.

The view out of the window no longer held his interest, so he
started looking around his office when the pictures on his wall caught
his attention. Each one meant something different to him, but they
were all equally special. There was the group photo of himself, Dave
Jacobson, Luke Smith, Will Dawson, Selak, Tonkin, and Klon. Next to
it was a photo Norton Parker sent him of all the Astrodyne pilots that
took part in the action on Gostis, plus yet another photo of Phil and
his son Michael on Gostis. Norton also sent Alice the same picture that
she referred to as her veterans.

Phil looked at the chronometer and decided that lunch was in order.
After leaving his office, he tapped on Gus's doorframe. Gus looked up
from his paperwork. Phil asked, "Eva's?"

"Best thing I've heard all morning," Gus said as he stood.

They took the platform lift to the plaza level and then the escalator to the second level where Eva's Café was located. Sitting at Phil's customary table was an unexpected surprise. Yuri Andropov, captain of the *William Burnside*, and Dave Jacobson, Captain of the *Atlantis Star*. Phil started to greet them with a smile, but the expression on his face changed midsentence. "Hey, guys, it's great to—you're frowning. Why are you frowning?"

"Because both of us expected to have our first meal on the station to be breakfast and not lunch. We certainly arrived early enough," Dave said with a bit of an edge in his voice.

Yuri nodded and said, "We are six hours behind schedule. I don't need to tell you, Phillip, how valuable those six hours are. We could be half unloaded by now."

Gus frowned. "Virginia Wells won't be pleased about this. A wrinkle in the schedule tended to get things out of shape quickly."

Phil definitely didn't like what he was hearing, but it was his main responsibility to make sure things ran smoothly. The freight operators would start looking for alternatives to using his station if it stopped being convenient. To solve the problem, he needed as much information as he could get. After Eva took his order, Phil asked, "Could you tell me exactly what your experience was when you arrived?"

Yuri said, "It appears you have a controller that gets completely rattled when there are more than two ships to handle."

Dave nodded. "That guy put us in two holding patterns before we docked.

There were some smaller vessels that he wanted to get out of the way first." Phil furrowed his brow. "That sounds reasonable to me."

Yuri replied, "Sure, but in the time it would take for our ships to be a factor, half a dozen or more shuttles could come and go."

Phil said, "Gus, could you look into this after lunch, please?" Gus nodded. "I'll see what I can find out."

Both Dave and Yuri knew Phil and Gus would resolve this problem one way or another, and there was no point in picking at it further.

Phil thought it might be a good idea to change the subject. "I checked the boards earlier and saw the *Morning Star* is arriving this afternoon."

That gave Dave and Yuri reason to smile. Dave asked, "Where has June been?"

"Flast," Phil answered.

Yuri nodded thoughtfully and said, "I've been told that there was a possibility of making cargo runs to Flast. Since they changed governments, they're free to develop markets."

Gus said, "That's got to be good for us."

While they were having their after-lunch coffees, two familiar faces approached. Phil knew immediately who it was. "Captain Hastings, Beverly, it's good to see you."

The first time Phil met Captain Hastings, he was decidedly shabbier looking. Now it looks as if the finder's fee Elias set aside for him and Beverly Ashton came through.

Captain Hastings smiled and shook Phil's hand. "Call me Greg."

Phil made introductions and invited Greg and Beverly to sit, then asked, "When are you going to take command of one of the new vessels your company purchased? I see you're still in the *Goldfield*."

Greg smiled. "Funny you should ask. We've just finished the last revenue trip in the *Goldfield*. A new ship called the *Spirit of 49* will be arriving tomorrow. I'll be taking that back to the Anna Mae system."

Phil said, "That's great! Congratulations." Dave asked, "What happens to the old ship?"

Greg shrugged. "A skeleton crew will take it back to New Oslo for decommissioning. It's always a sad thing, but that's the way of things. It was a good ship in its day. Actually, I was going to ask Mrs. Ross if there was anything from it she might want for her museum."

Phil nodded. "She might. You'll have to see the museum yourself and perhaps get an idea of what she may be interested in."

Greg said, "That's a fine idea. We'll do that this morning. There's one other thing I need to tell you about."

Phil raised an eyebrow. He was expecting to get more grief about the traffic situation at the station. "What's that, Greg?"

Greg was putting ketchup on his fries. "While exiting the nebula, we had a proximity alarm, so we followed established protocol and cut the light-speed engines. We approached the source of the alarm and discovered it was a vessel of a type I've never seen before. It's traveling at sublight speed, roughly in the direction of the station.

We pulled alongside and tried to establish communication without any luck, so we grabbed some images at multiple angles before moving on."

Gus furrowed his brow. "Are you telling us that it looks like it emerged from the nebula?"

"That's the only place it could have come from," Greg confirmed.

Dave leaned in. "What condition was the vessel in?"

Greg shrugged. "It was beat up and dirty. The nebula is a dense one in places.

Who knows what's in there."

"Could it be an unmanned vessel?" Yuri asked thoughtfully.

Greg shook his head. "It has a hatch and viewports. It may be some kind of probe, but it sure looks like it's designed for a crew. One thing is for sure, though, it's a hazard to navigation."

Phil exhaled. "I suppose that makes it up to us to deal with it. Could you do me a favor, Greg. Get those images to Jeremy Cole in vessel maintenance. It looks like we'll have to mount some sort of salvage mission."

Greg nodded. "I'll get those images to him right after I see Mrs. Ross." Phil looked at Gus. "It looks like our day is filling up nicely."

Having finished with their lunches, Phil and Gus rode the platform lift to the operations center. Gus went to his office to look into the traffic jams at the station and Phil to his office to do battle with more paperwork. After about two hours, Gus tapped on Phil's doorframe. "Hey, Phil, you need to hear this. I accessed the controller archive for this morning and found the source of our problem."

Phil leaned back. "Put it up."

Gus ordered, "SICOS, bring up controller archive, this date, period beginning 0800 Zulu ending twelve hundred Zulu."

Phil put the playback on his wall-sized display. The display showed the station as viewed from above. Phil could zoom out to any distance he desired to see the traffic coming and going. He scanned the image and said, "SICOS, start playback, eight times speed."

Just as the playback started, there was a tap on Phil's doorframe. Phil turned to see Dwight Needles there. "What can I do for you, Dwight?"

Dwight hesitated, "I really don't know if it's my place to say anything, Hoss, but I was doing a flight review this morning, and it was a confusing situation outside the station."

Gus raised an eyebrow. "Confusing?"

Dwight smiled. "I'm being kind, Hoss. I would describe it as more of a goat rodeo."

Phil chuckled. "Come on in, Dwight. You could give us a narration since you were there."

Dwight came in and sat, then Phil restarted the playback. At first, the traffic seemed to flow smoothly; the order started to break down as the number of vessels increased. Phil studied the flow, or lack of it, and said, "It looks like the Green Sector is the bottleneck."

The space surrounding Oasis 4 is divided into four sectors. During graveyard shift, all traffic was handled by a single individual, but during peak hours, there was a separate controller for each sector. Gus nodded. "Good eye, Boss. The problem is, if one sector gets screwed up, the problem snowballs."

Phil said, "Okay, now let's hear the Green Sector controller." Dwight smiled. "This is where it gets interesting."

Phil used SICOS to isolate the transmissions to and from the Green Sector controller. As Phil and the others listened, a pattern started to emerge. The moment a third vessel entered the Green Sector, the stress level could be heard to increase in the controller's voice. He became short with the pilots and captains over the radio. Worse of all, he couldn't coordinate the movement between multiple vessels. Phil leaned back after the playback finished. "We can't allow this to happen again."

Gus asked, "Do you want Dwight and me to stay, or do you want to talk to Virginia and Bret alone?"

Phil thought about it and decided that he didn't want to seem confrontational. He stood and said, "No, I don't want to set up a situation where it looks like pilots against controllers. Besides, Captain Hastings told me about what looks like a derelict craft near the nebula.

He sent imagery to Jeremy Cole. Why don't you two go down there and see what you make of it? I'll be down directly to check it out myself."

Gus looked at Phil. "Are you sure?"

Phil smiled. "You two go ahead and leave me to deal with this. I appreciate you looking into this, Gus, and your input, Dwight."

Phil left his office to look for Virginia Wells and Bret Pinkerton. He didn't have to go far to find Virginia, as she was in the operations center, trying to match cargos with ships and CargoMods. Phil saw Tillya was in the middle of it all, helping to resolve issues. He approached Virginia. "If you have a couple of minutes, I'd like to talk to you and Bret in my office in about ten minutes."

Virginia nodded, and Phil climbed the stairs to the control center. Looking around, he saw things were approaching something near normal. Phil spotted Bret across the control center. He took off his headset and let out a deep breath. Phil strolled over and said, "I need to see you and Virginia in my office, Bret."

Bret said, "Be right there, Boss."

Phil descended the stairs, cut through the ops center, and entered his office. He poured himself a cup and pondered whether he should sit at his desk for this or in the small sitting area. He finally decided the sitting area would be the least authoritarian, so he sat in the armchair. A very haggard-looking Virginia and Bret tapped on the door jamb and came in.

Phil said, "Do me a favor and close the door, then get yourselves a beverage and sit."

While Virginia made herself tea and Bret poured a cup of coffee, Phil asked, "It's been a couple of weeks. How is Tillya working out?"

Virginia smiled for the first time in a few hours. "She's doing a wonderful job. I was concerned that doing nothing but manual labor for a couple of years would dull her intellect, but so far, she's working out wonderfully."

Phil nodded. "That's what I like to hear. Now that the pleasant part of the conversation is done, tell me about Green Sector."

Phil was doing Virginia and Bret the courtesy of not rehashing the events of the morning. Bret shook his head. "I don't know what to tell you, Boss. I've never encountered anything like this."

"I listened to the record of this morning's traffic. I didn't recognize the Green Sector controller's voice. You know I'm not a micro-manager, but I have to ask why you would put someone new on during one of the busiest shifts," Phil asked.

Bret countered, "He's not new, Boss. Actually, he's eligible for retirement."

Phil frowned. "Then tell me why he's so terrible at handling traffic."

"I checked his personnel file. He's never worked a high-volume station before," Virginia offered.

Phil nodded slowly. "So he decided to bolster his retirement by working Oasis 4 for a couple of years, and he didn't realize the volume we do is way above anything he's used to. Or he was passed on to us in hopes that we could straighten him out or to get him out of everyone's hair until he decides to retire. Either way, he's going to pull his socks up or find himself out of a job."

Bret recoiled, "That's a bit harsh, Boss."

Phil kept his tone even. "We're not here as a charitable organization. We provide a facility and an environment for commerce to happen. If freighters and other vessels find it difficult to do business here, we fail. We can't afford to accommodate someone who's not up to speed."

"Point taken, Boss," Virginia and Bret said in unison.

Phil inhaled. "Give this guy remedial training or some kind of counseling, but definitely a dose of Charm School. He was pretty rude. By the way, what's this guy's name?"

Bret answered, "James Goodman."

Virginia and Bret left to work on a strategy for dealing with Goodman. Phil went back to his desk and received a page. Just as he sat, he pressed the intercom button. "What's up, Jay?"

Jay answered, "Captain Dixon of the *Morning Star* would like a word with you on Channel Six Alpha."

Phil acknowledged. "Thanks, Jay."

Phil turned to his SICOS. "Open Channel Six Alpha."

June's face appeared on the display. "Hi, Phil, don't worry. I'm not transporting fugitives this time, I promise."

Phil grinned. "That is cause for celebration. What can I do for you?"

June said, "I've got two VIPs on board. Their names are Yulona and Lytrina.

They're on the committee drawing up the new Charter of Rights on Flast."

Phil nodded. "I imagine that they're here to take that old Charter I've got in my vault home with them. Do they have some sort of entourage with them?"

June nodded. "Yes, they do, a historian and seven security officers."

"Okay, June, I'll have a reception committee for their arrival. See you then." Phil then signed off.

This was the part of the job that Phil felt he didn't excel at or feel comfortable doing. Meeting and entertaining dignitaries wasn't something he ever thought might be in his job description. He always managed to do all right in these affairs, but he wished he had some kind of protocol specialist for these occasions. Phil remembered his visit to Triptous and thought that the station manager there, Eric Hornsby, would be right at home doing that sort of thing.

Phil made a quick head count of people he thought should meet the VIP from Flast. A quick call to Maurice and Phil secured reservations for fifteen people. Maurice assured Phil that the number of diners could be kept flexible since Phil didn't have a hard number for him.

A check of the wall chronometer confirmed it was nearly lunchtime, so he left his office. Stopping in the ops center, he said to Virginia, "We have VIPs arriving on the *Morning Star*. I'm putting together a reception dinner for them at 1700 Zulu. I'll tell Dwight he'll be your plus one."

At first, Virginia was horrified that people in the office may be sniggering about her and Dwight seeing each other. Then on reflection, she realized that they weren't keeping their relationship a secret, and although they didn't vocalize it, their coworkers were generally supportive. She just grinned. "We'll be there, Boss."

*****

## Oasis 4, Upper CentMod

Phil took the platform lift to the plaza level, walked to the down escalator, and took it to the lower level where the museum was. He found Alice and a volunteer pushing a cart with an equipment box on it to a storage area.

Phil asked, "What have you got there?"

Alice gave the cart a final nudge into position and smiled. "Captain Hastings donated some equipment from the *Goldfield*."

Phil was curious. "What exactly did he give you?"

Alice shrugged. "The only thing really that was interesting was the equipment used to assay ore and sensing equipment used to determine if an asteroid is worth landing on."

Phil remembered, "Oh yeah, we used that on the Aurora. I'm surprised they're giving this stuff away."

Alice nodded. "It surprised me too, but apparently, their new ship is equipped with the latest equipment. This stuff is a couple of generations old."

Phil nodded. "Well, if you can tear yourself away for a while, let's get something to eat."

They took the escalators to the upper tier where Eva's Café was situated. They weren't there long when Gus arrived with Dwight, and Phil invited them to sit.

After ordering, Phil broke the news to them about the reception dinner. "We have VIPs arriving today on the Morning Star, and I'm scheduling a reception dinner for them at 1700 Zulu. Gus, you're invited. I expect you'll be having Brenda on your arm. Dwight, you're not invited, but Virginia is, so I expect you'll be on her arm." That made Alice grin.

Phil continued, "I'm also inviting Luke and the lovely Mrs. Smith for reasons that we'll get into later. I'll be stopping by the Flast Consulate to invite Lynuna and anyone on her staff that she may want there. Alice, of course, will be my date."

Alice put on a show of mock gushing. "Oooh, he finally asked me out." Gus smiled. "Where is the social event of the season taking place?" "Maurice's," Phil answered with a snicker.

After the chuckling ended, Phil changed the subject. "Did you look at the images of the mystery spaceship?"

Dwight nodded. "We shore did. Man, that thing is odd." Phil frowned. "What do you mean by odd?"

"Maybe 'unusual' is a better word, or perhaps 'unfamiliar,'" Gus offered. "Feel free to expand on that," Phil urged.

Dwight scratched his head. "It's a sublight vessel. That much is obvious unless someone has come up with a new light-speed engine design. There are markings on the hull that don't conform to anything we've encountered."

Phil leaned back. "I'm properly curious now. After I see Luke and Lynuna, let's see Jeremy and work out a plan.

After finishing lunch, Gus and Dwight retreated back to CargoMod 8, and Phil went to the security office to inform Luke about the evening's activities.

*****

## Oasis 4, Lower CentMod

After his visit with Luke, he took the platform lift to the lower section. Stepping off at the lower section plaza level, he walked to an escalator to the tier with embassy row. He made his way to the Flast Consulate and asked for Lynuna. An assistant paged her, and she came out of her office. "Mr. Ross, please come into my office."

Once in her office, she asked, "What can I do for you, Mr. Ross?" "I came here to invite you to a reception dinner tonight at 1700

Zulu at Maurice's," Phil answered with a smile.

Lynuna smiled back. "That's very kind of you. Who's the reception for?"

Phil furrowed his brow. "I would have expected you to know before I found out. Some of your fellow flastons are set to arrive at 1600 hours. They're on the committee that's drawing up the new Charter of Rights on your planet."

Lynuna brightened. "Oh my, this is wonderful! I wonder why I wasn't told?"

Phil thought a second. "There's a bunch of security with them. Perhaps they wanted to keep it quiet for safety. I hope I didn't overstep by planning the reception."

Lynuna frowned. "Do you know the name of the committee members?" Phil thought a second. "I think it was Yulona and Lytrina."

Lynuna brightened. "Oh, I see. I think they wanted to surprise me personally. I think you can relax, Mr. Ross. I'll be sure to meet the ship when it gets here."

Phil smiled. "Keep an eye on the boards. It's the *Morning Star*. By the way, is there anyone on your staff you would like at the reception?" Lynuna shook her head. "Actually, I think it would be more appropriate if Isnod and Feldon were there. After all, they did recover the Faldos Charter."

Phil nodded. "That's a fine idea. Will you contact them?" Lynuna smiled. "I certainly will."

*****

## Oasis 4, CargoMod 8

Phil took his leave and headed to CargoMod 8. Gus and Dwight were in Jeremy's office studying images of the spacecraft Captain Hastings found. Phil walked in and said, "So that's the mystery spaceship."

Jeremy nodded. "That's it."

"Any idea who it might belong to?" Phil wondered.

Jeremy shook his head. "I've never seen anything like this, ever. What I find strange about it is it's a sublight vessel, but it's hundreds of years from anything."

Phil studied the images. "Well, I suppose we'll have to get it. It's too large for the cargo hold on the *Aurora*. How do you propose we get it?"

Gus joined the conversation. "We'll strap it to the roof."

Jeremy nodded and said, "I have Chad and Helmut making a cradle to put on the roof of the *Aurora*. They'll put the mystery ship in the cradle and strap it all down tight."

Phil nodded. "When will you be ready to retrieve the ship?" Jeremy shrugged. "Everything will be ready to go in the morning."

Phil smiled. "I'd love to be in on this, but there's too much going on around here. Gus, Dwight, it's your job. Jeremy, who are you sending to do the hard part?"

Jeremy answered, "Chad and Helmut are still my first choice for this kind of thing."

Phil said, "Okay, we'll see what that thing is in a few days."

*****

## Oasis 4, CargoMod 2

After retreating to his quarters for a change into dress clothes, Phil and Alice went to meet the *Morning Star*. He and Alice were the first to arrive, but they didn't have long to wait before they were joined by Lynuna, Isnod, and Feldon. The umbilicals were connected, and a station worker checked the air lock seals then opened the hatch. In a few moments, the Morning Star's hatch opened, and a distinguished-looking flaston stepped out with a lady that was obviously his wife.

Lynuna could hardly contain herself as she rushed to them. "Father, Mother." While they embraced in the air lock, Isnod and Feldon exchanged looks with each other and Phil. Lynuna realized they were being stared at and started to giggle. She collected herself and made introductions. "These are my parents, my father, Yulona, and my mother, Lytrina. Father, Mother, I'm pleased to introduce Phillip Ross, the station manager, and this is his wife, Alice." Yulona and Lytrina shook hands with Phil and Alice. Then Lynuna said, "This is Isnod and Feldon the two who are responsible for getting the Faldos Charter safely back to us."

Yulona heartily shook their hands. "All of Flast is in your debt."

Two more flastons appeared at the air lock. One looked scholarly and, at first glance, left you with the impression that he wasn't a frequent traveler. The other was about Isnod's age and wore a uniform. Yulona smiled. "I'd like to introduce Rabot and Inspector Pindon. Rabot is an expert on Flast history and the foremost authority on the Faldos Charter. Pindon is an inspector with Flast law enforcement."

Rabot shook hands with Phil and the rest without much attempt at small talk. Pindon was a bit more gregarious. When he got to the bounty hunters, he had a broad smile. "Isnod! Feldon! It's so good to see you. If anyone was going to prove me wrong, it would be you two. To tell you the truth, I don't mind at all," he said, warmly shaking their hands.

Phil asked, "I understood you were bringing a number of security personnel with you. Are they going to be joining us for dinner?"

He saw the look on Yulona's and Lytrina's faces, then quickly added, "Oh, by the way, I've arranged a small reception dinner."

Yulona chuckled. "Protocol isn't always easy, is it, Mr. Ross? To answer your question, no, that wouldn't be appropriate. We're trying to create a classless society on Flast, but there are some standards that should remain."

Phil nodded and went to the closest SICOS terminal and paged Tiffany. "Hey, Tiffany, I know this is literally last second, but there are six flaston security officers that arrived on the Morning Star. It'd be great if you and some of the other off-duty security personnel took them to Eva's or Juans and Sparky's afterward. It's on the company."

Tiffany eagerly agreed, and Phil turned to the others. "Shall we go?"

They boarded the tram and rode to the CentMod. After getting off the tram, Yulona admired the CentMod interior and said, "So this is what the station looks like on the inside."

Phil was caught off guard again. He didn't realize that three of the five people he sneaked past Isnod and Feldon to get them from the Morning Star to the Bright Star were not only Lynuna, but her parents were with her. He smiled. "You're lucky. After your last visit, we decided to charge more for direct service." Yulona laughed. "The irony and coincidences concerning Isnod and Feldon and the fate of Flast are amazing. That day, they came so close to capturing my family and colleagues. It would have doomed Flast. Your intervention and their decision to become bounty hunters have shaped the future of my planet in ways that are impossible to calculate."

Phil was at a loss for words, so it came as a relief when they arrived at Maurice's. Maurice showed them to a private dining room where the rest of the guests were waiting. Phil made introductions, and waiters appeared to take their orders.

Yulona was interested in the events that occurred inside the station on the day that Phil and the rest helped them elude capture by Isnod and Feldon. Luke Smith provided most of the narrative, which he did with a comic flare that had everyone in stitches, including Isnod and Feldon, until he got to the part about the kortlax. At that point, Feldon solemnly stated, "I still can't laugh about that."

During dessert and coffee, Yulona asked the waiter, "Excuse me, Timothy.

You're a maldor, is that correct?" "That's right, sir," Timothy confirmed.

Yulona furrowed his brow. "I'm led to understand that's a human name, and maldors don't have names."

Phil put down his cup. "You know, that blew right past me. I knew full well maldors didn't use names, but why do you go by Timothy?"

Timothy shrugged his shoulders. "I had to go by something. I know what all of you are thinking. You're wondering how do maldors know who we're talking about when we discuss things among ourselves. Well, believe me, giving everyone a different name is just as baffling to us. At least until you get used to it."

Phil asked, "Since we're on the subject, how do flastons decide what to name their kids?"

Yulona nodded. "That's a better question than you think. The firstborn male child's name would consist of the first syllable of his father's name and the first syllable of his mother's name in that order. Then firstborn girls also use the first syllables of their parents' names, but it's the mother's name first. Second born use second syllables. With the third-born kids, the system gets a little complicated, but it works for us. In some cases, such as Lynuna, the second syllable isn't exactly the first syllable of the father. We modified it to sound more feminine."

As Timothy put a dessert in front of Phil, Phil asked him, "How is the food service study going, Timothy?"

"I think I've reached the end of what I can learn here on the station," Timothy answered. "I've booked passage on a freighter bound for Earth in two days. Before I leave, I have to ask if there is a type of restaurant you wished was on the station."

Phil scratched his head. "If I had my way, I'd put in a restaurant that served just meat and potatoes, so to speak. Maurice's here is great, but it's a little posh for every day. The other places on the station are great for breakfast and lunch, but a standard dinner is hard to come by."

Dwight said, "Come see me before you leave, Tim. There's a couple of places on Earth you should visit. I'll get you some addresses."

Yulona pushed his empty dessert plate away and smiled. "Mr. Ross, tomorrow morning, a passenger liner from Flast is arriving. After discharging a number of passengers. It's leaving in the afternoon. The six dragons in your jail and four security officers will be on it."

Luke asked, "Is the Charter going back on the same ship?"

Yulona shook his head. "No, I think you'll agree that would be too big of a security risk."

Pindon added, "We'll provide a series of feints designed to convince anyone who has an idea to steal the Charter again wouldn't know which ship it's on."

Luke asked, "Have you worked out which ship will be carrying the Charter back?"

Pindon smiled. "We haven't worked that out yet. It occurred to me that the best way to keep the criminals from finding out what your plans are is not to make them in the first place."

Gus said, "I'd love to take it back to Flast in the *Aurora*, except we'll probably be many light-years away clearing up a hazard to navigation." Pindon nodded. "Well, the *Aurora* isn't the only ship at this station." The reception ran its course. Yulona and Lytrina excused themselves, and Lynuna escorted the flaston party to the Star Lodge Suites.

*****

## Oasis 4, Morning Briefing

Phil checked off items on his pad as the different department heads gave their reports. He announced that Gus and Dwight, along with Chad and Helmut, were going to retrieve what looks like discarded space trash. Then he said to Luke, "Today promises to be a busy day for you and your department. What's the sequence of events?"

Luke glanced at his own pad. "First up, as you know, some of our flaston guests are going to meet in your office to examine the Faldos Charter. I'll be there along with two of my larger deputies. I'll post them just outside the door. They're bringing two of their own security officers with them."

Phil furrowed his brow. "That's overdoing it a bit, isn't it?"

Luke shook his head. "Normally, I would agree with you, but the flastons are taking this very seriously. I want to show that we're taking this as seriously as they are, so while the Charter is out of your vault, it gets every consideration. The Charter is actually more secure in your vault than the vault they kept it in on Flast."

Phil nodded. "That's good thinking. I want to do whatever I can to help the flastons be at ease with what we're doing here." The vault in Phil's office was used to store a supply of goaners for cases when hard currency was needed, along with anything else that needed to be kept secure. It was the most secure location at the station.

After the meeting, Phil went to his office to make sure he had enough tea and coffee and to make sure his desk was clear. Right on time, Lynuna arrived with Yulona and Lytrina. They had with them Palnit, Rabot, and Inspector Pindon. Then to Phil's surprise, Isnod and Feldon walked in. Yulona saw Phil's expression and said, "I thought Isnod and Feldon deserved to see this. They didn't get a chance to personally see the Charter."

Phil nodded, and Luke was the last to enter after giving the two deputies at the door instructions. When the office door closed, Phil said, "Luke, could you please give me a hand?"

He entered the combination and placed his thumb on the biometric secondary lock. A clunk was heard, and a green indicator illuminated. Phil turned the large wheel on the door to disengage the locking bolts, then pulled the door open. Luke entered the vault and picked up the Charter then put it on Phil's desk prompting Rabot and Palnit to open the case and remove the Charter. Rabot opened the folder and instantly nodded. "This is it! Oh, thank goodness. I thought I would never see it again!"

Lynuna shook her head. "That was remarkably fast, Rabot. Palnit and I examined it for the longest time before we were sure."

Rabot smiled. "I've been studying this document every day for my entire adult life. I know every crease, inkblot, and pen stroke."

The flastons each took turns examining the Charter. Phil tried to read the look on the faces of Isnod and Feldon as they looked over the Charter. He supposed he would have a similar expression if someone showed him a unicorn. Although that really wasn't accurate, there was a good amount of reverence also.

Yulona smiled. "That's a relief. Please put it back in Mr. Ross's vault. Mr. Ross, if we can ask for your indulgence for a little while longer, the next time the Charter is removed from your vault, it will be to transport it back to Flast."

As Luke put the Charter back in the vault, Phil assured Yulona, "It's no problem at all. Just let me know when."

"With your permission, Mr. Ross, we'll be sending replicas of the Charter case back to Flast at different times. If there are agents from the syndicate or the old regime on the station, it should throw them off the trail," Pindon said.

Phil nodded. "Of course, you have my permission. Work out any details with Security Marshal Smith."

After the flaston delegation left, Phil went to the ops center, where it looked as if Virginia was going crazy trying to match ships and cargos with docking ports. Phil furrowed his brow, and Virginia gave him an apologetic look. He headed to the stairs leading to the control center and climbed them. Bret had on a headset and was trying to bring order to a chaotic situation. Phil got his first glimpse of James Goodman. He was doing his part to deconfuse the situation, or at least he thought he was helping. The relief shift came on duty and started the task of getting ships to their destinations. Bret stayed put to finish putting the traffic right, but he made sure Goodman left. Phil caught Bret's eye, who nodded.

After a minute, to make sure things were indeed returning to normal, Phil descended the stairs to the ops center. Virginia and Tillya looked like they were successfully dealing with their problems when Phil approached them. He leaned toward Virginia. "When you and Bret get a second, Virginia, could I see you two?"

Phil went to his office and made a cup of coffee. He sat in the armchair and waited for Virginia and Bret. Both entered and had a "hang dog" expression. Phil gestured to the coffee corner. "Get yourselves a beverage. You both look like you could use one."

Both got themselves a cup and sat in a dejected fashion. They knew better than to try running excuses past Phil at this point, so they waited for Phil to start. Phil took a sip and asked, "Hey, can you guess what I wanted to talk about?"

Bret sheepishly said, "I'm sorry, Boss. We had a talk with Goodman, and he assured us that he was just having an off day."

Virginia nodded. "We thought we had it handled, Phil. Given his years with the company, I thought yesterday was a fluke."

Phil asked, "How long has he been here?"

Bret answered, "He arrived with the influx of personnel when we opened the station expansion."

Phil asked, "How is it that he got by so far?"

Bret shrugged. "He was always on night shift. He's never handled more than three vessels at a time.

Phil frowned. "Did he ask for day shift, or was he assigned?"

Bret nodded. "He was quite insistent that he got moved to day shift. We had to bump some pretty senior people to accommodate his wishes."

Phil took another sip. "He must know his limitations. Why would he want to go on the busiest shift?"

Virginia shook her head. "I'm not sure what his angle is. He might be trying to prove something to himself, or he's trying to put us over a barrel somehow."

Phil recoiled, "How and why exactly would someone do that?"

Virginia answered, "I'm not saying he is, but there's no other reason he would subject himself to that kind of stress unless he had to."

"It's possible that it's all subconscious," Bret offered. "It's possible that he's not aware that he's in over his head, at least on a conscious level. We can't force him to a quieter shift if he doesn't want to go because of his seniority and contract. We also don't have the personnel to supplement him whenever he's on shift."

Phil finished his coffee. "So what you're telling me is, we're in a bad spot with this guy."

Virginia nodded. "That's about the size of it."

Phil stood. "We can't have what happened the last two days happen again.

When does he go on shift again?"

"He has the next three days off," Bret answered. Phil nodded. "I'll figure something out."

As Virginia and Bret walked to the door, Phil asked, "Did the *Aurora* get underway all right?"

Virginia answered, "The boys lit out at 0830."

Phil held back a grin. "Lit out? You've been picking up some of Dwight's vocabulary."

Both Virginia and Bret were chuckling on their way out.

*****

## Oasis 4, CentMod, Eva's Café

Phil sat at his customary table. He was deep in thought about the events of the morning and the implications they may have on station operations. Alice, Brenda, and Tillya arrived and sat Phil's table. Brenda and Tillya looked frazzled. Not quite shell-shocked but close. Alice looked at them and shook her head. "What's Phil doing to you two to put you in this state?"

Brenda chuckled. "You can't blame the boss on this. One of our own is responsible for a good deal of chaos the last two mornings."

Alice said, "I really need more information for context."

Brenda proceeded to relate the events of the morning while the rest listened. Phil especially was interested in hearing the point of view of one of the controllers who wasn't Goodman's superior.

Before Phil could ask Brenda specific questions, Alice asked Tillya, "How badly did it affect operations?"

"The bulk cargoes weren't a problem. Issues arose when containers and palletized cargo were being transferred from ship to ship. The delays started to stack on top of each other," Tillya said.

Phil sighed. "Somehow, I've got to convince Goodman that the best thing for everyone is for him to go ahead and retire."

Brenda chewed her sandwich and swallowed. "Look in the employment contract. Every time Bret tries to resolve this, Goodman beats him over the head with the contract."

Phil slowly nodded. "Maybe I can find something in the employee handbook or the controller standards handbook."

"If there's anything I can do, just ask," Alice offered.

*****

## The *Aurora,* Astrodyne 65, Operated by the Stellar Logistics and Freight Corporation

Dwight set the velocity at LS 9 and made sure they were on course. Phil had set the policy that the cockpit would always be manned while underway, so the others kept him company.

They were marveling at the fact that they had launched in the nick of time. Chad chuckled. "Did you hear the radio chatter before we jumped to light speed?"

Gus just shook his head. "I wouldn't want to be in Bret's or Virginia's shoes right now, or Phil's, for that matter."

Dwight nodded. "You're right about that. That Goodman fella has 'em in a tough spot. Has anyone ever worked with Goodman before?"

"I did," Chad said. "The guy's a mess. Three vessels in his sector are all he can handle."

Dwight said, "An essential skill a controller has to possess is the ability to visualize where the vessels are going to be at any given time judging from the present situation."

Gus frowned. "Huh?"

Dwight laughed, then explained, "For instance, let's say that your sector currently has three freighters. Two arriving, one departing. Then let's complicate things a little by adding a cruise ship in there.

Now sprinkle in half dozen shuttles going in a half dozen different directions."

Chad wrinkled his nose. "No wonder controllers tend to be nervous and moody."

"Now consider they have to know the capabilities of each vessel," Gus added. "How's that?" Chad wondered.

Dwight explained, "Well, you have to know how controllable and responsive each vessel is going to be, freighters especially. Some are way easier to handle than others. Even two freighters that are identical like the Star Series. One loaded down with metal ore is going to be heavier than one loaded with wood products. Then cruise ships act differently because they're so light for their size. Shuttles and vessels under, say, a hundred foot are easy. You can pretty much treat them equal."

Helmut thought for a second or two and said, "Das it's a lot to keep straight."

Dwight agreed, "You're right about that partner, but not impossible. For some folks, it becomes second nature. Others have to work hard at it. Those that can't get it usually realize they're in over their head and find something else to do."

Gus asked, "How do our controllers stack up against others you have worked with?"

Dwight thought for a second, "Really well actually, but I've got to tell you, the best I've ever seen is on the station now."

Gus furrowed his brow. "Who would that be?" "Alice Ross," Dwight answered with a smile. "The boss's wife?" Chad asked.

"Yup," Dwight said with a nod. "When she was a controller on Earth Station 3, a flu virus hit the station. She was the only controller on duty during peak hours, and I have to tell ya, she was impressive."

Gus frowned. "They allowed traffic to continue with a flu outbreak?"

"The virus was contained by then. Those who were exposed were isolated, but they were still real short on personnel," Dwight answered.

"We'll see what it's like when we get back. Change of subject. Any ideas on what this thing is we're going after?" Chad asked the group.

"I believe it must be a discarded piece of equipment," Helmut offered.

Dwight squinted as he thought. "You mean like an exploratory vehicle designed only for a specific phase of a mission?"

"Ja, like the lunar landers in the Apollo program in the 1960s and 1970s," Helmut answered.

Gus nodded. "That could be right. Or it may be some kind of unmanned vehicle."

"You're forgetting about the viewports we saw in the imagery. Unmanned vehicles don't need those," Chad protested.

"It could be a manned vehicle converted into an unmanned vehicle," Gus said defensively.

Dwight raised an eyebrow. "Or we may look inside and find dead fellers in there."

The conversation continued for the rest of the day, raising all possibilities about the origin of the object they were after, its function, and so on.

*****

## Oasis 4, CentMod, Security Office

Phil wanted to make sure that all went as planned when they transferred the flaston prisoners from the security office to the passenger's vessel. He knew Luke and his Deputies were up to the task; however, he didn't want the flaston delegation to get the impression that he wasn't taking their situation seriously.

Yulona was there along with Lynuna, Pindon, and two flaston security officers. Luke saw they were ready and nodded to Tiffany. "Okay, Tiff, bring 'em out."

Tiffany pressed the cell door control button, and six cell doors slid open. She then ordered in a forceful tone. "Exit your cells, turn to your right, and enter the processing room!"

The six Dragons complied. They stepped into the processing room and stood on a line indicated by Tiffany. Pindon stepped forward. "Gentlemen, you are being transported to Flast for trial and prescribed punishment." He looked at the two security officers. "Put the restraints on the prisoners."

Just as it happened on Kassnins, the largest, and as it turns out, the most impetuous of the Dragons lunged at Tiffany. Tiffany wasn't surprised in the least and reacted instantly. Her baton was just a blur as she delivered one devastating blow after another. When the dragon was on his knees, Tiffany jammed the baton end in his ribs and pushed the button for the Tazer. The big flaston groaned and fell face-first to the floor. The remaining five dragons looked down at their partner with wide, unblinking eyes. Then at once, they held their wrist together to make it easier for the security officers to put on the restraints.

Once the restraints were in place, Tiffany called out of the door, "They're ready."

Four of the largest Oasis 4 security deputies entered and led the six dragons out of the room with the help of the two flaston security officers. Everyone followed the group to CargoMod 1, where the flaston passenger ship was docked. Isnod and Feldon were standing by the air lock when they arrived. One by one, as they passed, each dragon glared at them. For their part, the pair looked at each one with a look that could be best described as contempt.

The two security officers entered the ship, and the prisoners were now the responsibility of the Flast government. Luke furrowed his brow. "Are your two officers going to be able to handle those guys?"

Pindon chuckled. "Probably not, but the six additional officers that arrived with the ship will be able to. The ship will be met at Flast with the best security we can provide, and the trial will not be made public."

Isnod smiled. "Six down, many more to go."

Phil checked the chronometer and announced, "It's almost dinnertime. How would you folks like to try Mexican cuisine?"

Yulona smiled. "That sounds nice."

Phil smiled. "That's great. You can get Lytrina and Rabot, then meet us at Baja Juans in the Upper CentMod in, say, a half hour."

Phil called Alice, and they secured a table big enough for the whole group. Everyone arrived then Phil and Alice helped them make menu selections. At one point, Rabot thought the salsa was a bit mild, which Juan took as a personal challenge. He brought out a salsa that he called his personal reserve. Phil had to try some and swore he would never be able to taste anything ever again.

During the meal, Phil couldn't help but notice the way Isnod was looking at Lynuna, and he wondered if there was something brewing.

*****

## The *Aurora*, Astrodyne 65, Operated by the Stellar Logistics and Freight Corporation

After two days of travel at LS 9, they had reached the position provided by Captain Hastings. Dwight cut the light-speed engines and started the reaction engines. In a short time, the proximity warning system alerted them, and Gus checked the forward sensing plot. He found what he was looking for and started a tracking plot on it. Once they had solid data on position, speed, and heading, Gus entered it into the navigation computer, and Dwight used that information to maneuver the *Aurora* behind the mystery spaceship.

Once Dwight confirmed they were directly behind the vessel, he increased velocity to close the distance. This was always the nerve-racking part of this kind of operation because at the relative velocities they were traveling, it was easy to fly past a ship and miss it altogether, or worse. In terms of space, they would have to be ridiculously close to spot it. They calculated a kilometer-and-a-half would be the farthest distance they could ever hope to spot it.

Gus kept his eye on the plot and called out distance. When they were two kilometers apart, Dwight slowed the *Aurora* to a velocity just faster than the mystery ship. Gus started peering through a pair of binoculars. He was starting to wonder if there was enough reflective light coming from the nebula to allow them to spot the ship.

"There it is!" Gus excitedly exclaimed when he finally picked it out of the sea of stars. He then guided Dwight to it until he could get his own eyes on it. They crept up on the mystery ship slowly but surely until they could make out distinct features of the vessel. Getting abeam of it, they studied it from the viewport until they agreed on which side was up, and then Dwight rolled the *Aurora* to match. Gus activated the auxiliary viewers, which were normally used to dock the *Aurora*, and Dwight used them to position themselves directly under the mystery ship.

Chad stood up. "I guess we're up, Helmut."

They put the cradles they made at the space station in the air lock along with the tools they're going to need. With that done, they put on their PEWS and entered the air lock. Once outside of the *Aurora*, Chad used hand holds to get on the top of the hull, where he had Helmut hand up the cradles and tools. When Helmut joined Chad on the top, they immediately started to attach the cradles. This was as nerve-racking as any part of the operation since they didn't know if there was an onboard computer on the mystery ship that would start firing thrusters if it sensed it was going off course.

While they worked, the realization of the conditions they were in hit Chad. At that moment, they were traveling at a velocity of twenty-five thousand miles per second. Everything being relative in the vacuum in space, it was as if they were just floating there stationary.

They placed the cradles under the ship and attached a strap to one side. Then the loose end was tossed over to the other side and attached. Once that was done, the straps were tightened. The straps were only expected to keep the cradles in place until the whole thing was secured to the *Aurora*. They carefully lowered the ship until it was in contact with the *Aurora*, then they attached tension struts and tightened them. Once the tension was set, both vessels were essentially one. Chad and Helmut took the opportunity to see if they could see inside the mystery ship. They carefully used what appeared to be handholds to move up to the forward viewports.

Gus and Dwight were listening to the progress being made outside. "What are you seeing in there, guys?" Gus asked.

Chad let out a breath. "Well, it's definitely a cockpit. I see seats, controls, and instruments."

"I see an indicator illuminated," Helmut excitedly exclaimed. "Oh, okay! I see it!" Chad confirmed.

Dwight frowned. "You fellas certain there's no radiation leaking from that thing?"

"Vee checked it twice," Helmut answered. "Okay, guys, come back in," Gus ordered.

Once back in the *Aurora*, Chad and Helmut went forward to the cockpit. Gus frowned. "That went amazingly fast. After the *Prospector* experience, it seems like you two should have been out there longer."

Chad chuckled. "The *Prospector* was about a thousand times larger than this thing. We won't even know it's up there if we did our job correctly."

Dwight nodded. "Well then, let's put the spurs to this thing and get back to the ranch."

Dwight was fatigued from maneuvering, so Gus took the controls. They slowly increased speed until they were ready to make the jump to light speed. So far, Chad was right about the ship not having an effect on performance. They couldn't tell at all that there was a small ship strapped to the hull.

*****

## Oasis 4, Upper CentMod, Eva's Café

Phil was trying to enjoy his lunch. Today, he was eating with Virginia Wells and Bret Pinkerton. The topic was James Goodman and what to do about him. Phil wasn't encouraged by what he was hearing. He asked, "Could you say that again?"

Bret shrugged. "I told him that his performance was not to standards. He got angry and said we were asking too much from the controllers, and no one could be expected to handle that many ships."

Phil was doing his best to keep his temper in check. "Tell me, what did he have to say about his rude language?"

"He says if the captains and pilots were better at following instructions, he would be nicer," Virginia answered. "What do you say?" Phil pressed.

Virginia sighed. "I think he gets rattled way too easily and takes it out on the rest of the galaxy."

Phil took a deep breath. "So what we have is an individual in a position that's way over his skill set. He believes it's everyone else's fault that he's lousy at his job. To put a nice bow on this stinking mess, unless he agrees to step down or take another shift, he can handle we're stuck with him, and we don't have extra personnel to keep him company whenever he's on shift."

"You forgot about the rudeness," Bret said. "Thanks" was Phil's deadpan response.

Phil drank his coffee and mused. He furrowed his brow. "Somewhere, I heard that we actually didn't need as many controllers as we use."

Bret nodded. "That's right. We use four only during peak hours for safety and efficiency. Off-peak periods well go to two controllers, and graveyard shift, a single controller is all that's needed."

Phil was having an idea gel. "I've been going over the employee contracts. If Goodman cannot perform a duty to our satisfaction, he can be dismissed."

"We thought of that," Virginia said. "His little lapses are technically, by definition, minor enough that they don't warrant dismissal. Even if they snowball into a genuine mess."

Phil frowned. "So we need to convince Goodman that it's in his best interest to do us all a favor and retire. If we can demonstrate that his job not only can be handled by a single controller, but that controller can take on more than what we're asking him to."

Virginia frowned. "You mean, have a controller handle two sectors?" Phil shook his head. "Nothing quite so pedestrian."

Bret looked cornered. "I don't have a single controller capable of handling four sectors during peak hours."

Phil was holding back a grin. "Maybe not an active controller, but there's one on the station that could."

Bret was trying to catch up with what Phil was alluding to. Just then, Alice walked up, sipping a soda pop through a straw. "Hey, gang, what's happening?"

The three looked up at Alice. Then Virginia and Bret looked at a grinning Phil. Then thin smiles started forming on their faces.

Alice looked at the trio, "What?"

*****

## Oasis 4, Lower Section CentMod, Plaza Level

Yulona and Pindon had staged a series of False Flag operations. Two flaston security officers would emerge from Phil's office carrying a case like the one the Charter is in and take it to an awaiting ship bound for Flast. The operations were carried out with varying amounts of secrecy and stealth. The first one was obviously overt. For the one they just finished, they went to great pains to make it appear as if they were being careful and secret but not clever enough. Phil played his part well, acting like the bumbling but well-meaning station manager. As planned, Phil interrupted the procedure with a loud request for something pertaining to station business.

Looking around the Lower Section CentMod, he saw there was another business opening on the second tier above the plaza level. Curiosity was getting the better of him, so he took the escalator to the second-level tier. Above the door, there was a sign in flaston, which Phil couldn't read. As with all businesses on the station, the sign is in flaston, which is the norm for alien businesses on the station, but the business name is also printed on the lower half of the sign in the other known languages, English being the first. Phil read the sign 'Micton Studio.' What is that?"

He walked in, and there was a flaston fastening a rack on the wall. Phil watched for a few seconds, then said, "Two questions, what's Micton, and what's the rack for?"

The flaston continued what he was doing. "Micton is an ancient fighting style from Flast. It teaches us discipline, humility, and confidence. This is a display rack for some of the tools we use in our lessons when we learn how to defend ourselves. Weapons aren't used in micton, but we learn counter moves in the event someone attacks us with one."

Phil nodded. "I'm Phil Ross, by the way, station manager."

The flaston smiled. "I thought so. I'm Ivonorsic, micton master."

Phil was now genuinely interested. "How does one become a micton master?"

Ivonorsic smiled. "If a devotee of micton wins a battle against a formidable opponent, they can be pinned," he indicated to a pin on his shirt front.

Phil frowned. "That's it?"

Ivonorsic shook his head. "It's not that easy. There are only five thousand pins. They were made centuries ago. That's all that was made, and that's all that will ever be made. When a micton master reaches an age where he feels that stepping down is the best course of action for the order, he gives his pin to a micton master. Then the master is charged with the task of bestowing it on a worthy individual."

"Have you ever been tasked with bestowing a pin?" Phil asked.

Ivonorsic nodded. "I have two in my possession I have been given the honor of bestowing on worthy micton devotees, one belonged to my father, and one belonged to my uncle. It's not only an honor but a burden at the same time."

Phil nodded. "Well, I stopped by to wish you luck and to tell you if there's anything you need, don't hesitate to ask."

Ivonorsic thanked Phil, and Phil left the micton studio to see if Alice was ready for dinner.

*****

## Oasis 4, Operations Center

With the morning briefing being over, Phil and the rest retreated to the operations center where Alice was waiting with Bret Pinkerton. Phil and Virginia approached them, and Alice was trying to keep from grinning. Virginia asked Bret, "When does it hit the fan?"

"We're due for a rush in about ten minutes. We'll go up there in about eight minutes to give everyone a breather," Bret answered.

Bret went to the control center with Alice trailing. When they reached the control level, Alice put on headsets and gave Bret the thumbs-up. Bret waited until a controller had a pause. "Dave, get a cup of coffee."

A controller pulled off his headset and descended the stairs while Alice took over his sector. The controller at an adjacent sector was in a short lull. Bret said, "Take a break, Gail." Alice started handling both sectors.

Bret waited a few seconds. "Russ, you look like you could use a breather." Russ removed his headset and descended the stairs.

Goodman couldn't help but notice the control center was being abandoned.

Bret said, "Take a break, James."

Goodman cautiously removed his headset and started to the stairs. Bret stopped him. "Why don't you join us here in the observer area?"

Goodman joined Bret, and Phil then watched as Alice was starting to get into a rhythm. She was continually checking the plot while coordinating traffic. Phil and the rest didn't have headsets on, but while listening to Alice, it wasn't necessary.

Alice checked the plot. "*Clayborne*, continue approach to CargoMod 2, Docking Port 17. *Hatfield*, docking clamps released, thrust port until clear. *Shuttle 667*, pitch up fifteen degrees and thrust forward. *Shuttle 453*, follow *667*. *Hatfield*, pitch down ten degrees and thrust. *Clayborne* clear to CargoMod 2, Docking Port 17. Shuttle *Hoynosto*, continue to reporting point alpha..."

For the next fifteen minutes, Alice was controlling like she never took leave. The other controllers filtered back to the observation area with their beverages. Russ was watching and listening to Alice with professional admiration. "I never thought I'd get a chance to see the Legend in action."

Dave and Gail nodded in agreement; James Goodman was staring silently but open-mouthed. They were joined by the next shift's controllers, who were in awe of what they were witnessing. Bret looked at them. "Go ahead and take your shift."

The fresh controllers put on headsets and took over duties from Alice, who took off her own headset and walked to the stairs while Phil, Bret, and the offgoing controllers applauded, except for Goodman. In a half-hour period, Alice handled the controlling flawlessly. She guided freighters and countless smaller vessels. While the others were exiting the control center, Bret quietly said to Goodman, "Mr. Ross and I need to see you in Virginia's office."

Goodman had a defeated look as they descended the stairs and made their way to Virginia's office. Bret knocked twice, entered, and found Virginia waiting. Virginia had everyone sit in chairs that she had arranged.

Virginia sighed. "I'll come right to it, James. You simply cannot handle the pace that's required for the shift you want to be on."

Goodman looked like he wanted to object, but Virginia cut him off, "I think we've demonstrated that this shift can be handled by fewer controllers than what we're using. If you're unwilling to move to a shift you can handle, we'll have to come to some other arrangement."

Goodman was silent and downcast. Phil said, "Look, James, the bottom line is this, you can't do the job that's required. It's been demonstrated that the job we're having done by four people can be handled effectively by one individual. You're eligible for retirement. Why don't you go out gracefully?"

Goodman slowly nodded. "I don't want to leave you short-handed while you're waiting for a replacement from Earth. Could you please move me to an off shift until a replacement can arrive? I'll put in my retirement paperwork today."

Phil nodded. "That's reasonable. Virginia, Bret, you three can see to the details." Phil stood and shook hands with Goodman. "I really am sorry it couldn't work for all of us."

Goodman said, "Me too. I guess I was trying to prove something to myself."

Phil left the ops center and decided to tour the station. He really hated to do that to one of his employees, especially one that has given the company years of service. Even lackluster service meant something. Although Goodman really didn't leave him much choice.

*****

## The *Aurora,* Astrodyne 65, Operated by the Stellar Logistics and Freight Corporation

Gus cut the light-speed engines and started the reaction engines. A check of the navigation computer revealed that they were exactly where they planned to be. When they were at the outer reporting point, Gus contacted the station. "Oasis control. *Aurora* on the Yankee approach at the outer reporting point."

*"Aurora, continue approach. Report at reporting point Alpha,"* the controller that Gus recognized as Russ answered.

When they reached the reporting point, Gus informed Russ that they had to park next to CargoMod 8 so that vessel maintenance could remove the vessel from the Aurora. Afterward, they would need their normal parking at CargoMod 2. Chad used the vessel maintenance frequency to contact Jeremy and coordinate the removal of the mystery ship.

At reporting point alpha, they accepted vectors to CargoMod 8 and positioned themselves just off the maintenance hangars. Maintenance tugs with technicians on board descended on the *Aurora.* They disconnected the straps that were securing the mystery ship to the *Aurora* and attached a tug. The tug eased the mystery ship away from the *Aurora,* and Gus received clearance to CargoMod 2.

After docking and the umbilicals were connected, Gus powered down the reactor. Helmut opened the air lock, and the four of them grabbed their duffels and headed to CargoMod 8. Phil spotted them getting off the platform lift in the lower CentMod. Then after greetings, he joined them. Once in CargoMod 8, they went to the hanger bay and watched through an observation window as Jeremy and his crew examined the vessel. The maintenance crew was in protective garments in the event the vessel was emitting radiation that they didn't previously detect. There was a thick layer of dust on the vessel that the maintenance technicians started washing off.

Jeremy entered an air lock and pressed a button that started a decontamination sequence. He held his arms up while he slowly rotated, and soapy water was sprayed on him. Then rinse water washed off the suds. With that done, he pressed a button that opened the air lock, and he stepped through the doorway. After he pulled off the protective helmet, Phil asked, "So what do you think, Jeremy?"

Jeremy continued to pull off the protective garments. "We're defiantly looking at something we've never seen before. I can't wait until we get a better look at it without protective gear."

Dwight asked, "Why were you wearing protective gear in the first place?"

"In case there's radiation we haven't detected, and all that dust on it, I suspect it's from the nebula, has compounds in it that are of an unsavory nature," Jeremy answered.

Jeremy's crew finished their task and put away the cleaning equipment. When they were sure that all the remnants of the nebula were in the drain, they started removing their protective gear. Jeremy opened both air lock doors. "Well, let's see what we've got."

The mystery ship sat on the cradle that they built to bring it back. "Don't open anything until we know what we're dealing with," Jeremy cautioned.

They approached the ship and examined it. There were viewports on what they assumed was the front of the little ship. Jeremy and Phil used flashlights to peer inside. "Have you ever seen anything like this?" Phil asked.

Jeremy shook his head. "It's definitely not like anything I've ever experienced. I can tell you whoever built this is most likely bipedal and perhaps slightly smaller than us."

Phil nodded. "The seats give us a lot of clues. I see an indicator that's lit, so there's some kind of power source still operating."

"That's one of the reasons we have to be cautious," Jeremy confirmed.

Chad called from the side of the vessel, "Hey, Boss, we found the hatch."

Jeremy said, "You know the rules, Chad. Don't open anything until we've thoroughly checked it out."

As Phil and Jeremy walked around, Chad chuckled. "No worries here Boss. I said we found the hatch. I didn't say we found a way to open it."

They gathered around the hatch and examined it. They ran their hands around the edges, feeling for some kind of latch. The hatch door was perfectly flush with the outer skin and offered no clues as to how to open it. There was a small panel just above the hatch. Jeremy put his hand on it and found that it was hinged below the top edge a short distance, and he could open it by simply pressing on the top of the panel.

When the panel opened, Jeremy peered inside and furrowed his brow. "I expected to find the hatch release here, but all that's here is a row of indicators flashing randomly."

Phil saw there was a placard on the underside of the panel. The placard had rows of symbols that were unfamiliar. The thing that struck him as both odd and familiar was that there were only two symbols, but they were randomly arranged. All at once, Phil smiled. "How many indicators are there?"

Jeremy made a quick count. "Sixteen."

Phil pointed to the placard. "Do you suppose these symbols are ones and zeros?"

Jeremy's eyes widened. "Binary!"

He closed the panel cover, and Phil excitedly asked, "Why did you do that?" "I'm hoping that the sequence will start over when we reopen the panel," Jeremy answered.

He reopened the panel, and the indicators illuminated again. After it flashed a series of sequences, Jeremy grinned. "Binary confirmed. It's giving us prime numbers."

Phil nodded. "Whoever built this thing is actually pretty clever. So what's next?"

Jeremy looked at Chad. "Get me a stand-alone computer and optical reader." Chad nodded. "Come on, Helmut. I could use a hand."

"Whatcha doing, Jeremy?" Phil asked.

"You were right when you said whoever built this was clever but think about it for a second. If you built a probe and sent it out in hopes of it encountering an unknown intelligence, would you assume that they had compatible power systems? The one sure thing we do know is we can communicate optically using binary numbers. The optical reader also has an emitter that will attempt to talk back to the ship's computer. If we're lucky, both computers will figure out a way to teach each other their respective languages. We're using a stand-alone computer to prevent some weird alien computer program from doing unwanted things to the SICOS."

Chad and Helmut returned with the computer and optical reader. They attached the reader to the hull with adhesive and connected it to the computer. They started the computer and ran the interrogation program, which was the only program installed. Jeremy opened the panel cover, and the indicators started their sequence again. In a short time, the stand-alone computer recognized the binary numbers and responded. A light illuminated on the stand- alone computer, indicating they were now linked using radio transmission.

Jeremy said, "I've never done anything like this before, so I really don't know how long it's going to take."

Dwight couldn't stand it anymore. "I suppose no one else is going to say it. We haven't found a brand on this thing that we recognize. The reciprocal course it was on takes it back to the nebula. It's just my opinion, but I think we're going to meet some folks for the first time."

"I think you're right, Dwight," Gus agreed.

Phil nodded. "At the speed, it was traveling, how long do you think it was out there?"

Gus scratched his head. "Geez, we could be talking centuries."

Jeremy sighed, then said, "At any rate, it looks like this may take a while. We may as well let this run tonight and see what happens tomorrow."

*****

## Oasis 4, Operations Center Briefing Room

The next day, Phil thought the morning briefing was progressing nicely. Virginia was in better spirits. Will had the station's systems operating at peak efficiency, and Dr. Tillman's infirmary was as routine as can be. Phil looked at his pad. "We have that 'thing' later this morning, Luke."

The other meeting attendees suspected Phil was alluding to the continued intrigue with the flastons.

"Is there anything to report concerning that mystery ship, Jeremy?" Phil asked.

Jeremy nodded. "I checked before coming up here. The two computers finally learned to communicate with each other sometime last night. There's been an impressive amount of data exchanged so far."

"Good. Hopefully, it'll tell us how to get inside it," Phil said, putting down his pad.

*****

## Oasis 4, Upper CentMod, Plaza Level

Phil had just finished assisting in another false flag operation and was chatting with Yulona and Pindon. Lytrina and Lynuna were a short distance away, having a conversation of their own. Isnod stepped off the escalator and timidly approached Yulona. "Excuse me. May I have a private word with you Yulona?"

"Of course." Yulona motioned for Isnod to step a short distance away. Isnod quietly said, "I was wondering if Lynuna had suitors."

Yulona furrowed his brow. "I take it that you believe that the traditional ways should be honored in these affairs? You're seeking the approval of the father?"

Isnod was clearly nervous. "Yes, that's right."

Yulona frowned. "Then do me the honor, do Lytrina the honor, do Lynuna the honor of doing this the right way."

Isnod was staggered but recovered quickly. He faced the CentMod interior with his arms spread, and in a very loud voice, he got the attention of everyone. "I am Isnod! Son of Isdornac and Noduleic of Tobolor village!"

Yulona stood back with his arms crossed and held a scowl on his face. Isnod continued to address the CentMod. "As I have proved my mettle by defeating the common enemy of our people, I am coming to Yulona to ask if I may have his blessing to seek courtship with Lynuna!" Isnod stepped back away from the walkway railing and put his hands on his hips. Then he stood there with a resolute look on his face. Yulona uncrossed his arms and approached the railing. "Isnod has honored my house by coming to me with his plea in the ancient and honorable manner. Having found that he is a man of exceptional character, on behalf of my wife and myself, I am pleased to give Isnod blessings to seek courtship with Lynuna!"

Lynuna was, in turn, mortified and pleased as she covered her mouth with her hand. Lytrina was smiling broadly and nodded to Yulona who started smiling. Isnod approached Lynuna. "I would be most pleased if you considered allowing me to court you Lynuna."

Lynuna, trying to keep from grinning, said, "I am pleased that you are interested in pursuing a more personal relationship. Please contact me to arrange a proper activity."

Isnod smiled and slightly bowed to Lynuna. Next, he faced Lytrina and bowed deeper, then faced Yulona and nodded his head.

Isnod then turned on his heels and headed to a down escalator. From the other direction, Luke stepped off an up escalator with Gus and Dwight behind him. They eased up to Phil and Pindon while Lynuna was having a moment with her parents.

"What was that we just witnessed?" Luke asked quietly.

Phil looked at him and said while wearing a grin, "I should think that was obvious. Isnod asked for a blessing to court Lynuna, and Yulona granted his blessing."

"Is that how all courtships start on Flast?" Gus asked.

Pindon smiled. "Not anymore. It used to be very commonplace, but it gradually fell out of favor during the old regime. These days, it's actually making a comeback."

"A lot of troubled relationships could be prevented if more folks took the courtship process more seriously. I know I could have avoided a lot of heartaches if I had carefully considered each step in the relationship process. "Dwight said with a smile.

Phil furrowed his brow. "Why the shouting?"

"More tradition," Pindon offered. "The intention is to not only openly declare intentions but to inform other potential suitors that if they had similar intentions, they had better be ready for competition."

Phil nodded. "What about the exaggerated body language and expressions on their faces?"

"Again, tradition, the father tries to intimidate the young man. If the suitor isn't put off, it works in his favor. While the father makes his rejection or approval, the young man is almost daring the father to find fault while simultaneously telling everyone in earshot if they also have designs on the young lady, they'll have to impress a very exacting father."

Gus asked, "Has a father ever rejected a suitor?"

Pindon laughed. "I have witnessed it. As you humans might say, it's brutal." Gus nodded. "I'm happy for both of them."

Dwight added, "That Isnod's a fine fellow, and Miss Lynuna is mighty fetching herself."

Lynuna and her parents walked over to Phil and the others. "Mr. Ross, I hope that wasn't a disruption."

Phil smiled. "Not at all, Miss Lynuna."

"I'm going to spend some time with my parents. If you need us, please inquire at the consulate," Lynuna said with a sly grin.

After Lynuna and her parents left, Gus said, "We were on our way to CargoMod 8. Jeremy said the computers were done conversing. He sounded excited."

They parted company with Pindon and made their way to CargoMod 8.

*****

## Oasis 4, CargoMod 8, Maintenance Hangar 3

Phil, Gus, and Dwight walked into the maintenance hangar, and Jeremy smiled. "It's about time. There's exciting stuff happening here."

"What's up?" Phil asked casually.

Jeremy indicated to the computer screen. "We know who launched this, its mission, its origin, how to enter it, and how to revive the crew."

Phil nodded, then stopped suddenly. "Run that last thing by me again."

Jeremy nodded. "Yup. There is two crew inside, both males. They're from a system in the void inside of the nebula, not too far from Anna Mae."

"What do they call themselves?" Gus asked.

Jeremy checked the computer. "They're haldocs. The planet they call home is called Vestgut. Apparently, outside of the nebula was, or is, a complete mystery to these people. These two were sent to find out what's here and return with the data."

"That's exercising patience," Phil quipped.

Jeremy was anxious to get things going. "According to the computer, the crewmen are in individual pods that are similar to suspended animation units."

"I didn't think those could be used for anything other than keeping food fresh," Gus remarked.

Jeremy shook his head. "It's beyond me how they did it. They obviously have a technology we're not aware of. Once we get inside, we can remove the pods to a place where we can activate the reanimation sequence."

Phil stepped back. "Okay, get the medical information to Dr. Tillman. I imagine we'll need a couple of carts to move the pods. Luke, I think it would be prudent to have security standing by. We open this in a half hour."

The time ticked by as everyone carried out their assignments in preparation for opening the mystery spaceship. Phil walked to a communication terminal and punched in a code. Marie Tillman answered, "We're ready here, Phil."

"Okay, Doc. We're opening the ship now," Phil acknowledged.

He turned back to the others, then looked around. "Are we recording this?"

Jeremy pointed to cameras arranged on the hangar bay walls. "On and recording. Also, everyone who enters the ship will be asked to wear one of these."

He pulled a headband out of his pocket and put it on. Everyone recognized it immediately as a camera band.

Gus was fitting his own headband. "What kind of atmosphere can we expect in there? We would look stupid opening a hatch on a spaceship full of air that's poisonous to us."

Jeremy checked the computer. "They breathe a mixture of the same gasses we do. The percentages are slightly different but basically the same."

Phil took a breath. "Okay, Jeremy. Go ahead."

Jeremy reached into the open panel that concealed the binary code indicators. He pushed firmly on the center of the small display, and there was a click. The indicators slid to one side, exposing a latch handle. He grasped the handle, pulled, and there was a rush of air as the hatch was unsealed. Jeremy pushed the door inward, where it rotated slightly, and they could pull it outside. He then turned on a flashlight and went inside.

Phil followed him inside. "The air is very stale in here." Jeremy nodded. "It's cramped in here too."

"Judging by the size of the seats, I'd say that they were probably about a foot or two shorter than us on average," Phil observed while looking into what appeared to be a cockpit.

Behind the cockpit area, they found the two suspended animation pods. Jeremy looked them over and said, "According to the computer, we disconnect the power cable, and the pods will automatically switch over to an internal power source."

Phil was also examining them and saw they were fastened to the deck at each corner. Jeremy said, "I found the power cable. When I say go, release the locks on your side, and I'll get this side."

Jeremy disconnected the power cable. "Go ahead, Boss."

Phil and Jeremy released the latches on the first pod and gave it a nudge to see if it would move. They found that it slid easily. Jeremy studied it and announced, "It must have some sort of low friction coating on the bottom."

They pushed the pod to the hatch, where Chad and Helmut pulled it out and placed it on a cart. The next pod was removed from the small ship and placed with the first one. Jeremy and Phil climbed out, and Jeremy said to Chad and Helmut. "Let's get those to the infirmary."

*****

## Oasis 4, Lower CentMod, Infirmary

The pods were wheeled into the infirmary, and Dr. Tillman directed them into an intensive care room. She activated the SICOS and put the pod instructions on the screen. There was a small control panel on the pods that she studied for a few seconds. She would study the panel, then consult the SICOS until, finally, she said, "Well, here goes nothing."

With the touch of a button, an indicator lit. Then a panel slid down, exposing a clear plastic panel, allowing their first look at the haldocs. Phil looked them over. "They're like us, only…smaller."

Marie checked the SICOS, then pressed the pod control keys in a specific sequence. More indicators illuminated, and a screen came to life. She stepped back and said, "Well, the reanimation process has started. Their vital signs will be displayed on this screen."

"How long will this take?" Jeremy asked.

Marie shrugged. "According to the computer, the reanimation process will take about two and a half hours."

"I imagine that for Jeremy and me, this is going to be like watching paint dry," Phil observed.

"We missed lunch, and now my belly thinks my throat's been cut," Dwight quipped.

Phil laughed. "Let's grab a bite at Eva's, and afterward, we'll meet in the conference room number 1. Jeremy, is the data from the alien ship in SICOS yet?"

Jeremy nodded. "Did it this morning after checking for viruses."

"Good. All of us will put our heads together and learn what we can

before our new friends wake up," Phil said.

*****

## Oasis 4, CentMod, Conference Room Number 1

After a quick meal at Eva's, they gathered in conference room number 1. Phil said, "Okay, we don't have a lot of time before our guests wake up. First, where are these guys from?"

Jeremy leaned back in his chair. "SICOS, dim lights. Display holographic representation of our sector."

A star field appeared in the space above their heads, with the nebula in the center. "Highlight Oasis 4 and Vestgut," Jeremy ordered.

Two points glowed in the holographic display. Jeremy continued to stare over his head. "I had SICOS integrate the alien names for all the astronomical features in the database before you ask. SICOS, display course that was taken by the *Mystery Ship*."

SICOS drew a line from Oasis 4 to the point where the Aurora picked it up. The line was relatively straight, and Jeremy chuckled. "This is where it gets interesting."

The course line was anything but straight as it curved and looped until it reappeared in the void inside of the nebula. Jeremy said, "Remember, we're watching this in reverse."

The course was relatively straight in the void inside of the nebula until it reached a system that they identified as the Vestgut system.

Phil stared at the display and finally said, "SICOS, run it from beginning to end, starting at Vestgut."

The course line started at Vestgut and penetrated the nebula. Phil furrowed his brow. "Why does the course get so erratic in the nebula?"

"I'll bet it was pulled off course by stars and such in the nebula," Dwight put in.

Jeremey smiled. "Not bad, Dwight. It took me a while to figure it out. The onboard computer was programmed to keep the ship on a specific heading. When it was pulled off course, the computer would fire thrusters to put it back on course. They had no idea what was in the nebula or where anything was. The computer prompted more course corrections than they anticipated. The ship eventually ran out of fuel. They wouldn't be able to get home if they had to. It's lucky for them the *Goldfield* spotted them."

Gus asked, "How long were they out there?"

"Five hundred and twenty-two years," Jeremy answered.

It didn't come as a surprise to the group, but it still awed them. Gus nodded. "So what's the next step?"

Phil shook his head. "I don't know. We're treading new ground here. We're not a governmental organization, so we can't represent a country or world. Maybe that works in our favor. We'll just present ourselves as just who we are, employees of the Great Stellar Logistics and Freight Corporation. We can't plan anything until we see if our guest survives the reanimation process. When that's done, we'll contact corporate."

"How long would it take for us to get to Vestgut?" Gus asked. "At LS 9, we're looking at six days," Jeremy answered.

*****

## Oasis 4, Lower CentMod, Infirmary

After Phil and the others exhausted the usefulness of their conference room meeting, they made their way back to the infirmary.

Marie Tillman said, "They're close to being ready."

She then frowned. "I don't think it's a good idea if all of you are there when they wake up."

Phil furrowed his brow. "Well, someone needs to be there." "I'll be there with some of my staff," Marie stated.

She continued, "I don't want them overwhelmed with a lot of people hovering over them after they wake up. They're bound to be disoriented waking up in a different place from where they went to sleep."

Phil nodded. "Okay, I get that, but once they're awake and aware, I want to meet them."

Marie smiled. "Of course, I also think it would be prudent if there were a couple of Luke's deputies around."

Luke used his communicator on his wrist to summon deputies while Gus turned to the others. "We might as well find something else to do since we're not wanted."

Marie chuckled as she entered the intensive care room. The indicators on each pod were very active, with status bars crawling across the screen and symbols flashing that Marie learned was heart rate, respiration, and other vital signs.

The indicators suddenly turned blue, and the doors slid open. Marie had earpieces put on the haldocs. Then after a minute or so, each occupant spasmed and took in a huge breath. After breathing heavily for a few seconds, they slowly opened their eyes. When it was obvious that they were no longer aboard their ship, their eyes widened.

"Please stay calm. You're among friends. We found your vessel and brought it to our space station," Marie said in a calming tone.

The haldocs were at a loss for words at first, then one croaked out, "How do you know our language?"

Marie chuckled. "I don't know your language. Our computers taught each other our languages. We used that to program automatic translators. Before you became conscious, I had my staff put an auto translator earpiece on you. As long as you're wearing it, you can understand everyone on this space station."

Marie held a hand mirror, and the haldoc examined the earpiece. "Is this all I need?"

Marie shook her head. "No, you'll also have to carry this." She held up his auto translator and clipped it to his shirt front.

Marie smiled as he examined the auto translator, and she asked, "Do you think you can stand?"

He moved his arms and legs testing them. He looked up and said, "I think so."

She helped steady him with the help of an orderly while two orderlies assisted the other haldoc. Once the haldocs were on their feet, Marie had them walk about with the assistance of an orderly each. They were unsteady on their feet, which was completely understandable. She had them sit in chairs that were in the room. She smiled and said, "You two have been asleep for a long time. Naturally, it's going to take time to get everything working again."

Phil tapped on the doorframe. "Are you going to keep me waiting all day, Doc?"

Marie chuckled. "I think they're ready to meet you, Phil."

Phil walked the rest of the way in and introduced himself, "Hello, I'm Phillip Ross, the manager of this station. May I have your names?" The first Haldoc smiled. "My name is Votlormicuntox Hudixofon."

The second Haldoc said, "I'm Rokidosmor Remhifunos."

Phil felt like a deer in headlights. "That's a mouthful for us. Would you mind terribly if we called you Votlor and Rok?"

They both laughed, and Votlormicuntox said, "That's what we do on our planet. The impossibly long names are a throwback to an earlier time in our society. Of course, you may call us by those names. The doctor said, We are on a space station?"

Phil nodded. "Indeed you are. This station is called Oasis 4. It's owned and operated by the Stellar Logistics and Freight Corporation. One of our customers spotted your vessel after you exited the nebula."

Rok furrowed his brow. "Nebula?" Phil nodded. "The stellar cloud."

Votlor nodded. "Ah, we call it the Great Barrier." "How long have we been traveling?" Rok asked.

"By our calendar, 522 years. That's 360 years on your calendar," Phil answered.

The haldocs were stunned. Votlor shook his head. "Our mission wasn't supposed to last that long. Have you looked at our automatic log recordings to see what went wrong, or why we weren't awakened?"

Phil nodded. "We looked at the navigation data, but that's about all. We can look at the data together when you feel up to it. Until then, listen to Dr. Tillman."

Phil looked at Marie. "How 'bout it, Doc, does Votlor and Rok get a stamp of approval, medically speaking, any time soon?"

Marie shrugged and slowly nodded. "I think we should keep them here overnight. The medical database we downloaded from their ship says that about six hours after reanimation, they'll be ready for a full night's rest. We'll get them a meal and have them walk around some more, then we'll see in the morning. I predict that they'll be ready for a tour of the station after our morning briefing."

Phil smiled and said, "Okay, Doc, I'll see you tomorrow at the briefing."

There was some time left before the workday was over, so before leaving the infirmary, he went to a SICOS terminal. "SICOS, locate Jeremy Cole, Gus Condent, Dwight Needles, and Luke Smith?"

"Jeremy Cole, Gus Condent, Dwight Needles, and Luke Smith are in CargoMod 8, Maintenance Hangar 3," was the mechanical reply.

Phil left the infirmary and took an escalator to the plaza level of the Lower Section CentMod, where he walked to the CargoMod 8 connector tunnel.

*****

## Oasis 4, CargoMod 8

Phil decided to walk to the maintenance hangars after entering the CargoMod. There, he encountered Alice, Brenda, and Tillya coming out of Hangar 3 just when Phil was going to enter. Alice was holding a tape measure while Brenda was making notes on a pad with Tillya looking on. They didn't see Phil until Alice bumped into him.

"You do realize the alien's ship isn't ours to stick in a museum, right?" Phil quipped.

Alice grinned. "Just planning ahead."

Phil frowned. "Well, don't count your kortlax before they hatch. In the meantime, what do you girls say we get dinner later, then see what we can do at Sliders?"

Alice smiled. "That sounds fine with us."

"I'll tell Gus," Phil said as he turned to the hangar door.

Gus, Dwight, and Jeremy were in the alien ship, learning what they could. Phil stuck his head in the hatch. "Thinking of taking it out for a spin?" "No one is taking this out for anything anytime soon," Gus quipped.

Jeremy sat on the deck with his back against a bulkhead. "Out of fuel, reactor on its last legs, it's a wonder that the cabin could hold pressure. There's a supply of rations, but from the way they look, I don't think that they're good anymore. Those two would have been doomed if the Goldfield hadn't spotted them."

Dwight was on his knees, peering into the cockpit. "The flight deck layout looks pretty standard, except I don't dare try sitting in one of these seats. I might get stuck."

Phil furrowed his brow. "Does this have artificial gravity?"

Jeremy shook his head. "No, it doesn't, so it's better to be seated and strapped in. If you have to make course corrections, you won't get thrown around."

Phil nodded. "Yeah, that makes sense."

"Did you inform corporate about our new friends yet?" Gus asked. "Not yet," Phil said with a shake of his head. "I thought we could do that together before we knock off for the night."

Before they left the alien ship, Phil looked back at Jeremy and Dwight. "Don't let Alice or one of her minions take this to the museum."

That drew chuckles from Jeremy and Dwight.

Phil and Gus took the shuttle tram to the lower CentMod. On the ride, Phil said, "I told the girls we'd have dinner together tonight, then maybe some pool at Sliders."

Gus smiled. "That sounds like a good evening to cap a good day."

On the platform lift, Phil frowned, "I wonder how many people know about us discovering a new race and if that info has left the station yet?"

Gus scratched his chin. "That's a good question. We haven't made any efforts to keep it a secret. So far, the only people directly involved are you, me, and Dwight, Jeremy, and his crew, then there's the infirmary."

Phil nodded. "What gets me is how everyone who is involved in this isn't treating this like it's a big deal, but it's a very big deal."

When they reached Phil's office, naturally, they got a coffee each and sat down. They spent a half hour composing a letter to Elias Gilmore and the rest of the board. When they were done, Phil added it to the data stream packet that was scheduled to be transmitted at 1800 Zulu.

Back on the platform lift on their way back to the plaza level, Phil mused, "I wonder how long before we get a response?"

Gus took a breath. "Let's see. Today is Wednesday. It takes forty hours for a Space Interfold Transmission to get to Earth, which gets it there at 1000 Zulu on Friday, which is 0500 in Kansas City. That means it will be downloaded at company headquarters in time for Elias to read the letter at 0900. He'll call an emergency board meeting at 1300 local time. I would say he'll have a response on the next data stream, telling us he's coming here. We'll get that letter forty hours after it was sent, which will be Monday. Knowing Elias, he'll have that Pulsar 5500 headed here by morning. The Pulsar 5500 is the fastest ship model sold, so that puts him here three weeks from the time he leaves."

Phil frowned. "So we'll hear from him in about four or five days."

"Yup," Gus confirmed.

"You could have just said that," Phil said in an exasperated tone.

Gus chuckled. "Why don't we see if the girls are ready."

*****

## Oasis 4, CentMod, Plaza Level

The pair stepped off the platform lift on the plaza level and walked to the sitting area where Alice and the other girls were waiting for them. Phil and Gus sat down, and Phil asked, "What does everyone feel like tonight?"

Alice looked at Tillya. "Have you tried pizza yet?"

Tillya shook her head. "No, I haven't. When I walk past the restaurant, the aroma is so enticing."

Phil rubbed his hands together. "That settles it. We dine like college students tonight."

There were two sources of pizza at the station. One was a kiosk that sold by the slice, and the other was a franchise restaurant that also had delivery service available. Of course, they were headed to the restaurant to dine in.

Before they reached the escalator to the tier the restaurant was on, Phil spotted Feldon looking around the plaza level with a pensive look on his face.

Phil eased up to him. "Hey, Feldon, I'm not used to seeing you by yourself."

Feldon faced Phil and smiled. "Mr. Ross, I find myself casting about alone tonight due to Isnod's latest interest."

It took Phil a second to catch on to what Feldon was alluding to. "He works fast. Well, how about it if you join us? We're in the mood for pizza tonight and later a game or two at sliders."

Feldon smiled. "That's very generous of you, Mr. Ross. I would be delighted to join you."

After introducing Tillya to Feldon and then introducing both of them to pizza, they went up a level to sliders and shared a couple of tables. Feldon was thoroughly enjoying himself learning the game although he wasn't as good as the others who had played on and off for years. Tillya was the main surprise being the clear winner for the night.

Feldon and Phil were sitting on stools sipping beverages, watching Gus trying his level best to defeat Tillya. Feldon leaned toward Phil.

"I heard about the vessel you had salvaged earlier. There's a rumor that there were aliens on board. One rumor I heard was they're long dead, and the other rumor is they're alive and recovering in the infirmary."

Phil thought he would have some fun with Feldon. "Which rumor do you believe?"

"Given our distance from any inhabited system, I'd say you found a pair of corpses," Feldon said without hesitation.

Phil chuckled. "You'd lose that wager. We found two aliens in some kind of suspended animation unit. At the moment, they're under observation in the infirmary."

Feldon was indeed surprised. "Why are you keeping it a secret?"

Phil furrowed his brow. "We really aren't keeping it a secret. We just haven't made any announcements yet. I suppose the right thing to do would be to have some kind of reception for them and the consular generals to make introductions."

"What do they call their species?" Feldon asked. "Haldocs from the planet Vestgut," Phil answered. Feldon nodded. "I can't wait to meet them."

Tillya put the eight ball in a side pocket after caroming it off two bumpers.

She put her cue in the wall rack and said, "I've got to go to the powder room." Alice put her cue in the rack next to Tillya's. "Brenda and I will go with you."

As the girls walked off, Feldon said, "Huh, Earth woman go to the powder room in packs also."

Phil looked up from racking the balls. "I guess it's a universal female thing." "How long was Tillya a slave on Gostis?" Feldon asked while chalking his cue.

Phil stopped. "Now that is supposed to be a secret. Who told you she was a slave?"

Feldon grinned. "You just did. I wasn't sure until you confirmed it."

Gus nodded. "Pretty clever, Feldon. What made you suspect she was a slave?"

"Well, for one thing, she showed up the same night you returned from Gostis. I was told she was with two humans. Her arms and hands are scared from picking falta. Funny thing, though, she keeps to herself. I would think that she would want to be around her own people," Feldon said.

Phil shook his head. "She doesn't know who to trust."

Feldon nodded. "I can imagine why. Whatever village she comes from is probably controlled by the Syndicate. If word gets to them that she's free, they'll hurt someone in her family to send a message."

"That message would be, 'Keep quiet, or we'll go after the rest of your family,'" Phil finished for him.

Feldon nodded. "Her secret is safe with me. In fact, if there's a way to help her out, I'd be open to it." Then Feldon thought a second. "Who were the humans she arrived with?"

Phil answered, "One of the mercenaries and his wife." Feldon's frown slowly turned into a smile. "Corporal Evans?"

Phil nodded. "It's Sergeant Evans now. Tillya and Mrs. Evans became friends on Gostis."

"That made my night. I'm very happy for them," Feldon said.

Phil smiled and nodded. "I imagine there's been a lot of joyful reunions after the Gostis affair."

The girls returned to the tables, and they played one last game. On their way out of the pool hall, the man behind the counter said, "Oh, Miss Tillya, that cue you ordered should be in tomorrow."

Tillya smiled broadly. "Oh, I can't wait. Thanks, Slider."

The others stopped and looked at Tillya with bemused expressions. Finally, Phil said, "You've been practicing. That's why you've been beating up on us all night."

Tillya grinned. "It's a wonderful game. I've enjoyed improving my skills."

"I think Miss Tillya is good enough to enter tournaments," Slider offered.

They were all laughing while walking to the plaza level, where Phil, Alice, Gus, and Brenda headed to the HabMod 1 connecting tunnel.

Tillya and Feldon found themselves walking together to HabMod 4. To this point, Tillya avoided her fellow flastons because she couldn't be sure if they were part of the Syndicate or not, but Phil and Alice trusted Feldon, and she trusted their judgment. That was one of the reasons she felt very comfortable around him.

As they strolled, Tillya asked, "How come you're not on Flast anymore?" Feldon shrugged. "My partner and I were on Earth when the government on Flast fell, and we weren't sure if we would be welcomed home given our profession at the time. We've arrested so many members of the Syndicate it would have been unwise to return to Flast if the Syndicate had infiltrated the new government. As it turns out, they were entrenched pretty deep in the old government, and the new government is trying to eradicate the crime syndicate."

Tillya nodded. "I heard about you and your partner. You returned to the station with six dragons you captured."

Feldon chuckled. "I'm still sore from that experience."

Tillya smiled. "Mr. Ross said you brought back some kind of artifact that was important to Flast."

Feldon kept strolling. "I guess that sort of thing is hard to keep secret. The dragons stole the Faldos Charter. Isnod and I tracked them down and recovered it."

Tillya was trying to decide if she heard right. She stopped walking and stared at Feldon with her mouth open until, finally, she said, "They always told us it was a myth."

Feldon stopped, turned to her, and grinned. "It's real. I held it in my hands.

At least the case it was in."

Tillya was awestruck. "Did you get a chance to look at it?"

"Yes, I did, in Mr. Ross's office," Feldon answered with a hint of satisfaction in his voice.

Tillya could scarcely believe it. She shook her head and said, "The last couple of weeks have been a whirlwind of incredible events. First, I was freed from slavery on Gostis, then I was invited here to live with a job. Now I hear the Faldos Charter is real."

It was then she realized that she just told Feldon what she wanted to be kept a secret. She looked around with a panicked expression.

Feldon reassured her. "I already figured out that you were a slave." Tillya stared at him. "How…?"

Feldon smiled thinly. "I am a detective, you know. It's also reasonable to assume that the Syndicate is the reason you were made a slave."

Tillya nodded and said, "Yes, and I'm sure you know what will happen to my family if they find out I'm no longer a slave."

Feldon nodded. "Yes, I do. That's why I'm going to caution you not to trust just anyone on the station. However, you can trust my partner Isnod and myself, of course. Lynuna, the Flast consular general, although I don't know about her staff. The Rosses and the station employees are very trustworthy, in my estimation. However, there are so many people passing through the station I can't stress enough the importance of keeping your background to yourself. It's impossible to tell who can be trusted."

Tillya started walking again. "I'm not worried about myself. My family, however, would be in real trouble."

Feldon walked along. "There's a couple of things we have going for us. First, the Syndicate is busy trying to ensure its survival. Stealing the Faldos Charter is evidence of that. Second, the new government is active in rooting out corruption. Isnod and I didn't have any idea the government we worked for was as corrupt as it was. I suppose we didn't see what we didn't want to see."

Reaching the HabMod courtyard, Tillya smiled. "I'm on the sixth tier." Feldon smiled back. "I'm on three."

Tillya nodded and said, "It was a great pleasure getting to know you, Feldon.

Phil and Alice Ross like you, and I value their opinion."

Feldon bowed slightly. "I look forward to seeing you around the station."

*****

**Oasis 4, CentMod, Operations Center**

Phil had time before the morning briefing to check his correspondence. One letter stood out, and Phil opened it right away.

It was from Elias Gilmore informing him that he was departing Earth immediately for Oasis 4. There was some business he needed to discuss with Phil, and also, he wanted Phil to ensure that all company personnel who participated in the Gostis affair was on hand during his visit. Phil frowned. There was no way Elias could have received the transmission he sent him already. He must have planned on coming out anyway, which made Phil wonder what kind of business Elias wanted to discuss and why he wanted the personnel involved in the Gostis affair at hand.

Entering the briefing room, he filled a mug and sat at the head of the table.

Pulling out a pad, Phil tapped it and said, "Operations."

Virginia gave a quick outline of her upcoming day, and Phil nodded. "Station maintenance."

Will also had an average day planned. The reports were similar for security and vessel maintenance. Finally, Phil tapped his pad. "Medical."

Marie Tillman smiled. "Our guests had a good night's sleep, and they were enjoying breakfast when I left the infirmary."

Phil nodded and smiled. "After the briefing, I'd like to give them a tour of the station. Are they feeling up to it?

Marie answered, "I think we would have a tough time keeping them cooped up in the infirmary. They would welcome some exercise."

Phil put down his pad. "Great. I'll give them the nickel tour after the briefing. Virginia, I'll need a couple of things from you. First, I'd like to have a luncheon to welcome the haldocs. Please have the company cafeteria put something together in one of the banquet halls. Attending will be department heads and their 'plus ones,' consular generals and a guest, and the haldocs, of course."

Virginia was tapping notes on a pad. "I imagine you want quarters assigned to them also."

Phil smiled. "You bet, also a meal pass. They'll be with us for a few weeks at least. I received a communication from Elias this morning. He's on his way here as we speak."

"He couldn't have received our communication already!" Gus said with a flabbergasted tone.

Phil shook his head. "He said he had some things to discuss, and he wanted all company personnel who participated in the Gostis affair at hand when he arrived."

Virginia continued to make notes. "That's a bit cryptic, but we're used the way Elias runs things."

*****

## Oasis 4, Lower CentMod, Infirmary

Phil walked into the infirmary with Marie Tillman when one of her staff flagged them down. "Could I see you for a minute, Doctor, Mr. Ross?"

Marie responded, "Of course, Dr. Gilbert."

Reaching the small consultation room, Dr. Gilbert turned and smiled. "Whoever wrote the computer program for the haldocs really put a lot of thought into it."

Phil furrowed his brow. "What do you mean?"

"The haldocs realized there was a possibility that they would run into an alien culture so their computer instructed SICOS to design an introduction tutorial to educate the haldocs on a couple of subjects that range from interspecies protocol to how to use the facility's we provide for more of a personal nature. They're in their room now watching the presentation," Dr. Gilbert explained.

Phil nodded in understanding. "So they're learning acceptable ways to greet aliens and how to use the bathroom?"

Marie Tillman chuckled. "That actually makes more sense than you realize. Look at Earth's history. From region to region, the restroom facilities varied from porcelain flush toilets to holes in the floor. Hygiene standards were all over the place too."

Phil thought for a second. "Did it have a comparison of haldoc foods and what was available on the station?"

Dr. Gilbert turned to the SICOS and said, "SICOS, compare haldoc food with food on the station. Provide a list of foods that are comparable in taste and texture. Also, provide a list of foods that do not closely conform but may be acceptable to the haldocs palette."

The SICOS displayed a lengthy list after a few seconds of computing time.

Phil smiled. "Dr. Gilbert, could you please pass this along to Virginia in operations and have her pass it along to the cafeteria staff?"

Dr. Gilbert nodded. "Will do."

He then checked SICOS. "It looks like the tutorial is almost over." Phil and Marie entered the haldocs room just as the tutorial finished.

Votlor and Rok stood and enthusiastically shook hands with Phil and Marie.

Votlor smiled. "Are we doing this correctly?"

Phil smiled back. "Yes, you are. If you gentlemen are up to it, we can start the tour of the station."

"We've been very anxious to see your station. We're very excited," Rok said with a smile.

Phil nodded. "Well, let's get started."

Phil led them out of the infirmary onto the plaza level of the Lower CentMod. Votlor and Rok stopped and took the view while Phil pointed out various features. Finally, he indicated toward the platform lift. "This way, gentlemen."

On the trip up to the Upper CentMod, Phil continued to point out things that they might be interested in. Both Votlor and Rok were wide eyed as the lift entered the extension that connected the two CentMods. Phil explained they were now in the original CentMod, and he continued to point out items of interest.

*****

## Oasis 4, Upper CentMod, Operations Center

The platform lift stopped at the top, where Phil led Votlor and Rok to the operations center. They stopped, and Phil introduced them to Virginia, then he led them to the control center. This was the first time since their arrival they saw outside. Their attention was immediately drawn to the nebula, and Votlor asked, "Our home planet is on the interior of that?"

"Yes, it is," Gus answered.

They turned to face Gus, and he introduced himself, "Hi, I'm Gus Condent, the assistant station manager and one of the extraordinarily skilled pilots that went to retrieve your ship."

Votlor and Rok both grinned. "We are very much indebted to you," Rok said. Votlor asked, "Exactly where were we when you encountered us?"

Gus pointed in the direction of the nebula. "Do you see that particularly bright spot toward the bottom? We picked you up just this side of that spot. We have a presentation on this to show you later."

Votlor and Rok were fascinated with the activity both inside the control center and outside. Gus was kept busy answering questions mostly about the various vessels they saw. They were also very interested in the procedures that were being followed to control the traffic.

After a few minutes, Phil said, "Gus, why don't we go to the briefing room and see if we can give them more detail about their voyage?"

Votlor and Rok followed Phil down the stairs with Gus trailing. Entering the briefing room, Phil had the pair take seats, and then he put a full coffee carafe on a tray with cups, cream, and sugar. "Some people consider this to be an acquired taste. I like to drink it black with no sugar. Some folks like to add a little cream and/or sugar," Phil explained, pointing out the cream and sugar.

Gus grabbed a mug, poured some coffee, and added some cream and sugar. Then he mixed it with a stirrer. He went first to demonstrate and prevent Votlor and Rok from becoming concerned about committing a social faux pas and becoming uncomfortable.

Both Votlor and Rok tried some without condiments and declared that the drink was just fine the way it was. When everyone had something to drink, Phil leaned back in his chair. "SICOS, dim lights and display holographic representation of this sector."

The space over their heads filled with stars. Votlor and Rok were suitably impressed with what they saw. Phil continued, "SICOS, highlight Oasis 4 and Vestgut."

The two points glowed brighter, and Phil said, "SICOS, replay voyage of the *Mystery Ship* beginning at Vestgut."

They watched as a line traced from Vestgut and headed to the nebula. Rok asked, "Is there a way to see lapsed time from our launch?"

Gus nodded and said, "SICOS, attach time indexes in both Earth time and Vestgut time beginning from the commencement of the recorded journey."

The time indexes appeared below the *Mystery Ship*. They all watched as the *Mystery Ship* entered the nebula. Votlor nodded. "So far, it appears just as we planned it."

The course line started to veer. Slightly at first, then the curve became sharper as time went on. Votlor frowned. "The computer should have corrected it by now. In fact, we should have barely seen any anomalous course changes." "Could you please pause the playback?" Rok asked.

Gus nodded. "SICOS, pause playback."

Rok asked, "Did your computer download the data from the course correction input/output/net result calculator?"

Gus leaned back. "Yes, it did. However, we weren't sure what to make of the data."

"We knew we wouldn't be able to visually detect stars and planets once we entered the Great Barrier, so a system was developed to detect stars and their planets using the gravitational effect these bodies have on the vessel. As the measurements were made and cataloged, the computer would calculate the size, type, and a number of such things," Rok explained.

Phil shook his head. "That's amazing. How accurate is the system?" "Let's find out. SICOS, overlay data from input/output/net result calculator," Gus said with a smile.

The holographic display got more interesting. Votlor gasped and said, "That's denser than we thought it might be."

Rok stared at the display. "This is a most impressive system you have. As you can see, the system has calculated the position of stars and their attending planets.

Phil asked, "Why are the stars and planets surrounded by a halo?" "They're depicted in their probable location. The actual location is somewhere in the shaded areas," Rok explained.

Votlor couldn't take his eyes off the display. "We thought the number of systems in the Great Barrier would be the same as outside of it, and it is obvious that we were very much mistaken. I wonder if the Great Barrier was formed because there is an excessive number of stars here or the stars formed because of the Great Barrier."

Gus shook his head. "The stars were here first."

Votlor frowned. "How could you possibly know that?"

"Simple, they can be seen somewhat clearly from our home planet."

Rok shook his head. "That requires more explanation. How are you able to see through the Barrier from your planet, but everything is obscure at this distance?"

Gus smiled. "The nebula formed after the light from the stars was emitted. It'll be a long time before the reflected light from the nebula reaches Earth. Until then, we can see systems that are presently engulfed in the nebula as long as we're far enough away."

Votlor and Rok both chuckled, and Votlor said, "Of course, we should have guessed that. It's a very different way of thinking when you have to consider the vastness of it all."

Rok asked, "Can you get enough resolution to see planets in the Barrier?"

Gus shook his head. "I'm afraid not. At the distance, we would need to get to do that. The nebula has already thoroughly obscured the area."

"In that respect, your equipment has increased our knowledge of what's in there," Phil observed.

Gus straightened in his seat. "SICOS, use archival data with data currently displayed to update star charts."

SICOS made the update, and the holographic display changed once again. The SICOS mechanical voice warned, "The data inside the Great Barrier Nebula is not complete. It is not advisable to rely on this data for navigation."

Phil studied the display and finally said, "SICOS, resume playback."

The playback resumed, and Rok had Gus add thruster and engine data to the time indexes. After a time, Votlor said, "I see what happened. We were being pulled off course, and the computer kept correcting. The number of corrections needed was well beyond what we anticipated. You, gentlemen, were right. We were indeed very lucky we were spotted."

Gus nodded. "We had a chance to look at the data further. We found that your computer had a built-in instruction to prevent the pods from automatically waking you up if a set of conditions occurred that prevented your return to Vestgut."

Votlor and Rok absorbed the information. Finally, Rok let out a breath. "It's probably a good thing they didn't tell us about that feature before we left."

Gus restarted the playback then, in a couple of seconds, said, "This is where we picked you up."

The haldocs were interested in the salvage operation itself, so Gus ordered SICOS to display a holographic presentation of the operation. The Mystery Ship appeared over their heads, and they watched as the *Aurora* positioned itself under the *Mystery Ship*.

Votlor asked, "Did you have another ship recording this?"

Gus shook his head. "The *Aurora* has recording equipment, and the work suits our technicians wore while working outside the ship also have recording devices. All the data is put together, and the computer will create a composite presentation."

Rok nodded. "That's actually very clever."

When the recovery presentation finished, Phil said, "There's one more thing to show you before we tour the station. SICOS, display representation of this sector."

The stars reappeared over their heads. Phil continued, "Highlight Oasis 4 and Vestgut." Two points glowed, then Phil started naming the different inhabited planets starting with the closest. As he went through the list, the display would expand to accommodate everything. Soon, a very large portion of the galaxy was clearly discernable, which awed the haldocs.

"I see that we are a long distance from your home planet. In fact, we're a long way from any of the worlds. Why do you do business so far away?" Votlor asked.

Phil smiled. "SICOS, highlight the other Oasis stations."

Oasis 1 through 3 were highlighted, and Phil explained, "We maintain trading stations at locations we refer to as crossroads. As goods pass between worlds, we provide convenient locations for freight companies to store and transfer their products."

Rok frowned. "From what you've told us so far, our planet was about three or four hundred years ahead of yours when we began our journey. I wonder if our people have developed a means of propulsion that allows us to travel faster than light. If they did, why haven't they found a passage through the Great Barrier."

"We found a passage through it quite by accident. Your people probably haven't found a passage yet," Gus offered.

Votlor nodded. "That very well may be. I guess we'll never know for sure until we return to Vestgut.

After all the useful information they had for the haldocs had been gone through, Phil led them on tour. On the ride down on the platform lift, Votlor and Rok were again awed at the sight of the CentMod interior. Stopping at the plaza level, Phil pointed out various points of interest. They made their way to CargoMod 2, where a quick tour of the *Aurora* was in order.

While standing in the *Aurora* cockpit, Rok frowned. "We're experiencing gravity. How is it we're experiencing gravity?"

Phil smiled. "I was wondering if you were going to notice. We use gravity generators in the deck plating. They're similar to the inertia neutralizers that were installed in your suspended animation pods."

Votlor nodded. "You must have a very advanced design. Ours consume a great deal of power, which is why their use was limited to the pods."

Phil continued their tour of the CargoMod, where they watched a freighter dock, then the off-loading process started."

Noon came almost unexpectedly, and Phil led the haldocs to the banquet hall used for the reception. The cafeteria staff did an exceptional job, in Phil's opinion, being as they had seven separate races with different palettes. After a light lunch, everyone had a chance to meet the haldocs and give them their regards. To Phil's eye, it looked like the pretars were actually happy that the haldocs were roughly their own height.

At one point, Alice asked if they had anything else to wear. Votlor shook his head. "We hadn't considered the possibility of spending more than a few days taking scientific readings before getting back in the pods.

Phil grinned. "It's a good thing we have someone who likes to shop. Alice, why don't you spend an hour or two after lunch, making sure these two have something decent to wear while they're here? Afterward, we'll get them settled."

Virginia presented the haldocs with a meal pass each and explained how to use them. She also told them what their quarter's assignments were in HabMod 4.

Phil judged the reception a success, as did the attendees. Afterward, Phil and Alice took Votlor and Rok clothes shopping in the CentMod. There was a retail store on the station that was part of a chain of stores on Earth. It was a slightly smaller version of the rest of the outlets on Earth since a hardware and sporting goods department wasn't practical at this location.

Alice was a bit flustered at first until she discovered clothes made for boys in their early teens fit the haldocs nicely. Phil was relieved that he didn't have to keep Alice from overspending, being it was company money, although the company could more than afford it. Really he was trying to prevent the haldocs from getting overwhelmed. As it turned out, the retailer didn't stock a great deal of clothes in those sizes, but they managed to get Votlor and Rok a decent wardrobe.

The store manager sent the purchases to Votlor and Rok's quarters while Phil and Alice walked them to the HabMod. After stepping through the connecting passage into the HabMod central core, they took an escalator down to the first level, where the service area was located. They pointed out the fitness center and the cafeteria although they could eat anywhere with their meal passes. Finally, they showed them the laundry area and explained that there was an attendant assigned to this area during specified times if they needed assistance.

*****

## Oasis 4, Upper CentMod, Eva's Café

After acquainting the haldocs with their quarters, Phil and Alice took them to dinner at Eva's. Both Votlor and Rok found items on the menu that they thought weren't completely foreign to them. While having their after-dinner coffees, Votlor said, "Please don't misread what I'm about to ask, but what are your intentions towards us? Quite obviously, our ship is incapable of the journey back to Vestgut, and we would never ask you deliver us home, as it would be a tremendous undertaking. Please don't think us ungrateful. We're tremendously grateful."

Phil smiled. "I'm sorry if I left you with the impression that we weren't going to take you home. Right now, it's my number one priority. I'm kind of stumbling through this process because there isn't an established procedure for what we're doing here, at least none that I'm aware of."

Rok furrowed his brow. "What exactly will we be doing in the meantime?"

Phil chuckled. "Like I said, there's no established protocol for what we're doing, so we'll take it one logical step at a time. I'm not sure how much we can accomplish since you, gents, are a few centuries out of time. One thing that you must have a very clear understanding of is we don't represent any particular government, so we're not in a position to make any treaties. We can make trade agreements though. After all, that's what we're out here for. I've been giving it some thought, and I think what we'll do is have representatives from each of the conciliates give you a presentation of what kind of trade goods they have to offer and what kinds of goods they are interested in acquiring."

Votlor shook his head. "I'm afraid we're out of our element in these matters, Mr. Ross. Rok and I are scientists. I'm afraid trade negotiations are something we aren't trained for, and as you said earlier, we're centuries out of time. Our planet's needs and desires are bound to have changed."

Phil nodded. "We're not looking for binding agreements. Like it or not, you two represent the interest of Vestgut. It's going to be up to you to help make the introductions on your planet. The information about trade goods is a means to facilitate a dialogue. To be honest, my biggest concern is the initial encounter. You'll be arriving in a vessel very different from the one you left in. It may take a while to convince the folks in your world you are who you say you are."

Rok nodded. "I guess we are quite a bit overdue. When do you expect we can begin our return trip?"

Phil thought for a second or two. "The corporate president sent me a message saying he was on his way here starting today. It's a three-week journey from Earth, and he'll want to spend at least a week after his arrival personally getting to know you. There's also some corporate business he needs to deal with. I hate to ask you for patience being as you've been away from your home for so long already."

Votlor laughed. "After a few centuries, what's another thirty days or so? Besides, from our perspective, because of our slumber, it feels like we've only been away a few days."

Rok stifled a yawn, and Alice remarked, "You two have had a big day. Why don't you go back to your quarters and get a good night's rest?"

The haldocs smiled, and Votlor said, "That's a good idea. This has been an eventful day."

"Why don't you two come up to the ops center around 1000 Zulu, and we can start what we talked about."

Over the next couple of weeks, Votlor and Rok met with representatives from the conciliates at the station. All parties involved understood that the haldocs weren't in a position to even understand or anticipate the needs or desires of their home planet as far as trade goes. Most of the information they collected was statistical. For instance, they found out what kind of metals each planet used and the products they're known for. Also, they found the cultural information quite interesting and useful for preparing their own report, which they devoted a good deal of time on.

*****

**Oasis 4, CargoMod 8, Maintenance Hangar No. 3**

After two weeks, the haldocs had met with representatives from each of the conciliates and compiled as much information for their report for their home planet. Jeremy took the opportunity to have Votlor and Rok answer questions about their ship. That's when they found out that Votlor was the mission commander and chief scientist while Rok was the mission pilot. That's not to say they couldn't do each other's job; it was an excellent way to ensure that the mission would be a success.

Rok went through the cockpit controls while Jeremy and Chad looked on. Later, Votlor demonstrated the mission equipment they were going to use. Votlor thought it was a shame that he wouldn't get a chance to use any of it, but Jeremy assured him that he would be supplied with a database that far exceeds anything they could have gathered with the equipment they brought with them.

Chad was sitting on the floor of the haldoc ship when a thought occurred to him. He furrowed his brow and asked, "How did you get this in space? It doesn't appear to me that there's enough engine here to get it off a planet's surface."

"We assembled it in orbit," Rok answered.

Chad nodded. "You sent it to orbit in sections on rockets then?" Votlor frowned. "That would be wasteful. We used an orbital climber." Jeremy frowned. "You just lost me."

Votlor smiled. "Excuse me, I assumed that everyone had met the challenge of getting payloads into space in the same manner. Picture a space station in geosynchronous orbit, and the station is attached to the planet with a structure."

Chad nodded. "I've read about those, at least the theoretical concept. Personnel and cargos are loaded in a capsule, and the capsule quite literally climbs into orbit. I've always heard it called an Orbiting Tether."

Jeremy gave Chad a sideways look. "Where exactly did you read about that?" "Mostly science fiction," Chad said with a grin. He thought about it for a second and added, "The underlying theory is solid, though. We've always found it easier to send vehicles into orbit with reaction engines although an orbiting tether solves a lot of problems. There is one drawback is, though, building one is an enormous undertaking. How did you go about it?"

Votlor leaned back. "We did use a rocket to put a satellite into orbit. The satellite achieved geosynchronous orbit and lowered a fine cord from a spool. Once the cord was attached to the proper point on Vestgut, a miniature climber was attached and used to apply additional cords. When the cord is sufficiently enlarged, a larger climber is employed to apply larger amounts of cords. Eventually, there's enough structure and rigidity to add a framework and send sections up to construct a station."

Jeremy was impressed. "That must take a great amount of precision. How do you control the unwanted oscillations?"

"Thrusters mounted to the orbiter are used to dampen unwanted movement," Votlor explained.

Chad asked, "What material did you make the cord out of?"

"A material that you call Carbon Nanotubes. Once they're in place, the structure is reinforced with a metal I've learned that you call paxtite," Votlor offered.

Jeremy's eyes widened. "That's a lot of paxtite! We've only just recently discovered a source for paxtite ore in quantities that we can use in more standard applications and not just special projects."

Rok furrowed his brow. "I'm not surprised. It's not an extraordinarily common material on Vestgut, so it is carefully rationed. However, once it has been determined that a project is worthy, the metal is made available for it. In fact, this vessel is constructed of paxtite."

Chad examined some bare metal. "Oh my gosh! Why didn't I notice that earlier?" He then pulled a magnifier out of his pocket and a flashlight. After studying the metal, he handed Jeremy the tools and said, "You need to check this out."

Jeremy took the magnifier and flashlight. He looked at a couple of different patches of bare metal. "This is remarkable. I've never seen paxtite with a grain structure this perfect. You guys must have a very advanced refining and alloying process."

Votlor nodded. "We've spent a great deal of resources perfecting the refining process since it's a material found in limited quantities."

Jeremy smiled. "Well, if they haven't lost their skills on your planet, there's a commodity right there that's in high demand."

*****

## Oasis 4, HabMod 4, Food Court

Isnod and Feldon were having their after-breakfast tea discussing whether they were fit enough to return to their bounty hunting. Both were reluctant to admit their injuries were as difficult to recover from as they were. This morning's fitness training and micton practice told them they were indeed nearly back to their old selves. They were under doctors' orders to limit their activities, and both bounty hunters were careful not to push themselves too hard.

Feldon was taking a sip of tea when a flaston walked up behind Isnod. Before Feldon could swallow his mouthful of tea, Isnod put down his cup and said, "Ivonorsic, a human space station is an unusual place to open a micton studio. Don't you think?"

Ivonorsic walked around so that Isnod wouldn't have to turn around to see him, then he nodded slowly. "I'm grateful to see you've remembered that micton teaches us to be aware of our surroundings."

Isnod motioned to an empty chair inviting Ivonorsic to sit. As Ivonorsic took a seat, Isnod said, "We saw the micton studio and made subtle inquiries. I thought it would be interesting to see how long it would take for you to discover your finest pupil was living on the station."

Ivonorsic laughed at Isnod's "finest pupil" quip as he adjusted himself in the chair. After taking a sip of his own tea, he said, "I'm embarrassed to admit that I didn't know you were here until I spotted you a few minutes ago."

Isnod smiled. "Back to my original question, do you really expect a micton studio to be successful on a human space station?"

Ivonorsic nodded. "Actually, I do. Micton teaches us to make the most of an unusual situation."

Feldon furrowed his brow. "I thought micton taught us to be aware of our surroundings?"

"Micton teaches us a lot of things!" Ivonorsic shot back with a slight edge in his voice.

A thin smile formed on Feldon's face.

Ivonorsic instantly realized that he had just been baited successfully. He looked at Feldon and smiled. "Very good, Isnod's young friend. I suppose I should remember that micton also teaches us humility."

Isnod was grinning. "Ivonorsic, meet my partner, Feldon. Feldon, this is my micton teacher, Master Ivonorsic."

Ivonorsic continued, "To finish my answer, I do actually expect an adequate number of students. I have a partner due to arrive from Earth. He's an expert in several human martial arts disciplines. I expect we'll attract not only beginners but those who want to add new skills or perfect existing ones.

Ivonorsic continued, "I understand you have been keeping up with your micton practice. Our fellow flastons told me before I came over here that you two are hard at it in the fitness center whenever you're on the station. In fact, they said some weeks ago, you two captured six members of the Dragons. They tell me you were unarmed, but to be honest, I find it hard to believe given that among them was Hindor, Brinot, and Tonbor."

Feldon chuckled. "Two of the three you didn't mention were actually much more of a challenge."

"To put your mind at ease, we weren't armed, and yes, we used micton to defeat them," Isnod added.

Ivonorsic didn't try to hide how impressed he was. He nodded and asked, "Did they do any damage?"

Isnod chuckled. "That's what we were discussing before you walked up. We've decided that we've healed enough to restart our full training regime. We'll have to get the doctor's okay first, of course."

Ivonorsic stood. "Anytime you want to hone a micton maneuver, come see me. In fact, perhaps you two could give my students a demonstration. Seeing two former fugitive trackers and current bounty hunters in action would be invaluable. Watching micton in a studio is one thing but seeing a demonstration from someone who has used it in an actual situation is very instructional."

Isnod and Feldon promised that they would consider Ivonorsic's offer. After Ivonorsic left them, Feldon said, "I suppose we should use the SICOS to make a doctor's appointment.

Isnod finished his tea. "Let's go to the office and get it done."

*****

## Oasis 4, Upper CentMod, Station Museum

Alice had just opened the museum for the day when Votlor and Rok arrived. Alice smiled and greeted them, "Hi, guys. It's about time you two decided to pay the museum a visit."

Both haldocs smiled, and Votlor said, "Trust us. It's been on our list of things to do while we're here, but we've been so busy meeting representatives from different worlds. I think we're finally getting to the end of the useful information we can gather."

Alice nodded. "Well, take your time, guys. This time of day, we aren't particularly busy."

The haldocs indeed took their time. They found each display fascinating and made careful notes that they planned on using to put some polish on their report.

When they had finished touring the museum, they wandered into the gift shop. Votlor commented with a chuckle that it was pointless to shop here since anyone they might be inclined to buy a gift for was long gone. Just then, Rok spotted the book section. The selection of books had been steadily improving since the museum's opening. On Earth, most of the books were what would be referred to as coffee table books with topics that ranged from geography and zoology of each of the worlds they did business with, to books with art and ship recognition.

Alice had avoided asking what the haldoc's plans were in regard to their vessel, but she couldn't stand it any longer. Besides, she had an idea that she could make an offer that would be hard to turn down. She approached the haldocs. "What are your plans for your vessel?"

Votlor and Rok were caught flat-footed, as they hadn't considered what the disposition of their small ship would be.

Alice smiled in a manner that would give Phil anxiety although the haldocs weren't used to her mannerisms. She said, "I think it would be a great addition to the museum if only we had something to trade for it." Votlor and Rok looked through the door into the museum. Then they looked at the books in their hands. They looked up at a smiling

Alice and broke out in grins of their own. Alice had successfully traded a copy of each book offered in the gift shop for a once-used spaceship. The haldocs were pleased with the deal as they thought the books would make their report that much more complete.

*****

## Oasis 4, Lower CentMod, Plaza Level

Isnod and Feldon walked out of the infirmary with the doctor's blessings to restart their training in earnest. They have been exercising as part of their physical therapy and rehabilitation, but they were under the doctor's orders to limit themselves. Feldon checked the time. "It's about lunchtime. What do you say we go to the Upper CentMod and get a couple of slices of pizza?"

Isnod frowned. "I haven't tried it. Does it make a decent lunch?" Feldon shrugged. "It's not bad if you don't indulge too much."

Isnod chuckled. "You just described many things about the humans. Let's give it a try."

The pair took the platform lift to the Upper CentMod Plaza Level. Reaching the kiosk that sold pizza by the slice, Feldon discovered the pizza here was more convenient at the expense of variety. The kiosk only offered three varieties of pizza: pepperoni and cheese, deluxe, and Chicago style. The deluxe was like the pepperoni and cheese, except it also had green peppers and mushrooms. The Chicago style was much thicker, had pepperoni, cheese, ham, and this establishment was unique as they added a top crust. They decided to get a slice from each to see what kind they liked for future reference.

After purchasing their slices and a soft drink each, they took the escalators to the fifth-tier level and found a sitting area that offered a view of the nebula. Just as they sat, Yulona strolled up to them, holding a fruit cocktail he had bought at a different kiosk. He looked down and asked with a smile, "Can I join you?"

The pair looked up and smiled back. Feldon said, "Yes, of course. It would be a great pleasure."

"The humans can be curious people, don't you think?" Yulona asked as he studied a chunk of watermelon on the end of his fork.

Isnod nodded. "We're of that opinion, but I'm curious as to why you think so."

Yulona put the watermelon chunk in his mouth and nodded approval. While selecting another piece of fruit, he said, "I'm referring to their practices, where it comes to eating. They seem to be all over the place as to the amount of protocol that's appropriate. Right now, we're sharing a meal together in a fashion that's decidedly casual. At the other end of the scale, they'll have extensive and elaborate banquets for special occasions. I've seen Mr. Ross and his staff conduct business during meals, and I've seen humans who obviously preferred their own company while taking in nourishment."

Feldon thought for a second. "It looks to me like they've found a balance in such things. I've noticed that they observe proprieties appropriate to the occasion. That being said, they seem to enjoy eating in a communal fashion whenever possible."

At that moment, Pindon strolled up carrying a chili dog and fries basket and a root beer. After sitting, he smiled and said, "I see why you two decided to stay on this station. Human food is best described as fun." Feldon chuckled. "You should be more careful about what you eat. That stuff is okay every now and again, but too much, and you're looking for a tailor to let out your uniform." Pindon laughed. "Lucky I'll be leaving soon."

"I was wondering if you were going to take up permanent residence," Isnod quipped.

Yulona looked around to make sure there was no one near enough to overhear them. He said in a low voice, "I wanted to ask you if you would be of service to Flast one more time."

Isnod and Feldon leaned in closer, and Isnod answered, "Yes, of course. What can we do?"

Yulona kept his voice low. "We were wondering if you could take the Charter the rest of the way home."

Isnod frowned. "We would be proud to, but I thought you already had that operation worked out."

"We did," Pindon answered, "but our operatives on Flast have discovered that there's someone on the station passing information to the Syndicate. They've tried to grab all the fake Charters we've sent back."

Feldon felt a small surge of panic. "Do you have any idea who it is?" Pindon shrugged. "Not really. We've double-checked the consulate staff, but there are a number of flaston businesses on the station.

There are freight forwarders, brokers, and commodity dealers, just to name a few."

Isnod nodded. "You can probably cross Ivonorsic off that list.

Micton teaches us integrity."

Feldon suppressed a chuckle. "I'll have to add that to the list of things that micton teaches us."

Pindon smiled. "He's a bit overly dedicated to the mystique of micton, but there's an excellent reason the Law Enforcement Brigade hired him to instruct. There is one other flaston here that's a bit of a mystery. She works in the station's operations center."

"You can definitely take her off the list," Feldon interjected.

Isnod and Pindon were in the dark as to why Feldon said that with as much assurance as he did. Isnod asked, "What do you know that I don't know?"

Yulona leaned in. "This stays between us. The young lady working for Mr. Ross was up until, recently, a slave on Gostis. She was sold to a slave trader by the Syndicate boss that controlled her village. Apparently, that happens sometimes. If a crime boss needs capital or consideration within the organization, some villagers get sold."

Isnod frowned. "We flastons have always been told that we've never enslaved each other. Now we're finding out how common of a practice it really was."

Yulona nodded. "Entire villages would be taken over, the people terrorized into compliance. No one dares testify against them, or family members disappear. Our best hope in dismantling the Syndicate is to get one of the members to start talking. We just need one who wants to save their own skin. Then they start to unravel."

Pindon shook his head and said sarcastically, "Oh, is that all? From what we've experienced of the Syndicate, they would rather go to the grave than give testimony against their peers."

"That puts the young lady in a very ticklish situation," Isnod observed.

Feldon asked, "Has anyone made the Flast Criminal Database available to Security Marshal Smith?"

Pindon nodded. "We have."

Isnod frowned. "This station has state-of-the-art facial recognition equipment. If it hasn't alerted, then whoever the Syndicate informant is, hasn't been put into the system. That means they're new, low level, and probably looking for any opportunity to move up."

"I'm going to brief Security Marshal Smith about the informant. Technically if this person, whoever it is, doesn't break any station regulations, station security won't have legal authority to curtail his efforts," Pindon said.

Feldon slowly shook his head. "The staff on this station has demonstrated an unusual ability to get desirable results and stay within agreements. Also, I would think that they would want to know if a Syndicate agent was on the station."

Yulona nodded. "We'll have to rely on the resourcefulness of Security Marshal Smith and his staff on that issue. We'll give him as much support as we can, of course, but we have limited resources here. I suggest we concentrate our attention on getting the Faldos Charter back to Flast, where it belongs.

Isnod nodded. "What's your plan for doing that?"

Yulona looked around again to make sure no one approached them without their notice, then said, "We'll be returning to Flast in two days on a flaston transport. Rabot and I will have the Charter case. It will be empty, of course. You two will have an equipment case containing the Charter. After the flaston transport leaves, you two will use your Pulsar 1250 to bring the Charter home with Pindon. We'll take steps to give the impression that you two will be assisting Pindon in tracking down a fugitive wanted by Flast. With the speed of your Pulsar, I estimate you'll get to Flast just before we do."

Seeing that everyone had finished eating, Isnod stood. "Why don't we meet in our office where we can talk freely."

The four flastons relocated to the office of I&F Investigations and Retrievals to work out the details on how to safely get the Faldos Charter back to Flast.

*****

## Oasis 4, CargoMod 1, Docking Port 1

The day had finally come—that Elias Gilmore was scheduled to arrive. As Phil and Alice waited for the company Pulsar 5500 to finish the docking procedure, Phil looked around and realized that he hadn't been to CargoMod 1 since they finished converting it into a passenger terminal. It actually turned out quite nice. When it was announced that the conversion to a passenger-focused facility was going to take place, Phil had his doubts about how it would end up.

The umbilicals were connected, and the airlock seal safety was checked by a station worker. The airlock opened, and Elias Gilmore and his wife stepped out. Spotting Phil and Alice, he broke out in a grin. "There's my favorite couple."

Phil shook hands with Elias while Alice gave his wife a hug. "Veronica, it's so good to see you! I wish Phil had mentioned you were coming."

Veronica Gilmore, a short, pudgy woman with a kind face, was well aware of how Alice loved to give Phil grief, whether it was deserved or not. She smiled and said, "Don't blame Phil. I decided last minute to tag along."

Norton Parker and a pilot Phil knew, named Kyle Desmond, along with an Air Force colonel stepped through the airlock. Phil smiled. "Hey, Nort, how do you like the Pulsar?"

Norton grinned. "It doesn't haul like the Astrodyne, but it doesn't have to. I'll trade utility for that kind of speed any day."

He then motioned to the two at his side. "You remember Kyle Desmond, of course, and this is Colonel Fitzgerald."

While Phil shook their hands, Elias said, "Colonel Fitzgerald has a presentation tomorrow. I thought we would do it tomorrow at noon in the Upper CentMod Plaza Level."

Phil nodded. "I'll have Virginia set it up. In the meantime, let's get all of you fed up and bedded down."

*****

## Oasis 4, Upper CentMod, Maurice's

Phil had arranged to have dinner at Maurice's to welcome Elias and the rest. During the after-dessert coffees, Elias wanted to know how everyone was doing since he was at the station last. He asked, "How is Miss Tillya doing?

Phil smiled. "She's a wonderful addition to our team. I couldn't be more pleased."

Elias nodded and said with a smile, "I'm very happy to hear that. But I didn't spend three weeks in a shuttle to find that out. The reason I'm here is Oasis 4 is due to get another expansion."

Phil was floored. "We're not using the existing CargoMods to capacity yet."

Elias shrugged. "I know that, but we're not adding CargoMods. We're adding an ore storage module. It will mount below the Lower CentMod and have compartments for six different kinds of ore. Once we've completed our business here, I'm meeting with Space Habitat and systems Company to finalize the details."

Phil grinned. "I hope they use the same crew for this project that added the Lower Section."

Elias smiled back. "If it's an option, I'll insist on it. I'll also ask them to keep better control of their kortlax."

Phil nearly spit out his coffee. "You heard about that, did ya?" Elias laughed. "Earth is a long way off, but news does reach me.

For instance, right now, I'm wondering when you plan on telling me about the haldocs."

Phil was happy he didn't have a mouthful of coffee again. "I was wondering if the news caught up with you. I did plan on asking you if you received my communication."

"When were you going to ask?" Elias asked with a bit of mirth in his voice.

Phil looked apologetic. "Well, between the main course and dessert. When did my message catch up with you?"

Elias nodded. "We stopped at Raytheon for a meeting when I received the communication. Tell me, what are they like?"

Phil weighed the question. "Physically, they're much like us. If you didn't know better, you would swear they were pre-adolescent humans. A couple of minutes into a conversation with them you realize how intelligent they are. They've been away from Vestgut for 522 years. That means any information they have about their planet and their people is hopelessly out of date. We can get a general idea of what they're like, but five Earth centuries is a long time."

Elias nodded. "That's what the situation sounded like from your communication. We've got some business that needs to be done here. Then we'll take them back to Vestgut. We won't know if they're interested in commerce until we meet them. In fact, we won't know how they'll react to us until we're face to face."

Phil said, "We may be all right on that score. When they launched, they were open to the idea that they might encounter other species on their journey."

Elias nodded. "It sounds like they're open-minded. That is unless they've changed in the last couple of hundred years."

After dinner and coffee, Phil and Alice saw their guests to their quarters and retired themselves.

*****

## Oasis 4, Upper CentMod, Briefing Room

The morning briefing started at the usual time with the usual participants with the addition of Elias Gilmore. Phil started the briefing after pouring a cup of coffee. "Morning, everyone. Before we start our regular briefing, Elias has an announcement that affects all of us."

Elias smiled and stood and greeted everyone. "Hello, all. It's great to be back on Oasis 4."

Everyone answered back in unison, "Hi, Elias."

Elias chuckled. "I've missed that. I already told Phil yesterday that the station will be getting another expansion in the coming weeks. It won't be as extensive as the last one, but it will add a good deal of capability."

He dimmed the lights and activated the holographic projection system. An image of the station hovered over their heads. Elias had SICOS add the new section and gave everyone time to get an idea of the size of the structure. He then went step by step, explaining the sequence of events in the construction of the new section and its integration into the existing station.

"Phase one will be preparing the station with the necessary fittings and equipment needed to join the new section and the Lower CentMod," Elias narrated while the display added the items to the existing station.

Elias continued, "The new addition is being built by the pretar firm, space habitat, and systems Company, at their construction yards. It'll be shipped here and assembled at a position we designate then it will be moved into position and attached to the station."

"Are there any questions?" Elias asked, looking around.

Virginia raised her hand. "Looking at the new section, am I to assume it's strictly for storage of bulk material?"

Elias nodded. "Yes, that's right. According to the Superior Mining Corporation of Duluth, Minnesota, they'll put the capacity of the new unit to the test with the discovery of the Anna Mae asteroid belt."

"One more question, what size ships are we going to be seeing?" Virginia asked.

Elias smiled. "Intersystems shipping company has a new class of bulk carrier that will handle up to sixty thousand tons. They will be handling the iron ore, and smaller vessels will handle the paxtite."

Will Dawson asked, "What is the timetable for completion?"

Elias leaned back. "That's one of the things we have to work out with the pretars when I pay them a visit. However, they assured me it would take eight months to a year. They'll be starting work here within a month."

With no one else having any questions, Elias turned the meeting back to Phil. Virginia, Marie, Jeremy, and Will gave their reports. Luke pulled out his pad. "I had an interesting conversation with Isnod, Feldon, and that flaston law enforcement officer, Pindon. It seems there's a Syndicate informant on the station giving information about when the Charter is being moved. They're under the impression that the informant is flaston. I offered my opinion that the Syndicate didn't necessarily have to use a flaston informant, but they felt that the flaston Syndicate branch would want to keep things in-house."

Phil frowned. "I don't like the idea of a Syndicate member living on the station. What are you doing to find this guy?"

"I gave Isnod and the boys some ideas on how to flush out whoever it is. They were under the impression that we would be reluctant to arrest them if it didn't affect us negatively. I assured them that any members of the Syndicate, whether they violate station rules or not, will be arrested and sent to a planet that offers the longest prison term."

Phil interrupted, "Or shoved out the nearest airlock."

Everyone agreed they wouldn't be too fussed if a member of the Syndicate floated past their window. Phil adjourned the meeting, and everyone went to work.

*****

## Oasis 4, Lower CentMod, Office of I&F
## Investigations and Retrievals

Isnod, Feldon, and Pindon were busy working out a plan to smoke out the informant. Pindon leaned back in his chair. "This deception to find out who is passing information will strengthen our earlier plan to convince everyone that we were going to track down a fugitive. Now, where do you suggest we begin?"

Isnod furrowed his brow. "We have fifteen flastons on the station, who we can't substantiate or confirm they're not affiliated with the Syndicate. So we need the names of fifteen fugitives who have well-known ties to a single location."

"Why a single location?" Feldon asked.

"To limit the number of people we have to make inquiries to and to have a predictable baseline concerning the reliability of the information we get," Isnod answered.

Pindon laughed. "The sleaziest place I can think of that meets that criterion would be Kassnins."

Isnod shook his head. "There isn't anyone there we can rely on for dependable information."

Feldon chuckled. "I'll bet the guy at the shuttle port would be glad to help." Isnod shook his head again. "Let's keep things flaston. Our best bet is Treest.

There's more than enough bad characters on Treest to suit our needs, and we have an informant of our own there."

Pindon nodded. "I remember now that you had access to pretty reliable information on Treest."

Feldon nodded and directed SICOS to start a search for wanted criminals who frequented Treest. There were plenty of names to go through. The tricky part was finding a felon that would have had a plausible reason to have contact with the flastons on the station.

*****


**Upper CentMod, Plaza Level**


As requested, Virginia arranged for a presentation at 1300 Zulu on the plaza level of the Upper CentMod. There was a microphone stand and a small table setup. Announcements were posted on the news boards scattered throughout the station, and Virginia made sure all the consulates received a memo informing them of the presentation. Phil and the other company personnel who participated in the Gostis affair were on hand. He could see that a crowd was gathering that included the consular generals and much of their staff.

Elias stepped to the microphone. "Thank you for being here to help us recognize the company personnel who had a hand in our victory on Gostis. Please welcome Colonel Fitzgerald."

Colonel Fitzgerald stepped to the microphone. "I'll keep my remarks brief because I know all of you have important business to get back to. First, I have a letter from the president of the United States to the Stellar Logistics and Freight Corporation acknowledging the corporation's involvement in our victory on Gostis. I've given the letter to Mr. Gilmore, and he promised to post it on the SICOS. Also, the United States Air Force would like to present this plaque to commemorate the vital role Oasis 4 and all its personnel played in the Gostis invasion."

Colonel Fitzgerald picked up the plaque and handed it to Elias while shaking hands and posing for a photograph to commemorate the occasion. He then said, "Would the following personnel please step forward when I call your name? Norton Parker, Kyle Desmond, Phillip Ross, Gus Condent, Dwight Needles, Chad Kowalski, and Roy Engle." Phil and the rest stepped up to the area near Colonel Fitzgerald and Elias. Colonel Fitzgerald read from a pad. "For participation in, and exemplary conduct of the invasion of Gostis, the United States Air Force awards the following the Gostis Campaign Medal."

He picked up each medal and read the name for its intended recipient then pinned it on as he shook hands. When the applause ended, he said, "Could I have Captain Dwight Needles and Lieutenant Chad Kowalski step back up here?"

Dwight and Chad walked back up, and Colonel Fitzgerald read from a citation, "On July 23, 2586, during Operation Righteous Anger, Captain Dwight Needles and Lieutenant Chad Kowalski flew their Astrodyne shuttle in a manor calculated to disrupt the maneuvers of enemy formations. The flight was executed with skill in the finest tradition of the United States Air Force. For their skill and action, the Secretary of the Air Force, Secretary of Defense, and the president of the United States awards Captain Dwight Needles and Lieutenant Chad Kowalski the Distinguished Flying Cross."

Colonel Fitzgerald hung DFCs around the neck of Dwight and Chad. When the applause died down, Elias thanked everyone for being there and adjourned the gathering. Isnod and Feldon were with Pindon and Lynuna watching from the walkway one tier above the plaza level.

Feldon said to his companions, "Shall we put out some bait?"

Pindon nodded. "The quicker, the better. Where do you suggest we start?"

Isnod shrugged. "There's a commodities trader named Onustkay in the Lower CentMod. He works alone, so it'll be good practice."

*****

## Oasis 4, Lower CentMod, Office of Onustkay, Licensed Commodities and Bulk Merchandise Trader

They took the platform lift to the Lower CentMod Plaza, then took a series of escalators to the fourth tier.

The three of them approached the office of Onustkay, licensed commodities and bulk merchandise trader, and went inside.

Onustkay was sitting at a desk, which was cluttered, to say the least. There were pads strewn about, and they were surprised to see paper documents. A malnun was sitting across him, holding a pad of his own. Onustkay looked at the trio. "I'll be right with you, gentlemen." He did a quick double-take when he realized who the three were that entered.

He turned his attention back on the malnun. "Now see here, Kin Mos, the Kastian Pattern Tie Bolts are unequaled in clamping force, and I have a container full of them that I know you need. I'm offering them at a discount also. Two thousand goners is a very fair price."

Kin Mos shook his head. "They're a fine Tie Bolt, but it's a dated design. I know how much they're worth and how much you paid for them and how long you've been sitting on them."

Onustkay had an expression that gave him a defeated look. "Look, 1,500 goners is rock bottom. Any less, and my children will go shoeless this winter."

The malnun wasn't buying the "shoeless children" story, but he needed these Tie Bolts, and chiseling down Onustkay was entertaining. He sighed. "Is *this* container of Tie Bolts on *this* station?"

Onustkay nodded and held out a pad. "In CargoMod 4, ready to go." Kin Mos reached over to the pad and put his thumb on it.

Onustkay tapped some notes on the pad. "The container is now in your name. You can have station personnel attach it to a ship as soon as you can book space on one going to your destination."

Kin Mos nodded and left the office to arrange the transportation of his container of tie bolts.

Onustkay placed the pad on his desk and turned to the two bounty hunters and Pindon. "What can I do for you, gentlemen?"

Isnod smiled and produced a pad of his own. "Just a quick question or two. I understand that you attended a trading convention a while back on Raytheon."

Onustkay nodded. "Yes, that's right."

Isnod showed a pad to Onustkay. "Do you recall having contact with this man? He goes by Noglertlan."

Onustkay studied the photo on the pad carefully. "No, I would remember that face. You say he was on Raytheon at the same time I was?" He asked handing back the pad.

Pindon nodded. "We think so."

Onustkay slowly shook his head. "No, I'm sorry. He just doesn't look familiar. I have some images of that convention, keepsakes, and such. I can look them over tonight and see if he's in one of them. If I find him in one, I'll see you in your office or notify the consulate if you're not available."

Isnod and his companions thanked Onustkay and left his office. There were currently fifteen flastons living on Oasis 4 whom they couldn't vouch for, so they had fifteen different fugitives to use for bait. The fifteen fugitives had a couple of things in common. First, all of them were members of the syndicate. Second, they all had associates on Treest. Third, they would have to have had a plausible reason to have contact with the resident at the station. Isnod, Feldon, and Pindon visited the other flastons in question that afternoon and made their inquiries.

*****

## Oasis 4, Upper CentMod, Baja Juans

Elias finally got to meet the haldocs. He thought an informal setting would be best, and he had grown to like Juans a great deal on his last stay on the station. With him was his wife, Veronica, Nort Parker, and Kyle Desmond. Votlor and Rok were pleasantly surprised to learn that Elias planned to return them to Vestgut in just a couple of days. Elias smiled and nodded. "I'm afraid that I can't spend a great deal of time here. I have an important meeting with a construction firm on Pretna. We can be somewhat flexible about the timetable, but I don't want to put them off too long."

Rok nodded. "Again, we're very grateful for the effort you're putting into getting us home. I must admit that I have very mixed emotions about it. From our perspective, because of our time in suspended animation, it feels like we've only been away a few weeks. The reality is we've been absent for centuries. Our world is bound to be different, and our society may be completely alien to us."

Elias thought for a second or two. "I would be lying if I said I knew how your people would react. We just won't know until we get there."

Phil asked, "What are your plans for the next couple of days Elias?"

"Well, I thought I would make courtesy calls to the consulates. Also, I understand that Miss Lynuna's parents are on the station. I would like to make their acquaintance. Then I wouldn't mind seeing Votlor and Rok's ship," Elias answered.

Alice spoke up, "Drop by the museum anytime, Elias."

Phil shot a look at Alice. "You did it, didn't you? You stole a spaceship and put it in your museum!" He then turned to Votlor and Rok. "Guys, I am so sorry. I told her it wasn't hers." He then turned back to Alice and pointed a finger at her. "You are in so much trouble."

Alice stared back at Phil with a decidedly blank expression. "Are you done?"

He knew Alice must have bargained for the ship; he was just a bit put out that no one told him. He stared back at Alice and said in a more muted tone, "Yes, ma'am."

Everyone at the table was doing their best not to laugh out loud. Alice said in a voice so calm and reasonable that it gave him chills.

"I traded for it, then I had Jeremy and his crew move it to the museum with the help of Will and a couple of his guys."

Phil nodded slowly. "Oh. What did you have to give for it?" "Copies of every book in the gift shop," Alice answered.

Phil nodded. "It sounds like you got a good deal. I apologize." Alice squinted her eyes. "You better mean it."

Everyone knew that Phil and Alice's little exchange was put on for their own entertainment as much as everyone else's.

Phil made a show of changing the subject. "So, Elias, perhaps we can get together at Sliders one night."

Elias smiled. "That does sound like fun. Too bad, Rosanne Evans isn't here to give me competition."

Alice quipped in a low voice, "Nice redirection, Phil."

Phil ignored her. "Actually, we have someone who'll give you a real run for your money."

Elias raised an eyebrow. "Oh yeah, who would that be?" Phil grinned. "Why don't we let that be a surprise."

Elias chuckled. "I didn't think that my game made enough of an impression on my last visit for you to find a ringer. Okay then, tomorrow evening after dinner, let's do that."

*****

## Oasis 4, HabMod 4, Food Court

Isnod, Feldon, and Lynuna left the flaston serving line with their trays and found the table occupied by Yulona and Lytrina. After putting his tray down, Isnod held a chair for Lynuna so that she could sit. Lytrina couldn't help chuckling at Lynuna. "You look a little sore, dear."

Lynuna looked at her mother. "It occurred to me that living on a space station, it's too easy to let yourself get out of condition. Isnod and Feldon have volunteered to coach me and help establish an exercise routine."

Isnod smiled. "I know it sounds cruel, but you need to follow up with another session tomorrow. Eventually, you'll find yourself pushing harder.

Lynuna nodded. "You don't have to convince me that there's going to be moments where the last thing I'll want to do is exercise, but I'm committed to the process. One thing though, I watched you do your micton exercises. It looks fascinating."

Feldon chuckled. "You would learn a lot. I find it hard to keep up with all the things micton teaches us."

Isnod had to put down his spoon and said with a chuckle. "You need to stop doing that at meals."

Yulona laughed. "That Ivonorsic sounds like an interesting person."

Isnod collected himself. "As Pindon said yesterday, Ivonorsic, micton master is a little overly dedicated to the mystique of micton. Talking to him gives you the impression that there isn't anything that micton doesn't teach you. That being said, Ivonorsic is one of the finest micton instructors there is. I would highly recommend him."

It was at that moment everyone at the table looked up to see Tillya standing there with a tray in her hands. She asked timidly, "Would you mind if I joined you?"

Isnod, Feldon, and Yulona stood. Yulona said, "Of course not. Please have a seat," while Feldon held a chair for her.

Feldon sat back down. "I don't believe you've met everyone here, Tillya. This is Yulona and Lytrina from the committee drawing up the new Flaston Charter of Rights, and this I'm sure you know is Lynuna, our consular general, oh, my partner, Isnod. Everyone, this is Tillya. She works in the station's operations center."

Yulona smiled. "It's a great pleasure to meet you, Tillya. I understand that you've been doing exceptional work for your employer."

Without saying it out loud, Yulona revealed that he knew Tillya's circumstances and knew better than to talk openly about it.

Tillya smiled back. "Coming here was a dream come true. The work is sometimes challenging. My quarters are luxurious by any standards, and there are interesting diversions on this station."

Lytrina smiled. "What about friends? Have you made any?"

Tillya nodded. "The Rosses, of course, they've been more than wonderful. Brenda Gleason, she's a controller and Gus Condent. Then there's Virginia Wells and the gentleman she's seeing, Dwight Needles. He's funny. Recently, I struck up a friendship with Feldon."

Isnod was surprised. Feldon had alluded to knowing her, but he never elaborated. He asked, "When did that happen?"

Feldon answered, "You and Lynuna didn't want me hovering about that night. Mr. Ross happened to see me in the Upper CentMod trying to decide where to eat, so he invited me to tag along with his group. Tillya and I were introduced to pizza, and I was introduced to pool."

Yulona furrowed his brow. "Pool?"

Feldon nodded. "It's a human game played on a special table."

Tillya smiled. "Oh, I guess I could count Slider, the pool hall proprietor, as a friend also."

"I'm trying to figure out where you're from, but your accent is a little puzzling," Lytrina mused.

Tillya smiled. "That's because I'm from Velsra Provence, but my village is on the west shore of Trimlute Lake. Everyone's accent from that area is sufficiently muddled."

Lytrina smiled. "That would do it."

Yulona nodded and said in a low voice, "You'll see your village again one day, that much I can promise."

Tillya looked at Yulona and Lytrina and searched for something to say. She just smiled and nodded.

After breakfast, Yulona, Lytrina, and Lynuna went to the Consulate while Isnod and Feldon retreated to their office and Tillya went to the Operations Center.

One of the servers at the flaston serving line took particular interest in the group walking away.

*****

## Oasis 4, Lower CentMod, Flast Consulate

Elias walked into the Flast Consulate and was greeted by the receptionist and shown to Lynuna's office. Lynuna wasn't alone, as Yulona and Lytrina were there. Elias shook their hands and introduced himself. "I'm Elias Gilmore, president of the Stellar Logistics and Freight Corporation. I wanted to introduce myself before you had to leave. I understand you're on your way back to Flast this afternoon."

Yulona nodded. "That's right. The New Charter of Rights is nearly complete, and we need to be there to cast our vote for acceptance."

Elias smiled. "It's indeed a great honor to be conversing with some of the key people who are literally writing the latest chapter in Flast history."

Lytrina said, "At the risk of sounding melodramatic or trite but getting to know the people on this station has been an honor. The level of integrity shown by the people we've interacted with has been staggering, to say the least."

It was rare when Elias was humbled, but there he was, searching for the proper reply that expressed his appreciation for Lytrina's statement. Finally, he said, "Anything we can do to help create a more stable situation on Flast, we're willing to do. More than that, we encourage anyone's efforts to foster an environment that reflects the same principles we have."

Elias stood. "I'm sure you have important things to do before you depart. I just wanted to congratulate all of you on your success in changing governments and recovering your Charter. Also, of course, to wish all of you the best of luck with your new charter."

After shaking hands, one more time, Elias left to visit the other consulates.

*****

## Oasis 4, Upper CentMod, Maintenance Shop

A station technician named Ken Hancock left the maintenance shop with his tool kit and an equipment box on a two-wheeled cart. He walked to an escalator and balanced the cart on a step as he rode to the plaza level. After making sure his cart was secure on the platform lift, he pressed the button for the operations center.

When the lift reached the top floor, Ken stepped off while pulling his cart.

Virginia looked up from what she was doing. "The boss's office Ken." Ken smiled. "Right on it, Ms. Wells."

Ken wheeled his cart to Phil's office and tapped the door frame.

Phil could be heard. "Come on in, Ken."

Ken entered and was greeted by the sight of Phil, Luke, and the flaston named Rabot standing next to the vault. Ken asked, "Mind if I close the door, Boss?"

Phil said, "No, go ahead."

If anyone outside of the office was eavesdropping, they would be under the impression that Ken was performing a maintenance task best done with the door closed and nothing more. Phil nodded to Luke, who opened the vault and entered. In a few seconds, he emerged with the case holding the Charter and placed it on Phil's desk. Ken put the equipment case next to the Charter case and opened it. Rabot opened the Charter case and removed the Charter. He examined the equipment case and carefully placed the Charter in it, then fussed with some foam blocks to ensure it wouldn't shift about while in transit.

When Rabot was satisfied, Ken helped close the equipment case and put it on the cart. Luke wrapped one of the latches with wire and installed a lead security seal on it. Then held out a roll of tape with printing on it. "Would you do the honors, Mr. Rabot?"

Rabot took the roll. "I hardly think this is necessary since you gentlemen have been proven to be trustworthy."

Luke smiled. "We appreciate you saying that, but we want to offer every reassurance and security precaution available.

Rabot smiled, tore off a length of tape, and put it on the case in a place that it would have to be torn to open the case. Then Rabot used a permanent marker to sign the tape.

Luke nodded to Ken, who took his cart with the Charter in it out the door. Luke turned to Rabot. "You might as well relax, Mr. Rabot. Your party won't be here for a while."

Ken stepped onto the platform lift and pressed the button for the lower CentMod plaza level. As the platform lift descended, Luke's deputies on patrol noted Ken's progress and reported to Luke in a manner that wouldn't draw attention to the fact that Ken was being carefully watched.

The platform lift stopped at the Lower CentMod plaza level, and Ken made his way to CargoMod 6. As he passed security deputies, they would make discrete reports to Luke, who passed it on to Phil and Rabot. Reports from the deputies weren't actually necessary since Phil and Luke were watching Ken's progress on the SICOS monitor as he made his way through the station. The deputies, however, could see if anyone took particular interest in Ken's activities. He passed through the security gate and walked the passageway next to the docking ports. Feldon was at Docking Port 8 unloading rations and duffle bags from his own cart and stowing them away in their Pulsar. Just as Ken reached him, Will called from nearby, "Hey, Ken, do me a favor and hold this."

Ken held a fixture in place while Will tightened the mounting bolts. While they were occupied, Feldon took the equipment case from Ken's cart and replaced it with one from his cart. He was so quick and smooth. Even if someone was looking directly at him, they probably wouldn't have noticed the trade. Will asked Ken, "Are you taking that to the warranty container?"

Ken answered, "Sure am. Do you need me to take anything there?"

Will shook his head. "No, just hurry back to the shop when you're done."

Ken turned back to his cart and resumed his trip to the container that they used to store failed components that were being returned for overhaul or warranty claim. Feldon stowed the equipment case containing the Charter in a cabinet on board the Pulsar and locked it.

*****

## Oasis 4, Upper CentMod, Operations Center

The flaston delegation consisting of Yulona, Lytrina, Lynuna, Pindon, and a handful of flaston security officers arrived at Phil's office. Yulona waited until the office door was closed and asked, "Is everything progressing as we thought?"

Phil nodded. "I just got word that it's on Isnod and Feldon's shuttle." Yulona smiled. "I don't see any reason for delay."

Rabot pointed to the empty case on Phil's desk and said to the security officers, "That's the item, gentlemen."

One of the officers picked up the case while Phil shook hands with Yulona, Lytrina, and Rabot. After Phil assured them that he would make some effort to visit Flast, the flastons left the operations center with Luke leading the way.

They were met at the plaza level by half a dozen station deputies who escorted the group to CargoMod 1. A flaston shuttle chartered for the journey was docked at docking port 2. Reaching the docking port, Rabot entered the ship with the security officers and the case. Lynuna said her final goodbyes to her parents, who entered the ship and closed the air lock hatches.

When the shuttle disengaged the docking clamps and thrust away, Pindon said to Lynuna, "Let's go to CargoMod 6."

*****

## Oasis 4, CargoMod 6, Docking Port 8

Isnod and Feldon were waiting at their shuttle when Lynuna and Pindon arrived. Feldon was the first to spot them. "There you are. Did your parents get away all right?"

Lynuna nodded. "Indeed they did."

Feldon looked at Pindon. "Let's get aboard and start warming the systems that will give Isnod and Lynuna a moment to say goodbye."

Pindon chuckled as he stepped into the shuttle after Feldon. Isnod took Lynuna's hands. "I'm sure your mother and father will send word of our success."

Lynuna looked him in the eyes. "I'm already anxious for a word."

Isnod stepped aboard and closed the air lock hatches. After receiving clearance, the docking clamps were disengaged, and Feldon thrust away from the station. Lynuna watched until they were out of sight, then she made her way back to the Flast Consulate.

*****

## Oasis 4, Upper CentMod, Sliders Pool Hall

Phil and Alice, along with their party, which consisted of Gus and Brenda, Virginia and Dwight, Elias, and Veronica, and finally, the haldocs had dinner at Baja Juans, then made their way to Sliders.

Phil secured four tables then Gus and Elias helped carry the balls to the tables. Elias looked around. "Where's this 'pool shark' that's supposed to give me grief?"

"She'll be along in a minute," Phil assured him.

At that moment, Tillya walked in with Lynuna. Phil smiled. "There she is, you're right on time, Tillya, and it's nice to see you, Miss Lynuna."

Elias smiled. "Miss Tillya! Was hoping to spend some time with you before I left for Vestgut."

Tillya gave Elias a hug. "It's so good to see you, sir."

Elias introduced Tillya and Lynuna to Veronica, who took to them immediately. Phil thought they should get down to business. "Okay, we all know who the two finalists are going to be tonight. Tillya gets table 1, and Elias gets table 2. We'll record wins and losses. Then after we've determined who the top three are, we play for elimination. Then the final game to determine the night's winner, which will be played by Tillya and Elias, I'm sure."

Elias frowned. "Don't you think you're putting a little pressure on Miss Tillya?"

Tillya put a case on the table and opened it revealing a custom-made cue that she ordered with help from Slider, an old manufacturer in Maryland. As she removed the cue and assembled it, Phil shook his head. "No, not really."

Elias saw the cue, and it rendered him mute for a moment. Veronica grinned and leaned toward Alice. "Elias has been practicing since he returned from here the last time. In fact, he bought a table and had it put in the basement."

Phil actually went through great pains to make sure that no one got too competitive. Votlor sind Rok sat out the first round to study the game, then declared that the game was simple enough and easily mastered. Phil didn't want to deflate their egos, but when they got a chance to play, he gave them a short lesson on the importance of using

English to change the cue ball path and then controlling spin to draw the cue ball or keep it in place after striking the object ball. All in all, that was about the limit of Phil's pool expertise.

After a game, the haldocs backed off their original assessment and declared that the game was deceptive in that it appeared easy, but there were obviously subtleties that didn't necessarily have to be mastered but enhanced the game.

Slider overheard them and said they had the main idea.

Everyone had played enough games to satisfy their taste for pool. As predicted, Elias and Tillya defeated all comers. It was decided that they would declare a winner after the best three out of five. After the coin toss, Elias broke. It was very obvious that he had been practicing, as he had nearly run the table. He had one object ball left but no shot. The best he could do was leave himself a safety, which didn't put off Tillya. She managed to spin the cue ball around the eight ball and walk it down a bumper to sink one of her object balls. It was only by a stroke of bad luck that she couldn't sink all her object balls. The way was open for Elias, and he took it. After sinking his last object ball, he put the eight ball in a side pocket. He looked at Tillya. "Things just got serious."

Tillya narrowed her eyes. "Oh, it's on."

Tillya and Elias battled back and forth, making shots that the others swore were impossible. After the fourth game, they were tied with two wins each. It was Elias's turn to break, and he sent balls scattering over the table. A striped ball sank, and he set to pocketing the rest. A missed shot gave Tillya the opening she needed, and she cleared all of the solids. She pocketed the eight ball and put down her cue. Elias put his cue in the rack, smiled, and said, "I've had a great time, and I couldn't be more pleased that Miss Tillya was the one who defeated me.

Veronica put her arm around Elias. "We need to let these kids go back to their quarters. Everyone has a big day tomorrow." She then went to Lynuna and Tillya. "It was so nice visiting with you two."

Both Lynuna and Tillya said they also had a grand time, and they hoped that they'd have an opportunity to spend time with her again.

*****

## Oasis 4, CargoMod 1, Docking Port 1

Phil and Alice arrived early for their trip to Vestgut. Elias thought it would be a good idea if they appeared as benign as possible, and having their wives with them would achieve that goal. He couldn't order anyone to go, but Alice, being who she is, was up for an adventure. Veronica, however, was reluctant, but Elias managed to sweet-talk her into going. The news that Alice was going helped her make up her mind.

Phil took the opportunity to look around since he didn't have a chance to when Elias arrived. Just as it was back then, he was very satisfied with what he saw. Then he spotted some scuff marks on the floor that made him look closer. Everything still had a new appearance, but it looked as if it needed a broom and mop put to it. There were trash receptacles that should be empty or nearly so but were holding a fair amount of trash.

Phil frowned and went to a SICOS terminal. "SICOS, page Will Dawson."

In a moment, Will's face appeared on the monitor. "What's happening, Boss?"

"I need you in CargoMod 1 right away," Phil told him in a tone with enough edge to make sure Will didn't dawdle.

Will noted the tone and hurried to CargoMod 1 to find Phil scrutinizing the floor. He cautiously approached Phil. "What's going on, Boss?"

Phil didn't look up from his inspection of the floor. "What kind of schedule is the cleaning crew on?"

Will scratched his head. "The Trashbots and Sweepbots run every day. The other bots take more time to do an area, so every two weeks is the normal rotation."

Phil nodded. "The floor looks like it hasn't been swept in a while, and the trash is higher than it should be."

Will studied the scuff marks on the floor. "These look like they were made by bots. I wonder if one of them malfunctioned."

Phil frowned. "It's a bot. Isn't there a memory file you could download?" "Yes, I think there is, but since they had a software update, they've been… weird," Will said reluctantly.

Phil furrowed his brow. "Feel free to expand on that."

Will shook his head. "I'm not sure if I can. The bots have always been trouble-free. Each night, they set out automatically and perform their assigned task for the night. But lately, they've been showing signs of slipping up. If they were people, they would get a performance review."

Phil stepped back. "Are you saying they're developing some kind of personality problems?"

Will laughed nervously. "Oh, don't be silly, Boss. We'll have this worked out by the time you get back."

"Who is we?" Phil asked pointedly.

Will said, "Well, me and our programmer, Dan."

Phil nodded. "Okay, sounds like the right guys are on this."

Will went off to see what the progress was on diagnosing the Cleanbots just as the haldocs arrived. They were carrying their duffels, and there was a station worker behind them with a large case on a cart. Phil furrowed his brow. "What's in the case guys?"

Votlor smiled and said, "Supplemental reports."

Phil realized it must be the books Alice traded them for their ship. Norton and Kyle were right behind them, carrying their own duffels. Norton smiled and said, "You two are early. No point in boarding right now. It'll take a little while to warm the systems."

The Rosses and the haldocs sat in the waiting area while Norton and Kyle entered the Pulsar and started the preflight. Soon, Elias and Veronica arrived, and Elias grinned. "Morning, everyone."

Everyone replied, "Morning, Elias. Morning, Veronica." Norton appeared at the air lock. "We're ready to roll, folks."

*****

**Stellar Traveler, Pulsar 5500, Owned by the Stellar Logistics and Freight Corporation**

They loaded the baggage, boarded, and closed the air lock hatches. Kyle was the pilot in command for the first part of this flight, and Norton took the copilot's seat. Phil naturally wanted to sit in a cockpit observer seat, as did both Votlor and Rok. They received clearance to release docking clamps, and thrust starboard, then cleared to pitch and thrust forward until clear of the station. As they made their way to the point where the reaction engines could be engaged, Phil noticed that Votlor and Rok weren't looking in the direction of the nebula but in a direction that offered a clear view of stars. They stared unblinking until Phil asked, "What are you guys seeing that's so absorbing?"

Rok came out of his reverie and said with a smile, "You have to understand, Mr. Ross, our whole lives, we would look into the night sky, and we'd see stars, of course, but beyond them, there was always the Great Barrier."

Votlor kept his gaze on the vast vista laid out in front of him and added, "No one knew what was beyond the Great Barrier, or even if there was a 'beyond the Great Barrier.' There were those who speculated the stars that were in our view were all that existed, and there were those who, as it turns out, correctly postulated that the Great Barrier had an outer border, and we were simply in a pocket of clear space. In fact, there were dozens of outlandish theories of what lies beyond our vision, but in all of them, no one speculated about the awesome beauty of what's out here. It's truly breathtaking and humbling.

They were given clearance to fire their reaction engines, and Norton pressed the button warning everyone on board to brace themselves. Kyle engaged the reaction engines and accelerated to maximum velocity. After checking the navigation display, he engaged the light-speed engines and accelerated to LS 9.6.

Phil pulled the Pulsar 5500 Procedures and Data Handbook out of a pocket and started leafing through it. Norton looked back at him and asked, "Are you checked out in a Pulsar, Phil?"

Phil continued to thumb through the manual. "I have about five hundred hours in the 3500."

"This is just a bigger version. It handles about the same at sublight velocities.

The only difference is the addition of light-speed engines," Kyle offered.

Phil nodded, saying, "It might be easier on all of us if there were three of us to take shifts on this trip."

Norton said, "Sounds good to me. Actually, you technically don't even need an endorsement to upgrade to the 5500 since you have your light-speed endorsement."

Phil, Norton, and Kyle were too engaged in discussing the Pulsar to notice Votlor and Rok. They were transfixed by the view in front of them. Phil noticed their silence, looked at them, and smiled. "You guys all right?"

The haldocs came out of their reverie again, and Rok said while shaking his head, "Just the few minutes we've been talking, it would have taken us years to travel this distance in our old vessel. This kind of velocity was just a dream."

"We calculated it would take six days to reach Vestgut in the Aurora. What's our estimated time in route in the Pulsar?" Phil asked.

Kyle checked the navigation computer. "We're looking at just over three days."

Phil whistled. "This thing really 'hauls the mail.'" Norton nodded. "I told you the Pulsar was pretty sweet."

They arrived at the edge of the nebula after a bit more than a day's travel, and the haldocs were in the cockpit again for the event. Elias made the rare appearance in the cockpit himself. He was taking in the view when he frowned. "It seems to me that it would be pretty easy to have a collision in this relatively confined passage. After all, Superior Mining will be sending ships back and forth, plus the potential trade with Vestgut."

Norton pointed at the navigation display. "Superior Mining took the lead in establishing and publishing a passage procedure. They established lanes to stay in for each direction, separated by marker buoys at each end and at the turn. The buoys perform two functions, they mark the passage, and they incorporate communication repeaters so that messages can go back and forth."

Elias furrowed his brow. "Why is that last feature necessary?" "The compounds in the nebula prevent transmissions of any type from going any distance, both interfold and radio," Norton explained.

Elias nodded, and an idea came to him. "Do you think we'll have time to stop at the Anna Mae asteroid belt?"

Norton smiled and said, "Of course. In fact, I was hoping you'd want to stop.

I was curious about the mining operation myself."

When they reached the turn, Kyle cut the light-speed engines and idled the reaction engines. Phil was sitting in the copilot's seat at the time, and he checked the navigation computer. "Wow, Kyle! The marker is just off our nose. We'll make the turn in thirty seconds."

"The Pulsar has the best nav computer on the market," Kyle said with a grin. Kyle pitched up twenty-five degrees and yawed right forty-seven degrees.

Norton was watching over their shoulders and said, "That's really neat." "That's close to what our first reaction was," Phil said.

Kyle restarted the light-speed engines and resumed a velocity of LS 9.6. He furrowed his brow and said, "You guys navigated this and still thought it was a good idea to tow the Prospector through here?"

"You have to understand, Kyle, the crew that was originally planning to salvage the Prospector was the biggest collection of motley losers you ever saw. It became a point of pride for us to not shy away from a challenge that Fel Nos, Marcus Pointer, and crew were going try," Phil answered.

Elias asked, "Who was that fellow that you let go? I believe he was another malnun."

Phil smiled. "Brin Os. He wasn't wanted by anyone, and he hasn't broken any rules on the station that we couldn't ignore, so I gave him a way to straighten himself out."

"Have you heard if he's still walking the straight and narrow?" Elias asked.

Phil shook his head. "No, I haven't. I'll have to make a note to find out when we get back. Out of all of them, Brin Os was the only one who had what I would consider marketable talent. With our urging, he signed on to the *Odessa Dream* as a crewman. Probably a helmsman since he was a pilot with a light- speed endorsement."

"I'm beginning to wonder why the company bothers to pay you at all Phil since the entertainment value you get is nearly priceless," Norton said, laughing. Phil nearly missed emerging from the passage into the nebula void. He set the Anna Mae system into the navigation computer, and it provided a countdown to light-speed engine cut. The counter reached zero. Kyle cut the light-speed engines and idled the reaction engines. Phil used the navigation computer again to find the asteroid that Superior Mining designated as Asteroid 6753. Kyle adjusted his course and speed while Phil found the frequency to contact the Spirit of 49.

Phil keyed the microphone. "*Spirit of 49, Stellar Traveler,* we thought we'd drop by and see how you were doing."

They didn't expect to get an answer immediately since they weren't expected. In about a dozen seconds, Greg Hastings replied, "*Stellar Traveler, Spirit of 49, that sounds like Phil Ross.*"

Phil smiled. "Right the first time, Greg. Can we go to visual?" "*Why not?*" Greg answered as he switched to visual.

Phil smiled as Greg's face filled the monitor screen. "We were on our way to a system a short distance from here, and we thought we'd drop by and give our regards."

Greg nodded. "That's very kind of you. Who exactly are you with?"

Phil motioned to Elias. "This is my boss, Elias Gilmore, and his wife, Veronica."

He then introduced Norton and Kyle, and then he said, "You remember Alice, of course, and finally, I'd like you meet Votlor and Rok. They were the occupants of the vessel you reported on your last visit at Oasis 4."

Greg didn't try to hide his surprise. "Oh my goodness, gracious! If I had known you were in there, I would have made some kind of effort to get you myself!"

Votlor shook his head. "Please, Captain Hastings, there was no way for you to know we were in there. Also, we were certainly in no position to attempt to contact you."

Phil said, "We can get you caught up on what happened on your next visit to the station. For now, we're on a mission to return Votlor and Rok to their home planet, and we'd like to take a low pass and check out your operation."

Greg nodded. "Love to show it to ya. I'll stay on frequency to answer any questions."

Kyle positioned the Pulsar over the *Spirit of 49* and rolled the vessel to afford the best view for Elias and the others. Greg answered dozens of questions about the mining operation, which was actually more interesting than Phil thought it would be. After a time, Elias and the rest said their goodbyes to Greg and thrust away.

Alice came to the cockpit and asked, "Where's my planetoid?"

Phil chuckled as he found it in the navigation computer. He put it up on the nav display, and Kyle said, "Lucky for us it's on our way." Kyle adjusted his course, then idled the reaction engines. The planetoid came into view, and Kyle made a low pass. After passing Alice's Planetoid, Kyle resumed course to Vestgut and pushed the power levers to full. When they had exited the Anna Mae system, the light-speed engines were engaged.

*****

## *Stellar Traveler*, Pulsar 5500, Owned by the Stellar Logistics and Freight Corporation

According to the navigation computer, they were two minutes from dropping out of light speed in the Vestgut system. Kyle kept an eye on the nav display, then cut the light-speed engines when it prompted him. The view in front of the Pulsar came into sharp focus, and Kyle checked the navigation computer once again. "Our position is exactly where we wanted to be. We'll establish Vestgut orbit in one hour ten minutes."

It wasn't long before Vestgut came into view. Votlor and Rok were in the cockpit watching every maneuver. Finally, Rok said, "That's a welcome sight."

Votlor smiled and said, "Indeed."

Phil checked the Pulsars mapping feature. "I'm not seeing anything in orbit except a couple of satellites and some debris in a high geosynchronous orbit over the equatorial continent."

"Are you sure it's not an orbital climber?" Rok asked. "That should be where the tether is."

Phil shook his head. "I'm not detecting any space stations, no ships, nothing."

Norton tried several times to make contact via radio using frequencies provided by Votlor, but they had no luck.

Norton frowned. "Well, that answers the question of whether to dock at a station or land on the surface. Now the question is, where do we land?"

"Is there any way to display a map of the planet's surface?" Votlor asked.

Phil nodded. "We've just started the process now. With this system, it'll only take three orbits to get a high-resolution map of the surface."

Kyle completed the three necessary orbits, and the navigation computer created a map of surprising accuracy.

Phil showed Votlor how to operate the mapping system who rotated the image and centered a reticle on a geographic feature. "Our space program was headquartered here. There were facilities for aircraft there that should serve our needs."

Phil zoomed in on the map. "There seems to be a facility there still. It looks like it's still being maintained, unlike some of the things I'm seeing down there."

Rok frowned. "That disturbs me. Are you saying there are things there that appear to be in less-than-ideal condition?"

Phil nodded. "It looks like there are large sections of the city near that facility that's abandoned. See here. There are trees and bushes in areas they don't look like they belong. There are also some buildings that appear to be deteriorating."

"After 363 years, I didn't expect this," Votlor said, looking at the display.

To this point, Elias hasn't said anything. Finally, he thought he should add his two cents worth. "Well, with a lack of information, I think we should land there. In my mind, it's probably the one location that would be the most accepting of the unusual situation we're about to present."

Rok nodded. "Mr. Gilmore is correct. In our time, most of the people that worked in our program were very open to the idea of people living on other worlds."

"I think Votlor and Rok should be the first off of the shuttle to soften the shock, so to speak," Norton added.

Rok furrowed his brow. "I never considered our people might have a negative reaction. You're right. I think it would be very prudent for Votlor and myself to make the introductions."

Kyle, Norton, and Phil put their heads together and designed an approach and landing procedure that offered the least potential complications. When everyone was ready, they started the reentry procedure. Being as there weren't established procedures for this planet, they were unable to establish communication, everyone was on their toes. Phil had noted that there were aircraft in the area, but they weren't paying any attention to them.

When they were about fifteen kilometers from the facility, Kyle announced, "I have the visual."

In a couple of minutes, they were close enough to distinguish some detail of the facility. Rok said, "The layout has changed somewhat, but it's basically the same." Then he pointed to a substantial building with large windows that faced an expansive paved area. "I would land there."

*****

## Pulsar 5500, Owned by the Stellar Logistics and Freight Corporation, Final Approach to Vestgut Space Facility

As they neared the facility, Kyle slowed the shuttle and set up his approach profile to put them exactly on a point directly in front of the building. He brought the Pulsar to a hover precisely where he wanted to. Then he yawed to the left to face the building. Having done that, he remained hovering while he crept forward.

Phil could see some personnel milling about, giving them curious stares. It was very obvious when they realized the arriving craft was unusual. As the shuttle touched down, the personnel working outside at the facility stopped, then suddenly started running in every direction. Kyle secured the thrusters, then started an auxiliary power unit before he powered down the reactor. Two smaller vehicles charged toward them and stopped. As haldocs exited the vehicles, Votlor said, "They seem to be security personnel. They're carrying weapons, but their demeanor seems odd to me."

Phil furrowed his brow. "What do you mean by that?"

"If a spaceship landed on your planet, you weren't familiar with, wouldn't you expect that the security officers would take a more cautious posture?" Votlor answered.

Elias nodded. "Maybe you two should get out there."

Norton opened the hatch and lowered the stairs. Votlor exhaled. "Well, it's time to see if we're welcome back."

Votlor and Rok went through the hatch and descended the stairs. Phil and the rest could see the demeanor of the security personnel change and not for the better. The security officer that seemed to be in charge came forward. "You two need to explain yourselves!"

Votlor said, "I am Votlormicuntox Hudixofon, and this is Rokidosmor Remhifunos. We were sent from this facility 363 years ago to explore the Great Barrier."

The ranking security officer frowned. "There are one or two problems with that. First, you're overdue by several decades. Second, that's not the same class vessel that was used for that program."

"You must have some record from those days to verify who we are," Rok said. One of the men from the security detail said, "Excuse me, sir, but I've been studying history, and they appear to be exactly who they say they are, and there is a way to verify who they are."

The officer frowned. "How do we accomplish that, Joknot?" "Their photos and finger impressions were taken to prevent

unscrupulous people from arriving centuries afterward and perpetrating some sort of hoax or scam," Joknot answered.

The officer in charge asked, "Where do we get those items?"

Joknot thought a second or two. "Those files are kept in the base archives in the administration office."

The officer in charge took out a communicator. "Hopton, I need you to go to the archives and get a file for one of the Science Forward missions."

"Number five," Votlor offered.

The officer in charge rekeyed the microphone button. "Science Forward Mission Number Five. Also, bring out a finger impression reader."

In a couple of minutes, a vehicle pulled up with two haldocs in it. The ranking security officer turned and was surprised. "Supervisor Optic, you didn't have to come out here personally to do this."

The supervisor nodded. "I needed air, and I wanted to be here for this. I've heard about people trying to perform some sort of scam pretending to be returning members of the Science Forward missions."

He turned to the officer that accompanied him, "Get the impression reader, Hopton."

Hopton opened a case and pulled out a device that looked like a tablet. While he was getting it ready, Optic looked at the Pulsar. "Well done. That actually looks like it came from another world."

The impression reader was ready, and he had Votlor and Rok put their hands on it, palm down, one at a time. When that was done, he plugged it into a portable computer, then instructed it to identify the latest impressions.

In a couple of seconds, Hopton frowned. "According to this, these two don't exist."

Optic looked annoyed. "That's impossible! Everyone is in the system!" Hopton input more instructions into the computer, which made Optic frown.

"What are you doing?"

Hopton said, "I'm downloading the file from the Archives on the Science Forward Mission Number Five. I'm thinking we should consider the possibility that they are who they say they are."

Optic was starting to get really annoyed. "It's your time to waste, but for right now, I'm arresting these two!

Hopton was looking at his computer. "You shouldn't do that, sir."

"Why shouldn't I do that?" Optic demanded.

Hopton smiled. "Because they are who they claim to be."

Optic was ready to start unleashing wrath on everyone in the immediate area when he grabbed the computer from Hopton. He calmed considerably when he saw the screen. He looked over to Votlor and Rok, who were smiling broadly.

Optic shook his head. "Welcome home, gentlemen. Where did you get that ship?"

Votlor said, "It belongs to the people who found us." Optic frowned. "You need to say that again."

Votlor nodded. "We were found out there, and they brought us home."

Optic's reaction wasn't anything like what Votlor and Rok had expected. He didn't seem as surprised as he should have.

Optic asked, "Are these people in the vessel now?" "Yes, they are," Votlor answered.

Optic was silent for a moment, then he said, "Perhaps we should meet them."

Rok nodded and went to the open hatch. "They would like to meet you now."

Elias took Veronica by the hand. "Come along, dear."

They exited the Pulsar and faced Optic, who was looking up at the humans, speechless. Votlor made introductions, then after an uncomfortable pause, Optic finally sighed and said, "My name is Optic. On behalf of my people, welcome to Vestgut. We would be pleased if you would be our guests and make introductions with our leaders."

Elias smiled. "We'd be delighted to be your guests."

Optic frowned. "I'm afraid we'll need someone to translate,"

Elias took an auto translator out of his pocket and handed it to Votlor. Votlor handed it to Optic and explained how to use it. Once Optic put in the earpiece, Elias asked, "Can you understand me now?" Optic had a confused look. Votlor chuckled. "It actually takes a little while to get used to hearing both languages simultaneously. Also,

there are some words and phrases that don't directly translate." Elias nodded and said, "It's not perfect, but it does work."

Optic smiled. "We have similar devices. Did you bring more of these? It will take time to reprogram our own units, and these will make things easier when you meet my superiors."

Elias smiled. "Yes, we did, in the shuttle. In fact, if you would allow us to get our baggage, we have a case of auto translators on board you can distribute as you see fit."

Optic nodded. "Yes, of course, please. In the meantime, we'll put technicians to work programming our own translators with your language."

Norton, Kyle, and Phil busied themselves by removing baggage from the Pulsar, and Optic used his communicator to summon a transport large enough for everyone. Phil and Kyle were struggling with the last item, and Kyle asked, "What's in this thing?"

Phil put his end of the case on the ground. "It's supplements for Votlor and Rok's report."

Kyle stood straight. "Huh?"

Phil nodded. "Yup, the boys traded their spaceship for a copy of every book in the museum gift shop. They thought they would make an excellent supplement to their report."

Kyle thought a second or two, then nodded. "That's actually a pretty good idea."

Elias also had a sizable case that they unloaded. Elias explained it had the extra auto translators and a portable computer and holographic display projector.

A vehicle arrived that was nearly like a bus. After the baggage was loaded, they boarded and began their short trip to guest quarters. They immediately discovered their visit was going to have some physical challenges as the headroom and seat size in the vehicle were not calculated for humans.

*****

## Vestgut Space Facility, Guest Quarters and Meeting Center

After their arrival at their lodgings, they worked out what the sleeping arrangements should be. Elias and Veronica were given a room, then Phil and Alice were assigned a room. Norton, Kyle, Votlor, and Rok were given their own rooms. The haldoc that ran the guest quarters commented that if they found the beds too small, perhaps they could make some sort of arrangement.

Optic suggested that they go to their quarters and freshen up, then afterward, they would summon them for a light meal. Votlor suggested that they have the two large cases taken to wherever they were going to be giving the briefings. Before the cases were taken away, Elias removed three auto translators and handed them to Optic. "I'm sure you'll need these."

They were given about an hour then the haldoc staff escorted them to a dining room. Optic directed them to sit at a table then food was brought out. Phil was always wary of alien food, but he and the rest discovered that they had no reason for concern, as it was quite good. Optic pushed his plate away, "I took the opportunity to inform my superiors of your arrival. Representatives from the government along with some from the scientific and historical community will be heading here tomorrow to talk to you."

Votlor said, "That's good. We have a report that we're quite anxious to give."

Optic nodded. "That's what I wanted to hear. Until then, though, I'd like to hear the condensed version of your journey."

Votlor and Rok related the high points of their journey to Optic and Hopton, who listened intently. Votlor finished the narrative at the point where he and Rok woke up on Oasis 4. Optic and Hopton were completely rapt by the story, then Optic looked at Elias. "Your race is called human?"

Elias smiled. "Yes, that's right. We come from a planet called Earth."

"Your space station is located some distance from your home planet?" Hopton asked.

Elias nodded and explained, "Our corporation has four such stations located in such a way as to allow clients to take advantage of our convenient locations."

Optic nodded. "I have to ask. Besides humans and haldocs, how many races are there?"

"Five others," Elias answered.

Optic was starting to look a bit uncomfortable. "Do you get along with all of them?"

"For the most part. We have excellent relations with the home worlds of each race. Unfortunately, the same can't be said for some of the independent colonies. In fact, we just had a small war with a planet populated with a race called snoshin," Elias said.

"If I may ask, why did you go to war?" Optic asked.

Elias took a deep breath. "That particular planet had the institution of slavery. Normally, we wouldn't interfere with a planet's social order, no matter how repugnant we find it. But most of their slaves were individuals kidnapped from other worlds."

Optic leaned in. "What was the outcome of the troubles."

"After several weeks of combat, we finally got their military to dissolve the government and surrender. We are currently in the process of repatriating the former slaves to their home worlds. I get the general impression that there is a purpose behind your questions," Elias observed.

Optic nodded. "I think it's prudent to find out what kind of people we're dealing with. One of our greatest fears is an alien race showing up and denying us our basic freedom by force."

Elias frowned. "I still get the sense that there's more."

Optic was silent while he considered his answer, then he nodded and said, "You can add another name to the list of races. About eighty of our years ago, we developed space travel faster than light, and it didn't go unnoticed. We decided to investigate a system that we identified as a likely place to find a habitable planet. As it turned out, our observations with telescopes were very accurate. The planet was not only habitable. It's inhabited."

Votlor and Rok were stunned, and Rok asked, "These aliens have light-speed capability?"

Optic nodded. "Yes, they do. After we made contact with them, they're frequent visitors. In fact, they have diplomatic missions in each capital city."

Hopton snorted. "Calling them diplomatic is being kind."

"Hopton is quite right. They don't seem to be interested in diplomacy at all. From our first encounter with them, they persist in telling us they plan on invading our world. Apparently, it's part of their culture to conquer what they can where they can. After they discovered we existed, they've been busy making preparations for the conquest of Vestgut," Optic explained.

Phil frowned. "Why is it that you allow them to have diplomatic missions on your planet?"

"The hope is they'll reconsider when they know us better," Optic stated. Elias furrowed his brow. "Is it working?"

Optic shook his head. "It doesn't seem to be." "What do these people call themselves?" Elias asked.

"Plotors, and their planet is called Limdox," Optic answered.

Norton was trying to make sense of what the haldocs were telling them. His main problem was he was trying to use human logic to explain alien motivation and that rarely worked. Finally, he asked, "Have they tried to land troops here?"

Optic shook his head. "No, but they keep telling us that as soon as they've built enough troop ships, they're going to bring an army and subjugate us."

Norton nodded. "If they haven't invaded yet, I wouldn't count on them doing it anytime soon. Our own experience tells us that invading another planet successfully is nearly impossible."

"How can you say that? Didn't you just tell us you invaded a planet yourselves?" Optic asked.

Elias answered, "It took the resources of several worlds who brought different specialized capabilities to the operation. The only troops we could deploy and supply was light infantry. The various governments on Earth that participated had to use shipping from corporations as they're not oriented toward operations off our own planet."

Hopton considered what Elias said, "It sounds like the decision to invade was questionable from the start." Then he asked, "What factors contributed to your victory?"

"The first thing in our favor was the population on the planet in question was limited to a relatively small geographic area. Without getting into too much detail, the troops we needed to engage were situated around their capital city. The troops themselves weren't trained for the type of warfare we waged. They were mainly used for intimidating and controlling unruly slaves, so they weren't exactly up to the task of engaging in combat against other soldiers. The troops we used were elite forces and exquisitely trained," Elias explained.

Optic smiled. "That actually comes as a relief. We, of course, don't have firsthand knowledge of such things. So to clarify, you people don't represent any government body? Your interest is corporate?"

Elias smiled. "That's right. We do business with worlds that have signed on to the Universal Trade and Territorial Accord."

Optic was crestfallen. "I'm afraid we wouldn't qualify for such an agreement. You see, we're not a united world. We have seventy-two different nations on our planet."

"Only seventy-two?" Phil asked with a chuckle. "Actually, there are only a few worlds that are united. On Earth, for instance, only the countries with interest in doing business in space are signed on to the accord. Signers are agreed to only doing business with other signatories."

"What is the process if you find a world that has resources you want to extract or perhaps colonize? Is there a mechanism in place to ensure other parties don't encroach on a claim?" Hopton asked.

"As a matter of fact, there is. It's covered in the accord. In fact, some time ago, Phillip here helped claim a solar system not far from here that has an asteroid belt rich in minerals that are in high demand," Elias answered.

Optic frowned. "All parties are happy with that arrangement?"

"For the most part, there's enough unexplored space to keep everyone from getting greedy," Elias confirmed.

"So what happens if there's a remote mining operation, perhaps in this asteroid belt you have a claim on, and someone comes along and takes it over by force?" Hopton asked.

Elias nodded. "It does happen, and I wish it was rarer than it is. Usually, it doesn't happen to territory or property belonging to a recognized government. There have been corporations that have had remote facility's taken from them. In those cases, the corporations have the option of hiring paid soldiers to get their property back."

Up to this point, Votlor and Rok have been silent and wanted to change the subject. Votlor looked at Optic. "I couldn't help noticing before we landed that there were large areas of the city that appeared to be abandoned. Also, we were expecting to see the orbital climber, but its absence is quite obvious."

Optic nodded. "I keep forgetting you haven't been here for centuries and don't know what has been happening here on Vestgut.

We have had our challenges, to say the least. Events in the past have had a profound effect on our planet's development."

Rok furrowed his brow. "There must have been extremely significant events to have the effect you're alluding to."

Optic nodded. "Indeed there were, but I think it would be best if we let the historians fill you in on those."

"You can at least tell us if we still have a Space Ministry," Rok pressed. Optic smiled and nodded. "Yes, we do. It's small but up and running.

It's not nearly as big as it was when you launched, but still here." "Is this the only facility in the space program?" Votlor asked.

Optic nodded. "Yes, it is. We build our satellites here and launch them on rockets. We also store our light-speed vessel here."

Optic checked the time and said, "I'm afraid we've kept all of you up quite late. I'll have my staff see you to your rooms. Tomorrow promises to be a big day for everyone. I'm looking forward to your report, Votlor and Rok. Also, I'm given to understand that you have a presentation, Mr. Gilmore. I'm sure everyone is going to be very interested in that."

Everyone was shown to their rooms, where the length of the beds was put to the test, especially Kyle's, as he was six foot three inches tall. The beds were indeed short but not unusable. Kyle, however, had to get creative by asking for the Vestgut equivalent of a king-size bed and sleeping on the diagonal.

*****

**Vestgut, Space Center Guest Quarters**

In the morning, Phil and Alice were awoken shortly after sunrise and escorted to breakfast with the others. Votlor and Rok had already talked to the staff and educated them on what humans might find acceptable for breakfast, which was pretty close to what haldocs enjoyed for breakfast. Optic joined them and fixed himself a fruit plate and some bread.

As he sat, Optic said, "After morning meal, we should prepare the meeting room for your reports. Vice Minister Togglor and Science

Minister Jomit will be here soon. There will also be historians, scientists, and some of their staff that they deem appropriate."

Elias said, "That sounds good to us. We're looking forward to meeting them." Optic nodded and said, "Good, good." Then his expression changed. "You should be made aware that you may not be given the warmest greeting you've ever had. Our experience with the plotors has had an impression on our leaders.

After the initial introductions, the vice minister will want to meet with Votlor and Rok and specifically make inquiries about you."

"I expected something like that. Frankly, I think it's prudent that they should be somewhat suspicious and take some precautions," Elias said with a smile.

Optic furrowed his brow. "You don't think less of us for acting this way?"

Elias shook his head. "Absolutely not. I imagine if the roles were reversed, we would act the same way."

After the morning meal, they prepared a briefing room for the upcoming presentations. The briefing room was not unlike the briefing rooms found anywhere, with a large table and chairs arranged around it. There was a row of chairs behind the chairs around the table for the less important attendees.

Votlor and Rok had been shown beforehand how to use the holographic display projector and computer, and Hopton showed them how to dim the lights from the head of the table. They also arranged the books from the museum gift shop on a table in the back of the room, along with reading translators. A reading translator is a device that simply, as the name implies, translates the printed word into any language selected by the viewer and displays it on a screen.

Optic checked on their progress and was satisfied that everything appeared to be ready. Rok could see Optic was uncomfortable with something, so he asked, "What has you worried, Optic?"

Optic inhaled, let out a breath, and said, "I'm still concerned with the reaction we may get from the officials that are coming today. Vice Minister Togglor has been a vocal opponent to the Space Ministry because of our experiences with the plotors. I hope she and her staff aren't too hostile to you."

Elias nodded and said, "We'll do what we can to dispel any preconceived notions about ourselves. The only thing we can do is present ourselves as who we are."

Before Optic could carry on the conversation, an aide approached, "Sir, Vice Minister Togglor and the others have arrived. We've shown them into meeting lounge number one and distributed Mr. Gilmore's translation devices."

Optic nodded and acknowledged the aide, "Very good, Fitkel. We'll be along in just a bit."

Fitkel turned to inform the vice minister that their guests would be arriving momentarily, and Optic turned to the others, "Shall we?"

*****

**Vestgut, Space Center, Meeting Lounge Number 1**

They walked a corridor until they reached the lounge where Optic had them wait. He went inside and addressed the gathered officials, "Vice Minister Togglor, Science Minister Jomit, gathered dignitaries, I would like to introduce you to Votlormicuntox Hudixofon and Rokidosmor Remhifunos of the Science Forward Mission Number Five."

The ministers and the others started snapping their fingers, which the humans took as a round of applause.

Then Optic said, "Please welcome representatives from Earth who have brought our scientists back to us."

Optic introduced them as they entered, "Mr. Elias Gilmore and his wife, Veronica."

Elias and Veronica walked in and stood opposite the dignitaries, who were gawking speechlessly. Optic looked like he was becoming increasingly nervous as he announced Phil and Alice, "Please welcome Phillip and Alice Ross."

The haldocs were still speechless, then Nort and Kyle entered.

Optic continued, "Pilots Norton Parker and Kyle Desmond."

The haldocs looked near passing out when Kyle entered while ducking to avoid hitting his head in the doorway. Optic gave his superiors a moment to collect themselves, then introduced Vice Minister Togglor and the others.

Vice Minister Togglor politely greeted them, "Welcome to Vestgut, and the Republic of Sydnor. On behalf of my countrymen, I give you greetings. There are no established protocols for visitors from other worlds, so I must apologize if this seems awkward, but if I could talk with Votlormicuntox Hudixofon and Rokidosmor Remhifunos along with Optic and some of my staff."

Elias smiled and said, "Of course. We expected something like this." Togglor was taken aback. "Why were you expecting this?"

"If the roles were reversed, I imagine that's what we would do," Elias said with a chuckle.

Togglor was beginning to see they weren't all that different, and that didn't give her any comfort. Optic led Togglor, Votlor, Rok, and selected members of her entourage to a meeting room, not unlike the one they were in. The haldocs invited the humans to sit as there were comfortable seats arranged in a circle.

The haldocs that were conversing with the humans didn't tell them what their function was, but they could guess that there were a number of different specialties represented. They also had varying levels of cordiality. No one was downright hostile, but one could sense a certain amount of distrust from a couple of them.

As they chatted, Phil, Elias, and the rest started to sort out what the supposed roles were of the haldocs that they were chatting with. Phil definitely had the impression that some were sociologists or of psychological bent while the ones that were a little more hard-nosed were most likely from their version of the State Department or Defense Department, possibly even their Commerce Department. Elias was thinking along the same lines; in fact, he was convinced that was the case.

*****

## Vestgut, Space Center, Meeting Lounge Number 2

After everyone was settled, Vice Minister Togglor said to Votlor and Rok, "On behalf of everyone on Vestgut, welcome home. When the public learns of your return, the celebrations will last for many days. That is if they're not terrified by the people who returned you."

Rok recoiled, "I have to take exception to that. The humans have been especially accommodating, helpful, and generous."

"I have to agree with Rok. The behavior of the humans since they've been here has been wonderful. They've been an absolute delight, unlike the plotors," Optic interjected.

Togglor nodded. "I appreciate what you gentlemen are saying, but our previous experience with visitors from another world hasn't been pleasant. You, of all people, should know that Optic. We've been threatened with invasion and subjugation by an aggressive race. Now we learn there are more races out there, and these particular aliens are giants. You're going to have to work hard to reassure me that this isn't a problem."

Votlor chuckled. "If the size of the humans worries you, you should know that they're actually quite average height-wise. The only other race near our height is the pretars."

Togglor furrowed her brow, and Votlor put his hands up. "You will read about them in our report."

Optic could sense Vice Minister Togglor wasn't any closer to thinking that developing a relationship with the humans was a good idea, so he decided that he should try to guide the conversation. He interjected, "Vice Minister, I think we may be getting ahead of ourselves here. These people do not represent a government, and they cannot speak for any particular group."

Togglor frowned. "Then what do they hope to accomplish here?"

Optic shrugged. "From what I gather, they just wanted to establish a relationship with us and return Votlor and Rok, of course."

"If they're not representative of any particular government, who are they?" Togglor asked.

"They're employees of the Stellar Logistics and Freight Corporation," Rok answered.

"The Stellar Logistics and Freight Corporation is an organization that facilitates commerce in between worlds," Votlor continued.

Togglor thought for a few seconds, then asked, "What would their reaction be if we asked them to leave and not return?"

"I believe they would comply with our wishes. It would disappoint them, but they would respect our wishes," Votlor answered.

Togglor put her hands in front of her with the fingertips touching each other, and she closed her eyes. After what seemed like an uncomfortable amount of time, she slowly nodded and said, "We may be judging these humans too harshly. After all, we've just met. If they're not asking us to plunge into a relationship, I see no reason why we couldn't have some diplomacy. However, I think it would be prudent to proceed slowly and cautiously for now. Does anyone disagree?"

*****

## Vestgut Space Facility, Guest Quarters and Meeting Center, Dining Hall

The two groups gathered in the dining hall, where Vice Minister Togglor sat at the head of the table with Elias on one side of her and Optic on the other. The food was standard lunch fare and proved to be not unlike what the humans were used to. The conversation became so pleasant that Togglor had to be reminded that they should make their way to the briefing room.

*****

## Vestgut Space Facility, Guest Quarters and Meeting Center, Briefing Room

After everyone was settled, Votlor took his position behind the small lectern. Togglor was at the opposite end and was wondering how the report was to be made. She was further confused when the lights were dimmed.

Votlor cleared his throat then said, "Vice Minister Togglor, Science Minister Jomit, gathered dignitaries, on behalf of my crewmate and friend Rokidosmor Remhifunos and myself, I give you this short presentation on our findings during the Science Forward Mission Number Five."

Votlor engaged the holographic projector, and the Vestgut solar system appeared over the center of the table. The haldocs gasped at the sight of it, as there was nothing like it on Vestgut. Votlor continued the presentation. "As you are aware, we began our journey on the fourteenth day of Gounar, in the year 5622. Our original mission was to penetrate the Great Barrier and travel a given distance, where we would awaken and make scientific measurements."

As Votlor gave his presentation, a yellow line, representing the course of the little vessel, traced along. Votlor continued, "It was originally hoped we would emerge on the other side of the Great Barrier and begin a new era of space exploration for our people."

Science Minister Jomit put his finger up. "Have you determined why you weren't awakened and allowed to complete your mission?"

Votlor nodded. "Indeed we did. Rok can explain it better than I can."

Rok took his place behind the lectern while the display continued to play the small vessel's journey. As progress was made, the number of planetary systems increased, and the course line finally entered the Great Barrier. "As you can see, our mission progressed as planned until we entered the Great Barrier. As we traveled further, our course was altered by the effects of the gravitational pull exerted by stars and other bodies that couldn't be detected using other methods. When that happened, our computer would calculate the needed correction and instruct the guidance system to fire thrusters to bring us back on course. Unfortunately, we encountered more star systems than what we planned for, requiring more corrections which exhausted all of our fuel."

Science Minister Jomit asked, "Did your onboard computer calculate the positions of the stars and planets in the Great Barrier with the precision we're seeing here?"

Rok shook his head. "No, we had to put our data with data the humans had to get a composite of the features inside the Great Barrier.

As you can see, it's still far from being a complete and totally accurate representation of what's in there."

One of the science minister's assistants asked, "Did you awake from your suspended animation as scheduled?"

Rok again shook his head. "No, we didn't. The extended maneuvering exhausted all the fuel supply, which made returning home impossible. The computer was instructed not to wake us in the event that those conditions existed. As a result, the reanimation sequence of our suspended animation pods was not activated."

The course line exited the nebula and stopped. Rok said, "It was at this point we were spotted by a customer of Stellar Logistics and Freight Corporation. They reported our position, and Mr. Ross dispatched a vessel and crew to retrieve us. Mr. Ross has a short presentation to illustrate exactly how that was done."

Phil stood and stepped up to the lectern. "As Rok already said, it was brought to our attention that there was a small vessel near the nebula you call the Great Barrier. I tasked two of my pilots, Gus Condent and Dwight Needles, along with two technicians, Chad Kowalski, and Helmut Schultz, with retrieving the vessel and returning it to Oasis 4." Phil changed the presentation program, and an image of the vessel they referred to as the *Mystery Ship* on Oasis 4 appeared over their heads. It was the same program they showed Votlor and Rok when they were at the station. Phil continued to narrate as the presentation played on, with the haldocs giving it their full attention.

Phil's presentation ended with the *Aurora* arriving at Oasis 4, where he was assaulted with dozens of questions about the station and the *Aurora*. It was at this point that Votlor took over and reminded them that there were other materials concerning both of those subjects. Votlor resumed his position behind the lectern and displayed a star field just large enough to view the nebula and Oasis 4. Then working from notes, he started listing the different worlds beginning with those closest to the station. The scale of the holographic display increased as each world was added. This was a staggering revelation for the haldocs since they had no concept of what was beyond the Great Barrier.

At this point, there was only a small portion of the galaxy shown on the display. Votlor increased the scale to show the entire galaxy then kept increasing until the known universe was displayed over their heads. It was a humbling experience for the haldocs, who were quite unprepared for the realities of what was out there. Votlor turned off the projector and brought up the lights, then turned everyone's attention the books they had arranged on the back tables and explained their origin and how they came into their possession.

Togglor stood and said, "I think now would be an excellent time to take a breather and perhaps get some refreshments."

The haldocs descended on the books prompting Votlor and Rok to demonstrate how to use the reading translators. Phil looked at the collection of books and thought they would fill out a section of any public library on Earth. He also saw that the haldocs gravitated to the books that most closely related to their specific disciplines. For instance, aerospace types were poring over ship recognition books and space station books. Phil had a very pleasant conversation with a pilot who was leafing through a book about the recovery of the Prospector.

Phil left the haldocs looking at the books and got himself a beverage that Roc told him was called dolerye. Phil gave it a sip and nodded approval, as he thought it a close approximation of coffee although a bit richer. Togglor joined him, along with Votlor and Rok, with their own beverages. Togglor took a sip of her beverage. "We'll have to make copies of those books and include them in everyone's report. The originals should be kept in the Central Library."

Rok nodded. "I'm glad to hear that the Central Library is still in existence." Togglor frowned. "What do you mean by that?"

"On our approach to landing, we couldn't help but notice that the city had areas that were in disrepair. Also, there were a couple of things that Optic said that make us think there were significant events in our absence," Rok answered.

Togglor shook her head. "I don't think it would be appropriate to discuss our planet's shortcomings in front of our guests."

Votlor shook his own head. "I disagree. The humans have shared everything about their planet and culture, the good along with the bad. In fact, we know a great deal about all the alien races. It's only right they know us as well."

Togglor knew Votlor was right, but their experience with the plotors left them quite paranoid. She took a deep breath and let it out, "Very well, please forgive me for my caution. Mr. Gilmore and Mr. Ross here have been very candid, and I appreciate it. I just don't feel comfortable discussing our vulnerabilities openly. You may not be aware of the fact that during the era of your launch, we were at the peak of development, technological development, sociological development. By every measurable standard, we were at a level we can only dream of today."

"What happened to bring us down?" Votlor asked.

Togglor shook her head. "What didn't happen? That's going to be the subject of debate among historians for centuries. In my opinion, we had too much to maintain. People demanded that more services be provided, Transportation, medical, communication, education, the list goes on and on. It wasn't enough to provide these things. There had to be accountants, auditors, and over watchers to ensure public moneys weren't being wasted."

Togglor paused and took a sip of her beverage and let her last statement sink in. Then she carried on, "It wasn't just services that were costly. Every community clamored for spectacular public works like bridges, canals, dams, and roads. Politicians were more than happy to get funding for these things, regardless of whether they were needed or not. What they failed to mention was these things required constant maintenance, and very often upkeep was more than the revenue created by those modern wonders."

Phil furrowed his brow. "That sounds like what we went through on our planet to varying degrees."

Togglor nodded. "You have my sympathies if it was half as damaging to your planet as it was to ours. But that wasn't enough on its own to throw everything into chaos. Our universities used to be places where talented and qualified young people would go to learn important skills such as engineering and medicine. At some point, they were convinced that diplomas for subjects like philosophy should be given out. At first, it was argued that such a useless subject had no place in a university as it didn't contribute anything at all to the practical application of science, technology, or medicine."

Alice had joined them and overheard the conversation and was thoroughly caught up in Minister Togglor's narrative. She said, "It's been argued on our planet that those subjects help make a student a more rounded individual."

Togglor nodded. "I'm sure some would find such things interesting or useful, but a whole course on such subjects is only a means to itself. It doesn't help design a better bridge or aircraft or even plan a community event. Soon, there were degrees offered for a whole range of subjects that no employer would find useful. Many times, students who studied these things were loaned the funds to attend a university and wound up defaulting on their loans. The lenders would naturally make up their losses with higher interest rates. Soon, no one could afford to borrow, and as a result, goods weren't sold, and services weren't provided. All those wonderful public works started to crumble, so naturally, taxes were levied to pay for them. The more a person made or spent, the greater amount of tax they had to pay. Finally, it reached the point where everyone produced only enough to get along."

Votlor shook his head. "Surely, that doesn't explain everything. We saw huge sections of the city uninhibited. There was either a dramatic decrease in population or a population shift."

Togglor nodded. "You're right. It took much more than that. However, it made conditions right for disasters. Governments went so far into debt that financial institutions refused to do business with them. Institutions and agencies were rendered ineffective by bloated bureaucratic procedures, confusing rules, and lines of communication that often went nowhere, and slashed budgets prevented them from improving their processes. These were the very institutions established to safeguard us in the event there was an emergency. Influenza epidemics became pandemics that devastated populations."

"Was it just one event?" Rok asked.

Togglor shook her head. "There were two events. When you began your journey, our planet's population was eight and a half billion. About fifty years after you left, there was an influenza outbreak. It moved so rapidly that authorities couldn't contain it while it spread to every city and village on the planet. When it had run its course, the planet's population was four billion."

Votlor asked with a slight shake in his voice, "How long did the pandemic last?"

"About a year, it moved so rapidly that there was no way to predict where it would show up again," Togglor answered.

Phil couldn't help but draw comparisons to Earth's history. He asked, "What was the second event?"

Togglor replied, "Another outbreak of influenza, about five years later, even deadlier than the first one. When it was over, there were scarcely half a billion people on Vestgut. For a period afterward, we call the Rebirth Era. Vestgut was in a sort of preindustrial period. Things were thrown into a confused state as you may imagine."

By now, Elias had joined the group and said, "I can only imagine what kind of effect that would have. People have speculated for centuries about what would happen if this were to occur on Earth. I'm sure there's going to be a lot of people interested in how you dealt with it. How did your people react?"

Togglor smiled in a sort of contemplative way. "As I said, it was like a preindustrial period, but not quite. All the tools were there, but not enough people to run them. Imagine a factory that produced, let's say, kitchen cookers. Now there's only 5 or 10 percent of your workforce to operate it."

Phil interrupted, "On the surface, that doesn't look like a problem. After the planet's population was reduced, it seems that demand would also."

Togglor nodded. "That would be the case, except you have a factory that's designed and tooled for a given output and staffing level. You just can't simply resolve to cut your production. The whole process has to be redesigned, which is a task made difficult to impossible if the people needed to do that were gone suddenly."

Votlor frowned. "That's just manufacturing. I imagine every aspect of society was severely disrupted."

Togglor replied, "You're right. That was only one example. The truth is, there were constant challenges that had to be dealt with. The one thing we had in our favor was the collective knowledge of our world remained intact. There were still farmers, mechanics, craftsmen, tradesmen, doctors, teachers, and no shortage of enthusiastic laborers. Slowly but surely, we stabilized ourselves and started over."

Rok asked, "What about the space exploration program?"

"That's a fair question," Togglor said. "Naturally, we couldn't expend resources on something that didn't have an immediate payback. We couldn't even maintain the orbital climber and had to let it self-destruct. The program was restored as the need arose for satellites to be launched and maintained. Those efforts were taken up by the private sector. Scientists and engineers weren't satisfied with sending probes. They yearned to get in space themselves and make firsthand observations. Eventually, a team of brilliant physicists developed a method of traveling faster than light."

"That sounds brilliant," Votlor observed. "We're there many voyages?"

Jomit answered, "Thus far, we've made over two hundred voyages and have explored a large section of space inside the Great Barrier."

"So I take it that these plotors haven't objected to your continued exploration?" Votlor asked.

Togglor and Jomit looked shocked. Finally, Togglor said, "I see Optic has already briefed you about our other acquaintances."

Votlor nodded. "Yes, and the plotors sound like a challenge to say the least." Togglor explained, "I would have preferred to discuss the plotors a little later.

But it's out now, so I'll see if I can fill any gaps in what you know about them. The twelfth light-speed exploration mission took our explorers to the plotor planet called Limdox. There were some tense moments until they managed to find a way to link the computer on the light-speed vessel with a plotor computer. They quickly developed a translation matrix, and real communication could take place using devices similar to these you brought."

Phil interrupted, "That's pretty close to what happened on my station, but I have to give credit to your computer and whoever programmed it."

Togglor nodded. "Indeed, we've always had very talented technicians. Well, to continue, at first, it seemed the plotors were as keen about knowing they weren't alone as we were. Our explorers returned with the news of their discovery, and we were very excited about the new era we were entering. The plotors sent an envoy a short while later, and that's when things took an unexpected turn. Their so-called envoy didn't waste any time in telling us their intentions. As soon as they've made sufficient preparations, they were going to invade Vestgut and subjugate us."

Elias shook his head. "I would like to study how you've negotiated with the plotors. That information might be valuable if and when we have to deal with them."

Togglor nodded. "I'll see what materials I can get for you. However, I think meeting the plotors would reveal to you what we've been dealing with. I won't bore you with the details of our talks with the plotors. However, it was decided that the government should take control of the space program. There were those that argued against allowing any more space flights, lest we find another species out there that was even more difficult to reason with. Frankly, I'm in that group, although I've always felt that meeting aliens were a remote possibly. I just feel that the resources could be used in other areas."

Jomit smiled and said, "That was yesterday, Vice Minister. What's your opinion now?"

At first, Togglor looked like she was slapped in the face. Then a thin smile grew on her face. "Very good, Jomit. I must admit, I was very much against allowing alien access to us, and yesterday, I was actually wondering how to kill the space exploration program. But now I wouldn't say I'm enthusiastic about developments, but I am optimistic. I'm not saying we should plunge blindly into a new era of alien interaction. I think we should proceed with caution."

Elias said, "We wouldn't expect anything else. In fact, I was going to recommend easing into this process slowly and comfortably."

Togglor stood. "I believe you have a presentation, Mr. Gilmore. Shall we continue with our briefing?"

Optic got everyone's attention and had them retake their seats. Elias took his place behind the lectern and dimmed the lights. He activated the projector, and an image of Earth appeared over the table. "This is our home planet Earth. Our company headquarters are located on the

North American continent in a city named Kansas City." Kansas City glowed on the globe, rotating over their heads.

Elias waited for the globe to rotate at least once, then continued, "Besides our corporate offices, our assets include three space stations orbiting Earth." One by one, the stations glowed, then expanded to give a better view of them then they resumed their place in orbit.

"We also have a number of stations orbiting planets that we do trade with, along with managing stations for clients who don't want to do it themselves and have contracted us to do it for them." Elias waited for each planet to glow brighter and the scale of the holographic display to increase.

Finally, Elias said, "The most unusual thing our corporation does compare with other corporations is we maintain four space stations for the convenience of our customers. The stations are located at crossroads, so to speak, between trade routes."

The holographic display highlighted the Oasis stations, then a haldoc that Phil knew to be an aerospace technician raised his hand. Elias nodded, and the technician asked, "Does your corporation maintain and operate ships?"

Elias shook his head. "Traditionally, we've never got into shipping for revenue, but we have two ships that are used to supply the stations. Also, we have shuttles for moving personnel and freight from the stations to the surface of the planets. Also, just recently, we've added light-speed capable shuttles to our inventory."

A haldoc who Elias remembered was the commerce minister named Pidlute raised his hand. "Excuse me, Mr. Gilmore, but this is all very overwhelming. With all the worlds you do business with, I seriously don't know what Vestgut could offer. It seems you have access to any goods or services you may desire. I can't imagine we could compete with everything that's already available to you."

Elias smiled. "I think that's what every world said, and that's why I recommend that you proceed slowly and cautiously. But you know, while Votlor and Rok were giving a tour of their vessel to some of our technicians, they realized that a metal we call paxtite was used in the construction. In fact, they said it was the highest quality paxtite they ever saw, and that, my friends, is a product in high demand."

Pidlute frowned. "It's true we've developed very high-quality refining and alloying processes for that metal. It's centuries old, and somehow, we've retained the knowledge needed to work with it. However, there are limited quantities of the ore on Vestgut. I can't imagine it would be enough to satisfy the demands of all your customers."

Elias was grinning and said, "You remember I told you that Phil Ross here claimed a solar system that has an asteroid belt rich in minerals. Well, paxtite is one of the minerals in high concentrations there. The ore could be brought here for refinement and turned into finished products. It's actually a tailor-made and convenient industry for you to get into."

Togglor stood and said, "I must admit this has been a very pleasant and productive day. If the humans would indulge us a bit further, I'll arrange a meeting for you with our prime minister and representatives from other interested counties. This is just a meet and greet. We won't be expecting you to make any kind of presentation."

Elias asked, "Will the plotors be represented?"

Togglor shrugged. "I'm sure they will be. We'll announce tonight on media outlets the return of Votlor and Rok and meeting our new friends. The plotors will undoubtedly see the announcement and invite themselves to the meeting. Would the day after tomorrow work for you?"

Elias nodded and said, "Yes, it would. I'm not sure if you have anything planned for tomorrow, but the thought just occurred to me that we have a light- speed vessel sitting at your facility. I'm sure there are several individuals in your space exploration program that would jump at the opportunity to make a day trip to a distant system. I would be more than happy to make our shuttle and pilots available if that sounds like something you'd be interested in."

Togglor smiled and said, "That sounds like a dream come true for our people."

Optic interjected, "Indeed. If I were able to pass the physical examination, I would be the first aboard."

"Do I look like I would pass one of your physicals, Mr. Optic?" Veronica asked with a smile. She didn't give him time to answer, "If you can sit in a comfortable seat, you're more than qualified."

Optic looked stunned. "I can't believe I'm going to make it out there."

Togglor said, "We've had our differences, Optic, but I can't think of anyone more deserving."

*****

## Vestgut Space Center

Phil, Alice, Elias, and Veronica had spent the day being entertained by the security officer they met when they first landed, who they had since learned since then was called Unustous, along with Hopton, who they also met on their arrival. They were given a tour of the local sights and interacted with the citizens of the nearby city. At some point, someone realized the auto translators were not programmed with plotor or the other common languages of Vestgut. Word was sent to the government, and a team of technicians was put to work preparing a translation matrix for the human auto translators.

Veronica was helpful in this endeavor as her degree was in computer science. That task being done, they decided to wait for Norton and Kyle to return with the Pulsar and the handful of haldocs they took with them. They were waiting in a lounge area of the facility's main building, which would be called a terminal building on Earth. In fact, the Vestgut Space Center would make a very nice airport on Earth. It had a long runway for aircraft and a generously sized ramp area for parking aircraft and spacecraft. The lounge they waited in had large windows that overlooked the ramp area.

Phil and Elias stood at the windows watching the activities outside while they sipped from cups of dolerye, a little way away, Alice and Veronica sat with their own cups of dolerye, chatting with each other. Phil had a thought that made him smile. "Did you see how excited Optic was this morning?"

Elias laughed. "Yes, I did. I don't think I've seen that much joy on a person's face in a very long time."

Unustous entered the lounge with a smile on his face. "We just got word that the *Stellar Traveler* just entered the atmosphere."

Elias nodded and smiled. "Right on time. I hope they had a good trip." Unustous laughed. "I think I can guarantee they had a good trip." In a few minutes, the *Stellar Traveler* came to a hover over the runway. It turned toward the terminal and hovered closer, where it slowly descended and came to rest on the landing gear. The maneuvers were performed with a higher degree of precision than normal, which made Phil think Norton and Kyle were trying to impress their haldoc passengers. They waited until the thrusters were shut down and the hatch opened before they headed out to the Pulsar.

Kyle and Norton had just descended the stairs when Phil and the rest arrived. Optic descended the stairs and had to brace himself on the handrail. It was very obvious that he was having an emotional experience. As the other haldocs passed him, they each put out a hand and patted his back or gave him a squeeze on the shoulder. Unustous said to the group, "It's about time for the evening meal. You can tell us all about your adventure while we eat."

After starting their meal, Unustous asked, "Was the experience everything you thought it would be, Supervisor Optic?"

Optic smiled. "It was far more than anything I have ever imagined. Seeing videos and photos does not do it justice. We decided to visit a star system that was on our list of places to explore but had ruled it out because of its distance from here. The human vessel has made that a point of no concern whatsoever. What would have been a journey of several years took only three divisions. How long was that in Earth time, Kyle?"

"A little over two hours," Kyle answered.

"You were gone for over six hours. What did you do while you were there?" Elias asked.

Optic answered, "That particular system has a series of planets that we find fascinating. We spent some time carefully surveying the system using the systems on the Pulsar."

What kind of planets are we talking about?" Phil asked. Optic answered, "Kyle told us you called them Gas Giants."

Phil furrowed his brow. "I never considered the idea you never had a chance to study Gas Giants. Our own solar system has four of them."

Optic nodded enthusiastically. "That's what Kyle and Norton told us. That sounds fascinating."

"You'll have to visit sometime and see them for yourself," Elias added.

Optic nodded and smiled. "You can be sure I will." He then changed the subject. "Has the Capital contacted us yet?"

Unustous nodded. "Yes, they have. We'll escort our guest to the Capital in the morning via rail, of course. They'll meet with the prime minister and the Cabinet along with the Parliament Council of Elders. Afterward, the midday meal, then representatives from the foreign embassies will meet all of you."

Optic nodded. "Well, I've had a full day. I think I'll retire for the evening. I'll see everyone at the morning meal."

*****

## Vestgut, Rail Transport Pod

All the humans were taken to the city rail station after the morning meal and boarded a rail pod along with Unustous. The pod had adequate seating for all seven but not much more, so Optic and some of his staff, Votlor, and Rok took another pod, along with the computer, holographic display projector, and books brought back by Votlor and Rok.

The pod zipped along at high speed through farm and woodland, which made

Phil grateful the seats were larger than the transport at the Space Center, which allowed him to thoroughly enjoy the view. Elias and Unustous were making small talk when Phil overheard Elias ask, "What's the full story about Optic? I've never seen anyone so overjoyed over a six-hour space flight."

Unustous smiled. "Everyone on Vestgut knows Optic's story. No one has done more to earn a place on a Space Flight crew. He has the most knowledge of anyone in the Space Ministry, and it's well known he would make an exceptional space explorer. For reasons he mostly keeps to himself, he cannot pass the physical examination to become a space explorer."

"Do you have any idea what sort of thing would bar someone from the program?" Alice asked.

Unustous shook his head. "The physical requirements are stringent. Supervisor Optic is fitter and healthier than 95 percent of the population, but a space explorer candidate must have athletic health. It's said that less than half of a percent of the population qualifies based on the health standards."

Norton shook his head. "Why are the standards so high?"

"The standards had to be set somewhere. With a project as important as the space program, it was deemed vital that only the absolute fittest and intelligent among us were selected to go into space. There are a lot of us though that feel that some of the requirements are ridiculously high," Unustous answered.

Elias nodded and smiled. "I think it's probably going to be impossible to keep him on the ground from here on."

Unustous laughed. "I think you're right about that. Optics story is well- known. In many ways, he's the most qualified scientist in the Space Ministry. In fact, the Space Explorers petitioned the ministry to give Supervisor Optic an exemption on physical standards. Supervisor Optic heard about it and flatly said he would not accept an appointment under those circumstances. Vice Minister Togglor was quite correct when she said she couldn't think of anyone more deserving than Supervisor Optic, and that's the sentiments of many of us."

*****

**Vestgut, Trijulate City**

The transport pod entered a metropolitan area and slowed to a stop at a depot. The door opened, and they stepped onto the platform where they were greeted by Vice Minister Togglor. "Welcome to Trijulate City, our Capital."

"Thank you very much," Elias said after they exited the pod.

The pod-carrying Optic pulled into the station and stopped. Optic, Hopton, Votlor, Rok, and some assistants from the Space Center stepped out. Vice Minister Togglor smiled and greeted them,

"Welcome, gentlemen. We have transportation waiting if you'll follow me."

They walked through a lobby area and out to the street side, where there was a vehicle waiting that resembled a bus. All of them boarded, and Togglor sat next to Elias so she could have a word with him. After the vehicle started on its way, Togglor said, "I was wondering, Mr. Gilmore if you could give your presentation to the embassy representatives. There have been mixed reactions concerning your arrival, and I believe if they see the same presentation you showed us, it will go a long way towards relieving anxieties about the Space Ministry and your intentions."

Elias nodded and smiled. "I'd be happy to. How has your own government reacted?"

"Surprisingly positive. We've committed to asking you if there was a possibility that we could establish a presence on your space station. We believe it would make communications easier," Togglor said.

Elias smiled. "Yes, of course, we can work out the details later."

*****

## Vestgut, Trijulate City, Capital Building

The transport wound its way through ancient streets and stopped in front of an imposing building Togglor explained was the Capital. Walking from the transport to the building's front doors, a crowd had gathered and was cheering. Togglor said, "This reception is for you, Votlor, Rok."

Alice took a closer look at the people who were gathered. "There's a lot of girls out there."

Togglor chuckled. "It's a bit embarrassing, but a common fantasy among haldoc schoolgirls has always involved a returning Science Forward Explorer returning to Vestgut and reintroduced to society by a helpful young lady the brave explorer eventually falls in love with. Girls have always had their favorite explorer."

Veronica giggled. "Who was your favorite, Vice Minister?"

Togglor stopped and turned red. Then she grinned. "I'll keep that information to myself."

They entered the Capital building and found themselves in a large lobby. Togglor stopped and pointed to a corridor that led to one end of the building, "That end is for the ministry. The prime minister's office along with my own is there as well as the other ministerial departments and their support staff."

Then she pointed to a corridor on the opposite side of the lobby. "That leads to the parliament. There are stairs that lead to the upper floors where the parliament members have their offices. Then there are stairs to the lower level, which is the Parliament Debate Chamber. There is an additional chamber just under us for meetings. That's where we're going now."

*****

## Vestgut, Trijulate City, Capital Building, Diplomacy Room

She led them to a staircase at the end of the lobby, and they descended to the lower level and found themselves in another lobby just outside a set of double doors. Togglor stopped. "I'll make introductions."

She entered, and the conversations that were in progress suddenly ceased. Then she said, "Fellow ministers, parliament elders, I have the honor of introducing Science Forward Mission Number Five Space Explorers Votlormicuntox Hudixofon and Rokidosmor Remhifunos."

The gathered dignitaries started snapping their fingers as Votlor and Rok entered. Togglor then announced, "The humans that returned them to us, Elias and Veronica Gilmore, Phillip and Alice Ross, Norton Parker, Kyle Desmond."

As they entered, the haldocs snapped their fingers enthusiastically. Phil suspected they were forewarned about their height in an effort to mitigate the shock; however, there were some that had difficulty taking their eyes off Kyle. Togglor then introduced the prime minister, "I would like to introduce you to Prime Minister Bodlin."

Bodlin stood and shook hands with each of the humans. Phil realized they must have been given a short introduction to human protocols. Elias realized the same thing and appreciated the efforts the haldocs were going through to make them comfortable. Togglor then introduced the rest of the ministers and then the Parliament Council of Elders. Everyone was very cordial and polite. Apparently, they had time to read the reports and came to some positive conclusions. Phil noticed that everybody was wearing an earpiece similar to the auto translators.

The meeting room was arranged in the fashion that the humans were learning was the standard arrangement on Vestgut. There were seats that faced each other in the center of the room and more seats behind them for the attendees of lower rank. Bodlin had everyone sit and then addressed the room, "I would like to add my voice to those in welcoming our new friends to Vestgut and welcoming home Votlormicuntox Hudixofon and Rokidosmor Remhifunos."

Elias nodded and smiled, then said, "We would like to thank all of you for your hospitality and kindness. It's our sincere hope that this is the beginning of a productive and healthy relationship."

Bodlin nodded again and said, "We're all very excited about the new era we were entering into. We've discussed at length yesterday what the next logical step should be. We were hoping that we could position some of our people on that space station of yours that could act as liaisons between Vestgut and parties interested in doing business with us. We were thinking perhaps someone from our Diplomatic Ministry and someone from our Commerce Ministry."

Elias nodded and smiled. "I would recommend also sending someone who was familiar with paxtite."

Bodlin smiled. "Ah, excellent. Commerce Minister Pidlute took the liberty of contacting the firm that has expertise with that metal, and they have someone willing to go."

"That sounds like we're off to a very good start," Elias observed.

Bodlin's expression changed. "There are one or two things that I'm reluctant to mention, but I'm honor-bound to tell you. I'm sure you've been informed that we are not a united planet. I understand your own planet is not united. Later, you'll be meeting representatives from other countries. Our relationship with some of these countries is somewhat strained. One country, in particular, has been troublesome. Gatslon and we have been rivals for some time."

"It's not our intention to show favoritism," Elias stated.

Bodlin nodded. "We expected you wouldn't, but the representatives from some of the other countries may need reassuring, particularly the Gatslondors."

"I understand," Elias said with a smile. "Is that the only concern?" Bodlin took a deep breath. "You've been informed about the plotors

I've been told."

"Yes, I have. Vice Minister Togglor sent me a report about them. I think I have a handle on how to deal with them," Elias said with a grin.

Bodlin smiled and stood. "Well, I think this has been a very productive meeting. Please join us for the midday meal.

*****

## Vestgut, Trijulate City, Capital Building, Dining Hall

Bodlin and Togglor led the humans to the dining hall, where they were introduced to members of the full parliament. A light meal was served, and the haldocs were able to chat with the humans in a more informal setting.

Phil thought the haldocs he talked to were very cordial and keen to begin an official relationship with Stellar Logistics. He got into a conversation with Science Minister Jomit and asked about the devices that resembled auto translators, and Jomit told him that their computer experts managed to program a translation matrix for their own translators. Anyone entering the building will have their translator updated automatically, including the translators the plotors will be wearing.

After about an hour and a half of mingling and small talk, an assistant approached Bodlin. "Minister, the ambassadors have arrived."

Bodlin asked, "Have the plotors arrived as well?"

The assistant shook his head. "No, they haven't, Minister." Bodlin didn't expect the plotors to be there. They like to make a dramatic entrance on occasions like this.

A haldoc that Phil understood to be a combination of Sergeant at Arms and Herald, got everyone's attention, and summoned the

Parliament back to their chamber. Bodlin turned to Elias and the rest. "The ambassadors are waiting."

*****

## Vestgut, Trijulate City, Capital Building, Diplomacy Room

Bodlin made the introductions personally, and there was another round of finger-snapping. Bodlin waited for the finger-snapping to die down, then he said, "Mr. Gilmore has a presentation for all of us to explain his company's role among the community of worlds that have been revealed to us."

Elias stood, and the lights were dimmed, which confused the haldocs ambassadors. Elias activated the holographic display projector, and a holographic image of Earth appeared in the center of the room. The ambassadors gasped at the sight of it, and he continued with basically the same presentation he gave earlier for Vice Minister Togglor.

When Elias finished, he turned off the projector, and the lights were brought back up. The ambassadors snapped their fingers enthusiastically, except for one or two individuals. Elias made a mental note of which individuals were less than excited at the developments. He then asked, "Are there any questions you have for us?"

One of the less-enthused ambassadors put up his finger. Elias smiled. "Yes, sir."

The haldoc ambassador asked, "Why did you choose to contact Sydnor before anyone else? There are other countries on Vestgut with space programs. It looks to us like you're favoring one country over the rest."

Elias was expecting some friction, and there it was. He continued to smile as he explained, "We're not interested in favoring one country over the others. We were directed here by Votlor and Rok because their mission originated from Sydnor. Any country interested in doing business with us is more than welcome."

The ambassador looked like he was ready to lighten up but not quite. "Undoubtedly, you know about the plotors by now. How will your relationship with us change when they start making demands?"

Elias was about to answer when there was a sudden din from the entrance of the room. As planned, Elias eased to his seat and sat down. The humans were getting their first look at the plotors. They were gray with bald bulbous heads and dark eyes. Their height was about the same as the haldocs, but they were what could be described as bony looking. Phil thought they were the picture of what science fiction writers from centuries past imagined what aliens must look like.

There were three of them, and they were strutting down an aisle toward the center of the room. The lead plotor was raging as he walked and waved his arms. The plotors reached the center of the room, and the one in charge was yelling, "Do you think you can make friends with these aliens and then have useful allies against your future plotor masters? You should know that these aliens will eventually be brought to our subjugation as you will be!"

Kyle looked over to Elias, and Elias nodded. Kyle tried to suppress a grin as he stood and approached the ranking plotor from behind. The other two plotors were too busy glaring at the assembled haldocs to notice him as he approached the ranking plotor. Kyle tapped the plotor on the shoulder, who turned around and stared at Kyle's abdomen. The plotor slowly looked up as Kyle grabbed the front of his shirt. His eyes widened as Kyle lifted him off his feet to look him in the eyes.

"My name is Kyle Desmond. What's your name, friend?" he asked. The plotor's lip started to tremble, but he managed to croak out, "Riv." Phil could see the expressions on the faces of the haldocs were a mixture of amazement and amusement. Kyle continued to stare into Riv's eyes. "I'm new here, Riv, so I hope I'm not out of line. These haldocs are friends of mine, so I would take it as a personal favor if you didn't talk to them that way."

Elias stood. "Please put him down, Kyle."

Kyle lowered a relieved-looking Riv and returned to his seat. Elias faced Riv. "My name is Elias Gilmore, the president of the Stellar Logistics and Freight Corporation. We weren't intending to slight anyone here. The only reason we're talking to the haldocs first is because we met them first. Our only interest is establishing trade and commerce. If you're interested in that sort of thing, I've prepared an information and proposal packet for you."

Phil stood, reached into his pocket, and retrieved a haldoc data chip that some of Optic's technicians helped him prepare. He handed the chip to one of the plotors that were with Riv. "We asked the haldocs to put the information in a format you would be familiar with."

Riv looked over to the data chip, then he looked at Elias. "Don't think we can be tricked into lowering our guard!" He then turned to the haldocs in the room. "Be very careful who you make friends with!"

Riv and his companions strode to the door and left. Elias was left standing, watching the plotors leave. The haldoc Elias was engaging before the plotors arrival stood. "What kind of reassurances would we have that our dealings will be fair?"

"I've invited interested parties to open offices on our space station to see to the interest of their planet. Such an office would be required to see to the interest of all parties on your planet. In the case such as Vestgut, where the planet is not united, a cooperative can be formed between several countries. As long as all haldocs are treated equally under those circumstances, the system works quite well," Elias stated.

The haldoc mused for a few seconds, then he said, "My name is Wonjet, ambassador of Gatslon, by the way. How do we coordinate with you in initiating this?"

Elias indicated to Bodlin. "Sydnor has already committed to sending a representative to our station. Perhaps you can coordinate with them and send a representative of your own."

Bodlin stood. "We can get you in contact with our commerce minister and diplomatic minister. They're taking the lead on this for Sydnor. Perhaps we can form a cooperative."

Wonjet bowed slightly. "I have to contact my government, of course, but I believe they would be pleased to partake in this new adventure."

Bodlin smiled. "I'm so pleased you're looking at this so positively." Wonjet smiled back. "I don't think the plotors will be as pleased,

but I'm not as worried about that as I was a division ago."

The haldoc ambassadors started laughing and snapping their fingers enthusiastically.

Elias nodded and smiled. "This sounds like a very good start. I'm afraid we cannot stay here until you work out the details, as we have pressing business with another world. When we return, we'll dispatch a shuttle with communication equipment and transport the representatives you select. You can expect a vessel in, I'd say, ten of your days."

Bodlin nodded. "Could you return with our representative and perhaps with a representative from Gatslon if they can get someone ready before you leave?"

Elias smiled. "Yes, that would be wonderful."

Wonjet smiled. "We've had several volunteers the moment they heard about the possibility of establishing relations with spacefaring aliens. We can have a diplomat at the Sydnor Space Center by morning."

Bodlin beamed, "That's very good. We'll be expecting your aircraft.

The meeting was adjourned, and an evening meal was served in the dining hall with the ambassadors. Then there was a period afterward to mingle while enjoying dolerye. When the evening had run its course, the humans were taken to the rail station for the trip back to the Space Center.

*****

## Vestgut, Space Center

In the morning, the humans packed their things and stowed the baggage away on the Pulsar. There wasn't a time set for departure, so there wasn't a great hurry. An aircraft landed, and a passenger emerged, then crewmen unloaded baggage and put them on a transporter. The transporter drove to the terminal and let off the haldoc passenger. Then it drove the baggage to the Pulsar, where Kyle was doing his preflight checks.

Once inside, the new arrival introduced herself, "I'm Vimurnus, diplomatic liaison for Gatslon."

Optic greeted her and made the introductions. A few seconds after the introductions, another haldoc arrived with baggage. He introduced himself, "I'm Udlon, diplomatic liaison for Sydnor. Optic made more introductions, and Norton thought it would be a good idea to give the haldocs a briefing before boarding.

Elias had to be the one to say it. "I think it's time we should be leaving."

They said goodbye to Optic and his staff, then an unexpectedly emotional farewell to Votlor and Rok.

A transporter took them to the Pulsar, where they loaded Udlon's bags and boarded. After strapping into their seats, Kyle fired the thrusters and lifted off the ground. He moved to the runway and increased power to gain altitude and move forward. In a few moments, they were headed to the upper atmosphere, where he started the reaction engines and entered space. He then set a course for the nebula passage and engaged the light-speed engines.

During the journey, they were able to get acquainted better with Vimurnus and Udlon, which was an area that Elias continued to excel. There was also some business taken care of which kept them busy. The tricky part was preventing the haldocs from being overwhelmed too soon. Much of what they discussed was the infrastructure Vestgut would have to develop for commerce to take place.

The haldocs already had a good deal in place already with the space centers. The communication equipment was the first vital installment in making Vestgut a viable trading partner. To move goods to and from the surface, also paxtite ore to the surface and finished products to space, shuttles were going to be needed. At first, shuttles and pilots from the transportation companies could be used, but eventually, the haldocs would take over those duties.

The biggest item on the list of things that they'll need in the future is an orbiting space station of their own, but there was plenty of time for that. Elias had them stop at the mining operation on Asteroid 6753 in the Anna Mae system. Captain Hastings was grateful for the company and gladly answered a slew of questions from Vimurnus and Udlon. After about an hour, they were on their way again.

The transit through the nebula passage was uneventful, and Elias had them pause long enough to send a message to the station to give them their ETA and to have quarters assigned to Vimurnus and Udlon. While they were at sublight speed, the haldocs had an opportunity to view space without nebula clouds in the background. Both Vimurnus and Udlon weren't prepared for the vastness of it all and were quite overwhelmed. Norton restarted the light-speed engines after a time and resumed their journey to the station.

A day's travel after exiting the nebula, they were easing the Pulsar into the docking clamps on CargoMod 1. Phil busied himself, opening the airlock and getting the baggage ready. A station worker brought a cart for the baggage, and Phil made sure they were tagged so that they made it to the correct destination.

When everyone had exited the Pulsar, they cleared customs and walked the connector tunnel to the CentMod. When they reached the CentMod, Elias turned to the rest. "We'll take a day to recover, but we really need to get to Pretna as soon as possible. With that said, good night, everyone." He then took Veronica's arm, and they made their way to the elevator lift and HabMod 8 with Norton and Kyle in tow.

They passed Virginia and Tillya as they were stepping off the platform lift. There were quick greetings and pleasantries, and they went their separate ways. Virginia and Tillya joined Phil and Alice, who then introduced the haldocs. Isnod and Feldon strolled up, which surprised Phil, as he didn't expect them to be there.

Phil looked up. "Ah, Isnod and Feldon, this is Vimurnus and Udlon of Vestgut. They will be representatives of their planet. Vimurnus, Udlon, this is Isnod and Feldon of Flast. They have a business office on the station."

They all shook hands then Virginia said, "Why don't all of you go and get some rest and let Tillya and myself get the haldocs settled."

Phil and Alice bid Vimurnus and Udlon a good evening and walked to their own quarters in HabMod 1. They spent a little time getting settled down as it was always a bit of a trial reestablishing a routine after a journey. When they were finally in bed, Phil asked, "What is your opinion of future relations with the haldocs?"

Alice thought a second or two. "It looks like they'll be eager to do business if you ask me. I also get a sense that they're extremely curious people." "What about the plotors?" Phil said, smirking in the dark.

Alice chuckled. "Now there's a challenge." Phil nodded. "That's the sense I get."

The End

# BOT FIGHT

**Oasis 4, Trading Center Space Station, Owned by the Stellar Logistics and Freight Corporation**

Will Dawson was in the connector tunnel walking from CargoMod 1 to the Upper CentMod. He had just had a conversation with Phil Ross about the condition of the CargoMod. For the last week or so, the Clean Bots had been acting up, and it finally came to the boss' notice. Will was determined that one way or another, they were going to solve the Clean Bot malfunctions. He walked to the CentMod and took an escalator to a lower level and entered the Systems Center. About halfway down the hall, he came to a door labeled "Dan Harrington,

Systems Program Specialist" under that signage was a homemade plaque that said, "Galaxy's Best De-bugger."

Will chuckled. "We'll see."

He tapped on Dan's door and heard. "Come in."

After Will opened the door and entered, he was greeted with the sight of Dan working on a Clean Bot that was sitting on the workbench with a diagnostic computer connected to it via a cable assembly. Dan was too engrossed in what he was doing to look up, so Will finally asked, "What kind of luck are you having, Dan?"

Dan shook his head. "I honestly don't know. I think I've found what's causing the bots to act in an unusual manner, but it looks like it was done on purpose."

Will furrowed his brow. "Why would someone program a bot to misbehave?"

Dan was still staring at his screen, looking at lines of code. "They weren't going for bad behavior. They were trying to give the bots a sense of—oh, I don't know, Pride in Workmanship."

Will stared at Dan. "Huh?"

Dan leaned back in his chair. "It's a matter of establishing a set of priorities that the bot must follow. In fact, the bot would have a sense of failure if they fell short of programmed goals."

Will frowned. "It's a bot! Why would it care if it let us down?"

Dan shook his head. "I don't know, but they're programmed to stop at nothing to accomplish their mission. If they don't, it's almost like it's personal to them."

Will thought a second and said, "This sounds like artificial intelligence."

Dan nodded. "Yes, it does, but the level of AI we're talking about is illegal on an autonomous device without safeguards."

Will was trying to sort it out in his head. "So these new protocols were loaded in all the Clean Bots with the last programming update?" Dan nodded. "That's right, we added bots at the same time to the Upper Level to make up for the added area of converting CargoMod 1 into a passenger terminal."

"So we have an autonomous cleaning system with components that have emotional issues," Will flatly stated.

Dan nodded again. "That's about the size of it."

"If they have such a focus on mission accomplishment, why are their areas left undone?" Will mused.

Dan shook his head. "That remains a mystery. I suspect whatever's getting them beat up is preventing them from finishing their tasks before their 0700 Zulu return time. Unfortunately, the bots were never given the capability to play back what they did on previous nights. I think I'll submit a suggestion to remedy that."

Will examined the bot on the bench closer. "How did this get so banged up?"

Dan furrowed his brow. "I'm not the guy to ask. I was under the assumption that because of their function, they got beat up from accidents and such."

Will nodded. "You're right about that, but this looks excessive."

Dan continued going over lines of code, and Will asked, "If you can't find the problem, would you be able to uninstall the last update?"

Suddenly, the bot's indicators started flashing, and there was a stream of clicks and whistles coming from it. That alone would be surprising, but Will's auto translator interpreted the sound. "Please don't!"

Will stared at Dan, who shrugged. "The last update included communication protocols."

Will looked down at the bot. "You can understand me Sweepbot UL2?" There were more noises from the bot. "Affirmative."

Will furrowed his brow. "Why isn't the cleaning being done to standards?" The bot answered, "That data is not retained."

Will looked at Dan, who shrugged. "They're not programmed to record events that have occurred while doing their duties. At least in their long-term memories. We have the ability to adjust their programming using verbal commands, and then those commands will be shunted to their long-term memory. But we have to know what the problem is before we can try to tweak their program."

"So why was the voice interface added?" Will asked.

Dan furrowed his brow. "I think they thought it would be easier to input instructions."

Will frowned. "You mean change the programming?"

Dan shook his head again. "No, but it is possible to change the parameters of how they complete their assigned tasks or the order that they carry them out. We have to be careful because giving them the wrong instructions may make things worse."

Will started to chuckle. "So we can reason with them and get them to do their jobs better, but they have selective memory loss when it comes to what they did previously."

Dan smiled. "That's about the size of it."

Will thought about it for a few seconds. "I guess I'll have to check on them tonight and see what I can determine. Correct me if I'm wrong, but the Clean Bots start out in the same zone, but the Mop Bots and Dust Bots take the most time, so they do only one zone at a time. While the Sweep Bots and Trash Bots will do the whole station."

Dan nodded. "The Sweep Bots and Trash Bots actually begin their tasks fifteen minutes before the Mop Bots begin so that they're not in the way when the Mop Bots start."

Will thought he had enough to go on, so he left Dan and the bot to find something else to do to finish his normal workday.

*****

## Oasis 4, Upper CentMod

It was just after 2300 Zulu, and Will positioned himself on an upper tier overlooking the plaza level. Will watched as a small door opened, and the Clean Bots appeared one after another. He watched as a group of bots attached themselves to the walls and started to scrub them down. Dust Bots started cleaning handrails and other surfaces.

The Trash Bots went from refuse container to refuse container, emptying them into hoppers. When the hoppers were filled, the bot would race to a receptacle in the wall and empty the contents. The trash would travel down chutes to a storage area where equipment would separate the nonbiodegradable from the biodegradable elements.

The nonbiodegradable elements fell into two categories, trash, and reusable items. The reusable items were things like food containers and eating utensils from the food vendors. These items are washed, sorted, and returned to the vendors, and the trash is recycled. The biodegradable trash is broken down and mixed with the solid waste processor.

The Sweep Bots went into action while Utility Bots aided them by performing functions like moving seating benches and even entire vendor kiosks. This was accomplished by having a specialized Utility Bot access a maintenance plug-in point and turning off the gravity in a floor section, and another Utility Bot would move the object long enough for the Sweep Bot to do its job.

In a few minutes, the bots had a significant area swept and cleaned. The Trash Bots were the quickest, darting from thrash receptacle to trash receptacle. Fifteen minutes after the beginning of the cleaning program, the Mop Bots appeared. Two Mop Bots, attended by their own Utility Bots, raced to the section just completed by the Sweep Bots.

Will started paying particular attention at this point because now all the bots were in the same area. It happened so quickly he nearly missed the initial conflict. The two Mop Bots were both fighting to occupy the same area and started shoving each other. The shoving match quickly escalated to a ramming contest as both bots tried to make the other one give up its position.

One of the Utility Bots squealed loudly and rushed to the aid of the Mop Bot it was programmed to assist and started flailing away with its mechanical arms. Another Utility Bot spun around in preparation to join the melee, but before it could finish spinning and come to the aid of its assigned bot, another Utility Bot accessed a maintenance plug-in point and switched off the gravity. The bot started floating above the floor while tumbling, flailing its arms, squealing, and clicking excitedly.

The other bots joined the fight, and Will decided he should go down there and break up the melee just as Tillya came around the corner and stared at the fighting bots. It took her a few seconds to process what she was seeing, but when she did, she rushed toward the bots. Putting her pool cue case on a low wall, she started clapping her hands together. "Stop that at once! Stop it, I say!"

The bots suddenly ceased their fighting and faced her. The Utility Bot floating just over the floor was still clicking and squealing wildly. Tillya quickly looked around and spotted the Utility Bot plugged into the maintenance access. "Put him down!"

The bot reluctantly complied by restoring gravity, causing the hapless bot to fall to the floor. Tillya covered he mouth. "Oh my goodness!" She then rushed to the stunned bot and restored it to its upright position. "Are you all right?"

The bot operated its appendages and clicked. "Affirmative."

Satisfied with the bot's answer, she turned to the bot that controlled the gravity. "You should be ashamed of yourself!" She then turned to the other bots. "That goes for all of you as well!"

The bots had a visibly dejected reaction. Tillya put her hands on her hips. "Now what started all this?"

The bots started clicking and whistling excitedly all at once. Tillya covered her ears and shook her head. "One at a time!" She pointed at a bot. "You, Mop Bot UL1, what happened?"

Mop Bot UL1 started clicking. "This unit started today's cleaning program when Mop Bot UL2 disrupted this unit's cleaning process!"

Mop Bot UL2 protested, "This unit is programmed to clean this space! Mop Bot UL1 was preventing this unit from completing its assigned task."

Tillya put her hands up. "Quiet! Both of you." She then considered what she heard and pointed to a Sweep Bot. "Why did you take sides instead of trying to resolve the problem?"

The sweep bot responded, "We were trying to resolve the issue. The utility bots clear obstacles in the area to facilitate the cleaning, and the Sweep Bots remove loose debris from the surface. Then the Mop Bots can deep clean the floor then apply polish. If the Mop Bots fail, all bots fail."

Tillya frowned. "Then why are you fighting each other? The plaza level is big enough. Each team of bots can clean and not even encounter each other."

Mop Bot UL1 started clicking. "This unit is programmed to begin cleaning at section 1 and continue in sequence until the plaza level is complete. Continued failure to proceed cannot be tolerated."

Mop Bot UL2 responded, "This unit is also programmed in the same manner."

Tillya thought about it for a second, then said, "The plaza level has ten sections."

"Correct," the bots replied simultaneously.

Tillya smiled. "It's very simple then. There are two teams of bots. One team starts in section one and goes to section five. The other team starts in section six and goes to section ten."

Mop Bot UL1 asked, "How will we decide who does which section? It's all too confusing to us."

Tillya gave the bot a bemused expression. "It doesn't have to be confusing. The bots assigned to Mop Bot UL1 is Team 1. Team 1 will do the first half of the evening's assignments numerically. The bots assigned to Mop Bot UL2 is Team 2 and will do the second half of the evening's assignments numerically."

Mop Bots UL1 and UL 2 conversed with each other, faced Tillya, and simultaneously said, "That is acceptable."

Tillya smiled. "Good. See what can be accomplished if you work things out and cooperate?"

Mop Bot UL2 replied, "That sort of thing is very easy for a biological unit such as yourself. You have obviously been programmed to find solutions to problems, and you have never been in a position that required you to perform the same task every day."

Tillya bristled. "That's not true! When I was a sl—in my old job, we were required to only perform a single task. We couldn't talk while working, not even to coordinate our tasks. If we didn't do our tasks to standards, we were punished severely. Can any of you say that? I'll wager if any of you were unable to do your jobs, they would bring you in for servicing and make you better."

Sweep Bot UL2 asked, "Do biological units value mechanical units more than other biological units?"

The question caught Tillya off guard, but she slowly nodded and said, "Sometimes. The important people don't, but unfortunately, the people in control sometimes do." She thought for a few seconds. "The people who run this station value everyone and their mechanical helpers. We're all lucky to be here, and that's the reason I do my best every day to show my appreciation to those who are managing this station."

Mop Bot UL1 asked, "Will the cleaning units be reprogrammed or disassembled because of our behavior?"

There was a visible reaction from the other bots to the question. Tillya shook her head. "Not if you do your work properly. Now do all of you think you can work together and resolve your conflicts before they become a problem?"

There was a simultaneous response from all the bots. "Affirmative." Tillya smiled and nodded. "Okay then, all of you get busy."

With that, all the bots rushed off to perform their tasks. Tillya smiled and picked up her pool cue case, and Will said from the level above her. "Nicely done, Miss Tillya. You just saved us from a lot of reprogramming."

Tillya didn't realize there was anyone near to hear what happened. "Oh, Mr. Dawson. I hope I wasn't out of line just now."

Will smiled and shook his head. "Of course not, Miss Tillya. As I said, you saved us from a lot of work."

Tillya smiled back. "I'm glad I could help. I should be going back to my quarters now. Good evening, Mr. Dawson."

Will nodded. "Have a pleasant evening, Miss Tillya."

The End

# PUTTING THINGS RIGHT ON FLAST

**Pulsar 1250, Owned by I&F Investigations and Retrievals**

Isnod, Feldon, and Pindon were at the point where they had to cut the light- speed engines and start their approach to Flast. Isnod was at the controls, and he was watching the navigation display, waiting for the right moment to disengage the light-speed engines. An indicator started flashing, which made Isnod reach for the engine cut switch. When the indicator stopped flashing and remained steady on, he threw the switch, and the view out of the forward viewports came into sharp focus.

Isnod checked the navigation computer and verified their position, then said, "We're about an hour from the outer reporting point. An hour after that, we'll enter Flast orbit."

Feldon nodded and said, "Set the autopilot and come to the back. I'll get us some lunch."

After warming three rations, Feldon passed them out. Pindon looked down at his meal and sighed. Isnod furrowed his brow. "What's wrong? I thought you liked veslec stew."

Pindon shrugged. "You guys are living on a human space station. Couldn't you have stocked some chili dogs or cheeseburgers? I could get veslec stew at home."

Feldon laughed. "You'll be lucky if the brigade doctor doesn't put you on a diet."

Pindon put both hands on his middle. "You may have a point."

Isnod smiled and shook his head. "You know there's a reason I wasn't upset for very long when our careers with the Law Enforcement Brigade was over. If we could discuss the issue at hand, that would be nice."

Pindon stirred his stew. "You want to know what the plan is when we land." "Very astute," Isnod said with a wry tone.

Pindon put a spoonful of stew in his mouth and swallowed. "I've thought of three different ways we could do this. Idea number one, have the Law Enforcement Brigade assign an armed detail from the shuttle to the Archives. We land, have them meet us at the shuttle port, and if we're quick enough, the syndicate won't have time to put together a plan to counter us. Idea number two, land at the shuttle port and take ground transport to the Archives. Idea number three, land on the Archives courtyard and carry the Charter in."

Isnod nodded. "All three plans have some merit, but I think we can modify the second one and get this done."

"How do we change it?" Feldon asked.

Isnod put his empty bowl aside. "Actually, it would be a modification of the first two plans. We land at the shuttle port, but instead of getting a heavily armed and very noticeable escort, Pindon carries the Charter to the port security office. They have their own heavily armed reaction force who, if I remember correctly, has a particular animus toward the Syndicate, have them transport you to the Archives. You have the rank to get it done without a bunch of questions and avoid delay. The neat thing is, even if the Syndicate was tipped off, they wouldn't have time to react before you made it to the Archives."

Feldon shook his head. "The Syndicate is sure to have a team standing by, ready to go."

"They'll be waiting for Yulona and Lytrina if we did our deception groundwork back on Oasis 4 correctly," Pindon said with a smile.

"I don't like the idea of putting Yulona and Lytrina in danger," Isnod said with a frown.

Pindon leaned back and thought about Isnod's last statement, then a thin smile came on his face. "I can have a reporter from the 'Current Events Media' meet me at the Archives. I won't tell the reporter why I want her there. She'll report live that the Charter has been returned to Flast about forty-five sectors before Yulona and Lytrina land at the shuttle port."

Feldon frowned. "Media reporters are notorious for being untrustworthy. Are you sure you can control her?"

Pindon chuckled. "Actually, yes, I believe I can. She owes me a favor, and the idea of having an exclusive story to report will keep her in line."

Isnod nodded. "Okay, we have a plan."

*****

## Flast, Brintnonopek Shuttle Port

Feldon powered down the thrusters after touching down. Isnod opened the hatch, stepped out, and took a deep breath. "It feels good to breathe in the air from home again."

Pindon exited the shuttle holding the case with the Charter and a duffel bag.

Feldon was right behind him and said, "Well, so far, so good. If they suspected we had the Charter, we would have been attacked by now."

Isnod nodded. "I agree. I think we're in the clear."

Pindon shook their hands and then strode to the Shuttle Port Security Office.

Feldon secured the shuttle, and Isnod said, "Let's find a restaurant in the terminal that has media monitors."

*****

## Flast, Brintnonopek Shuttle Port, Security Office

Pindon walked into the security office, and the desk clerk looked up and recognized him. "Inspector Pindon! What brings you here, sir?"

Pindon was all business. "I need to see your commander immediately."

The clerk sensed Pindon wasn't in the mood for unessential interactions, so he pressed an intercom button. "Sir, Inspector Pindon is here to see you."

The commander entered the room and greeted Pindon, "Sir, we expected you to arrive with Yulona and Lytrina later today. What can I do for you?"

"I need a team and transport. Make sure the team is well armed," Pindon said with authority.

The commander recoiled a bit, "Sir, I'm going to need every team I have today. I'm expecting trouble from the Syndicate any time."

Pindon put the equipment case with the Charter in it on the counter. "Yes, I know. They're after this."

The commander stared at the case. "Is that…?"

"Yes, it is. It's the Faldos Charter, and it needs to get to the Archives before Yulona and Lytrina get here," Pindon said.

As far as the commander was concerned, there were too many unanswered questions, but enough of the blanks were filled in to do as ordered without hesitation. He opened the door he just appeared from. "This way, sir."

As Pindon walked around the counter, he tossed his duffle to the desk clerk. "Please make sure this gets to the Law Enforcement Brigade headquarters." Then he followed the commander.

They walked down a hallway and entered a room with a tactical vehicle and ten members of the reaction force. The commander went to the team leader. "Krondor, you and your team are tasked with transporting Inspector Pindon to the Archives."

The team stood there staring at the commander and Pindon, not sure if they heard right. The commander frowned and emphasized, "Now, gentlemen!"

The team leaped to action. Team Leader Krondor motioned Pindon toward the tactical vehicle and said, "This way, sir."

Pindon boarded the vehicle, which drove out the door as soon as everyone was settled. Krondor briefed his team as they drove out of the shuttle port gate.

*****

## Flast, Brintnonopek Shuttle Port, Diner

The waiter just put Isnod's and Feldon's beverages on the table and was walking away. Isnod was adding sweetener to his tea while looking out the window. He spotted the tactical vehicle passing through the gate and said, "There they go. How long do you think it'll take them to get to the Archives?"

Feldon looked at a chronometer and chuckled. "I was thinking it would take them about half of an hour, but then I realized I'm still using human time. I guess that would be about forty-five sectors."

Isnod nodded. "We'll have the staff here turn the monitor to a current events program when we're done with our drinks."

*****

## Flast, Reaction Team 1 Tactical Transport, Streets of Brintnonopek

Pindon had time to properly brief the reaction team on their sudden and unexpected mission, which put them properly on edge. Each team member knew of the attempts the Syndicate made to recapture the Faldos Charter. Pindon knew the team was the most elite law enforcement group on Flast, and they would even compare favorably with human law enforcement groups, which gave him a great deal of confidence.

The vehicle pulled to a stop in front of the Archives doors and the rear doors of the vehicle opened. Five of the team members exited and secured the short distance from the transport to the Archives door. Pindon exited with the Charter while the remaining team members formed a shield around him and walked with him. Reaching the door, two team members entered, with Pindon following, then the rest of the team. They made sure the immediate area was secure while Pindon told the desk clerk to summon the Archive director.

The director noted the tension in his clerk's voice and appeared almost instantly. He saw Pindon and his armed escort, "Inspector

Pindon! I thought you were with Yulona and Lytrina! Are you here to coordinate their arrival with the Charter?"

"In a way. I need a secure room and an expert on the Charter," Pindon answered in a no-nonsense tone.

The director stammered, "Yes, of c-c-course. Is there anything else?"

Pindon looked around. There was a group of visitors to the Archives who were there when they arrived. He spotted the one he knew would be there, and he pointed. "That lady with the camera recorder."

One of the team members motioned for the reporter to come forward. The director said to Pindon, "This way, sir." Then he said as they passed the clerk, "Have Lugron meet us in preservation room one."

They walked through a corridor to a door labeled preservation room 1 and entered. The room was well-lit, with a worktable in the center. There were cabinets along the walls with glass doors full of laboratory equipment and chemicals. Pindon placed the case on the table and said, "Let's wait for the expert to get here before we open this."

In a few seconds, there was a tap on the door. The team leader poked his head in. "Sir, there is a man named Lugron here. His identification checks out."

An older man, who was a bit shaken up over all the armed men and tension level, walked in. "You summoned me, sir?"

The director gave him a reassuring smile. "Yes, Lugron, please step over here."

Lugron stepped over to the table, and Pindon said, "Before we open this, could we have Sallday get a close-up of it?"

Sallday brought her camera closer and focused on the lead-sealed wire, also the security tape with Rabot's signature on it. When Pindon was satisfied that it was documented, he opened the case. Lugron gasped and pulled a pair of white gloves from his pocket and put them on. He carefully lifted the Charter, and the director took the equipment case out of the way. Lugron slowly opened the folder and nearly fainted. After he took a few seconds to collect himself, he went to a cabinet and removed a magnifier. A couple of seconds were spent scrutinizing the Charter, then he stood straight. "This is the Faldos Charter, and I can attest that it is genuine."

The director nodded. "Lugron, please put the Charter in secure storage."

Lugron closed the folder and carried it to a small hatch on the wall that looked like a wall safe. The director used his thumb on a biometric lock, and there was an audible clunk, and the director opened the door with some effort. That's when they could see that it wasn't a safe at all but a pass-through to the ultra-secure section of the Archives. When the charter was placed in it, the hatch was re-shut. Pindon let out a huge sigh of relief, then asked, "Did you get all that, Sallday?"

Sallday grinned. "Yes, I did. As soon as I get outside, I'll get the video to my production, guys, and I'll go live in front of the Archives for the setup."

"When will it be transmitted?" Pindon asked.

Sallday answered, "I'd say about ten sectors after I walk outside." Pindon smiled. "Please don't delay."

Sallday left the room, and Pindon had the Reaction team leader assign a couple of team members to make sure she made it safely.

*****

## Flast, Brintnonopek, Office of Syndicate Boss, Moliston

Moliston was patiently waiting for news of the operation he put into action. He had teams stationed to meet Yulona and Lytrina at the shuttle port. He received information that they had left the human space station with the Charter, and he was very determined to end this business once and for all.

He used the Dragons to steal the Charter in the first place. His colleagues warned him that it was risky to use them because they were about as unsophisticated as an organization could get. But in Moliston's mind, their ruthlessness was exactly what was needed. They were certainly very efficient at stealing the Charter, to begin with, but they weren't able to keep it.

The Charter somehow ended up on a human space station of all places. There was no information on how the Dragons lost the Charter or the fate of the six Dragons who carried out the operation, for that matter. He had suspicions about how things went sideways but no proof. After the Charter was destroyed, and the new government was overthrown. He swore he would even things with those who caused him so much inconvenience.

*****

**Flast, Brintnonopek, Capital Archives**

Sallday stood on the Archives steps and was ready to give her report. Her assistant gave her a countdown, and she started the report. "We have breaking news that the Faldos Charter has been recovered and returned to the Archives. The Charter was taken off-world several weeks ago by a branch of the Criminal Syndicate known as the Dragons. Flast law enforcement, working with unnamed agents, have recovered the Charter and returned it."

While Sallday gave her report, a video played of the tactical transport pulling up to the Archives and Pindon carrying the Charter into the building, then the events inside the preservation room. When the video finished, she concluded her report. "The Charter is now safe in the most secure facility of the Archives after experts have authenticated it as the genuine article."

*****

**Flast, Brintnonopek, Office of Syndicate Boss, Moliston**

Moliston switched off the monitor and did his best to keep from flying into a rage. He looked across his desk at his lieutenant and said, "Kimtol, call off the operation."

Kimtol wasn't convinced that was the best course of action. "Sir, this doesn't have to be a total loss. We can salvage something useful to us. Yulona and Lytrina will be most vulnerable at the shuttle port. We've expended so much putting things in place. It would be a shame not to use any of it."

Moliston thought about it for a second or two and shook his head. "No, that might work against us. We never calculated what would happen if we failed to destroy the Charter. You may well be correct,

Kimtol, but we've simply failed to factor in that particular variable. We mustn't act rashly. Please do as you're told, and cancel the operation."

*****

## Flast, Brintnonopek Shuttle Port, Diner

Isnod and Feldon watched the report on the diner's public monitor. The other patrons in the establishment displayed a general approval of the events. Some were overjoyed, some vocally hoped that it was indeed true, and some scoffed at the report. Isnod smiled. "Well, it's done. Let's go to the shuttle and send Yulona and Lytrina a coded message to report on our success."

As they calculated, Yulona and Lytrina's shuttle had just dropped out of light speed and were able to receive and acknowledge the message sent to them by Isnod and Feldon. Isnod could relax for the first time in quite a while. He looked at his partner. "We deserve a break. Both of us have family that hasn't seen us in a long time. Let's take eight days or so and wear out our welcome. I'll contact you when it's time to return."

Feldon smiled. "I was hoping you'd say something like that. Actually, I'm surprised you didn't want to go back to Oasis 4 right away."

Isnod frowned. "Why would you think that?"

Feldon held back a chuckle. "I was thinking you might want to keep the consular general on the station from issuing a warrant for your arrest."

Isnod smiled. "As a human might say, 'Oh ha-ha.' Let's get out of here."

Isnod and Feldon were from different provinces, so they parted company at the ground transport terminal at the shuttle port. Both men agreed on a day to get in contact with each other, then bought rail tickets to distant cities in different directions.

*****

## Flast, Tobolor Village, Home of Isdornac and Noduleic

Isnod woke early, did his exercises, then returned to his parents' house to clean up. After putting on fresh clothes, he made his way to the kitchen, where his mother was preparing breakfast. She looked up from her task and smiled. "Fine morning. Sit at the table and pour your tea. Your father will be down in a moment."

Isnod poured his tea and added sweetener. After he took a sip, he said, "I've missed your tea, Mother. No one brews a better tea than you do."

Isnod's father walked in and took his place at the table. He poured his own tea and said, "Fine morning."

Isnod and his mother said, "Fine morning," back at him.

Noduleic brought plates, heaping with the flaston version of omelets and toast. Isdornac ate a bite and nodded. "The fowl eggs are extra fresh."

Isnod remarked, "All the ingredients are fresh."

Noduleic finished her own bite. "Ever since the government got out of food distribution, we've had access to all kinds of food."

Isdornac asked, "What's the food like on that space station you live on?"

Isnod shrugged. "We have a flaston serving line in the cafeteria that serves nonhumans. It's not unlike cafeteria food here on Flast. The human food we've sampled is good. In fact, much of it is like ours."

He took a sip of tea. "There's one thing the humans have that I learned to like a great deal. It's a hot drink called coffee. At first, I didn't like it, but then it grew on me."

Noduleic nodded. "There's a café in the city that specializes in alien food.

Next time we're there, we'll try it."

A slight wry smile formed on Isdornac's face. "Have you had trouble out of the consular general on the station? We've heard that you and Feldon are holding a grudge against her for making you look foolish when she was a fugitive."

Isnod recoiled, "That's not true! Where did you hear that?"

"Word gets to us. In fact, it's much more reliable these days. By the way, the way you're defending her, it's almost as if you've declared your intentions to court her," Isdornac shot back.

Isnod looked like he was slapped in the face. Noduleic put her hands on her hips. "Isdornac, you've teased him enough!"

Isnod realized his father was having fun with him. "Okay, what have you heard, and how did you find out about Lynuna?"

Noduleic smiled and said, "Lytrina contacted us yesterday while you were visiting your friends. She thought since you two were courting, we should get together sometime."

Isdornac was laughing now. "I would have thought all those years chasing fugitives would have taught you some things. Some of the fugitives you caught were ladies, but the one you declare intentions to court is the one who got away."

Isnod was now laughing. "Good one, Father. When do you plan to see Yulona and Lytrina?"

"Sometime after the new Charter of Rights is signed, they voted on it yesterday. It passed, by the way," Noduleic said.

Isnod nodded thoughtfully. "I'll be back at work by then."

"Why didn't you tell us you declared intentions when you arrived?" Noduleic asked while pouring more tea.

Isdornac jumped in, "Yeah, boy, you've never had the ladies chasing after you.

I would have thought you would want to impress your mother."

Isnod was stumbling to find the words. "It's for that reason I've been reluctant to say anything. You know as well as I do I've never been someone who dazzled everyone with my ability to make the ladies swoon. I don't want to rush things with Lynuna, and keeping things to myself is one way to do that. I know it doesn't make a lot of sense, but it's my logic."

Isdornac was about to prod his son a bit more when Noduleic said, "Leave him alone, dear, or I'll start telling stories about you before we were married."

Isdornac's smile disappeared. "Maybe you and I remember those days differently."

"I doubt it," Noduleic said with a giggle.

Isdornac looked at Isnod. "What are your plans today while I'm out, making a better life for your mother?"

"I was thinking I would see Elvont at the police complex, then maybe later in the afternoon, I thought I would go on a hike. Perhaps the Mountain Lake Trail. I need a little alone time to think," Isnod said.

"Think about Lynuna?" Noduleic asked.

Isnod shook his head. "No, Feldon and I have discovered that there is a Syndicate informant on the station. We did some groundwork to try to get him to reveal himself. I need to try to think of a way to find him if our earlier efforts don't produce results."

Isdornac furrowed his brow. "You think wandering the woods in the Mountain Lake region will help you accomplish that?"

"I think better when I'm alone. Sometimes I need to say things out loud just to determine if it sounds crazy," Isnod said with a shrug.

Isdornac stared at his son. "You are crazy."

Noduleic frowned at her husband. "You obviously don't listen to yourself while you're in your workshop." Then she asked Isnod, "Did you want me to pack a lunch for you, dear?"

Isnod shook his head. "No, I'll try to time my visit with Elvont to make it convenient to take him to lunch at the village café."

After breakfast, Isdornac left for work, and Isnod helped his mother clean up the breakfast table. He then retreated to his childhood bedroom and put on a holster for his sidearm. A jacket to conceal the firearm completed his attire, so he said goodbye to his mother and went out the door.

His parents' house was situated on a hill on the outskirts of Tobolor Village, which is located in the foothills of the Utis Mountains. From the door, he could see the village rooftops and the beginnings of activity. He started walking toward the village center, down streets he had walked since he was a child. Occasionally, he would pass someone he knew, and there would be some small talk.

Near the Village center, there was a small grocery that had a small crowd gathering. Isnod knew the grocer who was putting signs on bins of fruit that were getting attention. The grocer looked up and saw him approaching. "Isnod, fine morning."

Isnod smiled back. "Humoldine, fine morning. What's causing the excitement?

Humoldine gestured to the bins sitting in front of his store. "I just got a shipment of fruit from Earth, but I don't know anything about human food."

Isnod came forward. "Well, I've been living on a human space station for a while now. Let me see if I can help."

He went to a bin. "These are apples. You can eat them just as they are if you want, or you can cut them into slices.

Humoldine retreated to the store and returned with a cutting board and a knife. He took an apple and cut it into slices, then his customers each took a piece and ate it. There were nods and general agreement that the fruit was pretty good. There were similar reactions for the grapes, peaches, and bananas.

The curious shoppers enthusiastically bought the alien food and thanked Isnod for tutoring them. Humoldine promised Isnod he would send a delivery of fruit to his mother for his help.

Continuing his walk, he made sure he said hello to people he knew and waved to those who didn't have time to stop. He didn't want to arrive at the police complex too early as he wanted to take Elvont to lunch. Before he saw Elvont, he needed to check for communication from Yesnic. The best place to do that was the Data and Knowledge Resource Center.

The Data and Knowledge Resource Center was a close relative of a public library on Earth. There was one in the village on the same road the grocery was on but at the opposite end of the village. The village wasn't very big, so it didn't take long to get there. Isnod walked in, and he was greeted with the sight of a familiar face. The old man that ran the facility looked up. "Oh, it's Isdornac and Noduleic's boy. Don't scribble in the books while you're here."

Isnod couldn't help but smile. "It's good to see you too, Minurn. I need to get access to a Central Computer System Terminal."

The old man checked a chart on his desk. "Cubicle four is available." He made a notation on a pad and had Isnod put his thumb on it.

Minurn turned his attention to some boys sitting at a table some distance from them, so Isnod went to cubicle four and closed the door after entering.

Sitting at the terminal, he entered the code that connected him to his communication account. Before leaving Oasis 4, he had sent a message to Yesnic on Treest to keep his ears tuned for any word about the bait they had set to uncover the informant on the station.

Isnod could have used the terminal in his parents' house, but he didn't want to take the chance that the Syndicate managed to trace the transmission. The main thing he wanted to avoid was the Syndicate tracing the transmission to his parents' house. It was bad enough that he was accessing the Data system Network from his home village, but he had made a number of precautions to make sure his communications were kept private.

First of all, he made sure his communication was bounced around through several servers before he accessed his account. The account itself didn't have his name attached to it, and the only recipient was Yesnic. Yesnic's account was likewise protected in the same manner. It was highly unlikely the Syndicate could hack into his or Yesnic's account, but he didn't want to take the chance of that happening.

Once his account was opened, he saw there were a number of messages from Yesnic. In the first message, Yesnic acknowledged Isnod's message about the plan to smoke out the informant. In the next three messages, Yesnic was letting Isnod know he hadn't heard any rumblings concerning Syndicate members being tracked by bounty hunters or law enforcement. In the last message Yesnic sent, he said he was hearing things from his associates that made him uncomfortable, but he didn't have specific information.

Isnod closed his communication account and thought for a few minutes. His mind kept going back to Oasis 4 and Tillya. When he and Feldon were in the Law Enforcement Brigade, they were quite aware that the Crime Syndicate not only existed but thrived in places they didn't expect. He got an uncomfortable feeling that there may be Syndicate members in Tobolor Village. He was born in this village and was reared here, so it stands to reason if the Syndicate had a presence, he would have heard about it.

Clearly, the extent of the Syndicate's activities and influence was largely kept from them by the old regime. It was just then he realized that he didn't have much of a clue as to what the Syndicate did for their main source of income. He was, of course, aware of some of the more onerous activities of the Syndicate that incurred the wrath of the Law Enforcement Brigade, but there must have been things they did for money that were low-key enough to allow them to continue to operate without coming to the attention of the authorities.

All this was relatively new to Isnod. His specialty was always fugitive tracking, so he was a bit out of his depth. He remembered that Tillya said her village was on the western shore of Trimlute Lake and that seemed to be a good place to start. He started by bringing up a map of Trimlute Lake on the Central Computer System Terminal monitor.

Flast had oceans and continents like Earth, but unlike Earth, the oceans made up less than just half of the planet's surface. The largest of the three continents had a huge freshwater sea named Trimlute Lake. The geographic location of the lake made it a major obstacle to transportation. Freight would arrive at one of the ports, where it's loaded on ships and floated to the opposite side of the lake. There was a major port on the western shore and a couple of smaller ports. Isnod frowned and asked himself, "What's there that would hold the interest of the Syndicate?"

Isnod decided that he would look into this further after he talked with Elvont and thought on it some more. He shut down the terminal and exited the cubicle after making sure he didn't leave anything behind to give Minurn a reason to get upset with him. Exiting the Data and Knowledge Resource Center, he bid Minurn good day, who just grunted acknowledgment.

Once outside, Isnod headed to the police complex, which was just down the road. In a few minutes, he was standing at the entrance of the Police complex, checking to make sure he had his credentials. Entering the building, he walked through a weapons detector embedded into the door jamb. The desk officer was immediately alerted, and he put his hand on his own sidearm. Isnod held up his credentials and the desk officer saw the symbol on Isnod's identification that marked him as  a person allowed to carry a firearm in areas where other citizens had to check theirs. The officer smiled. "Can I help you, sir?"

Isnod smiled back. "Could you inform Investigator Elvont, his intellectual superior, Isnod, is here?"

The desk officer grinned and pressed a call button. "Sir, your intellectual superior is here."

Isnod could hear a door open and footsteps getting nearer. When the steps were very near, he heard his friend Elvont, saying, "I don't think I heard that correctly, Uplad. In fact, I better not have…"

Just then, Elvont rounded the corner and saw who was there. Isnod grinned. "Nice to know what it takes to make your move."

Elvont checked the time. "I suppose you want to get a public servant to treat you to a midday meal."

Isnod shook his head. "The private sector pays more. I'll treat." Elvont looked over to the desk officer. "Make a note on the calendar,

Uplad, the improbable occurred today."

"Right away, sir," Uplad acknowledged with a chuckle.

The pair left together and headed to the village center. The village center would be called the village square on Earth and had all the typical features. This one was terraced because it was situated on a hillside and had a stream bisecting it. It was this feature that made this village an increasingly popular tourist destination. Now that flastons could become tourists.

They walked to a café at the high end of the center and selected a table near the stream. A server took their orders and left glasses of water. Elvont smiled at his friend. "I heard you were on Earth when the fugitive trackers were put out of work."

Isnod nodded. "That's right. They weren't supposed to let the criminal fugitive trackers go, but since we were after political fugitives at the time, we were lumped into the political division and given notice. The thing that really bothered us was we weren't aware of the nature of the supposed crimes of those we were chasing.

Elvont nodded and asked, "What are you doing these days?"

Isnod was surprised Elvont hadn't heard, so he explained, "Given our skill set, my partner and I decided to become to become bounty hunters. We have our office on the human space station Oasis 4."

The server brought their lunch, and while they were passing condiments back and forth, Elvont asked, "What kind of fugitives have you and your partner tracked down?"

Isnod shrugged. "We haven't been in business very long, but so far, we grabbed a human and a malnun who had escaped from a pretar prison, an assortment of criminals on Kassnin's trading colony."

Elvont chuckled. "I've heard there was no shortage of criminals on Kassnins."

Isnod laughed. "You're right about that. Let's see, we also managed to get a pretar who stole a lot of money from several banks using a computer. He wasn't very dangerous, but he was clever and gave us quite a chase. Then finally, we went back to Kassnins and brought back six Dragons."

Elvont frowned. Isnod was wondering if he was going to make the connection between what he just said and current events. Elvont looked up. "The Faldos Charter?"

Isnod grinned and nodded. "Yes, and my partner and I would appreciate it if it didn't become common knowledge among the Dragons, who managed to recover it and bring six of their own to justice, or the rest of the Syndicate, for that matter."

Elvont smiled. "I'm impressed, so that's what you're doing back on Flast."

Isnod nodded. "That's what brought us here, but we decided to visit family while we're home."

Elvont nodded. "Why do I get the general impression that there is a reason we're having midday meal together?"

Isnod grinned. "Why? Do I need a reason to visit a childhood friend and law enforcement academy classmate?"

Elvont laughed and said, "Probably."

"Well, I would have anyway," Isnod said with a grin. "For the moment, though, I've realized that I don't know a great deal about the Syndicate. I don't know how they operate or what their main source of income is. We discovered there was a Syndicate informant on Oasis 4, so all the intelligence we can gather about the Syndicate would be valuable."

Elvont nodded. "The old regime kept us in the dark about a lot of the Syndicate's activities. I've been to a number of Law Enforcement Brigade seminars on how they operate. Their reach into Flast society is staggering."

Isnod leaned back and asked, "Are they active here in Tobolor?"

Elvont shook his head. "There's nothing here for them to make money on." Isnod frowned. "What do they do for income?"

"Straight robbery, witnesses get intimidated to the point they refuse to testify. The merchandise they take is usually highly valuable or high volume. Extortion is a big earner for them. Basically, if the right people aren't compensated, bad things will happen," Elvont explained.

Elvont continued, "The type of criminal activity depends on the particular branch of the Syndicate. The more sophisticated crimes are handled by a branch known as the Top Tier. They're responsible for most of the high-level extortion, skimming profits, that sort of thing. They also receive tribute from the lower- level organizations."

Isnod frowned. "What incentive is there for them to pay tribute?"

Elvont shrugged. "If they pay tribute, they're allowed to exist. No one does anything without permission or giving proper consideration to the Top Tier. The lower levels handle ordinary crimes like robbery, narcotics trafficking, and, we're just learning, slave trafficking. The Dragons are the lowest level of that group. They provide muscle and violence to whoever requires it, and they're into a lot of street-level crimes."

Isnod thought for a few seconds. "So wherever high volumes of commerce are taking place, there is likely to be a Syndicate presence."

Elvont nodded. "Not just likely. You can count on it."

Isnod looked around and leaned toward Elvont. "This stays between us. I know a young lady who was a slave on Gostis. She was sold to slavers by the Syndicate branch that controlled her village."

Elvont thought for a second. "Where is this village?" "The western shore of Trimlute Lake," Isnod answered.

"That makes sense. There are all kinds of things they can exploit there. If they stole just half of a percent of the consumer goods that flowed through the lake ports, it would make millions in goaners. Add to that their other activities, and it's an impressive operation."

Isnod leaned back a bit. "So you see what I'm concerned about?"

Elvont nodded. "She can't go home without putting her family in danger. Add to that. You have a Syndicate informant on that space station you live on, and you have a lot of people in a tricky situation."

"Maybe I'm taking this too personnel, but I truly would like to see the girl free to return to her village," Isnod said.

Elvont frowned. "That's an uphill walk. The Syndicate was protected by the old regime. That means they kept a lot of information about them from us, and we're struggling to catch up with collecting intelligence about their operations."

The pair continued to discuss the Syndicate and the Law Enforcement Brigade's efforts to bring them to justice. After a while, Elvont said he had to return to the police complex, but he promised if he heard anything Isnod might find useful, he would get word to him.

Isnod and Elvont parted ways, and Isnod walked to the tram station, where he took an overhead cable car to the Mountain Lake trailhead.

*****

## Flast, Childhood Home of Feldon, North of Chimagian City

Feldon awoke early, as was his habit, and did his exercises. Feldon's father was a farmer and had a large building he used to store equipment and implements. It was also a great place to exercise. After he finished his workout, he left his father's equipment shed and walked to the house.

Entering the house, his mother smiled and said, "Fine morning, get cleaned up, and I'll have breakfast ready when you get back down." Feldon retreated to his childhood bedroom to clean up and change.

Coming back down to the kitchen, he was greeted by his father. "Fine morning, pour yourself some tea."

"Fine morning," Feldon said back as he sat and poured his tea.

Feldon's father sipped his tea then said off-handedly, "You know you wouldn't have to exercise before breakfast every day if you stayed home and worked the farm with me. Good hard work is what makes a man strong."

Feldon was about to rebut, but his mother beat him to it. "Kinfel, you know full well you're very proud of your son."

Kinfel nodded. "I was when he was with the Law Enforcement Brigade. When that came to an end, I would have thought he would come back to the farm instead of traipsing around the galaxy capturing monsters."

Feldon said, "Father, you know I love the farm, and I've always planned on taking over when you decide to retire. But right now, I think I'm needed, doing what I'm doing."

Feldon's mother brought over a platter piled high with their breakfast. The three of them started filling their plates when Feldon said, "You know the humans have a dish very similar to this. It's called French toast. Most of the time, they pour on a syrup made from tree sap that's been boiled down."

"What does that taste like?" Kinfel asked.

Feldon swallowed a mouthful. "It's very sweet, but it does seem to add that special touch to the meal."

Feldon's mother asked, "What are your plans today, Feldon?" Feldon was helping himself to more toast. "I thought I'd go to Chimagian and do some research."

Kinfel furrowed his brow. "Why, Chimagian, couldn't you use the terminal in the study?"

"I don't want to take the chance if I asked the wrong questions, it would attract attention and be traced back here. I have methods I use to confuse anyone who tries to trace the inquiries to a particular terminal. Using a public use terminal is an added precaution," Feldon answered.

After eating, Feldon went to his room to put on a holster for his firearm and a jacket to cover it up. He left the house and got on the two-wheel transport he had rented when he arrived in Chimagian several days ago. It was like the motorcycles he saw on Earth, except it was more utilitarian and not as flashy. Still, in all, Feldon enjoyed riding one whenever he had to.

After leaving the farm, he took a series of narrow roads until he came to the main highway. Turning toward Chimagian, he could give his task some consideration. Like Isnod, Feldon didn't know a great deal about the Syndicate. At any rate, it wasn't completely necessary for his immediate purposes. Tillya had told them that her village was on the western shore of Trimlute Lake. He didn't know which village, but he had an idea or two to figure out which one.

The countryside he was traveling through was made of a mixture of farm field and woodland on hilly terrain. As he was going over the top of a hill, Chimagian came into view. Although it was the biggest city in this region, it wasn't so big that getting around was difficult but big enough that it had a main Data and Knowledge Resource Center as well as smaller branches spread through the city, and it was impossible to know everyone.

*****

## Flast, Chimagian City

Feldon slowed his transport as he entered the city and then made his way to a branch of the local Data and Knowledge Resource Center. He pulled into a parking area and got off of his transport. Entering the building, he secured a terminal and got to work.

He was annoyed with himself when he realized that Tillya had never told him which village she came from. First task was identifying which villages would hold the interest of the Syndicate. He had the computer display a map of Trimlute lake. Then he zoomed in on the western shore. There was a city and a small handful of villages, so it wouldn't be an overwhelming task to figure out which one Tillya was from.

The city was called Yollour, and it was the main port that served the western shore. Feldon leaned back and thought about it. There were a lot of things the Syndicate could make money on in Yollour. There were goods that passed through the port that could be stolen, protection supplied for the right price, and organized labor to exploit.

Tillya definitely said she was from a village, so Feldon started studying them. The map told him volumes, in his opinion. All the villages on the lake naturally had ports, but the function of the ports varied. A few of the villages appeared to have only a commercial fishing port, and a data search using the computer confirmed that fact. He reasoned that there probably wasn't a great deal to interest the Syndicate.

There were villages that looked like they had more than a fishing port. A big clue would be a major road or rail service leading away from the village. Feldon nodded and thought he was on the right track. There might be enough commerce to attract the Syndicate but not draw attention to themselves.

He leaned back in his chair again to consider his next step. Everybody on Flast gets a photographic image every year. Adults have identification documents to make commerce and travel trouble-free. Before the fall of the old regime, it was mandatory by law, but now it's viewed as a convenience. Children were photographed once a year mainly for government records, but now it's mostly for proud parents to share with family, and the most convenient place to do that was school. Feldon was surprised to learn that both Earth and Pretna did similar things.

Under the old regime, all schools were under government control, so each village would have a school system database. Feldon searched each village's school database for the photographic records, and he was successful on the third village he checked called Resnon. The computer displayed all of Tillya's photos from each year, from first to her last year. He smiled, seeing pictures of her progression from child to teenager. The text with the pictures said, "Tillya, daughter of Yanoner and Tillmay."

Further searching yielded more information on her parents. Her father worked as a repairman in the boatyards, and her mother was an accountant at a local shipping company. Additional investigation told him where they lived.

Feldon spent the rest of his time in the Data and Knowledge Resource Center, trying to find out what branch of the Syndicate controlled Resnon. The simple fact of the matter was the old regime suppressed information about the Syndicate. So not only is the Law Enforcement Brigade struggling to catch up, both Feldon and his partner haven't been trained in recognizing the methods they use.

Making sure his notes on the pad he brought with him was encrypted, he left the Data and Knowledge Resource Center. There was a café across the road, so he walked over and had lunch. While he ate, he tried to work out what his next move should be. Anything he came up with sounded, in turn, like a rational, logical thing and, at the same time, something to avoid.

Having exhausted all the avenues available at the moment, Feldon reboarded his transport and headed back to the farm. As he rode, he considered the possibility of the Syndicate perhaps being active in Chimagian. The economy of the city is based on agriculture and supporting local farmers, along with facilities to handle grains and produce, and he seriously doubted if there was a Syndicate presence here. If they were here, he didn't think they would be heavy hitters.

*****

## Flast, Childhood Home of Feldon, North of Chimagian City

Pulling into the farm, Feldon saw there was a family transport in the parking area. He parked his own transport, got off, and went into the house. Suddenly, he was assaulted by three short flastons. "Uncle Feldon!"

Feldon looked down at his nephews and niece hugging his legs, then looked up to see his sister, Donfel, and her husband, Gombolk, grinning at him. He grinned back and said, "You know I could save everyone a lot of time later by just arresting these three right now."

The youngest of the three, his nephew, stepped back. "But we didn't do anything!"

The oldest, his other nephew, assured his brother, "He can't arrest us. He's not in the Law Enforcement Brigade anymore."

Feldon's brother-in-law laughed. "I'd be careful if I were you three. I'm pretty sure you're in the wanted bulletins. Your uncle could turn you in for the reward."

"I think they're teasing us," the oldest flatly stated. "They would have told us."

The youngest smiled at his uncle. "I want to be a bounty hunter like you."

Feldon smiled down at the youngster. "No, you don't. You would be better off selling seed with your father."

His niece asked, "Don't you think catching bad people is funner than getting seeds to farmers? I think it would be."

Feldon laughed. "Catch a bunch of Dragons, and you wouldn't think catching bad people is fun at all."

Donfel saw the look on their father's face. "Children, why don't you play outside until dinner?"

Kinfel stared at Feldon with an incredulous look. After the children went outside, he looked at Feldon. "They said the Faldos Charter was taken to a human space station after it was recovered from the Dragons."

Feldon really didn't want his parents to know every detail about his profession, but his father was good at solving puzzles.

"What are you into, son?" Kinfel asked cautiously.

Feldon was cornered, and he knew it. He slowly nodded as he considered how to explain without worrying his family. Finally, he said, "You're right. Isnod and I recovered the Faldos Charter and returned it. So far, the Syndicate has no idea who ruined their plans, so we would appreciate it if they didn't find out."

Kinfel frowned. "I'm glad you insisted on going to Chimagian to do your research today. By the way, if your role in this is over, what we're you researching?"

Feldon explained the events he was involved with to this point. He told them about Tillya and the complications with a suspected Syndicate informant on the station.

Kinfel nodded. "This is where I should ask if you're sure you don't want to work the farm with me. But there's a flaston who needs your help. If there was a way I could help, I'd be right there, son."

"Does that girl's family know that she's been freed from slavery?" Donfel asked.

Feldon shook his head. "Not that I'm aware of." Kinfel frowned. "Do you know who they are?"

Feldon nodded. "That's one of the things I found out today." "I think you should find a way to tell them," Donfel said flatly.

"I will, if I can do it without putting anyone in danger," Feldon confirmed. Kinfel asked, "When do you plan on doing that?

Feldon shrugged. "Isnod said he was going to contact me when he thought we should go back to work. When he does, I'm going to ask him to meet me someplace that won't draw attention. Then we'll see her parents together."

Kinfel nodded. "Well, that's worked out." He walked over to the kitchen door. "Donness, is evening meal about ready?"

Feldon's mother came out, "It will be shortly. Donfel, set the table. Kinfel, get your grandchildren. Gombolk, help me get the food to the table." Feldon asked, "What can I do?"

"Get cleaned up. Heroes who save the Faldos Charter and come to the aid of flaston girls in trouble don't have to do chores," Donness said with a smile and a wink.

The dinner was Donness's usual excellent fare, and everyone ate their fill. Feldon's sister and her family said their goodbyes and were only able to leave after Feldon promised the kids he would bring them presents from the Space Station the next time he came home.

Before retiring for the evening, Isnod contacted Feldon, and they agreed that their stay on Flast had run its course. Instead of meeting at the Brintnonopek shuttle port, Feldon suggested that they meet in the city of Trimlute, at a café that Feldon had already found using a city directory.

Isnod had an idea why Feldon wanted to meet there and agreed. Trimlute city wasn't on a direct line from his parents' home to Brintnonopek, and neither was it in a line from Chimagian to Brintnonopek. It may not be necessary to have a plausible reason for being there besides what they were actually planning, but it was always better to be prepared.

*****

**Flast, Velsra Provence, Trimlute City, Harbor Café**

Feldon awoke early, as was the norm in his parents' home. His mother made his favorite breakfast, and he had a tearful goodbye before he boarded his rented transport—a quick trip into Chimagian to the rail station where he turned in the transport and bought a high-speed ticket to Trimlute City.

After arriving in Trimlute City, Feldon walked to the Harbor Café and took a table. Isnod's transport was arriving shortly after his, so he just ordered some tea and waited. He was half through with his cup of tea when Isnod showed up. "So which ferry are we boarding?" Isnod asked as he sat down.

Feldon motioned to a waiter to bring more tea. "The late-morning express to Resnon. It's leaving in about a hundred and sixty sectors."

The waiter brought the tea and took their order. When he left, Isnod asked, "So what's the plan?"

Feldon shrugged. "There's not much of a plan beyond finding Tillya's parents and letting them know she's free."

Isnod nodded. "Okay, that sounds like a logical move. I have a pad with a list of some minor members of the Syndicate who have been seen in various places on the western shore in case someone asks what we're doing there."

Feldon smiled. "That's a good idea. I take it then that you've been looking into the Syndicate yourself."

"Yeah, I have," Isnod stated. "Mostly, what I found out was we have to do a lot of catching up to eradicate the Flast branch of the Syndicate."

Their meal arrived, and the pair ate while getting each other caught up on their families. After a while, Feldon checked his chronometer. "If we want to catch that ferry, we'd better get going."

*****

## Flast, Velsra Provence, Trimlute City/
## Resnon Cross Lake Passenger Ferry

They paid for the meal and carried their duffels to the ferry ticket office and secured passage to Resnon. After boarding the vessel, they looked for a seat that offered them some privacy in case they wanted to discuss the matter at hand further.

The bow of the ferry wasn't a popular place to sit being the temperature dropped once they were in open water. Finding seats that suited them, they sat and watched the crew go about their duties, getting ready to launch. Isnod gazed at the lake, then the surrounding countryside. "Have you ever been to Velsra Provence?"

Feldon shook his head. "No, I haven't. It's nice, though. Or it would be if it weren't so industrial looking in places."

Isnod thought about it, then said, "You know our fellow flastons have something we've never had before. Time to recreate. Remember those places we saw on Earth? Humans were catching fish for fun. It's a sport."

Feldon nodded. "What was that lake called?"

Isnod thought again. "Lake Erie, it's part of a chain of five fresh water lakes. It wasn't unlike this lake."

Feldon laughed. "How can you say that? That lake was frozen solid. They were hanging bait from hooks on a string through holes in the ice. I've never seen so much ice, and I've never been that cold in my life."

Isnod laughed back. "It's not frozen all year. In the warm season, sportsmen go out in boats or stand on the shore and catch fish. It's considered a relaxing way to spend your day."

Feldon furrowed his brow. "Do you think that will catch on here?"

Isnod shrugged. "Flastons are free to travel. If they go to Earth, there's a chance they'll partake in some of the more unusual recreations and perhaps start doing it here."

Feldon leaned closer. "There's a gentleman sitting behind you, over your left shoulder, wearing a blue jacket. He keeps looking over to us, and he looks familiar."

Isnod reached down and grabbed his duffel. After pulling out a pad, he set the duffel down. He went through these motions so that he could get a look at the man. Isnod nodded. "He does look familiar. We've been looking at so many images of Syndicate members. Maybe he's one of them."

Feldon shook his head. "I may be generalizing, but he doesn't look like a thug to me."

Isnod raised an eyebrow. "I recognize him. He's not a Syndicate member.

He's in the Law Enforcement Brigade. His name is Prendle."

Feldon frowned. "I've heard of him. He's an investigator, or at least he was.

He's either traveling undercover, or he's turned."

Isnod chuckled. "I can guarantee he hasn't turned. Although if he is undercover, it wouldn't do to go over and say hello. We'll let him decide if he wants to make contact with us."

Isnod had barely got the last word out when Prendle stood, walked over, and sat down. Isnod and Feldon's expressions made him laugh. "We've never met officially, but we have mutual friends. Many of them live on that space station you live on."

Isnod grinned. "I remember being at some briefings you gave at the Law Enforcement Brigade. In case you forgot, I'm Isnod, this is Feldon, and I remember you're Prendle."

Prendle nodded. "I have to ask, gentlemen, what's your purpose here?"

Feldon looked over to Isnod who nodded, then Feldon said, "We know a young lady who was sold to slavers by the Syndicate branch that controlled her village. She's free now, and we thought that her family might want to know that."

Prendle nodded. "I had the privilege of interviewing her immediately after her freedom was regained. I cautioned her not to try to contact anyone on Flast, lest they get put in danger."

"Putting her family in peril is the last thing we would want to do. We were going to use this ferry ride to work out a plausible explanation for why we're there," Isnod said.

Prendle rubbed his chin. "It may not be necessary to have a story ready, but it's a good idea. The Syndicate branch that controls Resnon is a little unorganized. They're brutal but not very smart."

"Maybe there's a way we can help each other," Feldon offered.

"That's an interesting idea," Prendle said. "Do you have a Syndicate suspect list?"

Isnod opened a file on his pad and handed it to Prendle. "This is what I've found on known Syndicate members with ties to branches on the western shore of Trimlute Lake."

Prendle thumbed through the list carefully and stopped. He held up the pad showing Isnod and Feldon the picture. "This is Covroynac. He sold some villagers to the slavers to pay back his debts to the Syndicate and make some capital."

Feldon furrowed his brow. "What's his standing in the Syndicate?" Prendle shook his head. "Shaky for a while, then Covroynac solidified his standing by selling the villagers. Their usual method of income is trafficking narcotics, theft, gambling, and anything else illegal to make money. The local Law Enforcement Brigade station was overwhelmed, and word has it they were purposely hampered to facilitate aiding the Syndicate."

Isnod frowned. "How is that information going to help either of us?"

Prendle started going through names on the pad again. "I'm getting to that." He found what he was looking for and handed the pad back to Isnod. "This is Pukontgore. There is currently a warrant for his arrest. He doesn't know that we know his name, but he's off-world. I suspect he's on Treest. If you two visited Covroynac and made some not-so-subtle inquiries about Pukontgore, it would explain why you're in Resnon and give you a cover story. That way, I can make inquiries and gather evidence while their attention is on you two."

Isnod smiled. "That might work better than you think. Before leaving Oasis 4, we made inquiries of our own. We're trying to flush out a Syndicate informant on the station, and Pukontgore was a name we used."

Prendle nodded. "Pindon gave me a briefing on your efforts in that area. Pukontgore was the street-level thug that was tasked with terrorizing Tillya's parents, among others. That'll give you a good cover story as to why you're seeing them. Again, it probably won't be necessary, but it's best to be prepared." Feldon asked, "Why isn't this guy on Flast?"

"He had to flee Flast for a time because some of his other activities came to our attention," Prendle answered.

Isnod nodded. "How aggressive do you want us to question this Covroynac?"

A grin formed on Prendle's face. "A colleague of mine from Earth would tell you to 'rattle his cage, hard.' If Pukontgore gets word his boss is taking heat because of him, it may make him more willing to make a deal with us."

Feldon smiled. "Consider it done."

Isnod nodded. "Do you have a list of people that have been victimized by this Pukontgore?"

Prendle furrowed his brow. "Yes, I do. Why?"

"I don't want Tillya's parents to be the only people we see. It would draw attention to them," Isnod replied.

Prendle got out his own pad. "That's good thinking."

Prendle supplied about a dozen names in the same section of the village Tillya's parents lived in. The ferry was approaching the dock by this point, so they stood up to get their circulation going again. Before going down the gangplank, Prendle turned to them, "We probably won't see each other today, so I'd like to wish you two the best of luck. If we have to contact each other, we can do that through Pindon."

*****

**Flast, Velsra Provence, Resnon Village on western shore of Trimlute Lake**

Prendle walked down the gangplank to the dock and blended in with the crowd. The bounty hunters were among the last passengers to leave the ferry. They found lockers that they used to store their duffels. Feldon went to a vending machine and purchased a map of the village. They could have used a pad with a map feature, but Isnod preferred paper for things like maps because he could see the village in its entirety without losing detail, as normally happens when you zoom out on a pad.

It was still early in the afternoon, so they weren't pressed for time. They walked to the section of town where Tillya's parents lived. On the way, they worked out a plan where they would visit a couple of Pukontgore's victims, then Tillya's parents.

They came to a humble little home and knocked on the door. A man a few years older than Isnod opened the door. "Who are you? What do you want?"

"We are bounty hunters, and we were wondering if we could ask some questions about a man named Pukontgore," Isnod answered.

The man's expression became a combination of anger, fear, and confusion. Then he looked at Isnod's and Feldon's faces for a few seconds. The man took a deep breath. "Come in."

A lady who was obviously his wife timidly looked in from the kitchen. "Who is it, dear?"

"They're bounty hunters, dear. They're asking about Pukontgore," he answered.

The lady looked shaken, so Isnod quickly said, "We understand you've had unpleasant dealings with him. We were hoping he had mentioned where he may have gone."

"Why would he say something in front of us about that?" The man demanded.

"Perhaps he mentioned a planet or colony in an off-handed manner that he does business with or has associates there," Feldon offered.

Both the man and his wife shook their heads, and the man said, "No, when he was here, he was all business."

His wife stared into space. "All business, very unpleasant business." Isnod put his hands together. "Okay then. Thank you for your help."

The man said, "Wait a moment, how could that have possibly been helpful, and what do we do if the goons show up asking what you were doing here?"

Isnod sighed. "It's more of a help than it seems. If anyone asks, tell them the truth, two bounty hunters asked about Pukontgore, but you didn't have any information for us."

The man suddenly understood. "This is for someone else's benefit, isn't it?"

Isnod nodded. "Only if our presence is noticed. If anyone asks what our purpose here was, just tell them exactly what happened. Two bounty hunters showed up and asked questions about Pukontgore that you didn't have answers for."

The man wasn't dumb, and he nodded. "I see. You're going to visit several more houses tonight that have had dealings with Pukontgore. One of those houses is the actual objective."

Isnod and Feldon were silent, which made the man smile and say, "Don't worry, gentlemen, whoever is brave enough to track down those criminals won't be betrayed by me."

"That's good to hear," Feldon said.

Isnod said as he turned to the door. "We've taken enough of your time, thank you."

The man's wife said, "Just one moment, gentlemen."

She dashed into the kitchen and returned with two pastries wrapped in paper napkins. "Red Swampberry tarts, fresh out of the oven."

Isnod and Feldon gladly took the tarts and thanked the couple, then consumed them before reaching the next house on their list. They visited four houses before going to the home of Tillya's parents, experiencing varying levels of welcome in each of the houses that ranged between concern and enthusiastic cooperation.

They stood outside the home of Yanoner and Tillmay until Feldon took a deep breath and knocked on the door. The door opened, and a man Feldon recognized as Yanoner from his research stood in the opening. He was a large man who was intimidating in his own right. He eyed Isnod and Feldon up and down, then asked, "What can I do for you two?"

"May we come in, sir? We have news of your daughter," Feldon answered.

They didn't know how Yanoner was going to react to the mention of Tillya. It looked as if the big man was going to start crying. Then he collected himself. Finally, he asked, "Who are you, gentlemen?"

"My name is Isnod, and this is Feldon. We're bounty hunters with an office on a human space station," Isnod answered.

Behind Yanoner, a woman's voice could be heard, "Who is it, dear?"

To the bounty hunter's relief, Yanoner motioned them inside, "This is Isnod and Feldon. They're bounty hunters, and they say they have news of Tillya."

Tillmay had to steady herself, causing Yanoner to take her arm and lead her to a seat at the table. He looked at Isnod and Feldon and motioned them to chairs. "Please have a seat."

Tillmay asked in a quivering voice, "Is she safe and healthy?"

Isnod smiled. "Oh yes, absolutely. She was freed from a falta farm on Gostis and has since been employed by the human corporation that owns the space station we live on."

Tears were welling up in Tillmay's eyes. "The Gostis ordeal happened long ago. We should have heard from her by now. Why hasn't she come home or contacted us?"

Yanoner put his hand on her arm. "She can't. Not until the Syndicate loses control of Resnon. We're safe as long as the Syndicate is unaware that she's free."

Feldon nodded. "Exactly correct. The station manager was sympathetic, so he offered her refuge and employment."

Tillmay was still in tears. "She must be very lonely."

Feldon shook his head and tried to reassure her. "It's true she misses both of you, but she has a lot of friends."

Yanoner frowned. "Flaston friends?"

"Mostly human. We don't know which flastons we can trust. However, she struck up a friendship with us and our consular general on the station and her parents," Isnod offered.

That news surprised them. Resnon was under Syndicate control, but news did reach them nonetheless. Yanoner asked, "Are you saying my daughter is friends with Yulona, Lytrina, and Lynuna? The revolutionaries?

Isnod nodded. "That's right."

"You cannot imagine how comforting that is," Yanoner said with a relieved tone.

Tillmay brought out tea service, and they talked while they drank the tea. Isnod and Feldon gave them as much information as they knew about Tillya's life as a slave, her rescue, and subsequent life afterward.

Feldon checked his chronometer. "We should probably be going, Isnod."

Yanoner said, "Wait a moment, could you take a message back to Tillya for us?"

Isnod frowned. "That wouldn't be a good idea. We have to pay Covroynac a visit and see what information we can beat out of him before we leave. If something goes wrong, I don't want anything to wind up in Syndicate hands that would put you or Tillya in danger."

Tillmay was on the verge of tears again. "Oh, please, it would mean everything to us."

"We can record a message on a data chip and get it to you at the rail station," Yanoner suggested.

"I wouldn't meet us in public," Isnod cautioned. Tillmay said, "We'll send it along with a neighbor boy." Feldon asked, "Can you trust him?"

Yanoner nodded. "Yes, we can. He hates the Syndicate because his father was also sold as a slave."

Isnod nodded. "Okay, how could we say no to that."

They left Tillya's parents to make their recording. Feldon asked, "Where do we find this Covroynac?"

"He has a warehouse by the docks," Isnod answered. Feldon chuckled. "Naturally."

*****

**Flast, Velsra Provence, Resnon Village on western shore of Trimlute Lake, Warehouse of Covroynac**

Isnod and Feldon examined the warehouse exterior in the growing darkness and found a series of windows with light coming from them. They positioned themselves to see inside and saw in one room three Syndicate members sitting at a table having a discussion. On closer examination, they watched Covroynac leading the conversation.

The pair went to a door, which they found unlocked, and entered. Walking past piles of stolen goods, they made it to the office door, looked at each other, and nodded. Feldon pushed the door open and entered with Isnod right behind him.

"Just who are these two dead men!" Covroynac demanded as his two companions came to their feet.

Isnod and Feldon strolled over to them, and the two thugs moved to meet them. The two Syndicate thugs were rendered unconscious by the bounty hunters without having to break their stride. Feldon walked up to a stunned and mute Covroynac, grabbed a handful of hair, and proceeded to slam his face into the desk top several times.

Isnod sat in one of the chairs, and Feldon held Covroynac's head up. There was blood flowing out of both nostrils and a split upper lip.

Isnod stared for a few seconds then he cleared his throat. Covroynac looked at him. "What do you want!? I would really like to know before my people kill you!"

Isnod chuckled and indicated to the two thugs unconscious on the floor. "Are they anything like these people? We're not all that worried. We're looking for a friend of yours. He goes by Pukontgore. We know he's off-world. We just don't know where."

"I don't arrange his travel!" Covroynac spat.

Feldon kicked Covroynac's feet out from under him. With his free hand, he opened a desk drawer and put one of Covroynac's hands in, then used his knee to slam the drawer closed. Covroynac howled in pain, and Feldon kneed the drawer an additional number of times.

Isnod stared at Covroynac. "Same question."

Covroynac glared at Isnod with pure hatred. "Go find comfort with your mothers!"

Feldon put Covroynac's other hand in the drawer and kneed it half a dozen times. There were renewed screams coming from Covroynac as additional fingers were broken. Isnod calmly said, "Wrong answer, Covroynac. Now one more time, where is Pukontgore?"

He continued to glare at Isnod through wide hateful eyes. Isnod nodded slightly at Feldon, who pulled Covroynac's head back by his hair. He muscled Covroynac's leg onto the desk and pulled the shoe off his foot. Then he picked up a heavy tool used for opening shipping crates. Before Feldon could bring it down on his foot, Covroynac screamed, "Treest! He's on Treest!"

Isnod suppressed a grin. "Treest is a big planet."

Feldon raised the tool, and Covroynac started screaming again, "He's in the capital! Where else would he be?"

Isnod smiled. "That wasn't so hard, was it?"

Covroynac stared at his broken fingers. "I've got powerful friends. There's nowhere safe for you."

Isnod smiled. "Okay, now that you mentioned it, you control Resnon, but who do you answer to?"

The look on Covroynac's face reflected the terror the question invoked. He implored Isnod, "You know I can't answer that! There's no way I can tell you!"

Feldon brought the tool down on Covroynac's foot, breaking more bones.

Covroynac renewed his screaming, "Please, I can't!"

Feldon continued to pound Covroynac's foot with the tool, making fresh breaks in Covroynac's bones. "Sure you can."

Covroynac was sobbing. "No, they'll kill me!"

Isnod simply said, "They're not here. We're here. Worry about us."

Feldon brought the tool down on Covroynac's foot again to drive the point home, causing him to howl himself hoarse. Then he pulled the shoe off Covroynac's other foot and worked it over with the tool. Finally, Covroynac couldn't take anymore. "His name is Dulpot. Everyone in Velsra Provence answers to Dulpot. He's in Trimlute City!"

"Very good," Isnod said. "It still sounds local, though. Who does this Dulpot answer too?"

Covroynac was sobbing. "I don't know! Please, I don't know!" Isnod nodded and quietly said, "I believe you."

Feldon gave Covroynac a chop on the side of his neck, which rendered him unconscious. The pair ransacked the office, looking for any information that might prove useful. A quick search of the office computer rendered a list of Covroynac's associates, which they copied. After copying everything on the computer and then destroying the computer itself, they pocketed a tidy pile of goaners they found. The pair left the warehouse and walked directly to the rail transport station.

The rail transport station was a section of the same facility that served as the ferry port. They entered and went to the lockers, where a teenage boy was waiting. The boy stood and approached the pair. "Are you the friends of Yanoner and Tillmay?"

Isnod nodded. "Yes, do you have something for us?"

The young man handed them a small duffel. "Please tell Tillya, Ubrose and his mother miss her."

Feldon took the duffel. "We'll be sure to."

The youngster turned and left the station without another word. After retrieving their own bags from the locker, Isnod and Feldon crossed the station and bought two tickets for an "on demand" rail pod to Raglont, and from there, they would get on another track to Brintnonopek.

After sitting, the rail pod headed out into the darkness. Isnod started chuckling. "You enjoyed what you did in Covroynac's office way too much."

A thin smile formed on Feldon's face. "I couldn't help it. That smug pile of useless garbage sold flastons to slave traders to line his pockets. Besides, he shouldn't have insulted our mothers. By the way, what was the line of questioning about his superiors for?"

Isnod laughed. "That ensures that he won't take his problems to his boss. He can't tell this Dulpot fellow about us without telling him what he told us."

Feldon chuckled. "That's not bad."

The ride to Raglont was going to be several hours, giving the pair plenty of time to sleep. They were nicely refreshed when they arrived, and there was a short wait until the train to Brintnonopek could be boarded. Instead of sitting around and waiting, they walked around the station. Isnod spotted a small gift shop. "There's something I'm not used to seeing on Flast."

Feldon nodded. "The humans are fond of these little trinket shops. I suppose flastons will too if they do a lot of traveling."

Isnod went into the shop and found a gift for Lynuna. It was a small music box that played a traditional tune. After a time, a multicar rail transport arrived and discharged its passengers. Isnod and Feldon boarded and found a seat among the other passengers that boarded with them. The rest of the journey to Brintnonopek was spent in turns napping and enjoying the scenery as they sped toward the capital.

On arrival in Brintnonopek, they took a local shuttle to the spaceport. It was now nearly time for midday meal, so they ate at the diner they had tea in when they first arrived. After eating, they stopped at a ration supply shop and chose a provision package from a standard catalog. They rode a courtesy tram to their Pulsar, stowed their bags, provisions, performed a preflight, and climbed aboard. After a few days, Feldon was at the controls when it was time to cut the light- speed engines. He watched the indicator as it stopped flashing and remained steady. He cut the light-speed engines and started the reaction engines, then verified their position.

Isnod brought a cup of coffee to Feldon. "This is becoming a habit."

Feldon took the cup and sipped the contents. "Not all habits are bad." He checked the navigation display and said, "We'll be at the outer reporting point in five minutes, and we should be engaging docking clamps in an hour after that."

The reaction engines carried them toward the station, and Feldon accepted vectors to their assigned docking port on CargoMod 6. The docking clamps engaged, and Feldon shut down the reactor while Isnod opened the airlock.

*****

## Oasis 4, CargoMod 6

They both grabbed their bags and looked at each other before stepping into the CargoMod. Isnod grinned. "I know we just came from home, but this feels like home."

Feldon chuckled. "I was just thinking the same thing. Come on, let's get something to eat, then turn in."

They stepped through the airlock and secured the Pulsar hatch. The security officers at the customs desk welcomed them back and allowed them to make their way to the Lower CentMod. The platform lift took them to the Upper CentMod, where they made a bee line to Eva's.

Eva welcomed them back with a smile. "We're closing in a little bit, guys.

What can I get for you?"

Neither bounty hunter wanted anything heavy anyway, so they each had BLTs and chips. They finished and started their walk to HabMod 4. Before they reached the connector tunnel, Phil exited the tunnel from CargoMod 1 along with everyone that went to Vestgut. With them were two haldocs they hadn't met yet, then Virginia stepped off the platform lift with Tillya and joined the group.

The bounty hunters approached them, and Phil looked up. "Ah, Isnod and Feldon, this is Vimurnus and Udlon of Vestgut. They will be representatives of their planet. Vimurnus, Udlon, this is Isnod and Feldon of Flast. They have a business office on the station."

They all shook hands, then Virginia said, "Why don't all of you go and get some rest and let Tillya and myself get the haldocs settled?"

When they had reached the HabMod 4, Central Core Atrium, Feldon turned. "Tillya, we brought something back from Flast for you." Then he handed her the small duffel from her parents.

She took the duffel with a puzzled expression. Isnod said, "Wait until you're in your quarters to open that."

Tillya looked up. "Thank you, guys. You really didn't need to bring me anything."

Feldon smiled and said with a chuckle, "Well, we really didn't have a lot of choice. We'll see you in the morning."

Isnod and Feldon turned and walked to the escalator, then back to their quarters while Virginia and Tillya finished showing the haldocs to their new residences. Afterward, Tillya went to her own quarters and placed the duffel on the coffee table then sat down. The duffel looked familiar, but she couldn't place where she had seen it. It wasn't of great importance since it was a very common item on Flast.

She opened the bag and extracted a well-loved stuffed animal with large ears. Tillya stared at the toy for a few seconds then hugged it tightly while bursting into tears. After a few minutes, she looked back in the duffel and drew out a data chip. She put the chip in a port on her SICOS terminal and played the recording her parents made.

After watching the recording several times, she went to bed, exhausted from the jumble of emotions she'd been through that evening. She finally drifted off to sleep, hugging her stuffed toy and with a renewed hope of being able to return to her home without fear.

The End

# REUNIONS

**Oasis 4, Trading Center Space Station, Owned by the Stellar Logistics and Freight Corporation**

Luke Smith was reviewing the previous days' shift reports. He didn't expect any surprises as he was briefed immediately when there was an unusual occurrence. Not finding anything that required his attention there, he decided to start reviewing the Multi-World Commerce Cooperative, or MWCC, Criminal Activity Reports.

While studying the criminal activity reports, Luke was always on the lookout for crimes that had a Syndicate connection. Most of the time, the activity was simply recorded as a crime and not specifically a Syndicate crime. Most law enforcement agencies were reluctant to tie crimes to the Syndicate unless there was solid evidence.

Point, in fact, the Syndicate was responsible for most mid- and high-level crimes. The tricky part for Luke was determining which crimes could potentially affect Oasis 4. To that end, the MWCC used a code system to rate the crimes according to the degree of probability they had a Syndicate connection.

Luke read the reports that were rated as definite Syndicate activity and highly probable Syndicate activity first. Then he read the rest as rated in descending probability. Every now and again, he would spot something in a report that would elevate it to a higher level, at least in his mind. Mainly, though, he looked for items that had a decent probability of effecting Oasis 4.

The intercom set on his desk chimed, and he reached over and pressed the answer button. Gus's face filled the SICOS screen. "Hey, Gus, what can I do for ya?"

Gus smiled, which reassured Luke that there wasn't an issue to deal with. "Hey, Luke, Phil and I need you at CargoMod 4, Docking Port 8."

Luke nodded. "Right away, Gus. Do I need to bring deputies?"

Gus shook his head. "No, it's not that kind of thing. There's an arrival that we think you would like to see."

Luke smiled and nodded. "Oh, I get it. You want me to be surprised. All right, I won't ruin it for you."

He left the security office, took the escalator to the plaza level, and walked to the connector tunnel to CargoMod 4. Once he reached the CargoMod, he could see Phil and Gus already, as Docking Port 8 was relatively close to the connector tunnel.

Luke was the kind of person who liked to be one step ahead of whatever situation he was in at the moment, so he was trying to figure out what Phil and Gus wanted before he arrived at the docking port. He could have checked the arrival boards or SICOS, but that would have been cheating.

He was quite close to the docking port and looked out a view port to see what ship was there. The ship was the *Odessa Dream*, and he was somewhat familiar with it. The captain's name was Fedir Makhno, and Luke was trying to recall the last time he saw the captain. Then it came to him. The last time the *Odessa Dream* was at the station, Brin Os signed on as a crewmember after Phil took leniency on him following his arrest for trying to steal the *Aurora*.

Luke continued to walk to the docking port, but he was having a harder time not smiling with each step. As he approached, Gus spotted him and nudged Phil. "I think he's figured out why we wanted him here."

Luke was now grinning. "I hope I'm not here in an official capacity."

Phil grinned back. "Not at all. I saw that the *Odessa Dream* was due, so I contacted Captain Makhno and invited him and Brin Os to lunch. After a conversation I had with Elias and Norton on our trip to Vestgut, I've been wanting to follow up on Brin Os."

Luke nodded. "That's nice of ya. Brin Os seemed like he was anxious to get his life on track, but a little encouragement is always nice."

The ship was completing the docking procedure when Luke arrived, but it was going to take a few minutes longer to secure the vessel's systems. They really didn't have long to wait as the ship was a fairly basic design, and Fedir Makhno's crew kept it in exceptional condition.

In a few minutes, Captain Makhno came through the airlock with Brin Os trailing. Fedir Makhno was one of those guys who was always happy to see you. He shook the hands of Phil, Gus, and Luke, then said, "I'm sure you remember Brin Os. He is now number one helmsman of Odessa Dream."

Phil shook hands with Brin Os and said, "It sounds like things are going pretty well for you, Brin."

Brin Os smiled back. "Better than I could ever have imagined. I'm finding that honest work is much more satisfying than scheming for riches could ever be."

Phil nodded. "I'm glad to hear you're doing well and put your life on a different vector."

They strolled to the customs desk, where Phil, Gus, and Luke waved their passes to get through. However, Captain Makhno and Brin Os had to follow procedures. Fedir was waved through with no difficulty, but Brin Os triggered a cautionary security alert. Luke was a little embarrassed. "Sorry, Brin, I should have told them you were coming."

Brin Os tried to shrug it off. "I'm actually getting used to it. I suppose I deserve harsher treatment for what I've done in the past."

Phil nodded. "Well, putting you on the cautionary list was part of the deal.

But I think your probationary period is about over. What do ya say, Luke?"

"I'll get right on it after lunch. By this evening, Brin Os will be off probation," Luke said with a nod.

Brin Os smiled. "That's very gracious of you."

Phil shook his head. "Not at all. Your probation was temporary in the first place. Come on, let's get some lunch."

They ate at Eva's, of course, and talked about the happenings on the station since the last time the Odessa Dream was docked. Brin Os was particularly interested in the Prospector recovery and asked a lot of questions. After hearing the whole saga, he decided that recovery of the Prospector was beyond the talents of his former associates.

At one point, Gus asked where they had been since their last visit, and Makhno said they had been making a lot of trips to Gostis. Phil was immediately interested. "What kind of cargo is going to Gostis?"

Fedir Makhno shrugged. "Nothing specific. They're not allowed to trade falta for goaners anymore. They have to accept trade goods as payment for falta."

Gus nodded. "That sounds about right. In fact, our company is going to put an office on Gostis to organize things better than they are."

Phil leaned back. "I remember reading that memo. Isn't the communication equipment for that project on the station?"

Gus nodded. "Yes, it is. It's in crates and containers in CargoMod 2. In fact, the last of the company personnel to set up the equipment and man the post arrived yesterday. Virginia was looking for space on a freighter for the equipment and the passengers together."

Phil thought a minute. "Is it the same package you and Dwight took to Vestgut?"

Gus nodded. "The exact one, except only set one is going to Gostis."

Phil had an idea telling, "How many people are going with the equipment?"

Gus had an idea where Phil was going with this line of questions. "Six, we can have the equipment loaded, and Dwight and I can be on our way tomorrow."

Phil shook his head with a grin. "Too fast. You and Dwight got to go to Vestgut. Now it's my turn for a junket. Besides, Mikey is still there, and Alice would love to go along and see him."

"You're still going to need a copilot. I'm volunteering," Gus protested.

Phil chuckled. "Nice try, Gus, but you're management. One of us has to stay behind and mind the store. I'll organize it this afternoon and get going in the morning."

Gus chuckled. "I knew it was a mistake accepting a management position."

Fedir and Brin Os thought the exchange was amusing and expressed their regrets that lunch was over when they shook hands with Phil, Gus, and Luke. Gus and Luke returned to their duties while Phil went to the station museum to see Alice.

*****

**Oasis 4, Upper CentMod, Museum**

Phil walked into the museum entrance and started looking for Alice. He finally tracked her down as she was finishing a guided tour of the displays and seeing the visitors to the gift shop. He approached her, and she smiled. "What brings you here?"

"How would you like to see Mikey?" Phil asked.

Alice could hardly contain her excitement. "Ooh, I'd love that!" "Well, pack a bag tonight because unless something comes up, we'll leave in the morning," Phil said.

He then explained what and who they'd be carrying there with them. She said she would see him when he got back to their quarters that night, and they would talk about it further. Phil gave her a kiss and left to make preparations for the journey.

The first step was getting in touch with Dwight to inform him that he was going to Gostis. Phil hoped Dwight's schedule was clear. It's not like there was a pool of pilots to choose from. He took the platform lift to the Lower CentMod and walked to CargoMod 8.

*****

**Oasis 4, CargoMod 8**

Dwight Needles was sitting at his desk working on a syllabus he was creating for flight training. It had occurred to him that the haldocs would need to be brought up to speed on space vessel operations. Phil tapped on the door frame, and Dwight looked up and smiled. "What can I do for ya, Hoss?"

Phil walked in. "How would you feel about going back to Gostis?"

Dwight slowly nodded while considering the question. "Sounds good to me, Hoss. I could use some time in the cockpit to clear my head. What's the mission?"

"Basically, the same task you and Gus did for Vestgut, accept instead of two crews and equipment, we're just taking one," Phil answered.

Dwight nodded and asked, "When are we going?"

Phil shrugged. "I'd like to leave tomorrow right after the morning briefing."

Dwight was taken aback. "No point in messing around. Why the rush?" he asked while turning to his SICOS.

"I just found out getting space for the equipment and passengers on the same ship is a problem," Phil answered. "It's been nearly a year since that whole episode started, and the company is anxious to get an operations center going there."

Dwight turned away from his SICOS terminal and looked at Phil, then said with a chuckle, "Not to mention your gal wants to see your boy."

Phil nodded. "Yeah, there's that too."

Dwight turned back to his SICOS terminal. "Well, there ain't nuthin' keeping me here that I can't reschedule. I'll get stores and rations onboard today and get a bag packed. Oh, by the way, get me the names of everybody going so I can file a flight plan."

"All right, Dwight, plan on a 0930 Zulu departure," Phil said as he turned to leave.

Walking from the CargoMod to the Lower CentMod, Phil had time to go over what preparations he needed to make before leaving. Truthfully, getting Dwight onboard was the biggest thing he had to do. Dwight would spend the rest of the afternoon prepping the Aurora. He already told Alice. Now he just needed to inform Virginia, who would make sure the equipment was loaded on the Aurora, and she would inform the passengers.

*****

## Oasis 4, Lower CentMod, Plaza Level

Phil reached the Lower CentMod plaza level and noticed some activity in the pedestrian open area. His curiosity was piqued, so he walked over to see what was happening. There were gymnasium mats laid out, and a human was in the center performing tai chi while Ivonorsic studied him with professional interest. Phil watched for a couple of seconds, then spotted Luke Smith a few feet away watching the same proceedings. He edged over and asked, "Hey, Luke, what's going on here?"

"Hey, Boss," he answered without taking his eyes off the man doing Tai chi. "Ivonorsic and his partner are going to put on a martial arts demonstration and try to drum up some business."

Ivonorsic walked over. "Mr. Ross, fine afternoon. I don't believe you met my partner. This is Xin Chen, from Earth obviously, and he hails from Taipei, Taiwan."

Phil looked over to Xin. "It's nice to meet you, Xin. What exactly are you doing?"

Xin continued his activities. "This is called tai chi. It is an internal martial art, practiced for its defensive training, its health benefits, and meditation."

Phil nodded. "Interesting."

Luke turned to Ivonorsic. "When is the demonstration going to end?"

Before Ivonorsic could answer, Xin said, "As in a circle, the end will be at the beginning."

Ivonorsic nodded. "That is what micton teaches us also."

While turning away, Luke muttered, "It's no wonder these guys had to learn how to fight."

Phil fought back the urge to chuckle. "I'll watch from over here."

Once the demonstration started, Phil couldn't help but be impressed with Ivonorsic and Xin's skills. Xin was obviously very skilled in a number of disciplines he recognized, like judo, karate, and tai khan do. Ivonorsic only knew micton, but it was very obvious that he was an absolute master in his discipline. Both martial artists thrilled the crowd demonstrating their disciplines until there wasn't anything else to show. When the demonstration ended, Phil walked to the platform lift while Ivonorsic and Xin worked to put away the mats.

*****

## The *Aurora*, Astrodyne 65, Owned by Stellar Logistics and Freight Corporation

Everyone who was going to Gostis boarded the *Aurora* after the morning briefing was adjourned, and they were thrusting away from the station by 1000 Zulu. Dwight was at the controls, and Phil was acting as copilot at the moment. Phil inputted the flight plan into the navigation computer and sent the data to the navigation display. Dwight checked the numbers. "Looks like we got three days to get there."

Phil chuckled. "Yep, hasn't got any closer."

Dwight chuckled himself, then said, "I wonder how different it'll be since the last time we were there?"

Phil shrugged. "Mikey tells us things are slowly settling down there. Griska is taking the lead in restructuring the social order and helping Gostis establish a suitable government. In fact, the Gostis general that opposed the Allied forces is taking the principal role in forming a new government."

Dwight frowned. "What's young Michael still doin' on Gostis?"

"The Army left a company of Rangers there with a multinational/ multiworld cooperative to make sure the snoshins there didn't try any monkey business," Phil answered. "They'll be coming home soon. The last of the freed slaves will be transported in the next couple of weeks."

Dwight nodded. "It'll be good to have that whole mess behind us."

*****

## Flast, Brintnonopek, Office of Syndicate Boss Moliston

Moliston was at his desk, going over revenue sheets on his computer. In addition to monitoring the production of income, he was responsible for the orderly administration of a global organization.

He made sure the activities of those below him didn't interfere or overlap with each other. As opportunities for profit arose, he would assign tasks and coordinate activities to maximize those profits. Occasionally, the need would arise to settle disputes within the greater organization, and his decisions were absolute. For all this administration, all he asked for in return was a percentage of the profits.

Something on a spreadsheet caught his attention. There was a dip in income from Velsra Provence. He had his computer graph the profit lines for each of the bosses that were under him. There were the expected dips from each organization, but they recovered after one or two collection periods, except one. He leaned back in his chair and stared at the monitor. After some consideration, he pressed a call button. "Kimtol, contact Dulpot in Velsra Provence. Tell him to be here tomorrow morning."

*****

## Oasis 4, Upper CentMod, Museum

Feldon stood in front of the toy selection in the museum gift shop. He had already selected two items for his nephews. The oldest was getting a model of the station he could put together. He picked out a toy freighter for the youngest, and now he had to find something for his niece. Brenda and Tillya walked up behind him, and Brenda asked, "How old is she?"

Without taking his gaze off the shelf of items in front of him, he answered, "She's just getting ready to start her second year of school." He then frowned. "Nephews are easy to find things for. How do I know what a little girl would like?"

Tillya scanned the shelves, then a grin broke out on her face. She walked over to the display and picked up a teddy bear and handed it to him. "Here, this is just the thing."

Feldon took the toy bear and frowned. "Don't you think she's a little old for something like this?"

Tillya smiled and shook her head. "Trust me. She'll treasure that for the rest of her life."

Feldon looked at the bear in his hands. "It's not flaston."

Brenda was starting to get flustered. "Isn't that the idea behind sending them gifts from the station? It's not as special if you can buy one on Flast."

Feldon nodded. "Maybe I'm thinking too hard about this."

Brenda laughed. "Come on. There are gift boxes for those bears in the back.

I'll get one while you pay for those."

After leaving the museum, Brenda left the pair because she had to take her shift in the control center. Feldon and Tillya took the platform lift to the Lower CentMod and made their way to the I&F Investigations and Retrievals office. When they walked into the office, Isnod looked up from his SICOS monitor. "So what did you find for the children?"

Feldon put his purchases on his desk. "You're looking at it."

Isnod stood and examined the gifts. He nodded approval of the space station model and toy freighter. Then he rolled over the box with the teddy bear. He looked at the bear through the clear plastic box front. "Are you sure about this?"

Tillya sighed loudly. "You're just like Feldon."

Isnod chuckled. "Which one do we put the data chip in?"

Feldon picked up the box with the teddy bear. "This one wouldn't be a good idea. Someone could possibly see it through the clear polymer." He then picked up the space station model. "I'm hesitant to put it in here. Gomdon could get excited and lose it before Donfel or Gombolk can find it." He then picked up the toy freighter. "This should do nicely."

He carefully opened the box the toy was in and extracted it. Looking over the toy freighter, he slid open the cargo hatch and smiled. "This is perfect. Have you got the data chip?"

Tillya pulled the chip out of her pocket and handed it to Feldon, who put it in the toy and slid the cargo hatch shut. He carefully put the toy back in the box and sealed it. Then he used a felt tip marker to put a small dot on the box lid. They all stood there and admired their work. Feldon picked up the toys and said, "Well, these aren't getting to Flast sitting on my desk."

Tillya thanked Feldon for his help and promised to see him that evening. Isnod and Feldon had worked out a system to get messages from Tillya to her parents on Flast. Tillya's parents would send messages back using the same methods. This time, Feldon was sending gifts to his niece and nephews. His sister Donfel would open the parcel and find the data chip. Then it was a matter of getting the chip to Yanoner and Tillmay.

So far, they've had Feldon's parents deliver a chip, then Isnod's parents. Yulona and Lytrina even got into the act of delivering a chip. Lynuna had the chip sent to them in the diplomatic pouch carried by a particularly trustworthy courier.

Feldon carried the gifts to the Lower CentMod plaza level, where Earth-based parcel delivery services had offices. He stopped short, midway between the Federal Express office and the United Parcel Service office. He found the next part entertaining as a FedEx employee came out. He said, "This way, sir. We'll get those packages to their destinations."

Then a UPS employee rushed out of her office. "We have the package services you need, sir."

Feldon said, "These are going to the same destination, but I didn't have a box that I could put all three in. Would one of you have an assortment of boxes in stock?"

The FedEx employee looked at Feldon's packages and realized his selection wasn't quite what Feldon needed, and he was crestfallen. Then he looked over to his competitor. "You win this one, Denice."

Feldon looked at the FedEx employee and shrugged. Then he followed Denice into the shop, where she helped him package the gifts and made a shipping label. In less than a half hour, Feldon's parcel was being loaded in a mini-container, and that would be loaded on the next freighter leaving for Flast.

*****

## Oasis 4, Control Center

The midmorning traffic rush had hit its zenith about an hour earlier, but there was still plenty of arriving and departing vessels to keep everyone on their toes. Russ Granger was busy coordinating the movement of two freighters and three shuttles. As two freighters passed each other, Russ keyed his microphone. "*Rising Star*, continue to CargoMod 7. *Pride of India*, continue to outer marker 4 for the Kastia one departure."

Both ships acknowledged the instructions and maneuvered accordingly. Russ checked the plot and saw the expected vessels depicted. Then suddenly, a vessel appeared at the outer edge of the plots range. Russ stared at the new target on the plot and waited for the transponder to link with the station systems and identify the vessel. When transponders linked with the station systems, a dialogue box would appear next to the return that provided a positive identification of the vessel. If the controller was unfamiliar with the vessel type, he or she could request further information with a press of a button on the vessel's speed, braking capability, maneuverability, and so on.

The vessel passed the point where initial contact should have been made, and Russ furrowed his brow. He let a few seconds pass, then keyed his microphone. "Unknown vessel on Great Barrier Approach, please contact Oasis 4 control on 124.8 MHz."

His request was met with silence, which made him frown. He moved a rotary switch that switched his headset to the intercom system, then pressed a button that alerted the chief controller. He heard in his headset. "*Whatcha need, Russ?*"

Russ continued to stare at the plot. "Hey, Bret, I hate to bug you, but we have an incoming on the Great Barrier approach, but they're not communicating."

"*I'll be right up,*" Bret answered.

Russ continued to attempt to contact the unknown vessel. Bret crested the stairs and walked up behind Russ. "Any luck?"

"Not yet," Russ answered. He checked the plot and saw the return. He noted the vessel's track and speed, then whistled, "That guy needs a refresher on approaching a space station."

Bret picked up the binoculars and linked them to the plot, then highlighted the unknown target. He put the binoculars to his eyes, and the plot provided directional information helping him find the vessel. It was still too far away to look like more than a dot against the nebula. He frowned. "It couldn't be a mining vessel. The Spirit of 49 has been gone only three weeks.

Russ handled two shuttles and a small passenger charter ship while Bret continued to watch the incoming vessel. The midmorning rush was quickly winding down, which relieved Russ given that there was a rapidly approaching vessel they weren't in communication with. He picked up his own binoculars and started examining the incoming vessel. It was now nearly close enough to start making out details. Knowing what kind of vessel it was would be helpful. He checked the plot and saw it had slowed down considerably.

Bret tried his hand at making contact, to no avail. He looked through his binoculars again for a couple of seconds, lowered them, then frowned. "According to our data, the haldocs haven't developed vessels capable of the speeds needed to make that kind of journey in a decent amount of time."

"That's what I've been given to understand," Russ agreed. Then he frowned. "You know, if the plotors left their home planet three or four weeks after the boss left Vestgut, they would be just arriving if the data on their ships was accurate."

Bret sighed. "I've heard these guys are going to be a challenge." He went to a SICOS terminal and recalled the data they had on known plotor vessels. "I had better tell Gus about our visitors when we get a positive identification of the ship."

As soon as the vessel was close enough to allow them to make out details, Bret and Russ started a comparison of known plotor vessels with what they were seeing. "That looks to me like an eight-seat plotor shuttle," Russ said as he lowered his binoculars.

Bret lowered his own binoculars and said as he punched a code into the SICOS. "It certainly looks like it."

Gus' face appeared on the SICOS monitor. "What's happening, Bret?" "There's an unidentified vessel approaching. They haven't made contact yet, but it conforms to an eight-seat plotor shuttle."

Gus rolled his eyes. "Oh, jeez. Alright, I'll be right up."

In a few minutes, Gus topped the stairs and sidled up to Russ and Bret. "Where are they?"

"Two hundred miles and closing in that direction," Bret said while pointing. "Where are you going to put them?" Gus asked.

"CargoMod 1, Docking Port 4, if we can ever establish contact," Bret answered.

Russ was continually attempting to establish two-way contact. He keyed his microphone. "Unknown vessel on approach to Oasis 4, please make contact on 123.0 MHz."

There was finally a reply, *Human space station, plotor shuttle waiting for instructions for docking!*"

Gus put down his binoculars. "Yep, they're just like I remember. I'll get Virginia and meet them in CargoMod 1."

He left Bret and Russ to deal with the plotor shuttle while he descended the stairs. Virginia was checking the dispatch boards, and he approached her. "We have a guest arriving."

Virginia furrowed her brow. "Funny. I don't recall any communications about arriving VIPs."

Gus chuckled. "I don't know how important they are. They're plotors." Virginia nodded. "How many are showing up?"

Gus shook his head. "Don't know, but their shuttle only holds eight." "We'll have a few quarters ready for them in HabMod 4 for the plotors who are staying with us. We'll put the shuttle crew up in the Star Lodge Suites. In the meantime, where should we put them on Embassy Row?" Virginia asked.

Gus thought for a second. "The haldocs are at one end, aren't they?" Virginia nodded. "That's right."

Gus chuckled again. "You would be doing the haldocs a kindness by putting them at the opposite end."

Virginia smiled and made a note on the SICOS, then said, "Done. Now let's go meet them."

*****

## Oasis 4, CargoMod 1, Passenger Lounge

Part of the conversion of CargoMod 1 to a passenger terminal involved installing larger viewports. Gus was sitting in the passenger lounge watching the plotor shuttle struggle to engage the docking clamps. Gus got a good look at the hatch of the plotor shuttle and saw that it had been modified recently. He remembered that the information packet and proposal that Elias gave them on Vestgut had dimensions and engineering drawings for standard design docking hatches.

He realized that the plotors had indeed read the packet, but he wondered why they couldn't be bothered learning the proper procedures for approaching a space station. Apparently, things had degraded to the point that Bret asked Jeremy to send a maintenance tug to go out and guide them to their docking assignment. After a good deal of maneuvering, the plotor pilot finally managed to engage the docking clamps. A station worker opened the hatch that exposed the power and communication hookups.

After the air lock seals were safety checked, the airlock was opened, and they waited for the plotor occupants to open the shuttle airlock hatches. After a time, the hatch moved a couple of inches, accompanied with the sound of air being expelled from pneumatic actuators. Another rush of air, and the hatch moved another couple of inches. This process repeated several more times until a set of grey, bony fingers gripped the edge of the partly open hatch and tightened. The owner of the fingers was obviously struggling to open the hatch further. When some progress was made, the plotor appeared and put his back against the hatch frame and pushed the hatch open with both hands and one foot.

Once the hatch was full open, the plotor straightened himself and stepped to one side. Another plotor appeared that Gus remembered was named Riv. He had subordinates behind him, and he was doing his best to project an air of importance. Before stepping into the airlock, he stopped and glared at the plotor who opened the hatch, then gave him a backhand slap. "So much for giving them a sense of our superiority!"

Riv composed himself and stepped through the airlock to the CargoMod. Gus put out his hand. "Hello, Mr. Riv, I'm Gus Condent. I'm sure you remember that we met on Vestgut." Then he motioned to Virginia. "This is our operations supervisor, Virginia Wells, and her assistant Fred Denkins."

Riv barely acknowledged Virginia and Fred, then he said while still refusing to take Gus's hand. "I am Riv, and these are my assistants, Fen and Bug. We are here to accept your company's offer to open a consulate on this space station."

"Yes, of course. How many of you will be staying here?" Gus asked.

"Just the three of us," Riv answered. "I trust we would be allowed to bring more if our needs change."

Gus nodded. "Absolutely. Virginia and I can show you to your quarters, and then once you've been given an opportunity to freshen up from your journey, we will show you to your consulate office."

"Our pilots will need accommodations as well. They will need a rest period before they return to Limdox," Riv stated.

Gus nodded again. "We'll put them up in the hotel. Tell you what, why don't you follow Virginia? I'll have a quick word with the crew, then catch up with you."

Virginia headed to the customs desk with the plotors in tow. Gus knew that process would take a little time, so he knew he had some time to try to attempt to at least gain a decent relationship with the crew. The crewman who struggled with the hatch was examining it with a sour, dejected look on his face. Gus approached him. "If you want, I can have technicians look at that for you."

The plotor pilot looked at Gus. "That would be helpful. Thank you. My name is Jot. I'm the second pilot."

A second plotor came out of the cockpit. "I am Vun. I'm the first pilot."

Gus smiled. To him, it seemed that the plotors who weren't diplomats weren't jerks. He nodded. "It's good to meet both of you. As a fellow pilot, I understand how aggravating it can be dealing with unreasonable people who don't know what kind of challenges we face."

Vun looked at Jot, then back to Gus. "That's a dangerous way of thinking."

Gus shrugged. "Perhaps in some cultures. Why don't you two follow Fred here? He'll get you a meal and get you checked in at the hotel."

Gus turned and rushed to catch up with Virginia and Riv while Fred summoned a baggage handler for the plotors luggage. Virginia and the plotors entered the CentMod, then they walked over to the connector tunnel to HabMod 4. Once in the HabMod, Virginia led them to an escalator and rode it to the tier their quarters were on. The luggage of Riv and his companions arrived as Virginia, and two of her staff were explaining the quarter's features.

Gus and Virginia left the plotor diplomats to unpack and freshen up. They went to the CentMod, purchased a cup of coffee each at a kiosk, then sat in a seating area to wait until it was time to get Riv and his companions. While they waited, Gus spotted the plotor pilots with Fred at Eva's Café. He could see they were eating soup, cautiously at first, then enthusiastically.

After a time, Riv and the others appeared at the connector tunnel leading to HabMod 4. Gus and Virginia walked over to meet them, where Gus said, "We were going to get you. You didn't have to rush."

Riv put up his hand. "We have plenty of time to unpack our things. We just ensured that our baggage made it to the correct quarters, and then we decided to see our assigned consulate office."

Virginia smiled and said, "Very well. Follow me, gentlemen."

They followed her to the platform lift and boarded it. Gus pushed the button, and the safety rail raised into place. Riv stepped up to the rail and loudly exclaimed, "All of you non-plotors will yield to our superiority! Your cultures will adapt to serve us, and we will demonstrate our benevolence by distributing the collective resources of your worlds!"

The platform lift descended into the extension between the CentMods, and Riv stopped raving. Gus and Virginia were both taken aback, and Gus was about to say something, but just then, they entered the Lower CentMod. Riv repeated his previous rant as they continued to descend while the people in the CentMod stopped to listen to him. Gus and Virginia exchanged looks, and Gus muttered, "Oh boy."

*****

## Oasis 4, Flast Consulate, Office of Consular General Lynuna

Lynuna was bothered by the fact that there was a Syndicate informant on the station that they hadn't managed to identify yet. She was beginning to wonder if the informant wasn't flaston as Security Marshal Smith suggested. Investigator Pindon thought the Flast branch of the Syndicate might want to keep their operations flaston. Isnod and Feldon were of the same opinion, and that carried a lot of weight with her.

The main reason she was leaning toward the informant being flaston was because of the well-deserved reputation for arrogance her people possessed. To be fair, the reputation comes from the way the ruling class acted in the old regime. The remnants of the Colavar regime were gone, at least officially, but the Syndicate was still there, and they had the same haughty mindset.

Going through the dossier of each and every flaston on the station was tiresome, to say the least. The consulate staff was her first task. She had known most of them personally for a very long time now, and she knew they would rather die than give the Syndicate any information that would help them. The staff members she didn't know beforehand had solid backgrounds and were vigorously vetted before being assigned to Oasis 4.

When Lynuna was satisfied that the consulate staff was thoroughly checked out, she turned her attention to the flastons on the station who wasn't on her staff. There weren't many in this group. A couple of freight forwarders and brokers rounded out this group. The first dossier she scanned was Onustkay, a commodities broker. Onustkay was in a position to be under suspicion due to his profession, but he avoided any Syndicate involvement by not dealing in merchandise that caught the eye of anyone who was looking to make a huge profit.

Some weeks earlier, Isnod, Feldon, and Pindon approached Onustkay looking for information about a criminal named Noglertlan. Their inquiry about Noglertlan was an attempt to draw out the informant. However, Onustkay came into the consulate with photos he had taken with friends and colleagues while he was attending a trade convention on Raytheon. Noglertlan was in the background, and an observant Onustkay reported it to Lynuna as he promised.

Lynuna continued to study the dossier of the flaston vendors, businessmen, and businesswomen on the station. Then there were the spouses of these folks that had to be checked into. Occasionally, something would pique her interest, and she would make a note to have her consulate security and intelligence officer, Palnit make inquiries. It was getting near midday mealtime, so she closed the files and left her office.

She made her way to HabMod 4 and walked to the flaston serving line. After selecting items and putting them on a tray, she looked around the tables and spotted Palnit sitting at a table alone. She walked over and put her tray down. "I hope I'm not bothering you, Palnit."

Palnit looked up. "Not at all, Consular. How is your review of personnel progressing?"

"Except for a few items for you to check on, I'm through," she said while removing her meal from her tray.

Palnit shook his head. "I simply don't think the informant is flaston. We've scrutinized every file for every flaston in the consulate, as well as the flaston tenets on the station. That's everyone."

Lynuna quietly ate her meal while thinking about their current dilemma. She finished eating and was finishing her tea when her eyes rested on the serving line, as she watched the cafeteria staff clean up the serving counter and put away the leftovers. Suddenly, she frowned. "Palnit, I don't recall the cafeteria staff being on the list."

Palnit shook his head. "The cafeteria staff is all employees of Stellar Logistics.

They already passed company security screening."

"I'm sure they're very thorough with humans, but they have to rely on the security services of other worlds with nonhumans. It would be too easy to falsify a dossier. Let's have a word with Marshal Smith when we finish our tea," Lynuna stated.

*****

## Oasis 4, Upper CentMod, Security Office

Lynuna and Palnit walked the connector tunnel to the CentMod and took the escalator to the first tier above the plaza level. They arrived just as Luke returned from his own lunch. He smiled. "Miss Lynuna, Palnit, what can I do for you?"

Lynuna smiled back. "We were going over dossiers of the flaston residents of this station, and then we realized there were more flastons on the station than I had files for."

Luke frowned. "How is that possible? Perhaps you two should come to my office."

Once in Luke's office, he offered them seats, and after they were comfortable, he asked, "Who did we miss?"

"The flaston kitchen staff in the HabMod 4 cafeteria," Lynuna answered.

Luke frowned. "Those are Stellar Logistics employees. We did a security screening on each individual before hiring them."

Lynuna nodded. "We realize that, but there may be something on their employment application that would point to them not being who they claim to be. Some nuance that could easily be missed by a non-flaston."

Luke furrowed his brow and slowly started to nod. "You have a point. We should look into this, at least in the name of thoroughness. Who do I send the files to?"

Lynuna answered, "Send them to Palnit. We'll go through them immediately."

Luke nodded. "I'll have SICOS send you the files. You'll have them before you step off the platform lift."

Lynuna and Palnit stood, and Palnit said, "Thank you, Marshal Smith. We'll inform you if we discover anything."

*****

## Oasis 4, Flast Consulate, Office of Lynuna

Palnit sent Lynuna copies of the files Luke sent to them. They opened the files in their respective offices and started poring over them. After a time, Lynuna was feeling that they went down the wrong path again. She was disappointed since she had high hopes they were finally on the right track. She had just closed the files on her SICOS when Palnit paged her. "Excuse me, Consular, but I believe I've found something interesting."

Lynuna answered, "I'll be right there, Palnit." She then rushed out of her office and went down a corridor to Palnit's office.

Lynuna entered the office, and Palnit said, "Please come in and sit. I don't have anything definite, but there is something I would call an anomaly."

Lynuna asked, "What have you found?"

Palnit shook his head. "It may be nothing, but if you may recall, Stellar Logistics didn't have the need for flaston kitchen staff in the past. However, right after your first visit here while eluding capture, the old regime tried to institute reforms to placate the people."

Lynuna smiled. "I remember, Palnit. Please continue."

Palnit nodded. "One of the reforms was allowing flastons to do business off- world. As flastons took residences here, Stellar Logistics hired flaston cooks. I was looking at the files for the staff that was hired before the change in government on Flast."

Lynuna was confused. "Why that group?"

Palnit smiled. "After your successful evasion of Isnod and Feldon, the old regime noted you may have had more than a little help from the staff here. Because of their cozy relationship with the Syndicate, they suggested that the Syndicate may want to position a spy here and used the opportunity as soon as it became available. This is all conjecture, of course, but it would be consistent with how the old regime and the Syndicate operated."

Lynuna chewed on what Palnit told her, and she asked, "So what was it that you saw that piqued your interest?"

Palnit put a dossier on his SICOS monitor. "Assistant Chef Gutroynod. His dossier looks like the others, except his birthplace is obviously a lie."

Lynuna read the report. "It says he was born in Drisloipid. What's wrong with that?"

Palnit held back a chuckle. "It didn't exist the year he was born."

Lynuna frowned. "I know it's not an ancient village, but perhaps they got his birth date wrong."

Palnit did chuckle this time. "Even if he was born the same year that the Mining Ministry established the village, that would make him an adolescent."

Lynuna leaned back in her seat and thought for what seemed to Palnit to be an eternity. She finally asked, "How do we proceed?"

Palnit took a deep breath. "I hate to say this, but I hesitate to make inquiries with Flast. I think we should make low-level investigations to avoid alerting the Syndicate that we're aware of one of their assets."

Without saying it, Palnit admitted that he didn't think the new government had gone far enough to tighten their own security. Lynuna tended to agree; however, keeping personnel from the old regime in certain positions was considered expedient and showed that the revolutionaries weren't vindictive, and the risk was considered negligible.

Lynuna asked, "Have you made any inquiries about where to look to see who this person actually is?"

Palnit nodded. "I have the planetary facial recognition database trying to identify him. So far, the computer hasn't identified who he actually is."

The computer announced that the search was done, and Palnit checked the monitor and frowned. "Well, whoever he is, he's not from Flast."

Lynuna nodded knowingly. "That makes sense. There are four worlds that have flaston populations. We eliminated one. Flast, where do we look next?"

"Treest is the most likely place," Palnit quickly offered. "Since Flast cut off support, Treest has struggled to get control of Syndicate activities there."

Lynuna was a bit deflated. "I suppose making inquiries on Treest is an even worse idea than making inquiries on Flast."

Palnit nodded. "Yes, it is."

A thought suddenly occurred to Lynuna, and she furrowed her brow. "Isnod told me he had a source of information on Treest. Get a photo of Gutroynod on a data chip with any more information you think is important, and we'll visit Isnod and Feldon."

*****

## Oasis 4, Lower CentMod, Office of I&F
## Investigations and Retrievals

Isnod and Feldon were planning a trip to Pentonos to track down a fugitive when Lynuna and Palnit arrived. Isnod invited them in. "Please have a seat. Palnit is with you, so I take it that this is an official visit."

Lynuna nodded. "That's correct, Isnod. We believe we've discovered the identity of the informant. We're not 100 percent positive, so we don't want to make accusations until we're sure."

Feldon furrowed his brow. "That's understandable, so let's start with why you suspect this individual."

Palnit handed Feldon the data chip they had prepared, and Feldon loaded it in the SICOS. They had just started to read the biographical data when Palnit suggested they look at Gutroynod's birthplace. Both Isnod and Feldon stared at the screen. Then it became quite obvious when they realized there was an anomaly.

Feldon leaned back. "That's kind of clever and kind of sloppy, all at the same time."

"I don't understand," Palnit said. "How could both be true."

"This was on an application for employment on a human space station," Isnod offered. "If the company had further inquiries to make, they would have gone through the Ministry of Alien Commerce, where it would undoubtedly be handled by a Syndicate operative."

Feldon put down a tray of tea service he brought over. "Even if the humans tried to go through the village of Drisloipid records department, they couldn't, so they would have no choice but to refer to the Ministry of Alien Commerce."

Palnit frowned. "Why is that?"

Isnod grinned. "Because the Mining Ministry closed that village three years ago."

Palnit took it all in, then asked, "What's the sloppy part?"

Feldon shrugged. "The fact that their little fiction could be quickly unraveled by a diligent clerk in an office. Humans would never have questioned the data, but a flaston should be capable of catching that little item." Lynuna shook her head. "I missed it."

Isnod nodded. "Indeed you did. However, Palnit has been trained to look for those sorts of things, and you haven't. I'm not saying that Palnit's discovery was inevitable. In fact, I'm not sure if Feldon or I would have found it."

"Lynuna and myself are of the opinion that Gutroynod is not from Flast. We think perhaps his most likely origin is Treest," Palnit offered.

Feldon nodded. "I gather that you've already processed his image in the facial recognition data base?"

Palnit nodded. "Yes, we did. Unfortunately, we don't have access to the Treest database."

Isnod smiled. "Well, we don't either, but we do have access to something a little better. We'll send an image to our contact on Treest along with a video."

Lynuna smiled and nodded. "Thank you so much, Isnod. You too, Feldon. Do you think it would be wise to inform Security Marshal Smith about our findings to this point?"

"Absolutely, if for no other reason but to maintain a quality relationship with him. Besides, he's a professional. He knows how to surveil a suspect without arousing suspicion," Isnod answered.

Feldon said, "We should get a reply from Treest by the time we return."

Lynuna was surprised. "Oh, I didn't realize you were going on a business trip."

"It just came up," Isnod replied. "One of our informants tells us there's a fugitive on Pentonos that needs to be relocated to Gostis."

Palnit reacted, "Oh my, was he part of the slave trade?"

Feldon nodded. "Apparently, he was a minister in the government." Lynuna was disgusted. "He made money on the misery of others."

Isnod chuckled. "Yes, and that's what gets us properly motivated. I'll make sure to see you before we leave."

*****

## The *Aurora*, Astrodyne 65, Owned by Stellar Logistics and Freight Corporation

They were a little more than an hour from dropping out of light speed. Dwight was at the controls, and Phil was acting as copilot. After Phil finished verifying the navigation data, he started to relax. He looked over to Dwight and asked, "Have you decided on the vessel to use in your flight training program?"

Dwight nodded. "Yup. The Pulsar 621 sounds like it'll do about right."

Phil nodded. "Not a bad choice. They can be taken from primary training to advanced light-speed cruise on the same platform although, I have to say, it's a bit much for a beginner."

Dwight smiled. "That's what I thought at first, but then I met their pilot pool. They have some really talented folks there."

"That was my experience," Phil agreed. "Other than Votlor and Rok's vessel, I never got a chance to examine their space vessels. Did you get a chance to get a look at one?"

"I shore did," Dwight answered. "That's why I'm pretty confident about their abilities to handle the Pulsar."

Phil mused for a few seconds, then asked, "How do their controls compare to ours?"

"Favorably," Dwight confirmed. "It's funny how two cultures who have never heard of each other but were struggling with the same issues and came up with the same solutions. Pitch and roll are handled like ours, but they control yaw differently. Instead of twisting the joystick, they use foot pedals like we used to on aircraft years ago."

Phil nodded. "Sounds like they should do all right. I'm not sure how involved they're going to get into spacefaring or how fast."

Dwight chuckled. "I don't think it's possible to go too fast for them. But that being said, I imagine that the situation being what it is, they'll get a shuttle fleet and pilots trained up. There'll be a mix of shuttles ranging from sublight shuttles to interstellar models. Then as the volume of cargo increases, container shuttles will arrive. Then if I read these folks right, freighters will be a popular item. I wouldn't rule out cruise ships either."

They spent a little while longer talking about the flight training program and its potential impact on the station. Before long, the point to cut the light-speed engines approached, and Phil provided a countdown. Dwight cut the Victor 150s, and the view in front of them came into sharp focus. He then started the Detroit 750s while Phil verified their position. They saw they were only a few minutes from the reporting point, so they brought up the planetary approach procedure for Gostis.

Shortly after the short war to free the slaves on Gostis, a unique system was established to control the traffic to and from the planet. The procedures were similar to those for approaching a space station, which was implemented by the allied coalition as control over the traffic to the planet. The procedures were necessary to prevent individuals from taking advantage of the chaos in a postwar environment.

At the reporting point, they were given vectors by the controllers on the orbiting station to establish orbit. Once they were in orbit, the station controller handed them off to a controller on the planet's surface, who provided vectors to a point where they were handed off to the shuttle port controller. In a short time, Dwight was settling the Aurora onto the pad assigned to them by the Capital City Shuttle Port controller.

After shutting down, everyone deboarded the *Aurora* and took a courtesy shuttle to the terminal to clear customs. In the morning, Dwight and the company personnel they brought with them would arrange to have the equipment on the *Aurora* unloaded.

The company manager for this new posting had his work cut out for him being as they had to arrange for facilities before they could do anything. Being as it was early evening, they decided that they would check into the hotel that they had made reservations in. Alice would have to wait until tomorrow to see Michael.

*****

## Flast, Brintnonopek, Office of Syndicate Boss, Moliston

Dulpot and his lieutenant sat in the anteroom, waiting to see Moliston as ordered. He had received word in the late afternoon that Moliston wanted to see him. As a result, he had to rearrange his own schedule and catch an on-demand rail pod to Brintnonopek that evening. He could have simply awoken early and caught the rail pod, but he would have more than likely slept on the journey, and as a result, his appearance would suffer. He managed to sleep on the pod, and on arrival in Brintnonopek, he rented rooms for himself and his lieutenant so they could get a decent amount of sleep and have an opportunity to freshen up before seeing their boss.

Moliston's lieutenant stepped into the anteroom, faced Dulpot, and flatly said, "Moliston will see you now."

Dulpot and his lieutenant stood, and Moliston's lieutenant put up his hand.

"Just Dulpot."

Dulpot looked at his lieutenant. "I shouldn't be too long."

Moliston's lieutenant motioned to a collection of beverages in the corner. "Please, help yourself to tea while you're waiting." Then he held the door for Dulpot.

Dulpot walked into Moliston's office, which never failed to impress. It was a large room with rich, exotic woodwork and what had to be the most impressive view in the city. Moliston had his back to the door and was staring at the view. Everything he did was calculated to leave his guest with a specific impression. Moliston getting up and warmly greeting Dulpot would have been the most desirable event. Had he been facing the door as Dulpot entered, it would have meant a number of things ranging from a request for support for an operation or even to ask for an opinion.

Moliston's back was to him, which meant he wasn't concerned that Dulpot might be stupid enough to try to harm him. Or Moliston was making sure Dulpot knew he wasn't in the best of graces at the moment. Either way, it wasn't good.

Moliston continued to gaze out the window. "Dulpot, please have a seat." Dulpot sat in a straight-backed chair opposite his superior.

"The box from Trimlute Provence has been light the last few cycles. Can you enlighten me as to the reason why the organization has to make do with less revenue?" Moliston said as he slowly swiveled in his chair.

Dulpot tried to hide how uncomfortable he was getting. He took a breath and answered, "I realize there have been shortfalls, but rest assured, I'll discover what the problem is."

Moliston kept his voice very even. "Somehow, I suspect you already know where your shortfall is, and you need to determine why."

Dulpot nodded. "As always, you can see through me."

Moliston rested his elbows on his desk and put his fingers tips together. "Where are your troubles?"

Dulpot squirmed in his seat a bit. "Resnon, revenue has dropped off from Resnon. I've made inquiries of Covroynac, and he informs me that he has had setbacks. However, he assures me that he's taking steps to correct the situation."

Moliston slowly nodded in understanding, but he was far from satisfied. "I think you should expedite the resolution of this. We cannot afford to be relaxed in the current climate of planetary reforms. One of the strengths we've enjoyed as an organization is the compartmental nature of our operations. Each branch will bear fruit according to its strengths. However, if there's a branch that suddenly stops producing fruit, we must find a way to make it healthy. If the branch cannot be mended, it must be removed before it infects the rest of the tree."

Dulpot solemnly nodded. "It will be done, sir."

Moliston leaned forward. "Just so you understand, Dulpot, if Resnon can be salvaged, by all means, do so. It seems that Resnon is a decent source of income. But if you determine there's the smallest possibility that the Resnon boss has been compromised, we'll have to close operations in that village and not return. I know that sounds, in part, counterproductive, but there is no way to determine how badly we've been compromised. Therefore, to preserve the organization, if need be, it would be best if everyone involved with Resnon disappeared."

Dulpot nodded. "I understand, sir. Everyone in the organization understands that is the way it must be."

Moliston smiled for the first time. "You've been more than an associate, Dulpot. You're a valued friend. If you say this task will be done, it gives me assurance that all is in good order. At least it will be after you've seen it. Have a pleasant journey home."

Dulpot stood and politely nodded. Then he turned and left the office. He walked straight through the anteroom, where his lieutenant fell in behind him, and they walked toward the elevator.

After Dulpot left, Kimtol entered. "It's not my place, sir, but are you certain that Dulpot will have the resolve to see this through?"

Moliston smiled in a contemplative manner. "Yes, I do. He didn't get in the position he's in being unwilling to do what's necessary to maintain good order. But there's something below the surface here, something I can't see that's threatening our organization."

Kimtol frowned. "Our new government is making things uncomfortable for us, of course. They've openly stated their desire to eradicate our organization."

Moliston shook his head. "That's to be expected. No, I'm sensing trouble coming from an unexpected direction. There have been too many occasions where a desirable outcome didn't happen for mysterious reasons. We'll discover the source of our misfortune and correct it in due course of time. Meanwhile, we must see to our affairs carefully and diligently."

Dulpot and his lieutenant strode to the elevator after leaving Moliston's anteroom. The building they were in was typical flaston architecture, being a tall building of seventy-five floors. There was a central core from the first-floor atrium to the top floor. Each floor had a balcony/walkway that faced the core, which had elevator lifts conveniently located at intervals around the core.

As the elevator descended, Dulpot's lieutenant noted his boss's demeanor and asked, "Do I dare ask how the meeting went?"

Dulpot slowly nodded. "You can ask. I suppose it could have been worse.

We'll discuss it in the rail pod going back to Trimlute City."

*****

### Gostis, Capital City, Hotel Yund

The Stellar Logistics employees and Alice were enjoying breakfast on the patio next to the Hotel Yund pool. Alice was about to experience guthar for the first time. She looked at the liquid in her cup, then gave it a sniff. "That doesn't smell like anything I would want to drink."

Dwight chuckled. "Well, you don't drink it like that. You add these," he said, pushing a bowl of crystals toward her.

Alice looked over the crystals. "How much do I add?"

Dwight picked up the small spoon in the bowl. "I like about three scoops from this. Some folks like more, some less. Be sure you don't get the spoon in the liquid. It'll have a chemical reaction with the metal and make it taste awful. Stir it with one of these wood sticks."

Alice added some crystals and stirred with a stick. She gave the liquid another sniff and raised an eyebrow. Then she sipped the guthar and made a yummy sound. "Mmmm, that tastes wonderful."

Dwight grinned. "Told ya."

Alice leaned back in her seat, holding her cup in both hands. "When do we see Mikey?"

Phil was adding crystals to his own cup of guthar. "Any time you want. He doesn't know we're here, so I don't know if he's available to entertain his parental units. We'll go to the Ranger Company Area and ask his commander if we can see him."

*****

### Gostis, Capital City Shuttle Port

All the Stellar Logistics employees, plus Alice, took a courtesy transport back to the shuttle port, where Dwight got off at the administration building. The company personnel who were going to be staying on Gostis to run operations were going to arrange for office space. Once that was secured, Dwight would supervise the unloading of the Aurora.

Phil and Alice stayed on the transport and had the driver drop them off at the Ranger Company Area. The rangers had moved into barracks that were formerly used by the Gostis Defense Forces garrison that was stationed there before the war. They stopped at the gate and showed a guard their identification cards while explaining why they were there. The guard picked up a field phone and conversed with a duty officer on the other end. After the guard put the phone down, he gave them directions to Company Headquarters.

They walked to a small office building adjacent to the barracks and entered. A soldier acting as a clerk stopped his activities and studied Phil, then he smiled and pointed. "Captain Ross."

Phil smiled back. "Not anymore. That ended when the war ended."

The clerk asked, "What can we do for you, folks? Are you trying to see your son?"

Alice smiled and said, "Yes, we are. Please tell me that can happen."

The clerk stood. "It's not up to me to say. I'll get the captain." He went to a door and opened it after tapping on it. "Sir, you're needed."

The ranger captain walked out and recognized Phil right away.

"Mr. Ross, it's good to see you."

Phil grasped his hand. "It's good to see you too, Captain Ferguson." He then introduced Alice. "This is my better half, Alice."

Captain Ferguson said, "Nice to meet you. I imagine you're here to see Lieutenant Ross. Your timing is pretty good. He should be returning with his platoon within the hour."

Phil had to ask, "Where did they go?"

"Every now and again, we get word of stubborn slaveholders who refuse to change their ways. When that happens, we send a platoon to convince them to see things our way," Ferguson answered with a smile.

Alice was instantly concerned. "Was there any fighting?"

Ferguson reassured them, "We didn't get any word of weapons play. Usually, when the taskmasters and reaction team realize who they're up against, they give up. Well, they should be along shortly. In the meantime, you can wait for him under the awning outside, and there are beverages in the dayroom."

Captain Ferguson went back to his office while Phil and Alice went outside and sat under an awning while watching the shuttle traffic. While they waited, they watched a group of container shuttles steadily landing and taking off, delivering containers from the orbiting station to the shuttle port.

Container shuttles were an odd-looking affair, looking like they were nothing more than a cargo container with a cockpit, engine, and thruster assembly attached to it, which was nearly the case. A shuttle would land and then release the clamps, detaching the container. Thrusters would fire, and the shuttle would rise, leaving the container behind. At that point, the shuttle was nothing more than a cockpit attached to a long, tiny fuselage.

The fuselage has an engine assembly on top, and four long awkward-looking projections that jutted out of each side and then angled downward. The projections supported thrusters used for maneuvering and landing, they also had clamp assemblies to attach to containers, and at each end, there were the landing gear assemblies.

A shuttle would land and detach its container, then hover taxi to a container headed back to the orbiting station. Straddling the container, clamps engaged, and thrusters fired, carrying the package to the orbiting station.

After some time, a column of vehicles entered the Ranger Company area being led by a Jeep. Soldiers came out of the barracks and waited for the vehicles to stop in front of them. Phil and Alice watched as the Jeep stopped, and Michael got out. His camouflaged platoon was exiting the troop transports and walked back to the trucks used to transport freed slaves. They helped the slaves get off the trucks, and soldiers led them to an area set up to process them and see about getting them home.

When the freed slaves were gone, Michael had his platoon fall in. Captain Ferguson came out and received a brief oral report of the operation, and Michael turned his platoon over to the captain. Ferguson congratulated the platoon on a successful operation and announced a three-day stand-down for the platoon.

Ferguson turned the platoon back over to Michael, where Michael, in turn, handed them over to his platoon sergeant. His platoon sergeant announced, "Weapons cleaning after mess, then stand down!"

He then yelled, "Attention!"

As the platoon came to attention, they replied, "Third Herd!" The platoon sergeant yelled, "Dismissed!"

Alice couldn't stand it any longer and run out to Michael. She was about twenty feet away when she made her presence known. "Mikey!" She grabbed a very surprised Michael and hugged him tight while kissing him all over his face. He said the only thing that came to him,

"Aww, come on, Mom, not in front of the fellas!"

Michael's platoon, along with Captain Ferguson, chuckled; however, it didn't put off Alice one bit. She held him at arm's length. "Let me look at you. Are you still in one piece? Are you eating enough? Are you getting along with the other boys?"

Michael was chuckling now. "All the big pieces are still there, I'm eating plenty, and most of them have to like me."

Phil gave his son a hug. "Are you too busy to have lunch with your folks?"

Michael grinned. "Absolutely not. Let me tell the captain where I'm going, and we'll grab a bite. We found a café within walking distance that's quite nice."

Michael had a quick word with Captain Ferguson, then the three of them walked to a café just off the shuttle port. They decided that Michael was right about it being nice. Michael caught them up with what was happening on Gostis and his duties here. Finally, he asked, "How long are you going to be here, and what are your plans?"

Phil answered, "Actually, we can leave anytime we want. But since you have a stand-down for three days, perhaps we can stick around, and you can show us around."

Michael nodded. "Be glad to. I have a report to write today, but tomorrow I can be all yours. Is there anything special you want to see?"

"Do you think you can take us to the farm where Roseanne Evans and Tillya lived?" Alice asked.

Michael nodded. "Yeah, sure. It's not too far from here."

Michael knew his mother well enough to know she had ulterior motives. For his part, Phil's hackles have been raised since they left Oasis 4. Whatever Alice had planned, it was probably something to do with the museum.

Phil said, "We'll rent a transport in the morning and go out there." Michael nodded. "I'll meet you at the hotel for breakfast."

*****

**Flast, Velsra Provence, Trimlute City, Office of Dulpot**

The moment Dulpot returned from Brintnonopek, he had sent word to Covroynac to meet him the next morning. The meeting with Covroynac could go either way for both of them. To that end, he sent his personal yacht to transport him from Resnon to Trimlute City. The boat was crewed by aids loyal to Dulpot whom humans would refer to as wise guys.

When the boat docked, he was given word that Covroynac would be there shortly, being as the dock was a short walk from his headquarters. His office wasn't as imposing as Moliston's. He obviously conducted a great deal of business there, but it did have a decent view of Trimlute Lake. There was a tap at the door, and his lieutenant entered. "Sir, Covroynac is here."

Dulpot looked up from his work. "Show him in Naplorn."

Naplorn disappeared and returned a second later with Covroynac being aided by one of his men. The man helped Covroynac to a chair in front of his desk and then helped him sit. It was very obvious that he had extreme difficulty walking. His fingers were bent at odd angles and showed signs of being not fully functional.

When Covroynac was settled, he turned to his aide. "Thank you, Jotlor, but I'm sure Dulpot wants to see me alone."

Dulpot nodded and smiled at Jotlor. "We'll only be a few minutes, Jotlor. Have Naplorn show you to the beverage service."

Naplorn showed Jotlor out and closed the door. Dulpot looked Covroynac in the eye. "I'll come right to the point Covroynac. The box from Resnon has been nonexistent for the last few cycles. That makes the box from Velsra Provence my superior light. My superior isn't a fool, and he's not near as patient as I am in these matters. I think you'll agree that the present situation is unacceptable and must be resolved immediately."

Covroynac squirmed in his seat. "Sir, we've had setbacks, and—"

"Are those setbacks the reason you can't walk without help or hold a writing tool?" Dulpot interrupted.

Covroynac had to fight back the urge to cry. He had no good answers for Dulpot, but lying would only make things worse. He inhaled deeply. "Yes, sir."

Dulpot frowned. "Don't make me ask endless questions." Covroynac swallowed. "Two men, flaston, came into my warehouse.

I was going over strategies to meet the upcoming projections with Jotlor and my other associate Gordlid when they just walked in bold as could be. Jotlor and Gordlid went to teach them manners, but the two strangers knew micton, and it was a short fight."

Dulpot nodded. "So what happened while Jotlor and Gordlid took their nap?"

Covroynac wasn't any more comfortable. "The two of them worked me over.

They wanted to know where one of my associates was." Dulpot frowned. "Who?"

"Pukontgore," Covroynac quickly offered. "They were looking for Pukontgore."

Dulpot frowned. "What did you tell them?"

Covroynac was now in a position he had desperately hoped to avoid. It was bad enough that he had to tell Dulpot what happened at his warehouse, but lying would only make things worse for him. Perhaps Dulpot would be understanding or even offer to help correct his problems. He looked down and answered, "I told them he was on Treest in the capital."

Dulpot rubbed his chin and nodded slowly. "Have you ever seen the two who visited you?"

Covroynac shook his head. "No, and I haven't seen them since. After knocking me out, they ransacked my office." He looked away and sighed. "They even stole a pile of goaners I was going to send to you."

Dulpot frowned. "Help me remember. Pukontgore is your lieutenant. Isn't that right?"

Covroynac nodded. "He's been with me from the beginning. We took over Resnon together."

"Yet he's not here," Dulpot interrupted.

Covroynac squirmed in his seat. "Pukontgore put together a crew and tried to rob a shipment of fur clothing, very high-end merchandise. The shipment's security was more robust than they anticipated, and they were fortunate to just get away. It gets worse. There were security monitors that recorded his image. They now have a face, but since Pukontgore had never been tied to any previous crimes, they didn't have a name. I sent him to Treest to wait until things settled down. He was thinking of getting cosmetic surgery to trick facial recognition software as a precaution."

"Who did you send Pukontgore to?" Dulpot inquired. "Jostorlac in the Capital," Covroynac quickly offered.

Dulpot considered what Covroynac told him. He looked out on the lake for a few minutes while Covroynac sat silent and uncomfortable. Finally, he turned back to Covroynac. "You brought Jotlor with you. How many of your aides are back in Resnon?"

Covroynac answered, "One other. His name is Gordlid. I'm looking for more that I can trust. Resnon is too valuable to leave to the locals. I also have some associates there who don't mind getting their hands dirty, but I don't believe they're candidates for rising in our ranks."

Dulpot nodded. "Perhaps I can help with your staffing problems. Go back to Resnon for now, and I'll consider what can be done. You can have the use of my boat for your return trip."

Covroynac thanked Dulpot and limped out of the office without another word. He didn't waste any time getting to the power yacht with the help of Jotlor, and after the boat's crew made them comfortable, they cast off.

*****

**Flast, Velsra Provence, The *Thrapmore*,
Power Yacht Owned by Crime Boss, Dulpot**

The boat was fast for its size. Dulpot selected the model while on Earth. He couldn't have a one-hundred-foot yacht transported from Earth to Flast, so he worked a deal with the Delaware boatyard, who supplied drawings and engineers to oversee the construction in a flaston boatyard on Trimlute Lake.

When they cleared the harbor entrance markers, the captain set a course for its 450-sector or five-hour voyage to Resnon. The communication set chirped, indicating an incoming encrypted message. A crewmember read the message and showed it to the captain, who made a course correction.

After reaching the deepest part of the lake, crewmen approached Covroynac and Jotlor who were at the aft end of the vessel. Three crewmen grabbed Jotlor, and a fourth put a shackle on his leg that had a four-kilogram weight attached to it. They picked up Jotlor and heaved him over the side before he had time to react.

Covroynac watched in horror as Jotlor disappeared below the water's surface. He knew he was doomed, as they were out of sight of land, and there were no vessels in sight, so screaming for help would do him no good. A weighted shackle was put on his leg. He was picked up and tossed overboard like Jotlor.

A crewman went to the captain to inform him the task was done. The captain nodded and resumed a course to Resnon. "We have one more, a man named Gordlid. We'll find him at Covroynac's warehouse. Let's get this over with.

*****

**Gostis, Capital City, Hotel Yund**

Alice and Phil were enjoying a Gostis breakfast on the patio with Michael. They were drinking guthar and planning the rest of the day. A low wall with greenery on top divided them from the adjacent tables.

They heard a group of snoshins sit at the table next to theirs, and the waiter came out to take their orders.

As the snoshins studied the menu, the waiter asked, "What brings you to Capital City?"

"We're looking for work," one of the snoshins answered.

The waiter casually pressed, "Were you in the defense forces?"

One of the snoshin answered, "That's right. We can't do that any longer since they don't need a large force. We didn't make the list of soldiers being asked to stay on."

"I'm glad I wasn't on the list," another added. "I feel very fortunate to just be alive."

The waiter asked, "You saw a lot of fighting, I take it."

The former soldier nodded. "Enough to last a score of lifetimes."

One in the group stated, "I'd be willing to pick falta for the rest of my life if it meant I didn't have to live through anything like the Battle of the Rondoli River Valley again."

That last statement caught Michael's attention. The first snoshin nodded. "Those are the same humans that we fought when I was in the Fifth Mechanized. We were searching the forest for them. They used techniques to blend into the landscape. A group of them just appeared right next to us. They were close enough to bury a knife in our guts if they wanted to. We had no choice but to surrender."

The snoshin who was in the Rondoli River Valley said, "You're fortunate you didn't have to fight them any more than you had to. Nothing could prepare you for that kind of viciousness."

One of the snoshins, who was silent up to this point, added, "I was in a reaction team. The humans we were against are called Ukrainian Spetsnaz. After they captured us, they started evaluating our equipment. The stun batons we used to control unruly slaves interested them, so they decided to test them."

One of the former soldiers gasped. "They didn't use them on their prisoners, did they?"

The ex-reaction team member shook his head. "That would be expected. What they actually did was more bizarre. They used the batons on each other. After everyone was zapped once, they had contests to see who could be zapped the longest without falling down. Believe me, watching them made an impression."

Phil looked up and said, "Are you two ready to go?"

Alice and Michael put their guthar cups down, and both said, "You bet."

When they stood, the snoshins at the next table realized the table next to them seated humans and it made them visibly uneasy. While Phil was putting a tip on the table, Michael approached them. "You gents may want to check with the shuttle port authority. They have job postings there occasionally."

The group of former soldiers was stunned at first and said nothing. Finally, one of them nodded and said, "Thank you. We'll do just that." Michael smiled, then showed his parents out of the patio area and through the lobby, where he had them get in a transport he had rented. Phil and Alice were settling in and getting comfortable while Michael pulled out onto the avenue. Phil said, "I was going to rent one of these.

You didn't have to get one."

Michael shrugged. "I already had it. When we have a stand down, it makes it a little easier to get around and see the sights. Besides, it doesn't cost very much."

Phil asked, "How far away is this farm we're going to?"

Michael checked a navigation tool installed in the vehicle. "About forty-five minutes away."

Alice had to ask, "Are we going to be seeing where you were in combat?"

Michael nodded. "Very close. I can show you where I landed in the drop zone. We'll be on the edge of the battlefield where we were engaged in fighting the Fifth Mechanized. Then, of course, we had that little dust up at the Zisros farm."

The scenery of Capital City gave away to woodlands and falta farms. They would occasionally pass a field with workers in it or a wagon used to transport falta pods. After about thirty minutes, Michael slowed to a stop and pointed to a field. "That's our drop zone. I landed about a hundred meters beyond that fence line."

Phil looked around to get his bearings. Then he said, pointing, "Okay, if I remember correctly, we flew from that direction to that direction."

Michael nodded. "That's right. After we landed and met at our rally points, we road marched toward the Rondoli River Valley in that direction," he said, pointing, "since our company wasn't tasked with attacking the Data Center or the military shuttle port."

Phil thought a second, remembering what the snoshin said a breakfast, "Do you think later we can see the Rondoli River Valley?"

Michael shrugged. "I guess so. In fact, I'm a little curious to see if nature has erased any sign of the battle."

Michael started the transport and continued their travels. While he drove, he pointed out different places he had been while engaged with the Fifth Mechanized Division. Before they knew it, they were passing through the gates that marked the Zisros property.

Michael had to slow down for the occasional wagon of falta or farmworker. Soon, they came to a group of buildings that had an appearance of once heavy usage but now had a semi-abandoned quality, kind of like an elementary school during summer vacation.

They got out of the stopped transport, and Michael started pointing out features that he knew. "Over there is the processing house. That's where the falta is removed from the pods and bailed." He pointed over the stone wall to the building past the little stone-paved courtyard. "Men's sleeping area on the right, ladies on the left, and in the center is the common area with a kitchen and dining tables."

Behind them, a woman's voice got their attention. "You there! This is private property, not a tourist attraction!"

When the woman got close, she stopped short and pointed at Michael. "I recognize you. You were in charge of some of the soldiers who fought the reaction team here."

Michael nodded. "Yes, ma'am. Lt. Michael Ross at your service, and you're Madam Zisros.

Madam Zisros looked at the three. "What are you doing here? I have no more slaves to take away."

Alice stepped forward. "I was wondering if I could talk to you for a few minutes."

A confused but compliant Madam Zisros followed Alice to the door of the slave quarters, and Alice looked back at Phil and Michael. "We'll be a few minutes. Find something to do in the meantime."

Madam Zisros was getting impatient. "What is it you want?"

Alice opened the door and said as she entered the slave quarters common area. "I'd like to bargain with you for some items."

Madam Zisros frowned. "What good is any of this to anyone?"

Alice ignored her question. "I'd like to purchase this table and benches." She looked in the kitchen area and selected some items, then looked around. "I'll take the dishes and cutlery also."

At that moment, a snoshin woman walked in. Alice saw that her hands were rough, and her arms had the marks of years of picking falta. The newcomer said, "Madam Zisros, we'll have three wagons for the processing house before sundown."

Madam Zisros looked at her. "Very good, Glinda. That means we should have enough for ten bales."

Alice could tell that being polite was something that didn't come easily to Madam Zisros, but she felt that making an effort was now required to maintain a harmonious relationship with the people who make their living, keeping her farm functioning. Alice smiled "Excuse me, Glinda, but did you live here?"

Glinda answered in a slightly defensive tone, "Yes, I did. I left after I got my freedom. Since then, I got a husband, and now we live in a small home that's ours."

Alice kept smiling. "Well, you must know Rosanne and Tillya."

Glinda was caught flat-footed but recovered quickly and broke out into a broad grin. "Oh yes, I certainly do! Do you know them?"

Alice nodded. "Yes, I do. Since they left here, they've both become two of my dearest friends. You're just the person to ask Glinda. Which beds belonged to Tillya and Rosanne?"

Glinda opened the door to the sleeping area. "Of course, it's just back here." Glinda threaded her way through rows of bunks in the cramped sleeping quarters, with Alice and Madam Zisros following. She stopped in front of a three-tier wooden bunk bed.

The bed had thin mattresses over rope suspensions and didn't look comfortable in the least. Then there was a small cabinet divided into three compartments next to the bunk. "Tillya slept here, Rosanne slept here, and I slept here," she said, pointing from top to bottom beds.

Alice turned to Madam Zisros. "I'll take this bunk bed and cabinet also." Madam Zisros was starting to get flustered in addition to her bewilderment.

"Tell me why you want any of these things? They're no good to anyone!"

Alice stared a Madam Zisros in a fashion that showed pity. Finally, she said, "Are you saying you would be unwilling to live in these quarters?"

Madam Zisros frowned. "Of course not. These accommodations aren't fit to live in."

"Yet you forced dozens to live like this," Alice retorted.

Madam Zisros wasn't expecting to be confronted with that reality again. Since her supply of slave labor vanished, she's had to manage the plantation herself, which meant she's had to do a good deal of labor for the first time in her life, giving her a new perspective on the value of work and those who do it. She was very obviously ashamed. "Well, that's over now, but you still haven't told me what you wanted these things for."

Alice answered, "My name is Alice Ross. My husband is the manager of a space station called Oasis 4. I curate a museum on the station, and we have displays that show significant events in the station's history. We were very involved in the invasion of this world, and I think it's important that people get an opportunity to see why we felt it was necessary to take the risks that we took." Madam Zisros frowned. "I'm not sure how I feel about letting the whole galaxy know what the life of a slave was like here on Gostis. On the one hand, I feel you're absolutely right. The plight of the people we held here should be on display to serve as a teaching tool to anyone who might be under the impression that being a slave wasn't so terrible. On the other hand, I'm horribly embarrassed we did this in the first place. I've had a lot of time to reflect on what we went through. At first, I was livid that our social order was called into question. Because I had grown up with the system, I thought it was the natural order of things. I still don't understand how the social order will function in the absence of the old system, but I'm not so old that I cannot change with the times."

Alice quickly negotiated for the items while Madam Zisros was in a reflective mood. In a short time, they agreed on a price that they both thought was fair. Alice said she would come tomorrow to take the things she had bought, and Madam Zisros said that would be acceptable.

Outside the slave quarters, Glinda asked, "That last day of slavery, things happened so quickly. Do you think you could get messages to Tillya and Rosanne for me?"

Alice smiled. "Of course, I can. I'll be here tomorrow to get the things I bought, and you can give them to me then.

Phil and Michael rejoined Alice, and they left the Zisros property in their rented transport. Phil felt his stomach growl, and he said, "It's about lunchtime. Is there anything near here?"

Michael thought for a second. "Yes, there is. There's a café in a village near here that was opened by former slaves."

*****

## Gostis, Rondoli River Valley

Michael Ross and his parents stood on Hill 567 in the Rondoli River Valley. He explained that Colonel Kline used this point as his headquarters during the battle. There were clear views of both the shuttle port and the data center that were attacked in the opening moments of the ground war. Michael pointed out where his position was during the battle and the sequence of events. Alice took in the view. "This is such a lovely little valley. It's hard to imagine that there was anything like the terrible events you described ever occurred here."

The trio boarded the rented transport, and Michael drove down the narrow lane into the valley. They came to the intersection of the lane and the road that went the length of the valley. The road had several bridges where it crossed the serpentine Rondoli River. Michael stopped at one that had a burned-out armored vehicle near it. He explained how his platoon used a missile to stop the vehicle and turn it into a roadblock. Then he explained how one of the other platoons did the same to a vehicle to prevent the Gostis unit from escaping.

After touring the battlefield, the trio got back in the transport and started heading back to Capital City. Phil's stomach grumbled, and he chuckled. "All that walking has made me hungry."

Alice checked her watch. "I guess it has been a few hours since lunch. By the way, how did you happen to stumble on that little village, Michael?"

Michael chuckled. "When that FBI guy, Tim Davis, found the shuttle owned by Borislav Lovanova, Sergeant Evans and his lieutenant had a chat with the ground crew, who told them Borislav had a local pal named Snit who worked for Yidlin Untocks, and Untocks supplied slaves to Toanin Zisros, among others. Snit lived in that little village. That's where we captured him. Later, we escorted Tim Davis back there to gather more evidence. That's when we found the café the former domestic slaves were running."

Phil nodded. "I thought they were doing a great job."

"Things were a little rough at first, but they're getting the hang of it," Michael agreed.

Alice frowned. "How do a bunch of former slaves get the capital to start a business or even the know-how to run one?"

Michael shrugged. "Their former owners were required to provide some sort of long-term provision for their futures. For many of the slaves that were used for domestic help, not much has changed except they get paid now. Some of the slaves wanted to step up socially, and their former masters are helping them, both with financial support and help understanding how to handle their businesses."

Phil furrowed his brow. "It doesn't sound like the slaves were treated equally at all."

"You're right about that," Michael agreed. "The slaves who worked in the fields or did other forms of hard labor had a grim existence and, in most cases, an even grimmer future. Once they were too old to do their jobs, they would be assigned less strenuous tasks or sold to job shops to do monotonous or hazardous chores. Finally, when they couldn't do that, they would go to government housing to wait for the end if they made it that long."

Alice shook her head. "What I can't get over is the absolute lack of opportunity slaves had to change their circumstances. How was the life of a domestic slave different?"

Michael laughed. "Night and day different. Domestic help, in most cases, was almost part of the family. In any case, any slave working as a domestic had to be a trusted member of the household. Some of them would even get a small allowance to do whatever they wanted. In fact, domestics had a better life in their golden years than their farmhand counterparts. They could look forward to a decent retirement when they were slaves. Now that's been thrown into confusion."

Alice said, "While talking to Madam Zisros, I met a snoshin woman named Glinda. She was a slave on the farm, but she still worked there. She said she has a husband and a house now."

Michael nodded. "Not surprising. The snoshins who were born into slavery had absolutely nothing to fall back on when they gained their freedom. The plantation owners were required to provide a home for their former slaves who decided to stay on and work, along with enough land to grow food for themselves."

"Let's have dinner at the hotel. I don't feel like going out tonight," Phil suggested.

Alice smiled. "Sounds good to me."

Michael laughed. "Speaking of former slaves, the waiter this morning was the property of the hotel owner. The twist is, they were good friends, and at the end of the war, the waiter was given part ownership of the hotel. It's not much, but it's enough to guarantee a comfortable life."

*****

## Flast, Utolon Provence, Home of Donfel and Gombolk

Feldon's sister and her family lived in a small village in close proximity to their parents' farm. Gombolk wasn't a farmer, but he managed to make himself acceptable in his father-in-law's eyes by working in the implement and farm supply industry.

A brown-colored package transporter slowed to a stop in front of the home, and a brown-uniformed flaston went to the vehicle's cargo area. Then after a few short seconds, he emerged with a carton. At the home front entrance, he pressed a button that alerted the occupants to his presence. As he stood there waiting, he stared at the button and snickered as he remembered his human training instructor called it a doorbell. He had always called it an occupant summons. Package services were a new feature on Flast, and most flastons were still getting used to the concept. In a few seconds, the door slid open, and Donfel asked, "Can I help you?"

The delivery driver smiled and held the carton. "Package delivery."

Donfel took the box and thanked the man. She carried the box to the dining area and placed it on the table. Finding the shipping label, she saw it was from Feldon and smiled. After opening the box, she removed some of the shipping paddings, then pulled out the gift box with the teddy bear. After examining the bear through the clear plastic, she smiled. "Aww, that's so sweet."

Next, she pulled out the box containing the space station model. She examined the box and remarked, "Gombolk will have to use the translator on the instructions for Gomdon. Then the two of them can do this project together."

Next came out the toy freighter, and Donfel spotted the dot that Feldon put on the box lid. She opened the box and removed the toy, then gave it a jiggle. She heard the data chip rattle around inside the toy freighter. Carefully, she opened the cargo door and removed the chip, then put the toy back in the box. Next, the presents went back in the shipping carton.

Donfel busied herself making dinner so it would be ready when Gombolk returned with the children. A short time after, she had their dinner simmering on the cooker when Gombolk entered the house with the children. After greetings, Gombolk saw the shipping carton on the table and furrowed his brow. "What's this?"

The kids were also very curious, as kids normally are toward anything new or unusual. Donfel smiled and said, "Uncle Feldon sent gifts from the space station."

Gomdon, Dongom, and Balkdon were instantly excited. Gombolk put his hands up. "Calm down. What did Feldon send, dear?"

Donfel reached into the box and pulled out the space station model. "This is Gomdon's."

Gomdon was overcome with joy. Gombolk eyed the model and saw it was made on Earth. "After dinner, we'll translate the instructions in flaston."

The next item out of the box was the toy freighter. Balkdon jumped up and down with excitement while Donfel removed the toy from the box.

Finally, Donfel picked up the box with the teddy bear and handed it to Dongom. The little girl turned the box until the clear plastic box front faced her. The look on her face made Donfel regret she wasn't recording the kid's reactions to show Feldon later. Dongom opened the box, pulled out the bear, and gave it a tight hug.

Gombolk pulled a pamphlet out of the Teddy bear box that the manufacturer provided to give a brief history of teddy bears. He found the flaston text and read the message. In a minute, he nodded. "That's very interesting."

Donfel reached into her pocket and pulled out the data chip and held it up. "There was something else in the box from Feldon."

Gombolk eyed the chip "Are we visiting Resnon?" Donfel smiled. "I've always wanted to see Trimlute Lake."

*****

## Flast, Brintnonopek, Office of Syndicate Boss, Moliston

Dulpot and Naplorn entered Moliston's anteroom, and Kimtol gave them a warm greeting. "Ah, Dulpot, Moliston is looking forward to seeing you." As he opened the door, he motioned to the beverage service. "Help yourself to tea, Naplorn."

Kimtol led Dulpot into Moliston's richly paneled office. Moliston was sitting at his desk facing Dulpot, which relieved Dulpot immensely. Moliston remained sitting, but it was a much-improved greeting than he got on his last visit. Moliston smiled. "Please sit, Dulpot. Kimtol, bring us tea, would you, please?"

Kimtol brought in a tray with tea service, and while he poured, Moliston asked Dulpot, "Did you resolve the Resnon situation?"

Dulpot nodded at Kimtol in appreciation as he took the cup of tea. "Yes, I did. Unfortunately, Resnon is no longer under anyone's control."

Moliston nodded. "What about Covroynac and his staff?"

Dulpot shook his head. "We won't be hearing from any of them any longer." Moliston frowned. "It's never pleasant when we have to trim our own ranks.

However, it's necessary from time to time for the greater good of the organization."

Dulpot nodded. "Everyone understands that is the way it must be. Loyalty and trust are maintained this way. If we don't have the assured loyalty or the trust of those over us, our existence is meaningless. It is the only way to conduct ourselves."

Moliston smiled and nodded. Dulpot fully understood the value of maintaining organizational personal but professional standards. He did want to make sure there were no, as a human would say, loose ends in this affair. "Have you considered what to do with Resnon?"

Dulpot put down his cup. "Indeed, there was one associate of Covroynac named Pukontgore who is still with us. Perhaps we can have him run Resnon."

Moliston frowned. "I thought you said everyone associated with Resnon is gone?"

Dulpot nodded. "Technically, they are. Pukontgore was Covroynac's lieutenant. He's been off-world for some time. Apparently, two bounty hunters showed up in Resnon looking for him, and to make a sad story short and bearable, they are the reason revenue from Resnon fell off suddenly. After Pukontgore gets cosmetic surgery, he can return to Flast. Since he has intimate knowledge of Resnon, it stands to reason that he could be making revenue for us there, especially if we can nullify the bounty hunters who were after him."

Moliston liked what he was hearing, but his experience was telling him to exercise caution. He asked, "Where is Pukontgore at this moment?"

"On Treest, with Jostorlac," Dulpot answered.

Moliston sat with his elbows on his desk and his fingertips together and thought about the new data presented to him. The fact that Pukontgore had a bounty on his head meant that he was not unknown to authorities and was, therefore, a possible liability. A liability that could possibly be negated with cosmetic surgery and perhaps a change in identity. Finally, he sat back in his chair and said, "Get word to

Pukontgore. Tell him to be sure he stays ready to return to Flast when ordered."

Dulpot nodded cautiously. "It will be done. If I may ask, should I mention the bounty hunters?"

Moliston nodded and said, "Yes, I believe we have an opportunity here to correct more than one unfortunate circumstance. I have an informant on a human space station. The same space station that, it seems, aided Yulona, Lytrina, and Lynuna in their escape from our former authorities. I used the chaos that ensued during the fall of the old regime and the rise of power of the present government to place him there. My informant tells me there are two bounty hunters who have based themselves at this station. Also, the Dragons I contracted to destroy the Faldos Charter were guests of this space station. The informant also tells me that one or two flastons freed from Gostis are now living on the station."

Dulpot felt a small wave of panic. "There is a great deal of coincidences concerning this space station. Also, the only flastons I know of that wound up as slaves were sold by local bosses. A former slave would potentially have a lot of information we don't want to be made public."

Moliston nodded and said, "Exactly correct. It's now impossible to determine if Covroynac gave up any information about the organization. Our compartmentalized nature prevents trouble from affecting the whole organization, but I think you should be motivated to see the successful resolution of this."

Moliston was right. Dulpot recalled how Covroynac told him that he gave up the location of Pukontgore to the bounty hunters. It didn't occur to him to ask Covroynac if he had given up information about the organization. He was going to have to take a more personal interest in this situation if he wanted to avoid going to a prison asteroid for the rest of his life.

Dulpot then nodded and said, "Pukontgore is either an asset or a liability. He can take an active role in cleaning up this mess. If we're successful, Pukontgore can go to Resnon and continue operations. If we're unsuccessful, he'll join Covroynac. It's the way it must be."

Moliston smiled and said, "If we get past this, you're going to rise to great heights in the organization. First, however, we need to bed down this current crisis. Remember, get word to Pukontgore while I organize the operation. It's going to have to be carefully planned and executed for us to prevail."

Dulpot finished his tea and left Moliston after assurance that he would get word to Pukontgore. If Covroynac did give his name to the bounty hunters, it meant his life in the organization was over, regardless of what Moliston told him. He had to distance himself from Covroynac's legacy if he were to have a future.

*****

## Gostis, Hotel Yund, Phil and Alice's Room

Phil was having a bit of a sleep-in at the moment. He figured this was a mini- vacation, and he was determined to make the most of it. Alice, however, was in a different frame of mind; she came out of the shower in her robe and stood next to the bed with her hands on her hips. Looking down, she said, "Phil, we've got things to do."

Phil made a couple of indistinct grunts and rolled over, pulling the blankets over his head. Alice frowned and took her hands off her hips. She knelt next to him on the bed and gave him a vigorous shaking. "Come on, Phil. Time to rise and shine, up and at 'em."

Phil poked his head out and squinted. "Mom was right. I married a crazy woman."

Alice frowned. "You know you say that all the time. I don't believe you. I don't think your mother would say that. She loves me."

Phil furrowed his brow. "I never said it was my mom who said that." Alice frowned. "Get up. Get showered. We have stuff to do."

Phil rushed through his shower and brushed his teeth. Then he dressed quickly to avoid incurring ire from Alice. After dressing, they both went to the hotel dining room for breakfast because the soft rain outside kept them from eating on the patio that morning. Dwight was with them as he didn't have a lot to do, having the previous day had

Aurora's cargo removed and taken to the facilities that were rented by the Stellar Logistics Gostis station manager.

Alice started adding crystals to her guthar then stirred it with the wooden stick. When she was done, she looked up, "Thanks for coming with us, Dwight. It'll be real handy with you along."

"It's no fuss, Alice. It gives me something to do," Dwight reassured her. "A fella like me would just get in trouble if left to my own devices."

Phil asked, "What's the plan for today?"

Alice took a sip, then answered, "Well, first, we go to the shuttle port and secure a small cargo transport and some day help."

"Did you look up that particular service already?" Phil asked.

Alice nodded. "While you were showering. I contacted them, and they said they had a transport, driver, and two helpers available for us. We'll have them follow us to the farm, and afterward, they'll take the items to their facility for crating."

Just as they were finishing their guthar, Michael entered the dining room. "Y'all ready to go?"

They stood, and Phil put down a tip, and Alice said, "You bet, Mikey."

*****

**Gostis, Zisros Falta Farm**

Michael pulled into the farm with the cargo transport right behind him. He stopped short of the courtyard of the slave quarters, and Alice got out to direct the cargo transport. The driver backed the transport to the slave quarters entrance, and after stopping, he got out, followed by his two helpers.

They recognized the helpers from the previous day, as they were two of the former soldiers looking for employment. The driver was clearly in charge; in fact, he owned the company that Alice contracted to do the work. Alice entered the slave quarters with the driver, Phil, Dwight, and Michael right behind her. The helpers busied themselves carrying shipping boxes from the cargo transport to the slave quarters.

Alice started giving everyone assignments on what items to pack in the boxes. They started their work when Alice said, "Don't load anything on the transport until Madam Zisros has inspected the boxes."

Just then, Madam Zisros walked in and said, "That won't be necessary. Take whatever you want to."

Alice furrowed her brow. "That's very generous. What's changed since yesterday?"

Madam Zisros picked up a metal food bowl and examined it with a look of curiosity and said, "Nothing really. I've been doing a great deal of thinking since yesterday. Things haven't been easy since the war. I've had to manage this farm myself without the benefit of my husband. Most of the former slaves who are native of Gostis have agreed to stay and operate the farm, but I cannot imagine carrying on like this forever. When my husband gets out of prison, I would like it if we could spend the rest of our time in peace and at ease. To that end, I'll have to explore different options to make enough revenue to be able to stay in my home."

Alice smiled. "In the meantime, you need to remove all the trappings of the slave workforce."

Madam Zisros smiled back. "Something like that." She then looked around and said, "This is a good-sized space. Perhaps I can rent it out to craftsmen for shop space."

Alice redirected the conversation, "Let's go outside, Madame Zisros, so I can give you the payment."

While following Alice, Madam Zisros said, "Perhaps you didn't understand.

I'm giving you the items."

Alice smiled and told her, "We negotiated in good faith, as we say on Earth, 'A deals a deal.' Besides, I'm sure you could use the money to explore other opportunities."

Alice pressed a tenth goaner coin in her hand, and Madam Zisros looked at it and then looked up to Alice. "Please call me Plinloo.

'Madam' is a title and trappings of the wife of a Teanon Council member and slaveholder. Please come with me to the house. I'd like to have further words with you." Alice started to object, pointing to the slave quarters, but Plinloo Zisros cut her off, "They'll be fine."

Alice followed Plinloo to a small vehicle that reminded her of a golf cart. As soon as Alice sat, they streaked off to the main house. Plinloo showed Alice to the kitchen, where she poured two cups of guthar, then they sat at the table and started adding crystals to their drinks. Alice was curious as to why she was invited here but didn't say anything. Plinloo Zisros saw the look on Alice's face and chuckled. "Today is your day to be bewildered."

Alice chuckled herself. "I suppose turnabout is fair play."

Plinloo raised an eyebrow. "That's a curious saying, but I suppose it's accurate. Yesterday, you told Glinda you were good friends of two of the young ladies she knew here."

"That's right," Alice said.

Plinloo nodded. "How are they doing?"

"Well, Rosanne, the human, is expecting their first child. Her husband's obligation to the Reynolds Planet mercenary unit is nearly over, and they'll be moving back to Earth to take over his family farm. They would have gone back to New Iowa, but he sold that farm after Rosanne was kidnapped. Tillya, the flaston, has been living on our space station," Alice answered.

Plinloo furrowed her brow. "Why doesn't she go back to Flast?" "The Syndicate," Alice answered. "She's a potential witness. If they

knew she was no longer in bondage and a source of information, her family would be in real danger."

Plinloo put down her cup and looked very downcast and said, "So much pain. I'd like to be able to say if I had known of the nature of my husband's associates, I would have insisted we stop doing business with them. But that would be a lie. The truth is, as long as our lifestyle was maintained, we felt justified in treating the slaves as objects. Did that young man who's with you tell you about the events that occurred here?"

Alice asked, "You mean Mikey, my son?"

Plinloo nodded and smiled. "I thought so. I could see the resemblance."

Alice answered, "Yes, he did. He said you had a tense interaction with Rosanne."

"Indeed, I did," Plinloo answered. "When she introduced me to her husband and slapped me across the face, the reality of what we did to people came into sharp focus in an instant. She wasn't just a harvester, a mere implement. She was a being with aspersions and hopes. Since then, with the benefit of hindsight, I've adjusted my attitude. You've met Glinda. I've known her for most of her life, as much as I cared to know a slave. Since she's gained her freedom, I've come to know her better, and I found out that she's a wonderful person. She's lacking formal education, but I've found that she possesses a depth of knowledge about things that, frankly, I previously thought were not worth learning but have since found worthwhile. You know, the old class system we had, prevented people of my former social class from the benefit of the collected lore of others."

Alice finished her guthar and put the cup down. "That's a familiar story. The same things have been recorded in history books on other worlds, including my own." She paused a few seconds, then asked, "Would you like me to convey your sentiments to Rosanne and Tillya?"

Plinloo smiled. "That would be nice." She stood. "Perhaps we should get you back to the slave quarters."

Alice stood, looked around, and said, "You know, if Gostis had a tourist trade, this would make a nice bed-and-breakfast."

Plinloo frowned. "What is a bed-and-breakfast?"

"A bed-and-breakfast is an establishment where someone turns their home into a country inn. It gets its name because guests rent a room, and breakfast is included. The guests are expected to find the other meals elsewhere," Alice answered.

Plinloo slowly nodded. "Interesting idea. I'll have to research that." In a few minutes, they were back in the cart speeding back to the slave quarters. Suddenly, she slowed the cart and said, "There are some things in this building that might be just the thing for your museum."

She pulled up to a building and stopped. "We used to process new slaves in this building, among other things."

Alice followed her inside, where Plinloo stopped at a locker and opened it. She reached in and pulled a pair of collars out, saying, "We used to make the slaves wear these. They have several functions. They can locate lost slaves. They are coded for each individual so that an electronic roll call can be taken; they even have translators built in them." As she handed one to Alice, she said in a shaky voice, "They were also used to discipline slaves."

Alice knew that meant an electric shock would be applied. Plinloo pulled the counter with the antenna attached to it out of the locker. "This was used to control and read the collars."

In a few minutes, they were back at the slave quarters, where Alice got out of the cart and said goodbye to Plinloo. She walked inside to find Phil and Dwight working to remove the legs from a table, and the rest were disassembling the three-tier bunk bed. There were shipping boxes that they had brought with them but were now full of items. Alice selected a box that had some room in it and put the collars in it with the counter. The cargo transport driver's hand unconsciously went to his throat when he saw what she put in there.

Phil put his hands on his hips and asked sarcastically, "Did you have a lovely visit while we were a work?"

Alice was a little embarrassed. "As a matter of fact, I did. Plinloo Zisros said we could take anything we want, so look around, see if there's anything that might look good in the museum." She looked at the hired workmen. "Follow me, gentlemen. We'll grab one more bunk and cabinet."

Everyone did as they were told, and another bunk was selected along with a cabinet. Phil and the rest scouted around and found some clothing, sandals, and a hat in the men's area. Alice gave the kitchen a second look and decided to grab everything, including the gas cooker.

When they had everything loaded and secured, a heavy piece of farm machinery pulling a falta pod cart rumbled to a stop. Glinda climbed down and walked over to Alice, holding a data chip. "This has a letter to both Rosanne and Tillya. I imagine Tillya can forward a copy to Rosanne."

Alice took the chip and smiled. "She sure can. Did you include an address for return correspondence?"

Glinda answered, "Oh yes, I did. Please be sure to tell Tillya and Rosanne, me and my husband, Hukron, miss them, and we're very happy that they're doing so well."

Alice smiled. "You can be sure I will."

Glinda beamed and said, "I would like to say I'm looking forward to seeing you again sometime, but I know that that's not very likely, so I'll just say it's been so nice meeting you."

*****

## Flast, Trimlute City, Ferry Docks

Donfel, Gombolk, and the children were sitting at the same diner that Isnod and Feldon visited on their stop at Trimlute City. The children were finding it difficult to focus on their lunch at the moment as there was so much here to distract them. For all of them, it was the most water they had ever seen, and both Gombolk and Donfel completely understood the excitement their children had. The waiter was having fun interacting with the children because, in the past, most of the patrons were people on business, but these days, tourism was an increasingly popular recreation on Flast, and he was getting used to vacationing families.

Gombolk's attention was on the activity in the harbor, as the boats and ships arriving and leaving intrigued him. The children were constantly pointing out things that were new and fascinating to the point that Donfel had to continually tell them to finish eating. In due course, it was time to make their way to the ferry docks. Gombolk paid for the meal, and the waiter bid them farewell with a smile.

Once on board, Donfel and Gombolk managed to find a place for all of them to sit that afforded them a view of the crew's activities while getting ready to be underway. Once the mooring lines were cast off and the ferry started to move, the children were beyond excited. The ferry was old, but the crew took a great deal of pride in its maintenance. The engines pushed the ferry to cruising speed shortly after passing the harbor entrance markers, putting distance between them and Trimlute City.

Eventually, the land behind them slid below the horizon, and the children grew restless. The captain and crew were still getting used to families and their unique requirements. To that end, stewards took interested parties on tours of the ferry. Gombolk accompanied his children on a tour while Donfel stayed put and relaxed with a book. All of them found the tour fascinating and learned a great deal, with the engine room being especially interesting for Gombolk, but the highlight of the tour for everyone was the bridge.

The rest of the voyage was spent spotting other vessels and the first hint of land. There was excitement as the hills and trees slowly came into view, and they could see the village of Resnon more distinctly as time went on. The ferry headed to the harbor entrance markers and slowed when they got near. Just ahead of the ferry, there was a small freighter making its way to the docks.

*****

**Flast, Resnon Docks**

There was a single dock, and the freighter headed for one side while the ferry headed for the other. Gangs of dock workers swarmed the two vessels and started handling lines to secure them to the docks. Once that was done, gangways would be put in place to allow personnel to deboard. The family was anxious to get ashore and stood at the guardrail, watching the activities on the dock.

Gombolk and Donfel watched as an officer from the freighter descended the gangway holding a small drawstring bag. They didn't think much of it until they saw the ferry's first officer descend their own gangway holding a similar drawstring bag. Both men met on the dock and exchanged casual greetings while looking about. It appeared to Gombolk and Donfel that they were waiting for someone.

A man came out of an office labeled Dock Supervisor and approached the pair. The ferry had a relatively low freeboard which allowed Gombolk and Donfel to hear the conversation between the ship officers and the dock supervisor. The freighter officer looked at the supervisor and said, "It's not like Covroynac to miss out on revenue."

The supervisor couldn't help but smile. "No one has seen him for some time.

In fact, his henchmen haven't been seen either.

Both officers broke out grins. The freighter officer pocketed the bag he carried; this is one bag of goaners that's not going to the Syndicate." With that, the supervisor and both ship officers returned to their duties. Gombolk and Donfel led the children down the gangway and to the baggage pickup. After claiming their bags, they were approached by a large man and his wife. When they made eye contact, the man smiled broadly. "We're Yanoner and Tillmay. You must be Donfel and Gombolk."

Donfel smiled back. "Fine afternoon, it's so good to meet you."

Tillmay said, "Yanoner, help get the bags into the transport. We need to get the children a good meal and a warm place to sleep."

The luggage was loaded, and everyone piled in for the short trip to Yanoner and Tillmay's home. Tillmay was indeed correct about the children needing a meal. The ferry trip lasted until well after their normal mealtime. The meal was excellent, and they finished it off with a Red Swampberry pie. Tillmay seemed especially happy to have children in her home and doted on them constantly. Soon, the children were stifling yawns, so Tillmay and Donfel took them to Tillya's old bedroom, where Dongom was put in Tillya's old bed while Gomdon and Balkdon were bedded down on a double wide air-mattress bed.

Once the children were asleep, Tillmay took the data chip and inserted it into a computer terminal, then said, "I hope you don't think us rude, but I cannot wait to see what Tillya sent us."

Gombolk started to stand. "Donfel and I can give you some privacy."

Yanoner motioned him down. "You deserve a look at who you were passing messages for. Besides, Tillya usually includes a sentiment for whoever delivers the message."

Tillmay started the recording as Gombolk and Donfel settled back down.

Tillya's smiling face filled the monitor. *"Fine day, Mother, Father. I haven't met Donfel and Gombolk or the children yet, but I cannot wait for that day to arrive. I want to thank you for agreeing to deliver this message to my mother and father. They expressed a desire to see a little of my life here on the station."*

Tillya pinned the camera to her blouse front and continued to narrate. *"These are my quarters. I still can't believe this is all for me."* She then did a quick tour of each room in her quarters.

Tillmay's mouth was agape, and finally, she said, "That looks lovely. I expected her to be living in a barracks type of arrangement."

Tillya exited her quarters and walked to the HabMod central atrium. She continued her narration, *"I'm just going to leave the camera on and edit the footage later. While I do that, I'll add narration. This is HabMod 4 Central Atrium. I like the plants and things here."*

Tillya walked the connector tunnel to the Upper CentMod and paused while she panned the camera. Her narration continued, *"This is the Upper CentMod. As its name implies, it's the center of Oasis 4. There are businesses here, and the operations center is located at the upper levels of this part of the station. I'll show you that shortly, but first, let me point out some things. Up there on the second level is Eva's diner. It's a fun place to eat. Then there's the security office. Security Marshal Smith and his deputies are very good at keeping order here. Freighter crews sometimes get a little rowdy, human term, after long voyages, so they sometimes need a firm hand. There is the Star Lodge Suites. I spent my first night here in their facilities and thought it was very luxurious.*

Tillya then changed positions and continued, *"Speaking of luxurious, there is Maurice's restaurant. It's very fancy, even by human standards. The pizza restaurant, then there's Sparky's Taproom, Alice Ross, and I will sometimes have a glass of wine there with friends. There's an establishment on an upper level that I frequent called Sliders. You go there to play a game on a special table that I quite enjoy."*

Tillya walked over to the platform lift and rode it to the operations center. As the platform lift came to a stop, Tillya walked to her normal work area. *"This is where I work. I can be found here five days in a seven-day human week. I make sure that cargos are matched with ships going to their destinations and occasionally other tasks that they need help with."*

She then took the platform lift to the Lower CentMod. As the Lower CentMod interior came into view, Tillya said, *"This is the Lower CentMod. You can spot the Consulates on Tier 5."*

As the platform lift settled on the Lower CentMod plaza level, she walked to an escalator and took it to tier two, then a second one to tier three. Stopping in front of a business, they could make out the sign written in both English and Flaston, as well as other common languages used on the station. Tillya said, *"This is the office of I&F Investigations and Retrievals."* She walked inside. *"These are my friends, Isnod and Feldon, obviously planning another adventure. You met them already."* Isnod and Feldon looked up and grinned while waving.

Tillya continued the tour of the station and ended it with a game at Sliders Pool Hall. Later, in her quarters, she sat down. *"I hope this answers any questions you may have about my life here in the station. Isnod and Feldon tell me that there are positive steps being taken to ensure that I can, one day, return home. They're not in the Law Enforcement Brigade any longer, so the information they get isn't always forthcoming. I'm just grateful that every day brings me closer to the moment we see each other again."*

Tillmay was wiping tears from her face. "I wish we could go visit her." Yanoner furrowed his brow. "Why don't we do just that?"

Tillmay frowned. "Don't you think that would be dangerous?"

Yanoner looked down and thought. Finally, he shook his head. "I don't think so. No one has seen Covroynac or his minions in a very long time."

"We overheard a conversation between the dock supervisor and ships officers that confirms that," Gombolk offered.

Donfel was skeptical. "Why would criminals leave riches like what passes through this village?"

Yanoner smiled. "It may have something to do with the time your brother and his friend Isnod paid Covroynac a visit."

Gombolk was incredulous. "They walked into their lair?"

Yanoner grinned. "Apparently so. The last thing they said to us was they were going to pay Covroynac a visit and see what information they could beat out of him. We didn't know what to make of that statement. Surely, they wouldn't be crazy enough to confront a syndicate boss and his muscle in his own warehouse. We sent the first data chip with a neighbor boy to the rail transport station but expected him to return it to us if they indeed met Covroynac. The boy said they took the chip and departed, so we assumed they missed Covroynac for some reason."

Donfel asked, "So now you think they confronted Covroynac?"

"Yes, I do," Yanoner replied. "After that day, Covroynac was never seen except once, and in fact, his lieutenants only made rare appearances. Then not long ago, a private yacht arrived from Trimlute City. Covroynac boarded with one of his men. He could barely walk, and his hands looked damaged. The yacht returned later that day, and Covroynac's other man boarded and left. No one has seen any of them since then."

Gombolk rubbed his chin. "I'd wager Feldon and Isnod touched a nerve in the syndicate, and now the syndicate is trying to control the damage."

"Do you really think we'll be able to see Tillya?" Tillmay asked hopefully.

Yanoner nodded. "Yes, I do. We have plenty of money saved for the price of passage and lodging, and I haven't used any of my relaxation period credits since Tillya was taken from us. We can do this. I think we should contact Lytrina and Yulona and see what they think."

Gombolk was having an idea growing. "You know, there are some dealers of agricultural equipment on that space station. We've talked about sending a representative there to see what kind of deals we can make for specialized or unique equipment. I'll wager that I can talk my supervisor into sending me. Bringing Donfel and the children would cost me minimally."

Donfel was getting excited. "Mother and Father would love to go also." Gombolk laughed. "I don't think your father would want to leave the farm."

Donfel had her own laugh. "Don't let him fool you. He would leap at the opportunity to see a space station.

Donfel, Gombolk, and the children spent the next day seeing the local sights. One of the things they did was visit a swimming beach that absolutely delighted the children. The following day, they said goodbye to Yanoner and Tillmay then boarded the ferry bound for Trimlute City. They had made sure that they had made tentative plans to visit Oasis 4, contingent on what Lytrina and Yulona advised, of course.

*****

## Oasis 4, Trading Center Space Station, Owned by the Stellar Logistics and Freight Corporation

Gus sat at his desk, making sure there were no more tasks for today. He was over feeling left out of the fun of a trip to Gostis, but since he just got back from Vestgut, he figured fair was fair. There was one last thing to do before he could relax for the rest of the day. The *Atlantis Star* was due to arrive within the hour, and it was carrying the pretar technicians who were tasked with getting the station ready for the addition of the expanded storage capability.

Leaving his office, he went to the platform lift to the Lower CentMod. At the plaza level, he walked to the connector tunnel to CargoMod 8. The tools and materials to begin the preparations for the station addition needed to be stored in a central location. As it worked out, the cargo area of CargoMod 8 was the ideal size, and there was the thought that it may be advantageous to have the ship repair facilities at hand.

The *Atlantis Star* was easing into the docking clamps when Gus reached the docking port. Virginia had tables set up at the docking port staffed with personnel who were going to assign quarters and ID badges to the pretar technicians. The ID badges would allow them to pass through customs without delay and also give them access to restricted areas to perform their jobs. He saw Tillya happily arranging the IDs on a table.

The station technicians finished connecting power and communication cables, along with connections to the potable water and wastewater systems. The gangway/airlock was extended to the ship's boarding hatch, and the seals were safety tested. Shortly afterward, the airlock hatches were opened, and the pretar technicians started filing off and walking down the gangway.

As the first pretar stepped onto the station, Virginia smiled broadly. "Mr. Selak!"

Selak smiled back. "Miss Wells, it's good to see you again."

Selak stepped to the table, and Virginia handed him his quarters assignment. "Phil Ross would have loved to be here to greet you, but he's away for a couple of more days. In the meantime, you'll have to make do with the assistant station manager."

Gus stepped up to the pair, and Virginia continued, "Mr. Selak, this is Gus Condent."

Gus stepped forward and put out his hand. "I'm very glad to meet you, Mr. Selak.

Selak grasped his hand. "I'm very happy to meet you, Mr. Condent. After my technicians have had a chance to settle in, we'll be ready to start work on the modifications to the station."

Gus nodded. "Would it be too much to ask you to make an appearance at the morning briefing to give us an idea of what to expect while you're here?"

Selak smiled. "Of course, I'll be there. I'm looking forward to seeing everyone again."

*****

## Gostis, Capital City Shuttle Port

The day of departure had arrived, and preparations were made to begin the journey back to Oasis 4. The *Aurora* was loaded with Alice's purchases for the museum, and goodbyes to Michael were said. Phil, Alice, and Dwight were required to have their vessel inspected before their departure. The three of them waited in the shuttle port administration building while two soldiers, a snoshin and a malnun, checked the *Aurora* for contraband or fugitives that Phil, Alice, or Dwight may try to take off of Gostis. The soldiers knew that was a remote possibility since they were familiar with Phil and Dwight. Everyone involved was of the mind to just let the humans be on their way, but proprieties had to be observed.

Before the soldiers inspected the *Aurora*, Dwight provided a cargo manifest and explained each item. As the soldiers walked out of the administration building, a Pulsar 1250 landed between them and the Aurora. The landing was unusual enough to draw the attention of most in the operations room of the administration building. Dwight even said it looked to him like the landing thrusters were running at full power. Phil thought the vessel looked familiar, and his suspicion was confirmed when he heard Feldon's voice on the communication set. *"Capital City Operations, I&F-1, request armed guard at this shuttle pad."*

That got the attention of the officer on duty. He looked out the window and studied the shuttle and asked, "Who is that shuttle registered to?"

One of the clerks put the registration number into a computer. "I&F Investigations and Retrievals, they're bounty hunters, and they're based out of— oh my, they must be friends of Mr. Ross."

The officer looked at Phil, who nodded. "Indeed, they are friends, and I wouldn't take their request for guards lightly."

That was good enough for the officer, who summoned a squad and sent them to the Pulsar. Then he contacted the civil law authorities to have them standby. Phil and the rest watched as the shuttle hatch opened just as the squad of soldiers arrived. Isnod descended the stairs, turned, and waited. A snoshin appeared in the hatchway with his hands obviously cuffed behind him. He was struggling against someone behind him, presumably Feldon.

The snoshin wasn't eager to come down the steps, but eventually, he was made to obey. Isnod had a word with the squad leader, who immediately positioned his men around the shuttle. Then Isnod and Feldon forced the struggling snoshin to the operations room. They entered the room on the ramp side at the same moment three Gostis law enforcement officers entered from the opposite side.

The eyes of the law enforcement officers widened when they saw who was being restrained. The snoshin in charge told his subordinates to put their own shackles on the hapless man Isnod and Feldon were struggling with. Then he smiled. "Treasury Minister Trendor Yolup."

One of the officers looked up from what he was doing. "We should follow protocol, sir, and verify his identity."

"Very well," the snoshin said. He then said, "Please open your mouth, Minister."

The former treasury minister had some select, well-chosen words for the law enforcement officers. Most were of a foul nature and questioned the parentage of everyone involved in his current predicament. Before a DNA verifier could be employed, he clamped his mouth shut.

Feldon looked annoyed. "Let's see. Snoshins have a nerve bundle right about here," he said, pressing his finger against Yolup's neck below the back of the skull.

Feldon's efforts weren't having an effect, which prompted Isnod to look over. "About a fingers width higher."

Feldon adjusted his finger placement and applied pressure. Their snoshin prisoner started screaming, and the law enforcement officer quickly used the instrument. When an indicator flashed, he checked the display: Verified. He turned to his underlings. "Take him to a cell and process him."

After the former minister was taken away, the officer looked at Isnod and Feldon. "Who do we give the bounty to?"

Feldon handed him a document. "All the information is here. The payment goes to I&F Investigations and Retrievals, and there's information here to make a direct deposit."

The officer took the paper, which had a miniature data chip embedded in one corner. As he studied the document, he quipped, "You didn't happen to ask him where the goaners are that he stole, did you?"

Isnod shrugged. "We didn't have to. They're in the shuttle now."

The mood in the room suddenly changed. The operations officer immediately picked up a handset on a landline communication unit and ordered a platoon into action and conferred with his superior officer. The law enforcement officer used his own communication set to request armed transport and extra men.

When that was done, the law enforcement officer pressed, "How much of it did you find?"

"There are one thousand boxes that hold one thousand goaners each," Feldon answered.

The officer was visibly shaken. "It's all there?"

"All the boxes have what looks like a security seal," a perplexed Isnod answered.

The duty officer asked, "Why didn't you two keep a few boxes for yourselves and blame Yolup?"

The law enforcement officer added, "Or just take the goaners and kick loose Yolup without any money."

"The events in our lives recently have reinforced the idea that the only way to conduct our affairs is with the highest level of integrity. If passing up an opportunity to become the richest two men in the galaxy marks us as fools, then that's the way it will have to be. Our honor is intact. We can hold our heads high, and we can sleep peacefully," Isnod said with a stern look and a very serious tone.

The duty officer nodded. "I salute you, gentlemen, and hope you can maintain those standards in these difficult times." He then turned to Phil, Alice, and Dwight. "You'll understand that we can't allow anyone to leave until the goaners are secure."

Isnod turned and saw Phil and the rest. "Oh, Mr. Ross, it's good to see you."

Phil smiled back. "Likewise. We were just leaving. Are you two going to be here long?"

"Just long enough to ensure our bounty gets deposited and give us a chance to rest up," Isnod answered.

Phil nodded. "We'd recommend the Hotel Yund." Isnod smiled. "We'll keep that in mind."

A flaston platoon showed up, and the duty officer rushed out to give them a briefing on the situation. Then the flaston officer immediately deployed his men. In a few moments, an armored vehicle arrived, and the law enforcement officer met it. The two groups coordinated, and the armored vehicle slowly made its way to the Pulsar. Everyone in the operations room watched as the Pulsar was unloaded and the boxes were put in the armored vehicle. Phil asked, "How did Yolup get off-world in the first place?"

"He used the chaos in the postwar environment. He put the gold in a shuttle during the fighting and bolted out when the offensive systems went offline," Feldon answered.

Dwight frowned. "That don't make sense. All the shuttle ports were under positive control. A shuttle would have to have had a valid flight plan to take off." Feldon grinned. "He had it all preplanned. He had a shuttle hidden on his property and transferred the gold during the fighting. The way it looks, I think he was planning on doing this all along, but he had to push up his schedule because of the war."

"Did I hear right? Did you say there are one million goaners on your shuttle?" Alice asked, exasperated.

Isnod nodded. "That's correct, a rather large percentage of the planetary treasury. Everybody was anxious to get that guy back. It'll go a long way towards stabilizing things here."

Dwight did some quick calculations in his head. "That's almost twenty-eight tons! No wonder your shuttle was working overtime to land."

Feldon nodded. "The thruster coils were getting warm. I can attest to that."

The loaded armored vehicle left the shuttle port with its gold and charge of guards. The duty officer said, "Mr. Ross, you and your party can leave. You've been cleared. Have a pleasant journey."

*****

**Treest, Flaston Colony (Self-Governed),
Capital City Shuttle Port**

The shuttle port was particularly busy this morning due to the departure of a passenger liner later. The liner couldn't land on the surface, so it docked at the orbiting station, and passengers were shuttled from the surface. A public address speaker made an announcement that a shuttle was ready to be boarded and a block of ticket numbers read off. Then Yesnic checked his ticket for the number. Seeing he had a matching number, he stood and made his way to the door that led outside and to the waiting shuttle.

Yesnic boarded the shuttle and showed his ticket to an attendant who directed him to his seat. He scrutinized the other passengers carefully as they boarded, as he had been doing since arriving at the shuttle port. The shuttle filled quickly as there were only people on this flight. The baggage was flown to the orbiting station on shuttles designated for that purpose. The shuttle he was on has a capacity of ninety passengers, and it was full. Shuttles were scheduled to ferry passengers between the orbiting station and the shuttle port for much of the day, as there were three passenger liners docked at the station. As a result, not everyone on this shuttle was going to the same liner.

Yesnic found the shuttle to be a little claustrophobic but tolerable. In human terms, the journey to the orbiting station took an hour and a half, and that included the time necessary to maneuver into the docking clamps. The passengers deboarded quickly, and Yesnic blended in with them. At first, he was concerned that he would draw attention traveling alone. Looking at the people rushing about, he relaxed, along with couples and families on relaxation period. There were plenty of people traveling alone, presumably on business.

After boarding the *Flying Norseman*, Yesnic received his cabin assignment from a purser and made his way there. This was his first time in space, let alone traveling thousands of light-years from his home planet, Treest. The *Flying Norseman* was a human liner that gave him some concern, not from a safety point of view but from a cultural point of view. Despite being very astute and skilled at reading the body language of flastons and interpreting what he saw, he's had limited exposure to humans and felt uneasy being thrown into a situation where he didn't have complete confidence in what he observed.

When all the passengers were loaded and the hatches shut and sealed, the *Flying Norseman* had the docking clamps released. Thrusters eased the big liner away from the orbiting station, and they began the journey to Oasis 4.

*****

## Treest, Prodicton (Capital City), Patio adjacent to the Office of Jostorlac

Pukontgore sat opposite Jostorlac and sipped his tea. The pair had become friends during Pukontgore's exile from Flast and spent a good deal of time together. Jostorlac reached over and gently pulled at Pukontgore's bandage and peered underneath. "When did the doctor say the bandages could come off?"

Pukontgore winced when she pulled a little too much. "A few more days, then I get to work on getting the skin looking normal."

Jostorlac frowned. "I don't understand."

"At the moment, the skin is quite agitated," Pukontgore explained. "It's discolored and raw-looking. Letting air and light get to it will do wonders."

Jostorlac took a sip of her tea and nodded. "I've used that surgeon for other occasions. He does very good work."

Pukontgore frowned. "That's not a medical discipline I've ever heard of.

Where did it originate?"

Jostorlac grinned. "On Earth of all places. Apparently, in centuries past, altering your appearance was a common practice for vanity reasons. If you felt your nose could have a more pleasant appearance or your chin, and you were willing to endure the discomfort, doctors could do whatever you need. Dr. Sonpurt went to a place called Beverly hills to learn the techniques."

"I hope they taught the doctor well. Dulpot said in his communication that I may be sent to a human space station," Pukontgore mused. "The humans use very sophisticated equipment to safeguard their space stations."

Jostorlac slowly nodded. "Dulpot's superior on Flast sent me a communication confirming that very thing. It seems there are elements on that space station that are making life difficult for the organization. We have an opportunity here to eliminate that threat, set the Law Enforcement Brigade's efforts against us back, and put you in a better position in the organization."

"I like the sound of that," Pukontgore said with a smile. "What do you mean by putting me in a better position in the organization?"

Jostorlac put down her teacup. "You must be unaware that Covroynac and his two lieutenants are no longer in the organization. You can return to Resnon and assume the position of boss."

Pukontgore frowned. "That's not possible. It's impossible to leave the organization unless you…oh…" He leaned back in his seat. "How did that come about?"

"Dulpot saw to it that they left. Apparently, there were inquiries made about you by bounty hunters," Jostorlac answered. "Along with telling his interrogators where you are, we believe he may have given information about the organization, revenue from that little village has disappeared after the incident. The short version is, Covroynac and his lieutenants were liabilities and had to be rendered nonthreatening."

Pukontgore thought about what he was hearing, then asked, "How is it that Dulpot and those over him have come to the conclusion that I would be the best choice to take over Resnon?"

"You know the operation in an intimate fashion," Jostorlac answered. "If you can restart the operation there and ensure the Law Enforcement Brigade is no longer looking for you, you can be a tremendous asset to the organization."

Pukontgore lowered his eyes and mulled over what Jostorlac told him. He slowly started to nod and said, "I would like that, but to be successful, there are a lot of people who have to assume the same condition that Covroynac finds himself in."

Jostorlac nodded. "It's safe to say that. Once you're in that space station, your image will be recorded. If you do anything to bring attention to yourself, everyone on that station must die and any computer memory with your image erased. Those higher in the organization will decide which method is safest and has the highest degree of probable success."

Pukontgore nodded. "This must be a situation of great concern to involve Dulpot and Moliston."

Jostorlac was surprised. "How do you know about Moliston? That kind of information is kept very secret. He's three levels over you."

"Some crew I recruited to steal the fur clothing were members of the Brintnonopek Clan. They were very low level and looking to build their reputations, but they were the type that soaked up every scrap of information that came their way. Unfortunately, they also didn't know how to keep it to themselves," Pukontgore explained.

Jostorlac shook her head. "Moliston has a well-deserved reputation for discipline in operational security. He would be horrified to hear there were so many people who knew who he was."

"That's why I don't plan to tell anyone else what I know about the organization over my level. However, you must agree that it's rare to have too much information," Pukontgore stated.

"In our chosen calling, information can current both ways," Jostorlac agreed. "It can create opportunities and, in dire circumstances, allow oneself to trade information for leniency. It's that last one that can put you on the short list of potential liabilities."

Pukontgore frowned. "That is painfully obvious at the moment, given what's happened to Covroynac, Jotlor, and poor Gordlid."

"Moliston should put more layers between him and the other levels," Jostorlac observed.

Pukontgore nodded. "There were indeed more layers before the fall of the Colavar Regime. However, these days adjustments had to be made. I do find it intriguing that Moliston and Dulpot think I would be the right person to run Resnon."

"Indeed," Jostorlac answered. "If you're successful in helping to eliminate the current danger to our organization, Moliston and Dulpot would show their appreciation. In the meantime, I've been asked to be ready to provide support for a various array of scenarios."

Pukontgore smiled. "Perhaps I should double up my micton practice."

*****

### *Aurora,* **Astrodyne 65, Owned by Stellar Logistics and Freight Corporation**

Dwight eased the *Aurora* into the CargoMod 2, Docking Port 1 docking clamps. The clamps retracted, pulling the *Aurora* into intimate contact with the station. Phil checked the safety seals on the hatch, which was easily done. Seeing all green indicators, he opened the hatch to the air lock. Alice walked up and handed Phil a duffel. "It's good to be back."

Dwight stepped into the air lock with his own duffel. "Amen, sister. Getting out and seeing places is fun. That's why I became a pilot, but it's always good to get back to where you hang your hat."

As they walked to the connector tunnel to the CentMod, Alice said, "I'll have the *Aurora* unloaded tonight and the cargo taken to the Museum."

Phil shook his head. "No hurry. If a trip comes up, there'll be plenty of time to do that. Leave it till tomorrow morning.

Dwight checked a chronometer. "It's gettin' close to supper time. I think I'll go my quarters and get slicked up a smidge, then see if Ginny wants to strap on a feed bag."

"You're such a romantic." Alice chuckled. Phil frowned. "Who's Ginny?"

Alice looked at Phil like he was a clueless dim child. "He's talking about your operations supervisor, Virginia."

Phil was a little embarrassed. "Oh, I never heard her called Ginny before." The three passed through the customs desk, then walked the connector tunnel to the CentMod. As soon as they walked onto the plaza level, they were greeted with the sight of a plotor running past them, waving his arms and screaming, "That creature is dangerous! Someone capture it!"

Dwight nodded and said in a very deadpan fashion. "Looks like the plotors found us."

Then a solo kortlax with blue feathers streaked past while it was being hotly pursued by a group of pretars with ropes and nets. Phil broke out into a grin. "The pretars are here to install the new storage module!"

The kortlax was having a difficult time getting traction on the plaza level deck, but it was learning how to cope with it. When the pretars got close, it would run straight for a wall and then use the wall to change directions suddenly, like a race car using a high banked track.

The kortlax opened an impressive lead when suddenly Tillya stepped in front of it. The kortlax was so surprised it stopped suddenly and went into a panic. Its confusion didn't last long as it realized Tillya was a flaston, and it started to snap at her. She recoiled and said, "Oh, you nasty beast!"

Tillya held her ground as the kortlax continued to snap at her. They were next to a coffee kiosk that had several small tables nearby. She grabbed a tablecloth and threw it over the surprised animal's head. The kortlax stood there inert and fell asleep on the spot. The pretars caught up and put a noose over the sleeping kortlax then pulled the cloth off. The kortlax recovered quickly and tried to make a getaway but gave up as soon as it discovered that it was properly restrained. The pretars thanked Tillya and then led the animal away.

Phil, Alice, and Dwight looked at each other and laughed. Tillya was handing the tablecloth to the coffee kiosk operator, and Alice asked, "Are you all right, Tillya?"

Tillya hadn't noticed them earlier, as she was busy with the kortlax. She faced them and smiled. "Oh yes, I thought it would react like typical fowls if it suddenly became dark. I'm happy to see all of you, by the way."

"Why don't you join us for dinner? We just need a little time to freshen up," Alice offered.

Tillya smiled "That sounds like fun."

Just as they were about to part company, Gus strolled up to them. "So that's a kortlax.

Phil nodded. "That's a kortlax. How many of them got loose this time?" "Just the one," Gus said with a shrug. "Have you folks had dinner?"

Alice shook her head. "We were going to get freshened up, then get something to eat."

Gus smiled. "Perfect. Brenda comes off shift in about forty-five minutes.

We'll meet you in the Lower CentMod in an hour."

Phil frowned. "There are no restaurants in the Lower CentMod." "There is now," Gus retorted.

"Well, we could use another eatery with the increased passenger liner traffic," Phil said with a nod.

*****

## Oasis 4, CentMod Platform Lift

Phil, Alice, Gus, Brenda, Dwight, Virginia, and Tillya descended to the Lower CentMod. When they reached the plaza level, they walked around the central column, and there it was. Gus said, "Ladies and gentlemen, the Circle T."

"Tell me that's a steak house," Phil pled hopefully.

Gus nodded. "You bet it is. Our young maldor 'food service student' came back from Earth with investor's money, chefs, and everything needed to open this place."

Phil was smiling. "Western theme." He looked at Dwight. "Did you have anything to do with this?"

"Dwight had a grin of his own. "You're looking at the proud owner of 10 percent of the Circle T."

Phil nodded. "I approve, Dwight. Now let's see if Timothy hired quality cooks."

Standing at the entrance was Timothy himself. He had a smile that grew larger when Phil and his party walked in. After greetings, Timothy showed them to a table and gave them each a menu. Phil looked around and saw many familiar faces. Among them, there was Lynuna and some of her staff.

Everyone was immensely satisfied with their meal and pronounced the Circle T a roaring success. For Phil's part, he was happy there was an establishment that really knew its stuff when it came to cooking a steak. As it turned out, Lynuna and her party were finishing their meal at the same time, so she suggested that they cap the evening with coffee at the kiosk in the Upper CentMod.

While in the sitting area, everyone broke into small groups and chatted in a seating area. Alice wanted an opportunity to tell Tillya about their experiences on Gostis and, in particular, meeting Madam Zisros. At first, Tillya wasn't sure what to think. Then she realized that having her friends see firsthand, what she lived with every day, was actually relieving her of a burden.

Tillya was further surprised to learn about Madam Zisros's new perspective.

Tillya giggled. "Did she really insist on you calling her Plinloo?"

Alice smiled. "Indeed. In fact, she wanted me to convey to you and Roseanne how much she regrets her part in what happened to you two. She seems very sincere. We also met a friend of yours and Rosanne's while we were there. A young lady named Glinda. She wanted me to give you this," Alice said, handing her a data chip.

Tillya smiled. "Oh, that's wonderful. I was afraid that we missed an opportunity to keep in touch with her in the confusion of those last days on Gostis. Rosanne is going to want a copy of this, I'm sure."

"In fact, Glinda asked if you would forward a copy to Rosanne," Alice confirmed.

Tillya pocketed the data chip. "I'll be sure to do that tonight. How did you meet her?"

"While we were dealing with Plinloo, Glinda walked in to give her a message," Alice answered.

Tillya nodded. "I thought she might stay on the farm. It's the only thing she knows. I wonder if she ever decided to get married. There was a snoshin slave who was keen on her, and unless I'm mistaken, she felt the same way."

Alice smiled. "Was his name, Hukron?"

Tillya grinned. "Yes, it was. I'll wager that she was very direct in telling you she was married."

"She told me that she was married now and had a house in a manner that was calculated to make sure that I knew she wasn't a piece of trash," Alice confirmed. Tillya nodded. "That sounds about right. Snoshin slaves were allowed to reproduce only under certain circumstances. The snoshins born into slavery have always viewed things like permanent relationships, homes, and other signs of a stable life to be things that were just out of their reach. Having a spouse and home meant that you weren't on the very bottom of the social order."

Tillya then said, "By the way, we heard from Isnod and Feldon. They said they ran into you on Gostis as you were leaving."

Alice grinned. "Yes, we did. As we were about to board the Aurora, Isnod and Feldon caused the shuttle port to close until they could secure the gold they recovered."

"They didn't mention the gold," Tillya said, surprised. "It must have been a substantial amount to take precautions that strict."

"I'll let Isnod and Feldon tell you that tale when they arrive," Alice said.

Tillya took a sip of her coffee, then said, "That probably won't be for some time. They said they had a lead on another bounty."

Alice nodded. "In the meantime, how would you feel about recreating sections of the slave quarters in the museum?"

Tillya furrowed her brow, then slowly nodded. "I had an idea you wanted to do something like that. I'd be happy to help."

"It wouldn't bother you to dredge up unpleasant memories?" Alice asked.

Tillya shook her head and smiled. "There's a saying on Flast, 'Look back at where you've been every now and again.'"

Alice thought about it and said, "If where you've been is not as nice as where you are…"

"Then there's no reason to complain," Tillya finished for her.

Alice nodded, then slowly furrowed her own brow. "Suppose where you are is not as nice as where you were?"

Tillya smiled again. "Then find a way to get back there or, if that's not possible, find someplace better."

Alice nodded. "It might sound overly simplistic, but there's a lot of wisdom there."

"Don't dwell on the past. Live in the present. Always work toward pleasant surroundings," Tillya confirmed.

*****

**The *Flying Norseman,* Passenger Liner belonging to the Viking Cruise Corporation**

The big passenger liner had large, clear observation windows on its main deck, which was now being crowded with people who wanted to gaze at the nebula after they dropped out of light speed. The ship's public address speaker announced, "Light-speed engine cut, in five, four, three…"

Everyone braced themselves in anticipation of transitioning to sublight speed. It was hardly necessary, being as the *Flying Norseman* had exceptional inertia neutralizers. The stars came into sharp focus, but every eye was drawn to the nebula, and there were auditable gasps at the sight. Yesnic allowed himself a few moments to admire the view, then he turned his attention to the forward direction and searched for Oasis 4.

The breaking thrusters fired and remained on to gradually slow the liner.

Oasis 4 gradually went from a dot lost in a sea of stars to the second most obvious feature in the area. Yesnic studied the space station with interest although he wasn't terribly informed, where it came to the nuances of space stations in general.

In fact, this whole experience pulled Yesnic out of his comfort zone. In addition to adding space travel to the list of things he has done, he's immersed himself in alien culture. Most of the passengers on this ship were humans, but the other races were represented in varying degrees. It actually came as a pleasant surprise that each group, barring nuances, could be read in roughly the same manner that flastons could be read.

Humans were the closest to flastons in mannerisms, with pretars being farthest. That's not to say a pretars body language and tone of voice couldn't be interpreted; in fact, Yesnic considered them to be the easiest. There were no pretenses with pretars. What you see is what you get. In fact, he thought it was amusing that they were as straightforward as they were, and it didn't occur to them that there were nuances to be interpreted.

The *Flying Norseman* slowed to a relative crawl and maneuvered to its assigned docking port on CargoMod 1. Yesnic returned to his cabin to arrange for his things to be taken to the station. A porter took Yesnic's baggage to the ship's off- loading belt, and he made his way to the air lock hatch. The docking clamps engaging could be felt throughout the ship, which meant it was only a manner of minutes before passengers would be allowed to leave.

At the passenger air lock, there were already people gathering, anxious to see the station. Yesnic blended in with them and made small talk with an industrial fastener salesman from Kastia. The air lock hatch opened, and everyone started filing off the liner. Once in the CargoMod, he followed the crowd to the customs desk. When it was his turn, he stepped up to the desk where the security deputy looked up and said, "Passport, please."

He handed over the document, which looked like passports that have been in use for centuries on Earth. A system had to be devised for identification when people started interstellar travel, and all the parties involved liked the human system. The pretars added a modern twist by putting the information on a data chip embedded in the passport cover.

The deputy opened the passport. "Mr. Yesnic." "Please, just call me Yesnic," he replied.

The deputy just smiled while opening the passport. He examined the picture and English text. Then he placed it on a pad that accessed the data chip. He had Yesnic look directly into a retina scanner then he ensured the information printed matched the information on the data chip and the database of passport holders in the Multi-World Commerce Cooperative. He then checked for stamps from other places he had visited. Finding none, he checked the passport itself and smiled. "This is your first time away from Treest?"

"Yes, it is," Yesnic confirmed.

The deputy nodded. "Is your visit to Oasis 4 for business or pleasure?"

The question caught Yesnic off guard. "Er, pleasure, I suppose. I'm here to see two acquaintances who make their home here. Isnod and Feldon of I&F Investigations and Retrievals."

The deputy grinned. "Two great guys. Everyone in the security department likes them a lot." He then pressed a button that retrieved Yesnic's suitcase. The suitcase arrived on a conveyor and was deposited at the custom desk. Another press of a button and the case was scanned for weapons and hazardous materials. The deputy checked the scanner display and nodded. "If you have any computer data chips, you may use the SICOS system to access them. They will, of course, be scanned for viruses and other programs that may damage station's systems."

"That is all very reasonable," Yesnic said with a smile.

The deputy tapped a series of keys on his SICOS, and a document appeared on the screen. The deputy turned the display to afford Yesnic a look, then he asked, "Did you review the station regulations on your journey?"

Yesnic nodded. "Yes, I did."

The deputy handed him a stylus. "If there are no questions, please sign as an acknowledgment of your understanding."

Yesnic signed the document and handed the stylus back. The deputy stamped the passport with an Oasis 4 entry stamp which also added a digital stamp to the data chip and the Multi-World Commerce Cooperative database. He then smiled and said, "Welcome aboard, Oasis 4. You can leave your baggage here until you make arrangements for lodging. Then the hotel will arrange for it to get to your room."

Yesnic thanked the deputy and took a pamphlet with the station layout and consulted it before entering the connector tunnel to the CentMod. Once in the CentMod, he stopped to take in the layout and get oriented with the help of his newly acquired pamphlet. He had to admit that he was a bit overwhelmed with the size and appearance of the CentMod. The station orbiting Treest was decidedly more utilitarian and, by comparison, downright ugly.

The Star Lodge Suites were situated on the other side of the CentMod and currently hidden from view by the central column. Yesnic decided that he wasn't particularly in a hurry, so he strolled at a very leisurely pace on the plaza level to the hotel. During his walk, he could see why many people chose to make this station a destination as well as do business here.

An escalator took him to tier two and the entrance of the Star Lodge Suites. After checking in, he went to his room and waited for his suitcase to arrive. He was surprised to only wait a few minutes before a bellhop arrived and delivered his case. On reflection, there was only one hotel at the station. With the arrival of the passenger liner, the hotel most likely simply took the initiative and fetched the luggage.

After the bellhop left, Yesnic powered the room SICOS terminal. The pamphlet only highlighted major features like the hotel and the security office. It didn't list individual businesses. The hotel SICOS terminal had a link to a very detailed station directory on its home page. He found the listing for I&F Investigations and Retrievals and saw it was in the Lower CentMod.

Not wanting to waste time, Yesnic left his room and made his way to the Upper CentMod plaza level, then boarded the platform lift for the ride down to the Lower CentMod. Once in the Lower CentMod, he took the escalators to the third tier and followed the walkway to I&F Investigations and Retrievals. Seeing the office was locked and a look through the window revealed a darkened vacant office that deflated him.

As he stood there considering what to do next, a security deputy approached him. "Can I help you find someone?"

Yesnic turned to face the deputy. "I was hoping to meet my friends, Isnod and Feldon. Perhaps I should have sent a communication letting them know I was on my way."

The deputy laughed. "It wouldn't have done you any good, they've been gone quite some time. Perhaps you can check with the Flast Consulate. Isnod and the consular general are good friends."

Yesnic nodded, and the thought occurred to him that any deception on his part while dealing with the humans would most likely work against him. He nodded. "I'll do just that. By the way, my name is Yesnic. I hail from Treest."

The deputy smiled. "It's nice to meet you Yesnic. It's especially nice to meet one of Isnod's and Feldon's friends. My name is Tiffany Waters. I'm the Lower Section security supervisor."

*****

**The *Brintnonopek Traveler*, Flast-Registered Passenger Liner**

Yanoner and Tillmay took their seats at their table in the main dining room. They didn't have a long wait before they were joined by Yulona and Lytrina, then Isdornac and Noduleic appeared. A waiter stopped by, and they begged him off, saying their party wasn't all here yet. In a few minutes, Kinfel and Donness arrived with Donfel, Gombolk, and the children.

After everyone was seated, the waiter returned and took their orders. This evening's meal was flaston, but the dessert was from Earth. The cruise line liked to mix cuisine from different worlds as a means to ease people into expanding their palate. Tonight's dessert was a slice of apple pie with a scoop of vanilla ice cream.

After the waiter explained to them what they were about to eat, Noduleic got a little excited. "Isnod did a small favor for our local grocer, and in return, he sent us samples of fruit from Earth. I remember the fruit called apples. They were very good just as they were. I didn't know they could be baked like this."

After everyone finished, the ladies decided to take the children and see a play that was scheduled to begin shortly. This was a popular activity in the hours between dinner and bedtime when they were underway. The men decided that a play wasn't for them that evening, so they went to a lounge for cocktails.

When they were served their drinks, Kinfel said, "I was put out that our journey to this space station was extended because they felt the need to stop and gawk at every interesting stellar phenomenon. But so far, Donness and I have been having a wonderful time."

Yulona took a sip and said, "Even with the side trips, we're still going to arrive two days earlier than we would have on one of the old transports."

Yanoner smiled. "I'm grateful to have the company. As badly as Tillmay and I want to see Tillya, it would be a nerve-racking journey if it was just the two of us."

"We're glad to be here," Isdornac said with a smile. "I never thought I would get a chance to take Noduleic on an adventure like this. When Yulona contacted us about visiting the space station, we couldn't say yes fast enough."

Yulona put down his glass. "Lytrina and I aren't just looking forward to seeing Lynuna, Isnod, Feldon, and Tillya but also seeing the humans we've befriended on our last visit. Have any of you had experience with humans?"

Isdornac nodded. "I've had brief exposure to them. The firm I work for bought equipment to maintain roads from a company on Earth, great big yellow things. They sent a team to assemble the machines, then teach us how to operate and maintain them."

The others acknowledged that they didn't have any experience with humans. Gombolk said, "I'll be spending part of my time laying the groundwork for purchasing farming equipment. What can I expect from humans as far as business dealings are concerned?"

Yulona shrugged. "I've never had business dealings with them. However, I can say that my dealings have been positive although I wouldn't take it on faith that all humans act as honorably. Remember, there were humans in the slave trade and other less-than-honest trades."

Isdornac laughed. "The technicians I worked with were highly skilled. They worked hard, and they played harder."

Yulona smiled. "They do like to enjoy themselves. That much is obvious. There's so much about them to appreciate, but there's also so much about them that's contradictory. During the invasion of Gostis, the military units from Earth distinguished themselves as some of the finest soldiers to be found. Their actions have been described as viscous and without compunction. On the other hand, humans show remarkable compassion and charity where it's needed."

Yanoner nodded. "That much is obvious from what I've learned from Tillya's correspondence. As soon as Michael Ross learned of her plight, he set about seeing what could be done about it. Then Philip Ross offered her refuge and employment on that space station, and the friends she's made seem to be of the highest quality. It seems to me that they didn't have to do any of that."

"It sounds like the way we used to be, or at least the way I feel like we should be," Kinfel observed.

Yulona nodded. "I think you'll find that humans and flastons are a lot alike."

*****

## Oasis 4, Lower CentMod, Tier 5, Flast Consulate

Yesnic timidly entered the Flast consulate and approached the receptionist, who looked up and asked, "Can I help you, sir?"

"My name is Yesnic. I'm a friend of Isnod and Feldon of I&F Investigations and Retrievals. I have some information that is potentially very important for them and, by extension, the consular general," Yesnic said with as much politeness as he could muster.

The receptionist studied Yesnic carefully and asked, "Is this a Flast security issue?"

Yesnic nodded. "Indeed it is. As a matter of fact, my information not only involves Flast but also this station."

"I detect a Treest accent," the receptionist observed.

Yesnic smiled. "Very good. I've been trying to lose my accent while away from Treest."

The receptionist, who was actually one of Palnit's operatives, was aware that they were awaiting intelligence from one of Isnod and Feldon's associates on Treest. He weighed the situation and pressed a button. A voice asked, "What can I do for you, Bokhun?"

"Sorry to interrupt, Palnit, but there's a friend of Isnod and Feldon, a Mr.

Yesnic, here to see the Consular," the receptionist answered. "Just call me Yesnic," Yesnic said.

Palnit asked, "Did he say why he needed to see her?"

"He's from Treest, and he has information for her, Isnod, and Feldon," he answered.

Palnit knew immediately this Yesnic fellow could have important information. "I'll be right up," he said, coming to a stand.

Exiting his office, he paused at Lynuna's office and tapped on the doorframe.

Lynuna looked up and smiled. "What can I do for you, Palnit?" "There's a man named Yesnic from Treest at the receptionist desk,"

Palnit answered. "He's a friend of Isnod and Feldon, and he says he has information for us."

Lynuna put down her pen. "Don't keep him waiting, Palnit. Please bring him in."

Palnit rushed to the reception area and quickly returned. Lynuna had him sit on the sofa in her office, and her assistant brought out tea service. After everyone had their tea, Lynuna smiled. "I understand you have some information for us, Mr. Yesnic."

"Please, just call me Yesnic. Isnod contacted me some time ago about a flaston he was suspicious of," Yesnic answered.

Lynuna leaned forward. "Were our suspicions justified?"

Yesnic nodded. "Indeed they were. His name is not Gutroynod. It's Nodroygut. The Treest Syndicate offered him an opportunity to make a name for himself in the organization, and he jumped on it. I have his dossier on a data chip."

Yesnic handed a data chip to Palnit, who took it and loaded it in Lynuna's SICOS terminal. After making a copy of the file, he gave the chip back to Yesnic and said, "I'll send a copy of this to Security Marshal Smith."

Yesnic nodded and said, "I have other intelligence that he should be made aware of. However, I would have preferred if Isnod and Feldon were there when I told him. Isnod has known me for a long time and can attest to my integrity."

Lynuna pressed a code into the intercom call system. Luke Smith answered, "What can I do for you, Miss Lynuna?"

"We were wondering if you had heard from Isnod and Feldon. We have some news that you should hear, but it would be better if the guys were there also," Lynuna answered.

Luke chuckled. "Funny you should ask. They contacted us just a little while ago. They'll be docking in about half an hour. They requested deputies, so they must be bringing in a fugitive. Why don't you come up then and give us your news?"

Lynuna smiled. "Excellent. We'll see you then, Mr. Smith."

Lynuna, Palnit, and Yesnic finished their tea and made small talk to avoid the appearance of being too eager to press Yesnic for information.

Half an hour had passed, and Lynuna stood. "We should go to the security office. Isnod and Feldon will be there shortly."

*****

## Oasis 4, Upper CentMod, Security Office

Luke welcomed the trio in the security office front desk area, where Lynuna introduced Yesnic. There was no time for conversation because, at that moment, a cuffed flaston was led inside by a deputy.

The deputy held the flaston against a wall face-first while Tiffany walked in and handed a data chip to Luke. "This is Noglertlan. The warrant for his arrest is on this chip. Isnod and Feldon will be up from the Lower CentMod as soon as they fetch a medic."

Luke frowned. "What happened?"

The deputy holding Noglertlan chuckled. "Mr. Noglertlan here just learned the hard way what not to do around Tiffany."

"He tried to get away while we were putting our restraints on him," Tiffany said with a shrug.

A flaston doctor walked in with Isnod and Feldon behind him. The doctor looked over the lump growing on Noglertlan's head. Then he used a small light to check pupil response. The doctor then extracted a pad from his med kit, peeled an adhesive backing off it, and placed it over the lump on Noglertlan's head. Next, while holding it in position with one hand, he slapped it in place with the other, causing Noglertlan to howl. The doctor said, "Leave that in place. It'll get cold in a few seconds."

Noglertlan retorted, "I'm not going to be able to get this thing off because you glued it to my hair!"

The doctor turned to leave, saying, "That sounds like the least of your problems."

Luke had to work to keep from laughing. "Take him to a cell. Who do we call to take this guy off our hands?"

Feldon answered, "They're standing next to you."

Palnit smiled. "I'll make arrangements as soon as we're done here."

Luke nodded. "Just out of curiosity, what did Noglertlan do to earn the wrath of the Flast government?"

"It looks like he was into stealing industrial secrets," Isnod answered.

Palnit asked, "Is there a syndicate connection with him?" "Some on the fringes," Isnod answered.

Palnit nodded. "Sounds like a few years in Velsra Prison. If there were more of a syndicate connection, he would go straight to Regorn Asteroid Prison."

Luke raised an eyebrow. "You have a prison on an asteroid?"

Palnit nodded. "It was established to operate along the same lines as the pretar maximum security prisons, except that it's inside an asteroid we hollowed out. It's for the most hardened of criminals."

"Are there programs to rehabilitate the inmates?" Luke asked.

Palnit shook his head. "That would be pointless. These particular inmates are never going to breathe free air again. It's a facility for warehousing criminals serving life sentences with minimal expense."

"This is all very fascinating, but we have pressing news for Marshal Smith," Yesnic quipped.

Isnod smiled. "We didn't expect to see you here, Yesnic. The information you have must be important to get you away from that lovely little colony."

Yesnic nodded. "Indeed, I do." He then looked around. "Is there a place we can talk in private?"

The group was a little large for Luke's office. He thought a second and said, "Let's go to my briefing room."

Luke led the group to the security office briefing room, where he held small meetings with his senior staff. When they arrived at the door, Yesnic pulled a device out of his pocket. "Excuse me, Marshal Smith, may I check the room first?"

Luke looked at Lynuna and Isnod, who both nodded slightly. He shrugged his shoulders and nodded. "Be my guest."

Yesnic activated the device and entered the briefing room. He held it in front of him as he waved it over the table in the room. Giving the display on the device his full attention, he carefully continued his scanning. The display changed indications suddenly, and Yesnic slowed his motion. After a couple of adjustments on the device, he got on his knees and looked under the table. Finding what he was looking for, he straightened himself and put his finger to his lips and then pointed to his ear.

Luke said to the group. "Wait here." He then edged past them and told the deputy at the desk, "Get Ian in here with the bug remover."

In less than a minute, Ian arrived with a small toolbox, and Luke pointed to Yesnic, who showed him where the listening device was. Ian opened the tool kit and extracted some tools, then disappeared under the table for a minute. When he reemerged, he held up a clear plastic cylinder with an electronic device that served as the cap. Inside the cylinder was a small device that Ian had removed from under the table.

Luke took the cylinder from Ian and examined it closely. "This looks Kastian to me."

Ian nodded. "That's where most Spyware comes from."

Lynuna stared at the object. "Won't the owner of this object be aware that it's just been compromised?"

Luke shook his head. "Not if Ian did his job properly. Right now, the container is feeding room noise. Whoever is listening at the other end will just think we're not bothering to use this room. The device itself thinks it's still attached to the bottom of the table."

"What's next, Boss?" Ian asked.

Luke frowned. "Get that to Carl and have him look at it right away. In the meantime, call in a Sweep Team and start looking for more bugs in critical areas. Begin with the Upper CentMod briefing room number 1."

"Right on it, Boss," Ian said, turning to leave.

Luke motioned for everyone to enter the briefing room. When everyone was in the room, Luke closed the door. No one bothered sitting, and Luke said, "I take it that Mr. Yesnic is here to verify the identity of the syndicate informant on the station."

Yesnic nodded and said, "Just call me Yesnic, but yes, that's right. I also have some further pressing information that's important to this station."

Luke nodded. "First things first, is that Gutroynod guy the syndicate informant?"

"His name is actually Nodroygut," Yesnic said with a nod. "He's an up-and- comer in the Treest Syndicate Information Cell."

Luke frowned. "I've never heard of it."

"It's a syndicate branch unique to Treest," Yesnic answered. "Like anything else, criminal activity requires intelligence and data. The more data that can be collected, the higher the probability of success for a given operation."

Luke nodded. "So they don't partake directly in criminal activity. They just gather information?"

"Most of the information they collect is of a sensitive nature. They use mostly illegal means to gather data, so their profession is not without its hazards," Yesnic answered.

Luke raised an eyebrow. "If we can link that listening device to Gutro...er, Nodroygut, then we can nail him to the wall." He then looked at Yesnic. "Would you mind going over this again for the boss, and we can discuss your other news."

Yesnic nodded. "That would be fine."

Luke told the group. "There's more room in briefing room number 1. That's why I had Ian scan it first. Tiffany, please show our guests there." When everyone was on their way, Luke summoned two deputies. "Mitch, go to CargoMod 8 and have Jeremy Cole meet us in briefing room number 1. Roger, you track down Will Dawson and do the same.

Don't say anything aloud, especially if they're in an office. Use a pad and pencil."

After Mitch and Roger left to complete their task, Luke went to the forensics lab. The technician was going through SICOS files, and Luke asked, "Any luck with that Carl?"

"It's a Kastian Corporation Model 483 mk2," Carl answered while pointing at a catalog page on his SICOS monitor.

Luke nodded. "Put that on a data chip and bring it to briefing room number 1 in the ops center."

Carl complied and the pair left together for the ops center. As the platform lift reached the top, Luke said, "Go to the briefing room. I'll get the boss."

Luke walked the corridor to Phil's office and tapped on the doorframe. Phil looked up from his work. "What's happening, Luke?"

"I need you out here, Boss," Luke answered.

When Phil was in the corridor, Luke held up a pad with a handwritten note that said, "Don't say anything until we get to briefing room number 1."

Phil nodded and headed to the briefing room. Luke repeated the performance with Gus, then Virginia. The four of them finally entered the briefing room, and Phil's eyes widened when he saw the crowd. Ian was putting tools back in his tool kit, and Luke asked, "Find anything?" Ian held up another plastic cylinder with a listening device in it.

"Just this one," he said, putting it on the table.

Phil picked up the container with the bug and examined it closely. He set it back on the table. "I take it that this is the reason you didn't want me to say anything in my office."

Luke nodded. "That's right. Our new friend from Treest, Yesnic here, found one in the security office briefing room."

Phil's expression changed. "So you think this belongs to the suspected Syndicate informant, Assistant Chef Gutroynod?"

Luke nodded again. "Most certainly. His name is actually Nodroygut. Apparently, our flaston assistant chef is part of a Treest Syndicate branch called an information cell."

Phil's expression was changing again but not for the better. Doing his best to keep his voice even and reasonable, he said, "Why don't you just tell me what our next step should be, just to keep me from flying off the handle?"

Everyone in the room knew what Phil meant by "flying off the handle." It probably involved a flaston screaming for mercy and an air lock. Luke tried to stifle a chuckle. "Our first step should be to tie these devices to Nodroygut and clear the station of any more bugs."

"There's a way to accomplish both goals," Carl offered. He stood and inserted a data chip into the SICOS terminal, then activated the wall-sized monitor. After he opened the file with the Kastian Corporation Catalog, he found the page he needed. "This bug is part of a larger system. The user distributes the bugs using whatever method becomes available. They're actually quite passive in function, as they will only activate when there are voices nearby. They won't even transmit a conversation unless there's a use of a key word input by the user."

Luke asked, "What does the receiver look like?"

Carl scrolled to the next catalog page. "This is the basic unit," he said, pointing to an illustration. "This receives signals from multiple sources and stores the data, then the operator can evaluate it at his leisure. Then he can decide whether to make a copy and pass it on to his higher-ups or not."

Will frowned. "How big is it? I mean its physical size."

Carl pointed to some text on the page. "Sixty centimeters by forty-five centimeters by forty centimeters."

Luke nodded. "Something that big can't be hidden in standard quarters, but really, there's no reason to hide it. It's not like we routinely look for spyware in quarters. Two things I don't understand, though, those bugs are way too small to transmit with any kind of power. How does it get enough range to reach the receiver, and how did he manage to put bugs in sensitive areas?"

Carl nodded. "Good questions. The transmitters use the VLF to the LF frequency range to compensate for the low power. The downside of that is it takes up to a couple of hours to transmit a ten-minute conversation. As to how they were placed, I have no clue."

Will frowned. "I think I know how that might have happened. He must have used clean bots to do the task. After a series of incidents with the Clean Bots, Dan Harrington has been monitoring their programming closely. He noticed some of the bots had been given instructions. Funny thing, though, once the task was carried out, the coding that made the instructions was automatically erased but not completely. We could tell something was done, but no idea exactly what was done."

Luke frowned. "Why didn't you bring that to my attention?"

Will shrugged. "Programming updates arrive on data streams all the time.

This just looked like it may have been random anomalies that corrected itself."

Phil shook his head. "I'm still not up to speed on how he used the clean bots to place these things. Wouldn't he need access to the bot's docking ports?"

Carl shook his head. "Not at all. All he would need to do is leave a bug hidden in a public space, perhaps under a bench, then leave instructions for a bot to retrieve the device and place it in any desired location."

Luke shook his head. "How did he get computer access to the bots?" Will shrugged again. "Anyone can access the program from any SICOS terminal. It's not a system that's considered sensitive."

Luke was about to comment, but Phil saved him some time. "Have Dan correct that."

Will made a note on a pad, saying, "It'll be done, Boss."

Phil nodded "Okay, we are now aware that sensitive areas have been compromised, and Luke's deputies need to do a station-wide sweep."

"That would take months," Gus said in an exasperated tone.

"Perhaps not," Carl offered. "As I said earlier, there's a way to fulfill both goals. We find that receiver in Nodroygut's possession that ties it to him. I can use it to locate all the other devices. Each bug would have to be cataloged in the system to help him keep track where the information is coming from."

Luke nodded again. "We have plenty of grounds to enter his quarters and search them. But if we come up empty, it'll tip our hand, and he'll likely warn his handler that we're aware of their efforts."

Will started to grin. "When we're done here, you and I will take care of it."

Luke didn't like the way Will said that, and Will didn't elaborate. He didn't have time to dig further, so he moved the conversation forward. "Mr. Yesnic said he had more information for us."

Yesnic couldn't help but smile. "Just call me Yesnic. I cannot be 100 percent sure, but the data I collected would indicate that the Syndicate has put an operation in motion that concerns Oasis 4. The Flast Syndicate boss contacted his counterpart on Treest and asked for several things. First, they wanted Pukontgore to meet up with an "under boss" from Flast. After a crew is put together, they are to stop a threat to the organization."

"Did they mention Oasis 4 specifically?" Phil asked.

Yesnic shook his head. "No, not specifically. However, some of the things I heard about and details about this station seem to overlap."

Isnod put up his hand. "I should mention that I've known Yesnic for most of my career, and the information I've gotten from him over that time has been absolutely accurate. If he gets twitchy, it's generally for a good reason."

Phil nodded. "We appreciate that you've made this journey for our benefit, especially since you don't have anything personnel to gain. So to summarize the situation, there may be Syndicate operatives on their way here. But the big question is, when will they arrive, and what do they plan on doing once they get here?"

Yesnic shook his head. "I thought perhaps they would try to kidnap or otherwise silence any former slaves on the station. But I heard mention of bounty hunters in some of the conversations. They didn't expand on what they were going to do about the bounty hunters, if anything, but I can imagine. The thing that really put me on a passenger liner was when they recruited assistance from the Dragons. I realize the safest place to be is not on this station, but Isnod and Feldon are my friends, and I wouldn't be able to sleep at night if I had information that was literally life and death but kept it to myself. Also, having associated with the Syndicate in one form or another for as long as I have, I've seen how despicable they are. They are whole without conscience or morals. If I can hurt them, I will. They can and should be destroyed."

"We have several advantages in that we know there is an operation in the works or possibly initiated. The number of goons it would take to overwhelm my deputies couldn't go unnoticed. We'll be able to screen passenger liners and charters for likely hazards before they engage docking clamps," Luke stated.

Phil nodded. "Okay, let's carry on with what we know. Thank you, Mr. Yesnic, for bringing us this information. Are you planning on staying with us for a while?"

"Please, just call me Yesnic. Yes, I'll be here until this situation resolves itself," Yesnic said with a nod.

Phil nodded. "Virginia, why don't you assign Yesnic quarters? The Star Lodge Suites are very comfortable, but quarters would be a bit more private, I think." He then turned to Luke. "Find that bug receiver. Then we'll talk about how to proceed."

Will looked at Luke. "I'll help you with that, Luke. You're going to love this."

*****

## Oasis 4, HabMod 4, Rooftop

Will, Luke, and Carl were in PEWS standing on HabMod 4. Will was used to working outside the station, and in fact, he quite enjoyed it whenever he had an opportunity to use a PEWS. Luke, however, was less enthusiastic. He stood between Will and Carl and said, "Will, I'm not liking this."

Will chuckled. "Just concentrate on the surface you're standing on. In fact, kneel down and take hold of the handholds, then use your safety clip on the rail. After you do that, turn off the microgravity generators in your boots."

The handholds were between the windows of the HabMod, and the rail was one of several tubular members that were on the exterior for the exact purpose of connecting the safety clip. Each PEWS safety clip had a reel that played out a cable to allow the user freedom of movement. If they reached the limit of the cable, they would simply attach to another safety rail.

When all three were ready, Will said, "Just a second, gentleman." He pressed a button on the control pad attached to his arm. They would be outside several quarters on this trip, so to preserve the privacy of those inside, an alarm would sound in each quarter, alerting the occupants that there would be workers outside.

Luke looked toward the bottom. "He's on Level 2."

Will started downward, headfirst, and Luke followed suit. As they descended, Luke glimpsed into a couple of quarters. From his perspective, everything was upside down. He shook his head in his helmet. "I don't know how you do this all the time."

Will laughed. "The lack of gravity doesn't help."

Carl laughed. "I'm having a great time. It'd be neat if there were more evidence to gather outside of the station."

"I'm glad you're enjoying yourself," Luke said wryly as they descended past a malnun child waving to them from the sitting room of his quarters.

They finally reached level 3, and Will said, "One more. Are you sure he's not in there?"

"I checked. He's cooking dinner at the moment," Luke answered. The trio eased themselves downward until they could see inside.

Will used the control on his arm to switch on the lights in Nodroygut's quarters. "That's about like the studio apartment I had after college," Carl observed.

Luke wanted desperately to get out of the PEWS and experience gravity again. "That's fascinating, Carl. Is that key piece of hardware in there?"

Carl nodded in his helmet. "Right there on the table." Luke was satisfied. "Let's tell the boss."

*****

## Oasis 4, HabMod 4, Quarters of Assistant Chef Gutroynod (Nodroygut)

Nodroygut entered his quarters and was greeted by the sight of Security Marshal Smith and Evidence Technician Carl Stewart sitting at his table. Nodroygut was angry at the intrusion and started to protest, "Excuse me! What is the meaning of this invasion of my privacy?"

"Don't act wounded, Nodroygut," Luke replied in a deadpan fashion. "I realize that I'm an alien on this space station, but I still have ri— what did you call me?" Nodroygut asked while backing toward the door. Nodroygut bumped into Security Deputy Marshal Ian Mackenzie, who was blocking the door. Luke looked at Ian. "Take him to a holding cell."

Ian put cuffs on a stunned Nodroygut and led him away. Luke then turned to Carl. "Did you figure that thing out yet?"

Carl nodded. "All it took was finding the menu and looking for the right page." He then made a couple of commands, and a list of locations came up where listening devices were located. He inserted a data chip. "I'll get this list to the Bug Sweep Teams."

Luke stood to leave. "After that, get your assistant and go through this place with a fine-toothed comb."

*****

**Flast, Velsra Provence, The *Thrapmore*,**
**Power Yacht Owned by Crime Boss, Dulpot**

Moliston sat in a lounge chair on the upper deck in the sunshine, and he took a sip of the cocktail that was given to him. As he watched, the bathing suit-clad girl who served him his drink walked away. He smiled then turned to Dulpot. "You certainly knew what I needed to help me relax. You know how to live Dulpot."

Dulpot stirred his own drink. "What would be the point in obtaining riches and power if one cannot enjoy the benefits and share those benefits with friends, of course."

Moliston nodded and said, "I sometimes forget that. I try to tell myself that work is its own reward, but that's not entirely true. Every now and again, one needs to leave their responsibilities with trusted associates and reenergize, as it were."

"I'm so happy you contacted me when you did," Dulpot said. "I've been meaning to take a cruise, and it's so much nicer to do it with friends."

The yacht was gliding slowly just off the shore to allow the passengers to take in the scenery. The shoreline on this part of the lake was mostly wilderness with forest-covered cliff tops, rocky beaches, and the occasional village. Moliston was indeed more relaxed than he'd been in years. He looked at Dulpot. "I contacted you for a reason, Dulpot. I have intelligence that Yulona and Lytrina are going to that troublesome space station, and I plan to take advantage of the situation. I've set events in motion. I've contacted Jostorlac, and I'm having her send a crew there. There are seventy-five Dragons, or more if they're available, going, and Pukontgore will be leading them.

Dulpot wasn't surprised, as he was anticipating this. Some quick math and he furrowed his brow. "By my numbers that's less than half the number of the security personnel on that station."

Moliston nodded thoughtfully. "That's true. However, they'll have some distinct advantages. First, they'll have surprise on their side. Couple that with the aggressiveness of the dragons, and human security will be no problem."

Dulpot frowned, then slowly started to nod. "I'll go there myself. I'll take Naplorn with me to ensure this episode is put away properly." Moliston smiled. "I'm feeling better already. When everything is settled, you can bring back Pukontgore and help him take that little village over again. If our associates have been compromised, you'll be in an excellent position to detect it and ensure corrective measures are taken."

Dulpot knew exactly what Moliston meant by corrective measures. Intelligence about the organization must be kept from those who seek to destroy it. He nodded and assured Moliston, "My thoughts exactly. Everyone knows that is the way it must be. It is the only way to conduct ourselves."

Moliston relaxed and said, "Knowing that you're taking action beyond a personal interest gives me a great deal of assurance. Your position in the organization is very secure. Now let's enjoy our current surroundings and work out the details later."

*****

## Oasis 4, CargoMod 1, Passenger Lounge

Phil had made sure there was a reception committee to meet the *Brintnonopek Traveler*. With him was Alice, Lynuna, of course, Isnod, Feldon, and Tillya. They watched as the passengers filed off and headed toward the customs desk. Isnod leaned toward Phil. "I'm glad you made sure Feldon and I were here to greet Yulona and Lytrina."

Phil nodded. "Well, there's more than just Yulona and Lytrina. They brought quite an entourage with them, I'm led to understand."

Isnod furrowed his brow. "Do you know who's with them?"

Before Phil could answer, Yulona and Lytrina appeared in the air lock. Lynuna rushed to greet them, and there were the usual hugs and kisses. Behind them, Isnod spotted two more flastons. Suddenly, he realized it was his parents, and in a low voice, he started saying, "No, no, no…"

Phil frowned. "What's wrong, Isnod?"

"You wouldn't need to ask if you had ever met my father," Isnod answered. As Lynuna's parents left the air lock, Isdornac and Noduleic rushed to Isnod.

Then Feldon was surprised to see his parents, along with his sister and her family. His parents had to wait until his niece and nephews got their hugs before they could give him their hugs. Tillya was enjoying watching her friend's affectionate greetings and was distracted by Yulona and Lytrina saying hello to her when her parents entered the air lock. She stared at them in disbelief then suddenly burst into tears and ran to them.

There wasn't a dry eye in the CargoMod as Tillya was reunited with her parents. The trio was beside themselves with joy as they tried to regain their composure. When Tillya was ready, she led her parents to Isnod and Feldon. "You've already met my good friends, Isnod and Feldon." They greeted each other then Tillya led them to Phil and Alice. "This is Phillip Ross and Alice Ross."

Yanoner grasped Phil's hand and shook it warmly. "We can't thank you enough for making sure our daughter had a secure and safe situation after she was freed from Gostis."

Phil assured Yanoner. "It was the decent thing to do."

Tillmay gave both Phil and Alice tight affectionate hugs while tears were streaming out of her eyes. It was very obvious that Yanoner and Tillmay were not without gratitude.

After they had composed themselves, Phil announced to the group, "We've organized a reception dinner at Maurice's. There are some more of the Oasis 4 family who wants to make your acquaintances."

The meal at Maurice's was excellent, as always. The new arrivals wondered if human food was always this fussy. They were assured that the usual fare from Earth was more like what they were used to. Maurice was told that there would be children there, so he did some research and provided a selection of items that flaston children would enjoy.

After dessert, coffee, and tea were served, they could have more relaxed conversations. Luke Smith had another opportunity to tell the story about how they snuck Lynuna, Lytrina, and Yulona past Isnod and Feldon. Naturally, he told it with as much comic flair as he could, which had Isdornac in stitches.

The conversations were so pleasant that everyone had lost their sense of time, and Maurice had to politely remind them that they had to close the restaurant. Phil stood and said, "On behalf of myself, Alice, and the Oasis 4 family, I would like to say how absolutely overjoyed we are to have been a part of this reunion if everyone could make sure that their respective parents get checked into their rooms all right. We're looking forward to seeing all of you around the station during your visit."

*****

## Flast, Brintnonopek, Shuttle Port

Dulpot sat in his first-class seat, watching out of the viewport as the shuttle docked with the Flast Orbiting Station. Naplorn sat next to him, watching over his boss's shoulder at the progress being made by the shuttle. This station was the oldest of two freight space stations orbiting Flast. There's been speculation as to when a dedicated passenger facility would be constructed, but that was a little way in the future.

When the docking clamps engaged, the air lock was opened, and the first-class passengers were allowed to enter the station. Dulpot and Naplorn walked through the air lock, and a station employee directed them to the docking port where the freighter waited that they booked passage on. Being as this station wasn't a dedicated passenger facility, they had to see to their own luggage, which Naplorn attended to.

The pair arrived at the proper docking port and presented their passports to the officer at the air lock. He examined the documents and nodded. "Ah, Mr. Dulpot and Mr. Naplorn, you made it just in time." At that moment, Ed Carlton walked up to the group. "There's our two passengers. Welcome aboard the *Bright Star*, gentlemen." He then looked at the officer. "Mike, show them to their quarters when you get a minute."

A flaston station worker walked to the air lock with a pad in his hand. He paused momentarily when he saw Dulpot and Naplorn but recovered quickly and acted like he didn't notice anything unusual. Ed edged past Dulpot, Naplorn, and the officer. "Is that the final items for the manifest?"

The station worker linked his pad with the one that Ed was carrying and transferred the data. Ed was examining the data, and the station worker said, "Oh, there's one other thing you need. Let me find it."

He started quickly tapping on his pad, then sent the short document to Ed, who frowned when he saw the short message. Then he tapped the translation button on the screen. The message was indeed short and simply said, "Those two men boarding your ship are in the Syndicate.

One is a major boss, and the other is his lieutenant." Ed looked at the worker. "Thank you, Enyont. That's indeed useful."

After ensuring his crew was closing the hatch and air lock, Ed walked to the platform lift and took it up to the bridge. After stepping onto the bridge, he went to his systems operations officer. "Clara, can I see you for a moment?"

Ed and Clara stepped into his cabin, and Ed said, "This is going to sound terrible, but I would like to record all conversations in our flaston guest's cabin." "I can imagine why," she said with a knowing nod. "It'll be done. I'll have the Ships Integrated Information Computer System record in discreet mode. "

Ed smiled as he opened the door to return to the bridge. "I knew I could count on you."

When the prelaunch checklist was complete, the docking clamps were released, and Ed put the *Bright Star* on a course to Kassnins Trading Planet.

*****

**The *Postup*, Passenger Liner Chartered by Jostorlac**

Pukontgore was given a private cabin on the *Postup* for their journey to Kassnins. They were going to meet Dulpot and Naplorn there, along with a number of dragons. There were already some members of the dragons on board, but given the numbers that were requested, they had to be recruited from two different locations. After arriving at Kassnins, he was to go to the surface and meet Dulpot, then return to the *Postup*, board the remaining dragons, then make their way to Oasis 4.

At the moment, he was studying the details of his mission. He felt fortunate that there was so much data available concerning Oasis 4. It stood to reason, though. It was simply a variation of other human commercial space stations, and therefore, the data wasn't considered classified. In his mind, the mission objectives didn't leave room for half measures. They had to neutralize the bounty hunters that were making things uncomfortable for his associates, along with any former slaves.

The difficult part of the plan was ensuring his or anyone else associated with the Syndicate didn't have their image recorded. Of course, there was a plan to correct that eventuality, and he wanted to be well prepared to execute it if need be. In his mind, it was an extreme plan. It involved the sudden loss of breathing air on the station and destroying any computer records.

The Dragons were easy to convince in partaking in this venture since there were millions of goaners worth of merchandise and commodities up for the taking once the job was done. Pukontgore privately wondered if the Dragons could be controlled long enough to ensure that the operation didn't crumble into chaos. He pushed those unproductive thoughts to the back of his mind and continued to study.

*****

## Oasis 4, Eva's Café

The flastons have been on the station for three days and were thoroughly enjoying themselves. Tillya was given time off while her parents were here. Isnod and Feldon only made visits to their office to check for messages. Lynuna was expected to be in the consulate during normal hours, but everyone understood that if they really needed to get a hold of her, they could get her in short order since there weren't too many places she could go on a space station.

Gombolk spent much of his time visiting farm machinery dealers on the station, and Kinfel was happy to tag along and give his opinion. At first, Gombolk was hesitant to bring his father-in-law, but Kinfel, being a farmer, had a unique understanding of the requirements of crops grown on Flast. After three days, Gombolk had enough data to recommend to his employer which machines they should offer.

Despite being on a space station with a limited number of activities available to them, they were not having a difficult time finding something to do. Phil relaxed his long standing rule about not allowing noncompany personnel access to work spaces like the control center, CargoMods, and vessel maintenance to allow tours for their flaston friends.

At the moment, everyone was enjoying their lunch at Eva's Café, especially the children. They were hesitant at first where it came to human food, but they discovered it wasn't so different from flaston food. They soon had meals that were their favorite and asked for them at every meal, but Donfel, with help from the wait staff in whatever eatery they were in at the time, made sure they got a variety, and it was relatively healthy.

After everyone had eaten, they made the short walk to a seating area after getting beverages from the coffee and tea kiosk. The children, of course, were sent to the ice cream vendor for their treats. Soon, they were joined by Phil and Alice, who sat with them and visited. After a time, a group of pretars led by Selak and Tonkin arrived. Selak approached Tillya. "Excuse me, Miss Tillya. I would like to thank you for helping us coordinate the movement of our equipment and materials these last couple of weeks."

Tillya smiled. "It was my pleasure, Mr. Selak. Please, I would like to introduce you to my parents."

Tillya introduced Selak and Tonkin to her parents, which made Selak and Tonkin beam in typical pretar fashion. Selak smiled. "Since you've been such a tremendous help to us, we would like to invite everyone here to a holographic performance of human music this evening." He looked around. "Shall I reserve fourteen seats?"

"I'm not sure the children would want to sit through something like that," Donfel said.

"I have a solution then," Selak said, beaming. "The daughter of one of my technicians is watching the children of some of my other technicians tonight. She would be happy to entertain your children, I'm sure. I'll be more than happy to arrange it."

Before Donfel could object, Gombolk piped up, "That sounds wonderful."

Selak smiled and said, "Very good. I'll make sure there are eleven seats for your party."

When Selak and his group resumed their walk to Eva's, Yesnic chuckled. "It was very good of him to invite us like that. But I have to say, I find pretars almost too polite."

Yulona looked in the direction of the pretars. "They are a unique people.

There is much to appreciate about them."

"What is it about humans where honorifics are concerned? I noted it when I first met Feldon, he called me Mr. Yesnic, a habit he obviously picked up from humans. I've heard 'Miss Lynuna' and 'Ms. Tillya.' Earlier this week, I heard someone refer to 'Mr. Selak.' Flastons and pretars don't do such things, and I find it a bit curious," Yesnic finished.

Yulona nodded. "In the Earth culture that this station springs from, it's considered polite and a sign of respect. I'm sure your friends can remember when they went from Mr. Isnod and Mr. Feldon to Isnod and Feldon. When that happens, it usually means the person has transitioned from acquaintance to friend. There are nuances, of course, but generally, that's how it works."

Yesnic nodded. "That's very interesting."

Lytrina smiled. "Indeed. There's another thing humans do with their names that's getting attention on Flast. I'm sure you've noticed they have several names."

Yesnic nodded. "I've noticed that. It seems confusing to me."

Lytrina shook her head. "It really isn't. Each family has a name, passed on through the father normally. When a child is born, it is given the first name, sometimes to honor someone they know or simply because they like the name. Then normally, a middle name is given, also mostly to honor a family member or friend."

"Three names?" Yesnic asked incredulously.

Yulona chuckled. "Or more. There doesn't seem to be any rules in this regard."

"It's not so different from what we did on Flast centuries ago. We only started coming up with names using the syllables of the parents' names as a fad. Even when they started doing it, they predicted the practice wouldn't last long," Lytrina stated.

Feldon laughed. "I, for one, am grateful that the system was flexible."

The flastons had a good laugh, which made Phil and Alice furrow their brows.

Phil shook his head. "I don't get the joke."

"Imagine sharing a name with the most notorious person in Earth history," Feldon answered.

Phil nodded. "Ah."

"There's actually an effort to reestablish family names on Flast. Some families have done research and discovered what their original family names are. For those whose family name is lost to history, they have the option to select a name," Lytrina stated.

Phil nodded. "That's interesting. How do they select a name for themselves?"

"The same way family names were developed on Earth, I've discovered after some research," Lytrina stated. "I've read that human names were adopted that reflected the profession of the family. Craftsmen who worked with metal were called smiths. As a result, a very common name in your language is Smith. Or their geographic location often factored into it. For instance, someone living near a river crossing would be called Ford."

Feldon smiled. "I suppose I would be Feldon Farmer."

"Don't you think 'Tracker' or 'Detective' would be more appropriate?" Kinfel asked.

Feldon slowly shook his head and furrowed his brow. "No, I like Farmer." "I'll take Tracker," Isnod said with a smile.

Kinfel didn't say any more on the subject, but he had a very satisfied smile on his face.

"Tell me more about this music. What are we going to be witnessing?" Isdornac asked.

Phil took a sip of coffee before answering, "The last time the pretars were here, they discovered music. As impossible as it seems, they never conceived of anything like it. When they were nearly finished with the station expansion, I arranged for Mr. Selak to receive a music collection that had a Holographic presentation."

Yulona nodded. "Earth is like a lot of other worlds with several styles of music. Are you familiar with what they have planned tonight?" Phil shook his head. "I haven't heard. Though I can tell you, whatever they choose, it'll be very tasteful. The collection they have is quite extensive."

Isdornac nodded. "I'm looking forward to it."

*****

## The *Bright Star*, Freighter Owned by the Intersystems Shipping Company

Ed Carlton had the *Bright Star* parked in geosynchronous orbit over the main shuttle Port on Kassnins. The *Bright Star* was dropping off a total of eight shipping containers and picking up six. As far as he knew, the cargo was legitimate, and the firms that arranged the shipping were of a reputable nature. However, because of the nature of the seedier elements of this planet, freighter crews rarely went to the surface. In fact, there wasn't even an orbiting station to dock with. Container shuttles brought containers from the surface and traded them with ones from the *Bright Star*. At the moment, an eight-passenger shuttle was easing into the starboard air lock. The shuttle's mission was to pick up the two flaston passengers. Ed stood and said to his first officer. "Carry on with the cargo exchange. I'll be in my cabin after seeing our guest to the shuttle."

He left the bridge and rode the platform lift down to the bottom deck. There, he found Dulpot and Naplorn waiting patiently for the shuttle to finish its docking procedure. Ed approached them. "I trust you, gentlemen, had a pleasant journey."

Dulpot turned his head toward Ed. "It was without incident."

At that moment, the hatch opened, Dulpot and Naplorn entered the shuttle with their luggage then crewmembers on both vessels closed the air lock hatches. Ed shrugged and turned toward the platform lift, saying sarcastically, "Geez, I thought they'd never stop yakking."

Back in his cabin, he accessed the file on the Ships Integrated Information Computer System that had a message he had composed for Phil Ross on Oasis

4. One final check of its contents, then he said, "Convert file into a compressed data stream and send to Phillip Ross on Oasis 4 via interfold transmission."

In a few seconds, the computer chirped, "Task complete." Ed returned to the bridge to finish the cargo exchange while hoping the information he sent was useful and on time.

*****

## Kassnins Trading Colony, Shuttle Port

After landing, Dulpot and Naplorn rode the courtesy transport to the shuttle station terminal. The maldor clerk pressed a button below the counter. When they reached the counter, Naplorn asked the clerk, "Is there a service that we can hire to take us to Morrok's Inn?"

Two maldors emerged from an office behind the counter, and the clerk sidestepped to allow the pair to get closer to the counter. The older maldor smiled in a decidedly condescending manner. "Most certainly, just outside the door. If one isn't there, just press the summons button, and one will arrive shortly."

Naplorn bent to pick up the luggage, and the older maldor said, "One other thing. Activities of visitors of this planet are subject to fees payable on departure."

Dulpot looked the maldor in the eye and said in a very deadpan fashion, "We'll keep that in mind." He then turned and left the terminal with Naplorn behind him.

*****

## Oasis 4, Eva's Café

Phil and Alice were sharing a table with Gus and Brenda, eating breakfast.

Gus said while buttering his toast, "I really liked the concert last night." Alice put down her juice glass. "It was wonderful, wasn't it?"

"What were the names of those singers?" Brenda asked. Phil fielded the question, "Patsy Cline and Brenda Lee." "I wish I had half of their talent," Alice mused.

At that moment, Tillya arrived with Yanoner and Tillmay. Then Isdornac, Noduleic, Kinfel, Donness, Donfel, Gombolk, and the children found seats. Phil looked over to the group after they ordered, and he mused, "We're a couple of flastons short, aren't we?"

"The others are having a working breakfast to discuss what Yesnic knows about the Syndicate," Tillya offered.

"What's the topic of conversation this morning?" Yanoner asked. "Patsy Cline and Brenda Lee," Gus answered.

Donness gushed, "I could listen to them all day."

Gombolk nodded. "I was blown down by Brenda Lee. I was not expecting a girl that young to have a voice that strong."

Tillmay asked, "Was that your first experience with human music, Tillya?"

"No, Feldon and I were invited to watch a presentation some weeks ago," Tillya answered with a shake of her head.

Brenda asked, "Who was performing?"

"The Righteous Brothers and a group named after a city on Earth, Chicago," Tillya answered. "They're from roughly the same era as what we heard last night, perhaps a little later. There must have been something magical about that time period."

Phil checked his watch. "Oops, Gus and I need to get our day started."

Phil and Gus hurried off to the morning briefing while Alice visited with the flastons. Their day actually progressed in a decidedly normal fashion, which made Phil wonder if there were any surprises waiting for him that afternoon.

Lunch found Phil and Alice at the pizza kiosk, where they bought slices and found a seat where they could people-watch. They finished their meal and sat there talking about the events of the day so far.

"Tillya finally brought her folks to the museum," Alice reported.

Phil nodded and asked, "How did that go?"

Alice shrugged. "They actually enjoyed themselves for most of it. Things changed, though, after they reached the Gostis exhibit. Tillmay was always on the verge of crying, and in fact, she did have a couple of breakdowns. Yanoner just had an angry look he tried to hide but failed to. Tillya gave them comfort until they could collect themselves. I'm telling you, that girl is made out of sturdy stuff."

They heard a familiar voice behind them. "There they are, sis."

Phil and Alice turned around, and they were greeted with the sight of Michael in his class A dress uniform, and he wasn't alone. Their daughter Amy was with him, and they were striding toward them. Alice jumped up and ran to them, squealing, throwing open her arms, ready to give them both mama bear hugs.

Phil waited for Alice to get her fill of their kids before he kissed Amy and gave Michael a hug. He asked, "Why didn't you two say you were coming here?"

Michael shrugged. "We're pulling out of Gostis, so Amy and I decided we should come here and see the parental units. I took leave and met Amy and the rest on Raytheon then we jumped on the passenger liner bound for here."

Phil furrowed his brow. "Who is the Rest?"

Before Michael could answer, another familiar voice could be heard. "They're right here, Henry."

Phil spun around and saw Alice's parents. "Mother Karen! Papa Henry!" Phil's mother-in-law threw her arms around him. "I see Alice is still taking good care of you. I guess her little lapses in sanity haven't got out of hand yet."

Alice was in midhug with her father, and she looked over to Phil and her mom. "Hey, that diagnosis was never confirmed."

Alice then hugged her mom while Phil shook hands with his father-in-law.

Then they heard yet another familiar voice. "They found them Doug." It was Alice's turn to spin around. "Mother Clare! Papa Douglas!"

After another round of hugs, Phil asked, "Why didn't any of you tell us you were coming?"

Phil's mother answered, "Michael wrote us and said his unit was redeploying to Earth, so he suggested that he could take leave and we could have a reunion here."

"It would have been nice to be in on the planning," Phil said with a grin.

Alice smiled and excitedly said, "Let's get everyone checked in, and then we can plan some activities."

Phil noticed there was a young man hanging around that he vaguely recognized. Before he could ask who he was, his father said, "Is that all that's involved in running a big space station?"

Phil frowned. "What do you mean?"

"Well, we strolled up, and there you were, hanging around the mall, like you did in high school," Douglas answered.

Clare shook her head. "Well, we did arrive at lunchtime, Doug."

Alice stopped. "Oh my goodness, after getting everyone checked in, we can get you some lunch."

They resumed walking to the Star Lodge Suites, and Phil said to no one in particular, "It's not called a mall."

They all trooped into the hotel lobby, where a smiling desk clerk greeted them. Alice's parents were the first to get their room. After getting the necessary information using an ID card swipe, the clerk had them state their names in a microphone. This provided a baseline for their voice print. To enter their assigned room, all they had to do was vocally instruct the door to allow entry.

Phil's parents were next. Then the clerk looked at his monitor. "Let's see, a Mister and Missus Kennet." Amy and the young man Phil tried to ask about earlier swiped their cards quickly one after the other, then registered their voice prints.

Phil was caught completely flat-footed and was quite speechless. Alice, however, put her hands to her mouth to stifle the squealing. When it finally gelled in Phil's head what was happening, he took a step toward his daughter and her husband. Amy put up her hands. "Now, Daddy, don't be mad!"

The young man edged slightly behind his bride. Phil stopped and shook his head. "I'm not mad. Just surprised."

Amy grabbed her husband by the arm and pulled him around to her side, which wasn't an easy task being that he wasn't entirely sure if it was a good idea to have no one between him and his new father-in-law. Amy said, "You remember Troy, don't you? You liked Troy. Don't you remember?"

Phil nodded. "I remember Troy. It would have been nice, though, to have some warning about this. Surprises are fun, but this is a little much. First, your brother joins the Army. Then you get married. All without telling us a thing." He then turned to Alice. "They learned this behavior from you, you know."

Alice's parents were nodding in agreement. He then walked to Amy, took her hands, and kissed her on the forehead. "Just do me a favor. Write to your mother and me before we become Grandpa and Grandma."

Amy smiled and hugged her father. "Deal."

Phil shook Troy's hand. "Welcome to the family, son." Phil then put his arm around Troy's shoulders and led him away. "I'm looking forward to getting to know you better, Troy, and letting you know how much I treasure my daughter. I'm looking forward to showing you the station, especially the air locks, best air locks in the galaxy…" Troy looked back at his wife with a plaintiff look, wondering what he had gotten himself into.

*****

**Kassnins Trading Colony, Morrok's Inn**

Dulpot pushed a plate away with half the breakfast he was served earlier still there. He looked around and said, "I hope the food is better on that charter ship."

Naplorn pushed his own plate away. "As do I."

Dulpot stirred the contents of his cup. "At least they have decent tea." In a few minutes, Pukontgore walked in and allowed his eyes to adjust. After spotting Dulpot and Naplorn, he approached their table. "You must be Dulpot. I am Pukontgore. The charter ship is orbiting, awaiting me to return with you and twenty-five dragons."

Dulpot motioned to a chair. "Have a seat Pukontgore." After Pukontgore took a seat, Dulpot motioned to his companion. "This is Naplorn. When the dragons get here, we'll go to the shuttle port and leave. In the meantime, have the waiter bring you some tea. The food here is questionable, but the tea is decent."

The waiter brought Pukontgore his tea, and Dulpot waited for him to return to the kitchen. Dulpot put down his teacup after taking a sip. He fixed his gaze on his cup of tea and said, "You've done things on Flast that have started a series of events that have the potential to destroy our organization."

Pukontgore was now very uncomfortable. He started to say something in his own defense, but Dulpot cut him off, "There's an opportunity here however to correct all that and leave our organization in a better position."

Pukontgore thought he should say something positive. "I'm willing to do anything to help the organization."

Dulpot nodded. "You sound genuine, and I think you mean it. However, I'm questioning whether you understand the scale of what the organization is trying to accomplish."

Pukontgore furrowed his brow. "I don't follow."

"Allow me to educate you," Dulpot offered. "Covroynac and his associates also did not understand what our long-range goals are. We do not exist for personal enrichment."

Dulpot took a sip of tea to allow Pukontgore to digest what he just said. He put his cup down and continued, "You had to leave Flast because you executed an operation that had monetary potential but did nothing to enhance the organization. If you were successful, the government authorities would be at a loss as to who they should be looking for. In the worst case, you and all your accomplices could have been captured. I'm uncertain what pressure they would bring to bear to get information from you, but any chance at all that you could give up information, however unintentionally, is completely unacceptable."

Pukontgore shook his head. "I would never divulge anything concerning my comrades."

Dulpot nodded. "You sound sincere when you say that. But as I said, one truly does not know how he would respond in that situation. Covroynac proved to be a disappointment in that regard. He told two bounty hunters where to find you. I'm uncertain if he gave up any information about the organization, and that's a concern."

"If Covroynac, Gordlid, and Jotlor were disciplined for their transgressions, why am I being given an opportunity to atone?" Pukontgore asked.

"Covroynac was disloyal. Gordlid and Jotlor's loyalties were in question as well and they were weak besides. You, however, are still somewhat of unknown quality, but there's an opportunity here to restore a damaged cell in the organization. Covroynac was introduced to these principles, but unfortunately, he didn't take the lessons to heart, and as a result, much of the organization was put in jeopardy," Dulpot explained.

Pukontgore shook his head. "I thought you said you weren't sure if Covroynac divulged information about the organization."

Dulpot smiled. "You heard correctly, but remember, he did sell you out. Loyalty works both ways. A leader must be loyal to those under him as well as those over him."

Pukontgore now realized that there were subtleties in their business that he hadn't bothered to pick up on. He resolved to learn as much as he could from Dulpot and, in the process, put himself in better graces with his superiors.

Dulpot could see Pukontgore was working things out in his head, and he decided to answer as many questions as he could before Pukontgore asked them. He finished his tea and put down the cup. "Covroynac knew these things, or at least he should have, being in the position he was in. It's bad enough that he yielded under pressure. His activities weren't low-key in the least. It was only a matter of time before the authorities were compelled to shut down his operation, and given his lack of discipline, organizational security would be compromised.

If that were allowed to happen, the goals we have been working toward would be hopelessly out of reach. Members of the organization that we are in must be prepared to go to any lengths to keep the secrets of the organization from being known by outsiders. If Covroynac knew this, he certainly didn't take it to heart. We should be prepared to take intelligence to the grave. It's the only way to conduct ourselves."

Pukontgore drank some tea to digest what Dulpot was telling him. At once, he realized that his activities weren't merely for personal enrichment. The Syndicate was actively seeking to reshape Flast society. He had to tread lightly to avoid looking too eager to know things that were beyond his level in the organization. However, Dulpot was gracious enough to educate him, and he wanted to make sure Dulpot wasn't wasting his time on him. He cautiously asked, "What are the long-range goals of the organization?"

Dulpot smiled thinly. He was beginning to realize that Pukontgore didn't contract Covroynac's ignorance. He refilled his tea from a pot that the waiter had thoughtfully left for them. "Our goals are to have a seat at the table when society is ordered properly, perhaps even at the head of the table. The galaxy is divided into three groups. The first group is those who espouse so-called personal liberty, and self-determination. The second group believes individuals cannot be trusted to see to their own affairs and see to the equal and fair distribution of resources. We are in the third group. We will do whatever it takes to position ourselves in places of power. We do that by making ourselves indispensable to the group in power at the time."

"Obviously, the current government on Flast is in the first group. Making ourselves indispensable to them may be impossible, and I can understand why the current government wants to curtail our activities, but what incentive was there for the Colavar Regime to allow us to operate?" Pukontgore asked.

Dulpot considered his response, as the reasons were a bit complex. Finally, he answered, "As long as we kept our activities low-key and didn't cause a public outcry, the authorities would pretty much allow us to do anything we want. Within reason. In return, we are often in a position to do favors for those who show us consideration."

Pukontgore furrowed his brow. "What kind of favors would a local official need?"

Dulpot laughed. "Not just local officials, but more than you could ever imagine. Framing political rivals, providing campaign funds, providing entertainment and recreational aids in the form of narcotics, women, and other things that polite society wouldn't find acceptable. All of which puts them permanently in our debt."

"In return, we can expect laws to be made that favor our activities. Law enforcement efforts against us hampered. The possibilities are endless," Pukontgore observed.

Dulpot nodded and smiled. "Now you're catching on. We provide a service, and the payoff is our organization becomes an integral component of the controlling element of our planet."

Pukontgore absorbed the information completely. He started to nod his head slowly, saying, "If I understand the relationship between the organization and the government correctly, we can exist in cooperation or friction. In friction, the organization has to expend considerable resources to conduct business and make a decent profit. Likewise, the government has to spend considerable resources to curtail our activities, depriving other government departments of those resources."

"In cooperation?" Dulpot asked with a smile.

Pukontgore smiled back. "The government only needs to expend a token effort to curtail our activities. As long as the proper people get compensated, we can do pretty much what we want."

Dulpot nodded. "I won't lie to you. Since the fall of the Colavar Regime, we've had to be very careful about our operations. We can still operate, but it's going to require that we take extraordinary precautions. Everything we do will have to be well-planned with unprecedented levels of intelligence and reconnaissance until we get a government that's more amenable to us, or we can compromise enough of the present government."

Pukontgore furrowed his brow. "I agree that a change in government would benefit us most. That seems unlikely to me, so our best course of action would be to compromise the present government. How would that be accomplished without the people demanding reforms or even noticing their freedoms starting to disappear?"

"The same way it was done with the Colavars," Dulpot offered. "First, the people will be divided into groups, which won't be difficult because these groups already exist along regional and ethnic lines. Then create mistrust and animosity between them to give the government a problem to solve. In fact, the more problems there are, the easier it'll be to erode their rights."

Pukontgore shook his head. "I find it difficult to believe that there would be enough people clamoring for solutions to problems imagined and ignore issues that will affect them for generations."

Dulpot laughed and said, "It's easier than you think. Most people, it seems, look for a crisis to wring their hands over. The problems to exploit are usually social, political, or scientific. Social and political problems are easy to spread. If you control the right institutions, you control the narrative."

Pukontgore furrowed his brow. "What institutions?"

"The government is currently banned from projecting undue influence on the media, but there are ways around that. Since the fall of the Colavars, the media outlets were separated into individual entities with corporate ownership. The good news is individuals who have the correct mindset can be put in influential positions in those entities. There has been some progress in this area but not near enough to get the full effect of what's desired," Dulpot answered.

Dulpot paused to allow Pukontgore time to soak in the lesson. He then continued, "Education is another critical area to control. The sooner we can start indoctrinating people in the way we need them to think, the easier our task will be. Finally, one of the areas that we enjoy considerable success is controlling trade guilds. If there's an organization that's troublesome, they'll find it difficult to get shipping, waste disposal, labor, and number of inconveniences until they see things the way we want them to."

"There's no possible way we can control all that," Pukontgore said in an exasperated tone.

Dulpot shook his head. "You would be surprised what can be accomplished with keeping your finger in key areas. We only need to provide pressure and resources in key areas."

Pukontgore's head was swimming. The scope of the organization he was a member of was being laid out for him. He had never thought about the long- range goals of the organization or his place in it, but now it seemed he had an opportunity to take a larger role that came with more rewards along with more responsibilities.

Dulpot couldn't help but smile, watching Pukontgore work things out in his head. He nodded his head slightly. "I can tell by the look on your face that certain realities are coming into focus. To be completely candid, back on Flast, you were a street-level thug terrorizing villagers into compliance. To be honest, you were a little better than a member of the Dragons. I blame Covroynac for your lack of education. I have to say, though, during this first meeting, I am detecting some of Jostorlac's influence in your current thinking."

Pukontgore smiled back. "I haven't really thought of it before. I guess Jostorlac has had an effect on me. Along with being very beautiful, she does have a subtle manner about her. She's learned how to get what she wants with cleverness and not violence. I can see why she's head of the organization on Treest. When our world is ordered, and the organization is providing tacit services to the benefit of those we are allied with, how will we control the 'less sophisticated' elements of the organization?"

"You mean the Dragons," Dulpot said with a laugh. "When their usefulness is no longer required, they will find themselves being scooped up by the authorities. Much like the idiots pushing for political reform in favor of our allies. Once their goals have been achieved and they're no longer an asset, they will be systematically removed from positions of influence."

Pukontgore nodded. "I just spent days on a ship full of dragons without telling them my name. I suppose that's to prevent them from telling the authorities who I am in an attempt to reduce any sentence they might receive."

Dulpot nodded. "Exactly correct. The Dragons are extremely expendable. There is much more expected of those at our level. I get the sense that Covroynac failed to teach you that lesson. In fact, he failed to live up to the ideals we venerate. That's why he's no longer with us. He did not live up to the ideals we aspire to. When pressure was applied, he did what was necessary to make the pain stop. A true member of the organization would rather go to the grave than give up information about ourselves. It's the only way to conduct ourselves. Everyone understands that's the way it must be."

Pukontgore nodded. "I understand. I also have an idea or two on how to deal with that space station."

Dulpot nodded slightly. "We'll discuss that on the journey. In the meantime, Pukontgore, I must say that when you were in Resnon, you were a little more than a street-level thug, not unlike our Dragon colleagues. Now that I've met you, I've come to the conclusion that you have the potential to be much more than that. I'm wondering if that's a result of your exposure to Jostorlac, or perhaps you've always possessed those desirable traits, but no one has seen the wisdom in helping you develop them to their maximum."

At that moment, a flaston walked in and headed directly to them. He had his shirt sleeves rolled up, exposing a tattoo of a dragon on his forearm. Dulpot eyed the new arrival and, in a moment, said, "You must be Mantonbid. My colleagues and I are ready to go if all your men are assembled."

Mantonbid nodded. "Our transport will follow you to the shuttle port."

They left Morrok's Inn, boarded transports, and went to the shuttle port. Dulpot, Naplorn, and Pukontgore got out of the transport when they arrived and entered the terminal. They made a line to the door that led to the shuttle ramp, but their progress was interrupted by the shuttle port manager and his younger partner. They stepped in front of them, and the manager held up his hand. "Just one moment, gentlemen. As you recall, when you arrived, there were to be fees to be paid."

Dulpot nodded. "As I recall, you said our activities here would be subject to fees. The only activity we partook in was staying at an inn."

"Do you think I'm so foolish to think you did nothing more than spend the night and have a meal? No one stays at Morrok's without being involved in a profitable venture. The proper thing to do would be proper compensation for using these facilities," the manager said resolutely.

The dragons started walking in, led by Mantonbid, which got the full attention of the manager's partner, but the manager was too invested in trying to squeeze Dulpot to notice them. Dulpot smiled and nodded. "Perhaps you're correct. See my colleague Mantonbid about any fees we owe you." He then walked around the manager and left the terminal with Naplorn and Pukontgore in tow. Mantonbid stayed behind a few minutes with some of the dragons to convince the manager to see things the right way.

*****

## Oasis 4, Office of Phil Ross

Phil waited until the afternoon to check his correspondence since he had other duties that day that were pressing. There were the usual company directives and memoranda that he quickly scanned for items that required his immediate attention. When he finished that, he spotted a correspondence from Ed Carlton. He quickly read Ed's message and said, "SICOS, save current file and attachments as security manager letter, add this date. Copy to Luke Smith, Security Marshal."

He then pressed a button on his desk. "Jay, have the department heads, Lynuna, Yulona, and Lytrina from the Flast Consulate, meet me in briefing room number one. Oh, Lynuna should bring Palnit, Isnod, Feldon, and their pal Yesnic should be there also."

Jay answered back, "What about Mr. Condent?" "I'll get him personally," Phil responded.

Phil left his office and tapped on Gus's doorframe. Gus looked up. "What's up, Boss?"

"We have a situation brewing. I've called a meeting in briefing room number 1 with the department heads and selected flastons," Phil answered.

Gus walked around his desk. "I can imagine what this is about."

Gus knew better than to press further until they were in the briefing room, and everyone was assembled. Walking past the reception desk, Phil said, "Thanks, Jay."

They didn't have to wait long before the department heads started walking in. Virginia was first, followed closely by Will Dawson. Jeremy Cole was the last to arrive as he had the longest distance to cover.

Once everyone was settled, Phil started, "I just received a communication from Ed Carlton, captain of the *Bright Star*. It seems two flastons booked passage to Kassnins. One is named Dulpot, a major boss in the Syndicate, and the other is his lieutenant, Naplorn." Isnod interjected, "Dulpot is the name we got from Covroynac.

He's the boss of Velsra Provence."

"It seems Ed took a couple of liberties," Phil said. "One of the cargo handlers on the Flast orbiting station told him who his passengers were, so he recorded as much of their conversations as he could, and the upshot is they're on their way here."

Yesnic put up a finger. "Did this Captain Carlton send a copy of the conversations he recorded? I would like to review them to see if there are any nuances that a human may not be attuned to. No offense."

"None taken," Phil assured him. "Of course, I'll make everything available to anyone who wants it."

"I can't imagine that they're coming here alone," Luke observed. "There are vessels that stop here direct from Flast. The only reason I can see for them to stop at Kassnins would be to pick up muscle."

Phil nodded. "Right you are. They're picking up a number of dragons on Kassnins, and there's someone else meeting them there from Treest."

Isnod smiled. "Let me guess, Pukontgore." "That would be the guy," Phil confirmed.

Feldon frowned. "That's a potential problem. Pukontgore probably had cosmetic surgery to change his features."

"I'd say that is very likely," Yesnic said. "The Syndicate boss on Treest makes use of an Earth-trained surgeon that specializes in that very procedure."

"What about that computer program you used to identify the dragons that stole the Faldos Charter?" Isnod asked.

Yesnic shook his head. "That program is actually still in development, and it's not nearly sophisticated enough to scan and evaluate individuals in real time, especially with the volume of traffic that boards this station."

"We'll have to rely on old-fashioned methods to predict their arrival," Luke stated.

Phil nodded. "I have every confidence that we'll see these guys coming when the time comes. What concerns me is, are we going to be able to protect their targets if they get here before we can get the flastons off the station?"

Luke nodded. "I think there'll be enough warning when they arrive that we can start an emergency evacuation of the flastons before the dragons step foot on the station."

"We can keep the *Aurora* in a quick launch configuration. Isnod and Feldon can do the same with their shuttle," Gus added.

"Our stay here will be ending in a couple of days," Yulona said. "If they don't know our itinerary, they could miss us."

Luke shook his head. "That leaves Isnod, Feldon, and Tillya in a tight spot, especially since it sounds like they're the primary targets."

Yulona looked a little embarrassed. "You're right, of course. I was thinking of their parents. The Dragons are whole without compunction. They wouldn't hesitate to use them to get to their targets. As I said, the *Brintnonopek Traveler* is set to arrive in two days. Another day, and it's returning to Flast. That would at least eliminate one of the potential tools they could use against us."

A thought occurred to Gus. "Did they mention a time frame on when they expected to be here?"

Phil shook his head. "Not that I could detect. They were pretty vague. However, given the distance they need to travel, the time they expect to depart Kassnins, it sounds like they'll arrive well after your party leaves unless they charter a super high-speed charter, and there simply aren't a lot of those around."

Luke nodded. "That at least gives us more options."

"Roger that," Phil said. "Virginia, you and Luke make this your number one priority. You know, we should have had Dwight here. He's the most versed on ship capabilities. Work with him also. In fact, don't hesitate to pester ship's captains for their opinion. Identify any likely vessel that could carry that much trouble."

Yulona didn't look any more comfortable, but he did manage to keep his voice even. "We'll be boarding the Brintnonopek Traveler in a couple of days. That will be a tremendous load off my mind to use a human aphorism. That still leaves Tillya, Isnod, and Feldon to worry about. Also, I'm not so sure if they're not after Lynuna."

Phil nodded. "I have family here also. Given our location and the nature of the vessels arriving and departing, it's nearly impossible to get everyone to a safer location. The *Aurora* won't be able to hold everyone, and it's an unattractive option for a variety of reasons."

Virginia smiled. "I can find a reason to send Tillya to Reynolds Planet, perhaps to give them a presentation on our enhanced ore storage facilities. I'll bet Lynuna could come up with a reason to go there herself. Dwight could have them there in a couple of days, and I suspect that even those dragons would be hesitant to go anywhere near the mercenary unit there."

Phil nodded and smiled. "That's not a bad plan. I like the idea of removing all excuses for showing up here in the first place. How does that sound to you, Lynuna?"

Lynuna looked troubled. "I'll do whatever you think is necessary for the safety of the station, of course. But I don't relish the idea of running away from danger."

"This may all moot in a few days," Lytrina said. "If Mr. Ross and his associates are successful in identifying their ship, I imagine that they won't be able to enter the station."

"If things go to plan," Phil confirmed, "that leaves Isnod and Feldon. Guys, it's completely up to you what you do. The number of dragons they would have to bring would be tall odds for anyone."

Both Isnod and Feldon grinned, and Isnod quipped, "You wouldn't be trying to keep us from earning bounties, would you?"

Phil chuckled. "Wouldn't think of it. All right, everyone has a rough idea of what they need to do. Let's see if we can spot them before they get here. "

Everyone started filing out of the room to do their part in trying to figure out when Dulpot and Pukontgore were going to get there. Isnod and Feldon left with Yesnic while Luke looked on and chuckled. "You know, I consider those two friends of mine, but I still think they're thumpers."

Lynuna grinned. "That's very true, but they're our thumpers."

*****

## The Postup, Passenger Liner Chartered by Jostorlac

Pukontgore was waiting at the air lock while a smaller charter vessel called the *Kodyan* docked. Dulpot waited with him to give him encouragement before they parted ways. He looked at Pukontgore. "I'm sorry I didn't mention this part of the plan at Morrok's. There were operational security concerns that were successfully dealt with en route. The *Kodyan* will dock, where you, along with the dragons with you, will enter the station. You should be able to easily overwhelm the security in the CargoMod, distracting them to the point I can enter the station with the rest of the dragons."

The air lock opened and allowed access to the *Kodyan*. The dragons who were accompanying Pukontgore started to file on board. Pukontgore turned to Dulpot. "Soon, this will be over. We will be successful, or we don't go home. It's the only way to conduct ourselves. I'll see you again in a couple of sectors."

A crewmember closed the hatches and ensured the seals were holding before the docking clamps could be released. Once that was accomplished, both vessels continued to their Oasis 4 destination although the ships took divergent paths to avoid approaching the station from the exact same vector. They wanted to arrive at the same time. However, it would look suspicious if they came from the exact direction.

*****

## Oasis 4, Lower CentMod

Phil was making his way to a maintenance access point located in a space below the station maintenance shop. The last tasks necessary to bring the ore storage bins online were being completed. Normally, he wouldn't put himself in a position where he might get in the way, but he suspected that someone was already making a nuisance of themselves.

He entered the maintenance shop and walked to a ladder that disappeared below the floor. Phil climbed down and looked around. This space was a maze of piping and ducting that carried everything that could flow through the station. In Phil's mind, it was best described as organized confusion. He stopped to listen to the various sounds in this space. Then he heard voices some distance away.

Picking his way through the passageways, he finally found the sources of the voices and approached the group. He put his hands on his hips. "Dad! Henry!"

His father and father-in-law both looked up from the work they were watching. Phil's father smiled. "Cildid here was showing Henry and me some welding techniques."

"I can't have you two pestering the technicians while they modify the station," Phil responded.

Cildid removed his welding helmet. "It was no trouble, Mr. Ross. In fact, that was the last weld in this project. Once we x-ray inspect the weld, this project is completed."

Phil smiled. "That is very good news. My operations director tells me that we're going to put the additional capacity to the test in short order."

Phil made his way to the ladder with his dad and Henry in tow. Reaching the ladder, he was greeted with the sound of an alarm. He climbed up the ladder and entered the maintenance shop, where the alarm was much easier to hear. Phil went to the nearest communication terminal and punched a code for the security office. The deputy at the duty desk saw the code on the comm set for Phil and decided that he'd better answer it.

The deputy answered the line, and Phil didn't give him time to finish the greeting. "What's going on?"

"Reports are a little sketchy, but a vessel docked at CargoMod 3, and a bunch of Syndicate goons got off, and they're making things interesting for the security deputies there," the deputy reported.

Phil frowned and asked, "Has the trouble gotten out of the CargoMod?"

"No, sir," the deputy answered. "Marshal Smith is sending every available deputy to CargoMod 3 to put a quick end to things."

Phil pressed the End Call button. He turned to his dad and Henry. "You two need to get to the others and make sure they stay safe." With that, the trio made their way to the platform lift and headed to the Upper CentMod before security protocols shut it down.

*****

## Oasis 4, CargoMod 1

The *Postup* had finished its docking procedure at CargoMod 1 at about the same moment the dragons accompanying Pukontgore on the Kodyan started being a problem in CargoMod 3. Dulpot put his hand on Mantonbid's shoulder. "It's time."

Mantonbid faced the assembled dragons and yelled, "Let's finish this!" He then ran into CargoMod 1 with seventy-five dragons. They ran directly to the customs desk, where the deputies saw what was coming and hit their alarm buttons that locked the entry gates as well as sounded the alarm. The dragons continued to run at the customs desks and the locked gates. In minutes, the gates were pried open, and dragons were making their way to the Upper CentMod. Dulpot and Naplorn casually stepped into the CargoMod and made their way to the connector tunnel.

As they strolled, Naplorn asked, "What is the strategy we're employing here?"

Dulpot continued strolling. "There's not much of a strategy. The dragons will neutralize the security force on this station using decidedly crude and brutal methods. Once that's done, all personnel on this station will be gathered to one location, probably a CargoMod, and we'll simply lower the oxygen levels in that compartment, and they'll gradually go to sleep and then expire. I suppose we could simply dump the pressure in the CargoMod and get it over with, but that seems excessive."

Naplorn nodded. "What do we do with the station itself? The computer will undoubtedly have data that we won't want to be retrieved. Also, there are ships docked that go into automatic lockdown during a station emergency like this."

"I looked into it," Dulpot answered. "Before we leave, we can go to the station maintenance control area. From there, we can release the locks on our ships so we can leave. Then we'll remove the safeties from the reactor and rig it to overload. The ensuing explosion will vaporize the station and any ships docked. When that's over, our problems will be over."

*****

## Oasis 4, CentMod

The security personnel from CargoMod 1 reassembled in the CentMod at the connector tunnel entrance to the CargoMod as protocol dictated in situations like this. None of the security deputies ever imagined a situation that required this tactic. The really unfortunate part of this tactic was the people trapped in the CargoMod were at the mercy of the dragons although it seemed that the dragons were far too interested in getting to the CentMod to pay attention to anything else.

Only a handful of deputies made it to CargoMod 3 to deal with the alert there before the alarm went up in CargoMod 1. Luke Smith assessed the reports coming from the CargoMods and quickly determined that CargoMod 1 was in greater need of deputies and used the communication device on his sleeve to divert deputies to the connector tunnel entrance to CargoMod 1.

Deputies started to arrive at the connector tunnel entrance to CargoMod along with Luke. The idea was to force the dragons to engage the deputies at a narrow point to limit the number of dragons in direct contact with the deputies at one time. Luke positioned his deputies in a fashion that would divide the dragons and prevent them from concentrating pressure at one point. Luke resized the situation and thought that no matter what he did, the CentMod was going to be filled with rampaging dragons.

He could hear the dragons in the connector tunnel racing toward them, yelling menacingly. Trying to conceal his nerves, he looked at the assembled deputies and exclaimed, "There are ten deputies in CargoMod 3 and about twenty-five here. What's holding up the rest?"

A deputy, out of breath from running, said, "The platform lifts from the Lower CentMod are on emergency lockdown. We have to come up one at a time through the neutral gravity tubes."

*****

## Oasis 4, Lower CentMod

Isnod and Feldon continued to do office work during their parents' visit. They just checked messages and scanned the Multi-World Commerce Cooperative Criminal Activity Reports, which only took a couple of hours. They had just finished and were heading to the platform lifts when the alarm sounded. They looked at each other, and Isnod said, "They're here!"

The pair ran to the nearest platform lift and punched the button, summoning the lift. A text message started flashing on the screen near the controls, saying, "Lift in Emergency Lock Down." Feldon pointed to the neutral gravity tubes. "This way!" He then bolted to the tube entrance labeled "Oasis 4 Personnel Only." He stepped in and pushed off, then Isnod followed.

The neutral gravity tubes were installed to allow maintenance and other personnel to go between the upper and Lower CentMods without overburdening the platform lifts. The most difficult thing about the tubes was keeping children from playing in them.

Deputies started lining up at the Lower CentMod central core. Each one entered a hatch that put them in a tube that led upward. The unique feature of the tube was the lack of gravity. Once inside, the occupant would push themselves upward by two handles in the side of the tube built in for that purpose. They would simply float upward to the Upper CentMod exit.

Arguably, the most difficult part of using the tubes is being careful not to push off too hard, which happened often. For that reason, the ends of the tubes were curved to prevent the user from smashing their heads at the top or winding up in a heap at the bottom. The curved tubes would direct the wayward individual into the Upper or Lower CentMod.

Shortly after Isnod and Feldon went up the tubes, security deputies started arriving. Tiffany Waters waited in the queue for her turn in the tube. She was approached by Ivonorsic and Xin Chen, who had very serious expressions on their faces. Ivonorsic asked, "Miss Waters, what's the nature of the emergency?"

"There's about eight dozen dragons on the station. Apparently, they're trying to take over the station," Tiffany responded.

Ivonorsic frowned. "You'll need our help."

Tiffany shook her head. "No way! You two need to get to your quarters or your studio until we resolve this."

Xin protested, "That is out of the question! We cannot cower in hiding while others are in danger! There is our honor to consider!"

Ivonorsic pushed past Tiffany. "This way, Xin!" He stepped into the tube and pushed himself upward using the handles with too much enthusiasm, which resulted in reaching the Upper CentMod much faster than he expected.

Xin was right behind him and pushed off with the same vigor. The curve at the top abruptly changed Ivonorsic's vector and deposited him unceremoniously on the plaza level. In true micton fashion, he rolled twice and assumed a defensive stance. Xin quickly followed, but having watched Ivonorsic, he was more prepared for the exit and landed with a bit more grace. They glanced at each other, then ran off to help the security deputies.

*****

## Oasis 4, Upper CentMod, Plaza Level

The dragons in CargoMod 3 pushed through the security barrier and raced through the connector tunnel to the CentMod. They started battling the security deputies, who were initially beyond their depth but were holding their own. Pukontgore entered the CentMod but didn't engage the deputies. Instead, he started searching for flastons who were not dragons.

## Oasis 4, Upper CentMod, Level 2, Eva's Café

Tillya, Yanoner, and Tillmay were having lunch at Eva's when the alarm sounded. They could see the commotion below them on the plaza level, and it seemed to them that there was a great deal of confusion. They stood there watching the security deputies take their positions while others scrambled about. The main problem was, the dragons had effectively blocked a good deal of people from CargoMods 1 and 3 and the relative safety of the ships docked there. Before they knew it, the dragons started pouring into the CentMod.

Eva and Burt joined Tillya and her parents at the railing to take in the scene below them. Burt quickly assessed the situation and said, "Eva, take Tillya and Tillmay to the kitchen and keep some of the knives handy. Yanoner, if you're up to it, you and I will stay out here and keep those animals away from the ladies."

"I would rather go down there and help Marshal Smith and his people," Yanoner shot back.

Burt understood Yanoner's need to pound syndicate goons senseless, but he shook his head. "We would just get in their way. Besides, if they make it up here, we'll get our share of trouble."

Yanoner furrowed his brow and mulled it over for a few seconds, then he nodded and said, "You're right, of course, but I would feel better if I had a club of some kind."

Burt nodded, reached behind the counter, and pulled out two axe handles. "I keep these handy in case some freighter crewmen get out of line and need to be dealt with before a deputy can arrive."

*****

## Oasis 4, Upper CentMod, Plaza Level, Donald's Garments and Haberdashery

Isnod and Feldon's parents and Feldon's sister and brother-in-law were clothes shopping at the start of the trouble. It was several seconds before they realized what the alarm was. Donfel started to panic and rushed toward the store exit to the plaza level. "The children!"

A sales employee stopped her with the help of Gombolk. Donfel was in a complete panic, and Gombolk wasn't much calmer. "If your kids are in the daycare, they're in good hands. You, however, could get hurt trying to get to them. It's best to let station security restore order," the sales employee said, trying to assure her.

*****

## Oasis 4, Upper CentMod, Level 2, Station Day Care

Gomdon, Dongom, and Balkdon spent part of their visit each day at the daycare playing games with other children and giving their parents some time for themselves. The games they played came from different worlds, and which one they played depended on how everyone felt about the rules. Today they were playing Duck-Duck-Goose. At first, Balkdon didn't want to play because he didn't know what ducks and geese were. The human kids explained what ducks and geese were, which satisfied Balkdon, who said, "We can play this at home, but we'll have to call it Stap-Stap-Trog."

The alarm sounded just as Gomdon was about to tag a malnun girl. The day care workers rushed to calm panicking children and restore order. Gombolk looked at his siblings and shouted, "The bad people are here to hurt Tillya!"

"We have to warn her!" Dongom cried out as she headed to the door with Gomdon and Gombolk right behind her.

*****

## Oasis 4, Upper CentMod, Plaza Level

Phil was in a genuine panic. He started to regret not ensuring that his father and father-in-law would do as he asked and find the rest of the family. It seemed to him that both of them wouldn't resist the temptation to get involved in the current crisis. For his part, Phil had no illusions about his ability to fight a professional syndicate thug. He hadn't been in a fight since high school. As he remembered it, he won the fight but at the cost of a shiner and a bloody nose.

Watching the increasingly chaotic situation, he worried that Alice and the rest of his family were in the middle of this mess. He was worried about Tillya and her parents, indeed, all his flaston friends. He rushed to the area where he thought Luke should be. His thinking was, at this moment, Luke was the best choice to be in command of the station. Any ideas he might have to resolve this that involved station systems might require Phil to implement them.

Phil finally reached Luke, who was engaged in a duel with a particularly nasty- looking dragon. Luke would swing his baton, which was skillfully deflected by the dragon, who would counter with a swing at Luke with a makeshift club. It looked to Phil like Luke was enjoying himself. Luke managed to crack the dragon in the head, dazing him long enough to allow him to jab the baton in his ribs and employ the stun feature. The dragon fell in a heap where station maintenance personnel descended on him and used plastic wire bundle ties, commonly called zip ties, to bind his wrist and ankles.

Phil admired the teamwork, then looked around. There were several dragons lying on the floor in the same condition that Luke's opponent found himself in. Unfortunately, there were also some station deputies lying motionless. Luke handed Phil a small piece of leather sewn into a tube about the size of an index finger and sewn closed at each end. The object was weighty for its size, making Phil look at it and frown. Luke saw that his boss was confused and laughed. "It's full of lead shot. Put it in your hand and make a fist. If you clobber someone, it'll keep you from busting your knuckles. I don't have to tell you the benefit of extra inertia in a punch."

At that moment, a pair of dragons rushed at Phil and Luke. Luke responded with his baton on one of the dragons bringing him down instantly while Phil put his fist in the face of the second dragon with every ounce of force he could muster. The dragon's forward motion was instantly halted, and he was lifted off the floor with the force of Phil's punch. While maintenance personnel were zip- tying the two hapless dragons, Phil opened his fist and looked at the item in his hand. "Where was this when I was in tenth grade?"

Luke couldn't help but chuckle. There was a shortage of opponents at the moment in their immediate vicinity, which suited Phil. Luke immediately started scanning the area for situations where he could be useful.

*****

## Oasis 4, Upper CentMod, Plaza Level, Connector Tunnel Entrance to CargoMod 1

Dulpot and Naplorn stood at the connector tunnel entrance gawking at the scene in front of them. They expected to see terrified station personnel running for their lives and dragons rounding them up. Instead, the dragons were fighting for their lives, and they didn't appear to be winning. Luke glanced at the connector tunnel entrance and got Phil's attention, "Do you recognize those two?"

Phil squinted in the direction of the connector tunnel. Suddenly, it occurred to him where he saw those faces. "Those were the two that Ed warned us about!" Luke smiled. "Let's get 'em!" he exclaimed as he bolted toward Dulpot and Naplorn with Phil close behind.

Dulpot continued to stare at the melee on the plaza level, and he still hadn't seen any reason to celebrate yet. Naplorn spotted Phil and Luke heading in their direction at a full run. When it was obvious that they were running at them, Naplorn got his boss's attention. "Those two humans are running for us!"

"Back to the ship!" Dulpot yelled as he turned and bolted toward the CargoMod.

As they entered the CargoMod and started squeezing through the wrecked customs gates, Naplorn asked, "What good would it do us to get back aboard? The ships are locked down, and we won't be able to release the docking clamps, not even manually!"

You don't believe that I would embark on a venture like this unless I had an emergency contingency in place, do you?" Dulpot answered, resuming his run. "They control their own docking clamps. I have a small two-man shuttle in the Postup cargo hold. We get in the shuttle and exit this unfortunate situation."

Phil and Luke had also pushed past the ruined gates and entered the CentMod with three deputies in tow. Luke spotted Dulpot and Naplorn sprinting toward the docking port occupied by the Postup. Luke yelled, "Roger, you and Ian run up the center aisle and get past those two. We'll box 'em in!"

Roger and Ian did as they were told as Dulpot reached the Postup docking port. Naplorn was deflated when the air lock hatch was closed and couldn't be coerced open. A red light flashed at the flaston Syndicate boss and his lieutenant, indicating the lockdown status. Both Syndicate members were now genuinely desperate.

Dulpot saw Phil and Luke closing the distance and decided to run in the opposite direction. They had sprinted a good distance when Roger and Ian appeared in the aisle in front of them. They were near an open-air lock hatch, so they rushed in.

Naplorn stopped and closed the hatch. He looked for something to use to jam the mechanism preventing anyone on the station from opening it. He pulled a tool off the rack full of tools kept there for emergencies. Then he shoved it in the gears of the latching mechanism.

He turned and saw why this air lock was open. The computer didn't bother securing this hatch because it was unoccupied. Dulpot stood, staring at the stars and the nebula beyond. Slowly, he turned to Naplorn just as Phil and the rest arrived and started pounding on the hatch. Naplorn ignored the commotion on the other side of the hatch while he removed another tool from a rack.

Phil pressed the intercom. "You might as well give up. As you can see, your situation is hopeless."

Naplorn still didn't acknowledge Phil and the rest as he slowly made his way back to Dulpot. When the two were facing each other at the hatch at the opposite end of the air lock, Dulpot took a deep breath. "You're more than a lieutenant to me, Naplorn. I trust you more than any other of my associates. In fact, you're my best friend and have always been such."

Naplorn wasn't given to emotional displays, but he found it difficult to remain stoic. "I feel the same. There isn't one thing I would change in my life, even knowing what's coming," he said with a voice that cracked and shook.

Dulpot smiled and said while nodding, "It's for the greater good of the organization."

Naplorn smiled back. "Everyone understands that is the way it must be.

Loyalty and trust are maintained this way."

Dulpot finished, "If we don't have the assured loyalty or the trust of those over us, our existence is meaningless. It is the only way to conduct ourselves."

Naplorn raised the tool that he had removed from the rack and smashed it against the window, separating them from the vacuum of space. The window, which was designed to withstand an impact, wasn't, however, able to withstand the sharp edge of the hardened tool steel. The window was ten inches by fifteen inches, which meant that at station atmospheric pressure of 14.7 pounds per square inch, there was in excess of two thousand two hundred pounds pressing on it. A crack formed and the window instantly shattered.

The air lock was approximately fifteen feet tall, fifteen feet wide, and thirty feet long. That means, when the window failed, 6,650 cubic feet of air rushed out into space in what seemed to be less than two seconds. Dulpot and Naplorn were caught in the rush of air, leaving the air lock and disappearing through the window instantly.

Phil and the rest stared in disbelief for a few moments until Phil broke the silence, "You know, I've made jokes before about sending people out of air locks. Sometimes I wasn't joking 100 percent. But you know, this gives me a whole different perspective of what that entails."

Luke just shook his head. "We'd better get back to the CentMod."

*****

## Oasis 4, Upper CentMod, Level 2

Gomdon, Dongom, and Balkdon were hunkered down behind a sitting bench while using a potted plant to hide themselves. They were some distance from Eva's, but from their hiding place, they could see Yanoner and Burt guarding the café. Gomdon whispered, "Tillya must be in Eva's. We'll stay here in case we're needed."

*****

## Oasis 4, Upper CentMod, Plaza Level

Phil, Luke, and the deputies that were with them walked into the CentMod. The fight with the dragons was still raging. In fact, it didn't look to them like there was much progress made by either side. Suddenly, a group of dragons appeared and rushed at Phil, Luke, and the others. Just as they took up a defensive posture, Ivonorsic and Xin Chen appeared from nowhere and engaged the dragons. After the dragons were lying on the floor with station maintenance personnel zip-tying them, Phil and the rest came forward, and Phil grinned. "Thanks for that, guys."

Just then, Xin pointed to Tiffany being surrounded by dragons. "That deputy needs our assistance!"

Ivonorsic and Xin started toward Tiffany, but Luke stopped them by putting his arm in front of them. "Let the girl do her job."

Ivonorsic and Xin were confused about Luke's lack of concern for Tiffany, but they quickly learned why he had a relaxed attitude toward Tiffany's situation. A series of well-placed, blindingly fast baton blows reduced the dragons to inert lumps on the floor while Ivonorsic and Xin watched in open-mouthed wonder. Once they saw station maintenance personnel applying zip ties, Xin came out of his reverie. "Let's find where we're needed!" With that, Ivonorsic and Xin rushed toward where they heard the sound of fighting.

Isnod and Feldon were near an escalator leading to Level 2 when Feldon spotted Pukontgore, who was near another escalator to Level 2 with a group of dragons. Feldon then spotted Yanoner and Burt guarding the café, which made him realize that Tillya must be in Eva's. "That's Pukontgore. It has to be! I'm going to Level 2! It looks like Tillya is up there!"

Isnod yelled back, "I'll stay down here. If they get on the escalator, we can cut off any escape!"

Feldon ran up the escalator near him while Isnod headed toward Pukontgore.

Pukontgore was indeed searching for Tillya but was growing more frustrated at his lack of success. He then spotted Yanoner on Level 2 and smiled. "I remember him." He then got the attention of a dragon near him. "Get some others and follow me."

*****

## Oasis 4, Upper CentMod, Level 2

The occasional dragon or two would challenge Burt and Yanoner but come out second best. Burt had had military training in his youth that served him well here. Yanoner didn't have any training, but he was an imposing individual nonetheless. The combination of working with the heavy tools in the little shipyard that employed him, and more than three years of rage worked to his advantage in this situation.

At the moment, there were two dragons engaged in fighting Burt and Yanoner. Burt's opponent made a tactical error, allowing Burt to swing his club freely and knock him out. Yanoner's foe wasn't quite as fortunate to just receive an incapacitating knock to the head. Every swing of Yanoner's club broke the dragon's bones. Yanoner delivered the final devastating knockout blow with such force that the dragons club flew out of his hands and landed a great distance away. The club came to a rest near a sitting bench where a small flaston hand reached out and took possession of it.

Pukontgore reached the escalator and started bolting up to Level 2. Before the dragons could follow him, Isnod literally flew in from the side kicking the lead dragon in the head. At that point, the dragons forgot about following Pukontgore and decided to punish Isnod. Isnod had taken up the classic micton defensive posture and smiled. "Ivonorsic, why don't you and Mr. Chen sit this one out?" Ivonorsic and Xin Chen had gone to Level 2 on the other side of the CentMod to afford them a better view of the fight. When they had approached Eva's, they spotted Feldon running to Eva's and Isnod engaging the dragons at the plaza level and rushed over with the idea of dropping onto the dragons.

Xin frowned. "How did he know we were up here?" "Micton," Ivonorsic replied.

Xin nodded. "Of course."

Pukontgore watched the same events and turned back around. After all, there were eight dragons against that flaston. At the top of the escalator, he strolled past Burt, stepped over an unconscious dragon, faced Yanoner, and the two started circling each other. Pukontgore sneered, "It was foolish of you travel here. You should have stayed in Resnon. Well, you and yours have seen the last of that lovely little village on the lake."

A voice behind him said, "Somehow, I don't think you're all that tough without someone to back you up."

Pukontgore spun around to see Feldon calmly approaching him and said, "Do you actually believe you're the challenge you're pretending to be?"

Feldon's smile disappeared. "There's only one way to find out." Pukontgore instantly rushed Feldon and sent a kick flying toward

Feldon's head, but Feldon expertly deflected it and sent a punch toward Pukontgore, who was also successful in avoiding contact.

The same moment Feldon and Pukontgore started their fight, Isnod launched into the dragons that faced him. Three of the eight dragons fell to the floor from well-placed strikes made by Isnod, causing a reaction from bystanders. Most of the dragons on the station have been rendered inert by now, and as a result, a crowd was gathering on the upper-level walkways.

Ivonorsic found it both irritating and convenient that both fights could be observed from his position, but he couldn't concentrate on one fight. Feldon and Pukontgore were busy trying to get the measure of each other while Isnod battled the five remaining dragons.

A lone dragon topped an escalator and stepped onto Level 2. He saw Feldon fighting with Pukontgore and started to sprint toward them. As he ran past a sitting bench, a club jutted out from under it and tripped him. The dragon fell face-first and sprawled out on the floor. Balkdon emerged from behind the bench as the dragon got back to his feet. The dragon dabbed at the blood running from his nose and looked at it in his hand. He looked up from his hand and stared at Balkdon. "You little troublemaker!"

Balkdon ran to the escalator with the dragon in pursuit. He was so fixated on chasing Balkdon that he didn't notice Gomdon and Dongom coming out from behind the bench. As planned, Balkdon made a sudden left turn as soon as he reached the escalator. As the dragon tried to change directions, Dongom yelled from behind him and on his left, "Stop chasing my brother!"

The dragon spun a little too quickly and had to work at keeping his balance. Suddenly, Gomdon jammed the club in his ankles again, causing him to fall backward onto the escalator, where he tumbled all the way to the plaza level.

The fall was bad enough, but this was an up escalator, which meant that he had to hit every step several times before he reached the actual bottom.

Gomdon, Dongom, and Balkdon were right behind the dragon, following him down. When the dragon had come to a stop at the plaza level, Gomdon cracked him in the head with the club. It was completely unnecessary since the dragon was in a stupor. Dwight strolled up, "You young guns shouldn't be horsing around here with all this going on."

The children all started pleading their case at once, and each repeated the same story over and over until Dwight put his hands up. "Hold up, y'all, one at a time." Dwight pointed at Balkdon. "You first. Why ain't y'all with a grown- up?"

Balkdon rattled off their story in one breath. "Tillya and her mother and father are in Eva's, and Uncle Feldon is outside there, fighting that bad man, and this man was going to sneak up on Uncle Feldon, and we couldn't let him do that."

Dwight smiled. "Well, you young guns have had a little adventure, haven't you?"

"We decided to be bounty hunters like Uncle Feldon. But we don't know if this one has a bounty on him or not. We don't even know how to find out," Gomdon stated.

Dwight pulled some tie wraps out of his back pocket and started to bind the wrist and ankles of the unconscious dragon. "Well, I suppose your Uncle Feldon could help you there. This fella looks mean enough. Bound to be paper on him."

Cildid saw the whole exchange from a short distance away and approached them while pulling a utility wagon behind him. He was smiling broadly. "Perhaps you can make use of this wagon."

Cildid lifted the portable welder off the cart and helped Dwight pick up the dragon and place him there. When that was done, Dwight said, "You kids stay here with me until your uncle finishes his fight. Then we'll go and see him."

*****

## Oasis 4, Upper CentMod, Plaza Level

All five of Isnod's opponents wielded clubs, and they were obviously very skilled at using them. That didn't put Isnod off even a little. The five surrounded him, cutting off any kind of escape. Isnod smiled at their foolishness and overconfidence. This was one of the scenarios that micton stressed training in.

Isnod did what was unexpected and lunged at one of his adversaries, then suddenly, he changed directions and attacked one of the Dragons behind him. The maneuver was done so skillfully that the four who weren't attacked just stood and stared in confusion. Isnod twisted the head of the first dragon and applied pressure to his neck. The crunch of the spinal column could be heard, and the dragon fell to the floor.

One of the other dragons looked at Isnod with pure hatred. "Did you have to kill him!?"

Isnod considered it to be a dumb question. "Of course I did. I'm sure you and your friends planned to kill everyone on this station.

You shouldn't act so outraged when it's turned back on you. Besides, I couldn't take a chance that he'd wake up and uneven the odds again."

Ivonorsic nodded. "Micton teaches us that," he said while he continued to watch from the Level 2 walkway.

One of the enraged dragons lunged at Isnod and, in seconds, was sprawled out on the floor, lifeless. Isnod didn't enjoy killing these men, and in fact, he had always found the idea of taking a life to be an unsettling thought. But in this case, there wasn't time to find an alternative solution to his situation, and the dragons were too skilled to attempt a nonlethal maneuver. If the dragons insisted on fighting him, he had to take the necessary measures to win.

There were now only three against Isnod. They charged him with clubs swinging and cursing in flaston. Isnod was lightning fast in his response, which left the three dragons unconscious. They were terribly hurt but still alive. Isnod gathered himself, then calmly walked to the escalator and rode it to Level 2. At the top of the escalator, he stood watching Feldon and Pukontgore as they faced each other, circling each other. Ivonorsic and Xin Chen quietly approached Isnod and joined him while they watched Feldon and Pukontgore.

Isnod and Feldon's families had come out to the plaza level and had an excellent vantage point to watch Isnod finish his fight and then watch Feldon Square off against Pukontgore. Feldon and Pukontgore were now fully engaged in trying to destroy each other. Each one would try and occasionally succeed in landing a punch. They weren't ordinary punches; they were punches with a micton nuance that was particularly damaging. Xin Chen observed, "Mr. Feldon's opponent is extraordinarily skilled."

Ivonorsic nodded in agreement. "One of the finest micton devotees I've ever seen."

Pukontgore launched a series of attacks at Feldon that bloodied and bruised him. The blows would have been enough to hospitalize most people, but Feldon's conditioning was exceptional. He certainly felt the punishment, but he didn't let it affect his performance. Finally, Pukontgore made a mistake. It was a small mistake, but it was enough for Feldon to launch into his own offense.

The mistake was so small that even Ivonorsic nearly missed it. In fact, he wasn't sure if he saw it correctly. Pukontgore wasn't a poor micton fighter by no means. Perhaps Pukontgore was exhausted and simply got sloppy. But the fact is, he made a mistake that Feldon immediately exploited.

Before he could correct his mistake, Pukontgore found himself in the air with his feet over his head. In the split second he had available, he decided to land and roll into a classic micton "swing, jump, and lunge" maneuver. Feldon, however, was thinking at least two moves ahead of Pukontgore.

Feldon could basically do anything he wanted to Pukontgore at this point. Whatever Feldon did to him, he had to counter with a prescribed counter maneuver. He knew full well that Feldon was going to use his own countermove, but he had to respond in the prescribed manner. He couldn't help it.

Finally, after several devastating blows, Feldon moved in for the kill. Before he could start his final attack, Pukontgore fell to his knees. "Please stop! I've had enough!"

Feldon stood straight and stared at Pukontgore. He was in rough condition from the fight, but Pukontgore was much worse to the point he collapsed to the floor. Feldon turned to Yanoner and quietly said, "I have a very important question for you, Yanoner."

Yanoner was confused at first, but he heard Tillmay behind him let out a small gasp. He looked at her standing next to Tillya. Then it dawned on him what Feldon was going to ask. He turned back and said, "Please ask."

Feldon stepped over Pukontgore and approached the railing. He faced the CentMod crowd, stretched out his arms, and in a loud voice said, "I am Feldon Farmer of Utolon Provence, son of Kinfel and Donness! Having proved my mettle in defeating enemies of our people, I have come to ask Yanoner and Tillmay, father and mother of Tillya, for permission to seek courtship with Tillya!

Yanoner followed tradition and put his hands on his hips and scowled at the start of Feldon's plea. He took his hands off his hips and slowly turned to Tillmay and Tillya. Tillmay was smiling and had tears of joy running down her face. Tillya was too stunned to have a response except for a nearly unperceivable nod. Yanoner grinned and nodded back. He then worked at putting a scowl back on his face, turned, and approached the railing.

Yanoner nodded at the gathered crowd and loudly said, "Feldon has honored me and my house by asking to seek courtship with Tillya in the ancient and time-honored manner! I have found him to be a man of courage, honor, and integrity! He has the enthusiastic blessings of myself and Tillmay to seek courtship with Tillya!"

Feldon turned and walked to Tillya. "I would be honored if you considered allowing me to court you Tillya."

Still in shock, Tillya answered, "I am pleased that you want to seek a more personal relationship. Please contact me to arrange a proper activity."

Feldon smiled and slightly bowed to Tillya. Next, he faced Tillmay and bowed deeper, then faced Yanoner and nodded his head. He turned and strode to the down escalator. Isnod and Ivonorsic fell in behind him, with Xin Chen following.

At the bottom of the escalator, they stepped off, and Ivonorsic said, "One moment, gentlemen."

Isnod and Feldon stopped and faced him. Ivonorsic nodded. "I have never seen a finer display of micton." He reached into a pocket and extracted a metal pin. "This belonged to my father." He placed the pin on Isnod's shirt. He then reached into his pocket again and took out another pin. "This belonged to my uncle." He pinned Feldon.

Both Isnod and Feldon looked at their pins and were at a loss for words. Ivonorsic understood and smiled. "There really isn't a lot of responsibility involved. You've already proved that you have the necessary skills and integrity." Isnod smiled. "I guess it's true what they say. They say that if you set out to become a micton master, you'll never become one. But if you dismiss the possibility, it's nearly a guarantee you'll have one."

Isdornac and Noduleic rushed to Isnod while Kinfel and Donness went to Feldon. For the first time Isnod could remember, his father hugged him. Then he said, "I've always known you were one of the best at what you do for a living.

I've always been very proud of you, but the words never came out. It's that way between fathers and sons sometimes."

Isnod smiled. "I've always known how you felt, Father. It's that way between fathers and sons indeed."

Noduleic grabbed Isnod and hugged him tightly. "I don't know how I should feel."

Isnod frowned. "What do you mean, Mother?"

She looked over to the dragons lying on the floor that Isnod had just fought. Station security was putting restraints on the wounded ones while medical personnel put blankets over the ones that weren't so lucky. She shook her head. "You seek out the most dangerous people in the galaxy. They are criminals who obviously have no conscious to speak of. But after seeing you defeat eight of them before my eyes, I feel better knowing how skilled you are. I still hate the idea of you dealing with such people. It's all too much."

Isnod regretted having his mother see the worst part of his profession. She was under the impression that his job was mainly sleuthing and using deduction. Indeed, she was correct; however, once all the clues had been analyzed, his quarry had to be tracked down and captured. As he struggled to find words to comfort her, a thought came to him that made him chuckle.

Noduleic frowned. "What's funny?"

Isnod shook his head. "You know it's a rare occasion that Feldon and I are faced with several dozen dragons at once."

Noduleic giggled. "I suppose you're right."

Kinfel and Donness were giving Feldon the same treatment. Donfel and Gombolk were nearby and still in a panic. Donfel grabbed Gombolk by the hand. "We need to find the children!"

Phil was nearby and thought to reassure them. "I'm sure they're fine. The day care has procedures for events like this."

From behind them, Dwight said with a laugh, "Don't bet the ranch on that, Hoss. I found three that jumped the reservation."

Everyone turned and was greeted with the sight of Dwight and Gomdon pulling a wagon with Dongom and Balkdon pushing. The part that truly shocked everyone was that there was a very upset dragon on the wagon, and he was swearing in flaston. When they stopped,

Dongom picked up the club that Gomdon used earlier. She swung it as hard as she could, making contact with the dragon's head. "We told you to stop using naughty words!"

The dragon winced and immediately stopped swearing. Gombolk and Donfel rushed to their children and checked them for injuries. Dwight thought he should make sure that they knew he had nothing to do with the kids leaving the day care. He related, "I was passing an up escalator when this feller tumbled down. I was going to put the boots to him, but the young guns had already made sure he wouldn't be able to move."

Gombolk was on one knee so as look them in the eyes. "Why did you leave the daycare? Why did you fight this dragon?"

"Because Tillya and her mother and father were in Eva's, and Uncle Feldon was outside there fighting that bad man, and this man was going to sneak up on Uncle Feldon, and we couldn't let him do that. We decided to be bounty hunters like Uncle Feldon. But we don't know if this one has a bounty on him or not. We don't even know how to find out," all three spouted at once although not in the same order.

Luke was standing nearby and said with a chuckle, "Tiffany, get out your DNA reader and see who this guy is."

Tiffany clamped the reader on the dragon's cheek. In a few moments, the display indicated that the task was complete, so Tiffany removed the reader and instructed it to link to the SICOS and search the database for his identification.

To fill the pause in the conversation, Dwight said, "Bound to be paper on him."

Tiffany smiled when a match was found "His name is Mantonbid. Oh my! Treest is paying five hundred goaners for him!"

Luke nodded. "Well, let's record who captured this guy and make sure these bounty hunters get the reward."

There was a small commotion approaching them, which prompted Luke to turn to see what was happening. The crowd parted as the commotion got closer, and Luke was greeted with the sight of Selak and Tonkin leading a group of pretars that were prodding a group of six dragons along who were tied to a long section of electrical conduit.

What truly surprised Luke was the fact that Yesnic was helping the pretars.

Phil took in the scene and chuckled. "That's an unusual team, but it looks like it's not one to bet against."

Luke looked the dragons over, who were bruised, cut up, their clothes in tatters, and each had a haunted look on their faces. The appearance of the dragons amused and alarmed Luke. He shook his head and said, "You, gents, are going to have to fill me in on how you managed this."

Yesnic, with wide, unblinking eyes, slowly shook his head, saying, "I've seen things."

Selak shook his head. "Oh my, dear, dear, dear. Perhaps we shouldn't have used Mr. Yesnic for bait."

"Bait?" Luke exclaimed.

Yesnic could only look down. "Terrible things." Phil asked, "What's he talking about?"

"Dear, dear, dear," Tonkin said, shaking his head. "Mr. Yesnic seemed so eager to help. We had already put a temporary barricade in the kortlax pen in CargoMod 2."

"Kortlax?" a wide-eyed Feldon uttered.

"That's right, "Tonkin answered. "There are four left. Mr. Yesnic got these criminals to chase him. He ran through the kortlax pen, and before the criminals could exit the pen, we closed both gates and raised the barricade. The kortlax must have thought they were getting a treat." "There were only six criminals," Selak stated. "We had planned for at least twice that number. Four kortlax were well beyond the abilities of only six men. On the plus side, it didn't take long for them to yield." Luke shook his head. "Remind me to never get you upset with me, Mr. Selak."

Phil chuckled, then he got serious. "Okay. Luke, make sure all these jokers are rounded up. Have teams scour the station looking for any dragons that we may have missed. Until we can determine if the crews of the ships that brought dragons have broken any laws, lock down their ships and keep the crews locked up on their ships."

Virginia had made her way down from the Operations Center. Phil looked at her. "Virginia, have some cargo handlers construct a pen in

CargoMod 2 to keep these guys in. I'm positive Luke's little jail is too small to fit all of them. Get with Will Dawson and have some of his guys help."

He looked around and saw Marie Tillman arriving with medic teams. "Doc, you know what to do, but I have to insist that dragons get treated after everyone else."

Will Dawson strolled up with Jeremy Cole, both carrying packages of tie wraps. "I'm sure you two know to assign some people to assist Luke's deputies."

Phil looked down. "Mr. Selak, I would like to purchase the remaining Kortlax. Animals that helpful should be allowed to live out their life. There are zoological parks on Earth that would love the donation."

Finally, he turned to the Flastons. "I imagine all of you have some celebrating to do after Isnod and Feldon get their cuts and bruises looked at. It would also be nice if someone got Yesnic a drink."

Selak stepped forward, beaming in typical pretar fashion. "We would be very happy to see to Yesnic."

Phil smiled. "Fine." He then saw Gus strolling up. "Could you see to things down here. I've got to check on my family."

Gus assured Phil that he had things well in hand, so Phil went in search of Alice and the rest. He tried to remember where they would be today. He then remembered they had talked about the museum gift shop and getting things for his and Alice's brothers and sisters and their families.

The escalator to the lower level was agreeably vacant. At the bottom, Phil stepped off and turned to the museum entrance, which was dark, but he could make out two bodies on the floor. The lights came up, and he saw Michael and Troy framed by the museum entrance. Troy was holding a handkerchief to his nose in an attempt to stem the flow of blood. Michael asked, "Is the trouble over?"

"It's all over," Phil answered with a nod. "Is everyone okay down here?" Michael nodded. "These were the only two to make it down here." Troy turned, saying, "I'll get the others."

As Troy was going back to the museum, Michael chuckled. "I had a hard time keeping Grandpa Henry and Grandpa Doug from going upstairs to help in the fight."

Phil shook his head and smiled. "That sounds about right."

In a moment, the others were coming out of the museum, each toting bags of gifts and being led by Alice. Phil saw them to the Star Lodge Suites saying they should stay there until Marshal Smith gave the all-clear.

*****

**Oasis 4, Trading Center Space Station,
Owned by the Stellar Logistics and Freight Corporation**

After the brawl with the dragons, there was a flurry of activity at the station. The first order of business was getting station personnel to erect a cage in CargoMod 2. Will Dawson showed a sadistic streak by having the cage abut the kortlax pen.

To celebrate their victory over the Syndicate, Phil, Gus, and Dwight organized a party in the Upper CentMod plaza level. It was done Fourth of July picnic style, with grilled burgers, hot dogs, and, as Dwight would say, all the fixin's. The eateries on the station provided the cooking talent. It's not that Phil asked them to, they volunteered to do it, and Maurice had a wonderful time grilling. They played games like the raw egg toss and the three-legged race. Later, the pretars set up 3D projection emitters around a stage and everyone enjoyed band music.

The next order of business was, of course, sorting out the culpability of the various players in the events that occurred. The captains of the charter ships that brought the dragons protested vehemently over their ships and crews being locked down. They claimed innocence by virtue of ignorance, but no one was buying it, though. After interrogation by Luke, both captains admitted they knew what was going to happen. The end result was each man lost their certification and would never be allowed to be an officer on a ship again.

A bigger challenge was the crew, being as it was plausible that they could be completely oblivious to the nature of their voyage. First, Luke checked to see if any of them were wanted felons, and as it turns out, a few were. Then through vigorous interrogation, it was determined which crewmen had some knowledge of what they were doing. These lost their union cards, and their names were added to the Multi-World Commerce Cooperative criminal database as known persons of an untrustworthy nature. The crew that was determined to have no foreknowledge of the events on the station was placed on probation by the union.

It still had to be determined what happened to the charter ships. For starters, Stellar Logistics had every right to confiscate the vessels since they were used in a nefarious enterprise. Phil didn't think much of that idea because it would make the corporation look vindictive. His judgment was to give the charter companies a hefty fine and put them on the Multi-World Commerce Cooperative list of Firms of Questionable Integrity.

Of the one hundred dragons that entered the station, ninety-four were captured alive. Since it was both obvious and admitted that their plan was to murder all the flastons on the station, as well as everyone else, they were all tried on Flast and sentenced to life imprisonment. Each one was sentenced to Regorn Asteroid Prison. It was highly unlikely that any of them would leave that asteroid alive. The isolation and lack of intellectual stimulation will wear down the inmates in surprisingly short order.

After a time, too soon in Phil's opinion, the time came for the flastons to leave. It was especially hard on Tillya and her parents, but she promised she would come home for a spell when she had saved up plenty of vacation time. Tillmay and Yanoner were surprised that she planned to stay with Stellar Logistics, but they thought about it and realized that staying there was actually the best option. For one thing, Feldon wasn't making plans to leave the station. Also, she felt a great deal of appreciation and obligation for the efforts made on her behalf by the station personnel, especially the Rosses.

Prendle of Flast law enforcement thought it was a good idea that Tillya stayed off Flast for the time being. They needed to determine if the Syndicate was looking for retribution after such a large part of it was destroyed. He thought the possibility was remote since it seemed the chain of Syndicate thugs from Resnon and up the line was either dead or in custody.

Prendle had arrived shortly after the melee with some additional investigators. The investigators busied themselves matching names with the captured dragons while Prendle interrogated Pukontgore. At first, Pukontgore was tight-lipped. His conversations with Dulpot were still ringing in his ears and the fact that both Dulpot and Naplorn demonstrated their commitment to the organization to the ultimate end. Pukontgore was struggling with the fact that he didn't have the resolve to show his loyalty to the organization like Dulpot did.

Prendle was very skillful at eroding a subject's resolve. He convinced Pukontgore that, deep down, the Syndicate didn't deserve his loyalty. Eventually, it was difficult to shut him up. He turned out to be a fountain of information that surprised Prendle. Most of it was disjointed information that seemed unrelated. In that respect, the habits of the Flast branch of the Syndicate worked quite well. The best piece of intelligence was the name of the leader of the Flast branch of the Syndicate, Moliston. Prendle couldn't believe his luck over this nugget of intelligence. They now had a subject to surveil.

Phil and Alice's families have returned to Earth, and it's left a hole in their routines. Nothing had really changed from before, but their visit only served to remind them how much they missed family. Presently, they found themselves sitting at Eva's Café sipping coffee after eating their lunch. With them were Gus, Brenda, Virginia, and Dwight.

Dwight stared blankly into the CentMod. "They're late." Gus checked his watch. "They've been later."

"There they are," Virginia observed.

A platform lift emerged from its journey from the Lower CentMod carrying the plotors. They watched as the plotors walked from the platform lift to an escalator to the second level. Riv approached the railing and announced, "All of you non-plotors will yield to our superiority! Your cultures will adapt to serve us, and we will demonstrate our benevolence by distributing the collective resources of your worlds!"

Phil shook his head. "They just won't give up."

Dwight nodded. "I've tried to get along with those fellas like you asked, but they don't do themselves any favors."

"With the pretars and their kortlax gone, these guys are the only entertainment," Gus lamented.

Phil chuckled. "I'm sure something will happen to liven things up around here. There doesn't seem to be a shortage of odd events in the galaxy."

The End

# FRICTION

**Oasis 4, Upper CentMod, Plaza Level**

Phil Ross just stepped off the platform lift and was strolling toward the escalator to Level 2 and Eva's Café. As he walked, he could hear a commotion coming from the area of his destination. That alone was reason to pique his curiosity, but seeing Luke Smith rush to the escalator and bound up the steps, he knew there was a situation that he might be involved in momentarily.

As he reached the escalator, the commotion from Level 2 changed pitch. The noise was less confusing, but there was still plenty of shouting. Near the top of the escalator, Phil could see the situation in Eva's although that didn't make anything clearer. Alice and Brenda Gleason were on either side of Virginia Wells, trying to calm her. Luke was holding back an irate Dwight Needles while Burt was restraining an equally upset Plotor named Riv.

Riv's aides, Bug and Fen, were standing together off to one side with looks on their faces that showed that they weren't expecting the series of events that they just witnessed.

Dwight strained against Luke's grip while yelling at Riv, "You ain't got no call to put hands on a lady!"

Riv was struggling against a slightly amused Burt. "Those that question my inherent superiority should expect to be corrected!"

Dwight pointed at Riv. "You'll sing a different tune when I put a branding iron on your belly!"

"That's a non-understandable and empty-sounding threat! You will not be on the protected roll list!" Riv shot back.

Phil stepped off the escalator and put his hands up. "What's going on here?"

Still restraining Dwight, Luke answered, "Apparently, Riv and Virginia had a disagreement. Then Riv gave Virginia a bit of a shove. Dwight took exception to it."

Phil looked at Dwight. "If Luke lets go of you, do you promise not to attack Riv?"

Dwight continued to glare at Riv. "I promise. But Luke should stay handy." "Riv, can Burt let go of you?" Phil asked.

Riv nodded but continued to glare back at Dwight.

Phil put his hands on his hips. "Gentlemen, I'm a little more than dismayed at both of you. Dwight, I appreciate the fact that you're coming to Virginia's aid, but Riv is a diplomat. Any breach in protocol should and would be handled by me.

Phil faced Riv. "Frankly, Riv, this can never happen again. I realize that your culture is most likely very different from our own. But you should know that once you put your hands on someone in a manner that is unwelcome or unwanted, expect a reaction. We'll talk about this later."

Phil looked at Virginia. "Are you all right, Virginia?"

Virginia nodded. "Of course. It just all happened very sudden." "Why doesn't Virginia come with Brenda and me for a cup of tea?"

Alice offered.

Phil smiled. "That's a good idea. Take all the time you need." He then looked at Dwight. "We're taking the rest of the day ourselves. We need to talk."

An older lady walked to the group with the aid of a cane. Phil turned to her. "Can I help you with something, Mrs. Jacobson?"

She nodded. "If it's all right with you, Phillip, I'd like to talk to these three," she said while pointing at Riv and his companions with her cane.

At first, Phil was hesitant, but he thought for a second and smiled. "That's a good idea."

Mrs. Jacobson looked at Riv, Bug, and Fen. "Well, come along. Don't dawdle."

They watched as Riv and his companions reluctantly followed Mrs. Jacobson to the down escalator. Phil chuckled. "If anyone can reach those three, it'll be Mrs. Jacobson."

Dwight was considerably calmer now. "Where we goin', Hoss?" Phil shrugged. "How does Sparky's sound?"

Dwight nodded. "Suits me down to the ground, Hoss."

*****

## Oasis 4, Upper CentMod, Level 3

Virginia, Alice, and Brenda stepped off the escalator onto Level 3 and started walking toward Kate's Tea Garden. Alice spotted Riv, Fen, and Bug following Mrs. Jacobson on the plaza level. "Look there. I think those three may be different after today."

Virginia nodded. "I almost feel sorry for those three." "Almost," Brenda agreed.

They found a table at the tea shop and ordered a pot and three cups. While they waited, Alice asked, "So what was the disagreement that led to all this?"

Virginia giggled. "Just Riv being Riv. Dwight and I were getting ready to leave Eva's when Riv and the Dumb Bell Brothers showed up. Riv started to demand a bigger office for their consulate. I told him we could discuss it later and he should contact my assistant for a time. When I turned to leave, he grabbed my arm and pulled me back around. That's when Dwight lost it."

Kate showed up with their tea, so they paused their conversation to pour their beverages.

*****

## Oasis 4, Connector Tunnel to HabMod 1

The structures that connected the HabMods to the CentMod were actually much larger than the actual passageway between the modules. The station designers cleverly used the extra space on either side of the tunnels for additional quarters. Mrs. Jacobson stopped at one of the doors in the HabMod connector tunnel passageway. "SICOS, allow entry."

An indicator went from red to green, and Mrs. Jacobson pressed a button. The door slid open, and she walked in with the plotors following her. She motioned to the sitting room. "Sit yourselves down. I'll be back with tea."

The sitting room had the standard furniture set, consisting of a love seat and a matching chair with a small table between the two that had a lamp on it. Additionally, there was a wing-backed chair located opposite the standard chair and love seat that was obviously added by Mrs. Jacobson. The last piece of furniture was a coffee table amongst the seats.

Bug and Fen sat on the love seat while Riv considered sitting in the wing backed chair since, in his mind, due to his rank and position, he warranted what was obviously the most honored seat. He reconsidered after he realized that he was probably still in a bit of trouble. So to avoid making another cultural faux pas, he sat in the standard chair.

Mrs. Jacobson was busy getting together the tea in the kitchenette while the plotors sat and took in their surroundings in the sitting room. There were some potted plants, bookcases with books, and pictures of presumably family, mainly grandchildren. There was one item that confused the plotors. It was a post with a series of platforms on it, starting about two feet from the floor to one at the top about four feet up. The first two feet of post were wrapped in thin manila rope.

While they were trying to work out what the object was, a black-and-white cat walked out of the hallway leading to the bedroom and paused in the sitting room doorway. Fen was the first to spot the cat, and he locked eyes on it. "What is that?"

Riv and Bug looked at Fen then looked in the direction he was staring. Spotting the cat, Riv said in a whisper, "Don't move. We don't want to provoke it."

Bug hissed. "Why would she keep a dangerous beast in her quarters?"

The cat stood and stretched, giving the plotors visions in their heads of their doom, making them shake uncontrollably with each movement of the cat. The cat approached the post wrapped with rope and sharpened its claws. A horrified Riv croaked out, "Look at it practice tearing the flesh off its prey."

The cat spotted the plotors and slowly walked to the love seat. At this point, the plotors were quite terrified and near passing out. The cat jumped up on the arm of the love seat, causing Fen, who was the closest, to clamp his eyes shut and start muttering, "Please, please, please…"

The black-and-white cat gently walked across Fen's legs, which nearly made him cry. He continued his journey and crossed Bug's legs, giving Bug a reason to have a similar reaction. The cat kept going, much to the relief of Fen and Bug, where he crossed the little table and onto the arm of the chair Riv occupied. Riv tried to keep his breathing under control while the cat got in his lap. Riv was starting to hyperventilate and wondered how he was going to survive this encounter. The cat started purring as it began rubbing on Riv's belly. A horrified Bug and Fen watched and marveled at how they had cheated death. Bug heard the purring and whispered, "That must be the sound it makes before it attacks."

Fen nodded. "Its bloodlust is obvious."

Mrs. Jacobson witnessed the entire encounter from the time her cat started sharpening its claws. She shook her head. "Give him a little pat on the head or a gentle scratch behind the ears."

Riv reluctantly did as he was told and rubbed the tomcat's head with a shaking hand. The cat purred louder than ever while Riv started scratching behind its ears.

Mrs. Jacobson walked over and picked up the cat, then put him on the top platform of the cat tree/scratching post. "You've said hello to our guest, so be a good kitty and stay here Chester."

Riv stared at Chester with fascination. "Why do you keep an animal in your quarters?"

"Many humans keep animals for companionship. They're called pets," Mrs. Jacobson answered while she made her way back to her tea cart. "What kind of animal is this?" Bug asked.

Mrs. Jacobson pushed the tea cart the rest of the way into the room. "Chester is a cat. There are many different kinds of cats on Earth. He is in a general category called a housecat. Housecat is a term used to describe domesticated breeds although there are dozens of breeds of domesticated cats."

Fen asked, "Are they all this size?"

Mrs. Jacobson poured the tea. "Chester is about average for a domesticated cat. There are breeds in the wild that will get to about three hundred kilograms. You can look this all up on your SICOS later." She handed cups of tea to her guest. "Now this is flaston tea. You don't put cream in it, but you can add a little liquid sweetener if you want. I think it's very good on its own, but take a sip and see what you think."

Riv and Fen thought it was fine on its own, but Bug used a touch of the flaston liquid sweetener and nodded approval.

*****

## Oasis 4, Upper CentMod, Sparky's Taproom

Lagers in frosted mugs were placed on Phil and Dwight's table. Dwight took a sip, which made Phil frown. "You know, Dwight, when you first arrived on Oasis 4, you had a bit of an issue with alcohol. I hope I'm not contributing to a bit of backsliding."

Dwight shook his head. "No worries here, Hoss. Believe it or not, I had the same concern after I first arrived. After our talk, I determined to stop feeling sorry for myself and clean up. I discovered something that surprised me. I really didn't miss crawling into a bottle. I thought about it and determined that I didn't need to drink. I wanted to drink."

"What's the difference?" Phil asked.

Dwight stared at the bubbles forming on the surface of his drink. "I've known genuine alcoholics in my time. They would do anything for a drink. They would lie to anyone about their condition. They would lie to their boss, friends, spouses, and themselves. The only time they tell the truth is when they say they need a drink."

Phil frowned. "So you never felt you needed to get drunk?"

Dwight shook his head. "Nope. I've always said that I wanted to get drunk. I was actually trying to run my life into a canyon. I truly believe that it was the grace of God that caused you and me to meet.

You have a genuine way about you, Phil, especially in the way you treat folks. I've noticed that you can size someone up in just a few seconds and know the best way to allow them to do what's best."

Phil appreciated the compliment but wanted to get back to Dwight's experience. "So you say you never had to have a drink?"

"Nope," Dwight said with a smile. "I don't know what makes some folks chemically or psychologically dependent, and some folks can walk away from bad habits. I just thank the Lord that I could leave it. I've only had a couple of beers since you and I talked that first time, and I simply don't miss it. Don't get me wrong. I still find beer a refreshing treat, but having one every day just doesn't appeal to me. I like having control of my faculties, and I like having folks respect me. I have that now. I have you to thank for herding me on the right trail and Ginny for believing in me."

*****

## Oasis 4, Upper CentMod, Level 3, Kate's Tea Garden

"We couldn't help but notice that when Dwight first stepped on the station, you took a chance and covered for his, shall we say, less than exemplary behavior," Alice said while pouring more tea. "What kind of history do you two have?"

Virginia blushed slightly. "I met Dwight when I first hired on to Stellar Logistics. I thought he was handsome, charming, and let's just say, unique. I developed quite a crush on him, but he was seeing someone else. We were always friends, but it seemed like neither of us was available at the same time."

Brenda put her cup back on its saucer. "The nature of this industry makes it hard on relationships."

"Phil and I discovered that it's worth the effort. The tricky part about relationships is finding out if it's a case of wishful thinking or if it's meant to be," Alice offered. "Too many couples get together for superficial reasons. Those relationships never last."

"What was your reaction when you found out Dwight was transferring to Oasis 4?" Brenda asked.

Virginia took a sip of tea to consider her answer. "I don't really know how to answer that. On the one hand, I looked forward to seeing him, but I heard he had personal problems and was spiraling down. I didn't want to add anything to his plate that he had to think about, so I decided I would just play it by ear and help him wherever I could."

Brenda smiled. "Gus said he had concerns about Dwight, and Phil had some real reservations. Gus said, judging by Dwight's performance his first day, he was sure Phil was going to dismiss him, but Phil saw something in Dwight when they first met."

"Phil does have some kind of weird ability to size people up with the least little bit of data," Alice said. "It's spooky sometimes."

*****

## Oasis 4, Quarters of Mrs. Jacobson

Mrs. Jacobson just poured everyone a second cup of tea. She had just listened to Riv's well-practiced oration about the planned plotor conquest of the known galaxy. She did note that he was very polite about it, which made her realize that the plotors had some sense of propriety. She wondered if they could see the illogic of their stated goal if they were to view it as non-plotors do.

While holding her cup and saucer, Mrs. Jacobson asked, "Is that the reason you wanted a larger consulate? Your species is superior. Therefore, you warrant bigger accommodations?"

Riv could sense that Mrs. Jacobson was going to try and convince him otherwise, but he determined to stick to his guns, so to speak, and make this human woman see logic. He politely nodded. "That is correct."

Mrs. Jacobson shook her head. "I don't see it. You've been on this station for some time now, and I haven't witnessed one superior thing. The haldocs have been here only a little while longer, and they've established a respectable amount of trade. The only thing you three have done is inform us about the impending reordering of galactic society."

"I believe you will find out soon enough that it would be wise to cultivate a relationship with your future masters," Riv stated.

Mrs. Jacobson smiled thinly. "I don't think so. In fact, after today, I wouldn't be surprised if Stellar Logistics asked you three to leave."

Riv recoiled, "That would be foolish! The wise course would be to appease your future plotor masters."

"The haldocs have been hearing that for the last 115 Earth years now," Mrs. Jacobson retorted. "If your people aren't prepared to invade Vestgut by now, you never will be. In that amount of time, your people could have made enough ships to move the entire population of Limdox."

Bug interjected, "Building the proper vessels necessary for such an endeavor is a very technical and difficult task. We wouldn't expect a human with no technical background to understand."

"I have more technical background than you know," Mrs. Jacobson shot back. "My husband is a freighter captain, and I was a systems technician. I traveled around the galaxy for over forty years on various ships, so you can imagine I'm a little more informed in these areas."

Fen shook his head. "It's not possible for you to know our capabilities from the little data about us we've allowed to be known."

"Small tidbits of information can be put together to get an accurate picture of your capabilities," Mrs. Jacobson retorted. "For instance, that little shuttle that brought you here had to be modified to be able to dock here. If you remember, the hatch nearly didn't open. The station technicians had to repair it before your people could leave for home. It seems the modification was done correctly but very roughly, and the alignment and adjustments were way off. Our technicians also noted your whole ship was constructed crudely. I can't imagine a people who can barely put together an eight-passenger shuttle capable of building anything bigger. Prove me wrong."

*****

**Oasis 4, Upper CentMod, Sparky's Taproom**

A waitress set down two fresh, frosted mugs of lager and took away the empty mugs. Phil took a sip of his and set it down. "So tell me about you and Virginia. She covered for you when you first arrived, and you two started seeing each other in short order. How well did you know each other before you were assigned here?"

Phil couldn't quite interpret the look on Dwight's face. "If that's too personal, you don't have to answer. I was just curious."

"Not at all," Dwight said with a shake of his head. "I knew her as well as anyone else I worked with. I was assigned to Earth Station 1 when she was a new hire in the operations department there. I thought she was pretty, but I was dating a little gal from Colorado at the time."

Phil smiled. "So availability is what kept you two from seeing each other?"

"Not 100 percent," he said with a smile of his own. "I always thought Ginny was sweet, and I suspected that she liked me some, but she was way different from the gals that I gravitated toward. Ginny's smart, refined, and focused. The gals I went after were usually a tad on the trashy side. I felt funny even thinking she'd be happy being with a feller like me."

"So what changed since you've been here?" Phil asked.

"Not sure," Dwight answered. "You suggested that I should apologize to Ginny for covering for me that first day. I did apologize, then offered to take her to dinner as an extension of that apology. One dinner led to two, and a movie or two, and so on. I'm still shocked she's still with me."

Phil chuckled. "To be honest, the rest of us were a little taken aback to see you two together. But I think I can speak for everyone; we're delighted to see the effect she's had on you. Also, I've noticed that Virginia has been a little different, in a good way."

"That's kind of you, Hoss. Now what kind of trouble am I in?" Dwight asked.

Phil laughed. "None. Everyone has wanted to take a swing at a plotor at some point, and Riv gave you genuine provocation. That's not to say we can have people punching diplomats in the face. But given the circumstances, we can forget it happened."

At that moment, Udlon from the Vestgut consulate strolled up with a tankard of ale in his hand. "Would you gentlemen mind terribly if I joined you?"

"Not at all," Phil said while Dwight reached over and pulled a chair out for the consular. As Udlon sat, Phil couldn't help but wonder how a guy so little could drink so much ale, but he put that thought aside for now.

"You've called it a day a little early," Dwight observed.

"As did you," Udlon responded. "Actually, Vimurnus and I heard about what occurred in Eva's Café, and we thought we could give you insight into the plotors."

Phil chuckled. "Anything you can tell me about them would be helpful.

Where's Vimurnus?"

"Oh, she's in Kate's Tea Garden," Udlon answered. "We decided that it would be better if the gentlemen got the male perspective and the ladies got the female perspective. I know it might seem hopelessly old-fashioned in some cultures, but I think it has merit."

Dwight smiled. "You ain't gonna get an argument from me on that."

Phil nodded. "Okay, why don't we give you our observations, and you could try to explain why they act the way they do."

"I'll try," Udlon said with a chuckle.

Phil frowned. "Okay, jeez, where to begin? Well, first, Elias Gilmore invited the plotors to open a consulate here as a courtesy. The hope was they would see opportunities to help themselves and realize that their obsession with planetary conquest was a nonstarter. So far, the only thing they've done is remind everyone in the CentMods of their plans. Then they pester our customers with more of the same. The only plotor vessel to arrive is the same eight-passenger shuttle that brought them here in the first place. Do they have any other vessels? Are all plotors as ill-mannered as Riv, Bug, and Fen?"

Udlon shook his head. "Your observations and questions are not without merit. I've been to Limdox, and I can tell you I don't believe they'll ever be ready to invade another planet. In fact, colonizing a planet without opposition, in my opinion, is quite beyond their abilities."

Dwight frowned. "What makes you think that's the case."

"They don't have the vessels needed for that kind of endeavor," Udlon stated. "You mentioned their shuttle. It's the same one that carries diplomats to Vestgut. In fact, there's no evidence that I've seen that they're in possession of any others."

Phil nodded. "My guys had a chance to do a couple of small repairs on their shuttle. They tell me it's about the crudest thing to meet their eyes. Jeremy Cole tells me that even brand-new. It must have been rough. The fit and finish was just terrible."

Udlon chuckled. "Imagine an entire planet like that." "You're kidding me," Phil said.

Udlon nodded. "It's an interesting set of circumstances that are contributing to the condition that Limdox finds itself in. Undoubtedly, you've noticed there are basically two classes of citizens with the plotors, the elites, and the rest. The elites are convinced of their own superiority, even with abundant evidence to the contrary."

"So if there are folks there that are brighter than the ones running things, what keeps them in control?" Dwight asked.

Udlon shook his head. "Sometimes I wonder, I believe it's a multilayered effort. From what I've been able to piece together, the elites gained power by doing several things. First, they made promises they couldn't keep or, more precisely, had no intention to keep. They simply blamed their opposition for promises that weren't kept. Of course, the whole thing would have collapsed if it weren't for their efforts in manipulating public opinion."

Phil laughed. "I think every world has experienced that same situation to some degree. Earth history is full of stories like that, and most recently, Flast is getting over some major abuses."

Udlon nodded. "Vestgut is also recovering from the effects of, shall we say, selective distribution of information."

"I've had a couple of occasions to talk to their pilots," Dwight said. "They actually seem nice although I have to say their range of what I would consider necessary knowledge for safe space travel to be a little limited."

"Believe it or not, that's by design," Udlon stated, "or, more accurately, a side effect of the education policies on Limdox. So much of their education system is dedicated to ensuring Limdox citizens understand their role in their society. There's very little room for practical subjects. Things like mathematics, chemistry, and so on are only given token attention."

Dwight frowned. "We have shop classes on Earth. Kids are taught things like woodworking, metalworking, plastics, systems labs, you name it. It was a place where young guns are allowed to develop skills. Even if you don't make a living with your hands as an adult, the lessons you've learned will serve you for a lifetime in other areas, if they're applied."

Udlon smiled. "That's very wise. The plotors have nothing like that, that I've found. Much of their efforts are geared toward identifying politically and philosophically reliable individuals for the elite class. The rest are prepared for a life of serving Limdox society in some menial capacity or another."

"So the reason their shuttle was so crude was because the people who put it together were unskilled?" Phil asked incredulously.

"That's the situation," Udlon answered. "I think they're capable of being skilled. They're just not encouraged to develop their skills. After all, what's the point in doing a better job if there's no reward for it? In many cases, plotor workers are performing tasks that they are not remotely interested in. Their jobs were assigned to them, and they have no choice but to do it."

Phil shook his head. "So for instance, that shuttle they show up in was built by people who weren't the least bit interested in building shuttles?"

Udlon nodded. "Most likely. Jobs are assigned to individuals using criteria like proximity of the individual's home and so on. There are some careers available for the nonelites where individuals are encouraged to excel, such as the shuttle pilots you mentioned. But all in all, they're not treated with the respect they deserve. The elites have no concept of what individuals have to do to be proficient in their respective trades, and they treat them as second-class citizens. The result is a lot of people who aren't very interested in doing anything beyond what's necessary to get along."

"So if I read the situation correctly, Riv and his companions will be reluctant to change the status quo," Phil observed. "I wonder what it would take for the nonelites to start pressing for more respect?"

"Seems to me they should figure out how to get the elites over a barrel," Dwight mused.

Udlon shook his head. "I'm not sure what it would take, but I do know trying to influence the natural development of their society would be a big mistake. The plotors will have to do it on their own. Perhaps if the nonelites become more affluent and perhaps have frequent exposure to different cultures, they would push for a more equal status."

A thought occurred to Phil that made him furrow his brow. "How much interaction do the plotor pilots have with haldocs?"

Udlon thought a couple of seconds. "There's some interaction with the ground crew, of course, but overall, haldocs avoid visiting plotors. The whole threat of invasion situation has made our people reluctant to engage with them."

Phil and Dwight exchanged looks, and a thin smile grew on Phil's face. "Maybe we need to consider there may be two reasons the plotors are constantly threatening your planet with subjection. First, it gives them a superior negotiating position if Vestgut feels there's some merit to the threat. Second, haldocs who come in contact with plotors will be sufficiently cowed by their bluster to take the chance they might upset one of them, so the haldocs will limit their exposure to them, thereby reducing the possibility that the nonelite pilots will develop their own opinions."

Udlon nodded and said, "That's actually a very reasonable assumption. In fact, it's the only thing that makes sense when you look at it."

"So just talking to their pilots when they're here goes a long way toward undoing centuries of the plotor social order," Dwight observed.

Phil thought for a couple of seconds. "It must frustrate them that we're not fussed about their threats."

Udlon laughed. "I think the events today will remove all doubt about how your people will react to their bluster, and I think it's wonderful. I wish my people had it in them to stand up to the plotors with a firmer hand sooner. Since your visits to our planet, there has been a noticeable change in tone when dealing with the plotors. My people have been slightly emboldened by the fact that we're not alone and your pilot picking up Riv in the Capital made an impression."

"Our purpose is not to affect change in plotor society, as welcome as that would be," Phil stated. "So the best course of action would be to engage their pilots or anyone else who's nonelite wherever we can. As far as Riv, Fen, and Bug are concerned, let's see how they get along with Mrs. Jacobson first."

*****

## Oasis 4, Upper CentMod, Level 3, Kate's Tea Garden

Vimurnus had roughly the same conversation with Alice, Brenda, and Virginia that Phil, Dwight, and Udlon had, and they came to roughly the same conclusions. Vimurnus asked, "Where's the plotors now?"

Brenda giggled. "Mrs. Jacobson cornered them."

"Oh my!" Vimurnus exclaimed. "Those three won't be the same."

Virginia smiled. "She does have a way of cutting through the nonsense. I've never met anyone as direct as her. When she's done, those three will be quite different."

"Mrs. Jacobson invited Udlon and me to tea some time ago," Vimurnus said with a smile. "She wanted to meet us and share some views. She would have made an excellent diplomat if she had decided to go that route. She really is quite a lady."

Alice put her teacup back on its saucer. "Phil had to give her special permission to keep Chester on the station."

Vimurnus smiled wider. "Udlon and I just loved Chester. The only animal we keep as pets on Vestgut are birds. The most popular ones are the songbirds that don't require cages to keep them from disappearing."

"Nothing furry that you can put in your lap and pet?" Brenda asked.

Vimurnus shook her head. "Oh my goodness, no. I can't think of any animals on Vestgut that could be domesticated in that manner. Both Udlon and I researched the pets people on Earth keep. I have to say, there was a lot of variety on that list, but the two most popular animals were the ones that held the most interest for us. I can personally say I spent a lot of time looking at videos of cats and dogs."

Alice smiled. "Phil has always had a dog, but that would be unfair to the animal, being cooped up on a space station. Cats are easier to keep happy in an environment like this."

"I sense the plotors are having another new experience right now," Vimurnus mused. "The plotors don't keep pets at all. They're quite terrified of all animals."

Alice smiled. "You know, when we returned from Gostis, one of the kortlax got loose. Bug was seriously losing it trying to get as much distance between him and the kortlax as he could."

Vimurnus smiled. "It may seem like a little thing, but exposing Riv, Bug, and Fen to a domesticated house pet will have an effect. They have so much invested in their own superiority when they learn that other races actually keep animals in their home, their opinion of themselves will start to crumble."

Alice shook her head. "Phil always said every culture has its own quirks. It'll be interesting to see if the plotors have a change in attitude after today.

"What does Limdox offer the rest of the galaxy when they do become interested in trade?" Virginia asked.

"They're actually very clever with fabrics," Vimurnus offered. "For whatever reason, they can take ordinary fiber and do fabulous things with it. I believe it's because there isn't a great deal of production of fiber-producing plants there, so they've learned to make the most of what they do grow. As far as wool goes, you can imagine their feelings about using the hair of animals."

Virginia nodded. "That's very interesting, I'll bet they could do something with a supply of falta, and with the system they have there, they probably have a shortage of consumer goods."

"I suppose we'll have to wait and see if Mrs. Jacobson can talk sense into our resident plotors before we can tell if the rest of them will come around."

*****

## Oasis 4, Quarters of Mrs. Jacobson

Riv and Mrs. Jacobson discussed the finer points of multiworld diplomacy and the benefits of friendly trade relationships. In other words, Riv was having his preconceptions on these matters picked apart one at a time. Riv was trying to digest what Mrs. Jacobson had just explained to him. It was painfully obvious that the approach the plotors used with the haldocs wasn't effective with the other aliens. "So are you telling us that no one believes that the plotors will subjugate the other races? In fact, you don't believe a plotor presence will be tolerated unless we have some mutual exchange in commerce?"

Mrs. Jacobson nodded. "That's generally how things work."

Bug shook his head. "The haldocs recognize our superiority, and there have been no demands or even requests for commerce."

"The haldocs are gentle people," Mrs. Jacobson retorted. "Once they see other races aren't fussed by plotor bluster, they may well change the way they deal with Limdox."

The plotors reaction belied the fact that it hadn't occurred to them that their efforts on Oasis 4 would have the opposite intended effect. Fen frowned and asked, "Just for the sake of argument, not that we're convinced you're correct, how should we proceed in partaking in commerce with other worlds?"

"That part is quite simple," Mrs. Jacobson assured them. "First, visit with the other consulates and find out what trade goods their worlds have to offer. It also would be a good idea if you went to the station operations center and acquired a list of goods that pass through here, or perhaps you can make inquiries on your SICOS. After you three have made your daily rounds to threaten the galaxy, you can visit some of the Licensed Commodities and Bulk Merchandise traders. Find out if there is anything your planet could use. There's thousands of products out there that your own planet may be perfectly capable of producing, but it's more expedient to import and trade for your products that may be unique or in some other way you can get a premium for."

Riv asked in a tone that belied his discomfort. "How are worlds accommodated that do not possess capabilities to move substantial amounts of freight off of the planet's surface?"

"There's a class of freighter that carries its own cargo shuttle," Mrs. Jacobson answered. "There are several that specialize in moving freight for planets without their own facilities."

Riv put his cup and saucer on the tea tray and stood. "Mrs. Jacobson, you have given us a great deal to think about." Bug and Fen also stood, and Riv looked at the cat napping on the top platform of the cat tree. "Also, thank you for introducing us to Chester."

*****

## Oasis 4, Lower CentMod, Limdox Consulate

As soon as the plotors entered the consulate, Riv turned to the others. "Fen, I would like you to use the SICOS to inquire about pets humans keep. Bug, I need you to look up something called a branding iron."

Bug and Fen nodded and said, "Right away." Then retreated to their respective offices.

Riv went to his office to do his own SICOS research. After two hours of staring at the SICOS screen, Riv's head was spinning. It occurred to him that if anyone had watched him over the last couple of hours, they would have come to the conclusion that he was the most random person in the galaxy. He had made several notations on a pad and saved references on his SICOS. He took a deep breath and pressed the intercom button. "Bug, Fen, I would like to see you in my office to discuss what you've found."

In moments, Bug and Fen walked into Riv's office. Riv waited for them to get comfortable, then he asked, "How have you progressed in your assignments? Fen, please give us your report."

Fen produced his own pad. "The varieties of animals humans keep for pets is indeed staggering. It's interesting to note that humans started keeping these animals to perform functions. Cats are one of the most common pets, and they are very good at hunting rodents. The rodents on Earth will often spread diseases among the humans, so they kept cats to control them."

Riv was intrigued. "Mrs. Jacobson said her animal was typical in size in the domestic varieties. Is this true?"

Fen nodded, turned, and said, "SICOS, display Riv research illustration one." The SICOS monitor brought up a chart illustrating cats. On the left were the domestic breeds, a human for comparison, then breeds in the wild on the right. He continued, "Indeed, Mrs. Jacobson's Chester is average in the household breeds. There are notable exceptions, though. There are several breeds slightly smaller than Chester." He tapped the illustration, and photos appeared of various house cats. "There's one notable breed that's larger." He tapped another illustration. "It's called a Maine coon."

The photo of the Maine coon cat being held by a human lady made them gasp. Riv asked, "Did you research the breeds in the wild?"

"Yes, I did," Fen answered. "There seems to be a staggering variety of those as well. To save us some time, I'll show you the two largest."

Fen tapped the tiger and lion illustrations, and photos of both large cats appeared. Riv studied the photos. "Is there an illustration to give us an idea of how big these animals are?"

Fen nervously said, "There's video that will accomplish that. SICOS. Play video Fen one." Videos started playing, showing both breeds of big cats in the wild. Then footage of circus lion and tiger trainers started playing.

Riv and Bug watched the video with wide eyes and with their mouths open. The video finished, and Riv finally uttered a question, "Are these beasts naturally tame?"

Fen shook his head. "Just the exact opposite. They are quite ferocious. This spectacle was designed to thrill audiences and allow people a look at exotic animals they normally would never get an opportunity to see."

Bug was so caught up in the moment. He broke protocol and asked a question before Riv gave him permission. At any rate, Riv didn't notice. Bug asked, "Are there any other animals they commonly keep as pets?"

Fen simply said, "SICOS, play video Fen two." As the video played, Fen narrated, "The other most common animal to domesticate is called a dog. Dogs have been bred to perform specific tasks, the most common being hunting dogs. In fact, there are breeds that are for specific animals to be hunted. Some dogs chase their quarry. Others assist in finding birds then retrieving them after they've been dispatched."

Riv interrupted, "How common is it for humans to hunt?"

"I haven't done an in-depth study on that subject. However, hunting was often a necessary avocation for food. But humans continue to hunt for recreation," Fen reported.

"Recreation? You mean to say they go into the wild where the animals live and risk being mauled by a beast?" Riv exclaimed.

Fen nodded. "That is correct."

Riv looked shocked. Finally, he said, "Please continue, Fen."

Fen restarted the video. "There are breeds used for guarding facilities or aiding soldiers in warfare. Some were bred to pull sleds through snow. One interesting group of dogs I've found were helper dogs. Humans that have physical handicaps often get one of these specially trained animals to perform tasks for them. For instance, blind humans will get dogs that are capable of safely guiding them from one destination to another. Others are trained to assist humans with limited mobility."

Riv nodded. "Those were the most common pets. What others are there?"

Fen ordered, "SICOS, play Fen video three." As the video played, Fen again narrated while Riv and Bug became more horrified and had trouble hiding it. "Birds are very popular, turtles, snakes, rabbits, rodents of every description. Then there are those that are too large to keep in a household, most notably, horses."

Riv and Bug stared at the picture on the SICOS screen. It showed a human couple riding horses while smiling and laughing. Riv stared at the screen. "Now I understand why these people aren't intimidated easily," he said it aloud before he realized it. Then he asked, "Bug, what did you discover?"

"Believe it or not," Bug started, "it is also related to animals. Food animals, called steers, were allowed to mature in vast grasslands. There were no barriers to prevent the steers from one herd separated from other herds. A device called a branding iron was used to mark the steers with a symbol to identify the owner of the steer."

"That doesn't sound so bad," Riv observed.

Bug almost smiled. "SICOS, play Bug video one."

A video played, showing cowboys branding a steer. A wide-eyed Riv watched the spectacle as his hands subconsciously went to his belly. Bug said, "There's more. These men are called cowboys. They were responsible for gathering the correct steers and getting them to market. The horses Fen showed us were an important tool used by the cowboys. Naturally, they developed specialized skills for this profession. An interesting competition developed to showcase these skills called a rodeo. SICOS, play Bug video two."

The three watched in awe as the different rodeo events were explained. At the end, Riv said, "Turn off the SICOS. I did my own research while you did yours. I was curious about something Mrs. Jacobson said. She said that she felt the haldocs would start thinking of us in a different light when they see the other races aren't intimidated by our presence."

"Something like that is hard to qualify," Fen observed. "What kind of data could you use to verify that assertion?"

"Just my own observations," Riv answered. "Also, I took the time to read the reports from our replacements on Vestgut. It seems Mrs. Jacobson is quite correct in her assessment of the haldocs attitude toward us."

"What of her opinion of our abilities to subjugate other worlds?" Fen asked.

Riv looked downcast. "Her observations and analysis are sobering and accurate. There is much that you don't know about our spacefaring abilities. Indeed, the ship that brought us here and brought us our diplomatic pouches is our only operating vessel."

"That can't be right!" Bug interrupted. "I've seen the spaceport maintenance shop with a dozen ships inside!"

Riv nodded. "Indeed you have, but none are operational. Another one of Mrs. Jacobson's observations that is painfully accurate is the quality and standards that our spacecraft are built to are indeed poor."

"That doesn't sound right," Fen protested. "Our spacecraft is faster than the haldoc spacecraft. Ours is obviously superior."

"Speed isn't the only measure of quality in a spacecraft, the haldoc vessel is slower, but according to our pilots, who have been afforded a look, it's much safer. Our machines are quite crude in comparison," Riv explained.

Bug shook his head. "If we don't have the necessary ships to subjugate Vestgut or even the technical expertise to build them, we're in the process of losing the skills necessary to maintain what we've already built. Why are we constantly telling the other races to prepare for the impending plotor reordering of galactic society?"

"That's a fair question for a non-plotor," Riv said. "But I would think the answer would be quite obvious to you. Our constant rhetoric is designed to accomplish two things. First, it distracts the nonelites and aids in keeping them in line. The thinking is they're too concerned about what their role would be in such endeavors to ask any questions that would bring them unwanted attention. Second, if the haldocs had a mind toward invading us, they would probably reconsider if they thought that we thought we could invade them."

Bug shook his head again. "So all this time, we not only had no intentions to subjugate the haldocs, but we didn't actually have the ability."

Riv hung his head. "That is correct."

"I feel like such a fool," Fen groaned. "What happens to us when the other aliens realize we're just noisy nuisances?"

"I suspect they've known it all the time," Riv admitted. "What led you to that conclusion?" Bug asked.

Riv nodded. "I knew the moment that human pilot lifted me off my feet in the Sydnor Capital. Their size is imposing. They're not intimidated by us at all."

"They certainly aren't like the haldocs," Fen agreed.

"Why should they be?" Riv asked. "They keep animals in their homes to keep them company. They ride on animals that are ten times heavier than themselves. In fact, the whole human and animal dynamic is far beyond anything in our experience."

Bug observed, "There doesn't seem to be much that intimidates them."

"A people with that kind of nerve has nothing to fear from us," Fen added.

"There's more," Riv stated. "Undoubtedly, you've heard of their recent invasion of a planet."

"That effort took the resources of several worlds to accomplish," Fen interrupted.

"That's very true," Riv confessed. "But did you study the human performance in that conflict? The humans have earned a reputation for being a warrior race. I can only imagine what they think of our bluster."

"So what do we do next?" Bug asked. "If we carry on as we have been, the nonelites gradually become aware of how tenuous the elite position is, and our status is lost. If we change our policies suddenly, just as suddenly, the nonelites become aware of how tenuous the elite position is."

Riv smiled thinly. "You have a keen grasp of the situation we find ourselves in Bug. Our superiors on Limdox have reached the same conclusion. It seems we have few options available to us in light of what's happening. My instructions were to come here, evaluate the alien races, and determine if they can be intimidated like the haldocs." "I think that question has been answered today, without a doubt," Fen stated. "Now that we know what the other races are like, did our superiors indicate how we should proceed?"

"They left that decision up to me," Riv stated. "With the circumstances we find ourselves in, it's been decided that we should make efforts to engage in trade and commerce with these other worlds. If we do our tasks properly, perhaps the nonelites will get a sense that they're improving their position in our society."

"What happens if we do our tasks poorly?" Bug asked.

Riv looked down and frowned. "The distinction between the elites and nonelites narrows and possibly disappears."

"How do we proceed?" Fen asked.

Riv inhaled deeply. "Tomorrow is the first day of the period the humans call the weekend. They have a secession of business activities for two days. When they begin the new workweek, we will do the unthinkable. Then we will set about determining what goods and commodities Limdox would likely buy and sell."

*****

## Oasis 4, Operations Center, Briefing Room 1

Phil walked in and filled a coffee mug, as was his habit. After sitting, he took out his pad and prepared to start the morning briefing. There was a knock at the door, and Phil said, "Come in."

Phil's office assistant, Jay, poked his head in the door. "I apologize for the interruption, Mr. Ross, but these gentlemen insisted that they needed to see you right away."

Phil furrowed his brow. "Who exactly needs to see me, Jay?"

Riv poked his head around Jay. "Please indulge us for a few moments, Mr. Ross. This won't take long."

Phil raised an eyebrow as he noted the change in tone from Riv. He nodded. "Please come in, Mr. Riv."

Jay stepped out of the way and allowed Riv and his companions to enter. When Riv, Fen, and Bug were inside, Jay left, closing the door behind him. Riv approached the conference table and, after clearing his throat, said, "I would like to sincerely apologize to Miss Wells for my behavior in Eva's Café. Also, I feel I owe apologies to Mr. Smith and Mr. Ross. Please forgive my behavior. If you will excuse us, we need to give our regrets to Eva and Burt, then finally, Mr. Needles."

Riv bowed and left the room with Fen and Bug in tow, leaving the Oasis 4 management speechless. Phil broke the silence. "I am now regretting not starting a betting pool."

"I was convinced that humility in those amounts would do permanent damage to a plotor," Luke observed.

*****

## Oasis 4, Connector Tunnel to HabMod 1

Riv pressed the call button on Mrs. Jacobson's door and waited. Presently the door opened, and Mrs. Jacobson smiled for her guest and said, "Please come in, gentlemen."

"I must apologize for arriving unexpectedly," Riv stated as he entered with his companions.

Mrs. Jacobson smiled. "There's no need for an apology. You three are always welcome."

That statement caught Riv and the others off guard. He recovered quickly and came to the point of his visit. "We appreciated the kindness you showed us and your candor. It would be most helpful if we could ask for advice from time to time. It seems we have a great deal to learn about interacting with other races."

"I would welcome the opportunity to share what I've learned over the years," Mrs. Jacobson said.

Riv smiled. "Excellent. We'll have to have you as a guest in the consulate for tea very soon."

"I look forward to it," Mrs. Jacobson assured him.

Fen spotted the cat napping on the cat tree top platform. "Excuse me, Mrs. Jacobson, may I say hello to Chester?"

Mrs. Jacobson assured him that it would be all right, so Fen approached Chester and timidly scratched him behind the ears. Chester opened his eyes then closed them again while rolling slightly to the side to allow Fen better access while purring vigorously. Fen smiled. "He's wonderful."

The door chime rang, and Mrs. Jacobson opened it and was rewarded with her son. She hugged the newcomer. "Oh, I was wondering if you forgot about your mother."

"It'll never happen, Ma," he assured her. He looked in the sitting room and saw the plotors giving Chester reason to purr. "Oh, you have guest."

Mrs. Jacobson made introductions, "Riv, Fen, and Bug, this is my son David.

He's the captain of the *Atlantis Star*." Dave smiled. "Nice to meet you fellas."

Riv bowed. "Pleasure." Then Riv and his companions went to the door, and Riv turned. "Again, thank you for your advice, Mrs. Jacobson. We look forward to learning much more from you."

Riv turned to leave, and Mrs. Jacobson stopped him, "Can I give you some advice in the meantime?" "Of course," Riv said.

Mrs. Jacobson grinned. "Don't try to reinvent yourselves overnight. Take it one step at a time."

Riv smiled and nodded. "Let's hope the others will be as patient with us as you are."

*****

## Oasis 4, Upper CentMod, Eva's Café

Phil, Virginia, Gus, and Luke had just sat and picked up menus when Dwight strolled up. "Mind if I join y'all?"

Phil chuckled. "Would it matter?"

"Possibly," Dwight replied with a laugh. He said as he sat. "I had an odd experience this morning. Riv, Bug, and Fen paid me a visit. Riv actually apologized for what happened on Friday."

Phil nodded. "They expressed their regrets just before we started the morning briefing."

"Mrs. Jacobson must have made an impression," Virginia observed.

Gus saw the plotors arrive on the platform lift and step onto the plaza level.

He grinned. "I guess we'll see in a minute."

Everyone at the table watched as the three plotors walked from the platform lift and cross the plaza level to an escalator to level 2. Riv stood at his customary spot and announced, "The planet Limdox is preparing to engage in free commerce! The other races should prepare to bargain for the superior goods and services we are preparing to offer!"

Phil slowly nodded. "Well, that's certainly different."

The End

# SPEED



Chad Kowalski packed away his tools after making sure the calibration unit he was using was properly powered down, and the cables were stored in the equipment case. The maldor ships engineering officer downloaded the maintenance record logbook entry to permanently record the work that Chad performed. When that was done, he picked up his tools and calibration kit and headed back to the maintenance office. After putting away his tools and storing the calibration kit, Chad went to Jeremy Cole's office and used the SICOS to finalize and turn in the work order. Jeremy walked in carrying his own paperwork. He looked over to Chad. "How did it go on the maldor ship?"

Chad stood. "Actually, it went very well. I didn't even need any parts. I know I'm generalizing here, but the maldors are really good at putting ships together but not so great at making the adjustments necessary to get the most out of their machines."

Jeremy sat and thought about that for a second or two. "I've noticed that. I wonder why that is?"

Chad shrugged. "Cultural thing, I guess. They just don't have the instincts other cultures have in regard to making machines run at their best. All I did was adjust flow rates here and there. Then made sure all the clearances were correct. When I was done, reaction engine efficiency increased 8 percent, light-speed engines up 4 percent, and reactor efficiency up 5 percent."

"You've been doing a lot of tune-ups," Jeremy said. "You're getting quite a reputation among the gypsy freighters."

Chad nodded. "They're usually pretty happy when they get a performance boost without having to spend a bundle."

"Well, we're making the pencil pushers at corporate happy, so let's keep doing what we're doing," Jeremy said with a nod.

Chad finished his paperwork and stood. "If you don't have anything else, boss, I'm knocking off for the day."

Jeremy smiled. "Fine with me. I'll see you in the morning."

Chad left the office and headed to the maintenance department exit. Before he made it to the cargo handling section of CargoMod 8, Helmut Shultz ran up to him, out of breath. Before he could ask what was wrong, Helmut pointed back in the direction he had just come from. "Der last component needed to complete our project is available!"

Chad stopped in his tracks. "Don't play with my emotions, Helmut."

Helmut grinned. "It needs work, but we can use it. In fact, it's better than we hoped for."

Chad forgot about the after-work plans he had made. "Why are we wasting time here?"

Helmut led Chad back to the shop area and then to the maintenance docking ports. The maintenance docking ports we're used when a hangar bay isn't needed. When they reached their destination, Helmut stopped at a tarp-covered object and smiled. "The last major component." He then reached down and pulled the tarp off a cylindrical metallic object, about ten feet long, eighteen inches in diameter, with fittings at each end.

Chad's smile disappeared. "Helmut, this thing is way too big! It needs to be about a third this length."

"I know that," Helmut said indignantly. "But this one is made of thicker material than the ones in the size range we need."

Chad slowly nodded. "Thicker is better, but what about the length? This looks new. Why is it available? How would we integrate this into our system?"

Helmut grinned. "All excellent questions. This had a partially blocked ion injector, which eroded the wall in the center at one location. We will cut out the center; join the ends by welding, making it shorter. We can use material from the center to make reinforcing bands."

Chad stared off into the distance, as was his habit when he was working things out in his head. He nodded slowly. "We can shorten it to the optimum dimension for our application. We won't have to make it workable for a wide range of conditions. The thicker metal helps there."

"Ja," Helmut said with a nod. "We can be ready for test flights in under a week."

Chad frowned. "Won't the owners of this wonder what happened to it?"

"It's eroded beyond specifications," Helmut assured him. "It's also beyond practical repair."

"Let's get this to the container before we change our minds," Chad said with a bit of sarcasm.

They used a utility cart to move the object from the docking port to a container in the cargo section of CargoMod 8. After locking the container, Chad said, "Tomorrow, I'll do the calculations, and we'll start the modification after work."

*****

## Oasis 4, Upper CentMod, Eva's Café

Jeremy didn't often have breakfast at Eva's, but his wife would make an exception if he did something nice for her or if she was in an especially good mood. Phil Ross walked up smiling. "Hey, Jeremy, could you stand to eat with the Boss?"

"Please, be my guest," Jeremy said, motioning to a chair.

The pair ate mostly in silence, which was unusual at any table Phil sat at. Phil could tell that Jeremy had something on his mind, but he thought it might be a personal issue, which made him reluctant to inquire about what he may be troubled by. Finally, he couldn't take it anymore. "What's bothering you, Jeremy?"

"I'm not sure," Jeremy said, pushing his empty plate away. "I saw a couple of my guys putting a used plasma/ion intermix chamber in a container."

Phil took a sip of coffee and raised an eyebrow. "Three questions, first, should we be concerned being that the part is used? I mean, is it really our business? Second, whose container is it? Third, which two technicians are we talking about?"

Jeremy nodded. "The part looked like it was in excellent condition on the outside, but you have to see the inside to determine its space-worthiness. It's probably beyond economic repair, so it would actually cost more to scrap it than the metal is worth in that quantity. I'm not sure whose container it is, but it's in space 8-22A. The two technicians were Chad and Helmut."

Phil frowned. "I can't imagine those two would be involved in anything dishonest or shady. I'm sure there's a reasonable explanation." Jeremy smiled. "I'm sure you're right. I just don't like 'not knowing.'

Maybe I'm nosy, but I'm properly curious."

Phil got up. "I'll see you at the morning briefing."

*****

## Oasis 4, Upper CentMod, Operations Center

Having finished with his company duties for the day, Phil stared out the window at the shipping traffic. A freighter from the Star Series came into view while maneuvering to a docking port. The containers attached to the side of the ship caught his attention. He remembered his conversation at breakfast, and that rekindled his curiosity. He turned to his terminal. "SICOS, who does the container in 8-22A belong to?"

The SICOS monitor displayed the information. Phil read the information and was a little surprised to see it did actually belong to Chad. Regulations required that the container contents are listed and on file. He checked the contents column and frowned. The file only said there were personal items on board. "How much personal items does Chad need?" Phil mused.

The intercom buzzed on Phil's desk, and he gave it an annoyed look. "What do ya need, Jay?"

"Jeremy Cole from ship maintenance on one for you," Jay answered.

"Thanks, Jay," Phil acknowledged almost apologetically before pressing the line one button. "Jeremy, what can I do for you?"

Phil could see on the monitor that Jeremy was grinning and had trouble starting a sentence. He finally shook his head. "I can't explain, Boss. If you have a couple of minutes, could you meet me at container space 8-22A?"

"Your timing is perfect. I was looking for an excuse to get out of the office," Phil answered cheerfully.

He headed out the door and made a left. Passing Gus's open office door, he saw him staring absent-minded out of his window. "Hey! Feel like going to CargoMod 8 with me? Jeremy has solved a small mystery."

Gus jumped with a start but recovered quickly. He then smiled and said, "Just what I needed."

The pair walked to the platform lift and boarded it. As the platform started downward, Gus asked, "What kind of mystery are we talking about?"

On the way down, Phil got Gus caught up on events. Gus agreed that there wasn't enough information to form an opinion about what may be going on. Both agreed that Chad and Helmut were both of good character, and it would be hard to imagine either of them doing anything shady.

*****

## Oasis 4, CargoMod 8, Container Space 8-22A

Phil and Gus arrived at Container space 8-22A to find Jeremy, Chad, and Helmut standing outside the container there. Jeremy was trying to conceal a grin, but Chad and Helmut had neutral expressions with a hint of concern. Jeremy nodded at their arrival. "This is something you need to see for yourself."

Chad and Helmut unlatched the doors and pulled them open. The five of them stood there and stared at the contents after Helmut switched on the battery-operated lights. At that moment, Dwight Needles rounded the corner. "Hey, Jeremy, have you heard any word about the Pulsar Training Manuals we ordered? We should have received an order confirmati—gall dang!"

Dwight joined them in, staring into the container. Finally, he broke the silence, "What did y'all do to your escape pod?"

Phil and Gus both comprehended what they were looking at the same moment. It was indeed an escape pod, but Chad and Helmut had obviously made extensive modifications. They entered the container and took in the atmosphere, so to speak. Chad had obviously been in possession of this container for some time. There were shop tools that he owned, as well as small containers of parts and hardware bins. The walls were covered with posters and memorabilia from the last five hundred years of motorsports.

"Has anyone ever heard of the Raytheon Challenge?" Chad asked, in an effort to answer as many questions as possible in one question of his own.

Dwight nodded. "I have, and I even seriously considered entering. Then I sobered up."

"I've heard of it, but I don't know anything about it," Gus said with a shrug. Phil nodded. "Same here."

"It's a race calculated to push spacecraft design to its limits," Jeremy offered. "Vessels have to fly a course that challenges the versatility of the vessel and the skill of the pilot."

Phil interest was definitely piqued. "What kind of course?"

Chad flipped on a portable computer and accessed a file. The file was a representation of the Raytheon Challenge course. He explained each part as it played out on the screen. "It's a 'time trial' format. Racers start at a starting line on the planet. The first leg is a standing start to orbit. One complete orbit is made between an altitude of 100,000 meters and 110,000 meters. When that's done, it's an unlimited light-speed run to the Endeavor Asteroid Cluster. The tricky part about that is there's absolutely no margin for error in your navigation. An error of less than one-tenth of a percent will put you through a star or a very bad part of a solar system."

"Tell 'em the best part about the navigation system," Dwight urged. Chad grinned. "It's all old school. You have to input beginning coordinates and destination coordinates by hand. There can be no automatic systems or automatic flight control systems, so the vessel is completely hand-flown."

The Endeavor Asteroid Cluster appeared on the monitor with its course highlighted. "The destination is the Endeavor Asteroid Cluster. It's about twenty minutes from the time we break orbit. This is the most efficient route through the cluster. The only tricky part is you have to go through a series of gates in the correct direction and order. All with the reaction engines only."

"How much movement is there in the cluster?" Gus asked.

Chad shook his head. "The smallest rocks have recorded movement of ten to eleven centimeters in one Earth year. The larger ones, much less than that. The rocks are quite stationary, but the whole cluster is extremely dense. The Anna Mae Asteroid belt is considered dense, but it really has nothing on the Endeavor Cluster. If you stood on one of the asteroids in the Endeavor Cluster, you can see at least a third of the whole cluster with the naked eye. Which is what makes it unique and a challenge."

"I have a feeling that there are even more challenging aspects to this race. Not that there has to be since I've already added it to my personal list of things to desperately avoid," Phil quipped.

Chad chuckled. "After leaving the cluster, we go as fast as we can to the Hedron system and touch down on a moon orbiting the fifth planet for a mandatory pit stop. Technically speaking, it's completely unnecessary being as we don't need to refuel, but the engines and reactor can be adjusted for efficiency or power. The pilot and crewman are barred from making adjustments themselves."

Gus shook his head. "Please tell me this is near the end of the race." "Oh, you wish," Chad said with a grin. "There are two gates located

in deep space, not associated with a solar system or other feature. It'll take about twenty minutes of flat-out travel to reach the first one. The gates are horribly difficult to locate, and races have been lost looking for them. The second gate is another twenty minutes, and the leg back to Raytheon is about thirty minutes."

"That gives the pit crew time to get back to Raytheon on the last lap to see the finish," Dwight put in.

"The final challenge is my favorite," Jeremy said with a grin.

Chad grinned back. "That's everybody's favorite part." He saw that further explanation was necessary. "Arriving back at Raytheon, we fly a five-hundred- kilometer course. It has to be done at subsonic speeds and at altitudes that maintain a level of difficulty appropriate for the terrain while still leaving room for safety. The inspiration for the final leg was a combination of the old Isle of Man TT Race and the ancient military low-level training routes. Particularly, the routes in Death Valley and the Mach-Loop in Wales."

Phil was familiar with both military training routes from his interest in Earth aviation history, but he was less familiar with the Isle of Man TT Race. He nodded, then furrowed his brow. "Two questions. What was the Isle of Man TT Race? What sort of restrictions are on the machine for this leg?"

Chad was a little reluctant to answer the first question, but he took a breath and gave it a try. "The Isle of Man is located in the Irish Sea, between Ireland and England. In 1907, they started a cross-country motorcycle race called the Tourist Trophy. The course ran through the island's villages and mountains on the existing roads."

A wide-eyed Gus said, "That sounds insane."

"Insane doesn't do it justice," a laughing Helmut said. "There are archive videos of the race. The only safety equipment they had was a helmet and full- body leather suits. Race organizers put energy-absorbing barriers in places where they thought they would do the most good, but these madmen would race on roads bordered by stone walls, farm fences, and trees."

Phil nodded. "Okay, I get it. You start your low-level run and fly in canyons, river valleys, and so on."

"For five hundred kilometers," Chad confirmed. "It's a real crowd-pleaser." Phil asked, "What are the requirements for the leg?"

"It all has to be subsonic through the start gate, so the stretch from atmospheric entry to the start gate is used for deceleration. The whole course is flown using aerodynamic controls only, and navigation is visual with only a gyro compass and paper map," Chad answered.

Dwight nodded. "Then you get to do it again. Only now everyone is a little more familiar with the course, and that makes for faster times."

"Unfortunately, familiarity breeds contempt," Chad added.

Gus looked at a calendar on the wall of the container. "When does this nightmare start again?"

"September first," Chad answered.

Dwight was scrutinizing the little vessel in the container while simultaneously keeping up with the conversation. "What all is left to do?"

Chad pointed to the plasma/ion intermix chamber sitting in a cradle on the floor of the container. "We need to optimize this for our application and install it. Then we can do our tests."

Phil looked at the chamber, which looked like a camper's propane tank to him. It had markings on it that Chad had made earlier. He studied it for a few seconds. "So I take it that you're going to cut out the middle and use the ends."

"Ja," Helmut answered. "Ve vill use der good sections from ze middle to reinforce der seems, injector locations und mounting flanges. Some machining for zee injectors, then ve install zee device."

"That will take three or four evenings," Chad added. "Then we can start flight trials."

Dwight smirked and said, "Maybe I'm not as much of a cowboy as I thought I was, but I'd like to be considered for the pit crew."

Phil and Gus looked at each other, then both said, "Us too." Jeremy grinned. "You need a fourth."

Chad and Helmut looked at each other, then toward the four in front of them. Chad nodded and said, "We have a team."

They agreed to having a team meeting when the little racer was ready for test flights. As they walked away from the container, leaving Chad, Jeremy, and Helmut, Phil chuckled. "Have you noticed that Helmut's German gets a little more pronounced when he's excited about something?"

Both Gus and Dwight laughed, and Gus nodded. "I believe you're right."

The next couple of days was spent modifying the intermix chamber and installing it, then Chad's skills were put to the test in balancing flow rates and tuning the machine. Once that was done, Chad and Helmut decided it was time to paint their creation. At first, they couldn't agree on a paint scheme, but Chad gently reminded Helmut that the racer was his project. Helmut was a little embarrassed as he realized he was taking unwarranted liberties. He put his head down and nodded. "You're correct. I'm a little out of line."

It was Chad's turn to be embarrassed. He didn't realize Helmut was starting to think of the racer as part of his. He wasn't sure why, especially since he himself started thinking of Helmut as co-owner. He put his own head down and nodded. "I don't know where that came from Helmut. Of course, you're an equal partner in this. I only started the project, but it would have been impossible to get this far without you. From now on, there's no question about it. You and I are equal partners in this."

They decided to give the racer an overall white paint job with a pair of blue racing stripes from front to back, parallel to the long axis but to one side. When that was done, they admired their work, and Chad said, "We need a name."

Helmut grinned and said, "I was thinking along the same lines. How about *Schnellmaschinemitvorgesetzterentwurfubergegner?*"

Chad was quite used to Helmut's sense of humor. "Translation, please."

"Fast machine with a superior design over adversaries," he answered. Then added, "That's a rough translation."

Chad nodded. "That's pretty elaborate. Don't you think a name with a little mystery would be a little more appropriate?"

Helmut nodded, and his expression belied the fact that he was impressed with Chad's ability to keep a straight face. "We probably don't have the space on the fuselage to paint a name like that anyway."

"Why do Germans string together a whole gaggle of words to give something a name?" Chad asked flabbergasted.

"It's fun," Helmut answered. "What name would you suggest?" Chad didn't hesitate. *"Vanishing Point."*

Helmut gave it some thought. "I like it. How did you come up with it?"

"There was a movie from the mid-twentieth century of that name. The main character was named Kowalski. Tell you what, let's get cleaned up. Meet me in my quarters. We'll order a pizza and watch it," Chad suggested.

While Chad was paying for the pizza, Helmut scrolled through the Entertainment Packet. He found the proper title and frowned. "There are four movies with that title. Which one are we watching?"

"The one from 1971 is the one I like best," Chad answered as he put the pizza on the coffee table.

As they watched the movie, both marveled at the machines that we're featured. In the end, Chad wondered if he would ever get tired of watching this movie, but Helmut was at a loss for words. Finally, he shook his head. "I hope our fate isn't like the Kowalski in the film."

"You don't have to worry about that," Chad assured him with a chuckle.

*****

## The *Aurora*, Astrodyne 65, Owned by Stellar Logistics and Freight Corporation

Stellar Logistics officially became the corporate sponsor of what became known as Schnellmaschine Racing, much to Chad and Helmut's relief. It gave them resources that they wouldn't have otherwise. For starters, a pit crew. Since Phil, Gus, Dwight, and Jeremy had enthusiastically volunteered to be pit crew, that was one requirement they didn't have to worry about. Stellar Logistics also paid for team uniforms that. Surprisingly enough, Virginia Wells insisted on designing. At first, the team was reluctant, but in the end, they thought they looked quite snazzy in them.

*Vanishing Point* was loaded in a container along with the tools and supplies they would need. The container was attached to North Star, a new sister ship to the existing star series. It would be dropped off at Raytheon, where the Schnellmaschine Racing team would remove *Vanishing Point* and ready it for racing.

Phil was at the controls of the *Aurora* and just settled into an LS 9 cruise. The whole team was crowded in the cockpit at the moment. Not for any particular reason. It seemed wrong to be anywhere else. This was Jeremy's first experience in the *Aurora*, and he was thoroughly enjoying himself. He sat at the systems station and marveled at what he saw in the various displays. After a few minutes, he turned to Chad. "I see what you've been going on about with this ship. It's quite addictive." Chad grinned back. "Told ya."

"What kind of competition are we going to encounter at this thing?" Gus asked.

Chad solemnly shook his head. "Stiff. Huge corporations spend bundles on this competition. Racers are designed starting with a blank sheet, so to speak. The crews are full time, and there is a lot of prestige being on a winning team."

Dwight interrupted, "Even the losing teams have all kinds of girls hanging off 'em."

"Disgusting," Jeremy said in mock agreement.

Phil furrowed his brow. "Are you sure we're going to be competitive?"

Chad nodded. "We are decidedly home spun. But yeah, after running the numbers, we have a better than even chance of winning."

"Who do you reckon is going to be your biggest headache?" Dwight was curious to get Chad's opinion.

Chad leaned back and answered after weighing the question, "The entrants are a 'who's who' in the performance machine industry. Team Kawasaki is always a strong contender, Textron, as ever is a threat."

"BMW always finishes well," Helmut put in.

Chad nodded. "It's fair to say our biggest adversary is corporate money.

Independent teams like us haven't placed in the top ten in the last fifty years." "How many independent teams do you think will enter this year?" Gus asked.

Chad shook his head. "Probably about half or a little less. Besides the obvious disadvantage of not having access to corporate funds, you'll find we'll be the target of plenty of ridicule."

Gus frowned. "But we do have a corporate sponsor. Our employer." "That's different," Chad said, shaking his head. "Stellar Logistics is supporting a team. Those other guys are wholly owned and controlled by their corporations."

Jeremy nodded. "As long as they do well for themselves, they can expect a better-than-average lifestyle."

"I wouldn't mind being the guy to hand them their first disappointment in decades. I don't expect to win first place. It would be nice, but top ten would do me just fine," Chad solemnly stated.

*****

## Raytheon, Waltham Shuttle Port, Freight Receiving Ramp

The six-man Schnellmaschine Racing team watched as a container shuttle placed their container on the ramp. A vehicle called a container mover, simply enough, nosed up to the closed end. The mover had a set of wheels on an axle affixed to the front. The driver inched forward until the attachment gear clicked into place, securing the assembly to the container. He then reversed, leaving the wheels in place. Next, he drove to the opposite end, where he reversed and engaged a probe into the container. Once that was secure, at the push of a button, the probe lifted its end while simultaneously, the wheel and axle lifted the opposite end.

The mover scanned a label that was affixed to it back on Oasis 4. This gave the driver all the information he needed to deliver the container. The scanner read the label and transmitted the data to a dispatch computer that consulted a database. The dispatch computer sent the mover the destination and any special handling instructions. Before they knew it, the Schnellmaschine Racing container was on its way to the pit area located on the opposite side of the shuttle port.

Chad, Helmut, and the rest took ground transport to the pit area. Most of the other team's containers had arrived, and they walked past them. The team containers were brightly painted and decorated with the team names and sponsor logos. When they reached their own container, Phil sighed at the sight. Their team container was a standard Stellar Logistics unit. The only thing that distinguished it was the hand-stenciled "Schnellmaschine Racing" on the door. Chad started working the latch when a voice behind them got their attention. "So, Helmut, you have decided to leave the safety of that maintenance shop. Father always said you were best suited to that sort of work."

Everyone, except Helmut, turned to see two blond men who bore a striking resemblance to Helmut. They were wearing Fokker Racing jackets, and there was a gaggle of girls a short distance away giggling, acting starstruck and silly. Helmut nodded and said while slowly turning. "Wolfgang, Hans, I see you two are still humble as ever."

The second brother, who turned out to be Hans, smiled. "We don't actually have reason to be humble."

"Chad, Mr. Phil Ross, Gus, Jeremy, and Dwight. These are my brothers, Wolfgang and Hans," Helmut said, introducing his brothers to his teammates.

Both Wolfgang and Hans clicked their heels and bowed slightly in a very "German" fashion. Wolfgang smiled and said, "We'll catch up with each other at the reception tonight. Right now, we have to see to our fans."

Wolfgang and Hans turned to the swooning girls and left with them. Team Schnellmaschine stood there starring, then after a little bit, Chad said, "They're your brothers, Helmut, but I would really like to beat those guys."

At the moment, Helmut regretted getting involved in this. No matter where he and Chad placed, he would be a target of ridicule at family reunions. He finally nodded. "They've been that way since we were children. I suppose I should have expected this, coming from a racing family. On the surface, it's always been good-natured. But deeper, I think it gives them a feeling of self- satisfied superiority over their little brother."

Jeremy brought them back to the present task. "Come on, let's see if *Vanishing Point* survived the trip."

*****

**Raytheon, Waltham Convention Center,
Raytheon Challenge Pre-Race Reception**

The reception was typical of receptions for this type of event. Speeches by race organizers and various dignitaries, a dinner for the teams, and a cocktail hour to allow the participants an opportunity to mingle. Old friendships were revived, along with old rivalries, and acquaintances were made.

Dwight caught up with some of the former students that he hadn't seen in quite a while. Helmut's brothers sought him out, and they had a catch-up themselves. Mostly, they talked about family and plans to get together for Christmas, that sort of thing. Every now and again, Wolfgang or Hans would get in a little dig to annoy Helmut. Once, Hans said that Grandpa wouldn't be disappointed if Helmut lost as long as he did everything he could to finish in a respectable position.

Chad fell in with other independent teams to get as much advice as they would offer. The corporate teams did whatever they could to avoid talking to him. Their reaction to him ranged from rather polite brushoffs to overt snubbing.

Phil, Gus, and Jeremy chitchatted with anyone who would talk to them. In Phil's case, some of the corporate executives attending the race in an effort to show support for their own teams. Being the station manager of one of the more important stations made Phil quite popular. They had switched from cocktails to coffee to prevent fuzzy-headedness in the morning. Just as they were finishing their coffees, a voice behind them said, "Jeremy! You found a team that would take you. That's fantastic!"

They turned to see a group from one of the other teams. Jeremy's eye was drawn to the smiling individual who was front and center. He nodded. "Hi, Roger, that would be obvious. Everyone, this is Roger Denton, the pit chief of Delta Racing. This is Chad Kowalski and Helmut Shultz, our pilots. This is Phil Ross, Gus Condent, and Dwight Needles, our pit crew."

Roger cast a critical eye on the pit crew. "Are you the pit chief?" "That's right," Jeremy answered with a nod.

Roger grinned. "Well, I see you went for maturity and experience over youth and energy."

"They'll get the job done," Jeremy assured him.

Roger looked like he was holding back a laugh. "Well, I might have to make sure I get my guys to bed early. There's going to be some real competition this year. Well, we'll see you in the morning."

Roger and his entourage turned and left. They could hear Roger make a comment that they couldn't quite make out, but the others found it amusing and had a chuckle. Jeremy continued to stare at Roger and his team as they walked away. "Roger has always been that way."

"You mean a condescending, passive-aggressive, arrogant jackass?" Phil asked.

Jeremy nodded. "Yup, ever since school. Everyone who knows him would like to be the one who serves him a slice of humble pie. The problem is, he is very talented. He wins because he's skilled. I just wish he wasn't so insufferable. When he took the position as one of Delta Racing Pit Chiefs ten years ago, his racer has consistently finished in the top three. In fact, his racer has finished first, three times."

Dwight brought everyone's attention back to matters at hand. "We ain't gonna win no races standing here grousing about old rivalries. I suggest we bed down and get some rest."

*****

## Raytheon, Waltham Shuttle Port, Raytheon Challenge Pit Area, Prep Day

In the morning, the Schnellmaschine team met at their assigned pit area. There were some items leaning against the container door that they stared at for a few moments. Among the things, there was a box of tissues along with a note saying it was for when they came in last—a stack of pamphlets for trade schools and other items meant to be an insult.

Chad pushed the items out of the way and unlocked the container. Phil and Dwight started picking up the items while Dwight said, "They're just trying to put a burr under our blanket. Don't let 'em put you on the prod."

Once inside the container, Phil and Dwight put the items on a shelf. Gus asked, "Why are you saving that junk?"

Phil frowned. "To be honest, I don't know. Maybe partly to remind us who our competition is."

"Or to rub it in the faces of those who put it there," Dwight added.

Gus furrowed his brow. "Don't you think it's just some good-natured ribbing?"

Chad shook his head. "Some of them perhaps, but there's an element here that genuinely doesn't think we belong here. If you doubt me, think back. How warm of a welcome have we been getting since we arrived?"

"Chad's right," Jeremy said. "We might get some respect if we place well. But I wouldn't count on it."

Ready to change the subject, Dwight asked, "What's today's schedule?"

Chad pinned a sheet to the bulletin board. "Conformity and Safety Inspections until noon. One to three, briefings for the flight crew and pit crew. Five to six, public time. That's time for photos, interviews, garbage like that."

Jeremy directed them while they pulled *Vanishing Point* out of the container and into the semi-enclosed awning area in their pit area. Everyone thought it awkward that although Chad was clearly the leader in this particular endeavor, Jeremy was giving orders. He was simply fulfilling his function as Pit Chief, so it wouldn't be right to remain silent during this task. For his part, he felt odd about the relationship in this situation with Chad and Helmut, being as once they were back on the station, he was their boss again. No one anticipated any of this would be an issue. It just felt odd.

Once *Vanishing Point* was out of the container and positioned under the awning, there was a tap, tap, tap at one of the corner posts. They turned to see the pit chief of the independent team next to them. The man smiled. "Hi there, I'm Vernon Waltz of Waltz Racing. I just wanted to welcome you to this year's Snob fest."

That drew a chuckle from the Schnellmaschine team. Jeremy introduced himself and the rest of the team, who was relieved to finally meet a friendly face. Vernon eyeballed *Vanishing Point*, and his expression belied the fact that he was impressed. "Say! That's some machine you have here. Some say that using modified escape pods is a no-starter. But I have to say this looks fast just sitting here."

"I'm familiar with Waltz Racing," Chad stated. "Who do you think is the team to beat this year?"

Vernon didn't hesitate. "Everyone always talks about Team Kawasaki, and they actually don't look bad this year. But I have to say that Fokker Racing is a real contender this year. Of course, Delta Racing is expected to win, as always."

Jeremy couldn't help himself. "What has been your best finish?"

"We finished number twelve three years ago," Vernon answered.

Phil nodded. "Twelve, out of a field of sixty or so. That's respectable in anyone's book."

"Most would agree with you," Vernon agreed. "But here, unless you're on the podium, any accomplishments are brushed off."

There was another tap at the corner post. They turned to see a pair of racing officials standing there, holding clipboards. They entered and introduced themselves. "I'm Amit Gupta, and this is Carlos Ramirez. We'll be inspecting your racer for conformity."

Vernon started backing away. "Well, I guess I'll be next. We'll get a chance to talk later."

"We'll see ya," Chad said as Vernon went to his own pit area.

The inspection proceeded at once, with Amit checking the racer for conformance to race rules and Carlos inspecting for safety. Both technicians had a checklist that they carefully followed, marking off each item once they were satisfied the appropriate requirements had been met.

When the last items have been checked off each list, Amit and Carlos had trouble concealing their surprise that all the requirements had been met. As they left the Schnellmaschine pit area, Phil observed, "Those two actually looked disappointed that they couldn't find a reason to keep us from racing."

Chad nodded. "I suppose the snobbery extends to the officials."

The team kept themselves occupied organizing the tools and supplies they would need for the race. After sorting their equipment, they practiced their individual pit crew tasks. When noon rolled around, Schnellmaschine Racing went to lunch, where they endured a new round of insults.

The briefings were held in a facility near the dining hall, so they didn't bother to return to the pit area. There was a briefing for the teams as a whole, then a briefing for the pilots, the pit crew as a whole, finally, separate briefings for the pit crews on the moon and pit crews remaining on Raytheon.

Back in the pit area, the team donned their uniforms. The cowlings and cockpit door were opened on *Vanishing Point* to afford the public a better view of the racer's interior. Race fans would stop and gawk, make comments, and occasionally a fan would get Chad and Helmut's attention and have them autograph a program.

Every now and again, a knowledgeable fan would spot something about *Vanishing Point's* hardware that would cause a reaction. Vanishing Point's systems were perfectly ordinary; however, Chad and Helmut did an extraordinary job putting them together. There were design details that both technicians had come up with that looked normal, but a trained eye would spot a detail that belied its uniqueness. Those design elements were made to allow rapid replacement of components and adjustments.

A photographer arrived and took a series of candid photos as well as group photos. When that was done, they talked to fans until it was time to put *Vanishing Point* back in the container and get dinner.

*****

## Raytheon, Waltham Shuttle Port, Raytheon Challenge Pit Area, Race Day

Team Schnellmaschine met in the pits after breakfast and readied *Vanishing Point*. They performed a careful preflight check and waited for the race officials. Just after 9:00 a.m., a group arrived who had armbands on that said "Raytheon Challenge Official." They were accompanied by a young lady who wore a sash that proclaimed her as Miss Raytheon. She carried a fish bowl with folded slips of paper in it. The lead official, who identified himself as Ben, had Chad reach in and take a slip and hand it to his assistant, who went by Ned. Ned read the slip, "Eleven-twenty-two."

A third official, named Thomas, entered the time on a pad which transmitted it to a display board and to interested parties who weren't in the grandstands on their own pads. When a popular team drew a time, there were cheers and cat calls. One interesting similarity to Earth was the fact that Raytheon had a nearly identical orbit and rotation. In fact, the residents used earth time standards. They would simply stop the clocks at midnight for twelve minutes and twenty- three seconds. There were plans to develop their own standards, but they didn't feel the need to do so immediately.

Once the board was complete with teams and times, the excitement level increased by the minute. Dwight and Gus shuttled to the *Aurora* and started their short trip to the moon, orbiting the fifth planet of the Hedron system. At just before 10:30 a.m., the racer that drew the first time slot taxied to the start line. The official, named Ben, made sure the racer was in the proper position and waited for the timer to reach the proper time. At precisely 10:30 a.m., he waved a flag. The Sukhoi Racing team applied full power, immediately left the ground, and accelerated toward the upper atmosphere while Miss Raytheon waved. Race officials went up and down the pit area, making sure the racers queued up in the correct order. *Vanishing Point* was pushed out of the awning area, where Chad and Helmut boarded and strapped in. Jeremy and Phil had their own helmets on while they stood by for the engine start. The engine started, then Chad and Helmut went through their checklist while Phil and Jeremy checked items they were trained to check both on the racer's exterior, under cowlings, and access panels.

Phil gave Jeremy the thumbs-up, who acknowledged the gesture.

He then waited for Chad and Helmut to finish their checklist. Finally, Chad looked out the window where Jeremy gave him a thumbs up, and Chad returned it. Jeremy and Phil moved off to one side and waited for the racer to join the queue. A race official appeared and stood in front of Vanishing Point. The racer from Team Mitsubishi taxied past, and the official made sure he had Chad's attention. He had *Vanishing Point* taxi forward, then make a turn to the left to get in line.

Jeremy and Phil loaded tools and parts on a motorized utility cart and left to set up the midrace pit area. The pit assigned to Schnellmaschine Racing was close to the start line so they could observe the start of

*Vanishing Point's* run. Team Mitsubishi taxied into position and an exhaust deflector raised behind it. Then Ben, the official, checked to make sure they were positioned properly and watched the start clock tick down. At 11:20 a.m., a green light illuminated, and Ben dropped a white start flag and Team Mitsubishi was off with a roar.

The exhaust deflector lowered, and Chad taxied into the start gate, and the official motioned him to a stop at the start line. The exhaust deflector raised behind them, and they waited for 11:22 a.m. Chad set the parking brakes to hold *Vanishing Point* stationary, and he brought the reaction engine power lever up to put out as much thrust as they could without the parking brake slipping. At 11:22 a.m., the green light illuminated, and the start flag dropped. Chad shoved the power lever full forward while simultaneously releasing the parking brake.

*****

## *Vanishing Point*, Schnellmaschine Racer

*Vanishing Point* rocketed forward and climbed toward the upper atmosphere. Maintaining the optimum climb angle, heading, and leveling off at the right altitude was a much harder task than imaginable. At 90,000 meters, Chad started to pitch *Vanishing Point's* nose down. Orbit was established at 103,000 meters. Helmut noted the point where they crossed the 100,000 meters point and started entering that coordinate in the computer.

Chad had the reaction engine at its maximum output. He was adjusting the variable vector exhaust nozzle to give Vanishing Point a constant nose-down pitch as they orbited the planet. It was tricky balancing their speed and the pull of gravity, along with varying their pitch to maintain a constant altitude.

The easy way to do it would be to calculate a velocity that would balance the pull of gravity with the centrifugal force created by their orbit. In this situation, it wasn't possible, though. The racers were all capable of speeds much faster than the velocity needed to keep the vessel in orbit at the desired altitude; therefore, they had to go as fast as possible if they wanted to win the race. That meant keeping the reaction engine power lever at maximum, vectoring the thrust to hold them in orbit.

Chad was finding out that he needed every bit of the ten-thousand-meter tolerance they were given for this part of the course. Helmut cautioned Chad. "You're getting close to the upper limit."

"I know that, Helmut," Chad retorted. "This isn't the easiest thing I've ever done."

After Chad had some time to get a handle on things, he let his altitude get near the one hundred thousand meters limit. Helmet input the coordinates for the Endeavor Asteroid Cluster into the navigation computer, and the displays indicated the proper course. Then Helmut provided a countdown to the point they could break orbit.

When he reached zero, he said, "Now!"

Chad abruptly changed the thrust vectors to pitch the nose up until he was happy with the new course. Then he rolled *Vanishing Point* twenty-three and a half degrees left with the thrusters and used vectored thrust to fine-tune his new course. They were very close to the desired course but not good enough. A mistake here could prove to be disastrous and even fatal. He locked the exhaust nozzle in the nominal position and used the thrusters in minimum output to finalize his vector. Races have been won or lost at this point, as some pilots get overexcited and start overcontrolling their machines.

Chad was now sweating a storm as he eased *Vanishing Point* in the proper direction. He stared at his navigation displays and said, "How's that look to you, Helmut?"

In Helmut's mind, Chad did that remarkably fast. He scrutinized the display and said, "Ja. You've got it on the money!"

Chad nodded. "Engaging the light-speed engines." Then he flipped on the light-speed engine's power master and engaged the Start Sequence Initiator.

Helmut consulted a systems display. "Bubble formed." Chad slid the light-speed power selector forward.

The light-speed acceleration was nothing less than remarkable.

Helmut called out the velocities, "LS 1, LS 2, LS 3…"

Then they reached LS 12. The count slowed, "LS 12.1, LS 12.2."

*Vanishing Point* topped out at LS 12.6. Helmut brought up the light speed systems page, and he studied it with Chad. He nodded.

"I believe you are correct, Chad. LS 12.2 gives us the best chance to preserve our engine for the second half of the race."

Chad immediately pulled the power level back to give them a speed of LS 12.2. The light-speed capability of the racers is actually a well-guarded secret. There were rumors and leaks to the press on such things, as well as some very educated guesses. Chad did some research and determined that teams will push their machines hard in the first part of the race to get ahead in the field early on.

The problem was they could probably get LS. 12.3 or 12.4 in the first lap. But pushing their machines that hard had negative effects. Excessive heat would tend to warp and erode components in their reactor chamber, and power output coils would lose their effectiveness and require degaussing or replacing, which is not an operation they can undertake at a pit stop.

Usually, the final lap is made at a velocity under LS 12. It doesn't sound like much, but at these speeds, the difference is massive. Chad and Helmut's strategy was to run the engines at the fastest level that didn't deteriorate the performance level later in the race. They would make up for any shortcomings in the sublight sections.

*****

## Drummond, Raytheon Challenge Pit Area

Drummond was a moon orbiting the fifth planet of the Hedron system. Race officials had speakers in each pit area that were used to hear the race announcer, Ted O'Danials, and his co-announcer, Bud Johnson. Dwight and Gus had just finished setting up their pit area and were listening for news concerning *Vanishing Point*. The announcers were doing what announcers have been doing for centuries. In the absence of reportable events, they prevented dead air by presenting facts and figures along with some trivia. Presently, O'Danials said, *"There's Tatsu of team Mitsubishi dropping out of light speed at a very precise one thousand kilometers from the gate."*

*"Pilot, Hideki Nagashima has this machine dialed in for his style of flying. His copilot/navigator, Tomouki Kuroda, once again left them enough room to maneuver and set up their profile for entry into the gate,"* Johnson added.

*"Nagashima is firing his thrusters furiously, getting Tatsu aligned with the gate,"* O'Danials reported.

Johnson excitedly added, *"It looks like he has it nailed, and there he goes! He's fired his reaction engine, and he's through the gate, dead center!"*

*"Tatsu is through the gate, and Nagashima has started to pick his way through the asteroids. He's got to be the smoothest pilot I've ever seen. He makes it look so effortless,"* O'Danials gushed.

*"Kuroda has a talent for plotting a route through the asteroids. Not necessarily the shortest, but a route that allows them to get to the exit gate at the highest speed. Watch how he went a long way around the first asteroid instead of slowing to take the more restrictive passage. This way, Nagashima can keep the power level… We just had a racer drop out of light speed just outside the start gate!"* Johnson excitedly reported.

*****

## Vanishing Point, Schnellmaschine Racer

They were a few minutes from the Endeavor Asteroid Cluster start gate, so Helmut brought up the course on the standby portion of the navigation did display. The instruments told him when to start the countdown to light speed engine cut. Helmut stared at the display. "Cut light-speed engine in five, four, three, two, one, cut!"

Chad already had the reaction engine powered when he cut the light-speed engine. When the scenery outside came into focus, they got their bearings. They actually came out of light speed at the distance they had agreed upon during prerace planning, but it was still a little closer to the Endeavor Asteroid Cluster start gate than Chad liked. After he made some fairly aggressive rolling and pitching maneuvers, they were aligned with the gate. The gate was actually a holographic image of a circle that was projected from a series of emitters. There was a vessel nearby that had race officials on board who ensured everyone went through the gate without touching it. Touching the gate incurred a ten-second penalty.

*****

**Raytheon Challenge Announcer Booth**

O'Danials quickly checked a pad. "That's *Vanishing Point* of Schnellmaschine Racing! Pilot Chad Kowalski is working overtime getting aligned with the gate." "It looks like Copilot Helmut Schultz may have miscalculated their light-speed cut," Johnson agreed.

O'Danials brought up information on his pad that he had prepared. "This is the first year for Schnellmaschine Racing along with first-timers Chad Kowalski and Helmut Schultz. Kowalski and Schultz are technicians and pilots for Stellar Logistics and Freight. One interesting note about Helmut Schultz is he's from a family with a racing heritage. In fact, his brothers represent Fokker racing in this event."

"Wow! *Vanishing Point* is through the gate, and Kowalski didn't slow one bit. In fact, it looked like his reaction engine was at full output," Johnson exclaimed while trying hard not to sound impressed.

O'Danials added, "Let's hope they respect the asteroid belt more than the start gate before they decide to see if any of the rocks are solid."

"Maybe that would save them the embarrassment of coming in last or near to it," Johnson said, chuckling.

*****

***Drummond,*** **Raytheon Challenge Pit Area**

Gus shook his head. "Even the announcers have it in for us." "Don't let it get to ya," Dwight offered. "I'll bet Chad ain't. "Space

Interfold Transmissions are faster than standard radio, so what we heard had some delay but not much. Let's make sure we're ready when they get here."

*****

## Vanishing Point, Schnellmaschine Racer

Chad and Helmut had taken the time to carefully plan their route through the asteroids. It was Helmut's job to continually monitor their position and give Chad directions. As they passed through the first gate, Helmut started a timer.

"Roll right twenty-three degrees and pitch up seven degrees, in four, three, two, one, now!"

Helmut consulted his notes and verified that they were on the desired track.

Seeing that they were indeed where they wanted to be, he waited for the next check point and said, "Roll left ninety-two degrees and pitch down fifteen degrees, in three, two one, now."

Chad performed the maneuver crisply. "I see the gap."

Most teams plan a route that allowed them to make their course changes without an extremely high degree of precision. The gap they were headed for was well within the skill set of every team, but most will take the long way around the asteroid. They were confident enough in Chad's skills to shoot the gap, as they were far enough from the gap to allow Chad to align *Vanishing Point* properly. Chad will be able to keep his velocity up while he adjusted his vector. After doing the math, they had determined that they had a small advantage using this strategy, and Chad was determined to take every advantage. Helmut provided vectors around several more asteroids and got them aligned with the next gate.

*****

## Raytheon Challenge Announcer Booth

"*Tatsu* is through the final Endeavor Asteroid Cluster gate with Nagashima and Kuroda setting a course for the Hedron system," O'Danials reported.

Johnson added, "They're making that long sweeping left turn to align themselves on course."

O'Danials chuckled. "Whoever laid out this course wanted to make sure the racers had to work as hard in open space as they had to in the asteroid belt. It's hard enough getting the proper alignment for light speed, but doing it after making a turn like that, at the velocities they're traveling, is a real test."

"It looks like they're ready to engage their light-speed engines… Holy cow! *Vanishing Point* just rounded the Endeavor 376 asteroid and shot through the exit gate!" Johnson exclaimed.

"They are practically on top of *Tatsu*!" O'Danials agreed. "They've nearly made up the two-minute difference in start times!"

"It looks like they'll keep it that tight also," Johnson agreed. "Kowalski is avoiding making the sweeping left turn because of the angle he shot through the gate."

O'Danials nodded. "Everyone takes it for granted that you have to pass through perpendicular to the gate. Kowalski went through the angle he needed for the Hedron system. It'll save them precious seconds."

"*Tatsu* has gone to light speed, and there goes Vanishing Point after some quick fine adjustments," Johnson reported.

*****

## Vanishing Point, Schnellmaschine Racer

After engaging the light speed engines, Chad checked the engine parameters. After ensuring everything was as it should be, he smiled. "Did you see what was just in front of us when we passed through the gate?"

Helmut shook his head. "I was too busy getting us aligned with our course."

"*Tatsu* of Mitsubishi went to light speed about five seconds before we did," Chad reported.

Helmut smiled. "I wonder if we'll have little close competition."

Chad shook his head. "There are too many variables. Who knows, there might be a lot of us bunched up. Especially toward the end of the race."

*****

## Drummond, Raytheon Challenge Pit Area

*Tatsu* entered the Drummond atmosphere, landed at the moon's racing center, and taxied to its assigned pit. One Mitsubishi pit crewman ran to the engine cowling and opened it. Then he plugged in the headset he was wearing so he could communicate with the pilots. Then he started plugging in an engine monitor/analyzer. The other pit crewman opened the cockpit door and talked to the pilots.

To Dwight and Gus's eyes, everything was being handled in an efficient and professional manner. Suddenly, a sonic boom announced the arrival of a racer. Dwight raised binoculars and spotted Vanishing Point in time to see it land. He knew that the pit crews all monitored the race announcers and passed information to the pilots, which made him wonder what their reactions would be. He turned to Gus. "Get ready!"

They barely had time to get their helmets on when Chad stopped *Vanishing Point* in the pit. Gus rushed to the engine cowling and opened it, plugged in the engine monitor/analyzer, then plugged in his headset. Dwight opened the cockpit door and handed sports drink bottles to Chad and Helmut. While Chad and Helmut replenished important elements they had been sweating out, Dwight looked in the Mitsubishi pit. They hadn't noticed *Vanishing Point's* arrival right away. While Dwight waited for Chad and Helmut to finish their drinks, he saw *Tatsu's* pilot discover *Vanishing Point's* presence. Suddenly, there was a lot of yelling in Japanese and a noticeable increase in the tempo of the pit activities. "It looks like we need to tighten injectors three and five one flat each, and six and eight two flats," Gus said over the intercom from the engine bay.

Chad nodded in his helmet. "I concur. That's what I see on my gauges."

The injectors were designed to give optimal performance at a given depth in the mixing chamber. The injectors Chad designed were threaded. To fine-tune the injectors, the pit crewman would disconnect injectors he needed to adjust with the quick disconnect fittings. Then he marked the position of the injector to be adjusted and then loosened a jam nut. He would now turn the injector to the desired amount. Normally, some sort of measuring device would be employed for this procedure. However, Chad came up with a different system. The injectors used threads with a thread pitch of thirty-two threads per inch, which meant a full turn increased or decreased the depth by one thirty seconds of an inch or three hundred twelve and a half ten-thousandths of an inch. The injectors had six-sided wrench flats for installation and adjustment. Turning only one flat meant the injector would move in or out fifty-two ten-thousandths of an inch. It wasn't the most precise way to do the job, but it was fast, and they reasoned precise enough. At least well within an acceptable tolerance. Incidentally, Chad and Helmut butted heads more than once over measuring standards. Metric or imperial, not that one was better than the other. They just needed to pick one and stick to it.

Gus made the necessary adjustments and checked his monitor. Satisfied with what he saw, he disconnected the monitor and closed the cowling. Dwight took the empty drink bottles, gave Chad and Helmut fresh ones, and secured the cockpit hatch. Dwight and Gus rushed to the safety zone so that Vanishing Point could taxi out of the pits. *Tatsu* just managed to leave the pits just ahead of Vanishing Point while Dwight and Gus looked on. Then both racers took off one after the other. Gus could feel eyes on him. He looked over to the Mitsubishi pit area and saw the crew staring at them. Dwight saw Gus was staring back at the *Tatsu* pit crew, chuckled, and said, "Those guys are some of the best in the business, and they know it. The fact that we pushed *Vanishing Point* out at least a minute quicker than they did will give them a little self- doubt."

*****

## Vanishing Point, Schnellmaschine Racer

After establishing orbit, Helmut provided the navigation system with the proper vectors to the first gate. Chad aligned *Vanishing Point* with the information on his display and engaged the light-speed engines. Helmut slowly shook his head. "I think we may be way behind Tatsu after these last two legs. If they saw us, it would just motivate them to press harder."

"That will probably work in our favor," Chad agreed. "Human nature being what it is, the possibility they'll make a mistake is greater. Plus, if they push their engines harder, their last lap will be slower than they planned for."

Twenty minutes later, Helmut provided the countdown to the light-speed engine cut. Chad cut the engine, and the stars came into focus. Helmut scanned the stars, and the navigation system provided an exact position. Helmut smiled. "Pitch up 2.2 degrees. Yaw left one point 4 degrees. LS 5 for three minutes."

Chad carefully adjusted *Vanishing Point's* course and pushed the light-speed engine to LS 5. A lot of races were lost at this point. In an effort to pass through the gates as quick as possible, most racers do two things that have the potential to work for them or against them. First, they set their course in a hasty fashion so that they can go to light speed as soon as possible. The obvious flaw is if their calculations are off by even less than one degree, they could find themselves a race losing distance from the gate. The second thing they do is delay the light- speed engine cut until the last possible moment. Again, if their calculations are off by just a little bit, they end up over shooting the gate. Then they have to backtrack and try to find the gate, then maneuver to pass through the gate.

Chad and Helmut reasoned they could avoid the first mistake by being extra cautious before jumping to light speed. A few seconds delay would most likely pay big dividends. Stopping short of the gate ensured that they wouldn't overshoot. The shorter distance allowed them to arrive at the gate with more precision and closer than they ever could otherwise.

Again, Helmut gave a countdown to light speed engine cut. The stars came into focus along with the gate. Chad and Helmut grinned, seeing as they were perfectly aligned to pass through the gate. Once they were on the far side of the gate, Helmut calculated the course to the next gate. After double-checking his figures, Chad adjusted his course and engaged the light-speed engines. Passage through the final gate went just as smoothly, causing both Chad and Helmut to wonder if they were doing something wrong. Chad put it out of his mind as he set course to Raytheon and went to light speed.

*****

**Raytheon, Waltham Shuttle Port, Raytheon Challenge Pit Area**

Phil and Jeremy had been listening to the announcers, as did all the pit crews. Competing racers have been arriving for some time now. Some alone without much fanfare and some in clusters that thrilled the crowd. The fans and the pit crews used a simple technique to gauge who was doing well and who wasn't. The order the racers started was posted on a scoreboard. They would simply compare the times a racer finished the first lap with the time posted for a rival racer. For instance, if the second racer to start the race crossed the line in less than two minutes from the time the first racer crossed, the number two racer was ahead.

Jeremy was clearly more enthusiastic about keeping tabs on Vanishing Point's progress in comparison to the competition. Phil furrowed his brow. "I don't really understand why you're bothering to pay attention to that stuff right now. The guys are holding back on the light-speed sections, so it stands to reason they'll be a little behind at this point."

Jeremy pulled his gaze away from the scoreboard, looked at Phil, and gave him a thin smile. "You'd be surprised. The other teams are indeed pushing hard right now. However, they're making mistakes. *Vanishing Point* is actually ahead of some of the others, and they're surprisingly close to the ones they're behind. The pit chiefs will report to their pilots how things are stacking up with their competition. If they report that an independent newcomer is giving them a run from their money, they'll push harder. That's when mistakes are made."

*****

***Vanishing Point,* Schnellmaschine Racer**

Chad killed the light-speed engine, and Raytheon appeared shockingly close in front of them. Helmut gave Chad coordinates to the start gate to the five-hundred-kilometer atmospheric low-level section. Chad entered the coordinates in the navigation system and was rewarded with vectors to the start gate.

Entering the atmosphere was visually dramatic. If it weren't for the navigation shields, *Vanishing Point* would burn away in seconds. The racer smashes into the air molecules so hard they explode into a white-hot plasma. Chad could adjust the strength and focus of the shields to change the rate of deceleration. It took several minutes to emerge from the ball of plasma and allow Chad to switch off the deflector and engage the aerodynamic controls. The start gate was located where a river flowed into a sizable lake in a mountainous region.

The center of the lake was about ten kilometers from the gate. Chad passed over the center and adjusted his heading to the gate at an altitude of five meters. *Vanishing Point* was now cruising at subsonic velocities although not much slower than the speed of sound, causing water mist to rise behind the racer. Chad and Helmut were far too engaged in operating *Vanishing Point* to notice the crowds of fans cheering wildly as they blasted through the gate.

Helmut had his paper map open and concentrated on directing Chad. He divided his attention between the map and the terrain under them, looking for landmarks and terrain features, then relating that information to Chad while telling him what to expect around curved sections of canyons and the far side of ridges. Chad, for his part, was concentrating on staying at the proper altitude and, of course, avoiding colliding with the tesrrain.

From the gate, the course followed the river for a short distance in a wide valley. The course then veered off into a canyon they were expected to fly through, remaining below the top of the canyon rim. The canyon eventually started to get smaller and fade out. Once they passed a tiny waterfall, they could fly above the rim, much to Chad's relief. At that point, the canyon became a draw that continued up hill. Helmut had Chad follow it up to a ridge where they pointed the nose down and followed another valley with steep sides.

There were around twenty-five minutes of this kind of flying, which had both Helmut and Chad exhausted. The sight of the exit gate came as a relief, and they passed through happily. Chad immediately throttled back the reaction engine and pitched the nose up while turning to the right to enter the downwind leg of the landing pattern at Waltham shuttle port.

*****

## Raytheon, Waltham Shuttle Port, Raytheon Challenge Pit Area

Phil and Jeremy stood by with their helmets on and tools at the ready. Jeremy looked over to the Delta Racing pit. The Delta racer had just pulled in, and he watched as Roger Denton and a pit crewman went to work. *Vanishing Point* touched down on the runway and taxied to the pits. Chad stopped on the mark directed by Jeremy and set the brakes. Jeremy threw chocks under the nose wheel, then opened the cabin hatch. Phil had the cowling open and started disconnecting the injectors from the intermix chamber. Handing sports drinks to Chad and Helmut, Jeremy said, "You guys have them worried. Stick to the game plan, and you'll finish this thing in pretty good shape. I'll give Phil a hand."

Jeremy rushed to the engine cowling on the opposite side of Phil and opened it. While climbing up to the engine deck, he saw Roger give him a look and grin. Phil had the old injectors removed and the new ones were lying out on the engine deck. Jeremy took a tool that looked like a modified depth micrometer. He looked at Phil. "Plasma first." He inserted the tool in an empty injector hole and turned the thimble. When the spindle bottomed out, he read the measurement. "This one is plus twenty-two-tenths."

Twenty-two-tenths meant Phil had to set the stop on the injector to allow it to go twenty-two-ten thousandths of an inch deeper into the chamber. Running at the speeds they were, parts became slightly eroded. The racer could actually operate for hundreds of hours like that but not at the performance levels needed to win. Phil placed the injector in a homemade fixture and started adjusting the depth stop until a digital readout told him he had the correct adjustment. The injector replacement continued until they were all installed and connected. Jeremy had Chad perform an integrity check. At the press of a button, high- pressure nitrogen was ported to each system. There was a chemical added to the nitrogen, which would appear as a puff of smoke if there were even the smallest of leaks. Happy with the results, Phil and Jeremy closed the cowling doors. Jeremy passed two more sports drinks to the cabin and closed the hatch while Phil pulled the chocks. Chad taxied smartly to the runway and went streaking to the upper atmosphere.

Jeremy and Phil started putting away the tools and used injectors. Roger Denton closed up the cowlings and hatches on his racer while his pit crewman pulled the chocks. The racer taxied out while a smiling Roger watched it leave. Roger looked over to the empty Schnellmaschine pit, and his grin instantly morphed into an open-mouthed gape. Jeremy tried not to laugh while the color drained from Roger's face. It was a treat watching Roger realize he had been beaten—badly.

*****

### *Vanishing Point,* **Schnellmaschine Racer**

Chad pushed *Vanishing Point* to 100,000 meters and leveled off at 105,000 meters. After the orbit, they streaked off toward the Endeavor Asteroid Cluster. Both Chad and Helmut were finding it easier the second time around in some ways. That made them take an aggressive approach to resist the urge to relax. Incentives for staying alert came in the form of Team McLaren. They dropped out of light speed in the same manner as their first time through. As Chad was lining up to the gate, the McLaren *F1* passed them and shot through the gate just ahead *Vanishing Point.* Helmut consulted a note he had made. "Those guys left Raytheon just before us."

"That means they're losing some light-speed capacity," Chad confirmed. "They probably have a slight edge at sublight speeds, but we can beat them in the stretches."

Helmut navigated the team through the asteroid field along the same route they had used before. Both Chad and Helmut had to constantly remind themselves not to get too confident, but they did find that it was much easier the second time around, being as if they knew what to expect. Vanishing Point and the McLaren *F1* emerged from the asteroid field at roughly the same moment but at different points. The McLaren *F1* was slightly ahead of Vanishing Point and passed through the gate, then started making his long sweeping left turn to align with the course for the Hedron system. As with the first lap, Chad didn't need to make that tricky turn because he was already aligned roughly on course. Passage through the gate was at an angle, but that wasn't a big deal. In a few seconds, they were aligned and engaged the light-speed engines.

*****

## Drummond, Raytheon Challenge Pit Area

Gus and Dwight had the tools ready as they did the last time. Both thought they could shave off a few seconds from their time although the first pit was more than acceptable. Watching how the other pit crews conducted themselves was an education. Some crews ran about in a frenzy carrying out their assigned tasks in an exaggerated fashion. Dwight thought there was a lot of unnecessary movement for what they needed to do. He supposed that it was human nature. There was a sense of urgency and excitement that tended to breed that sort of behavior.

Then there were the crews who didn't seem to think it was worth their while to hurry. It's as if they knew they were defeated, so what's the point in knocking themselves out? They got the job done, but there was plenty of room to shave off a few seconds from their pit times.

Then there were the professional full-time race technicians. Things were at a much higher pace but with no unwanted motion. Every action is deliberate and precise. Watching them was a real treat. Dwight noticed something about them; however, that would probably make for an interesting study in human performance. On the second visit to Drummond, the full-time professional teams acted a bit more panicked. He even overheard pilots berating the pit crewman for making an incorrect adjustment.

The teams that had crews that had a more relaxed attitude toward their jobs actually picked up the pace on the second visits of their racer. For the teams that had the spastic pit crews, there didn't seem to be any appreciable change. They were all getting the same updates from the announcers, and an image of the scoreboard was in each pit. Dwight couldn't help but notice that there were several independent teams that were giving the big teams something to worry about.

A racer from an independent team pulled into the pit next to theirs. The pit crew fell into the spastic category. Dwight and Gus watched for a few seconds while a crewman would open a cowling door and ran to a cart for a tool. He would get halfway back and realize he needed an additional tool, then run back to the cart. It wouldn't be so bad, except it happened over and over. Dwight looked away while shaking his head. "It's like a pretar fire drill over there."

A sonic boom announced the arrival of a racer. Dwight checked a display and saw it was *Vanishing Point*. He and Gus put on their helmets and gathered what they needed for *Vanishing Point*. Chad taxied into the pit where Dwight chocked the front tires and opened the cockpit hatch while Gus opened the cowling doors and plugged in the analyzer. Dwight handed sports drinks to Chad and Helmut. Chad drank half the bottle in one long pull, then asked, "Have you been able to figure out how we're doing?"

"Best I can calculate, you're pretty close to the top," Dwight answered. "Just fly the way you've been, and you'll do okay."

While looking at the analyzer, Gus said, "The readings I'm getting tell me that any adjustments are a waste of time."

Chad checked his own instruments. "That's the reading I get." "Okay, closing up," Gus said as he stepped off the engine deck.

Dwight closed the cockpit hatch and pulled the chocks. Chad restarted the engine and taxied to the runway. In a few seconds, *Vanishing Point* was off with a roar and on its way to the first of two deep space gates. Dwight and Gus started packing their things, and Dwight said, "Let's hightail it back to Raytheon."

*****

## *Vanishing Point,* Schnellmaschine Racer

Chad had *Vanishing Point* settled into a comfortable LS 12.2 cruise. Both Chad and Helmut were pleasantly surprised to see the engine performance wasn't degraded at this point in the race. If the other racers pushed their machines hard in the first lap, it was likely the best most of them could do is LS 11.8. They used the same strategy of stopping short of the gates to get a more accurate read on their position. The passage through the deep space gates went flawlessly. Chad inhaled deeply. "One more challenge, Helmut."

*****

## Raytheon, Waltham Shuttle Port, Raytheon Challenge Pit Area

Dwight and Gus had just returned with the Aurora and hurried to the pits. There have been racers returning for the last hour or so. The finish times were posted on the scoreboard, which made the crowd cheer. Gus studied the board for a few seconds and observed, "The times are all over the place."

Jeremy shook his head. "Those numbers are useless. They haven't added the time penalties yet."

Dwight nodded. "Touching a gate or an altitude incursion, as well as a speed incursion in the atmospheric portion, will get you pinged."

Jeremy smiled. "There's a lot of stuff that gets you a penalty in the atmospheric portion. The spectators love to watch the competitors battle it out, but it's too easy to crowd another racer off course."

Dwight nodded again. "Actually, it is allowed, but only in certain situations."

"That's why pilots would rather not be in a pack in the atmospheric portion," Jeremy agreed.

"Why is there a huge difference in the fastest and slowest times?" Gus asked. "I would think it would be tighter than this."

"The longer times were most likely when someone misses a gate, they have to go back and find it," Jeremy offered.

Phil studied the board and asked, "Why is Team Triumph in red?" Dwight looked grim. "Red means they're out of the race. A little while back, we got word that the Triumph guys bounced off an asteroid.

There's no word about them yet, but we're hopeful."

*****

### *Vanishing Point,* Schnellmaschine Racer

Helmut gave the countdown for the light-speed engine cut, and Chad killed the engine and fired up the reaction engine. Raytheon came into sharp focus, and they saw that they were in the middle of a swarm of racers they had caught up to. Chad had been watching power sports all his life, and he remembers being thrilled as anyone watching racers battle it out, vying for position in a crowded field. He even fantasized about this situation more than once. Now that he's here, he wished he was anywhere else.

One racer entering the atmosphere was an impressive sight, but seven racers was a spectacular event. Chad aligned with the aim point in the center of the lake and made sure there was no one directly in front of them. Once the white- hot plasma formed, there would be no way they could detect anything in front of them. They emerged from the ball of plasma, and Chad could work on getting *Vanishing Point* below the speed of sound and aligned with the gate. They leveled off above the lake with four competitors ahead of them. All the racers aligned themselves one after the other. They actually couldn't pass here even though they were capable because they were moving at the maximum allowable velocity.

The racers shot through the gate one after the other, to the delight of the fans that were nearby. Chad had to constantly remind himself that he couldn't trust the navigation of the racers in front of him; after all, everyone made mistakes. Helmut's workload increased as well because he not only had to guide Chad, but he had to also advise on the best line to take to put them in the best position to make the most of the next turn or challenge. Chad did an exemplary job mixing it up with the other racers. At one point, he actually had the lead. After some aggressive flying, he was second in the group of seven.

They passed through the exit gate and turned to the finish line, which was the race start line. The racers were prohibited from going to an altitude of over twenty meters. This rule made for interesting results at times. The finish line gate was actually just wide enough for two racers to pass side by side. This time, there were three racers side by side with wings overlapping to prevent them from touching the gate and incurring a penalty. Chad managed to get next to the leader's left while another racer was on the leader's right. To make things more interesting, three took position over the first group.

All the ships were capable of powering past their competition, but that would earn them a time penalty for exceeding the speed of sound. The best they could do was the speed of sound and hope someone made a mistake. Race officials would have to examine data to determine that the times were accurate. There wasn't room for the seventh racer, so he trailed the group, thinking that if someone made a mistake, he would ease ahead of the wreckage and win this immediate contest.

It was long decided at the Raytheon Challenge that times would be to the hundredth of a second. Four of the six racers that crossed the finish line as a group had precisely the same time stamp with the other two just one-hundredth of a second later. It didn't actually matter in a time trial format since the start times were staggered. They now had to separate themselves without smashing into each other. The top three racers climbed and eased themselves away from each other. Then the lower group did the same while spacing themselves for landing. On reflection, Chad thought it was the craziest part of the race.

After landing, they taxied to their individual pit areas. After *Vanishing Point* shut down and the chocks were in place, they opened the cockpit door and helped Chad and Helmut get out. The pressure suits Chad and Helmut wore came off next, revealing the clothes they wore under the pressure suits were soaked with perspiration. They sat there with fresh sports drinks trying to rehydrate when Chad asked, "How does it look for us? I know we're not last, but that was so much harder than I thought it was going to be."

Jeremy smiled. "I don't want to get your hopes up, but you two just turned in a very respectable finish. According to the board, you're in the top twenty."

Chad looked at the others. "We're in the top twenty. We're a team, all of us.

There's no way Helmut and I could have come this far by ourselves.

No matter how we do, I'm extremely grateful." "Ja, me as well," Helmut added.

*****

## Raytheon, Waltham Shuttle Port, Raytheon Challenge Grandstand

The Schnellmaschine Racing team made their way back to the grandstands to watch the last of the racers finish. A little more than half the field started after *Vanishing Point*, meaning they would be watching the field end their race for about an hour or so.

Helmut avoided checking the scoreboard, then Dwight brought it to his attention. "Your brothers haven't finished yet, Helmut. They started after you."

Helmut studied the board and saw that they had indeed finished in a very good position. He had to remind himself that the penalties for various offenses still have to be announced, and he wasn't 100 percent sure they didn't have at least one incursion. There were thirty-five more racers left to finish, and a quick look at the board told them the last racer should be there in half an hour. In the short few minutes since they sat, there had been three racers streaking across the finish line. Each time, the crowd would ooh and ah at the time posted on the board.

There were two clusters of racers that managed to bunch up like they did when *Vanishing Point* was on the last challenge. As they crossed the finish line, Chad had to admit that it was pretty exciting watching them even though he had just experienced the same thing himself. A lone racer crossed the line to the cheers of the fans. Helmut saw it was Fokker Racing, and he checked the board for their finish time. A smile formed on his face when he saw *Vanishing Point* ran the course nine minutes and fifty-six seconds faster than his brothers. It was too early to celebrate, but he couldn't wait to see the look on Wolfgang's and Hans's faces.

The last racer crossed the line, and the fan excitement didn't suffer. The next part was by far the most nerve-racking for everyone. The results of the race were announced. The unique twist was they would announce the results in reverse order. Usually, roughly half the field would make an error that would add so much time. They would be knocked completely out of contention. For instance, missing a deep space gate and searching for it could add as much as ten minutes to their time.

When the team from the last racer made it to the grandstands, announcer Ted O'Danials addressed the fans, "Ladies and gentlemen, we have the results for the fifty-third running of the Raytheon Challenge."

The fans erupted in cheers. O'Danials continued, "We only have one that didn't finish this year. The Triumph team bounced off an asteroid and couldn't limp in. The crew has been recovered, and they're in the hospital for observation." His co-announcer Bud Johnson added, "We just got word from the hospital that Team Triumph pilots are in good condition except for some rather large bruises."

"That's good news," O'Danials stated. "Now the race results."

While O'Danials read the results, Helmut was watching his brothers. They hadn't given the board a look since sitting in the grandstands. Hans studied the board while Helmut watched from his seat. It was very obvious when he read the Schnellmaschine results. He immediately got Wolfgang's attention and pointed at the scoreboard.

Wolfgang's smile disappeared while he worked out things in his head. He then leaned over to Hans and said something while Hans nodded. Helmut thought he must have said something like their little brother couldn't possibly have run the course without ringing up a pile of incursion penalties.

Jeremy was looking for Roger Denton of Delta Racing. He finally found him a short distance away, talking with the pilots. To Jeremy's eye, Roger didn't look like a man that was convinced his team did well. Perhaps he was still remembering his and Phil's performance in the pits. Also, it was his understanding that Dwight and Gus turned in two incredibly fast pit stops themselves. He was sure that his Hedron pit crew was given instructions to report on how the Schnellmaschine crew did.

When O'Danials got to the twentieth place, Chad gave him his full attention. Indeed, it was becoming more interesting for everyone. Getting into the top third of the field was actually quite prestigious, even if the other competitors didn't act like it if you didn't get to the podium. Any top twenty competitors are good enough to be a thorn in their side in any race.

"Coming in at number twenty, *Fantasma*, of Santiago Powersports. Raw score, 4 hours, 3 minutes, 12.56 seconds. Ten-second penalty for incursion at the start gate of the Endeavor Asteroid Cluster. Final score, 4 hours, 3 minutes, 22.56 seconds," O'Danials reported.

Chad and the rest expected *Vanishing Point* to be the next announced, but it wasn't happening. Experienced contestants knew the faster contestants tended to make more incursions than the others. They tended to think that a ten-second penalty here or there was worth it if it meant they shaved off more than that incurring the penalty.

The teams that haven't been announced yet were getting anxious. O'Danials continued, "Number six, *Shock Wave* of Delta Racing. Raw score, 3 hours, 58 minutes, 4.46 seconds. Two incursions, 10-second penalty at Endeavor exit gate, and a 10-second penalty at deep space gate number two. Final score, 3 hours, 58 minutes, 24.46 seconds.

It took Jeremy a few seconds to realize that his team beat Denton's team. At this point, he really didn't care as long as Schnellmaschine was ahead of Delta Racing. O'Danials moved on to the next place. "Number five, *Teufel* of Fokker Racing. Raw score, 3 hours, 58 minutes 12.29 seconds. Clean run. No incursions or penalties. Final score, same as raw score."

O'Danials announced the number four finished, but no one on the Schnellmaschine team heard who it was. They just knew it wasn't them. Chad and Helmut realized they were going to be on the podium, and they had a hard time believing it. Just as Chad thought there was a terrible mistake, O'Danials said with increased excitement in his voice. "Now the three you've been waiting for."

There was an uproar in the grandstands, and everybody could see clearly who the top three were. O'Danials continued, "Number three, *Banshee* of Dublin Speed Merchants. Raw score, 3 hours 55 minutes, 48.84 seconds. One incursion, altitude incursion on the atmospheric leg, a 20-second penalty. Final score, 3 hours 56 minutes, 8.84 seconds."

Everybody cheered as the Dublin Speed Merchants made their way to the podium. "Number two, *Vanishing Point* of Schnellmaschine Racing. Raw score, 3 hours, 48 minutes, 16.25 seconds! Clean run, no incursions!" Chad and Helmut made their way to the podium and stood in the second-place tier and shook hands with the Dublin Speed Merchants.

"That leaves just one left! With a raw score of 3 hours, 46 minutes, 58.26 seconds, no incursions or penalties! *Greased Lightning* of Waltz Racing!" The pilots of Waltz Racing, who turned out to be Vernon's son and nephew, went to the podium and stood on the top tier after shaking hands with the Speed Merchants and Schnellmaschine pilots.

The official named Ben approached the podium, Miss Raytheon was with him, and the official named Ned pushed a cart with three trophies. The trophies were distributed to the cheers and fanfare from the fans then the traditional champagne bottles were passed out. The three teams on the podium were all independents, which was unique in this contest. Chad and Helmut didn't mind one bit coming in second. In fact, standing on the podium was actually a crazy fantasy earlier that day. Everyone felt that the Waltz Racing team deserved to be number one after putting in their dues for so many years. When the champagne was consumed, actually most of it was sprayed out, soaking everyone in close proximity. They posed for photographs and finally were allowed to go back to their pits.

There was a postrace dinner afterward, where the Schnellmaschine Racing team was treated with a little more respect. They were actually becoming good friends with Vernon Waltz and his team. In fact, all the independents got along quite well. The corporate teams were a bit more contrite than they were before the race. Roger Denton avoided running into Jeremy that evening. In fact, Jeremy made somewhat of a game out of circulating through the crowd, making sure to get close enough to Roger to cause him to make an excuse to move to another part of the ballroom. Some of the other attendees figured out what Jeremy was doing and did what they could to help Jeremy out. After a little while, Roger made his excuses and left the party early.

Helmut tracked down his brothers, who suddenly decided to treat their little brother with a bit more deference. When they said their goodbyes, Helmut smiled and said, "Tell Mama and Papa to expect to see me sitting around the Tannenbaum this Christmas.

The next day, there was a full day of promotional tasks to be carried out. The three podium teams were interviewed as a group and individually, then clean uniforms were put on for photographs. The day after that, Vanishing Point was rolled back into the shipping container along with the tools and other materials that belonged to the team. The container was shuttled to orbit and attached to a freighter bound for Oasis 4.

Chad and Helmut's heads were swimming from the excitement and attention. It was nothing in comparison to how the Waltz Racing team felt. Vernon, his son, and nephew became very good friends with the Schnellmaschine team. The Speed Merchants were also very friendly, but they all drank more than a comfortable amount in Chad's opinion although, while shaking hands, their pilot said to Chad while grinning from ear to ear. "Kowalski, now there's a good Irish name. You needed that kind of luck to beat us. We'll see next year. We'll make sure we're not hungover like this year."

✶✶✶✶✶

## The *Aurora*, Astrodyne 65, Owned by Stellar Logistics and Freight Corporation

The Schnellmaschine team was on board the *Aurora* with Gus and Dwight at the controls. Again, everyone was in the cockpit talking about their experience on Raytheon. Phil noticed that Chad wasn't contributing to the conversation and was just absent-mindedly staring off into space. Phil smiled. "What's on your mind, Chad?"

Chad was caught off guard but recovered in a few seconds. His lips formed a thin smile. "Ever since I was a kid, I've always dreamed of standing on the winner's podium. What kid hasn't? I came into this thing not expecting to even place in the top twenty. I know I said we were good enough on paper to get in the top ten or even win. But I never really expected to do as well as we did. I wonder if this is how Henry Ford felt when he won his race in 1901, which helped jump-start his company. One thing is certain, however, this experience is something no one will be able to take away. If I never race again, I'll never forget how I feel right now and the friends who helped make that happen.

The End

# FUGITIVES

**Oasis 4, Trading Center Space Station, Owned by the
Stellar Logistics and Freight Corporation**

Brenda Gleason was midway through her shift in the control center coordinating the movement of freighters and other various vessels to and from the station. They were coming off a rush where dozens of vessels arrived and departed in a short period. The rest of her shift would be considerably less hectic. There was a lull in the activity, so she checked the plot. The outer edge of plot coverage was one million kilometers. Approaching vessels didn't have to contact the station until they reached the five-hundred-kilometer point.

*****

***Langyous Mining Shuttle 265***

Ubtel was looking over the shoulder of the maldor flying the shuttle. They had just cut the light-speed engine and verified their position. He saw they were precisely where they wanted to be, but Ubtel had doubts and shook his head. "Are you sure it's necessary that we stop here, Bagpin?"

"Only if we want to eat," Bagpin answered. "Besides, this shuttle is on its last breaths."

Ubtel leaned back in his seat. "I just don't want to end up a slave again. I don't know anything about humans or their feelings about slavery."

Bagpin furrowed his brow. "We'll just have to hope our forged passports and identification are up to the task of concealing our identity."

"This vessel isn't designed for venturing this far from its home port," Ubtel observed while looking around. "I wouldn't want to trust it any further than this space station. How do you propose we continue our journey?"

Bagpin shrugged. "Perhaps we can sign onto a freighter and simply leave the shuttle here."

"Perhaps fortune will stay with me, and I can find a freighter going to Flast," Ubtel said hopefully.

Bagpin frowned. "I don't think it would be a good idea if you went to Flast right away. Once you determine what the situation is on Flast, and you've made some money, you can arrange to get your family off planet."

Ubtel stared out into space. "Perhaps you're right. Getting recaptured wouldn't do anyone any good. I miss my family more than you can imagine. I have to be careful. It's not my undoing."

Bagpin nodded in understanding. "I feel the same about my family. Fortunately for me, I'll be welcomed home by the authorities. Your situation is admittedly more difficult."

Ubtel used a translator to find the approach procedures for Oasis 4. Bagpin adjusted their course to intersect a course at a reporting point. Ubtel nervously asked, "Are you sure you can pass yourself off as a qualified pilot?"

"I've listened to my former master do it enough. I think I can make a passable effort," Bagpin assured him. "It's the docking that has me concerned."

*****

## Oasis 4, Control Center

Brenda tapped the blip that represented the incoming vessel on the plot. A dialogue box appeared that provided data on the vessel. She read what was presented and saw it was a maldor short-range shuttle, the registration number, and the general specifications of the vessel. A quick inquiry of the computer determined that there wasn't a flight plan. That actually wasn't all that odd. There were always shuttles arriving without flight plans. She should find out in a few minutes who these folks are in a few minutes anyway.

*****

### *Langyous Mining Shuttle 265*

Bagpin checked his position on the navigation display and took a deep breath. He keyed his microphone. "Oasis 4, *Langyous shuttle 265* on the Prospector Alpha approach outer reporting point. Inbound for docking."

*****

### Oasis 4, Control Center

Brenda keyed her microphone. "*Langyous 265*, continue inbound, observe velocity step-downs at established points. Will you need passenger facilities, or will normal facilities be to your liking?"

*****

### *Langyous Mining Shuttle 265*

"Oasis 4, *Langyous 265*, normal docking facilities will do just fine," Bagpin answered. They carried on toward the station, slowing at the prescribed points. When they were in visual range, Brenda assigned them CargoMod 2, Docking Port 18. Bagpin carried on toward the station and slowed to a relative crawl when he reached the final position fix reroute to the station. The approach procedures feature of the navigation system had a translation that helped them identify the number two on top of CargoMod 2 and a diagram to help them find docking port eighteen.

Brenda's voice came over the radio. *"Langyous 265, Oasis 4, will you need vector assist to find the docking port?"*

Bagpin keyed the microphone. "Negative Oasis 4, we have the directory displayed."

"Very well, *Langyous 265*, proceed direct to docking. Welcome to Oasis 4," Brenda directed.

Bagpin carefully bumped the thrusters edging the ten-meter-long shuttle closer to the docking port. When they reached 18, he came to a stop. He engaged the viewer used to align with docking clamps. Bagpin was learning that moving a shuttle sideways wasn't as easy a maneuver as it should be, in his mind. He needed to constantly adjust the roll to prevent the top or bottom locking lugs from engaging before the others. Having the viewer that was intended to assist in moving sideways face forward made things awkward.

The docking clamps engaged then retracted, pulling the shuttle into contact with the station. Ubtel checked the seals at the hatch and found them to be behaving acceptably. A station worker connected umbilicals and opened the station air lock. Ubtel opened the shuttle air lock and was greeted by the station worker. "Good afternoon. My name is Andy. I see on my pad that you've been here before. We still operate in the same manner, any cargo handling requirements you may need, you can make a request on the SICOS. To visit the rest of the station, you'll have to clear customs at the end of the CargoMod. Do you have any immediate questions or needs?"

Ubtel shook his head. "Not at the moment. My partner and I will be enjoying the hospitality of this station. We may have needs later. We'll have to wait and see."

Andy bid them a good day and left to attend to other duties. Bagpin came out of the cockpit, laughing. "You did that remarkably well. Are you sure you weren't an actor or a spy before being sold as a slave?"

*****

## Oasis 4, CargoMod 2, Customs Desk

There were two security officers at the customs desk, meaning Ubtel and Bagpin didn't have to wait. Both officers motioned the pair to seats. The officer opposite Ubtel asked, "Passport, please?"

The officer took the document and opened the passport. He examined the picture and English text. Then he placed it on a pad that accessed the data chip. Then he had Ubtel look directly into a retina scanner. He then ensured the information printed matched the information on the data chip and the database of passport holders in the Multi-World Commerce Cooperative. There were small telltale signs that the passport was a well-crafted fake. He casually pressed a series of buttons that directed SICOS to start identifying the individual in front of him using facial recognition. "I take it that you're here for business?"

"Yes, I am," Ubtel confirmed.

The deputy tapped a series of keys on his SICOS, and a document appeared on the screen. The deputy turned the display to afford Ubtel a look, then he asked, "Did you review the station regulations on your journey?"

Ubtel nodded. "Yes, I did."

The deputy handed him a stylus. "If there are no questions, please sign as an acknowledgment of your understanding."

Ubtel signed the document and handed the stylus back. The deputy stamped the passport with an Oasis 4 entry stamp, which also added a digital stamp to the data chip and the Multi-World Commerce Cooperative database. He then smiled and said, "Welcome aboard Oasis 4."

The conversation the other deputy had with Bagpin went in roughly the manner. Ubtel and Bagpin were allowed to enter the station. After they disappeared into the connector tunnel, the two deputies looked at each other. The deputy that handled Bagpin asked, "Was yours also a fake?"

"Yes, it was," he answered with a nod. "Weird thing, though, facial recognition has him as Ubtel. He was sold into slavery about three years ago."

The deputy nodded. "My guy had a similar thing going on. The difference is he's maldor. I wonder what the deception is for?"

"There are several possibilities," he mused. "I think they're afraid we might return them to their slave owners. Unfortunately, they don't pay us to figure out their stories. I'll call the boss."

He tapped a code into the intercom and was rewarded with the sound of Luke Smith's voice. "What do ya need, Jonesy?"

"Edwards and I just had two guys come through with fake passports," Jones answered.

Luke frowned. "Why did you let them on the station?"

"Facial recognition identifies them as victims of the slave trade," Jones answered.

Luke relaxed. "Oh, I see. Good job, guys. Send me the data on these two. I'll take it from here."

*****

## Oasis 4, Upper CentMod, Security Office

Luke accessed the files Jones and Edwards sent to him. He quickly scanned the data. "A flaston and a maldor." He was very aware that escaped slaves would be very hesitant to announce who they were to people they didn't know. He pondered about how he should approach this situation, then decided that the direct approach was best.

Luke turned in his seat. "SICOS, where are the new arrivals, Ubtel and Bagpin?"

SICOS replied, "Upper CentMod, plaza level." "SICOS, where is Lynuna, Flast consular general?" "Lynuna is in Sliders Pool Hall" came the digital reply.

"Where is Walzticor Raffdon, Pintex consular general?" Luke pressed.

SICOS didn't hesitate. "Walzticor Raffdon is in Thunder Lanes Bowling Alley."

Walzticor had a reputation for dawdling, so he called him first, "SICOS, connect me to Thunder Lanes desk, please."

The Thunder Lanes Saturday manager answered, "What can I do for you, Marshal Smith?"

Luke was to the point. "Could you please have Consular General Walzticor meet me in Eva's in thirty minutes?"

The manager assured him he would pass the message. Then he had SICOS connect him with Slider. "Hey, Slider. Could I speak to Lynuna?"

Lynuna appeared on the screen, "What can I do for you, Marshal Smith?" "We have two new arrivals traveling on fake passports," Luke explained. "One of them is flaston."

Lynuna was puzzled. "If they're fugitives, you don't need my permission to arrest them."

"I'm afraid you don't quite understand, Miss Lynuna. They appear to be escaped slaves," Luke explained.

"Oh, I see," Lynuna said. "You want me to reassure them? Where do you want to meet?"

"I asked Walzticor to meet me in Eva's in thirty minutes," Luke answered.

*****

## Oasis 4, Upper CentMod, Plaza Level

Ubtel and Bagpin were quite overwhelmed by what they were experiencing. For the last three years or so, Ubtel spent his time in the dark and noisy mines of a mining planet when he wasn't sleeping. Bagpin, for much of his life, lived in the back of the shuttle he stole to bring him here. The brightness of the CentMod dazzled them. Standing there looking at the meal choices made their heads swim.

Bagpin appeared as normal as anyone else on the station, but Ubtel felt subconsciously uncomfortable in his tattered and worn mining clothes. Both men had an uncomfortable thought while surveying their surrounds. Bagpin asked, "Do you think we have enough money to get anything here?"

A wide-eyed Ubtel shook his head. "I wish we could have stolen more than a few coins. Perhaps it'll be enough to get us a slice or two of those flat pies over there," he said, pointing at the pizza kiosk.

From behind them, a voice said, "I'd be happy to buy you gents a meal."

Ubtel and Bagpin turned to see Luke strolling over to them. The uniform concerned them, but there was nothing they could do about it now. Bagpin asked, "That's very generous of you. But I have to ask why?"

"I'm surprised you have to ask, Bagpin. You and Ubtel deserve a good meal after your ordeal, and it's an honor to be the one who provides it," Luke explained.

The look on Ubtel's and Bagpin's faces bemused Luke. "Our computer used facial recognition to identify you. We knew your real names before you left the customs desk." He motioned to an escalator. "My name is Luke Smith, the security marshal here. Let's get you that meal."

Bagpin and Ubtel followed Luke up the escalator to the second level and took seats in Eva's. Luke smiled and said, "I'm sure you're not familiar with human food, so if you don't have any objections, I'll order for all of us.

"I'm sure it will be better than anything I've eaten in the last three years," Ubtel stated.

Luke smiled and ordered three Selaks. He explained that Selak was a friend of his, and the two cheeseburger, cabin fries, and strawberry soda pop were his favorite human meal. Eva brought the meals, and Luke explained what condiments when with what and reassured them that it was all down to personal taste. Ubtel and Bagpin had a difficult time eating at a civilized pace, being as they were quite hungry.

A busboy cleared the dishes, and Eva brought coffee. Bagpin sipped his coffee. "What are your intentions regarding us?"

Luke put his cup down. "We make sure you two get home, reunited with your families."

Ubtel nervously stated, "I'm not sure if it's a good idea for me to go back to Flast. It might put my family in danger. I don't expect you to understand."

A voice behind them said, "Marshal Smith understands better than you think."

They turned, and Ubtel stammered, "You're Lyn…Lyn…Lynuna!"

Lynuna smiled. "That's right, and I'm led to understand that you escaped from bondage."

Ubtel nodded. "Yes, so clearly, I'm not current in my knowledge of how things are on Flast."

Lynuna sat and added cream to the coffee Eva put down. "Well, the high points are. The Colavar Regime has been overthrown. The Flast branch of the Syndicate is being dismantled as fast as the Law Enforcement Brigade can manage it. If you're from a village that has had the local arm of the Syndicate destroyed, there shouldn't be a problem getting you home."

Another voice cried out, "Ubtel! I can't believe you're here!"

Everyone at the table spun to see Tillya standing with Isnod and Feldon.

Ubtel gasped. "Tillya! Is that you?"

"Yes, it is," Tillya answered with a smile. "I honestly thought I'd never see you again."

Ubtel had trouble containing his happiness. "Oh, it's so good to see you." Then he looked confused. "We were taken at the same time. Are you still a slave? If these people own you, why are they so anxious to get me home? If you're free, why don't you go home?"

Tillya sat at the table while Isnod and Feldon sat at an adjacent table. She looked him in the eyes. "I was a slave. I was forced to pick a fiber product called falta on a planet called Gostis. The planet was invaded, and the slaves were freed."

"Why don't you go home then?" Ubtel asked.

Tillya took a breath. "For the same reason you can't. Until very recently, Resnon was still under Syndicate control."

Ubtel nodded. "But if Resnon is no longer under Syndicate control, why don't you go home?"

"We're trying to determine if any of Covroynac's old associates are still there to make trouble," Lynuna stated. "I'll have to get a briefing from my security liaison, Palnit. The head of the Flast branch of the

Syndicate is on the run, a man named Moliston. If it's falling apart that rapidly for the Syndicate, I think very soon Resnon will be safe."

Ubtel frowned. "I remember Covroynac, his lieutenant, Pukontgore, and two henchmen named Jotlor, and Gordlid."

"Well, Covroynac is dead," Lynuna reported. "As is Jotlor and Gordlid." Ubtel leaned in. "How did they expire?"

"Apparently, his boss decided that he was a liability and decided to make sure that he couldn't do any more damage to the organization," Lynuna reported.

Ubtel smiled. "That is indeed good news. How did they go?" Lynuna shook her head. "I assure you it was quite grizzly.

Covroynac's boss in Trimlute City, a man by the name of Dulpot, had the crew of his yacht put weights on their victims and dumped them into the deepest part of Trimlute Lake. The water is so cold there. The bodies are remarkably well-preserved. We wouldn't have known about it but for one of the yacht's crewmen who pled to a reduced sentence. The Law Enforcement Brigade divers have recovered about a dozen victims of Dulpot."

"What did Covroynac do to this Dulpot person to earn that kind of treatment?" Ubtel asked.

"He told us where Pukontgore was," Isnod answered from the adjacent table.

"He also told us who his superior was."

Ubtel stared at Isnod for a couple of seconds. "I don't imagine that made this Dulpot happy. What is your name, please?"

"I am Isnod, and this is Feldon of I & F Investigations and Retrievals," Isnod answered. "We paid Covroynac a visit to find out where Pukontgore was hiding. With some carefully applied persuasion, he gave us the information we were after. Apparently, that demonstrated a certain lack of commitment to the organization they belonged to."

Ubtel nodded slowly, then asked, "What happened to Pukontgore?" "Moliston sent him here, along with Dulpot, his lieutenant, and with a hundred dragons, to kill everyone on this station," Lynuna answered. "Is he dead?" Ubtel asked hopefully.

Isnod chuckled. "No, but I'll wager he wishes he was.

"What happened to him?" Ubtel asked with growing interest.

"My parents were here at the time," Tillya stated. "Pukontgore spotted Father up here during the fight. He came up here to face him, and Feldon challenged him."

Ubtel was wide-eyed. "Pukontgore knows micton. How did you survive the fight, let alone beat him?" He thought for a second. "You did beat him, didn't you?"

Feldon chuckled and pointed over to a piece of the floor near the railing. "Right over there. He begged me to quit. My micton was a little sharper than his. Not by much, but sharper."

"Where is he now?" Ubtel asked.

"Regorn Asteroid Prison," Lynuna answered.

Ubtel looked at his coffee cup. "What's the next step in getting me home?"

Lynuna thought for a second or two. "You may well be part of the final step in determining if it's safe to return to Resnon. There was some question concerning Covroynac's thugs that weren't in his organization. I understand that they have been identified, but there have been too few collaborating witnesses. We'll see my Security Liaison Palnit directly."

Walzticor Raffdon, Pintex consular general, walked to the table. "I'm so sorry I've kept you waiting. I had to finish my match against the grunst consular general."

"Please have a seat, Mr. Raffdon," Luke offered. As the consular sat, Luke motioned to Bagpin. "This is Bagpin Dront. He recently escaped from slavery."

Consular Walzticor gasped. "We need to get you home. How long have you been in bondage?"

Bagpin shrugged. "Since I was a child. My classmates and I were on a trip when we were taken. I don't know where everyone else went, but I was sold to a man called Fillgan, who kept me on board his shuttle. I would load and unload the cargo, keep the shuttle clean, and even some maintenance duties."

Walzticor was intrigued. "Did your master teach you to operate a vessel?"

Bagpin shook his head. "Heavens no. I learned by carefully watching him. I had to be very careful, as he would have suspected I was going to do what I did."

"How did you two manage to escape?" Luke asked.

Ubtel laughed. "It came as a surprise to both of us. One of the few times that I've been tasked with something out of the mines, I was sent to the shuttle port to move some of the supplies from shuttles and containers to the warehouse. I saw Bagpin take a beating for some perceived transgression. I don't know what it was precisely, but something stirred in me. If there was a way to leave, I decided I would try, no matter the risk. I looked down, and there it was, sitting on a work table, a tool kit for the tracking collars. I found a pile of coins in a desk drawer and a pallet of shuttle rations that I grabbed two weeks' worth for two people."

Luke furrowed his brow. "They let you wander around the facility unsupervised, with collar tools lying about?"

Ubtel smiled. "A portion of good fortune for me. The shuttle port has always been known among the slaves as a place of relaxed diligence. Besides, they could track us with the collar. I made sure to throw my collar in a transporter that was heading to the most distant mining facility. After that, I simply waited until a cargo tram was going past Bagpin's shuttle and used it to conceal my movement there."

Walzticor interrupted, "I can imagine the decision to flee was difficult for you, Bagpin, being as you've been a slave since childhood."

Bagpin smiled thinly. "The beating helped in that regard. I admit, I was feeling quite sorry for myself and wept a little. The human slaves I've met had a saying that has stayed with me. I was at the end of my rope. Quite an accurate summing up of my condition. I looked up, and a flaston slave was standing at the door of the shuttle. He just looked at me and said we would be better off away from that place. I showed him where to put his belongings, where to sit, and closed the hatch."

Ubtel interrupted with a laugh. "Then you performed the worst, most frightening, and wonderful takeoff I've ever hoped to experience."

Luke laughed at that, as he was very sure he would probably feel the same way. A thought occurred to him. "Do you know the name of the planet you were on?"

Bagpin shook his head. "My former master called it mining planet three. I can tell you it's the only mining planet we visited with an atmosphere. I know very little about navigation. In fact, we had to orbit a deserted planet until we could figure out the navigation computer. We decided to come here as it was on the way to Flast, and it's also convenient for Pintex."

Luke frowned. "Have you been here before?"

Bagpin nodded. "Oh yes, we picked up a consignment of fasteners for customers, but I wasn't allowed off of the vessel."

Luke hated to hear that there was an opportunity to make someone's life better if he had just known. He put that aside for now, "If you don't mind Bagpin, I'd like to have one of my deputies go aboard your vessel and download the navigation history records."

Bagpin grinned. "If I never see that shuttle ever again, I won't miss it. You may do whatever you wish to it. Besides, it's not really mine is it."

Luke grinned back. "Actually, it is your shuttle. There's a little clause in the Multi-World Commerce Cooperative Charter that says any vessel confiscated by a slave from a slaveholder for the purpose of escape is now the property of the former slave."

Bagpin thought and nodded. "Perhaps I can sell it. It'll help me start my new life."

"You know," Luke said. "I think I might know some folks that would be eager to purchase that shuttle."

Bagpin shook his head. "It's quite worn out. I'm not sure how much I'll get for it or if it's even ethical to burden someone with it."

"I wouldn't worry about that," Luke stated. "As long as there's full disclosure at the sale."

Lynuna stood. "For now, let's get Ubtel checked in at the Star Lodge Suites and then some decent clothes."

Walzticor smiled. "That's an excellent notion. We'll do the same, Bagpin. I'll take the rest of the day and get you somewhat settled. Then tomorrow, we'll work on getting you home."

"Yes, one step at a time," Lynuna agreed. "Is Mr. Ross expected soon? He usually loves to welcome special guest."

Luke grinned. "He's expected tomorrow. Team Schnellmaschine came in second place by the way."

"Oh that's wonderful!" Lynuna gushed. "Everyone talks about how talented Chad Kowalski and Helmut Schultz are. Now we have proof."

*****

## Oasis 4, Upper CentMod, Plaza Level

Virginia had spread the word that the Schnellmaschine Racing Team had docked, and anyone who wanted to greet them should be in the Upper CentMod. Phil, Gus, Jeremy, Dwight, Helmut, and finally, Chad walked out of the connector tunnel into the CentMod to the cheers of everyone who gathered. Chad and Helmut held the Raytheon Challenge Second Place Trophy over their heads.

Will Dawson led the group to the Central Column, where he had built a trophy case. Each side of the case had photos of their racer, Vanishing Point, taken at various points during the race. Chad and Helmut placed the trophy in the case, and Will secured the door.

The crowd began to disburse, and some came forward to shake hands and offer personal congratulations. Phil was smooching with Alice when Lynuna approached them. "Please accept my congratulations, Mr. Ross, to your team!"

Phil smiled back. "Thank you very much, Miss Lynuna, but it certainly isn't my team. Chad and Helmut are more properly the team leaders."

Chad heard what Phil said and looked over his shoulder. "We learned from the best, Boss," he said while Helmut chuckled.

"Well, congratulations to all of you," Lynuna corrected herself. "May I give you another reason to celebrate?"

Phil smiled. "Anytime."

Lynuna pulled Ubtel to her. "This is Ubtel. He just arrived yesterday. He escaped from slavery with a maldor, and we're working on getting him home."

Phil and Alice smiled broadly at the news. Alice said, "We're taking the Schnellmaschine team to dinner. Why don't you and Ubtel join us at the Circle T? Oh, and Isnod, of course."

Lynuna smiled. "We'll be there. You should know, Ubtel was a neighbor of Tillya."

"Oh my goodness," a shocked Alice said. "You'll have to make sure Tillya and Feldon are there too."

Phil frowned. "You said there was a maldor with him. Is he here?" At that moment, Walzticor strolled up with Bagpin in tow. "Ah, Mr. Ross! I have someone here I would like to introduce you to." He introduced Bagpin, "Mr. Ross, this is Bagpin, former slave."

Phil smiled. "I'll give you the same invitation we gave Ubtel. Why don't you and Walzticor join us for dinner at the Circle T to celebrate? Walzticor, please bring your lovely wife. We'll meet you there at eighteen hundred hours."

*****

## Oasis 4, Lower CentMod, The Circle T

Everyone was enjoying the meal and atmosphere of the Circle T. It was hard not to. There was no shortage of topics for conversation at their table as everyone was very interested in Chad and Helmut's perspective on the race and Ubtel and Bagpin's experiences as slaves. As everyone conversed, Phil saw that both Isnod and Feldon were a bit preoccupied.

After dinner, they all went to the Upper CentMod for ice cream. The conversations that were started in the Circle T were continued well into the early evening. Everyone was preparing to call it a night although there was still quite a crowd in the CentMod. Unexpectedly, Isnod stood and hollered, "Is there a man here who wishes to court Lynuna? I have to know now, or you will be silent on this matter forever more!"

Feldon stood. "Anyone who wishes to court Tillya, show yourself now! I will not remain patient in this matter!"

The CentMod was silent while Isnod and Feldon stood there looking very intimidating. Finally, Isnod walked over to Lynuna. "I declare an end to our courtship. Would you enter into eternal bonds with me?"

Lynuna stood. "It would be the pinnacle event of my life."

Feldon walked to Tillya. "I declare an end to our courtship. If you agreed to enter into eternal bonds with me, I would be joyful."

Tillya stood and looked Feldon in the eyes and answered in a quivering voice, "I would share in that joy."

The whole CentMod was silent for a few seconds. The silence was broken with a splattering of applause from different directions. Alice asked, "So how does this work? Do we get invitations to the wedding?"

Ubtel leaned over. "That's not how weddings work on Flast. You just witnessed the most public part of a flaston wedding. The next step is to go to Flast and record their commitment to the proper authority. Or there may be an authority here in the station consulate. At any rate, as a practical matter, they are married."

*****

## Oasis 4, Operations Center, Briefing Room 1

Phil walked into the briefing room and filled his mug, took his seat, and brought the meeting to order, "Nice to be back. First up, operations."

Virginia looked at her pad. "Everything is as normal as can be, especially now that upper management has come back from his junket."

It took Phil a few seconds to pick up on what Virginia was alluding to. Phil had made a point of setting the policy where now that he had Gus as an assistant, one of them should be there if the other went off station. Now here, both Phil and Gus went off to be pit crew for Chad and Helmut. There was no graceful way to excuse their departure from protocol. He just nodded. "I'm picking up on what you're saying. You're right, of course. I guess we got caught up in the moment."

Virginia laughed. "I wasn't saying that it was an imposition. I just couldn't help myself. Actually, I don't have anything to report other than everything in operations is fine."

Phil got the reports from medical and facilities maintenance. Then he turned to Luke. "How's everything in security?"

"Nothing to report except we're waiting on a response from Flast law enforcement on the status of Resnon. That's the Village Tillya and Ubtel are from. Walzticor is in the process of booking passage for Bagpin on a Pintex bound freighter."

Phil made a note on his pad, then asked, "What sort of information do you need from Flast?"

"Apparently, the Syndicate thug in Resnon would hire street-level muscle when needed. These local yoyos aren't technically in the Syndicate, but they could make things very uncomfortable for certain people if they were trying to get into the organization," Luke reported.

Phil frowned. "It sounds to me like the Flast branch of the Syndicate is imploding. I would expect that Ubtel could go home anytime."

Luke nodded. "That's what I'm expecting. In fact, I'll bet Tillya and Feldon will go back with him."

That caught Phil off guard. "Oh yeah, you know, I'd love to be there when she sees it for the first time in this many years. On another note, what's the status of the shuttle Ubtel and Bagpin arrived in?"

"I had my evidence technician download the navigation history, then go through the ship with a fine-toothed comb," Luke reported. "We gathered a ton of data about Bagpin's former master and passed it to Tim Davis of the FBI. One of the more interesting things we found was a kit made for constructing fake passports. It's a nice one too. If Bagpin and Ubtel knew how to use it properly, we would have likely never known they were fakes. They even had software that added the fake data to the MWCC database."

"Two questions," Phil said. "Was there any cargo on the shuttle?

Also, what's the disposition of the shuttle and its cargo?"

Luke nodded. "There were cases of fasteners on board of various sizes and styles. They are on consignment with Onustkay, licensed commodities and bulk merchandise dealer. The plotors are very interested in buying the shuttle, contingent on the vessel maintenance report."

Phil made a note on his pad. "Jeremy, I don't expect you to know what's happening in your department on your first day back."

Jeremy nodded. "Well, I have some idea of what's happening in vessel maintenance, as I've asked the lead mechanics about the happenings for the last week. The only notable thing today is the maldor shuttle. I'll put Chad on it. He's pretty good at identifying genuine problems in maldor equipment. He'll tell us if any maladies have to be corrected with overhaul, or parts, or with a simple adjustment."

*****

## Oasis 4, Lower CentMod, Flast Consulate

Luke entered the Flast Consulate and was directed directly to Lynuna's office. He walked in, and she smiled. "Ah, Marshal Smith, please come in. Palnit says he has news that concerns all of us."

Luke looked around and saw Lynuna, Palnit, Ubtel, Tillya, Isnod, and Feldon. He took a seat and smiled. "By the look on Palnit's face, I'll bet it's good news."

Palnit nodded. "Indeed. With the Syndicate on Flast crumbling and in disarray, Resnon has been declared clean of Syndicate influence, including informants. As an added precaution, the Law Enforcement Brigade staffed the local office with new personnel."

Ubtel could hardly contain his jubilance. "I'm going to see if a freighter will sign me on for the journey to Flast."

"Why go through all that?" Isnod asked. "You can go back with us in our Pulsar."

"Four of us have to record our commitments, you know," Isnod answered.

Lynuna and Tillya's expressions belied the fact that they hadn't even considered they had to complete their weddings. "I hadn't even thought of that," Lynuna uttered.

Tillya stared blankly into space. "I'm going home."

Feldon smiled. "For a few days at least. Remember, it's traditional that we spend three nights at your parents' house, then three nights at my parents' house."

Tillya shook her head and grinned. "This is moving too fast, wonderfully fast. I thought when the time came, I would just move back with my parents, but I have a life here."

Feldon smiled. "Well, Isnod and I plan on staying here for the time being, and you've made a place for yourself here. There's no reason you can't continue your career after visiting home."

Luke smiled. "By my math, you've earned a couple of weeks' vacation time by now. Go ahead and use some. You may be surprised how some time off will reenergize you, and you may even look forward to coming back."

Ubtel frowned. "What's vacation time?"

"Oh, sorry," Luke apologized. "I believe it's called relaxation period credits on Flast."

Ubtel anxiously asked, "When can we leave?"

Lynuna smiled. "If it's all the same to Isnod and Feldon, I'd say as early as tomorrow. I need to do one or two things at the consulate before I can leave. But I have to say. I think Tillya should probably give her employer more notice."

Tillya was about to say something, but Luke cut her off, "I think, under the circumstances, they'll be happy to let her go. I'll tell you what, Tillya, we'll go to Virginia together after this, and I'll help you explain things."

"That's very kind of you, Marshal Smith," Tillya uttered.

Tillya left the consulate with Luke to see Virginia. Lynuna set to prepare the consulate for her absence. That left Isnod, Feldon, and Ubtel to look for something to do. The trio decided to go to the Upper CentMod for coffee.

Isnod, Feldon, and Ubtel caught up to Luke and Tillya and rode the platform lift to the Upper CentMod with them. The platform stopped at the plaza level, and Tillya spotted Virginia and Phil in Eva's, waving them over. They walked to the up escalator and rode it up, then strode to Eva's.

After they took seats, Virginia said, "Tillya, I need you to go to operations today and sign your vacation request."

A bemused Tillya frowned. "How did you know I was going to need time off?"

"Isnod and Feldon's hollering yesterday was our first clue," Phil said with a laugh. "We talked with Ubtel here for a while longer after the declarations, and he told us what the expectations were afterward.

Virginia continued, "I have you down for two weeks. If you need more time, we can work something out. When are you leaving?"

"We were shooting for tomorrow," Feldon Put in.

Virginia smiled. "No point in messing about. Congratulations, you two."

Tillya smiled back. "I can't tell all of you how I feel. I've been blessed with two families, and I'm finding out leaving this one, even if it's just for two weeks, is harder than I can imagine. Maybe I'm being silly."

"Just a little," Phil said with a laugh. Then he said, "No one deserves to feel that way more than you do. When all of you see your folks, say hello for Alice and myself."

At that moment, Bagpin came out of the bank with Riv, Fen, and Bug. Riv was clutching a bill of sale. "Thank you, Bagpin. My government authorized me to purchase a vessel, and it's our good fortune you had one for sale."

Bagpin bowed slightly. "The good fortune is mine. I just wish it was in better condition."

"Ba," Riv said with a wave of his hand. "Chad, the technician, assures us the vessel needs some adjustments and some minor parts to get it in top condition again. In fact, he said we could upgrade the systems for minimal expense."

Bagpin smiled and bowed again. "I'm very happy you're satisfied with the transaction."

They parted company, and Bagpin spotted Ubtel in Eva's. He walked over, and Phil waved him to a seat. "Join us for coffee."

Bagpin grinned. "Thank you very much. I'm glad I caught you all. I needed to see Ubtel."

"What did you need me for?" Ubtel asked.

Bagpin reached into his pocket and produced an envelope with a First Galaxy and Trust Bank logo. He handed it to Ubtel. "This is for you."

Ubtel opened the envelope and pulled out a paper. He found the flaston text and read it. "This is a bank draft for five hundred goaners in my name!"

Luke was looking over his shoulder. "That's what it is, all right. It even has the electronic chip embedded in the corner with the particulars on it."

A shocked Ubtel looked at Bagpin. "What? How?"

Bagpin smiled. "I sold the shuttle, and Onustkay found a buyer for the cargo.

Half is yours."

Ubtel protested, "The shuttle was in your name."

Bagpin shook his head. "It wouldn't have been under my name in the first place if you hadn't shown up in the hatch that day. No, it's every bit yours as it is mine. I don't know much about finances, but it sounds like we may have put our futures in a better spot."

Ubtel put the envelope in his shirt pocket. "I never expected this. Speaking of better spots, have you secured a passage home yet?"

Bagpin nodded. "One of the human Star series is headed to Pintex this evening. How about you?"

"My friends leave for Flast tomorrow morning on their shuttle," Ubtel answered with thinly concealed elation.

Bagpin stood. "I had better get ready." He looked about the group. "I do hope our paths cross again one day." Then he turned and left.

*****

## Pulsar 1250, Owned by I&F Investigations and Retrievals

They left Oasis 4 without delay and made an uneventful journey to Flast. The navigation computer was providing a countdown to light speed engine cut. Tillya and Ubtel were in the cockpit when Feldon cut the light-speed engine.

The view in front of them came into sharp focus, and Flast was directly ahead and growing larger. Tillya and Ubtel were having difficulties keeping their emotions in check as they approached their home planet.

They received clearance directly to Brintnonopek shuttle port. Feldon followed established, published procedures for approaching and landing at the capitol shuttle port. In what seemed like no time at all, the Pulsar was settling into their assigned parking pad.

Isnod opened the hatch while Feldon secured the cockpit. A transporter arrived, and the ladies climbed aboard while Isnod, Feldon, and Ubtel loaded the baggage. Ubtel scrutinized the luggage. "These bags look brand-new."

Isnod laughed. "They're a gift from the Rosses. Apparently, there's a tradition on Earth, where newly wedded couples are gifted with items that are designed to help them establish their lives together."

Ubtel thought and nodded. "That's actually a nice tradition."

The transporter took them to the terminal, where they were greeted by Yulona and Lytrina. After they had their hugs and kisses, they introduced Ubtel. Naturally, Yulona and Lytrina couldn't help but fuss over him. After a bit, Feldon said, "If we want to catch the rail service to Raglont, we need to go now."

Lytrina laughed. "We have a couple of minutes, Feldon. Besides, all of you still need to record your commitments."

"They don't have time to go to the registration office," Lynuna blurted out.

A voice behind them said, "There's no need for that. I have everything set up here."

"Everyone, this is Veltinyette of the registration office," Yulona announced. "We have some influence there."

Veltinyette giggled. "If Isnod and Lynuna would please come forward." Isnod and Lynuna complied, and Veltinyette continued, "I have prepared the papers. Sign both copies and put your right thumbprints in the indicated areas."

The paper was made of a material that resembled parchment on Earth. The pens used to sign the documents were handmade and old-fashioned. Even the ink was a traditional recipe and would never fade. The thumbprints were made with ink made with a different formulation. It was just as durable, but it was better at showing the detail of the print. One copy of the document would go with the married couple, and the other went into the archives. When Isnod and Lynuna finished, Feldon and Tillya signed and printed their copies.

After the signing, they didn't waste any time. Isnod and Lynuna went off with her parents while Feldon, Tillya, and Ubtel boarded the rail service train to Raglont. Tillya was a bundle of emotions on the train. There were sights, sounds, and smells she was certain she would never experience again. Although it's been a relatively short period since the fall of the Colavar Regime, she could see evidence of improvement in certain things. The buildings looked more cheerful. The roads were in better condition. Even farmer's fields looked healthier.

When they reached Raglont, they boarded an on-demand rail transport pod to Resnon. The pod sped off toward Resnon, and the mood in the pod gradually changed as they got nearer to their destination. Feldon was taking the journey in stride, but Tillya and Ubtel were growing increasingly apprehensive. They didn't know why they were feeling the way they did. It's just that they've been away for so long.

The pod crested a hill and slowed, giving them their first look at Trimlute Lake. Both Tillya and Ubtel had to wipe tears from their faces at the sight. The pod descended the hill and entered the village, then stopped at the rail/dock terminal. They exited the pod. Feldon grabbed the luggage while Ubtel carried his small duffel bag. They crossed the terminal, and there was the welcoming party they were expecting.

Rosetta and Ubrose rushed to Ubtel, and all three were quite beside themselves with joy. Tillya and Feldon also enjoyed warm greetings from Yanoner and Tillmay. Once everyone had collected themselves, they made their way back to their respective homes. In the days to come, they were celebrities in Resnon. Everyone in Resnon wanted to welcome home the former slaves. The role Feldon played in bringing down Covroynac and defeating Pukontgore in hand-to-hand fighting was somehow made public. As a result, he was very popular in the village.

*****

## Oasis 4, HabMod 1, Quarters of Phil and Alice Ross

Phil was watching a baseball game that was included in the entertainment packet of the weekly data stream. The Toledo Mud Hens were playing the Lansing Lugnuts. Phil took a sip of his lager and wondered. "I wonder how Ubtel and Tillya are doing. After being away from home for so long, I would expect that it's in some ways different and familiar."

Alice looked up from her knitting. "I get the impression that Ubtel might have a harder time. Tillya's parents were here not long ago, you know. I think that will help take the edge off. Besides, she was freed from slavery a good while ago. Ubtel has only been a free man a few days. It may take a while for him to decompress."

Phil thought about it. "I think you're right. I just hope Tillya doesn't decide to stay at home. We need her here. That sounds a bit selfish on my part."

"Yes, it does," Alice agreed. "I don't think you have anything to worry about there."

Phil smiled. "You're right, I think. She'll fit in great with the company's proposed expansion. We need to get her trained up in other areas."

Alice smiled. "It's funny how things work out sometimes. Only in our circle of friends will be a former slave girl who marries a bounty hunter and becomes one of the most valued employees of a corporation headquartered thousands of light-years away."

Phil smiled back. "Yeah, funny."

The End

# LETTERS

The following are selected correspondences to and from Oasis 4 associates. It should be noted that these letters have been written over a period of several years.

Dear Phillip Ross and Oasis 4 family,

It has been some time since I visited the space station. My only regret concerning the last visit was that I was only there long enough to collect the fugitives Fel Nos and Marcus Pointer. Besides my friends, the fondest memories I have is the time I spent in Sliders Pool Hall. You may be surprised to learn I have ordered and received a pool table from an earth manufacturer. I've set it up in my home, and I practice most every night. It's also an excellent activity during get-togethers.

I am considering taking a cruise for my next vacation, and I've been looking for one that stops at Oasis 4. To that end, it would also be terrific if Slider held one of his tournaments while I was there. I'll keep an eye on Slider's internet page for tournament announcements. I've been wanting to talk to Slider about a pool hall business model here in Pretna. It occurred to me that it may be a pleasant way to spend my time in my retirement. Not that I'm ready to retire, but I'm approaching mandatory retirement age. Speaking of my profession, we have been kept very busy tracking down members of the Pretna Syndicate.

The events on Gostis and Flast have shaken loose a lot of terrible people doing terrible things, in a lot of places. I am happy to report that Syndicate activity on Pretna has fallen 83 percent in the last solar cycle.

I really must sign off now. I look forward to hearing from all of you soon.

Your friend,<br>Klon

Dear Mom, Dad, and Janis,

I hope everything on Ashbury is going as well as it was when I left for Reynolds Planet. To bring you up to date on what's happening in my life, I have been accepted into the Reconnaissance Platoon. You'll remember it was the Reconnaissance Platoon that fought the Reaction Team on Gostis.

The training is the most challenging I've experienced so far although I've done well in every stage of the training, except for tasks that require reading and mathematics. My lack of education has been a source of inconvenience, to say the least. There is a learning center here that has been an immense help in that regard. My reading has improved to an Earth tenth-grade level, and my mathematics skills are now college level. Speaking of training, you'll remember our fellow slave on Gostis, Rosanne Evans, was here with her husband, Sergeant Evans. He finished his obligation to the Mercenary organization and moved back to Earth. He was one of my training sergeants, and I can see why he was highly thought of by the other soldiers. Rosanne Evans was expecting their second child when they went back to Earth. Her first baby was a little girl.

Being in the Reconnaissance Platoon, I'm sure to be deployed on more than my share of missions, especially since the unknown purveyors of the slave trade are being discovered. There are always rumors about being sent off to fight some band of criminals or an illegitimate company's private army, but I found that it's best to ignore those things.

I must end this letter here as it's time to sleep. I hope to hear from all of you soon, and I'd like to hear how the food harvest went this season.

Your loving son,<br>George

Dear Tillya and Glinda

Another year has passed since our liberation on Gostis. Hardly a day goes by that I don't look back on those days with mixed feelings. What surprises me is I don't tend to look back in bitterness but with a fondness for the friends I've made. I did run into that young man, George, who was in the last batch of slaves that joined us. They were from Ashbury. If you remember, his father was a strange guy, Oliver. George was accepted into the Reconnaissance Platoon and was in training while Charlie was a training sergeant.

We have since moved back to Earth, where Charlie has taken over running his family's farm. We had discussed going back to New Iowa, but he had already sold the property. I'm not at all upset by it, as we thought the move off Earth was questionable in the first place. Charlie keeps quite busy growing corn, wheat, oats, soybeans, and barley. He has expressed an interest in trying sunflowers, canola, and he has a likely place on the farm to grow cranberries. Recently, I received the correspondence from Madam Zisros that she sent to all the former slaves from her farm. I was surprised when she said that she'd dropped the title "madam," and she prefers to be called Plinloo. She sounded quite sincere and contrite in her letter. I've always thought that I wouldn't want anything to remind me of those years picking falta. In some ways, that's very true, but I miss my friends a great deal.

I'm still trying to imagine the Zisros estate as a bed- and-breakfast. It doesn't surprise me that she got the idea from Alice Ross. But I was really surprised to see that she leased the old slave quarters to an investment group that turned it into a fancy restaurant. It sounds like Gostis has changed a great deal since our departure, except falta is still the number one product.

I was very happy to hear that Hukron was chosen to manage the Zisros farm while Plinloo operated the Bed and Breakfast. I have to admit I'm very curious about the social order on Gostis. Perhaps we can get together for a reunion sometime when the children are old enough to appreciate something like that.

Well, I really should be getting my chores done. Charlie doesn't do all the farm chores. As always, I look forward to hearing from you two and give my warmest regards to Feldon and Hukron.

Love, Rosanne

## Limdox Consulate Oasis 4
## Office of Riv

To: Limdox Commerce Ministry
From: Consular General Riv
Regarding: Trade goods

My fellow functionaries,

In response to your concerns that demands for our superior textile products will be greater than the current system can supply. As requested, I've made a survey of potential suppliers of raw materials among the members of the Multi-World Commerce Cooperative. It seems there is a wide variety available from each world. I have taken the trouble to secure samples of fabrics from common fiber sources.

Falta is a fiber that's in high demand, as it has some versatility in that it's durable and has a natural quality that makes it rot-resistant. Cloth made from it is used wherever toughness is a requirement. There are several worlds that grow the plant, so supply shouldn't be an issue, and multiple sources should foster a spirit of competition among suppliers, keeping prices low.

Earth has multiple fibers available, the most common is cotton. It has the same qualities as falta, but it's not as durable or rot-resistant; however, it's better suited for making bedding and clothing.

Flax is another natural product, and it's used to make a cloth called linen.

There are other fibers that are derived from, believe it or not, animals. The humans call it wool, and it's quite remarkable. The main source of wool is from animals called sheep. Cloth from wool is very warm and has a unique quality in that even when wet. It will continue to retain heat. Wool can come from other animals, some of which are considered exotic.

The most unusual exotic fiber comes from, I hesitate to say, worms. A thread called silk is secreted from the worms and gathered. Cloth made from this fiber is extraordinarily luxurious and durable.

I have assurances from the other consulates on Oasis 4 that fabric samples will be forthcoming. Of course, if there are any questions, I can be reached at the Oasis 4 Consulate office. You can order raw materials from any one of the bulk commodities dealers here. One dealer, in particular, has been very accommodating, a man named Onustkay, who does business as "Onustkay, licensed commodities and bulk merchandise dealer." He has sold some of our products and has been proven to be very trustworthy in his business dealings although I have to stress that there are other bulk commodity dealers here that enjoy equally positive reputations that will be more than happy to procure raw material for you or sell your finished product.

Please contact this office for any questions.

Consular Riv

**LIMDOX CONSULATE**
**OASIS 4**
**OFFICE OF Riv**

To: Limdox Ministry of Diplomacy
From: Consular General Riv
Regarding: Acquired shuttle

My fellow functionaries,

After responding in the affirmative to my request to acquire a serviceable craft to supplement our existing fleet, I have purchased a shuttle from maldor construction. The machine is preowned, but in acceptable condition. The technicians on Oasis 4 have submitted a written report as to the condition of the vessel. I have attached the report to this letter.

I will attempt to summarize the technical report for you. The vessel is in generally good condition except for minor items that require adjustments to operate at better efficiency.

There are mechanical items that require replacement, but the parts are very common, therefore, not very expensive.

This model of vessel is what is referred to as a short- range design. It is adequate for journeys to Oasis 4, Vestgut, and Limdox in its current configuration. However, the technicians have informed me that some components can be upgraded and our new vessel will be better able to serve us and also give us a better margin of safety. Many of the components in question are worn parts that need to be replaced anyway. Therefore, I have given permission to start the work.

It should be noted that the seller allowed the price to be adjusted to reflect the needed maintenance. I have been informed by third parties that we still paid substantially below what the vessel is worth. The seller was motivated by personal circumstances.

If you have concerns about the human technicians we've been working with, please let me put your mind to rest. The technician that is performing the work is quite possibly the best in the Stellar Logistics system. In fact, he and others have modified a ship's escape pod into a racing vessel. They recently returned from a very prestigious race they participated in and came in second position. I have included an information packet on this race and attached it to this letter. That is one of the many reasons I have confidence in using humans for this purpose.

We have made arrangements with the station chief flight instructor about getting our pilots checked out in the new machine. He also suggested a course in space flight operations to make up for gaps in their education. That sounded prudent, so I have agreed to have him design a program for our personnel.

Given the state of our fleet, it's my recommendation that we obtain alien-built vessels for our use and put our efforts into areas we excel in. If our pilots have a positive opinion of the new vessel, perhaps we can continue to acquire maldor vessels. I have been assured that they are well-designed and constructed. Although, it seems the maldors aren't the most skilled at adjusting and tuning their machines. It seems odd to me, but I'm learning every race and culture has interesting quirks like that.

I have been assured our new vessel will be ready for crew training when the next crew arrives from Limdox. The chief flight instructor assures us he can handle any class size we care to bring, so I would expect our next shuttle to arrive full, with pilots eager to master our new machine.

Consular Riv

Dear Charles and Rosanne,

Thank you for the kind letter I received recently. I truly enjoy hearing from my former soldiers from time to time. I'm grateful that my assessment of you as a farmer was accurate. I had no evidence to support that assumption except your behavior and work ethic as a soldier. The photos of the farm are indeed impressive as they are heartwarming.

Seeing your first daughter, Tillya, in her school attire makes me wonder where does the time get off to. Your second daughter, Glinda, is as adorable as can be playing in the yard while your son, Thack, watches on. He looks as if he's determined to learn how to walk so he can join in the fun. By the way, I was brought to tears to learn you named your child after me. It's an honor I never expected. Let me see if I can answer some of your questions in your letter. After the affair on Gostis, I was sent back to Pretna to recover from my wounds. The recovery took some time as the wounds were extensive. Nevertheless, I made a full recovery and assumed duties in the Pretna defense forces. There were those who wanted to fold me into a unit and assume the duties of a superior sergeant, which I was happy to do. Then there were those who clung to the old caste system and wanted to quietly usher me out of the military. Then there was a third group who thought my experience with an elite military group could be of value.

I was assigned to a committee to establish a reconnaissance and special operations element. It was a much harder task than we initially thought it would be. First, we had to determine what kind of missions such a group would be asked to do. From that, we could calculate what kind of physical conditioning a soldier in such a unit had to have and what intelligence level. That would help us in the selection process for prospective members in such a unit.

Next, we had to design a training course that challenged the soldiers enough that we could determine early on those who weren't going to make the cut. Those who finished the early stages were still challenged physically and mentally, but their earlier successes gave them the motivation to continue.

The program is up and running, and I'm proud to say that it's very successful. It still needs some adjustments in places, but the soldiers are the best Pretna has ever fielded. Detractors have complained that there was no need for such a strict unit. I always remind them that the humans have been training like this for centuries and were the single most important part and the reason the Gostis invasion was a success.

I have one more committee yet to participate in before my retirement. NCO development in the defense force is nonexistent. We are starting a process to identify soldiers of lower ranks who have leadership potential. I've always been quite good at selecting soldiers for promotion. However, I'm finding it difficult to articulate what kind of qualities to look for. Among mercenaries in a mostly human organization, I learned what to look for. Culturally, pretars are different than humans, so nuanced behavior is far more difficult to detect. One of my colleagues, who has served the Pretna defense forces all his adult life, is much more attuned to reading our people than I am. We laugh about it whenever it comes up, but he's of the same opinion I have about the importance of this project. There are too many poor examples of sergeants in our organization. I understand there are similar efforts underway for officers.

Perhaps one day, we can have a reunion of the members of the reconnaissance platoon who participated in the Gostis invasion. There, we can raise a mug of lager and say huzzah to the fallen comrades. As always, I look forward to hearing from you.

Your friend,
Superior Sergeant Thack

## The Office of President Peintoc Gostis, Capital City

Pursuant to Gostis law, set forth in the Articles of Federation, this is the president's annual report.

The most impactful series of events is the formation of a separate country on Gostis by citizens of our world who have felt marginalized by their treatment under the Founding Regime. They have established borders on the Western continent, which, as you know, was previously uninhabited. We will, of course, make every effort to maintain a cordial relationship with them.

The formation of another country on Gostis has had unexpected consequences. For instance, we have to have a name for our country. Then there are the challenges that come with not being a united world.

As always, we will meet these challenges and find a way to make things work out for the best.

The Allied authority that has been ensuring that our affairs are kept within established cultural norms has established the conditions that we must meet to end the era of supervision we are currently under. The parameters are reasonable and quite obtainable. As a planet, we have met most of the requirements, and what's needed to end our supervised existence is time.

Members of the Teanon Council who were also members of the Syndicate have all been tried and convicted for their crimes. Simply belonging to the Teanon Council or owning slaves does not constitute as a crime since the Teanon Council was a proper branch of government and slaveholding was legal at that time. Councilman Toanin Zisros was sent to prison on a moon in the Griska system. Unfortunately, he escaped with the help of Syndicate operatives. There are appropriate bounties posted for his capture, and his likeness has been widely distributed so as to ensure his recapture. An interesting quirk in the legal system allowed his wife to file for divorce so as to sever any ties he has with her, and any assets he may have possessed is now his ex-wife's.

In the area of economics, we continue to steadily improve our standing. Falta production has actually increased over the prewar levels. It goes without saying that the standard of living of the former slaves has been improved many times over. The standard of living has slightly improved for the former taskmaster class. The only group in the old class system not to enjoy an improvement in living conditions is the privileged and ruling class. This is not to say that all in this category are worse off than they were. The fate of those who were in government and politics depended on their position and title. Among the falta growers, some are very successful, as they found ways to employ their former selves. Their profit margin is generally lower. However, the workforce is more motivated. Therefore, production is greater as a result. Growers who could not make the transition to using a paid workforce haven't been as fortunate although it has introduced opportunities for people of limited means to obtain property and advance economically.

Falta will continue to be the majority cash crop for our world for the foreseeable future. However, it has been determined that producing food crops should be given a higher priority. In addition to agriculture, manufacturing and service-related industries should be considered.

In conclusion, the state of affairs on Gostis is very good and improving. Our people have demonstrated the ability to overcome difficult situations, which is what makes me optimistic about our future.

As always, it continues to be the honor of my life to serve my people.

Your president,
Uldoor Peintoc

## Stellar Logistics and Freight
## Office of Philip Ross
## President

To: Management-level employees Oasis 4 and
Flast Orbiting Station 1 From: Philip Ross
Date: September 4, 2601
RE: Company Personnel assignments

I would like to announce my retirement will be effective at the end of December 31, 2601.

My wife, Alice, and I would like to spend time with our grandkids in our golden years. Employment by the Stellar Logistics and Freight Corporation would be the highlight of any career. It's certainly been a blessing to me, my flying assignments, and later my management assignments, have been challenging and rewarding. Also, I have my career to thank for introducing me to the love of my life.

The years spent managing Oasis 4 will be ones I remember and will always remember with fondness. The friends I made there are the best anyone could hope to make. That includes the vendors, freighter crews, dignitaries, and employees, both human and the other races.

Naturally, my departure will leave room for advancement in the Stellar Logistics system. My recommendation for Virginia Wells- Needles to replace me as president was unanimously approved by the board of directors. To that end, Tillya Farmer will replace Virginia Wells-Needles and assume the duties of station manager of Flast Orbiting Station 1. There are a number of flastons who are suitable to assume the role of operations manager of Flast Orbiting Station 1. It's our goal to put as many flastons there in management positions as we can, and we're on track to do that.

Gus Condent informs me that Oasis 4 has moved a record amount of freight. A good amount of that freight is the raw material from the Anna Mae system in the form of iron, copper, nickel, gold, and platinum. Paxtite ore is sent directly to Vestgut, and the finished products are processed through Oasis 4.

The efforts to end the slave trade have paid dividends many times over for millions, including our corporation. The fact that Stellar Logistics and, in particular, Oasis 4 played such a large role in the biggest event of the anti- slavery effort fills me with pride.

Alice and I are ending our official association with Stellar Logistics and Freight Corporation, but the friendships we've made over the years will endure forever. If any of you feel the need to decompress and visit old friends, our home in the Missouri Ozarks is an ideal location. Alice and I look forward to seeing each of you. God bless, and take care.

Philip Ross

The End

# ABOUT THE AUTHOR

Dale Chamberlain is an aircraft mechanic and maintenance inspector with over forty years of experience. He started his career in the Army right out of high school. After serving in the Army, he obtained his civilian certifications and worked on aircraft ranging from two-seat Cessnas to four-engine cargo planes to jets. Somewhere in all that, he found time to get his pilot's license. Currently, he is the director of maintenance for a university flying club. He makes his home in Southeast Michigan, where he enjoys the outdoors and his hobbies.